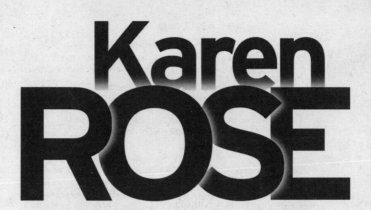

Karen ROSE

every dark corner

HEAD

D0227303

First published in Great Britain in 2017 by
HEADLINE PUBLISHING GROUP

First published in paperback in Great Britain in 2016 by
HEADLINE PUBLISHING GROUP

1

Cataloguing in Publication Data is available from the British Library

ISBN 978 0 7553 9007 6 (B format)
ISBN 978 0 7553 9008 3 (A format)

Typeset in Palatino by Avon DataSet Ltd, Bidford-on-Avon, Warwickshire

Printed and bound in Great Britain by Clays Ltd, St Ives plc

Headline's policy is to use papers that are natural, renewable and recyclable
products and made from wood grown in well-managed forests and other
controlled sources. The logging and manufacturing processes are expected to
conform to the environmental regulations of the country of origin.

HEADLINE PUBLISHING GROUP
An Hachette UK Company
Carmelite House
50 Victoria Embankment
London EC4Y 0DZ

www.headline.co.uk
www.hachette.co.uk

Karen Rose was introduced to suspense and horror at the tender age of eight when she accidentally read Poe's *The Pit and the Pendulum* and was afraid to go to sleep for years. She now enjoys writing books that make other people afraid to go to sleep.

Karen lives in Florida with her family, their cat, Bella, and two dogs, Loki and Freya. When she's not writing, she enjoys reading, and her new hobby – knitting.

To my friend, Amy Lane, because your stories soothed my heart when I was afraid and grieving, and because your characters helped me fall in love with my own characters all over again.
PS: Thanks for the knitting :-)

To Aunt Maurita. You've demonstrated true strength and grace in the midst of great sorrow. Thank you for allowing me to be your honorary kid.

To the memory of Reverend Richard Wertz, aka Uncle Dick. You married us, you laughed and lived with us, and when your time on earth was through, you faced the end with dignity and great faith. We wish you were here.

And, as always, to Martin, for our thirty-five amazing years together (so far). I love you.

Acknowledgements

Marc Conterato for all things medical. Thank you for always making time to answer my questions.

Amy Lane for reintroducing me to the art – and the therapeutic benefits – of knitting. It really does help quiet my over-active mind.

Mike Magowan for your firearms expertise.

Terri Bolyard and Kay Conterato for talking me through the rough spots.

The Starfish – Cheryl, Chris, Kathy, Sheila, and Susan for the encouragement and discipline. Time to write!

My sweet husband, Martin, who takes care of our family while I'm in my cave working.

My amazing readers all over the world – you allow me to have the best job ever. Thank you!

As always, all mistakes are my own.

Prologue

Cincinnati, Ohio,
Saturday 8 August, 12.45 P.M.

Cookies. Chips. Fruit Roll-Ups. Mallory Martin gritted her teeth harder with every package she tossed into the grocery cart. Crossing the fruit snacks off his list, she made her way to the frozen food section of the store. *Frozen pizza. Ice cream.* Then on to the toppings – one of each type on the shelf at the end of the aisle. Chocolate syrup, candied walnuts, peanuts, caramel. *No store brands,* he'd said. *Get the most expensive.* Bile burned her throat. *Only the best, Mallory dear. Only the best.*

She dropped her gaze back to the list, double-checking that she'd gotten all that he'd specified. *Don't forget anything, Mallory darling,* he'd said, his smile tight as he'd run his finger down her face. *You know how I hate to have to punish you.*

'Looks like somebody's having a party.'

Mallory jerked at the deep male voice, her grip tightening on the jar of cherries she'd just pulled off the shelf. *Because we must have cherries.* She could hear the lilting, mocking words inside her mind.

Always inside her mind. *Always. Everywhere.* She hated that. She hated him. She stared at the jar of cherries in her hand. She hated herself.

'Are you all right, miss?' the man standing in front of her cart asked with concern.

Mallory shoved the hated voice from her mind, lifting her eyes to the stranger standing in front of her. He was about thirty, with wide

1

shoulders and a slight paunch. Looked like a used-to-be football player, once upon a time. She knew the type. She knew *all* the types. He was watching her, his expression wary. Like she was a lunatic just waiting to do something crazy.

And he'd be right, she thought.

'I didn't mean to startle you,' he said. 'I'm sorry.'

'I'm fine,' she said quietly. 'Thank you for asking.' She tried to move her cart, to get around him, but the man took a step to the side, blocking her movement before it had a chance to become an escape.

She took a step back, but once again he mirrored her movement, stopping her. 'I know you,' he said, his eyebrows bunching as he studied her more closely.

A shiver ran down her spine. Fear. Disgust. Despair. She forced herself to smile. 'No, I'm sure you don't. I'm new in town.' A lie, of course. But after so many, what was one more?

He tilted his head, eyes narrowing. Mallory pulled the cart backward a few paces, gritting her teeth when beefy fingers closed over the metal, keeping her in place.

She could tell the exact moment he recognized her, his lips curling in a Grinch-like smile. She didn't know this man, but that smile? *That* she knew. Once again bile burned her throat, but this time it was mixed with desperate fear.

'Let me pass,' she said, hearing her own panic. 'I have to get out of here.' She yanked her cart from his hands and careened around him. Briefly she considered abandoning the cart and running like hell.

Running as far as she could. As fast as she could.

Running until she reached a place where no man would ever wear that smile.

But that wasn't possible.

Because the Internet was everywhere. Mallory was everywhere. Even though she wanted to be nowhere. Which also was not possible. So she pushed her cart to the dairy section and opened the door to the milk. For a moment she stood there, the cold air of the fridge a blessed relief to her overheated face.

Her heart was racing, her pulse pounding in her head until it was all she could hear. Still holding on to the door, she carefully glanced over her shoulder. Her stomach pitched.

The man stood at the very end of the aisle, texting, his phone small in his big hands. He looked up, saw her watching him and smiled that Grinch smile again. Fluttered his sausage-sized fingers in a wave.

And took her photo.

No. No. No. Not again. Please, she wanted to scream. *Not again. No more.*

But she didn't scream. Didn't cry. Didn't run. Instead, she chose a gallon jug of milk with as much dignity as she could muster, placed it in the cart, and checked his list once again.

Whipped cream. It was the last item on the list and her hand shook when she reached for the red can. It should be a normal thing, buying a can of whipped cream. But she knew why he wanted it. Knew he'd use it for far more than topping an ice cream sundae.

Tell someone. For the love of God, Mallory, tell someone.

Shut up, she wanted to snap. How many times had she told herself to tell? But it wasn't that simple. Nothing was ever that simple. *If it was simple, I'd've done it by now*, she thought wearily. The red can went in the cart and she made her way to the lanes of cashiers.

The used-to-be football player with the deep voice was in the checkout line to her left, trying to catch her eye with flirtatious winks. Mallory ignored him, keeping her head down. She paid the bill with cash, as she always did.

Can't be leaving a trace now, can we, Mallory dear?

No, she thought dully. *We can't. But I did.* She'd left a trace that could be seen from goddamn space. She'd never meant to. *It wasn't my fault.*

Which was the truth, but who the hell cared?

She shook her head mutely when the cashier asked if she needed help with her bags. She was eighteen years old, after all. She could load her own damn car.

Well, not her car. It was his. Everything was his.

3

Even Mallory. And he never let her forget it.

The intense heat of the August noon slapped her in the face as she pushed her cart out of the store. On edge, she glanced both ways before crossing the street to the car. The used-to-be football player was gone. 'Thank you,' she breathed softly.

Quickly she loaded the groceries in the trunk, making sure to put the ice cream in a freezer bag so that it didn't soften on the drive home. He got angry when the ice cream softened. It was never good when he got angry. Mallory had the scars to prove it. Not that anyone would believe her.

He'd seen to that, she thought bitterly, slamming the trunk shut with both hands. For a moment she stood there, her palms flat on the blisteringly hot metal, holding herself up because her legs were trembling. *No one will ever believe me again.*

A shadow fell over her shoulder. 'Well, if it isn't Sunshine Suzie!' the deep voice drawled.

Mallory froze, her hands clenching into fists. She didn't move away from the car. She wasn't sure that she could.

The used-to-be football player was back. Standing behind her. She could see his wide shoulders reflected in the car's rear window. He held a phone in front of his face. 'I told you it was her,' he added smugly, then turned the phone in her direction. In the window, she could see the fuzzy reflection of another man's face. *A video call. Shit.* 'Turn around, Suzie. Say hi to my friend. He's a big fan, too.'

Mallory slid her hand into the pocket of her jeans, her fingers closing over her keys. *Just a few feet. Get in the car and you'll be safe.* She bolted, only to have those beefy fingers close over her upper arm in a grip tight enough that she'd have a ring of bruises. This she knew from experience.

'Let me go!' she cried. 'Please, just let me go.'

'Not a chance,' the man said, cruel laughter in his voice. 'Nobody's seen you for a few years, sweetheart. Now that you're back, I'd like an encore performance. What do you think, Justin? Don't you think Sunshine Suzie owes us a show?'

'Oh, man,' the guy on the phone whined. 'I think you'd better be fucking making a video.'

'Abso-fucking-lutely.'

Mallory fought the bile that was rising once again. 'No!' Keys in her hand, she whipped around, grazing the big man's cheek and startling him into dropping his phone on the asphalt. The screen shattered and the face of the man on the other end of the call splintered into a hundred different pieces.

Mallory tried to run, but Mr Football grabbed her tighter, his face grown dark. 'That was a new phone, bitch,' he snarled. 'You'll pay for that, one way or another.'

'Excuse me,' a female voice said quietly. 'Is there a problem here?'

A lady cop. In uniform. Mallory wanted to scream *YES!* Instead she heard herself saying, 'No, ma'am.'

Mr Football abruptly dropped his hand and Mallory was free. 'No problem, Officer,' he said with an easy smile. 'Just a misunderstanding. No harm done.'

'None,' Mallory agreed. She gave the policewoman a fast nod of gratitude, then ran to the driver's side of the car, pressing the key fob to unlock the door.

'Wait!' the cop ordered.

Mallory froze again, her hand clutching the now-open car door. 'I need to go,' she said, her panic out there for all to see. 'My ice cream will melt.'

'What happened here?' the cop asked sharply.

Tell her. Just tell her. Tell her everything. For a moment Mallory teetered, but then she remembered the last time she'd tried to tell, and the time before that. Nobody listened. Nobody believed her. And the punishment for trying to tell was far too severe to ever try again.

'Nothing happened,' Mallory insisted. 'Just a case of mistaken identity. He thought I was someone else.' She locked herself in and started the engine, grateful there was no car parked in front of her, because the cop and Mr Football still stood behind her. She pulled straight through the parking place and made her way to the exit, expecting the lady cop to follow. Breathing a sigh of relief when the woman did not.

5

Her grip on the steering wheel white-knuckled, Mallory drove . . . *home*. The word stuck in her throat. Hurt to even think it. But it was where she lived, no matter how much she hated it. When she pulled into the driveway, her hands ached from clenching the wheel.

You should have kept going. There was enough fuel to get her to Columbus, or maybe even Toledo. *Then what? Don't be stupid, Mallory. You came back here because you had to.* There was nowhere else to go. No way out.

Not that she'd run even if she could. Because of Macy. Always Macy. *Macy who runs at the sight of me. As if I'm the monster.* Macy didn't know the monster. Would never know, just as long as Mallory behaved. So Mallory would behave.

She sat in the driveway, staring at the pretty white farmhouse that was her prison. Trapped. She was trapped. And if she sat here much longer, she'd be whipped, too. The last time she'd made him angry it took two weeks for the welts to heal.

But her hands still shook and her gut still clenched over the encounter in the grocery store parking lot. *Sunshine Suzie.* Mallory hated Sunshine Suzie.

She closed her eyes, fighting not to throw up. It wasn't the first time she'd been recognized. It wasn't even the first time a man had tried to drag her away for an 'encore performance', but this was the first time a cop had become involved.

Should I tell him about the cop? she asked herself tentatively. The answer came swiftly. *No. No way.* Even if the cop noted the car's license plate, it would never lead back here. Never to him. He was untraceable. Invisible.

He was Satan. *And I'll never escape his hell.*

Wearily she climbed from the car and gathered the grocery bags, the words 'encore performance' whirling around in her mind. The aroma of grilled burgers came from behind the house, nauseating her as she climbed the back stairs to the kitchen door.

Hamburgers, hot dogs, and ice cream. What more could a kid want?

Freedom.

6

Mallory looked in the window before reaching for the doorknob. She could see the kitchen table from where she stood on the outside looking in, and her stomach lurched again.

Oh God. There were four of them this time. Four sitting around the table. Usually there was only one, or maybe two. But today . . .

Four of them. Two girls and two boys. All young. Thirteen years old, maybe. All awestruck at their apparent good fortune. Hamburgers, hot dogs, and ice cream.

So pretty. All of them. Wide-eyed and innocent.

Not for much longer. He'd use them until they were used up. *Until they're me. And then people will recognize them in the grocery store.*

No. Something within her broke. *No more.* She could feel the snap. Could feel the bile rising and could no longer hold it back. Her knees gave out and she fell against the stair rail, her head hanging over the side. The little she'd eaten that day came up and she was too weary to try to stop it.

Four of them, innocents. Sunshine Suzie. Encore performance.

She crumpled into a heap on the landing, shaking, the words tornadoes in her mind. Today he'd give them free ice cream sundaes. Next week free pizza. But the week after . . . Mallory wiped her mouth on the sleeve of her shirt.

There would be payment required. There was always payment required.

She lifted her head. *But not this time.* There would be no more Sunshine Suzies. No more encore performances. *No more.*

But what about Macy? Her resolve faltered. And then she heard the laughter in the kitchen. Four young kids, laughing at a joke. Mallory couldn't remember the last time she'd laughed. If she ever had. But Macy laughed, and Mallory needed to keep it that way.

Encore performance. She closed her eyes. There had to be a way. To stop him. To end this nightmare once and for all without sacrificing Macy.

The door opened with an almost soundless creak. He stepped out of the kitchen, his shadow covering her. 'Mallory, dear,' he said silkily. 'Please come inside. The ice cream will melt.'

Mallory made herself stand. Locked her knees so they wouldn't give out beneath her. Nodded without meeting his eyes. She never met his eyes. She hated what she saw there. Power. Smug, because he knew he held the cards.

'Let me introduce you to our guests,' he continued, and Mallory forced herself to meet their eyes. 'Guys, this is my daughter.'

This has to stop. Mallory had to make it stop. She *would* make it stop.

Even if I have to kill him to make it so.

Even if I die trying.

One

Cincinnati, Ohio,
Wednesday 12 August, 5.30 P.M.

Run. Run. Faster. Stop him. Please, God, let me stop him this time.

Kate took the stairs two at a time, her heart beating wildly. But not from the running. It was the fear. Fear so thick that she could smell it. Taste it. Feel it coating her skin as she charged up the stairs that never, ever seemed to end.

Because she knew she'd never stop him. She was always too late.

She reached the door and stopped. Can't do it. Can't do this again. Please, don't make me do this again. *But her hand moved as she watched, turning the knob.*

Her hand always turned the knob. The door always swung open like it weighed five hundred pounds. Slowly.

Revealing him sitting in her easy chair, his head resting on the brightly colored afghan her grandmother had crocheted just for her when she was six, a mocking smile on his face.

And the barrel of a gun in his mouth. Her gun.

She flinched, closing her eyes a second before the gun went off. Because she knew what would happen. She knew how bad it would—

'Kate?' The voice was muffled but insistent, then became abruptly loud and clear, followed by a soft smack on her cheek. 'Kate? Special Agent Coppola, you need to *wake up*.'

Kate woke with a start, her heart racing faster than it had in the dream. She'd been too late again. But she'd always be too late, because he hadn't wanted to be stopped.

He'd wanted her to see.

9

She blinked, her darting gaze taking in the hospital room, the chair in which she sat – fucking uncomfortable – and the deep, rhythmic breathing of the man lying in the bed next to her – Special Agent Griffin Davenport.

But mostly the unusual eyes – one blue and one brown – staring up at her from a woman's face framed with bold white streaks that contrasted starkly with the rest of her inky black hair. Kate reached out a tentative hand to nudge Dani's shoulder, just to be sure she wasn't still dreaming. The shoulder was solid and real.

Kate exhaled sharply. 'Dani,' she said, just to hear her own voice. It was raspy, like sandpaper. Like she'd been screaming. *Oh God, don't let me have been screaming.*

Dr Dani Novak spoke calmly, like one might speak to a feral animal. Or a wild-eyed woman just coming out of a nightmare. 'Yes. I'm real. And yes, you're awake.'

She was kneeling in front of Kate, holding the cord to her earbuds in one hand and her laptop in the other while Kate clutched the blanket she'd been knitting to her chest like a shield.

'You nearly lost your computer,' Dani explained in that same calm voice. 'I came in as it was slipping off your lap. You were dreaming.'

Kate let the knitting fall to her lap so that she could press her fingertips to her temples. 'Yeah,' was all she could muster. She hated waking up from that dream. Hated feeling fuzzy and disoriented. Hated the pounding of her pulse in her ears. Hated that the last thing she'd seen was a man's head exploding. 'Wish you'd come in a few seconds earlier,' she muttered.

Dani made a sympathetic noise. 'Me too. You were . . . talking in your sleep.'

Kate's eyes widened, a different kind of fear giving her a hard jolt that woke her right up. 'What did I say?' *Please don't let it have been too much.*

Dani's voice dropped to a whisper. 'Just "I'm sorry, Jack. So sorry."'

'That's it?'

A single nod set Kate's mind at ease, because even though she didn't know Dani all that well, she did know the woman didn't lie. Dani Novak was the sister of Kate's close friend and former Bureau partner, Deacon, who was as honest as any man she'd ever met.

Deacon Novak was a rare find – a male colleague who was simply a good friend. And that was all. There had never been a hint of anything else, not even once. The attraction hadn't been there for either of them, and Kate had been so very glad. She hadn't needed a lover then. She might never need one again. But she had desperately needed a friend, and Deacon had been one of the best.

When Deacon had transferred to Cincinnati from Baltimore, Kate had missed him – his professional skill along with his sarcasm and blunt honesty. She'd missed her friend. So when a position opened up in Cincinnati, she would have taken it even if it had meant a demotion. Luckily it had been a move up the ladder. She'd told everyone that she'd taken the job because of the promotion, but the real reason she'd chosen Cincinnati out of all the possible transfers was because of Deacon Novak.

They'd no longer work side by side – Deacon had been assigned to a joint task force with Cincinnati PD, while Kate was squarely owned by the FBI's field office – but just knowing he was close by, that she had a friend watching her back again . . . that was enough.

The news that Deacon had found love here in Cincinnati soon after he'd arrived had made Kate incredibly happy. She'd found her soulmate once upon a time, long before she'd ever met Deacon Novak. Deacon deserved his turn now, and Kate heartily wished him and his fiancée Faith the happiness she'd once known.

But she hoped Deacon and Faith would know their happiness for a whole lot longer than Kate had known hers, because the few years she'd actually been happy wasn't much in the grand scheme of a life. Heartbroken and lost when she'd moved to Baltimore three years ago, she hadn't realized how much she'd needed a friend until she'd met Deacon. Now—

Mocking smile, barrel in his mouth, gunshot—

Stop it. Viciously she shoved the image away. But it would be back. It never went far, a nearly constant taunt. But also a constant reminder of exactly how much she needed friends. And pathetically

11

needy as it was, Kate hoped that Deacon's sister might become one, too.

The Novak siblings had always seemed carved from the same rock, so Kate believed Dani when she murmured, 'I don't think anyone else heard what you said. You were more mumbling than speaking. Are you okay?'

Kate nodded, still shaken from the dream. From the knowledge that she'd spoken in her sleep, when she couldn't control her words. At least 'I'm sorry, Jack' wasn't so bad. It could have been much worse. *At least I didn't scream.*

But was she okay? *Hell, no.* She might never be okay again.

'I will be,' she lied. Pasting a smile on her face and willing her hands not to tremble, she relieved Dani of the computer and earbuds. 'Thanks for saving my piece-of-shit laptop.' She put it on the floor under her chair. 'As much as I want a new one, this one can't break until I've at least backed up my notes on the audio files I've been transcribing all afternoon.'

Dani shrugged. 'The audio file was either finished or it was just a lot of dead air.'

Kate stared at her. 'You *listened*? It was private.'

'Not intentionally.' Remaining calm, Dani grabbed the earbuds' cord and held up the tail end. 'It came unplugged when I grabbed your piece-of-shit computer.'

Now Kate felt bad. 'I'm sorry. Thank you again,' she said humbly. 'I was being surly. I don't wake up very nice.'

Dani waved the apology away. 'Neither do I. Anyway, all I could hear was static.'

'Because the speaker's a piece of shit, too,' Kate grumbled, grateful nonetheless that she hadn't inadvertently shared the contents of an ongoing investigation with every nurse, patient, and family member in the ICU.

'What were you listening to?' Dani asked curiously.

'Recordings he made while he was undercover.' With a quirk of her head, Kate indicated the man in the hospital bed.

Special Agent Griffin Davenport had been placed in an induced coma the week before so that he could heal after a bullet had bruised his lung, cracked a rib, and filled his chest cavity with blood. He'd been in intensive care all that time, a ventilator breathing for him, the steady rise and fall of the man's massive chest evidence that the machine was doing its job.

Telling Dani that Davenport had made the recordings wasn't an issue. The man's cover had been blown sky-high while rounding up a group of human traffickers who'd retaliated by putting him here in ICU. It had been an ER nurse who'd found the envelope full of CDs in a pocket sewn onto the inside of his pants and turned them over to the police.

And truthfully? The contents of the CDs themselves hadn't been terribly damning so far, and Kate had been listening to them for days. *Only days? Feels like weeks.* There had been a lot of thug chatter, but most of it wasn't anything new. Nothing to warrant Davenport getting shot over, certainly.

'Why you?' Dani asked.

Kate jerked her gaze away from Davenport down to Dani, who was still watching her carefully from her kneeling position. 'What do you mean, why me?'

'Why are you listening to his recordings?'

'Because there's something important on one of those CDs.' Of that she was certain. 'Davenport took a huge risk trying to get them out.'

The envelope containing the CDs had been addressed to his handler in the event that he was unable to deliver them personally, which, in the end, was exactly what had happened. Except they hadn't gone to Davenport's handler, because he was dead, shot by members of the same ring. So Kate had listened while Davenport healed.

'No, I mean why are *you* listening? There are a lot of agents in that office and Deacon said that you're one of the bigger fish in the pond now. Why not have a smaller fish do the listening?'

Kate shrugged uncomfortably. 'I'm the new kid on the block. A week in the job and I don't have a caseload yet. Besides, I do have a few of the smaller fish listening, too.'

Dani tilted her head thoughtfully, just like Kate had seen her brother do a thousand times. 'Why do you visit every day?' She chuckled at Kate's look of consternation. 'You think the ICU nurses haven't noticed? You think they didn't just try to pump me for information the moment I walked in the door?'

That the nurses would ask Dani questions wasn't a surprise. The woman was an ER doctor in this very hospital, although currently on a leave of absence. That they'd ask about Kate was the mystery. 'Pump you for information about what?'

Dani rolled her eyes. 'They all but have you two as star-crossed lovers, tragically separated but reunited when he got shot and you raced to his aid.'

Kate's eyes widened. 'You are kidding me, right? Me and Davenport?'

'You *do* visit every day, Kate.'

That was true. Some of the time she'd listened to the recordings from the privacy of her desk at the Cincinnati Field Office, but she had made a point of visiting him every day. She thought she was the only one who did, and that bothered her. She hated the thought of him being so alone after being deeply undercover. The life of an operative tended to be very lonely.

So sometimes she talked to him about trivial things – the unrelenting heat and humidity, her search for an apartment. A few times she'd shared her frustration at not hearing anything of value on the damn CDs. She'd played him tunes from her iPod and read to him from the book she'd thrown in her carry-on when she'd left for Cincinnati last week. But mostly she simply sat with him and caught up with her knitting while she listened to the recordings he'd risked his life to share.

'I met him for the first time less than an hour before he got shot, and that's the truth.' She sighed when Dani just waited for more, saying nothing. 'Deacon was on the team who breached the traffickers' compound and he brought me in as one of their snipers.' She'd been in town all of two days, but had jumped at the chance. She didn't get to use her sharpshooting skills as often as she would have liked, and Deacon's case had been right up her alley. 'I was doing recon and saw Davenport attempting to slip away. He was trying to get the CDs out, but I didn't know that then. I dropped down on him from a tree.'

Dani moved to sit in the chair beside her, her delighted grin surprising Kate more than the nurses' gossip. 'You *dropped* him? Took him down? Goddamn, girl. You really are a super-chick. I thought Deacon was exaggerating.'

Kate's cheeks heated at the praise. 'I didn't actually drop on him. I don't think I could have taken him down, even from a tree.' Because Griffin Davenport was built like a freaking tank.

'Hell, maybe not even from a helicopter,' Dani murmured. 'So what did you do?'

'I landed behind him, stuck my rifle in his back, and took him by surprise. But he wanted to be found, so he cooperated, which was a good thing. I would have hated to have to shoot him. Unfortunately the traffickers didn't have that concern.'

Dani nodded soberly. 'I haven't had a chance to thank you yet.'

Kate frowned. 'For what?'

'For saving Deacon's life. He was standing next to Davenport when the bullets started flying. If you hadn't stopped the shooter the way you did, there might be more patients filling these ICU beds. Or bodies in the morgue. So thank you.'

Kate fidgeted. 'I was just doing my job. Any of the other agents there would have done it.'

Dani lifted one dark brow. 'The way I heard it, none of the other agents there had the skill with a rifle to stop a speeding car half a mile away.'

'Deacon exaggerates,' Kate mumbled, now very uncomfortable even though it was true. She was a skilled shot, but she wasn't a fathead. 'Besides, they were already fleeing the scene by then. I didn't mean to kill them. I wanted them alive for questioning.' She'd stopped them, but she'd also taken out the shooter and one of his trafficking partners. The only passenger who'd survived knew so little about the trafficking business itself that he was all but useless.

Dani shook her head. 'You may have wanted them alive for questioning, but I'm glad my brother is alive *period*. I owe you one, Kate. Seriously.'

Kate started to laugh it off, but then she realized that Dani Novak really was very serious. 'He's my friend,' she said simply. 'I would have done the same for any other agent, but the fact that it was Deacon made it easier to sleep that night.'

Except that she hadn't slept. She'd woken with the dream. She hadn't had the dream in almost a month prior to coming to Cincinnati, but she'd had it every single night for the past week. It might have been triggered by the gunfight with the traffickers or the fact that she'd been bunking down in a strange hotel bed. Or that she was plain exhausted because she really hadn't slept at all. Or that she'd strained her back sitting in the uncomfortable chair in ICU.

Kate rolled her head, hearing her neck crackle. 'I hate falling asleep in chairs.'

'Then maybe you should go home to bed,' Dani said mildly.

'So,' Kate said brightly, 'I didn't expect to see you here checking on Davenport.' She didn't care that her subject change had all the finesse of a clubbing from a baseball bat. 'Are you back on duty?'

Dani's leave from the ER had started a few months before. Kate knew the bare bones of the story, partly from phone and email conversations she'd had with Deacon over the past nine months and partly from the news she'd read online. Dani was HIV positive – and Kate figured that however that had occurred was Dani's business and Dani's alone.

But someone else hadn't agreed, because Dani's status had been leaked to the media, leading to negative press and finally to Dani going on leave. Again, Kate didn't have details, but she knew the Novaks well enough to be sure that Dani had taken every sensible precaution on the job. Hopefully her presence here today meant that the hoopla had died down enough for the woman to resume the career she'd worked so hard to achieve.

But a shadow had passed over Dani's face. 'No. I resigned.'

Kate's mouth fell open. 'What? But why? And when? You mean just now?'

Dani took a deep breath and let it out. 'I'm not actually here to check on Agent Davenport,' she said, her subject change equally clumsy, her tone so bright that it was brittle. 'Deacon asked me to check on you. He's worried you're spreading yourself too thin keeping vigil.'

Kate wanted to ask why Dani wasn't suing for discrimination. She wanted to ask if Dani had another job, because she hated the thought of the woman not being able to pay her bills. She wanted to make sure that Deacon's sister would be okay.

But Dani had made it clear that she wasn't willing to discuss it any further, so Kate drew a deep breath of her own and made herself smile. 'You can tell Deacon that I'm okay.'

Dani's eyes filled with a gratitude she didn't voice. Instead she made her reply sharp and tart. 'I'll tell him that you were asleep in your chair and that you probably haven't been eating properly. He'll be here soon enough to yell at you in person.'

Kate made a sour face, just for form. 'You're supposed to be the nice Novak.'

Dani grinned. 'Surprise! Well, since you're okay, I guess I'll just see you later.' She started to stand, and Kate found herself reaching for the woman's arm to yank her back.

'No, Dani, wait.' She didn't want to be left alone with her post-dream thoughts. She didn't want to fall back to sleep. She didn't want to hear that gun go off again. 'Can you stay, maybe talk for a little while?' She tried for a brave smile. 'You can keep me awake.'

Dani frowned at her gently. 'If you're that tired, maybe you should go home and go to *bed*,' she said, repeating herself.

'I can't go home. I'm staying in a hotel until the movers bring my stuff.' But she didn't want to go to the hotel either. *Because I will dream again, and I just* . . . A shudder passed through her, and that she didn't even try to control it told her something. Either she was exhausted, or she simply felt comfortable enough with Dani to reveal her vulnerable underbelly. Or maybe a little bit of both. 'Besides, I need to sit here with Agent Davenport, in case he wakes up again. I was one of the last people he saw before he was shot, so I'm hoping that I can calm him down if he's disoriented when they try waking him again.'

'Again? They tried waking him up already?'

'Yeah, but it didn't end so well.' Suddenly antsy, Kate stood up to stretch her back and to better see Davenport's mask-covered face. A lock of the man's blond hair had slid down his forehead, and she gently pushed it back. 'They tried to bring him out of the induced coma this morning before I got here, but he became agitated. He was thrashing and trying to pull out his breathing tube, so they sedated him again right away.'

'He's way too big a boy to be thrashing,' Dani murmured. 'He could injure someone.'

She wasn't wrong about that. Davenport was over six feet tall, his enormous feet nearly hanging off the edge of the bed. He had to weigh at least two-fifteen, and there was not an ounce of body fat anywhere that Kate had seen.

That she'd actually *looked* was something between her and the four walls. She wasn't in the market for a man to share her life, but that didn't mean she couldn't appreciate the scenery while she made the journey. And Griffin Davenport, even in a coma, was very nice scenery. Apart from the chest full of muscles, he had a strong jaw, golden hair, and pleasing features, even though most of his face was still covered with the ventilator mask.

Like all the Avengers rolled into one. With liberal helpings of Thor and Captain America, her personal faves. Of course, she also knew he was going to wake up. The doctors had all but guaranteed a speedy recovery. If his life were in the balance, then looking would be just wrong.

'The nurse said it took three people to hold him while a fourth sedated him.'

'Agitation while coming out of sedation isn't uncommon,' Dani said. 'It can be a disorienting experience. Kind of like waking from a really vivid nightmare.'

The shrewd tone of Dani's voice had Kate glancing over to see that the woman had stopped looking at Davenport and was now watching her. It was then that Kate realized she'd been stroking Davenport's forehead. Tenderly, actually.

And it wasn't the first time. She had found herself touching his face several times over the last week. She told herself it was because she knew that comatose patients had some sense that people were with them. She told herself it was because she didn't want him to be alone or afraid, that touching him was simple human compassion, but deep down it was still disconcerting seeing her fingertips stroking another man's skin, and she wasn't exactly sure why.

Maybe because a caress that should have felt rusty with disuse felt so . . . natural? Or because she hadn't recoiled in disgust at the feel of him?

'The doctor said that they weaned him off the paralytic that was keeping him immobile and they've started weaning him off the narcotics again. He could wake at any time.'

'I'm sure he'll appreciate a friendly face,' Dani said softly.

'I thought so. I'd want someone to be there when I woke up.' She gave Davenport's brow a final stroke, then sat back down, frowning when her stomach growled. 'I need to eat or I'll get mean. Meaner, anyway,' she added and saw Dani smirk. 'I've eaten all my protein bars and the food in the cafeteria sucks. Do you hear that, Davenport?' she said tartly to the man in the bed. 'You need to wake up *right* next time so I can leave this hospital for some real food.'

'Does he have family? Someone else you can call who'd be familiar to him?'

'None that I've been able to identify so far. He's been undercover for a couple of years. Usually those guys get picked for the deep undercover jobs *because* they don't have families. He listed his handler as his emergency contact, but the handler was killed last week by other members of the trafficking group. The line for a second contact was blank.'

'How lonely,' Dani murmured.

Kate had thought the same thing. It made her feel an odd sort of bond with him, because she no longer had an emergency contact either. But at least she had a few people she could ask. Which she needed to do ASAP, because HR had been on her case about it for the last week.

'Listen, Dani, you remember that favor you said you owed me? I'm ready to collect. Of course, if you don't want to do it, I totally understand.'

'Just ask,' Dani said patiently.

'I went to fill out all the transfer forms in HR and realized that my emergency contact was . . . no longer available.' *Don't think about the dream. Don't—* She flinched when she heard the echo of that gunshot once again. 'I'd ask Deacon, but . . .' She let the thought trail with a shrug.

Dani tilted her head. 'But?'

Kate sighed. 'But he'd ask me why I needed a new contact and I really don't want to get into it with him right now.' *Or ever.* 'He doesn't mean to be nosy, but . . .'

'But he is,' Dani finished. 'So am I, actually, but I'm a bit more discreet.' Her voice softened. 'Your old contact, was it Jack?'

She'd asked so kindly, so compassionately, that Kate felt compelled to nod. Her voice didn't want to work and the nod was all she could muster. But at least it was the truth.

Jack Morrow had been her emergency contact. Until he'd blown his brains out all over the chair in her living room. And the wall, and the carpet, and the ceiling. And the afghan her grandma had crocheted just for her when she was six.

'Then I'm sorry for your loss,' Dani said gently.

'Thank you.' Kate forced the words out, knowing she should feel guilty for allowing Dani to believe that Jack was someone she'd cared for, but she couldn't muster that either. And it wasn't entirely untrue. She *had* cared for Jack as a treasured friend, but that had changed.

Jack had changed. And so had Kate. In many ways not for the better. *What if Johnnie could see you now? What would he think of the woman you've become?*

If Johnnie could see me now, then he'd be *here, which means that Jack would* be *here and I wouldn't be having this idiotic conversation with myself, so shut the fuck up.*

A sharp pain in her neck made her realize she was grinding her teeth hard. And of course Dani had noticed. 'You gonna be okay?' Dani asked soberly.

'Yeah. Peachy.' *I just can't fall asleep again. Not until I'm alone.* Because the nightmare always returned. She might not dream again for a week or two, but it always came back, usually when she least expected it.

Like when I'm fucking asleep, she snarled to herself.

'Call me if you need anything,' Dani said.

'Same goes.' Kate's brain kicked into gear just as Dani got to the door, and she remembered what she'd most wanted to ask about Dani's resignation. 'Dani, wait. Do . . . do you have another job lined up? I know Deacon won't let you starve, but I just want to make sure you'll be okay.' Her voice broke, mortifying her. She lifted her chin. 'I need to know that you'll be okay.'

Dani's smile bloomed, a sweet smile that reached her incredible eyes. 'Yes, I'll be okay. Thank you. I've been working part-time for the free clinic that's part of the Lorelle Meadows shelter. The board just approved the creation of a full-time position and they offered it to me. Frankly I resent the hell out of being pressured into leaving emergency medicine by the media and general bigotry, especially when I followed all of the AMA guidelines to the letter. But I'll be an important part of the community at the clinic and that makes me feel very okay. I start on Monday. When you get settled, come down and I'll show you around.'

'I will.' When Dani was gone, Kate let her gaze fall back on Griffin Davenport, whose chest continued to rise and fall. 'No offense, Griff, but I wish you'd hurry and wake the hell up. I really need to sleep and that's not happening here. Not again.'

She straightened abruptly, thinking she'd seen the quirk of one of his fingers against the white sheet. She even called the nurse in to check, but the woman found nothing to indicate he was waking up. In the end, she patted Kate's hand and advised her to go home to sleep. Told her that she was starting to imagine things.

Biting back what would have been a completely unacceptable reply, Kate sat back in the chair, set up her laptop, retrieved her knitting, and prepared herself for another rousing evening of listening to Davenport's undercover tapes.

She paused, holding her earbuds in one hand. 'You realize that if you'd just wake up, you could tell me what I'm looking for. So come on, Davenport.' She watched again, but there was no further response, so she put the earbuds in and got to work.

Cincinnati, Ohio,
Wednesday 12 August, 10.30 P.M.

Long ago he'd learned that the best place to hide anything was in plain sight. It was for this very reason that he'd pulled his car through the broken gate at the back entrance of King's College and was now waiting for his informant to arrive. No one would raise an eyebrow about a car parked here – it was the closest that King's College came to a lovers' lane.

Well, maybe a little bit of lovers' lane crossed with drug-buy-central.

And there were no cameras. None that worked, anyway. The students themselves had made that happen. Anyone who said that today's youth grew dumber every year had obviously never met any crafty college kids bent on getting high or laid or both.

There had been some brouhaha about campus security early the semester before after two young women were abducted. The college administration was *shocked* and *appalled* that their safety record had been blemished and had replaced every light bulb and camera on the campus proper. Then they'd patted each other on the back for their good deed and never looked back. The camera here at Lovers' Lane was the first one to go. It hadn't even lasted a week.

He'd learned all this from his clientele. College kids tended to get really chatty when they were high and his stuff was among the best. Everybody knew it.

However, if the camera was actually working for a change, that was okay too. It would see exactly what he wished it to. But that didn't mean he was keen on sitting here, risking observation. Eventually somebody would come by. It was still Lovers' Lane, after all.

He glanced at his watch – yes, he still wore one even if it made him an old man – and frowned. She was late. He did not appreciate tardiness. It showed a general disrespect that could not be tolerated. But it didn't really matter. She wasn't going to survive long enough to get to her next appointment, wherever that was.

He heard her before he saw her. Sidney Siler drove a motor

scooter that was in severe need of an exhaust repair. She slid in sideways, sending gravel everywhere. He rolled his eyes. Killing her was going to be a public service. She was a road menace.

She climbed into his passenger seat. 'Sorry I'm late. I know you don't like that.'

She didn't make an excuse and he appreciated it. Not enough to let her live, but whatever. 'Well? Did you see her?'

'I did, and she totally bought that I was her attorney's assistant. I wore my black suit, the one I only wear to funerals. That and the authorization on her attorney's letterhead got me past the front desk at the jail with no issues. I really owe you one for that.'

Of course the authorization had passed muster. He'd forged it himself. That she'd worn her funeral suit was just delicious irony. 'So? How did it go?'

Sidney made a face. 'I will be extra-special careful about my drug buys from now on. That jail is nasty dirty. I would *not* like to end up on the other side of the glass.'

'I would hope the cleanliness of the facility wouldn't be your only deterrent,' he said dryly. 'How was Alice?'

'Cool.' A genuine shiver shook Sidney as she grimaced. 'I mean glacially so. I'm glad she believed I was on her side. I wouldn't want to be on her bad side.'

That had to have been one of the smartest things Sidney had ever said. 'And?'

'She was a little surprised that I was there, because she thought she'd fired her attorney for being a pussy. Her words, not mine. I got the impression that she wasn't very confident about his ability to get her off. In the legal sense, of course.'

His lips twitched. He really did like Sidney. 'Of course. Although Alice was never very hard to get off. In that sense, anyway.' On the job, Alice was stone cold. Hell, she'd been caught on a roof with a sniper rifle in her hands, firing at a group of federal agents who'd been escorting a key witness. But off the clock, the woman had some serious bedroom moves. He'd almost enjoyed it, but she'd been *way* too old for his tastes. He suppressed a shudder. Sex with Alice was part of playing the game. You wanted her product, you fucked her.

And for a time, he'd wanted what she'd been selling. So he'd taken it for the team.

Sidney grinned slyly, her teeth white against her dark skin. 'I can't imagine the two of you, you know, *together*. I mean, she's my age. And you're . . . not.'

He scowled at her. This was what happened when he socialized with his college-aged clients. They became far too familiar. 'Any togetherness we might have experienced is ancient history. What I meant was, Alice is going to do a long stretch of hard time.'

Sidney snorted back a laugh. 'Long and hard. Sorry, sorry.' She forced her expression to sober. 'She says she was set up.'

'Of course she does. They all say that. Did she mention me? You know, kisses to her old boyfriend or anything like that?'

'Nope. I didn't mention you either.' She frowned at him. 'I'm not stupid, Professor.'

He felt a little quiver of relief and hid it well. That had been the only weak spot in his plan, but he'd been a little desperate to get someone into the jail to speak with Alice – someone that couldn't be traced back to him.

'Good,' he said with a smile. 'Like you said, I wouldn't want her on my bad side. And if she finds out I helped you get in there to do an interview for your journal article . . .'

'She won't. No one will. I didn't even tell my faculty advisor yet. I wasn't sure if I'd get in, and I didn't want to disappoint her if it didn't pan out. But when I tell her, she's gonna flip. It will be the perfect lead for our article on sociopaths. I'm ahead of schedule and the semester hasn't even started yet.'

'Did you ask Alice about her handing over her records to negotiate a deal?'

'Yeah. I told her that my boss said he thought he could get the death penalty off the table if she produced records implicating her customers and suppliers, just like you said. She went *ballistic*. She said that only idiots, imbeciles, or old farts with faulty memories kept records anywhere other than in their heads. It was too dangerous. She said she's saving everything she knows until she gets an offer of full immunity. I'm supposed to take my boss's imbecilic plea proposal back to him and shove it up his ass. It was an amazing moment. It was . . . like . . . *seeing* her. Truly seeing who she is. Right there. A sociopath in full meltdown.'

Another wave of relief swept through him. Alice hadn't kept records. If she had, he would have needed to find them and destroy them. This made everything so much simpler. He'd only communicated with Alice when he'd purchased product from her, so he didn't have to worry about anyone else having his information. He could destroy her without worry.

The only remaining loose end was a formerly undercover federal agent, currently in a coma. He'd already made arrangements for the snipping of that loose end as well.

'Well, Alice *is* a sociopath.' He smiled at Sidney. 'I promised you one and I delivered.'

'Did you *ever*. I can't wait to write it up. It was a total rush, I gotta say.'

He lifted his brows. They were heavier than normal – the August humidity tended to weigh down the facial prosthetics he used when he made his rounds of the college campuses. He'd come up with the disguise years ago, when he'd been an undergraduate himself and sold coke to his friends. Small scale, nothing huge. Just enough to pay for his books and put gas in his car. But his business had grown quickly as he became known as having access to 'really good shit'.

He made it all himself in his basement lab, a real-life Walter White a decade before *Breaking Bad* ever graced a Hollywood storyboard. He still sold to individuals like Sidney, but it was more to keep his ear to the college-aged group than for the money. His serious money in recent years had come from selling to the big operations, drug trafficking rings like Alice ran for her father. Now that Alice had been shut down by the damn Feds, he was going to have to find another outfit to sell to. He had expenses, after all.

Alice had never known that he'd been both a customer and a supplier. He'd sold her his good-quality shit as the Professor, and he'd bought other assets from her as himself. Luckily he'd already found other sources for his purchases. Way cheaper than Alice's product had been, and as a bonus, he'd been able to stop fucking her.

Either way, he was glad Sidney hadn't mentioned him.

'You want a *real* rush?' he asked.

Sidney's black eyes sparkled. 'I thought you'd never ask.'

He handed her a small bag filled with white powder. 'My special blend today.'

She looked at the product doubtfully. 'How much for the special blend?'

'Same as usual. I thought you might want to celebrate a little.'

She beamed. 'Absolutely.' She drew her kit from her backpack and set it up on the console between the two seats. Mirror, straw, razor blade. With efficient movements she readied the sample, forming three good-sized lines. She bent over to take her first snort, but he stopped her with a touch to her shoulder.

'I have a bonus today – something new I've been playing with. You want to try it?'

She eyed him warily. 'Is it safe?'

She was snorting cocaine. He wanted to roll his eyes, but he controlled himself. 'Very safe. I've tried it myself and given it to a few of my best customers. You'll like it. I promise.'

She lit up like a Christmas tree at being included with his best customers. 'What do I do?'

He held up a small vial containing one capsule. 'Snort your line, pop this in your mouth, then bite down. It will make your high amazing. Orgasmically amazing.'

She giggled. 'I don't think that's a real word, Professor.' Leaning forward, she inhaled, drawing the line up through the straw, then leaning back to close her eyes as the coke hit her brain. 'Oh, wow. This alone . . . Amazing.'

He grasped her jaw gently, pulled it down, and transferred the capsule straight from the bottle into her mouth. No contact. No fingerprints. 'Now bite. Hard. And swallow fast.'

She obeyed. For a minute nothing happened. She frowned. 'I don't feel anything.'

'You will. Don't worry.' He pulled two latex gloves from his pocket and put them on. Sweeping the unused coke into the baggie, he sealed it and put it in his pocket. He put her kit back together, dropped it into her backpack, then drew out her phone.

'What are you . . .' She grimaced. 'I'm not feeling so . . . Oh God, what was in that pill?'

'Cyanide.'

'*Wha?*' Her eyes grew wide with helpless panic, as her mouth failed to fully form the word.

'And ketamine was mixed with the cocaine. That's my special blend. You're not going to be able to move, so don't try. For the next few minutes, you'll wish you were dead. And then you will be.'

Unlocking her phone's screen required her fingerprint, so he took her hand and pressed her right index finger to the start button. *Presto.* He flipped through her photos, just to make sure she hadn't taken any of Alice. He didn't want any connection whatsoever.

Excellent. No photos. He'd throw her phone in a dumpster the first chance he got.

Sidney was hunched over, hugging herself. *Cramps*, he thought. It wouldn't be long now. He leaned around her, pulled on the door handle, and shoved her out, tossing her backpack on the ground where she fell. 'Sorry,' he said apologetically. He really was.

He pulled the door closed and drove through the broken gate and away from Lovers' Lane. Then he removed the SIM card from her phone and tossed the phone into the first dumpster he saw. Driving another few blocks, he pulled to the curb, stopped, and dropped the card into the storm sewer. *Next stop, Ohio River.*

The river made disposal so very convenient. And on the minuscule chance the SIM card was found, the river itself would have destroyed any data stored there. He grimaced. *And people still eat fish that comes out of that river. Oh my God.*

Speaking of fish . . . He hadn't had dinner yet. He wondered what Mallory had prepared, hoping it would taste as good warmed up. *Better not be fish.*

TWO

Cincinnati, Ohio,
Wednesday 12 August, 11.30 P.M.

She was clacking again. And humming, really, really off-key. But Decker didn't mind. The sounds she made were real. He wanted the real. He kept clawing to get to the real. But the dark kept pulling him back and he was so damn tired of fighting.

But she was clacking and humming so he held on to that. What was the song? He knew that he knew it. Even as off-key as she hummed, he knew it. The name of the song hovered in front of him, too far away to grab. And then, words. She was singing.

'How I wish . . . how I wish you were here.'

Ah. Pink Floyd. Still really off-key. And so damn sad. *Why's she sad?* He needed to know, but he couldn't . . . couldn't ask. Couldn't make his body move. A surge of fury pulsed through him, but it fizzled quickly. Just not enough energy to fuel the mad.

Then the clacking stopped. The singing stopped, her voice breaking as she sang about the two lost souls swimming in a fishbowl. He panicked when he heard the rustle of her movement. *Don't go. Please don't go. Touch me again. Please.* That had felt so nice and he'd wanted to tell her so. It had been so long since anyone had touched him like that.

A wet sound found its way into the dark, followed by her ragged sigh. She was crying. *Don't cry. Please.* He relaxed when the clacking began again. She was still sniffling, but at least she wasn't leaving.

'Fucking Pandora,' she muttered. 'Throw me sad songs. Make me cry like a damn baby. Like I need that today. What I need is some

28

happy.' The clacking paused. 'Hey, Griff, you want some happy too? Maybe it'll help you wake the hell up and tell me what I'm looking for.'

Music flowed faintly and he wanted to get closer, to curl into it. He could barely hear.

There was a slight pressure on his pillow and the music got louder. *Yeah. That. Thank you.* She'd put her iPod next to his ear. Then he wanted to laugh. He knew this song, too. *Zip-a-Dee-Doo-Dah.* She was playing him Disney songs.

'This is my secret playlist, so you gotta promise not to tell,' she murmured as her fingers brushed his forehead. *Yes. Please. More.* But her touch disappeared and he wanted to scream. Wanted to beg. *Touch me again. Please.* 'It's labeled "Death Metal", just in case somebody gets a peek at my iPod. I got a reputation as a badass to uphold, you know. But sometimes even badasses need some happy, and everybody loves the Mouse.' She was standing close, her voice a quiet murmur in his ear. 'Even freaking big tanks like you.'

The clacking resumed and he relaxed again. What was she doing? *Open your eyes. Find out.* But his eyelids were too damn heavy. He wanted to tell her to talk to him. He needed to hear her, needed to find his way back. She'd talked a lot before. When he was awake before. Almost awake, anyway. She'd talked and talked.

Sometimes to me. Sometimes to that other woman. Decker didn't care about the other woman. Didn't care about the music. He wanted to hear *her.* Needed to hear *her.*

Need to tell her . . . His mind stilled. This was important. He needed to tell her . . . *What?*

The music kept flowing. Kids' songs. Happy songs. *Turn off the music and talk to me.* He needed to hear her more than he needed the music. But the music went on.

Then he remembered, and it was like a shock to his brain. *I need to tell her about the kids.*

She sighed again and the clacking stopped. 'Break's over, Griff.' He heard the rustle, felt her by his bedside, and the music stopped. 'I gotta get back to your damn recordings, which you should know are really boring so far. But don't worry. I'm not giving up.'

Wake up. She's going back to the chair. Wake the hell up! Do. It. He forced his eyes open and— *Holy fucking God, that hurts. So bright. Too bright.*

But he wasn't about to close his eyes again, because she was there, her face inches away from his, brown eyes wide and mouth open in shock. Then she smiled at him.

He knew her. Red hair like a sunrise. Pretty pale skin. Freckles across her nose. *Kate.* Her name was Kate. He tried to speak, but he couldn't. *Fucking mask. Fucking tube. Need it out.*

'Welcome back, Agent Davenport. It's about time you woke up.' She caught his wrist before his hand made it to the mask. '*Don't.* Do *not* touch this tube. I'm ringing for a nurse.'

Kids. He needed to tell her about the kids. Desperation grabbed at him and he struggled to shake off her hand, but she tightened her grip.

'Griffin, *stop.*' She was calm, but firm. 'If you try to pull out that tube again, they will put you back under. Do you understand?' Her expression softened even though her grip didn't. 'Don't be afraid. You're going to be okay. I promise.'

He believed her, so he stopped struggling. Still he didn't drop his hand, just in case.

She smiled at him again. 'Thank you. You might not remember me. My name is Kate.'

I knew that. He relaxed a little more. He'd gotten that right.

'Special Agent Kate Coppola,' she continued, her voice calm. 'I was with you when you were shot. I need you to settle down and listen. I don't want them to sedate you again. You're on a ventilator, but you're going to be okay.'

He nodded. At least he hoped he had. He let his hand fall to his side, too tired to fight anymore. She brushed his hair off his forehead and his eyes slid shut. *Don't stop. Please don't stop.* But her touch disappeared and he panicked again. *No. Don't leave. Stay!*

He forced his eyes back open and relaxed again. She was still there. *Need to tell her.* He blinked hard.

'I was just pressing the call button. I'm here, Griff.' He frowned, and she frowned back. 'That's your name. Griffin Davenport.'

30

He shook his head, surprised when it moved. He'd been stuck . . . frozen for so long. He hadn't thought he'd ever find his way out. His eyes teared up and he blinked hard. *Shit.*

But she was there to wipe away the wetness with her fingertips. He reached up with the arm that moved – the other one had tubes in it – and gripped her wrist when she would have moved her hand from his face. Again she smiled, and it was sweet. *So damn sweet.*

She stroked his forehead and he fought to keep his eyes open. 'I'm not going to leave you, Griff. Not just yet anyway. At some point I have to leave so I can sleep. But I'll be back.'

He frowned again and shook his head. *Not Griffin. Not Griff. My name is Decker.*

'I wish I didn't have to sleep, too,' she said with a little laugh. 'But I have to.'

He rested back against the bed, frustrated. Too exhausted to do more than stare at her.

She narrowed her eyes. 'Wait. What were you shaking your head about?' She looked up and over toward the door. 'He's awake. And calm.'

Seconds later a nurse was at his side, smiling at him. 'So he is.'

Kate looked back down at him, brows arched. 'And he's not planning to yank out the tube. Right, Agent Davenport?'

Decker wanted to snarl, but he couldn't even do that. *Goddammit.* It was almost better in the dark. *No, it wasn't.*

The nurse was busy fussing over him, but Kate stayed, her eyes never leaving his. 'You've been here a week,' she said. 'They will take out this tube. Right, Nurse?'

'Absolutely,' the nurse assured him.

He didn't need the nurse to say so. He trusted Kate and tried to tell her so. She gave him a little nod and another smile, so he must have communicated something right.

'Keep talking to him, Agent Coppola. You're keeping him stable and calm, and that's a good thing. I'll get the doctor in as soon as possible.'

Kate grasped his hand as soon as the nurse was finished with him. 'They had to put you into a coma for a week. The bullet did a

31

lot of things that I'm too tired to try to pronounce, but basically it messed up your lung. If they'd left you to heal on your own, it would have hurt like a motherfucker every time you drew a breath. So, the coma. Got it?'

He blinked. *Keep talking, honey*, he thought. *You're doin' fine.*

'You had a chest tube, which they took out, but the ventilator is still breathing for you. As soon as they're sure you can breathe on your own, they'll take out this tube too. Don't worry.'

He wasn't. Not about that. But he *was* worried about something. What was it?

Right. The kids. What about the kids?

Dammit. He couldn't remember. He couldn't remember and it was important.

'Sshh.' Kate squeezed his hand and stroked his forehead with her free hand. 'You just tensed up again. I need you to stay calm. If they think you're about to go all batshit on them, they'll knock you out again. One, I don't think you'll like that, and two, I need you to be able to talk to me. I gotta know what's on those CDs that's so important.'

Yes. Kids. On the CD. His hand went for the tube again and she tightened her grip.

'Oh come on, Griffin. Really? Do not make me get tough with you. I guarantee you won't like it.' She pushed on his hand until it was flat on the sheet. 'That's better. I get that you want to talk about the CD. Once the doc comes in, we'll figure out a system. I promise.'

He relaxed. She'd promised. *Hurry, Doc. Please.*

Cincinnati, Ohio,
Thursday 13 August, 12.15 A.M.

The ringing of a phone woke Mallory out of a sound sleep, but she was okay with that because she'd been having bad dreams of men with sausage-sized fingers chasing her around the grocery store. Peering at the clock on her nightstand, she shuddered, her skin all clammy with sweat. It was only midnight. Plenty of time to go back to sleep and dream some more. *Yay, me.*

But wait. The phone had rung and it had been answered. After midnight. Blinking hard, she comprehended the significance of this, because he subscribed strictly to the 'nine to nine' adage. No calls before nine in the morning or after nine at night. Any other calls were not answered, the numbers blocked for supreme rudeness. Except for his two sisters, of course. Their calls he answered, but he still got angry with them for calling after nine.

Nell, his older sister, tended to be more respectful, calling him only in the worst of emergencies. Gemma, on the other hand, routinely called whenever she wanted, no matter how early or late. He always answered, though, because she might be calling about Macy.

Because he'd given Macy to Gemma to legally adopt, to raise as her own child. But Mallory he'd kept. Kept and used and abused until she had no hope of rescue.

Gemma usually called him for help when Macy was sick, which had been a lot in the very beginning, but not so much nowadays. It had always been in his best interests to keep Mallory's baby sister healthy and safe, because it was only his threat to take custody of Macy and turn her into the next Sunshine Suzie that kept Mallory in line.

At first Mallory had thought that Gemma would be an ally, that his little sister would want to save Macy. She thought Gemma would listen when she told her what he'd done to her. What lay in store for Macy. What lay in store for Gemma herself, because for him to get custody of Macy now, something terrible would have to happen to Gemma.

Like she'd have to die. He'd kill his own sister. He'd bragged to Mallory about how he'd do it – which would be the same way he'd killed Mallory and Macy's mother.

But Gemma hadn't believed Mallory back then. Instead she had tattled, telling him exactly what Mallory had told her.

Things had not gone well after that for Mallory. He had brutally taught her the price of honesty. And that had been the moment she'd lost all hope of ever being free again.

But this call came far later than Gemma usually called, and it had been answered, so it was most likely business. Mallory carefully climbed out of the princessy poster bed he'd bought for her when she'd first come to live with him and picked her way across the hardwood floor, taking care to avoid the boards she knew creaked.

She pressed her ear to her door. He was downstairs, so she could only hear a murmur. If she opened her bedroom door and he heard her . . . Well, she hadn't been beaten in a while, so at least he wouldn't be thrashing into fresh cuts. But calls after midnight were never good, and Mallory decided the risk of discovery was outweighed by the foreknowledge of what he'd throw her way next, because allowing him to catch her by surprise always ended badly.

She grabbed an empty plastic bottle from her dresser, thinking she could pretend she was filling it with water from the bathroom sink if she was heard creeping about.

She slid the door open until the gap was just wide enough for her to slip through, and tiptoed past Roxy's bedroom. The door was closed, but it didn't matter either way. Roxy wasn't going to tell a soul that Mallory was up. Roxy could barely draw breath anymore. She needed a hospital, but he wouldn't allow it. His wife would die at home.

But not because he cared. Just because he was afraid someone would find out the truth. Poor Roxy. She'd been trapped in this life, same as Mallory.

But Mallory couldn't spare the distraction of compassion. If he heard her . . . well, she'd beat Roxy to the afterlife. And some days Mallory yearned for that. If it weren't for Macy, she would have sent herself into the afterlife a long time ago. Because that was the only way she was getting out of here.

She tiptoed past the guest bedrooms. All were empty at present, but they'd been tidied and prepared for the next round of . . . *victims*. The very word made her queasy, but that made it no less true. The rooms were decorated out of every kid's dreams, but would become the core of their nightmares. And that would happen soon unless Mallory thought of a plan to stop him.

'When?' he was asking sharply. 'When did he wake up?'

From her vantage point at the top of the stairs she could see him for only a few seconds at a time as he paced the living room.

'Did you take care of him?' he demanded. 'I don't give a shit if J. Edgar Hoover himself came back from the dead and is sitting there guarding him. Get rid of him before he has that tube pulled out. However you need to.' He growled low in his throat and Mallory backed up a step, her hand over her mouth to keep herself from squeaking in alarm. But he hadn't seen her and continued to pace. 'Do I *care* if you're off duty? Get back in there and *fix* this or *you'll* have a breathing tube down *your* throat.'

Carefully she backed away, slipping into her bedroom while he was still yelling downstairs at whoever had been so foolish as to disobey his direct order. *At least he's not setting up any dates for me. Or video shoots.* Which wouldn't have been for her, so that was something at least. One benefit of growing too old. If he'd been setting up a video shoot, her timetable to save the four kids she'd seen on Saturday would have had to be moved up considerably.

Forcing her into action that would end up with her dead. She really did not like that plan.

Mallory got into bed and stared at the ceiling, thinking about what she'd heard. Specifically how she could utilize the information, because this could be the break she'd been praying for.

Whoever was about to get 'taken care' of was probably in a hospital, because tubes were going to be pulled out. She'd watched enough TV to know that. But what had grabbed her attention was his mention of J. Edgar Hoover. She'd watched enough TV to know that name too.

Hoover used to be the boss of the FBI. Her heartbeat took off on a little burst of speed. Did that mean that the FBI was involved? Were they watching him? Had he sounded so angry because he was scared? He never sounded scared. Well, not often. It had been almost a year since she'd heard fear in his voice. She'd prayed then, too, but nothing had happened and life had gone on.

But if the FBI was involved . . . The implications left her downright dizzy. That meant someone suspected him. *And that someone will believe me this time.* That alone was enough to make her want to cry, but she'd learned long ago not to cry at night. Or any other time.

Oh Mallory. The whisper in her head was his, and she hated it. *No one will ever believe you.*

That's not true. Whoever suspected him would. *I just have to find him. Or her.*

Oh Mallory, Mallory, Mallory. You mean the 'someone' who's guarding 'someone' else in a hospital 'somewhere'? You mean all those names you don't know and whose locations you don't know – and don't have the first idea of where to even start looking?

Mallory clenched her jaw. *Yes. That's exactly what I mean.* That 'someone' was exactly who she had to find. She would figure out where to look. She would.

She couldn't use his computer, because he monitored everything. He'd put a block on nearly every website. She could use a recipe website when it was her night to cook. Any site related to news or current events, though . . . all were blocked.

But she'd find a way. Because if someone believed her it meant that someone would stop him. *Somebody other than me.* Which meant that she might not have to die trying.

Cincinnati, Ohio,
Thursday 13 August, 6.30 A.M.

'Good God, woman. What happened to you?'

Decker woke abruptly, eyes flying open to see a man in the doorway. Blinking hard, he wondered if he was awake or still asleep, or maybe even back on the morphine drip and having hallucinations, because the man looked . . . strange. Bright white hair stood in sharp little peaks all over his head, but he wasn't old. He looked like he was Decker's age.

Which was thirty-four. He stopped to do a quick mental check, pleased when his mind was clear, the information readily accessible. Yeah, that was right. He'd just had a birthday a few weeks ago. *Alone.* Because he'd been undercover then, and Gene Decker's birthday was in April.

He steered his mind back to the weird man in the doorway. The guy's goatee was also white, as were the eyebrows arched high over

36

the wraparound sunglasses he wore. Inside. They *were* inside, right? Decker's eyes darted upward. *Ceiling, check.* Yeah, they were inside. *So what the hell?* The guy's fists were on his hips, his mouth grim.

Decker blinked a few more times. The guy was still there.

A throaty chuckle came from the chair on the other side of his bed, accompanied by quiet clacking. *Kate. Good. She's still here too.*

'Yeah, Griff, he's real. You're awake again. You've met him before, actually, the night you got shot. This is Special Agent Deacon Novak. He made sure you didn't bleed out before the medics showed up. Deacon, stop scowling at me and show Griffin your manners.'

Deacon. Decker had heard the name. He searched his mind, pleased once again that his brain made a quick, painless connection. Kate had talked about him before, when the other lady was with her. When he'd still been trapped in the dark.

He frowned. But Kate had also said, *I'm sorry, Jack.* Who the hell was Jack?

He put Jack on the growing list of the things he'd ask Kate as soon as they took out the damn tube. Why hadn't they? She'd promised they would. He started to tense, then made himself relax. She'd tell him why, but for the moment he was lucid enough to know he couldn't pull it out himself. That would be bad.

Agent Novak came to stand at the side of his bed and Decker squinted up at him. Yeah, he remembered him. Kind of. Except that he had a weird memory of . . . eyes. But that couldn't have been real. That had to have been the morphine. Morphine hallucinations were the worst.

Novak nodded at him now. 'Agent Davenport. I'm glad to see you're coming around.'

Slowly Decker lifted his hand, shocked at how hard it was to do so. A week? It felt like he'd been asleep for a month. He tapped the corner of his eye and Novak's mouth quirked up in a smirk, but he complied and took off the sunglasses.

Shit. Decker flinched back against his pillow, earning him another chuckle from Kate. Those eyes were freaky. Like cat eyes, but bi-colored. Blue and brown. Both of them.

He remembered the eyes staring down at him as a voice demanded that he not die. He seriously thought they'd been part of the morphine hallucinations. *Hell.*

'Luckily, Agent Novak uses his witchy eyes for good and not evil. Mostly.'

Novak sneered at her. 'This coming from the woman that looks like something the cat dragged in. Or maybe even threw up. What the fuck, Kate? Dani said you weren't taking care of yourself, but I didn't think it was this bad. For God's sake, get the hell back to your hotel and go to sleep.'

Don't you yell at her! Decker had to curb the urge to rip out his breathing tube and shove it down Novak's throat. Novak couldn't even see Decker's killer glare because he was staring across the bed at Kate, wearing a killer glare of his own.

The clacking started back up and Decker cautiously turned his head to see what it was. *Ah. Knitting.* She was sitting in the chair knitting something that was green and brown and . . . *Camo,* he realized. It was patterned just like his combat uniform back in the army. He added a question about that to his list, then lifted his gaze to her face.

She did look tired. But her face was still the only one he wanted to see.

'Are you finished yelling?' Kate asked Deacon mildly. 'Because if you're not, I suggest you finish your tirade in your indoor voice. It's not like we're, y'know, in ICU or anything.'

Deacon's cheeks grew red. 'Dammit, Kate,' he whispered loudly. 'You're going to make yourself sick. Get your things. I'll take you to your hotel myself, right now.'

'No.'

'No?' he echoed in disbelief. 'Then come home with me.'

Decker had stiffened in protest, but he calmed at Kate's next words.

'I'm sure your fiancée would have something to say about that.'

'Yeah, well, Faith said to tell you that you're welcome to stay as long as you want. We have a spare room and she wants to get to know you. Come on, Kate,' he wheedled.

'I'll go back to my hotel when they take his tube out. I promised him I'd stay.'

Decker felt a satisfaction that crossed well over the border into territorial, then frowned. She'd also promised that they'd come up with a system to communicate, but they hadn't done that. *Because I fell back asleep*, he realized. *Dammit*. He hadn't told her any of the things he needed to.

That his name was Decker, not Griff.

Oh shit. The kids. He tapped the rail weakly, but Kate heard him over her clacking, which stopped. In seconds she was leaning over the rail, her fingertips brushing his forehead again.

Yes. That. Don't stop that. She gave him an amused smile. *Don't stop that either*. He liked to see her smile.

'I'm sorry. I had to be mad at Deacon for a minute. I guess you want to know why you still have the tube in. You were too tired last night to pass the breathing-on-your-own test. You fell asleep halfway through.' She gave him a long-suffering look. 'Probably because you wore yourself out by trying to yank out the tube yourself.'

He narrowed his eyes at her and she laughed softly. 'You'll get your chance at a witty comeback later today. The doc said he'd be back mid-morning and he'd try again. Until then, you ready to try blinking your way to communication? Once for yes and—'

He blinked hard once, interrupting her, and she laughed again. 'Okay. I guess that's a yes. Deacon, did you make those charts I asked for?'

'Yep.' Novak slid a backpack off his shoulder and searched inside it.

'In case you're confused about who works where,' she said, 'Agent Novak and I used to work together when we were assigned in Baltimore. Now we're both here in Cincinnati, but he's attached to a CPD joint task force. I work the Bureau's task force on human trafficking. I'm here to follow up on the traffickers you spent the last three years with. My new partner is Agent Troy, and I know he'll want to talk to you too. We need associates, suppliers, customers. I've been listening to your recordings hoping to follow the money trail. Novak is here because he was on the team that identified your traffickers and brought them in. He needs answers to a few questions so that he can close out his report. I imagine he's also here because he saved your life, so he's invested. Oh, and he came to yell at me.'

'Damn straight on that last one,' Novak muttered as he unrolled a piece of paper the size of a small poster to reveal an alphabet chart with an image of a QWERTY keyboard below it.

'We can do this a couple ways,' she said. 'You can write with a pen, but that will tire you out and you might have to sleep before you tell us everything you want to say. Tomorrow or even later today – once they take that tube out – you'll feel strong enough to write.'

She spoke as if she had experience with this. Another question added to his list.

'Or,' she said, 'we can scribe for you. You can point to the letters and we'll record. When your arm gets too tired, Deacon will point to the letters, you blink, and I'll record. However we do this, it's gonna be slow, so be patient with us, okay?'

Decker blinked once.

'Good,' Kate said. 'I have a few yes/no questions before we begin. First, is your name Griffin Davenport? It seemed to bother you last night when I called you that.'

He blinked once, then moved his shoulders experimentally in a shrug. Which hurt. But not as badly as he'd expected.

'Yes, but?' Kate said, and he blinked again. She held up her pencil and he shook his head, relieved when the room didn't spin as it had the night before. He raised his right hand, wiggled his fingers, then brought them together in an O. 'You can't use your right hand? Oh, you're a leftie? Which is of course the hand that they've turned into a pincushion,' she added wryly. 'Okay, then. Keyboard?'

He blinked, and Novak held the paper so that he could reach it. *DECKER*. He pointed to each letter and watched her frown.

'Gene Decker was your undercover name,' she said. 'Decker's your real name, too?'

NCK.

'It's a nickname,' Deacon guessed, and Decker blinked hard.

40

'Must have made being undercover a little easier if you were using a familiar name.'

He blinked once, then looked up at Kate, brows cocked.

She smiled at him. 'Decker, then. Do you remember the night you were shot?'

He did, in blindingly clear detail. *God*. He'd expected to hate the people he'd been sent to expose. They were drug runners after all, transporting and distributing cocaine, heroin, and OxyContin up the I-75 corridor from Miami to Detroit. But it was way worse than that. They'd branched out, selling people in addition to drugs. People. *Children*.

He hadn't just hated them. He'd wanted to eviscerate each and every one of them, then hang them by their innards. But he'd had to play nice. Had to mitigate what evil he could without blowing his cover. Had to act like he fucking *admired* them.

'Hey,' Kate murmured. 'Your heart just took off like a rocket. Maybe we need to wait until later for this.'

He blinked twice. Hard. Then closed his eyes and willed himself to relax. She stroked his forehead again and relaxing became much easier.

'What?' Kate asked sharply. He opened his eyes to see her and Novak glaring at each other.

Novak shrugged. 'I didn't say anything.' But he wanted to, Decker could tell.

He waited until Novak looked down at him to narrow his eyes. *Back off, boy.*

Novak grimaced. 'Wow,' he said sarcastically. 'I didn't need any blinks or letters to understand that, Davenport. Message received, loud and clear. Ceasing and desisting.'

Decker had time to nod before a nurse came through the door and pushed Novak aside. 'You two have to leave,' she said, forgoing any preamble. 'You're upsetting my patient.'

Novak pulled his badge from his pocket, but the nurse waved it away. 'I know who you are,' she said, not budging an inch. 'Who you both are. And I don't care. You have to go.'

Decker's shoulders came off the mattress in mute protest,

but Kate gently pushed him back down while the nurse took his vitals.

'Ma'am,' Kate said quietly. 'He's a federal agent with something he needs to share. If you make us go, he'll become more agitated. Let him get it out and we'll go so he can rest. All right?'

The nurse frowned at all of them. 'I know he's a federal agent *out there*, but *in here* he's my patient, and I'm here to make sure he survives to get back *out there*.' She huffed a frustrated sigh. 'Five minutes, and that's only because he's managed to calm himself down. But if his pulse rises again, I'll throw you both out if I have to drag you out myself, and don't you think I can't. I raised four sons who were as big as Mr Davenport here. I have skills you do *not* want to experience for yourselves. Am I clear?'

'Yes, ma'am,' Kate said respectfully, her lips curving in a genuine smile. 'Thank you for making him your priority. We won't make you throw us out.'

'All right then,' the nurse grumbled. 'I'll tell his doctor he's awake.'

Novak looked over his shoulder to make sure she was gone, then rolled his eyes at Kate. 'Suck-up,' he muttered.

'Yeah, and who bought us five more minutes, huh, hotshot? You don't fuck with the nurses. They will *own* your ass.' She met Decker's eyes. 'And you, mister, you keep it together. We'll talk about the night you were shot later. For now, what am I looking for on the CDs?'

The CD. The kids. Decker closed his eyes for a moment, trying to remember where and when he'd heard that. He sequenced locations and dates until he figured it out. *Okay, right.* Opening his eyes, he began jabbing at letters the moment Novak put the chart within his reach.

TU AUG 4. He paused a second. *7 8 9 PM?*

'Tuesday, August fourth?' Novak asked when he was finished. 'So somewhere between seven and nine that evening?'

Decker nodded, dropping his hand back to his side.

'That was the day before you were shot,' Kate said. 'Hold on.' He shifted his body so that he could watch as she turned away, but then she bent over to retrieve a bag under her chair and Decker's mind temporarily shorted out.

Kate Coppola had a *very* nice ass and her slacks were just snug enough to show it off. Hunger rose within him, feral and blistering hot, and the fingers of his free hand flexed and tightened into a fist as he imagined touching her, praying that she'd let him.

'Watch it, asshole,' Novak warned next to his ear in a near-silent growl.

I am, Decker thought, following every move Kate made. *Don't you worry 'bout that.*

Novak's fingers grabbed his chin none too gently, forcing him to look away from Kate and up at him. 'She's not yours,' he mouthed silently.

Decker lifted his brows, returning the man's stare. *Not yet.*

Novak's glare became glacial. He released Decker's chin and straightened to a rather impressive height only seconds before Kate returned with a plain canvas bag with a picture of kittens and a ball of yarn printed on the side. 'My knitting,' she explained, setting it on the mattress beside him. 'What now?' she asked Novak, exasperation in her tone.

Novak shook his head. 'Your knitting bag's not very secure,' he grunted.

She blinked, surprised by his tone, not understanding that Novak's sour attitude was directed at Decker. 'No less secure than my computer bag. I kept both bags secure.'

'Unless you'd fallen asleep in that chair,' Novak snapped.

'Shut up.' Kate shot Novak a quelling look that left Decker feeling smug, then pulled out a ball of camo-green yarn from the bag with one hand and dug around with the other. 'I have five CDs with me. Hopefully it's one of these. I've already listened to Outer Office I, II, and III.' She produced the CDs in the sleeves in which he'd stored them and held them up, one at a time. 'Outer Office IV? Kitchen? Garage? Master Bedroom? Home Office?'

He blinked hard and she put the four rejects back under her yarn. 'Home Office, then. I'll check it ASAP. Now Novak and I are going to let you rest.'

Decker grabbed her arm when she moved to leave and, ignoring Novak's growl of disapproval, tapped her wrist where a watch would be if she wore one. 'What time is it now?' she asked, and he shook his head. Her eyes registered understanding. 'When will I come back?'

He let go of her arm with a nod.

'It'll be a few hours,' she said.

'At least,' Novak grunted. 'She's going back to her hotel to sleep. Right, Kate?'

Her mouth tightened in annoyance. 'Yes. God. But first we are going to find out what's on the damn CD, okay, Novak? We'll get the info to Zimmerman and then I'll go to sleep.' Her jaw clenched when Novak didn't respond. 'Back off, Deacon,' she said very quietly, and Decker could only hope she never used that tone on him. 'I don't know what bug has crawled up your ass, but evict it. Now.'

Novak nodded, lips thinly pursed. 'Got it. You ready to go?'

'Wait for me at the elevator, please. I'll be right out. *Go*,' she barked when Novak didn't immediately move. 'Our five minutes are almost up.'

Novak left without a backward glance, and Kate looked at Decker, still annoyed. 'I don't know what that was about, but I suspect you do.'

Decker widened his eyes and blinked innocently, but she wasn't fooled.

She rolled her eyes. 'I had four brothers, ace. Don't even try.'

Had? Who was Jack? He had too many questions, but only one answer that was important at the moment. He grabbed the chart Novak had left behind and began to point. *KIDS*. Then he pointed to the CD in her hand and watched her pale, the freckles on her nose standing out in stark contrast.

'What kids?' she asked urgently.

He shrugged helplessly, because he didn't know their names. He didn't know who had them. He only knew two things – first, that they were in danger. He tapped her wrist again, then, with his forefinger, he mimicked the ticking of the hand of a clock.

44

'Whoever they are, their time is running out,' she said grimly.

He nodded, closing his eyes. *That was the second thing.* He'd done what he could for now. He was going to have to trust her to take the baton and run with it. For now, at least.

He heard her gathering her things, then felt her fingertips on his face, stroking down the side of the mask, sending a shiver racing across his skin. 'Rest now,' she murmured.

He opened his eyes, staring up at her stubbornly, and one side of her mouth lifted. 'Yeah, I get it. You don't want to rest. You want to be out there, doing your job. Tough shit. For now anyway,' she added when he narrowed his eyes. 'The doctor said that once they get you off the ventilator, you'll bounce back pretty quickly. A week, tops. You'll get up and you'll walk out and you'll go back to work. But not today. Today your job is to pass the breathing tests so that the doctor takes out that tube. I'll be back later when I have something to tell you.'

He traced a cross over his heart, clumsily, and the other side of her mouth lifted.

'Yeah, I promise.' She cupped the side of his face, sliding her fingers into his hair, and he wanted to sigh. But he couldn't, so he gripped her wrist lightly and turned his head into her hand. Heard her breath catch. But she didn't pull away. Not for another few seconds that he greedily hoarded, not knowing when she'd be back.

Someone cleared a throat from the direction of the door.

'The nurse is giving me the evil eye, so I'll say goodbye for now.' Tugging her hand free, she wrote a phone number below the printed keyboard before folding the paper and slipping it into his hand. 'That's my cell. Call me if you need me, but rest now.'

Cincinnati, Ohio,
Thursday 13 August, 6.30 A.M.

Dr Meredith Fallon loved her peeps. But she respected them almost as much, if not more. The women she called her friends had been through the crucible, had come out so damn strong. But their strength was tempered with compassion and a commitment to making the world a better place for everyone around them. Not a selfish heart in the bunch.

Unless it came to pancakes, especially when Bailey Beardsley wielded the spatula. Then it was every girl for herself. At the moment eight women were crowded around the prep island in Bailey's country-style kitchen, arguing about what filling should go in this morning's batch.

Meredith stayed out of it, preferring to watch her friends interacting from the quiet comfort of the Beardsleys' kitchen table while she sipped from a large mug of coffee.

'Are they always like that?'

Meredith turned to the young woman sitting next to her, flashing her a quick grin. This was Audrey O'Bannion's first introduction to Meredith's growing circle of friends. Meredith had met Audrey through Dr Faith Corcoran and Detective Scarlett Bishop. Faith had joined Meredith's counseling practice nine months earlier and Scarlett worked with Faith's fiancée, Deacon.

Audrey and Faith were step-cousins, their family tree just a little bit warped. *Okay. Really warped*, Meredith allowed, because Scarlett was now dating Audrey's oldest brother. Meredith, Faith, and Scarlett had taken Audrey under their collective wing.

The O'Bannions were wealthy, but Audrey struck Meredith as incredibly lost. She'd already been arrested three times for her involvement in protests ranging from animal rights to the plight of the homeless. She also worked tirelessly to raise funds for those causes, so she did good things. Still, she seemed rudderless. And so lonely.

Meredith was all about changing the lonely. 'They're just having fun,' she told Audrey. 'At least there's no wine involved. Movie night with wine? Choosing which flick we were going to watch once took three hours. By then I'd run out of wine and all their men had come to get them.'

Audrey's smile was small, but real. 'That sounds like fun, too. Maybe more fun than the actual movie. Do you always meet here, at Bailey's house?'

'Movie nights are at my place, but breakfasts are always here because Bailey is an awesome cook. In fact, Bailey and I are step-cousins too, just like you and Faith. Bailey's stepsister, Alex, is my cousin. Bailey and Alex grew up near Atlanta, but Alex came to live with my family when her mother . . . well, she was murdered.'

Audrey's smile faded. 'How horrible,' she whispered.

Meredith knew Audrey understood, because her younger brother had been murdered nine months before and she'd nearly lost both of her older brothers just a week ago. There was a lot of pain happening behind Audrey's polished facade. Which was why Meredith had mentioned it. Audrey needed to know that she wasn't alone.

'It was horrible,' Meredith said. 'For Bailey, too, because she loved Alex's mom. You would never guess it to look at her now, but Bailey became an addict. Heroin.' Meredith nodded at Audrey's shocked gasp. 'Alex went back to Atlanta a few years back to help Bailey and her daughter, Hope. Alex fell for a cop down there and stayed. Bailey met her husband, Ryan, down there too, but she needed a new start after finishing rehab, so they came up here to live with me until they got this house. Bailey finished her nursing degree and is now a substance abuse counselor. She works for Wendi Cullen, the blonde who's currently shoving berries into her mouth like a rabid squirrel. Sometimes it's hard to believe Wendi is the director of a halfway house for adolescent girls and not one of the residents. But the girls love her.'

Audrey chuckled. 'Wendi is why I'm here, right? Her halfway house needs funds.'

'No, sweetie. *You're* why you're here. I think you'll like this group of ladies. We're an amazing support system.' Something Audrey desperately needed. 'You should totally hang out with us. Second Thursday is breakfast, fourth Wednesday is movies. You're invited.'

Audrey eyed Meredith with wary gratitude. 'Thank you. But when you invited me to breakfast you said the house Wendi uses was being taken away from her and she needs funds for another property.'

'Her house is getting knocked down, actually. It's targeted for demolition in six weeks – a new road's going through. But we can't afford to lose the services she provides.'

'She takes in young women who've been forced into prostitution. She gives them a safe, nurturing environment where they can heal and be reintegrated into the community.'

Meredith was impressed. 'Somebody did their homework.'

'I always do when I'm asked to do a fund-raiser,' Audrey said a trifle defensively.

'Then that explains why you're so successful at it.' Meredith smiled and watched Audrey's ire visibly recede. 'I get the feeling that people underestimate you, and dismiss you as flighty or silly or maybe even dumb. I won't be one of those people.'

'Thank you. But I read Wendi's bio, that she was a victim too. That her abuser took obscene photos of her and distributed them back in the early days of the Internet. I'm impressed that she's made something so positive out of something so horrific. I want to help with that.'

'And we will gladly take your help. We really wanted you to join our group, but you kept blowing off our invitations. And don't tell me that you're busy. We're *all* busy. Faith, Wendi, Bailey, and I are all counselors or therapists. Dani's a doctor. Delores runs an animal shelter. Corinne is a college student and interns with me, doing art therapy with the really little ones. And Scarlett and Kendra are cops, so they only join us when they're off duty.'

Truth be told, Scarlett Bishop hadn't joined them very often at all, even when she'd been off duty, and the few times she had, her guard had been up, as if she'd been afraid to show her true self. That Scarlett had shown up this morning had been a very pleasant surprise. That she was openly laughing with the others was a development that made Meredith's heart happy – and one she attributed directly to the detective's new relationship with Audrey's oldest brother, Marcus. *Whatever you're doing, Marcus, keep it up. Please.*

Kendra's presence, while not a surprise, was troubling because she wasn't laughing with the others. And she kept throwing furtive glances at Meredith over her shoulder when she thought no one was looking. Something was wrong.

'Is Kendra a detective too?' Audrey asked.

'Oh no, not yet. She's just out of the academy. She and Wendi are sisters, by the way.'

Audrey blinked, but her good manners allowed her to say only, 'Oh?'

Meredith chuckled, because Wendi was five-two, blond, and rail-thin, while Kendra was nearly six feet tall and muscular, her skin ebony. 'Foster sisters,' she explained. 'They love getting a reaction, so when they tell you, pretend to be surprised again, okay?'

'O-kay. So . . . should I bring wine to movie night?'

'Sure, but nothing too expensive. It just has to taste good with chocolate.'

Kendra abruptly broke away from the larger group to join them at the table. 'I didn't get a chance to say hi and welcome, Audrey. So hi.' She smiled. 'And welcome.' She put the bowl of berries on the table. 'Wendi was gonna make herself sick. Woman needs a frickin' keeper.'

Meredith popped a berry into her mouth. 'You do a good job of it, Kendra.'

Kendra smiled fondly. 'I know. I've had a lot of practice.' Then her smile dimmed. 'I have a small confession. I came specifically today because there's something I wanted to talk to you about, Mer, if it's okay. I didn't mean to interrupt if you two are talking serious stuff. I waited until it sounded like you were done.'

'No,' Audrey said with a genuine smile. 'You two talk. I think I'll dive into the fray.'

Meredith waited until Audrey had joined the noisy group around the island, then turned to Kendra, quickly sobering because she looked upset. 'What's up, hon?'

Kendra opened her mouth. Closed it. She looked down at her clenched fists. 'I've been having fantasies. About doing things to perpetrators. Especially the ones who do the sex crimes.'

Oh. Poor Kenny. 'Violent things?' Meredith murmured.

Kendra nodded grimly. 'Oh yeah. So violent that if I admitted them to anyone in the department, I'd be in a shrink's office so fast my head would spin. I'd end up on traffic detail for the rest of my life. I'm a little scared myself. I have a trigger temper sometimes.'

49

She turned beseeching eyes to Meredith. 'I don't want to ruin my career. I don't want to end up in jail. I should say I don't want to hurt anyone, but I can't make myself go that far.'

'I'd have called you a liar if you had,' Meredith said mildly. 'I want to strangle them with my bare hands, eviscerate them and feed them their own guts. I want them to die a thousand painful deaths for every child whose life they've ruined. I'm glad I don't have direct access to the DMV license plate database. It would be too serious a temptation to get their addresses.'

Kendra almost hid a double-take and Meredith knew she'd hit a nerve. 'You always seem so . . . level. Even when you're talking about eviscerating people. You're . . . serene.'

Meredith laughed softly. It was a common misconception. 'No. I'm not. I'm really not. But I don't dwell on those violent thoughts, either. That's one of the reasons I'm so diligent about social gatherings like this. If I'm busy and if my heart is happy, there isn't room for the anger. I have a lot of anger, so I make, keep, and cultivate a lot of friends. Keeps me grounded. I also exercise. Do yoga. Meditate. If you want, I can give you tips.'

'God, would you?' Kendra looked grateful – and so young. She was normally such an old soul that Meredith sometimes forgot that she was barely old enough to legally drink.

'Absolutely. Let's compare calendars after breakfast. Which smells like it's about ready.'

They were all serving themselves, buffet style, when Bailey's husband came into the kitchen, dressed in a suit and tie. He snuck a pancake, rolling it up to eat with his fingers like a burrito.

'Ryan!' Bailey gave him an exasperated look. 'Get a plate.'

'Can't.' He dropped a kiss on her mouth. 'Gotta run. I'm late. Hope's still asleep.' He looked over at Delores. 'Angel's lying at the foot of her bed, if you wonder where she went.'

Angel was Delores's huge dog – it looked to be a wolfhound crossed with a Great Dane with a bit of St Bernard thrown in. The dog also doubled as a security blanket and bodyguard after a killer had left Delores for dead. She rarely went anywhere without Angel.

Delores looked dismayed. 'I'm sorry. I didn't know she'd wandered upstairs. I'll go and get her right now.'

'You'll do no such thing,' Ryan said gently. He was a big man, a former army chaplain, and he always struck Meredith as incredibly gentle. 'She's keeping Hope company.' He glanced at Bailey meaningfully. 'We have to get her one. You know that.' He looked back at Delores. 'Hope's been asking for a dog for a long time. She's nine now – that's old enough to take care of one, so I think we'll be visiting your shelter soon.'

Bailey rolled her eyes, but it was with affection. 'You just want it for yourself.'

He grinned. 'Not untrue. Blame your in-laws for that. I have to get to work. Love you.'

'Love you too.' Bailey smiled when he stole another pancake and blew a kiss to the women as they *awwwed* in unison. 'That man is as big a kid as Hope. My sister and her husband visited from Georgia a few weeks ago and brought their basset hound. Ryan and Daniel took Hope to the park and threw a ball with that dog for hours. Now all Hope talks about is dogs.'

'I've got a few you'll like,' Delores said. 'Well trained and low maintenance.'

'How many animals do you have?' Wendi asked Delores once they'd all sat down.

'Thirteen cats and ten dogs, but only half of the dogs are adoptable right now. Why?'

'Well, assuming I find another house, I'm thinking of introducing a new vocational training program for our older girls,' Wendi said. 'We've already got a culinary training program and one for web design, but I think working with animals would be a good addition. The demand for vet techs is growing – and working with the dogs would be good therapy for all of our girls, no matter what they decide to do with their lives.'

'It sounds amazing,' Delores said. 'A win for everybody.' She hesitated. 'How is the house hunt coming along?'

Wendi shook her head. 'Not good. Any property that anybody wants to donate is one step away from being condemned, and I haven't found one with affordable rent – no place that's safe and nice. Or big enough. But I've still got six weeks, so it's a long way from over.'

From the corner of her eye Meredith saw Audrey's eyes narrow thoughtfully, but it was Scarlett Bishop who spoke first. 'Don't discount those properties too quickly. We can mobilize a fixer-upper crew. Marcus and his friend Diesel build houses for worthy causes. I'll ask them.'

Audrey nodded. 'And they're nice houses, too. We could do a fund-raiser for materials and furnishings. I've done them before. I know who to ask.'

'She does,' Dani confirmed. 'She has raised some serious cash for the free clinic.'

'And I may have a lead on a house for your girls,' Faith added. 'I've made a few calls, but I have some more work to do before I can give you details. It's a fixer-upper, but it's . . . well, it's got character. Don't get your hopes up just yet, but know that we're trying to help.'

Wendi's eyes lit up. 'God, anything you guys can do . . .' She choked up. 'Thank you.'

They spent the rest of the breakfast planning until Scarlett got a text. 'Sorry, girls,' she said as she pushed away from the table. 'Gotta roll.'

'Is everything all right?' Bailey asked, concerned.

'Yeah. It's work. My partner needs me to meet him.'

Meredith frowned. 'I thought you were still on medical leave.' Scarlett had bruised ribs from a case she'd worked the week before.

'I've been back on desk duty for a few days.' She rolled her eyes. 'Don't worry, Mom.'

Her departure broke up the meeting, and the group made quick work of the dishes, restoring Bailey's kitchen to rights before saying goodbye.

'Are you free tonight?' Kendra asked as she walked Meredith to her car. 'I'd like to get started on those anger management techniques as soon as I can. I can bring dinner.'

'I don't turn down food. Say around eight?' Meredith got out her phone to plug in the details, only to see that she too had received a text while she'd been in Bailey's kitchen. It was from Special Agent in Charge Zimmerman, who managed the local FBI field office, asking her to call him ASAP. She was normally contacted by CPD, not the FBI. *This should be interesting.*

'Eight is good,' Kendra said. 'I'll see you then.'

'Until then, do not let yourself give in to your anger.'

Kendra nodded. 'I'll try.'

'Try hard.'

Three

Cincinnati, Ohio,
Thursday 13 August, 8.50 A.M.

Kate had returned to her hotel room, but only long enough to shower and change her clothes before hurrying into the office. Now she understood Decker's urgency, his frantic need to tell someone. Had he been cognizant the whole time he was in a coma?

God, I hope not. To have the knowledge bouncing around in his head for a week and not be able to tell anyone? To know that children were in danger and be helpless to stop it? That he'd been able to calm himself the way he had was testament to a very strong will.

God. Kids. She'd given up asking how anyone could target children years ago. She just accepted the existence of pure evil masquerading as walking, talking, breathing human beings. And then did her damnedest to put them in a little box. Usually that box was a steel cage in a prison, but if it was a pine box six feet under so that they were never able to walk and talk among the innocents again? That was deeply satisfying, though it was nothing she'd ever tell anyone in the Bureau, because it'd have her ass in a shrink's office before she could blink. Although odds were good that the people she respected the most were thinking the same thing and also vowing to never tell anyone either.

The atmosphere in Special Agent in Charge Zimmerman's office was grim when she arrived, but she figured that her new boss had just cause. He'd had a really shitty week.

Zimmerman stood staring out the window, arms folded over his chest, his mouth tight and his expression drawn. She'd only known him for a week and this had been his expression at least eighty percent of the time. He'd lost two of his agents the week before, both shot by the traffickers. And that didn't include the near loss of Decker.

Kate had delivered notifications to many families over the course of her career, on behalf of both the FBI and the US Army. Each left her heart shredded, her soul drained. Zimmerman looked like that now, standing at the window. He'd get past it. *We all do, one way or another.*

At least the two fallen agents had family and friends to grieve them. If Decker had died, who would have grieved him? *I would have.* Because he'd hooked her attention the moment he'd looked up at her the week before, on the ground with her rifle in his back.

But last night, when those blue eyes had popped open, focusing on her face like she was his lifeline . . . he'd hooked her imagination at the very least. As for the rest, they'd have to see.

Deacon Novak had already arrived and was sitting at Zimmerman's small round table staring at his laptop, earbuds in his ears. He looked up at her, his impossible eyes unwitchy at the moment. They were weary and bleak and she hated to see it. She far preferred him sarcastic and irreverent.

He pulled the buds from his ears. 'I played it for him,' he said quietly.

Meaning Zimmerman, she understood. She and Deacon had listened to Decker's recording of August fourth while sitting in his SUV in the hospital parking lot. Silently Deacon had driven her to her car, no longer nagging that she should sleep when she said she'd meet him here in an hour.

'I figured that out myself,' she said, relieved when one side of his mouth quirked up.

'Smartass.'

Zimmerman turned then, heartache still written on his face, but his eyes were determined. 'The others will be here momentarily. We'll play it for them and come up with a plan of action. Have a seat, Kate. There's coffee in the pot and bagels if you're interested.'

She was interested. She'd felt nauseated when she'd first listened to the CD, but now she was hungry. Ravenous, actually. 'No to the coffee, but a bagel would hit the spot.'

Zimmerman gave her a look of horror that she wasn't entirely certain was in jest. 'You don't drink coffee? Are you human?'

She smiled at him. 'I drink coffee, but not after an all-nighter. I get too jittery.'

Deacon snickered. 'And then the human part comes into question. Especially if she's hungry, too.' He feigned fear, quailing when she lifted her brows at him. 'I'm just giving him fair warning that you can be . . . intimidating when you're hangry and sleep-deprived.'

Her tendency to become intimidating was a symptom of the ADHD that had gone undiagnosed until she'd been in the army for a year. That doctor had damn near saved her sanity. He'd certainly saved her military career. She'd been a bare step away from the very brig she guarded as one of the MPs.

Now she knew what to watch for. Don't get too tired. *Ha*. Don't get too stressed. *Double ha*. Don't let your sugar drop too low. And always have something to do with your hands. The first two came part and parcel with a career in law enforcement, but the final two she could and did manage pretty well.

Zimmerman sat next to Deacon, his own coffee cup full. 'It's okay. I get hangry, too. I keep an emergency stash of protein bars in my desk if you ever get desperate.'

'I usually do too, but thanks.' She got a bagel, then took the chair on the other side of Deacon, glancing at his screen to see that he'd been listening to Decker's audio file. 'I called Agent Troy on my way from the hospital to the hotel, so he'll be here. Who else is coming?'

'We are.' A woman Kate's height with a long black braid came through Zimmerman's door, followed by a man in his early fifties with thinning hair and a face that had been beautiful once, but to which age had not been terribly kind.

Detective Scarlett Bishop was Deacon's new partner in the joint task force with CPD, and Kate liked her very much. Scarlett was tough, but she had heart. And she had Deacon's back.

The man was Kate's new partner, Special Agent Luther Troy, and based on what she'd observed so far, she was going to like working with him, too. Troy was smart and funny, possessing a rapier-sharp wit that she'd already learned could cut deep or skillfully whittle. A wit that expressed itself as a verbal swagger that would have earned him a slap across the face from Kate's mother. Her father wouldn't have been that gentle, because Troy was a member of one of the many, many groups her father despised.

Troy had broached the topic himself when they'd initially been paired up the week before, looking her squarely in the eye. 'I'm gay,' he'd said. 'Is that going to be a problem for you? If so, tell me now. I need to be sure you've got my back.'

'Not for me,' had been her quick and truthful reply. 'You watch my back, I'll watch yours.'

He'd seemed mostly satisfied, but Kate had detected a hint of wary I'll-wait-and-see in the way he'd nodded. She supposed he'd had to be hyper-vigilant. Not fair, but it was reality, especially in law enforcement, where it was still a challenge to be anything other than a straight, white male.

Kate had to forcibly stop herself from running her tongue over her capped front tooth, a little souvenir of the time she'd voiced her disapproval of the blatant prejudice that had been the cornerstone of the house in which she'd grown up. To this day she wasn't sorry about what she'd said. She was only sorry she hadn't been fast enough to duck her father's fist. Or her mother's resounding slap across the face once she'd managed to pick herself up off the floor.

And you are thinking about them, why? Because she'd slipped when she'd told Decker that she'd grown up with four brothers. She'd been rattled at the wordless, hostile exchange between Deacon and Decker. She'd told Decker that she hadn't known what it was about, but she had. Tired, emotionally raw, and rattled, the fact that she had brothers had just . . . escaped. Word vomit.

She hated word vomit. She hated thinking about her family even more. *So don't. Think instead about the way Decker turned his face into your palm there at the end.* As if he'd been parched earth and her touch was rain.

She drew a deep breath, her pulse beginning to race. *No, don't think about that, either. Think about the two people that just sat down at the table who are giving you strange looks because you look like you've lost your fucking mind.*

'Good morning,' she said to both of them, proud that her voice gave away none of what she'd been thinking. 'Scarlett, you look like you feel better.' Part of the team that had apprehended the traffickers, Deacon's partner had bruised a few ribs in the process.

'I do. I can at least breathe again.' Scarlett put a plastic bowl full of cookies in the middle of the table. 'And I'm going insane on desk duty, so here y'go.'

Troy's eyes lit up. 'Tell me those are chocolate chip.'

Scarlett nodded. 'With pecans. Please eat them. I have another six dozen at home, just waiting to leap onto my butt and say "Honey, I'm home."'

Deacon had already dug into the bowl and sent it around the table. 'Nine months as partners and I just now find out she can bake. These are amazing.'

'Because I just got a new oven. It makes a huge difference,' Scarlett said, studying Kate intently as she spoke. 'How are *you*, Kate?'

'I found an apartment and arranged for my stuff to be moved, so I'm settling in.' It wasn't what Scarlett had meant, but Kate didn't want to go there. 'How is Marcus?'

Marcus O'Bannion was the publisher of the *Ledger*, one of the city's major newspapers. He'd been a critical resource in the apprehension of the traffickers – but in exactly what capacity, Kate wasn't entirely sure. She'd been surprised at how much he had known about an ongoing investigation – and that he'd been included in the final op. The man could totally handle himself around weapons, but he was a civilian – and a media person, which was even worse.

Deacon hadn't been terribly forthcoming with the details, which made Kate think they hadn't run the case exactly by the book. Scarlett wasn't talking either, but she'd fallen head over heels for Marcus so she was in no way an unbiased source of information. Marcus seemed like an honorable man, though, and Deacon trusted him. That meant a lot.

Whatever the case, Marcus had paid dearly for the exclusives that had covered the front pages of the *Ledger* for the last week. He'd lost too many people he'd loved when one of the traffickers went on a shooting spree at the *Ledger*'s main office.

'He went back to work today,' Scarlett said. 'It's better for him to be busy. He's had some trouble sleeping, but that seems to be getting better.' She'd looked like she wanted to ask if Kate had had trouble sleeping too, but had decided not to at the last minute.

Kate was grateful. She didn't need anyone else telling her how tired she looked.

Troy brushed the crumbs from his fingers, then leaned in to whisper, 'Bishop's being kind. I won't be. You look like shit, Coppola. Why aren't *you* sleeping?'

'Strange hotel bed,' she whispered back. 'I'm looking forward to sleeping in my own bed.'

Troy's brows rose in reluctant admiration. 'Wow. You lie really, really well. Now don't get me wrong – I count that as a benefit in a partner. Just don't lie to me.'

She sighed quietly. 'Bad dreams, okay? Backstory not relevant. I'll be all right.'

'Better,' he said. 'You tried to sneak in a zinger with the "I'll be all right" at the end, but nine points from the Russian judge for the effort.'

She had to laugh. 'Shut up,' she said with no heat.

'That I can do.' He turned his attention to Zimmerman, who was brushing his own crumbs away. 'Has everyone else heard this recording?' Troy asked him. 'I still haven't.'

'We're still waiting for two people,' Zimmerman said.

'One of them is finally here and very sorry that she's late. The sky just opened up as I was parking my car.' A redhead hurried in holding a dripping umbrella, her face flushed and dewy. Not sweaty, Kate noticed with a little envy. No freckles, no sweat. Porcelain skin. And dewy.

She had met Dr Meredith Fallon the week before, but only in passing. She knew the woman was a child psychologist and very well respected by Deacon's task force. And if she hadn't already known that, the look on Deacon's face at the moment would have been testament. It was admiration and . . . maybe even gratitude, which Kate didn't understand. Yet, anyway.

'Meredith,' Scarlett said, surprised. 'I didn't know you'd be coming.'

'I invited Dr Fallon,' Zimmerman said. 'Meredith, come in, sit down. I'm glad you could make it at all, considering I didn't give you much notice this morning.'

'Not a problem,' Fallon said with an easy smile. 'I was able to shift my first appointment to my partner. I'm glad you called me.'

'Deacon recommended you for this case. Have you met Agents Coppola and Troy?'

Meredith nodded. 'I met them briefly last week when they were interviewing the Bautista family.' Just one of the many families victimized by the traffickers with whom Decker had been embedded. 'The Bautistas send their regards, by the way. They were my first appointment and I stayed long enough to introduce them to my partner. They're in good hands with Faith.'

Kate blinked in surprise at that. 'Deacon's fiancée works with you?'

'She does indeed. Dr Corcoran brings a great deal of expertise in working with victims of sexual assault. I was lucky to convince her to join my practice.'

'Which means that Faith no longer works directly with the sex offenders,' Deacon said, his relief bare for all to see. Then one side of his mouth quirked up. 'Which means my hair won't go any whiter worrying that another one of her patients will try to kill her.'

Ah. That explained his gratitude, Kate thought, before delivering the punchline he'd deliberately set up. 'D, if you went any whiter we'd *all* be wearing wraparound shades indoors.'

It had the desired effect, making everyone smile for another few seconds before they got into the grim reality of Decker's CD.

Zimmerman checked his phone when it buzzed. 'We're waiting for one more, but Detective Kimble just texted that he's on his way up. Set up the clip, won't you, Deacon?'

From the corner of her eye, Kate saw Meredith Fallon stiffen.

It was only a fleeting movement, and within seconds her expression was once again smilingly serene.

Troy leaned into Kate's space again. 'You two must have had fun together,' he said with a hint of wistfulness, indicating Deacon, who was cueing up the CD.

'Gotta laugh sometimes,' Kate murmured, 'or you start crying and can't stop. I hope you laugh sometimes, too, because I have a feeling we're really going to need it.'

'It's been a while,' he admitted, then tilted his head toward Meredith. 'What's with her?'

'Not a clue,' Kate whispered back. 'I'll ask Dea—'

She was interrupted by a knock at the door and turned to see a tall, dark-haired man coming through the doorway, wearing an abashed smile and a dark suit that was dripping wet. Detective Adam Kimble and Deacon had grown up together. They were family.

'Hi, everyone,' Kimble said. 'I'm sorry I'm late. One drop of rain and traffic comes to a screeching . . . halt.' So had Kimble's powers of speech as soon as he'd seen Meredith Fallon at the table, but he'd recovered quickly, his smile reappearing.

'Good morning, Detective,' Zimmerman said. 'You haven't missed anything. We're about to review Agent Davenport's audio file. Everyone, this is Adam Kimble. He's on the MCES team with Deacon and Scarlett.'

'Backstory?' Troy murmured.

'MCES is the joint task force. Major Crimes Enforcement Squad.'

Troy rolled his eyes. 'I knew *that*. Backstory on *Kimble*.'

'He's Deacon's cousin.'

Troy blinked. 'No shit? I wouldn't have guessed that. What else?'

Kate tried to remember more. 'I met him last week when we took down the traffickers, but before MCES he was working Personal Crimes.' Which was the CPD's nice way of referring to sex crimes. 'No clue on what's going on between him and Dr Fallon.'

Kimble had taken off his drenched suit jacket and was giving it a little shake. 'Where can I hang this? And maybe something to dry my head? I feel like a drowned rat.'

'There's a hook on the back of the door,' Zimmerman said. 'Paper towels on the table by the coffee. Do you know everyone, Adam?'

'Not everyone.' Kimble hastily scrubbed his wet head with a paper towel, then scanned the table, taking the only vacant chair, right next to Meredith. But he'd hesitated first. Just for a second, and only noticeable if one had been looking, but of course everyone present was looking.

That was the trouble with working with a bunch of cops. Everybody was trained to spot the tiniest bit of behavior. The smallest facial twitch. It made keeping your private life private a real challenge. Kate thought she did a pretty good job most of the time. God, she hoped she did. She had private shit that she did not want anyone to know. Ever.

Kimble met Troy's eyes across the table, all business now. 'I'm assuming you're Agent Troy. I read about the trafficking ring you shut down last week in Cleveland.' His eyes took on a hardened, almost angry defiance. 'That was good work.'

Troy looked uncomfortable. 'Thank you, but now I feel like a slacker because you did the homework and I didn't even know the assignment.'

Kimble's smile was wry. 'Hey, D, looks like I get to be the straight-A student for a change,' he said with self-deprecating humor.

Deacon looked up from his laptop with an eye roll. 'You would have always been if you hadn't been too busy warming the bench in the principal's office. Boss, I've got this clip about as cleaned up as I can with the software I've got. The sound quality is still crap, but it's ready to play. Do we need a set-up for Adam and Meredith?'

'I'll give you the CliffsNotes version,' Zimmerman said, 'and answer any specific questions you have after the clip. Agent Griffin Davenport was undercover for three years with a human trafficking ring that was initially on the Bureau's radar for its drug trade – heroin and oxy were its bread and butter. Davenport was known to them as Gene Decker. He started out as personal security for the ring's leadership, but realized pretty quickly that something more was going on. He wasn't getting access to the information we needed as a bodyguard, and we were thinking of pulling him out, but then he got dinged by a bullet a few months ago – nothing as serious as his injury last week, but enough to put him on disability for a while. Griff has an actual accounting degree and luckily we'd added that in when we built his profile. He was able to convince them to assign him to assist the ring's CPA. He'd gleaned that human trafficking was happening but wasn't getting access to the real books because he wasn't part of the inner circle. So he and his handler . . .' Zimmerman faltered, closing his eyes for a few seconds. 'Excuse me, please. Agent Symmes and I were friends.'

And Agent Symmes was dead. Kate tried to remember if Decker would have heard about that before his coma, and then realized that his handler's body hadn't been found at that point. *I'll have to tell him.* She dreaded the thought.

Zimmerman cleared his throat and resumed. 'Davenport and his handler had a prearranged plan for "Gene Decker" to make himself part of the inner circle, and were waiting for the right time to spring it. They got their break last week when one of the victims escaped her captors. Davenport incapacitated the ring's head of security and his right-hand man and delivered them to the place Agent Symmes had set up. Symmes went to bring the two men in and . . . well, there was a struggle. Symmes killed them both, but was fatally injured in the process.'

Zimmerman faltered again, pain tightening his features, and he pursed his lips hard. Kate didn't let him see her compassion because she didn't think he'd welcome it. Instead she took up where he'd left off, giving him an opportunity to regroup.

'Once Agent Davenport made the two men disappear,' she said, 'he assumed some key security responsibilities. There was apparently enough confusion in the ranks that nobody questioned him and he was able to bug the inner circle's offices. Davenport tried to wake up yesterday morning, but he was so agitated that the doctor had to re-sedate him. When he woke this morning, one of the first things he communicated was the date and time of this clip that Deacon's about to play.'

'What was the *first* thing he said?' Meredith asked quietly.

'Well, he didn't actually *say* anything,' Kate said. 'He's still on the ventilator. He pointed to letters on a keyboard to tell us his name was Decker. Apparently it's a nickname, so he used it as part of his cover ID.'

Zimmerman looked surprised. 'I've known him for three years and I've always called him Griff. So did Richard Symmes.'

Kate shrugged. 'Maybe it's a post-coma thing.' Or maybe it was just personal. She really wanted it to be personal. 'The last thing he typed before the nurse threw me out was "kids".' Everyone around the table seemed to deflate. 'Which is why we're all here.'

'You'll hear two clips,' Deacon said, 'both from a conversation between the leader of the ring and his daughter, Alice.'

Scarlett Bishop's jaw went taut. 'Bitch,' she muttered, and no one corrected her. Alice had been arrested while trying to kill a witness. Had she succeeded, her next target would have been Scarlett's boyfriend, Marcus.

Kate thought that Scarlett was controlling her temper admirably under the circumstances.

'They also mention a guy named Woody McCord,' Deacon went on. 'McCord was arrested for possession of child pornography after an anonymous tip to the Internet Crimes Against Children hotline.' He looked directly at his new partner when he said this and Scarlett's jaw tightened again, but this time apprehension flickered in her eyes rather than rage.

But she didn't say a word. Just stared back at Deacon until he sighed.

Troy nudged Kate and she shrugged. 'No clue,' she said, but loudly enough to be heard by the entire table. 'We *will* have a clue, though, won't we, Detective Bishop?'

Scarlett nodded once. 'Yes. But not at this moment.'

Kate leaned forward, propping her elbows on the table, keeping her tone mild even though she was seriously pissed off. Scarlett was protecting Marcus, she was sure of it. 'What part of "kids" is less important than whatever secret you're keeping, Detective Bishop?'

Scarlett looked miserable. 'Dammit, Kate. They've been through so much.'

Oh for God's sake. Kate rolled her eyes, her patience strained. 'K-I-D-S, Scarlett. The anonymous tip was from your boyfriend's newspaper, right? Blink once for yes, twice for no.'

Scarlett didn't blink at all. 'I'll get the information you need,' she said rigidly. 'ASAP.'

Fucking hell. Kate reined in her temper, her hands going for her knitting bag. 'Thank you.'

Troy raised his brows in surprise when she dug her project out of the bag and began to knit furiously. 'I remember McCord's arrest,' he said calmly. 'It was news for weeks because he was also a teacher in one of the local high schools. He was found dead in his jail cell – he hanged himself. But that was almost a year ago. Why is McCord significant now?'

Scarlett's answer was crisply professional. 'According to McCord's attorney, he was planning to reveal his suppliers to the DA in order to get his charges reduced from possession of child porn to pandering. He was found dead the next day. His wife was found dead of an apparent suicide a few days later. His attorney died soon thereafter in a fire. Suspected arson.'

'So McCord most likely had help hanging himself,' Troy said dryly.

'That was my assumption, yes,' Scarlett said.

Kate lifted her gaze to Scarlett's. 'He was found with child porn on his home computer, right? But pandering insinuates that a profit was made. He must have been willing to admit to some kind of commerce for him to believe that the DA would negotiate. Was he a pimp?'

'I don't know.' Scarlett had fully regained her composure. Any indication of misery or anger was gone. 'Maybe. But my guess was that the kiddie porn they found on his computer was for more than his personal use.'

Troy frowned. 'You think he was selling it? That would have given him an even longer sentence than possession. Pandering wouldn't have applied.'

'Not unless the suppliers he was giving up were really big fish,' Scarlett said quietly. 'Deacon and I had already connected McCord to someone known to have purchased victims of trafficking for labor.'

'Big fucking fish,' Troy muttered. 'Why haven't I read about this? Your boyfriend's paper printed everything else.'

Scarlett's eyes flashed. 'Not even close to everything else, Agent Troy.'

Zimmerman intervened. 'We asked Mr O'Bannion to hold that information out of the *Ledger* and he has been very cooperative. ICAC has been reviewing the files taken from McCord's PC nine months ago.'

Scarlett sighed wearily. 'And McCord's dead, so whatever commerce he may or may not have been engaged in is defunct. The threat has passed.'

Kate's sigh was silent. *Not as defunct as you think, sweetie.* 'Play the first clip, Deacon.'

'This one is Alice speaking.' Deacon tapped his keyboard and a faint, tinny voice emerged from the speakers, female and angry.

'O'Bannion runs a newspaper. They investigate stuff. I shouldn't need to draw a diagram here. He nearly brought us down nine months ago, when he exposed Woody McCord's kiddie porn collection. If he'd dug a little deeper, he would have realized that he hadn't even touched the tip of the iceberg with McCord.'

The clip ended and Troy whistled. 'Okay. Got it. McCord's significant.'

'But he's dead,' Kimble said quietly, and there was something in his voice that had Kate setting her knitting down and studying his face. He was as tense as she was, she realized. And he was expending an enormous amount of personal energy to contain it.

'And he can't hurt kids ever again,' Meredith said so softly that it was almost a caress.

Kimble nodded grimly. 'Right. But he's the tip of the iceberg. Where's the rest?'

'Second clip,' Deacon said. 'Alice and her dad. The Sean they mention was the IT guy, Alice's half-brother.'

'Are you still monitoring McCord's partner?' the man asked.

'Yes,' Alice said. '*He seems to be in control and to have learned from Woody's mistakes.*'

'*Has he added any assets?*'

'*A few, but not from us. We're still taking a cut of his profits, though. Not huge profits, but steady, and there's promise for future expansion. McCord's partner welcomed Sean's e-commerce expertise. Locating his server offshore and teaching him about proxies was also . . . appreciated. His appreciation increased the profit trickle to a steady flow. We haven't made personal contact in months. He knows I watch his progress, but as long as the deposits are made every month, I don't bother him.*'

The clip ended and a hush hung over the table like a dark cloud until Zimmerman cut into the silence. 'The tip of the iceberg. And since this mystery man and McCord were partners, we can only assume these assets were the same ones that McCord was about to plea to pandering.'

'Kids,' Kate said grimly.

Cincinnati, Ohio,
Thursday 13 August, 9.00 A.M.

'Well, Agent Davenport?' The doctor set the breathing tube on the tray held by his assisting nurse. 'How does that feel? Better? Just a nod is fine.'

Fuck the nod. Decker needed to know that his voice still worked. *So that I can talk to Kate.* 'Like you ripped a fuckin' tube out of my throat,' he rasped, then coughed, which fucking *hurt*.

The doctor, a fifty-ish man with graying hair, a thick mustache, and gentle hands, rolled his eyes. 'I told you a nod would be fine, but you cop types never listen. He can have ice chips,' he said to the nurse, then pressed his stethoscope to Decker's chest. 'Breathe. Nice and slow.'

'Open up,' the nurse said, and popped an ice chip in his mouth when he obeyed.

And yeah, the ice did feel good. His throat still felt like a dozen cats had been dragged out of him, every one with their claws dug into his tracheal walls, but he could live with that. He'd had far worse.

The doctor listened and seemed satisfied with whatever he heard. Decker was just happy that it didn't hurt his chest to draw a breath on his own. He'd be able to get up and move around now, the sooner the better. Because as soon as he could walk without falling down, he was walking out of this frickin' hospital and going back to work.

Kids. Assets. Steady flow of profits. McCord's partner was still operational. *Not for long.*

The doctor narrowed his eyes. 'Whatever you're thinking about, stop. Your pulse just rocketed. Unless you *want* the nice nurse to sedate you again?' he asked with false sweetness.

The nurse pursed her lips, obviously as irritated with the doctor as Decker was. But she said nothing and the doctor either didn't see her expression or ignored it. *Asshole.* As Kate had said that morning, you did not mess with the nurses. They could fuck you up.

Concentrating on lowering his pulse, Decker bared his teeth in an intentional parody of a smile. 'No, Doctor.' *Dickhead.* 'That won't be necessary.'

'Good. Your chest sounds are clear. We'll be moving you to a regular room soon.'

'Excellent,' Decker grunted. 'I want out of here. I have to get back to work.' *Because . . . kids. Goddammit to hell. Breathe. Keep that pulse normal.*

'Of course you do.' The doctor crossed his arms over his chest and gave Decker what was probably the guy's most serious expression. 'So here's the drill, Special Agent Davenport. Once you're in a regular room, we will put you to work – the work of healing, which is hard. You do your lung exercises, eat your meals, take walks around the ward, and you *cooperate.* And then *maybe* you'll see daylight in a week. But going back to work? Try a month. At the earliest.'

Breathe. Decker's pulse remained steady, but it was a challenge. *A week for fucking daylight? My fucking ass. And a month to return to duty? What're you smoking, Doc?* But he just nodded. 'That sounds fine, Doctor.'

The doctor stared at him for a second, then snorted a laugh. 'If you think I bought *that* . . . A week, Davenport. I mean it.'

Or? Decker managed not to roll his eyes. 'I believe you,' he said, with a nod for effect.

The doctor rolled his eyes for the both of them. 'Whatever.'

'Doc, wait,' Decker called out when the doctor turned to leave. 'I've been out of it for a week, right?'

'Right,' the doctor said warily.

'Well, I can read, right?'

The doctor lifted one gray eyebrow. 'I don't know. Can you?'

Decker narrowed his eyes. *Asshole.* 'I'm allowed to read. Is that correct?'

The doctor nodded. 'That is correct, yes.'

Now was that so hard? 'I had a lot of balls in the air when I got here and I'd like to know where they fell. I need access to a newspaper. Please. At least give me that much.' That way he could get caught up on what the public knew before Kate returned.

'You are in ICU, Agent Davenport,' the doctor said, exasperated. 'You're breathing on your own for the first time in a week. You'll be moved as soon as possible. That's all I can promise.'

Decker swallowed his frustration. 'Thank you,' he said, and tried to sound civil.

'Thank me by cooperating. I really don't want to see you back in here.'

That makes two of us. Decker glared at the man's back, drawing a deep breath once he was gone. *Okay, fine.* He *was* breathing on his own. *That's a start.*

'I'll call down for a tray so you can eat,' the nurse said, and Decker thought he heard sympathy in her voice. 'Here's a cup of ice chips. Your throat must be sore.'

'Your tongue must be bleeding from biting it,' he said quietly, sucking on an ice chip. 'I thought they taught the docs sensitivity and respect?'

Her lips twitched. 'They do. Sometimes it takes.'

He dug deep for his most sincere tone. Unfortunately his throat made everything he said sound like he was a kidnapper making a ransom call. 'Is there any way for me to catch up on a specific news event? I promise I will eat everything on my tray and not complain even a little bit. Even if it's gray and nasty. Even if it's Jell-O with pieces of fruit in it. I will be the best patient you ever had. I promise. But I really need to see the news.'

She chuckled softly. 'I know who you are, Agent Davenport, and what you were up to. Dr Dani Novak is a friend of mine. We had a chat about you yesterday.'

He blinked, confused. 'Novak as in Agent Novak?' *Another irritating asshole.*

'Yes. Brother and sister.'

He wondered if that was the second voice he'd heard the day before. 'Does she have the . . . y'know, the eye thing going on?'

Another chuckle. 'Only kind of. But she said you were a hero. I'll see if I can scare up a tablet for you or something. But you can read for a little while only.' She shook her finger.

He smiled at her. 'Does this mean I can complain about the Jell-O?'

'Nope. I'm going to hold you to that one.'

'Rats. Then I'll have to hold up my end of the bargain.' He swallowed a yawn. Damn, he hated getting tired so easily. This sucked. 'Is Dr Novak one of my doctors?' He hoped not, because that meant he'd have to be nicer to Deacon.

She looked sad. 'No. Dr Novak resigned yesterday. I can't go into details, but the long and short of it is, she got shafted and we're going to miss her a lot. No, Dr Dani was here to see the other agent who was camped out in that chair beside you. Kate Coppola.'

His chest warmed. She'd camped out here. He liked that. Then a detail clicked. Deacon Novak had thought Dani was exaggerating how tired Kate had looked. His shoulders sagged a little from simple relief that he was remembering things more easily. 'Can I ask one more favor? Can you inform Agent Coppola that I'm able to speak and ask her to come as soon as she can?'

He looked at the little table next to his bed, then frowned, because the only thing on it was the cup of ice. 'Someone took a piece of paper from my table. It had Coppola's number on it.'

'No problem. She left her number at the desk, so I have it.'

He did, too, because he'd memorized it the moment Kate had

written it down. 'Good. Thank you.' He maintained a grateful smile until the nurse left the room, then let his lips loose to frown. It wasn't *no problem*. He didn't like people touching his things.

He'd slept after Kate had left that morning. Someone must have come in then and taken it. It was only a piece of paper, but the thought that someone had been in his room, that close to him . . . It left him unsettled.

Get a grip, Decker. You're in a hospital, for God's sake. People will be that close to you. Resolutely he pushed the paranoia away and focused on what was important. He'd be able to catch up on the news. And Kate would be coming back soon.

Cincinnati, Ohio,
Thursday 13 August, 9.20 A.M.

Kate studied the faces of the team sitting around Zimmerman's table as Deacon replayed the clips that Decker Davenport had nearly died smuggling out. She saw revulsion and rage, but also resolve to stop the mystery man who procured children so that he could exploit them for profit.

'Assets,' Meredith murmured. 'That they can speak about human beings – children – as assets so coldly . . .'

'What else does Agent Davenport know about this mystery client?' Troy asked.

Kate shrugged. 'I don't know for sure. We'll have to go back to the hospital and ask him. Hopefully they'll take his breathing tube out today, but he still won't be able to talk a lot right away. I think this is all he knew, though – what we've just heard. I mean. I think we should focus on getting Alice to tell us who this guy is.'

Scarlett's dark eyes flashed. 'You really think you can make her talk?'

'No,' Kate said with a shake of her head. Both she and Scarlett had interrogated the trafficking ringleader's daughter, but the woman was not going to crack easily. 'Not unless we have some leverage. Right now we don't have anything that'll either tempt or squeeze her. She's an attorney, and she's demanding full immunity because . . . y'know, why not? She's going to make us show every card in our hand before she makes a move.'

'So we find a way to peek at her hand even if we have to cheat,' Kimble said. 'She's lived here in Cincinnati for how long?'

'Three years,' Deacon said. 'Ever since she graduated from law school.'

Kate opened her laptop to review her notes. 'We got her transcripts on Monday – no flares there. Troy and I also interviewed several of her old professors via Skype. Everyone says basically the same thing – she was a quiet student. Did her work, got decent grades, nothing exemplary. She didn't make friends easily and wasn't involved in any outside clubs or associations.'

'Kate's being too modest,' Troy said with a mild glare. 'I was wrapping up my last op in Cleveland most of the last week. Kate did the legwork here – hours of it. Plus listening to the tapes? No wonder you haven't slept,' he said in a loud aside.

'Say it a little louder, Troy,' she shot back, irritated. Nobody got on the male agents when they didn't sleep. It was sexist and damn annoying. 'I think there are a few people in the building next door who didn't hear you. The point is, nobody in Alice's academic past knows anything about her. She's practically non-existent on social media. The only thing we know is that she visited Marcus O'Bannion in the hospital nine months ago, then joined a gym so that she could keep an eye on him after he was released. She chatted him up, asked about his news stories. Pretended to be his friend. She and her father didn't want Marcus digging any deeper into Woody McCord, his arrest, or his subsequent death.'

Deacon nodded. 'But what really worried her was the possibility of Marcus uncovering McCord's partner.'

Scarlett glanced at Deacon, troubled. 'And now I know why you asked me to come to this meeting. You were right to, of course. You're going to need to talk to all the guys at the *Ledger* – Marcus, his brother Stone, and their friend Diesel Kennedy. They discovered McCord's collection of child porn.' She looked at Zimmerman, her gaze defiant. 'I'm going to advise them to have an attorney present.'

Then the *Ledger* guys had broken a law or two while investigating

Woody McCord, Kate thought. Probably hacking, since it involved McCord's computer. She found herself looking forward to meeting these guys herself.

'I figured you might,' Zimmerman said, confirming Kate's suspicions. 'For the hacking alone. That's why I asked Detective Kimble to be here. I want a strong bridge with CPD on this case, especially as this guy appears to be local. Kimble, you know the area?'

Kimble nodded warily. 'I grew up here. Same as Scarlett and Deacon.'

Zimmerman looked pleased. 'Good. You may be able to ferret some things out that we transplants might not pick up on right away. Detective Bishop, I value all the work you've done, but you're too close to the case. Given the potential for a conflict of interest, I'm going to have Kimble and Novak work this one. It's not a reprimand. You get that, right?'

Scarlett's lips thinned and her cheeks grew red, but she only nodded. 'I am too close,' she agreed. 'I take it that my lieutenant concurs?'

'She does,' Zimmerman said. 'Nobody wants to put you in a bad spot,' he added kindly. 'Lieutenant Isenberg was adamant that we protect your career.'

Scarlett smiled at him – a small smile, but it was genuine. 'I know. I appreciate that.'

Deacon's eyes had widened with stunned dismay before narrowing to glare at Zimmerman. 'I didn't know they were going to pull you off the case, Scar. I would have warned you.'

Scarlett gave Deacon an even warmer smile. 'I know. Now if it's okay with you all, I'm going to drive out to the *Ledger*'s offices and talk to Marcus and Diesel. Stone hasn't returned to work yet. If you want to interview him, you're going to have to go up to his dad's house in Indian Hill. He's recuperating there.'

'Tell them we'll need to talk to them within the hour,' Kate said. 'And thank you,' she added, much more graciously than the last time, when she'd all but barked it. She waited until Scarlett left the room before turning to Zimmerman. 'There's one other lead that we can amp up. Right before he got shot, De . . . avenport' – she corrected herself at the last moment, not wanting her growing familiarity with the agent to show – 'mentioned the trafficker's accountant, Joel Whipple. Joel had made noises to Davenport about wanting to get out of the trafficking business. Davenport thought he might turn state's evidence.'

'But?' Kimble asked.

Zimmerman scowled. 'But when the agents I sent got to Whipple's house, he was gone. No evidence of foul play. I've got a team trying to track him down, but I'm betting the accountant had a Plan B, with a new ID and travel papers all set up just in case they were ever caught. The ringleader did – he had a passport in his pocket when he was taken down.'

'And a plane ticket to Tahiti,' Deacon added glumly. 'I'm sure you're right about Whipple having a way out. I wonder why he let Davenport believe he'd turn state's evidence.'

'Whipple might have suspected him,' Kate said thoughtfully. 'Again, this was before he was shot. Davenport said he wasn't allowed access to any of the good stuff while he was in the accounting department. He did the legit books and Whipple did the real ones. There were no signs of any of either kind of books in Whipple's house.' She thought back to the day Decker had been shot. 'Right before he took the bullet, he said that he'd gotten the data he'd needed, that most of it was stored in his head. He was in a hurry to debrief with you, sir,' she told Zimmerman.

Zimmerman's lips curved in a ghost of a smile. 'Good. Griff's got an eidetic memory. If he got a chance to look at the real books, he'll be able to give us a lot of good information.'

'So we get at what's in his head,' Kimble said, 'and hope that the steady flow of profits that Alice mentions on the tape was recorded somewhere in a way that lets us follow the money.'

'I don't know how long that'll take,' Kate cautioned. 'He was still grasping for small details this morning. He'd remember something, but then you could see how frustrated he'd get when it wisped away. It's the anesthesia on top of the whole physical trauma.' And God, did she remember that. It had been one of the hardest things to watch when Johnnie— *No. Not now. You will* not *go there now.* 'It wipes the brain cells clean,' she added quietly.

'Pull what you can out of him as soon as he's able,' Zimmerman said. 'And ignore the doctors. They'll want to keep him quiet so he can heal, but you need to push as hard as . . .' He sighed. 'That sounds wrong and it's not what I mean. Hell, *I* want him to heal, but . . .'

'He said the clock was ticking on the kids,' Kate finished. 'He knows this. I won't have to push him. He'll push himself.'

'*You* won't have to push him?' Troy said, mildly rebuking her, and Kate felt her cheeks heat.

Yeah, she had a partner again. No, she hadn't forgotten. Not really. But she didn't picture anyone else sitting at Decker's bedside. *No one but me.*

'We. Me. Whoever debriefs him. Anybody but Deacon, that is.' She gave Deacon a pointed glare. 'Mr Congeniality got off on the wrong foot with Agent Davenport. They had words.'

'I thought Davenport was on a ventilator and couldn't talk,' Troy said, amused.

'Silent words,' Kate said flatly.

Zimmerman looked surprised. 'Deacon?'

'It was nothing, sir,' Deacon said, returning Kate's pointed glare and turning it up a few degrees. 'Agent Coppola was mistaken.'

'This is gonna be interesting,' Troy murmured, then chuckled when both Kate and Deacon turned their glares on him. 'It's good to see that Old Partner has a flaw. Makes New Partner feel better.'

Kate found she had to laugh, and the tense mood was broken, which was what she suspected Troy had been trying to do. 'Okay, New Partner. See, you can laugh too. It's not so hard. Do you know anything about accounting?'

Troy's pleased grin shrank to a horrified grimace. 'Hell, no. I joined the Bureau before you had to be all smart and everything.'

'Bullshit,' Zimmerman said amiably. 'But they let you in anyway.'

Troy blinked at their boss for a second before his lips began to twitch. 'Damn, that was a good one. I did not see that coming.' He rolled his eyes. 'Old Partner is a bad influence on our boss, Agent Coppola.'

'Don't I know it,' Kate muttered. 'But seriously, who here – besides me – has an accounting background?'

Kimble's brows lifted. 'You do? Really?'

'Math degree with an emphasis on forensic accounting,' she confirmed with a businesslike nod, but her heart had started beating harder. She was uniquely qualified to debrief Decker, which meant she got to spend more time with him and do her job at the same time. *Kids.* She had in no way forgotten about the kids. *The assets*, she thought bitterly, and cursed every last one of their abusers to a dark hell. 'I was a licensed CPA when I joined the Bureau, so I'll work with Agent Davenport.' She glanced at Troy. 'You in, New Partner?'

Troy's lips curved. 'Yeah. I'd like to meet him, at least. After that, I'd like to dig into Alice's movements during the years she's lived here. Everyone leaves a footprint somewhere. She had to have had some extracurricular activities or a lover or something. Somebody has to have some insight into what makes her tick – and what secrets she might have that we can use as leverage.'

Deacon nodded. 'We also arrested the son of one of the traffickers. He and Alice had some kind of a relationship.'

Kate grimaced. 'I interviewed him once. He either knows nothing or he's really good at playing dumb. I'm not sure which.'

'I haven't interviewed him yet,' Deacon said. 'Let me see what I can get out of him.'

'I want Woody McCord,' Kimble said, very quietly. He hadn't cracked a smile when the rest of them were teasing one another. Kate had noticed. So had Meredith Fallon, who kept glancing at him from the corner of her eye when she thought no one was looking. 'I know he's been dead for nearly a year, but with all the notoriety around him, he would have been a topic of conversation among his neighbors and fellow teachers. If he and this guy were partners, somebody might remember seeing them together.'

Meredith drew in a breath. 'Are you sure?' she asked, her voice nearly inaudible.

Jaw taut, Kimble nodded and looked at Zimmerman. 'That's why I'm here, isn't it, Agent Zimmerman? You wanted someone who'd worked with ICAC in the past to go through the files found on McCord's computer, to see if there's anything that leads to this mystery man.'

Kate flinched. It was the one job that had to be done that she'd avoided even thinking about. Nobody liked to view picture files involving kids. They ripped out your guts and left a deep, mawing hole of black ooze where your heart and soul used to be. That Kimble faced it straight on, even though he was clearly dreading it too . . . *Wow*. Respect for him tightened her chest.

Zimmerman nodded. 'Your lieutenant thinks you're the best person for the job. Is she right?'

Meredith sighed softly. 'Yeah, she's right. You are, Adam. I just . . . I'm sorry. I shouldn't have said anything.'

Kimble looked at her, really looked at her, for the first time since he'd sat in the chair beside her. 'I have to do this sooner or later,' he said with a gentleness that was startling. He turned to the group. 'I was in Personal Crimes last year and had a . . . well, a bad experience. I had to take leave to straighten out my head. But I know the guys in ICAC and I know what to look for in McCord's picture files. I . . .' He blew out a breath. 'Yeah, well, better me than anyone else.'

'Why?' Kate asked him, and his lips twisted in an excuse for a smile that hurt her heart.

'Because it's already broken me once. No need for it to break anyone else.'

Meredith swallowed hard. 'I can come with you,' she offered.

Kimble's twisted smile untwisted, becoming almost . . . sweet. 'No. If I need to unload, I know where to come.'

Kate looked at Deacon, found him staring at the pair with undisguised pain in his eyes. But the pain was softened with hope. Whatever had happened to Kimble had been really, really bad. Whatever solace Meredith had provided must have been . . . healing.

Kate cleared her throat, suddenly feeling very guilty over her delight in getting to spend more time with Decker. 'Agent Davenport will only be able to debrief for short periods of time at first. He'll have to sleep frequently until he gains his strength, especially if I'm pulling information out of him. I'll go to the hospital and check on him, maybe take him a tablet or something so he can write things down as he remembers. Then I'll go to the *Ledger* office and meet with Scarlett and Marcus and hopefully find out what I need to know about the newspaper's investigation into McCord. After that, I'll connect with you, Adam, and we can . . .' She drew a breath, shuddered it out. 'You shouldn't have to bear that burden alone.'

'We'll see,' Kimble said, then closed his eyes, looking weary and . . . *real* for the first time since he'd walked through Zimmerman's door. 'Jesus, this sucks.'

'I can get someone else,' Zimmerman said. 'There will be no negative repercussions.' One side of his mouth lifted sadly. 'No notes in your permanent record.'

Kimble opened his eyes and laughed, a rusty sound. Like he hadn't laughed in way too long. 'Thanks, Principal Zimmerman. But my permanent record already has a note in it.'

Zimmerman shook his head. 'No it doesn't. Just a brief notation that you took some leave.'

'I wasn't talking about my personnel file, sir. I was talking about the record in my own mind. Besides, how many times does a man get a chance to right a wrong?'

'You didn't do anything wrong,' Meredith said, quietly but firmly. 'Do you *hear* me?'

'Yes, ma'am,' Kimble said dutifully but with a mild edge. 'I hear you.'

Meredith sighed. 'But you don't believe me.'

'I don't know if I do or don't,' Kimble said, his sarcasm now gone. 'But I do know that I need to do this. My lieutenant knows it too,' he added to Zimmerman. 'Or she wouldn't have recommended me for the job. I'll go to ICAC straight from here.'

'Anything else?' Zimmerman asked.

'Maybe,' Meredith said, a thoughtful frown wrinkling her brow. 'The pictures McCord had were taken at least nine months ago. Probably further back. We don't know when he began victimizing children. Those kids may have grown up. Moved on.'

'Or they're dead,' Kimble said grimly.

Meredith acknowledged his point with a nod. 'Not all, though. Many live to grow up.'

'And they usually continue to work the sex trade as they get older,' Kate said, guessing where the psychologist was going with this. 'It's the life they know, so they go from abuse to hooking.'

'Exactly,' Meredith said. 'Up until recently, these victims were charged with prostitution and then had criminal records on top of being abused. McCord's victims – and those of this unknown partner – will be working the streets or, if they're lucky, will be in counseling. I know a lot of these young women, and a few young men as well. One of my associates manages a halfway house for the young women coming out of the life, to help them build new ones. I'll find out if any of them knew McCord. If none did, I'll hit the street. My associate, Wendi Cullen, knows where they hang out. She'll come with me.'

Troy nodded his agreement. 'I know Wendi. She's sharp and she has a way with kids. I placed some young women with her last year. She's built a strong program.'

'Which is in danger of being shut down,' Meredith said. 'But for the moment it's serving some of the very victims we need to talk to.'

'I'll assign an agent to accompany you, Meredith,' Zimmerman said, then his hand sliced at the air to cut off her protest. 'Not negotiable. We will choose someone who will not hamper your efforts to talk to these women, but you will not venture out alone.' His shoulders sagged. 'That goes for all of you. I know I don't have to tell you to be careful, but I'm going to say it anyway. Make sure Dispatch is on speed dial. Call for backup before you go into a dangerous situation. Do not wait until bullets are flying. If you leave this facility without a vest, you will be on leave without pay. No exceptions and no excuses. No more funerals. Everyone be back here at sixteen hundred for a debrief. Dismissed.'

Four

He checked his watch. Didn't anyone value punctuality these days? Everyone was so damn connected online that they forgot common courtesies. Like being on time for a drug buy.

Come on, Roy. I've got places to go, things to do. Nurses to threaten. Because Roy's girlfriend had not cooperated last night when he'd told her to go back and finish Davenport.

So now he was going to finish Roy. In the end it was probably deserved, so he wasn't going to feel bad about it. He might feel bad about losing a steady customer, though, especially one like Roy who paid without trying to haggle the price. Not like Roy cared about money. Or male pride for that matter. He'd met his little nurse and cheerfully settled right in to his role as a gigolo. Or boy toy. Or whatever the kids were calling it these days. Whatever the term, Roy was a kept man, comfortable living off the nurse's salary.

He really hoped Roy had been good in bed at least, because this relationship was going to ruin the nurse forever. She'd either kill Davenport or have her addiction exposed to the hospital administration. He might have felt bad about that, except that the nurse knew exactly what she was getting into when she'd started sleeping with a college kid half her age.

Women who liked bad boys had always baffled him. Regardless, Roy certainly fit the bill, with his curled lip and his swagger and his muscle car, complete with the actual muscles that went with it –

thank you, steroids. *I really hope he was good in bed, honey, but I kind of doubt it.*

Roy's recreational drug use had been an enticement. A way for a single, middle-aged woman with a teenager to add a little spice to her life. Now she would pay the price.

Roy, of course, was just the warning shot over the bow. A way to demonstrate that he *would* kill without compunction or hesitation. He didn't think Roy's untimely death would bother her all that much at this point. She'd grown tired of the poor bastard but hadn't been able to make him leave her house or her bed. *Hell, she might even thank me.*

Until she got his next message, because then she'd understand the true consequences of her non-compliance.

The growl of Roy's muscle car assaulted his ears and he glanced up in the rear-view to make sure that Roy was alone. It hadn't really been a concern, because Roy didn't share well. He'd only shared his stash with his nurse long enough to get her hooked. Roy had become her dealer because God only knew she wouldn't want to be caught *buying* drugs. Using them was bad enough. She'd give Roy money and he'd buy drugs for both of them.

He had no idea if the nurse knew that she was financing her boyfriend's drug habit too. He suspected that she did. He was pretty certain that she didn't know it had been Roy who'd provided the photographic proof that the nurse had been stealing narcotics from the hospital.

She'd started supplementing the coke with stolen opiates after realizing how much their drug habit was costing her. Stealing from the hospital had been so easy to start. So hard to stop.

A little narcotic for the patient, a little for the nurse. Slip the vial in your pocket, take it home and shoot up. Roy wouldn't have cared, except she didn't share with him, which pissed him off enough to snap a series of photos of her sitting on her bed with a needle in her arm and the clearly stolen vial in her hand. Photos Roy had shown him when he was high as a kite, happily texting them to him for a few free hits of the Professor's special blend. Roy probably didn't even remember sending them. He'd been really high.

He also didn't know that his little nurse was being blackmailed. All the better, because rocket scientist or not, even Roy might have put those details together, and his nurse losing her job meant Roy would lose his meal ticket. Something Roy was in no hurry to do.

The nurse didn't want to lose her job either, because her kid was sick and they needed her health insurance. He didn't know what ailed the kid and really didn't care. If the nurse did his bidding, it would be a moot point. He wouldn't expose her and her life could go on.

She hadn't instantly capitulated, despite his photographic proof of her drug use. She had actually tried to talk her way around his threat to make her drug use public. *I might get fired*, she'd said, *but I'll get a job somewhere else. That shit never follows you. I have lots of friends who got jobs after being fired for using.*

To which he'd calmly informed her that he would personally see that every hospital in the country knew about her drug use. So she'd finally agreed, but only with her words. She still hadn't finished the job. *And now Davenport's awake, dammit.* If Davenport said one damn incriminating word . . . *I'll eviscerate the bitch and make sure she feels every slice.*

'Dude.' Roy slid into the passenger seat with a goofy smile that he probably thought was charming. 'Sorry I'm late. Things were crazy on campus. Some girl got found dead. Did too much blow, I guess.'

Roy always reminded him of Ted 'Theodore' Logan from the *Bill and Ted* movies. If Ted lived in a young Arnold Schwarzenegger's body. God, the guy was fucking huge.

Only an idiot would cross Roy when he was sober – or even conscious. *I am not an idiot.* However, he also knew that he'd have to time this properly or he'd have to deal with hauling Roy's heavy ass back to his own car. The brute had to weigh at least two-fifty.

He smiled indulgently at Roy. 'I know. I saw the story on the news this morning so I knew to avoid the campus area.'

Roy bobbed his head in a happy nod. 'I figured you did when I saw the coordinates.' He looked around at the trees that closed in on them. He'd sent Roy the GPS coordinates rather than an address, because this clearing didn't have an address. 'Real rustic, Professor. I feel like I should be wearing a flannel shirt and hiking boots.'

He chuckled. 'I found this place when I was your age. I've had a pot plot here for years.' That wasn't a lie, actually.

Roy looked intrigued. 'There were rumors that you grew your own. Maybe I'll try it sometime.' He patted the pocket of his shirt. 'I brought the stuff. Did you?'

'Of course.' He lifted his brows in challenge. 'You want to try it now?'

Just like Sidney's had last night, Roy's eyes got big and excited. 'Oh yeah.' But then he frowned. 'Why do you want this?' He patted his pocket again. 'I figured you'd have your own.'

Good question, Brutus. The kid had surprised him. 'I do, but lately my supply's been off quality. I've had some complaints. I want to run a check in my lab, to do a comparison.'

Roy seemed to buy it. 'Okay. I was just curious. So what about this new formula?'

He gave Roy the packet. 'It might be a little low-strength for your body size. If this doesn't give you enough of a high, I'll send more home with you. Just spread the word.'

'Oh, I will. Don't worry.' Roy prepared the powder and snorted it all up at once.

Just as he'd known the kid would.

Roy sat in the seat, a frown dimming his features. 'It's . . . okay. Honestly, I don't see what the fuss is about. Sorry, Professor. This one's a dud.'

He'd known Roy would say that, too. Unlike Sidney's blend last night, he'd mixed Roy's so that there was far more ketamine. It would be taking effect in a minute or two. This was where timing was going to be key in avoiding a hernia.

He sighed heavily. 'I was afraid of that. That's why I wanted to try it on someone of your size. It works on the tiny guys, but your metabolism is different.'

'I know,' Roy said proudly. 'When you get it fixed, call me, okay?'

'You can count on it.'

Roy got out of the car and paused, his hand on the door. 'I forgot to give you the vials.' He fished them out of his pocket.

Seconds were ticking. *Get in your car, asshole*. He kept his smile rueful. 'Keep them. I wouldn't feel right about taking them.' He got out of his car and followed Roy to the muscle car, waiting until he was in his seat with the door closed to knock on the window. 'I forgot to give you this,' he said when Roy lowered the window. He handed over another packet of white powder. 'For your trouble.'

'That's not gonna do anything to me, Professor. Sell it to a scrawny guy, make yourself a few bucks.' He smiled, put the key in the ignition and turned it, filling the air with the roar of the engine that was his pride and joy. He started to put the car into drive, then paused, a puzzled frown wrinkling his forehead. 'Shit. I don't . . . I don't feel so . . .' He swallowed hard. 'So good.'

He stood there quietly and watched as Roy's muscles began to deaden and freeze. Roy made a last grab for him through the window, but he sidestepped easily. He'd known the kid would do that, too.

It had actually taken longer than he'd expected for the paralytic to kick in, and he'd mixed in enough to take down a rhinoceros. Thank God that Roy was back in his car, because he would have had to leave him on the ground otherwise. No way was he throwing out his back moving two hundred fifty pounds of dead weight.

He gave it another few minutes, then gloved up and took the vials from Roy's shirt pocket. He pulled a syringe and tourniquet from his own pocket and deftly prepared the man's ham-sized arm for the injection. Roy had brought five vials of Dilaudid, the opiate the nurse had stolen, just as he'd been instructed.

He proceeded to inject the contents of two of the vials. Because the nurse had given her patients part of each vial, neither was full. He waited, keeping the needle in Roy's arm and his fingers on Roy's wrist, measuring the man's pulse until it slowed to a mere whisper. And then nothing at all.

He pocketed the vials he hadn't used, positioned the empties on his gloved palm, then snapped a photo with Roy's phone. He found 'Nursey' in Roy's contact list and texted her the photo.

He followed it up with another of Roy dead in the driver's seat, a needle in his arm.

Then he waited for the call. He didn't have to wait long.

'What is this?' the nurse whispered harshly. The sound bounced. She was in a restroom stall or a small closet. 'Who is this?'

'It's your boyfriend, ma'am,' he said politely. 'Or what used to be your boyfriend. And I'm the man who doesn't appreciate being lied to. When someone promises they'll do certain things, but only makes excuses . . . Well, ma'am, that just pisses me off.' He dropped the polite act. 'So listen and hear. Do what I told you to do.'

'Or what?' she said hysterically. 'You'll kill him? You already did!'

'And with the drugs *you* stole from the hospital. The next photo you get will be of this guy.' He found a photo of the nurse with her teenaged son and texted it. He knew when she'd received it, because she moaned.

'Why? Why are you doing this to me?'

'It's not personal. It's really not. I need you to do this job. If you'd simply done it when you had access and opportunity, no one would have been the wiser. But you didn't, so you've forced me to resort to this. I do not make idle threats. I will not only make sure that your son ends up like poor Roy here, but I'll arrange for the vials you've touched to be found on their bodies.'

A gasp. 'You can't.'

'I can and I will. Now, if you cooperate with me, I'll do something for you.'

A long, long silence. 'What?' she huffed, like she'd had trouble getting the word out.

'I'll make sure that when poor Roy is found, he has a different vial in his hand. It'll be oxycodone and it will not be traceable to you. But I have to hear from a reliable source that Davenport is dead. Do you understand me?'

'Yes.' A hard, audible swallow. 'I hate you.'

'So many do,' he said mildly, and that was true, too. He simply didn't care. 'Get to work, Nurse. I'll be waiting to hear good things.'

Cincinnati, Ohio,
Thursday 13 August, 11.45 A.M.

Decker still hadn't gotten a newspaper or a tablet, so he still had no idea what had happened with his fucking case. The ICU nurse who'd promised him so nicely had dematerialized and her replacement had just scowled at him. 'Do you realize,' she'd said in a nasal voice that grated, 'that it's only been ten minutes since the last time you asked for a newspaper and nine minutes fifty seconds since the last time I said no?'

'No,' he'd roared, his temper loose, 'I was not aware that it had only been ten minutes because I don't have a fucking phone! I just want a fucking newspaper! Is that so difficult?'

She'd shut the door to his room with the first bellow, folding her arms to glare nastily. 'Are you *aware* that this is an intensive care unit? Are you that selfish? Or maybe you're mentally disturbed and I should call for security? We'll happily calm you down.'

Fucking witch, he thought, then felt really bad for shouting. 'I'm sorry. You're right. I was wrong to yell.' He remembered what Kate had said to Novak that morning when chiding him for the same thing. He gave her his best smile, the one that had caused his foster mother to forgive him time and time again. 'I'll use my inside voice from now on.'

The nurse had accepted his apology begrudgingly. 'You still can't have a newspaper or a tablet or a phone, or even two cans tied together with string. You're in ICU.'

He sighed. 'Can you at least get me out of here? Please?'

'Gladly. I will make it a priority.'

And she had. He was now in a regular room at least, but he'd had no contact with the world outside the hospital since Kate had left hours before, and he was losing his fucking mind.

A new nurse entered the room, but he was afraid to ask her for a tablet. By now he'd figured out that the more he asked, the longer they were going to make him wait. So he closed his eyes and breathed deeply, stifling the urge to ask again. He'd waited until the new nurse had finished changing the IV bag and had left before opening his eyes and cranking the bed up forty degrees. She'd left him at an angle that wasn't good for anything but staring at the ceiling. At least now he could see the TV. Which was fucking useless.

He switched the TV channels like a squirrel on crack, spending a second on each one. Which was a fucking second too much. The TV news was worse than useless. No wonder the country was going to fucking hell in a hand basket. People thought the pablum served up on the 'news' stations was actually news.

No, he did not want to know about the latest sexcapades of whatever Hollywood couple was the latest ridiculous thing. He did not care about cute babies or paternity tests. He did not want to buy jewelry or even see highlights from last night's baseball game. He paused an extra second on a home improvement show before moving on. That might be worth another look later.

He'd need to find somewhere to live now that he was no longer under, and anything he could afford would probably need fixing.

But he wasn't even sure where he'd end up within the Bureau. He could be transferred anywhere, but he wanted to stay here. For a little while, anyway. At least until he'd finished the job he'd started.

Wherever he landed, he wanted to put down some roots for the first time in forever. He wanted a house. Nothing huge or fancy. Somewhere he could have a vegetable garden and a dog. A really big dog. A smile curved his lips at the thought of it, because he hadn't had a pet in forever either. He might even grow some roses. Mama Davenport had grown roses, all different colors. He'd built her a trellis, and how she'd smiled at him …

His throat thickened at the memory. She was gone now. Long gone. God, he missed her, but a part of him was relieved that she hadn't lived long enough to see him now. To see the hard man he'd become. He chuffed a laugh that sounded far too unsteady for a decorated soldier. She'd have taken a slice outta his hide if she'd heard the way he'd spoken to the nurse in ICU.

That had been her totally empty threat. *I'll take a slice outta your hide, boy!* But a gentler woman he'd never known. She'd no sooner have laid a hand on him in anger . . .

He drew a deep, deep breath and let it out slowly, his eyes

stinging. *I'll make you proud, Mama D.* He'd said the words to her as he'd waited on that train platform, the tie of his new uniform snug around his throat. God, he'd been young. But her words . . .

Decker hadn't allowed himself to think of them in far too long. *You already make me proud, Decker McGee. Every day you lived with us, you've made me proud.* She'd leaned up on her toes to press her finger to his lips, cutting off his denial. *I was proud when you were Decker McGee. You changing your name to Davenport don't do anything but make me love you more.* She'd never said that she loved him, not until that moment as he'd waited for his train. But he'd known. Every day he'd lived under her roof, he'd known. *Be safe, Second Lieutenant Griffin Davenport. And come home to us, boy, all in one piece.* She'd dragged him down to press a hard kiss to his cheek. *You come home to us, y'hear?*

And then she'd turned tail and run with a speed surprising for a woman of sixty-five, leaving him standing on the platform alone with Old Griff. The burly man had simply sighed big. *What she said, Decker. What she said.* Then he'd shaken Decker's hand, pulled him into a hard embrace and whispered gruffly, *You always have a home with us. Don't ever forget it.*

Decker's hand shook as he scrubbed the wetness from his face. He grabbed the TV remote and began changing channels with all the focused intensity he'd used in preparing for a battle. Because . . . yeah. The feelings weren't that different.

He'd come back to the home show later. When his heart didn't feel like it had just been crushed in his chest.

An image on the TV screen caught his eye a few seconds too late, yanking his mind back from its wandering. He surfed backward until he found the channel, then squinted up at the screen, grateful for the distraction.

He knew those people. The man and the woman. Both had dark hair, both were tall. They'd been there that night. At the traffickers' compound. When he'd been shot.

But their names hovered frustratingly out of reach.

The channel was a local 24-hour news station and it was now the top of the hour, so he was finally getting real news. The pair were being followed down a city street by a reporter with a mike, her questions peppering the screen with closed captions. He turned up the volume in time to hear the reporter call, 'Mr O'Bannion! Marcus!'

Marcus O'Bannion. Media guy. He ran a newspaper, the *Ledger*. He'd exposed Woody McCord. The traffickers had hated this man. Decker considered that one of the most glowing endorsements imaginable.

The woman was . . . well, very pretty. Not as pretty as a certain redhead, but still striking. *Red*. Her name was something red. 'Scarlett,' he said aloud, pleased with himself. Last name was religious. Priest, Vicar . . . 'Bishop,' he said with a nod.

'Mr O'Bannion! Detective Bishop!' The reporter had started chasing them because the pair did not appear to be slowing down. Then Bishop tugged on O'Bannion's sleeve, leaning in to tell him something when his steps faltered. She grabbed O'Bannion's hand, threaded their fingers together, then they turned as a unit.

'Yes?' O'Bannion said quietly.

'Is this your first day back after the shooting?' the reporter asked, a tad breathless.

Decker frowned, the questions piling in his mind faster than they piled up on the screen. *Shooting? Where? When? Who got shot?*

Oh. Right. It came flooding back to him. One of the traffickers had walked into the *Ledger*'s office and started firing. They'd lost several people. *God.*

O'Bannion looked . . . exhausted. Heartsore. *I get that*, Decker thought.

Bishop looked . . . Decker's lips curved at the belligerent tilt of the detective's chin, the fire in her eyes. She looked like a lioness, like she'd claw anyone who dared hurt the man at her side. *I want that*, came the sudden thought. *I want someone to look at me that way.*

No. After being alone for so damn long, he knew that he'd long ago bypassed 'want'. It was a deep-seated need. A hunger, even. He was almost afraid to admit to it. It was this huge thing that had started to consume him in his last days undercover. Perhaps it was being forced to keep such close quarters with the kind of depravity that was commonplace among the traffickers. He'd needed something to counteract it. Or at least something strong enough to keep it away from his soul, because he'd felt like he was slowly corroding. If he hadn't gotten out when he did . . . He'd been afraid that nothing would be left of the man he'd been.

The real Griffin Davenport, who'd taken him in and given him a home, had been a damn good man. Honorable. Hard-working. Kind. Not the sort of man to shout at a nurse in an intensive care unit, for sure. Decker had tried to be like him every day of his military career. And during his three years under.

At the end, remembering the real Griffin Davenport had been the one thing that had kept Decker sane. He hoped he had gotten out in time, that there was enough of Griffin left inside his soul to allow Decker to have a life. To share a life with someone else.

To deserve to have someone look at him the way Bishop was looking at O'Bannion.

'Yes,' O'Bannion was saying. 'This is the first official day back for many of us. For many of us, the media is our life. We understand that you're going to poke and prod and put us – our grief – on display. I suppose that's only fair, because we make our living doing the same thing. But many of our employees aren't accustomed to the intrusion of cameras. I ask that you leave them alone to grieve in peace. I'll be happy to give interviews if you'll respect the privacy of my people. For now, I have to get to work. Thank you.'

He pushed through his office door, but Bishop lingered a moment to give the reporter the eye, ensuring that the woman did not follow them. The reporter turned to face the camera, spouting her wrap-up. The next story was about the body of a student discovered on the campus of King's College, dead of an apparent overdose. Her friends had gathered in shock to say what a great person she'd been. What fun she'd been.

Decker muted the TV, rolling his eyes. Stupid, stupid kids. Throwing their lives away like that. For 'fun'. They'd been having fun while he'd been in Afghanistan, dodging bullets. He had very little sympathy for them. If they didn't use the drugs, there'd be no market for them and guys like the traffickers wouldn't be in business.

They wouldn't have expanded their business to traffic humans. *Children, for God's sake.*

He began channel-surfing again, but nothing was on. Not even the home improvement show now. He eyed the phone on the little table, wondering how much Kate had been able to discover about McCord's nameless partner.

Even if she hadn't found anything yet, maybe she could bring him something that he could use to get online. Gritting his teeth, he stretched out his arm, anticipating pain, pleasantly surprised when it wasn't that bad. He'd make the call, leave her a voicemail if she didn't answer, then he was getting his ass out of bed.

The doc had said he needed to walk. That the sooner he was fit, the sooner he could walk out the door. The doc had also said it would be a week. *Fuck that.* And fuck a month to get back to work. In the desert, they got shot, they got patched up, and they got sent back into the fray.

Other men might need a week to get out of here. Decker was planning to do it in four days. Tops. And that was if he lasted that long without killing someone out of sheer bored frustration.

He dialed Kate's number from memory expecting her voicemail, but she answered. And his twitchy body seemed to settle as soon as he heard her voice.

'Coppola,' she said.

'Da . . .' His own name stuck in his throat and he cleared it. 'Davenport.'

'Decker.' He could hear her smile and he had to smile back even though she couldn't see him. 'He speaks!' she added, teasingly. 'When did you get the tube out?'

'Hours ago. They were supposed to call you.'

'Huh. I didn't miss any calls from the hospital, so they didn't. That's rude. Although maybe they got busy, but still. Are you up to visitors?'

'Depends,' he croaked. 'Hold a sec.' He tossed back a few ice chips and cleared his throat again. 'Damn tube was like broken glass coming out. Which visitors?'

'Well, me and my partner for one.'

91

Decker grimaced. 'Novak's coming?'

She chuckled. 'No. My new partner is Luther Troy. I told you that this morning, but you might not remember. We're actually just about to get into the elevator in the hospital lobby.'

'Oh.' He was torn between excitement and disappointment. *She's on her way up.* But not alone. And he was too late to ask her to bring him a gadget. 'I'd hoped I'd caught you before you left the office. I need a laptop or phone or tablet or something that connects to the Net.'

'I brought you my old tablet. It might run a little slower than the new ones, but it works.'

Relief mixed with something else. Something more. 'Thanks. They moved me. I'm on the fourth floor. Four-twenty-six.'

'Got it. I'll lose the signal in the elevator, so I gotta go.'

He hung up, relaxed into the pillow, and closed his eyes, sudden fatigue hitting him like a rogue wave, dragging him under. *Shit.* So much for taking his first lap around the hospital floor. He couldn't even keep his eyes open. *Can't fall asleep. Kate's coming.*

Cincinnati, Ohio,
Thursday 13 August, 12.00 P.M.

Kate pocketed her phone and frowned. 'The nurses in ICU were supposed to call me as soon as he got his breathing tube out. He's on four.'

Troy pushed the correct button. 'They probably got busy, like you said.'

'I know, but . . .' She glared at him when his lips twitched. 'What?'

'You must have been hell on wheels in the army. The look on your face, well, it promises swift and painful retribution. I wouldn't want to cross you.'

He'd said it lightly, his go-to tone for constructive criticism. Kate consciously wiped the scowl from her face. 'Better?'

'Much. What did you do in the army?'

'I was an MP.'

'Why am I not surprised?' he said dryly. 'I bet there are dozens of military men and women who still cry in their sleep when you visit their nightmares.'

She smiled ruefully. 'More like hundreds. Sorry. I hate hospitals. Lots of shitty memories. I'm mostly okay once I get to the person's room, but walking through the corridors gives me hives.' She'd kept her cool while sitting with Decker by knitting.

'Because of your husband,' Troy said quietly. 'I'm so sorry for your loss.'

Her eyes widened in shock, both that he knew about Johnnie and that he'd bring it up. 'You had to dig for that.'

He shrugged almost apologetically. 'I like to know who I'm dealing with. What your vulnerabilities are.' His mouth twisted bitterly. 'I've been burned in the past. And your family doesn't exactly wave the rainbow flag.'

'No,' she agreed. 'Tolerance is not in their vocabulary, but hate sure is.'

Troy shook his head. 'How did you avoid getting tarred with that brush?'

'I moved out and away,' she said wryly, and found herself probing her front tooth with the tip of her tongue once again. 'Almost twenty years ago. Never went back. How about you? Did your family accept you?'

'Yeah,' he said with a small smile. 'Except for one brother, but the rest of them are great.'

They both got quiet after that, an awkward quiet that was broken by the buzzing of both of their cell phones at the same time. Grateful for the distraction, Kate pulled hers from her pocket.

And stared at the screen in disbelief. *No way. No fucking way.*

'Goddammit,' she hissed, then glanced up to find Troy looking both horrified and furious as well. 'How could that possibly happen?'

'I don't know,' he said flatly. 'Let's call him and find out.' The elevator doors opened and they both sped to a family waiting room. 'I'll call you on your phone, then patch Zimmerman in. That way we can both hear without using the speakerphone.'

He was already dialing, connecting the three of them up as he and Kate moved to the window of the thankfully empty waiting room. 'Kate's on the line with me,' Troy said when their boss answered. 'What the fuck, Z?'

'I told you,' Zimmerman said, his own fury apparent in the way his voice shook. 'Someone got to Alice Newman. She's dead.'

Cincinnati, Ohio,
Thursday 13 August, 12.00 P.M.

The ringing of his cell phone cut through the sound of the shower. Luckily he was just finishing up – removing the remnants of his Professor face took a while sometimes. The August heat made it necessary to use a stronger prosthetic glue, otherwise his disguise might peel off. Which would be very bad indeed.

He turned off the water and picked up the ringing phone, vowing that if this call from the prison didn't give him better news than the call he'd received from the hospital, he was going fucking ballistic. *Excuses.* Griffin Davenport still breathed because his person inside the hospital kept making *excuses.* Now the man was awake. And soon he'd be talking. He'd already passed CDs to the Feds. At least his person inside had been connected enough to know that much. God only knew what was on the CDs, but since Davenport had been spying on Alice's people for *three fucking years*, it didn't take a rocket scientist to assume they contained information that Alice would not like others to know.

He wasn't terribly worried about his own exposure. He hadn't dealt directly with Alice since McCord got himself caught. Fucking idiot. But if whatever those CDs contained was enough to pressure her into working a deal with the prosecution?

She'll give me up in a heartbeat. Less than a heartbeat. So Alice had to go.

Toweling off his freshly shaved head, he hit ACCEPT. 'Yeah?' he answered brusquely.

'It's done, Professor,' Rawlings said, keeping it short and sweet.

He let out a silent sigh of relief. Rawlings always came through.

Having to kill him was going to be a shame. 'You're sure?' he asked, keeping his tone casual.

'Yep. Saw her body myself. You'll make good on our deal?'

He slathered on moisturizer because the glue dried his skin. 'Meet me tonight. You know where. Once you cut this brick a few times, you'll be the richest guard on the prison block.'

A dry chuckle. 'I'd settle for staying alive, Professor.'

He froze for a moment, a mere split second. 'What's that supposed to mean?' he asked quietly, injecting just the right note of personal outrage.

'It means that my mama didn't raise a fool. I just took care of an important prisoner for you, and before I did, I took the extra precaution of checking the people who'd visited her over the last few days. She's had a lot of visitors – detectives, Feds, lawyers. I don't know why you want her dead, but I've worked the prison system for a long time. You wouldn't have taken such a risk if she hadn't been very dangerous to you.'

His blood went cold, but he kept his tone casual as he carefully set the moisturizer bottle in its place in the medicine cabinet. 'Has nothing to do with me. I told you. I'm just a middleman. That's it. I was hired for this job because I had contacts in the prison system. That includes you.'

'Do your contacts also include Sidney Siler?'

Rage bubbled up from his gut. *Oh Rawlings, you were going to die painlessly. Now? You're gonna hurt.* 'I know her. Why?'

'Yeah, well, I know she visited Alice yesterday, using a fake ID. I also know she was found dead of an apparent overdose this morning. Rumor is dirty coke.'

There is nothing dirty about my coke, fuckhead. 'That's a shame. I liked her. She should have bought from me. She wouldn't be dead.'

Rawlings chuckled again. 'Well, I have to hand it to you. You're a cool sonofabitch. I hope you won't be offended, but I've added you to my list of people I've done favors for. That list is somewhere safe. If I show up dead of anything, even a hangnail, my representative knows to make the list public. It's just a little insurance. I'm sure you understand.'

Oh yeah. I understand that you're a dead man. Or you'll wish you were. 'Of course. I make sure I'm equally insured.' *Because I'm not a moron, asshole.* He knew things that Rawlings didn't know. *Like even if the Professor is outed, nobody can connect him to me.* He'd been taking that precaution for nearly two decades. But he also knew that Rawlings's oldest kid had a problem with drug use. Little Timmy Rawlings Jr really liked coke. A lot.

He wasn't going to make any threats. He'd take action and Rawlings Senior would figure it out. Rawlings Senior was smart that way. 'So we're still meeting tonight?'

'Absolutely. See you then.'

He hung up and blew out a breath. The Alice loose end was now snipped. He'd take care of Rawlings's kid later. He had time before tonight's meeting.

For now, Special Agent Davenport was his chief concern. He had a few other people inside the hospital, but those he didn't want to risk. He needed them exactly where they were. If he couldn't prod the one he already had in there into action, he might just have to take care of Davenport himself. And that would suck.

He needed to eliminate Davenport so that he could focus on planning the upcoming video shoot. His newest customers had very specific requests for the acting talent and were willing to pay for his trouble. And if they liked what they saw, they'd be a source of business for years to come.

The individual drug sales, like to Roy and Sidney, didn't bring in enough cash to pay his bills. Up until last week, his sales of coke, heroin and meth to Alice and her father had been his primary source of income. He needed to secure a new distributor who'd buy the same volume, but that would take some time. Until then, the porn videos and the sale of their starring actors would have to pay the bills.

A year ago he would have had trouble providing the actors his porn customers wanted, only because the actors had been expensive and relatively hard to come by. McCord hadn't believed in buying American, choosing instead to source their assets through Alice and her father. It was supposed to have added layers of security to their operation – no one could trace the teenagers because no one knew them. No family would search if they disappeared. And if anyone got caught, it would have been Alice and her father, and they supposedly had the resources to evade the cops.

He'd gone along with it at the beginning, because he'd been the student, McCord the expert. McCord had all the contacts for the porn – both supply sources for the actors and distribution channels for the videos and the actors themselves when he'd been finished with them. They'd come from a myriad of countries, speaking different languages, all of which made grooming them a lot harder than it needed to be.

He wanted his actors happy on camera, not scared and crying. It was bad for business.

But then McCord got himself caught and everything had unraveled from there. *Now* I'm *the expert*. He'd made a lot of changes and everything was much better. Now his assets were home grown. Given the time, he could groom the actors to perform as directed. No coercion required.

He could still buy assets when he needed to, and for a lot less money than McCord was paying, so his profits were considerably increased. A mother would sell her own soul for a hit – but usually she parted with her kid first. He should know – he'd been cultivating his personal group of addicts for years. He kept up with many of them, scratching their names from his list when they got clean. Or died. Mostly they died.

Personally he didn't want to be in the same room with a skeezy addict who'd sell her own kid for drugs, but he did what he had to to get by. Just like everybody else out there.

I just do it better.

Five

Cincinnati, Ohio,
Thursday 13 August, 12.15 P.M.

'Details, please, boss,' Kate said into her phone from behind clenched teeth. Alice was dead. Their key lead – the only one who knew for sure the identity of McCord's partner – was dead.

'How did they get to her?' Troy added into his own phone. 'We had her in a secure area.'

The light from the hospital's fourth-floor waiting room window highlighted the angry red flush rapidly spreading across Troy's cheeks, the snap of his dark eyes, the grim set of his jaw. Her new partner looked just as stunned as she felt. And just as furious.

She hadn't seen him furious before. Good. Troy had fire. She'd hoped he would.

'Not secure enough, obviously,' Zimmerman said curtly.

Kate dragged a plastic chair close to the window and sank into it, her knees suddenly wobbly. *I'm tired*, she thought wearily, but shoved the exhaustion aside. She'd sleep later. Maybe. She blew out a breath. Tried to rein in her temper.

'Part of me wants to find Bishop and throttle her,' she said honestly. 'If she'd simply told us when she found out last week that McCord didn't commit suicide, instead of protecting the *Ledger* folks' privacy, we might've put a heavier guard on Alice.'

'That was my first response as well,' Zimmerman said, sounding just as weary. 'I had actually dialed all but the last digit of her LT's phone number before I calmed down. We thought we'd gotten all the pornographers when we took down McCord. Bishop thought so too.'

Kate rubbed her forehead. 'Cause of Alice's death?'

'Appears to be poison. May have been in her breakfast. The ME's there now, checking her out. Alice was taking her meals in her cell, so she wasn't among the gen pop. She was apparently a celebrity,' he added, his voice cold.

'So whoever did this had access to her food,' Troy said. 'Depending on how tight security is, this could be a narrow field or wide open.'

'I'm thinking it'll be the second one,' Zimmerman said grimly. 'The warden did take some precautions, like feeding her in her cell, but there's some major covering-up going on, so I don't know what or who we can believe right now. Dr Washington will, of course, expedite the autopsy, but her initial time-of-death estimate was earlier than the warden's. It looks like Alice was dead for over an hour before the warden called me.'

'Dr Washington is good?' Kate asked.

'Yes,' Zimmerman said. 'If there's a COD to be found, Carrie Washington will find it. Alice got her meal around nine and was dead by ten, so the poison was fairly fast-acting.'

'Someone didn't want her to talk,' Troy said. 'Could be McCord's mystery partner, but who knows how many people she could have incriminated? I'm actually surprised someone hasn't taken her out before now.'

'Whoever it is, they're snipping off . . .' Kate trailed off, her body jerking like she'd touched an electric fence. *Oh God*. 'Shit. Decker. Decker woke up and now Alice is dead.' She saw the flicker of understanding in Troy's eyes and together they started running for Room 426. 'He's snipping off loose ends and Decker is the critical one. Gotta go, boss. Call you in a few.'

Kate hung up and dodged an orderly pushing a food cart. 'Shit. It's meal time.' She flashed her badge in the air as several nurses came out from behind the desk, shouting at her to stop, threatening to call Security. She ran faster, dodged a few more carts, then took a hard right into Room 426 and skidded to a horrified stop.

Decker was breathing, but his breaths were jagged. He was blinking hard and irregularly. His skin wasn't just pale, it was ashen, and his lips . . . *Holy God*. His lips were blue.

A woman in green scrubs stood at the foot of his bed, holding a lunch tray. Her badge identified her as a nurse's assistant. She'd frozen in place, staring at Kate, fear in her eyes.

'Put that tray down!' Kate ordered, and the woman dropped it immediately. It fell to the floor with a clatter, food going everywhere. The woman put her hands in the air and backed up, her face pale.

'Kate.' Decker reached out for her, his voice raspy. 'Wrong. Something's wrong.'

'I know.' It didn't look like he'd touched any of the food on the tray. 'Has anyone given you medicine? Anything?'

'Just the IV.'

It was possible. Kate ran around the bed and clamped the IV bag to stop the flow, just in case, then turned to the nurse who stood in the doorway, glaring at them. Her badge said she was Jen Choi, RN.

'What do you think you're doing?' Choi demanded, marching to the bed. About fifty, she managed to be intimidating despite being quite petite. 'This is a hospital, not a—'

'His lips are blue,' Kate snapped, interrupting her tirade. 'Do something.'

'Dammit,' the nurse hissed out. She called the desk to have them summon the doctor, then began taking Decker's vital signs. 'What did you do to him?'

'Me?' Kate stared at her.

'Yeah, you.' The nurse's eyes popped wide when she saw the IV. 'You *clamped* his IV? I don't know who you are, lady, but Security's on their way to haul your ass out of here.'

The woman's outrage had a strangely calming effect, and Kate was able to shove her own panic aside so that she could think. 'I'm Special Agent Kate Coppola, FBI. This is Special Agent Davenport. He's been given something. Or he's having a reaction, or something.'

Don't let it be poison. He couldn't have fought so hard to live, only to be taken out by doctored hospital food. She leaned over the rail so that she could hear him. 'Did you eat lunch, Decker?'

'No.' He was fighting hard to stay with her. 'Not yet. Breakfast, yes.'

Shit, damn, fuck. Alice had eaten breakfast, too. 'What time?'

He blinked at her. 'After . . . after they took out the tube. Don't know the time.'

Kate looked at the nurse. 'When was that?'

The nurse was frowning at her. 'I don't know exactly. Sometime before ten.'

'So two hours.' Alice had died in one. 'What's in the IV?'

Choi glanced up at her, her irritation clear. 'Saline and antibiotics. Same as he was being given in ICU. In fact that is the bag he came down with.'

'Nurse Choi, it *cannot* be the same thing he was being given in ICU. His lips were not *blue* in ICU. Now, either give him something to reverse the effects of whatever's causing this, or get someone in here who can.'

The nurse, bent over Decker's bed, looked up, stunned. 'You think *we* did this?'

Kate drew a breath. 'Three minutes ago we were given reason to believe that Agent Davenport may be a target for someone who wanted him dead. We come in his room and find this. What do you think?'

'Kate.' Decker struggled to meet her eyes, blinking rapidly. 'Don't fuck with the nurses. They'll own your ass.'

Kate snorted a surprised laugh. 'You're right.'

He nodded, once. 'You are too. Someone did change the bag. Not her.'

Drawing another breath, she sobered and faced the nurse, whose expression was now horrified. 'I need to take this IV bag as evidence. Please get a fresh one.'

The nurse just nodded. 'We've called the doctor. He should be here within the next minute. This looks like an opioid overdose. Mr Davenport will be given something to counteract it.'

'Okay.' Kate looked around the room and realized that Troy wasn't there. He was probably dealing with Security, but she directed her next request at the nurse because she had too much energy and felt like she was going to supernova any goddamn second. 'We'll need a copy of any security videos of this floor and a list of anyone who's touched his IV bags.' She looked at the nurse's assistant who'd been holding the tray. 'You can leave that on the floor. I'll be taking it as evidence too. Please wait outside in the corridor. Do not leave. I will come and find you.'

The woman nodded, her eyes huge in her thin face, and hurried from the room.

'Badass,' Decker whispered.

'You'd better believe it.' Kate brushed her fingers over his face. 'How's the breathing?'

'No tube. Please.'

'If they think you need one . . .'

'No. No damn tube.' He blinked hard and looked up at the nurse. 'You hear that?'

'Your lips are blue, sir. You are oxygen-deprived. If that continues, you'll have brain damage. Is that what you want?'

Decker gave Nurse Choi a dirty look. 'No.'

'I didn't think so. Tell me how you felt immediately before your friend Speedy tore up my floor, jumped hurdles over my staff, and caused a general panic trying to get to you.'

'Only general panic?' he asked between labored breaths. 'Not utter chaos? Slacker.'

'You stop it,' Kate scolded. 'Save your breath to answer her.'

Decker turned his head toward the nurse. 'Sudden fatigue. Trouble breathing. It was like a wave, dragging me under.' His brow furrowed as he stretched his non-IV hand toward Kate, almost absently. She grasped it without hesitation, giving it a slight squeeze. 'Metallic taste, too,' he added. 'Nasty. Just want to sleep.'

The doctor rushed in then, frowning as he saw the food on the floor. 'Somebody clean that up,' he said and then scowled at Kate. 'You touched a patient's IV.'

'It may be tainted.' She lifted an eyebrow that dared him to disagree. 'Humor me, Doctor. Start a new one. Fresh. And don't even think about asking me to leave.'

Rolling his eyes, the doctor did many of the same checks the nurse had already done. 'If you could move to the other side of the bed and give me room to work,' was all he said to Kate before turning to Decker. 'I'm going to give you a drug called Narcan.'

'Show her,' Decker said, closing his eyes. Trusting Kate to keep him safe.

Kate let go of his hand to walk around the bed, giving the doctor room, but Decker reached for her again, and again she didn't hesitate. The man seemed to crave tactile sensation, but that might be a side effect of having been in a coma for a week. The doctor held up the vial so that Kate could read it. 'Assuming it hasn't been tampered with, it's what he says it is.'

'Then just do it,' Decker said wearily.

The doctor talked as he worked. 'Narcan will reverse the effects of opioids in your system.'

'And if it's something else?' Troy asked from behind Kate. He'd slipped in so quietly she hadn't heard him. Or maybe she was that focused on Decker. Which meant she was too focused. She needed to be more vigilant about anyone coming through that doorway.

'Then it does no harm.' The doctor injected the drug into Decker's vein, then watched him intently. 'It's safe enough that it's being given to first responders to treat heroin overdoses in the field. If they're wrong and it's not heroin, then no harm. Why is there food on the floor?'

'We have reason to believe that a person associated with one of Agent Davenport's cases was poisoned through food in an institutional setting,' Troy answered.

'I was taking no chances,' Kate added. 'I told the assistant to drop the tray and she unfortunately took me literally.'

'I don't blame her, the way you came charging in here.' The doctor hadn't taken his eyes off Decker. 'Will you scrape it into an evidence bag or something? Somebody's going to slip on it.'

'In a minute,' Kate said quietly, squeezing Decker's hand. 'Decker? You okay?'

He nodded slowly, then about fifteen seconds later gasped in a huge breath. 'Yes. I can breathe better now. No tube.'

'He just got one removed this morning,' Kate told the doctor.

'I know.' He tapped his pocket where an iPad Mini poked out. 'I read his history on my way to his room. Sometimes the opioid OD symptoms recur. I'll wait and give him Narcan again if that happens.' He looked over Kate's shoulder to Troy. 'And no, he can't OD on the Narcan.'

'Thank you,' Troy said. 'I was going to ask.'

'Everyone does. Did you touch the equipment panel, Detective?'

'Special Agent Coppola,' Kate corrected him. 'Behind me is Special Agent Troy and this guy here is Special Agent Davenport. And no, I did not. I only clamped the tube. Why?'

'Because someone's set this drip to maximum flow,' the doctor said grimly. 'Based on the amount in the bag, it wasn't dripping long. Ten, fifteen minutes, tops.'

At least the doctor was a believer now. 'I was on the phone with Agent Davenport about five minutes before we got here. He sounded alert at that time.'

'Felt it right after I hung up,' Decker said, his eyes still closed. 'Feeling better now.'

'That's what they all say when they don't want a breathing tube,' the doctor said.

'Your lips aren't blue anymore at least,' Kate told Decker. 'That scared me.'

Decker's lips quirked up for a brief moment. 'Me too. Nurse set up the bag and left. I watched some TV. It was near the end of the hour, because after that the news got less stupid.'

The doctor nodded. 'The timing works then. Jen, who was on duty in this room?'

Nurse Choi frowned. 'I was. I still am. But I didn't change his IV. He came with one from ICU and it was about half full, just like that one. The flow settings were on minimum, too. He shouldn't have needed a new bag for at least another hour.'

'What did the other nurse look like?' Kate asked Decker.

'Forty or so. Blonde. Thin face. Like a rabbit.'

'A thin face like a rabbit?' Kate asked.

'No. She twitched. Facial tic.'

'We need a list of all your nurses,' Kate said. 'Blonde or otherwise.

We'll question them. We should have put the whole hospital on lockdown.'

'I did,' Troy said. 'Not a complete lockdown, but we have officers at each exit and Security is making copies of all the video in the entire hospital. Davenport, how tall was she?'

Decker closed his eyes again. 'Five-six. One-twenty at the most. She was thin all over. Hair was buzzed short.' His brows furrowed slightly, as if thinking hurt. 'That twitch . . . Now that I think about it, she might have been high.'

'Shit,' the doctor muttered.

'Buzzed hair?' Nurse Choi grimaced. 'Could be Eileen Wilkins. But she's not on this floor.'

'She's ICU,' Kate said grimly. 'Or that's where I saw her. She changed his IV a few times while he was in the coma.'

'I'm calling downstairs,' Troy said. 'They can monitor the exits and catch her if she hasn't gone yet.' He stepped away from Decker's bed and made the call.

Decker's expression had gone completely neutral. 'I don't remember her.'

Kate leaned over the rail to speak in his ear, keeping her voice calm even though she was so angry she could spit. 'Because you were in a damn coma. She could have killed you at any time and you wouldn't have even known she was there. I could have watched her do it and never have known. So if that freaks you the fuck out, I'm right there with you.'

His jaw tightened, then relaxed. 'Yeah. It does.'

'If she's still in the hospital, we'll find her.'

His chest rose and fell as he drew a deep breath, then exhaled. When he opened his eyes, she saw the full extent of his fury. And his understandable fear. 'And if there are others who have poison IV bags?'

'We'll work on that. We'll figure out how to keep you safe. I promise.'

His nod was curt, but she didn't take offense. It was difficult to be in a helpless situation when you were used to being in charge. And being confined to a hospital bed made you feel as helpless as a child anyway. Perhaps even more for the person standing by and watching than for the patient himself. This she knew well.

But this time it's different. She let herself breathe, just a little. At least Decker would live.

Cincinnati, Ohio,
Thursday 13 August, 12.35 P.M.

He answered the phone on its third ring, after checking the caller ID. 'This had better be good, Nursey. I'm tired of your excuses.'

'It's done.' Roy's girlfriend choked out the words. 'It's done, you bastard. Now leave my son alone.'

'How did you do it?'

'I gave him enough Dilaudid to kill an elephant. Put it in his IV, set it on max drip.'

'And then you walked away?'

'Yes. Would you prefer that I'd been caught?' She hissed the words through her teeth.

His phone vibrated as a text came through, this one from one of his indispensable contacts inside the hospital. *Nurse failed. Fed lived.*

Of course he had. He clenched his teeth. *Goddammit. Now he'll be even harder to kill.*

'Of course I don't want you to be caught,' he said to the nurse calmly. 'You're out of the hospital, then?'

'Yes.'

'That's good. Did anyone see you?'

'No. The Fed was asleep. I slipped in and slipped out again. I didn't swipe my keycard either. I just followed people in and out, so there won't be a record of my having been there. I'm supposed to be off shift, so that would have been hard to explain. We had a deal. You were going to fix it so that I couldn't be connected to Roy, that he wouldn't have my vials in his pocket.'

She sounded nervous as she made her demand. He noticed that she didn't sound terribly devastated that poor Roy was dead, which meant she wasn't that stupid.

'I don't break my promises,' he informed her icily. *Unlike some people.* 'Roy's death will not be connected to you.' Because she'd be dead, too.

'Thank you,' she said, trying for dignity. 'I won't hear from you again, correct?'

'No.' *You won't hear me coming, or see me either, sweetheart.* 'I'll do you one better. I'll tell you where Roy is so that you can get the vials yourself. That way you'll know for sure that it's all taken care of.'

She released a relieved lungful of air. 'That would be perfect.'

'I'll text you the coordinates.'

He ended the call, sent the coordinates to Roy's nurse, then texted a reply to his trusted contact. *Any suspects?*

He had to wait a minute for the answer. *The Fed saw her.*

'Of course he did,' he muttered, then texted back. *Who knows? Everyone. Feds. Staff. Word spread like wildfire.*

Leave it to the staff grapevine, he thought sourly, then texted his reply. *Thx. TTFN.*

No prob. Love you. XOXOXO.

Which was a damn good thing. A contact who loved you was one who wouldn't sell you out. Until they didn't love you anymore. But he always killed them before that happened.

Whistling, he grabbed his keys, unlocked his basement door, and jogged down the stairs, past his lab, and past the locked door to the storeroom where he kept his best coke, heroin, and meth, as well as the steroids that made him so much money with the gym rats. He unlocked the door to his armory, where he kept his rifles and handguns and a few new weapons he'd made himself but had never tested. He had the proper elements to create a few quick and dirty car bombs on an as-needed basis – and he had needed them over the years, usually as a not-so-friendly warning to a client who hadn't paid.

Locked away in a special cupboard was what was left of the ricin he'd made just to see if he could. After all, Walter White had done it on television. How difficult could it be? Turned out, not so difficult at all. He'd been disappointed that it hadn't been more of a challenge, so he'd used some of it to try something different – a twist on a flea bomb that would kill a lot more than fleas.

He kept the result – two canisters of aerosolized ricin – fully contained in a special airtight safe. Not because he worried they'd be stolen. Nobody had a key to this room but him. But if they went off by mistake? That would be bad indeed.

But he didn't need anything like that to deal with the nurse. He grabbed an ordinary semi-automatic rifle and his favorite handgun, complete with a silencer, just in case. There was no need to try to mask the death of Eileen Wilkins as anything more than it really was – the elimination of a contract employee whose services were no longer required. Because she'd failed. He wanted people to know about Eileen. He wanted any future contacts to know that he did not suffer fools. Needed to ensure that the next time he ordered a hit, it would be done quickly and done right.

Now he'd have to figure out what to do about Griffin Davenport. That the man would have a guard 24/7 from here on out was a given. That he'd spilled important information to his fellow Feds was also a given.

He briefly wondered if Davenport was worth killing at this point. Alice was dead, so she couldn't corroborate anything he said. And she'd left no records. *So I'm good there.*

But it bothered him, leaving that loose end unsnipped. He needed the man gone, simply for his own peace of mind.

He locked the basement once he'd finished. 'I'm leaving now!' he called up the stairs to Mallory. 'I'll be back for dinner.'

Mallory appeared from the laundry room, carrying a basket of clean clothes, size tween. Everything an adolescent boy or girl would want to feel special. 'I'll have it ready.'

'I feel like steak. Make sure we have steak.'

'I may have to go to the grocery store, then.'

He didn't worry about letting her run free – within limits, of course. He knew that she knew better than to run away or to tell or to do anything that would endanger him. He held her sister's health and happiness in the palm of his hand.

He tapped her nose with his finger, realizing that she'd grown taller yet again. She'd been such a cute kid. His first star. She'd made him and McCord a hell of a lot of money, even with all the pirating bastards who'd played their videos without paying for them.

'Get some fresh strawberries while you're at it,' he said. 'And make that shortcake that you do so well. I'll be in the mood for that later.'

Cincinnati, Ohio,
Thursday 13 August, 12.35 P.M.

'Those breaths were normal, Doc,' Decker said after drawing several deep breaths at the doctor's request, each one lowering Kate's blood pressure a little more. That the Narcan worked meant that they'd identified the problem correctly. He'd been drugged, not poisoned like Alice. 'I don't think I'll need any more of your wonder drug, and you really don't have to stay any longer. I'm good now. Thank you.'

The doctor gave him an exasperated look. 'I'll make my own decisions, Agent Davenport. I'll leave when I believe you're stable.'

'I figured you'd say that,' Decker muttered. He focused his blue eyes on Kate, and her heart tripped a little. He had the most beautiful eyes she'd ever seen. 'Who was poisoned?'

Giving the doctor a wary look, she bent down to whisper in his ear. 'Alice.'

Decker's wide shoulders sagged. 'Goddamn it to hell. She was a loose end.'

'I know.' She swiped her thumb across his knuckles. 'We were afraid you'd be considered a loose end too.'

He huffed a hoarse chuckle. 'So you jumped the staff like hurdles.'

'Yeah.' And it was worth it, because he was okay. She tugged her hand free. 'I need to get that food on the floor bagged and tagged. I'll be back.'

'I'll do it,' Troy said, coming back into the room. 'You stay with Davenport.'

'Thank you,' Kate said to her partner. 'Had Eileen Wilkins left yet?'

Troy scooped the spilled food into an evidence bag. 'Yeah, dammit.'

Kate sighed. 'You put out a BOLO? I know you did. I'm sorry. I'm still shaken up.'

'Don't worry. I didn't take offense.' Troy sealed the evidence bag. 'Hospital security is getting us a copy of the photo on her ID badge. I'll amend the BOLO when I get the pic.'

'This is your partner?' Decker asked. 'He's not an asshole like the other guy.'

Troy laughed. 'You really didn't like Novak, did you?'

'Asshole,' Decker pronounced.

'Deacon's a good guy.' Kate kept her reproof gentle. 'We've been friends for years.'

'Still an asshole.'

Troy stood at the foot of Decker's bed. 'I'm Luther Troy. It's nice to meet you, Agent Davenport. Should I call you Griff or Decker?'

'Either is fine.' Decker took several large breaths, then opened his eyes wide and fixed his gaze on Kate. 'You said something about bringing me something I could use to get online?'

Kate sucked in one cheek. 'I think he really is feeling better now, Doctor.'

'Or he's obsessed,' the doctor said. 'He made a major fuss up in ICU.' Again he tapped the iPad in his pocket. 'Pissed off the nurses.'

Decker's cheeks darkened. 'I apologized.'

'It was noted, which means the nurse accepted it. You must have done some serious kissing up to charm Mary Jean. She's a tough one.' The doctor handed the tainted IV bag to Kate, set up a new one, then pulled what looked like EpiPens from his pocket. 'I'm leaving these with you, Agent Coppola. They're auto-injectors. Same active as Narcan, different name. Aim it anywhere. You can't hurt him. If he feels another wave of exhaustion or his breathing becomes erratic, dose him. Don't hesitate. Then call the nurse. I'll stop by in a little while to check on him.'

'Thank you.' Kate put the injectors in the pocket of her jacket. 'What are we going to do with you, Decker?' she asked when the doctor had left the room.

He flashed her a quick, wicked grin. 'In what context, Kate?'

Her cheeks heated. 'In the context of keeping you alive.'

His blue eyes twinkled at her. 'Oh yeah. Well, I guess that would be nice, too.'

'I'm beginning to understand Agent Novak's issue with you,' Troy said tartly.

'Stop it,' Kate said when Decker opened his mouth to reply. 'I'm afraid to leave you here.' She gave Troy a troubled look. 'Anyone can get to him, even with an armed guard at the door.'

Troy sighed. 'I know. It's not like they'd know if the medical staff were doing the wrong thing, any more than we would.'

Decker's expression went stony once again. 'I need to get out of here. They told me to walk, that I could leave if I walked.' He abruptly tried to sit up, then sank back to the pillow with a groan. 'That was really dumb, wasn't it?'

Kate gave him no quarter. 'It really was. How long did they say you'd have to stay?'

'They said a week. I was aiming for four days. Now . . . I need out of here faster.'

'Exponentially faster,' Kate agreed. She studied the pieces of equipment monitoring him. 'What are they worried about? Infection? Relapse?'

'Pneumonia. The bullet wound's mostly healed, but pneumonia's a risk if I'm not moving.'

'So you can't be guarded in here 24/7. You have to leave this room sometime to walk.' A thought occurred to her and she turned to Troy. 'Is it possible to get him a private physician we can trust and set him up in a more secure location? Like a hotel room or a safe house?'

'I actually like that idea,' Troy said, sounding surprised.

Decker nodded. 'So do I,' he said, but didn't sound surprised at all, which was nice. 'You got an idea for a doctor we can trust?'

Kate nodded. 'Yeah, I do. Dani Novak. Deacon's sister. She just quit this hospital and doesn't start her new job for a few days. If she's available, we can trust her.'

'She visited you yesterday,' Decker said, and Kate blinked down at him.

'You heard that?'

'Bits and pieces,' Decker acknowledged.

'I'll see if we can make that happen.' Troy opened the door, then looked back over his shoulder. 'Guard's here. His name is Agent Triplett. I'll call you when I know something, Kate. Good meeting you, Griff.' He closed the door behind him, leaving the two of them alone.

Decker fumbled for the bed control and slowly raised himself so that he was sitting up. 'Now, that tablet you promised me . . .'

Kate shook her head. 'You know you're a single-mindedly stubborn man, right?'

'I consider that one of my strengths.' He held his hand out. 'Please.'

Kate dug the tablet from her yarn bag, but hesitated before giving it to him. As soon as he went online, he'd look up the status of the case that had gotten him shot. He'd see the obituaries and read about the death of Agent Symmes, the only name he'd given as his emergency contact. Notification of his handler's death should be more personally delivered. 'I need to tell you a few things first.'

His eyes immediately shuttered, hiding his emotions. 'I'm listening.'

Cincinnati, Ohio,
Thursday 13 August, 1.00 P.M.

Decker was listening, but he didn't want to be. It didn't take a genius to know he wasn't going to like what was coming.

To her credit Kate didn't mince words, didn't try to make it better with euphemisms and platitudes. She just said it, plainly but gently. 'Agent Symmes is dead.'

Closing his eyes so he didn't have to see the sympathy in hers, he clenched his teeth against the growing tightness in his chest that had nothing to do with his physical injuries. For a few heartbeats he remained silent until the worst of the emotion had passed. When he spoke, it was evenly. Carefully. 'I figured as much.'

'Because he didn't come to you when you were in the coma?'

Decker nodded. 'He was my emergency contact.'

'I know. Your only one. That's why I hated leaving you alone.'

He swallowed hard. 'Good thing, I guess. Symmes wouldn't have sat with me for the hours you did. He has a family. *Had* a family,' he corrected, his voice still level. 'No wife or kids, at least, but his parents were old and he took care of them.' His throat grew thick and he had to clear it. 'Nurse Evil would have probably put a pillow over my face if you hadn't been there.'

'Maybe,' she murmured. 'Doesn't make his loss any easier.' His hand that clutched the bedrail was suddenly warm. Her hand covering his. It was comfort, pure and clean and . . . sweet. And it gave him the courage to ask the questions he needed to ask even though the answers were ones he really didn't want to know.

'How did he die?' Because it shouldn't have happened. Decker clearly remembered overpowering the traffickers' head of security and one of his men. It had been the day before he got shot. He remembered every second of that day. *I tied them up. Securely. I made sure their pockets were empty and I disarmed them. I know I did.* But something had happened, because Richard Symmes was dead.

'The head of security had a blade hidden in the hem of his pants,' Kate said. 'We were able to piece the scene together. It looks like the second guy helped his boss rip his pants leg and get to the blade. They cut the ropes on each other's hands and were almost free when Symmes entered the room. They stabbed him, but he was able to shoot them before they got away. All three were dead before we got there.'

Decker wanted to sigh, but he held it in. 'I should have checked them better.'

Her hand squeezed his. 'The blade was thin, Decker. If you'd stripped them naked and taken their clothes, then maybe . . . But you disarmed them, and from the knots I saw on those ropes, you'd tied them well. Maybe you should wonder how Agent Symmes let them get the jump on him. Symmes was armed. He knew he was walking into a potentially deadly situation. Maybe he wasn't being careful.'

'Symmes was a good man.'

'From what I can see, so are you,' she said, and he could hear the smile in her voice, even though he steadfastly refused to meet her eyes.

The corners of his mouth, however, had a mind of their own and curled upward, pleased at her compliment. 'At least he got 'em,' he said gruffly.

'How did *you* get them?' she asked, not moving her hand away from his. 'We wondered.'

He appreciated the topic change. 'I was so damn frustrated that all they'd let me see was the legit books, no matter how much I hinted to the head guy.'

'Joel Whipple.'

'Yeah, him. Joel is a weasel. He's brilliant with numbers, but he's got a streak of mean in him even though he was too scared to do anything with it. Like he wouldn't push you off a boat himself, but if you tripped and fell overboard, he'd stand there and watch you drown. Watch him closely. He said he wants to deal, but he'll be sneaky.'

Kate shrugged. 'It's moot. He's gone. In the wind.'

Decker wasn't really surprised. 'Foul play?'

'None that the investigating agents could find. He bailed. He's probably sipping Mai Tais on a beach somewhere. Could he have suspected you?'

'Of being a Fed? I doubt it. If he had, he would have told his partners and I'd have gone to sleep one night and not woken up the next morning.' A twitch of her fingers on his was the only indication that the thought of him not waking up bothered her. Otherwise, she was silent, letting him answer the question she'd asked. He liked that. Too many people asked a question, then jumped in to help answer it. 'But he did think I was gunning for his job. That's why he kept me focused on the legit books. He knew I was bored out of my skull. I think he was biding his time, waiting for me to blow a fuse so that he could have an excuse to end me.'

'What happened the night you abducted the two security guys?'

'Partly luck, partly preparation. As soon as they transferred me from being a bodyguard to an accountant, I started setting up a plan in case I got a break. Which happened that night.'

'The escape of one of their trafficked victims.'

'Yeah. It set off the alarm in the security control room. I'd already made friends with the guy manning the room. I'd work all night and take my break up there with him. I started bringing coffee, doughnuts, getting him comfortable with me being there. I also kept a syringe of sedative in my pocket, just in case I had to make a quick escape. When the alarm sounded, I injected him with the sedative and then added some to his coffee, in case someone checked up on him. It made him woozy enough that I was able to walk him out to his car without him raising another alarm.

'I contacted his boss, told him that I thought his guy was using, but that I thought he should take care of it directly and not involve the rest of his team. The boss appreciated that – he was a former cop who really didn't trust the traffickers. They trusted him, though, and that was their mistake. He met me, I injected him with sedative, then tied them up and dropped them off in the apartment that Symmes had set up as our meeting place. I called Symmes from a landline in the apartment, let it ring once, then hung up. That was our code.'

'Why didn't you just tell Symmes who you'd brought to your meeting place?'

'Because at that point, both of the security guys believed I was just trying to stage a coup. I'd been in the security department before they stuck me in Accounting. I wanted them to think I was a crooked opportunist, not that I was Bureau. I did call Symmes on my burner phone once I'd left the room. He was on his way to pick them up already. I tossed the burner after I called him – I never used a burner more than once. Rich Symmes knew what he was walking into.'

So why did you let them take you down, Rich? Why?

'Then you shouldn't feel guilty that he's dead,' Kate said quietly but firmly. 'It was a good plan, Decker. It worked, except for Symmes getting surprised by them. That's not on you.'

He nodded once, grateful for the words. Someday he might actually believe them. 'Anything else you need to tell me?'

'The guys that shot you . . . they're dead too. Everyone is dead now who was in any position of authority or who knew anything.

Only people left standing are the low-level flunkies.'

There was something in her voice, a reluctant regret that had him turning his head to look at her. 'Who killed the guys who shot me?'

Her chin lifted slightly. 'I did. They shot you through some trees, then hopped in their car and drove away. I chased, I shot, the car wrecked into a tree, and . . . no more shooters.'

Decker considered the layout of the compound where he'd been shot. If the shooters' car was on the road, driving away, she'd had to run down a long driveway just to have a clear shot. If they were driving fast, they would have gotten a huge head start. 'How far away were they?'

She shrugged. 'Half a mile, give or take.'

His eyes widened. She'd hit a moving car at half a mile? 'Are you fucking serious?'

Her mouth tightened. 'I'm good at my job, Decker.'

He remembered she'd been carrying a rifle with a scope when she'd dropped out of that tree behind him. 'Holy hell, you must be. I mean . . . wow.' She looked uncomfortable with his praise, so he dialed it back. 'Thank you. You kept them from hurting anyone else.'

She looked away. 'Yeah. But now we can't question them.'

'Who knows if they'd still be alive by now anyway? Whoever got Alice may have gotten them too. What's going on with that anyway?'

'You know what I know, basically. Novak's following up. How are you feeling now?'

'Tired. Frustrated. Hungry.' He slid her a sideways look. 'But otherwise, better than I might have been. Thank you for jumping the staff like hurdles. You may have saved my life.'

Her auburn brows arched, her cocky attitude thankfully re-appearing. '*May* have? I'd say I definitely did. I'd say you definitely owe me.'

Suddenly he was no longer tired, but he was very frustrated and very hungry. Only in a different way now. He owed her. He liked the sound of that. He liked it so much that he had to shift his hips, bending one knee slightly to hide the sudden tenting of the sheet over his groin.

He smirked to hide what would have been a heated look that both her old and new partners would have heartily disapproved of. 'Can I go online now?' he asked, giving the tablet she held a pointed look.

She huffed a short laugh and put the tablet in his hands. 'I turned all the locks off so you don't need my password. Knock yourself out.'

'Thanks.' He wondered if her password would have been *Jack*. 'Anything I should avoid?'

'No. I only use it for e-books, knitting patterns, and games, and not very often at that. In fact I can't remember the last time I even turned it on.'

But she'd turned him on. He kept his gaze on the tablet, feeling uncertain for the first time in a long time. Because she was the first person in a long time to have gotten close enough to matter. She'd held his hand and had sat with him for hours and had definitely saved his life. He knew that her voice was the one he'd listened for the whole week he lay helpless in that damn ICU bed. He knew that she was the one he trusted.

But he didn't know why she'd stayed. She'd said it was because Symmes was dead and he had no other emergency contacts. If that was all it was, he wasn't interested. He didn't want her pity. He wanted her to be as turned on as he was.

'Decker? Is something wrong?'

He drummed a tattoo on the tablet's cover, his fingers needing something to do. Something to touch. *Just ask her. Ask her and be done with it*. 'Who was Jack?'

Her gasp was barely audible, even in the quiet of the room, and for a long moment she didn't say a word. Finally she blew out a breath. 'How do you know about Jack?'

He kept his eyes on his still-drumming fingers. 'I heard you,' he admitted. 'You talked to him. When I was . . . out of it. You said you were sorry.'

Another silence, longer this time. Then she reached over the rail to cover his hand. 'Please, stop the drumming. You're making

117

me crazy.' Her hand, which she hadn't retracted, was visibly trembling.

'Who was he, Kate?'

'How do you know he *was* anything? Maybe he *is*.'

'The other woman – Novak's sister – you told her that you needed her to be your new contact because your old one had died. She asked if it was Jack, then said she was sorry for your loss. That usually indicates a death.'

'Jesus,' she whispered, her voice trembling too. 'What else did you hear?'

'Later, you were humming "Wish You Were Here", then you cried.' One side of his mouth quirked up. 'Then you played Disney songs for me and made me promise not to tell. That you had a badass rep to protect.' Taking a chance, he flipped his hand over so that he could lace their fingers together. She didn't pull away and he summoned his courage again. 'Who was Jack, Kate?' he asked as gently as he could.

She drew a deep breath. 'My husband's brother,' she said on the exhale.

What the fuck? He whipped his head around to stare at her. 'You're *married*?' he demanded, regretting his tone immediately.

She was pale. Stricken. Like someone had slapped her. *That someone would be me. You idiot.* Because a verbal slap could hurt more than a physical one.

She shook her head. 'No,' she whispered. 'Not anymore. He died, too.'

Decker let his head drop to the pillow, calling himself twelve kinds of fool. 'I'm sorry.'

'For what?' she asked, her voice too quiet. Too sedate. 'For accusing me of cheating on my husband, that I lost my husband, or for poking into my personal life?'

'The first and second ones. I accused you of something terrible and I'm sorry.' He turned to look at her again, the guilt stabbing him worse than any real-life knife he'd ever taken in his gut. But he needed to be honest. 'But not the last one. I needed to know.'

She gave his hand a weak squeeze before pulling away. 'It's

okay, I guess. I would have wondered, too. Um, I started charging the tablet in the car on the way over. It's at about twenty percent now.' She pulled a charging cord from her bag along with a wireless card. 'You can get Internet here in the hospital, but if you want to do anything secure, use my Wi-Fi card.'

'Thank you.'

She leaned over to plug the charger into the wall outlet near the floor and he bit the inside of his lip. Damn, but the woman was built. *Such a pretty butt.* He wanted to reach out and touch so badly . . . *But not here. Not now.*

But definitely not 'never'. He adjusted the tablet so that it covered his erection, which had found its second wind after hearing she wasn't married. Not anymore, anyway. His heart could feel sympathy that she'd lost someone she'd loved, but his cock didn't have any such feelings. All it knew was that it wanted her. A lot.

She straightened and shouldered her bag printed with the picture of kittens and yarn, the movement making her jacket swing back to reveal the service weapon in her shoulder holster.

God. The soft woman who knitted with camo-colored yarn was a better shot than he was. Far better. The disparity was . . . hot. So hot that the tablet on his lap popped up, then slid down the sheet, nudged by an almost painful pulse of his completely unsympathetic cock. He reset the tablet in place, then realized that she'd grabbed her laptop bag as well.

She was leaving. 'Wait,' he said. 'Where are you going?'

'Not far. I need to follow up with Agent Troy on getting you a private doctor.'

'You can call him from here,' Decker said, studying her face. She was still rattled.

'I need a little space,' she said softly. 'Don't worry. I'll be back and Agent Triplett is just outside. I'll tell him that nobody is to give you anything. Can I get you some water or juice while I'm out? I'll get it from the drink machine in the cafeteria.'

'Yes, that would be nice.' He frowned as his stomach growled. He was suddenly starving. 'And a cheeseburger. Maybe two. And chicken. Not soup or nuggets. Wings, with hot sauce. Or maybe not hot sauce just yet. I'll save that for tomorrow.'

She laughed. 'Anything else?' she asked.

Relief had him sagging back into the pillow. She was smiling at him again. 'Peanut M&Ms,' he said. 'And pie. Apple. Or cherry, whichever they have. Maybe some Cheetos. And a brownie. Or cake. Chocolate.'

She shook her head. 'How about an appointment with a dentist because of all that sugar?'

'I'll floss.' He lifted his hand in a three-fingered salute. 'Scout's honor.'

She looked surprised. 'Were you a Boy Scout?'

'Eagle.' Thanks to Mama D and the real Griffin Davenport.

Her expression grew pensive. 'Good for you. I'll see what I can do about the food.' She started to open the door, then stopped short. 'Oh. I completely forgot why I came to see you to begin with. We need to get everything you can remember from the traffickers' ledgers. Customers, suppliers, profits, losses – anything you can recall. Hopefully there will be something in there that points to McCord's mystery partner.'

Decker nodded, grateful for something tangible to do. 'I'll get on it.' He waited until she was gone, closing the door behind her, before turning on the tablet and opening a browser page.

He stared at it for a full minute before giving in to the need to know. With one hand he hunted and pecked his search terms: *survived by Kate Coppola*, *husband*, *death*, and *Jack*. Then he held his breath and hit ENTER.

Six

Cincinnati, Ohio,
Thursday 13 August, 1.25 P.M.

Mallory had been giving a lot of thought to her plan as she drove to the Kroger and she'd thought she knew exactly what she needed to do. But now that she was here, parking the car, she wasn't so sure.

What if he finds out? What if people still don't believe me?

He'd take Macy. He'd get custody of her, even though it would mean murder.

It's not like he hasn't done it before. So many times. What's two more?

But . . . they were his blood. His sister. Her husband.

He'd still do it. Of that Mallory had no doubt. He'd nearly done it once before. *Just to teach me a lesson.* And if he got custody of Macy? He'd make her into Sunshine Suzie.

So what do I do? Mallory sighed. She'd had this argument with herself so many times. 'Shit or get off the pot,' she murmured, remembering her mother saying the words a lifetime ago.

It was the thought of her mother that got her moving. No way would she ever be like that, surviving from one fix to the next while her children cried themselves to sleep, hungry and cold. *Not gonna happen. I really would rather be dead.*

She locked the old non-descript car he'd given her to drive, noting that he'd changed the plates again. He did that every time she returned from running errands and she often wondered where he got all the license plates. But she didn't ask because she really didn't want to know any more of his secrets.

She was having enough trouble with the secrets she already knew.

Keeping her eyes to herself, she made her way into the Kroger, crossing her fingers that it still had a pay phone. Pay phones were really hard to find these days, so she made a point of remembering when she saw one because she had no cell phone. He'd never allow that, even though he'd be able to track her every call.

Mind games. He loved to play mind games.

She breathed a sigh of relief at the sight of the old-school pay phone. *Still here.* She stared at it, then forced herself to remember the clothes she'd folded. He was preparing for the kids to return. On Saturday. He'd already begun the process the Saturday before. Making them feel welcome. Valued. Loved.

On Saturday he'd take the next step. He'd make them feel pretty. Handsome. Sexy.

Her throat began to burn as her stomach churned acid. *Make the call, Mallory. He won't know. How could he possibly know? He thinks he has me scared, too afraid to act.* Because of Macy. Always because of Macy.

If you don't make that call, he'll be right.

She forced her feet to move until she stood in front of the pay phone. Hands trembling, she pulled out the heavy phone book that hung below so that it perched on the booth's little shelf. She'd never used a phone book before, but she could read, so how hard could it be?

Harder than it looks. There were so many numbers and she only had so many coins. She'd found them in the sofa cushions, but she never kept all she found. She returned most of them to him because he'd know otherwise. He always knew because he had cameras in every room. He watched her. All the time.

She let the phone book drop, closing her eyes to fight the wave of nausea that swept over her. He always knew.

He'll know, he'll know, he'll know.

She dug her nails into her arm, the pain distracting her mind from its never-ending litany.

If you let him hurt those kids, you are no better than he is. So pick up the book and make the call. She obeyed, breathing through her nose, hoping to control her racing heart.

She picked the number with the address closest to where she'd been shopping on Saturday. Because she didn't know how to find out who the Fed was that was in the hospital, the one he wanted killed. But the policewoman would know. The one who'd been kind. Who'd realized something was wrong and helped stop it, even though she probably didn't know it.

Mallory fumbled the coins, her hands were shaking so badly. Finally she put in the right number and dialed, swallowing back the bile as she did so. She'd want to throw up if she did call and if she didn't, so she might as well call and make being sick worthwhile at least.

'Cincinnati Police,' a crisp female voice answered. 'How may I direct your call?'

'I'm . . . I'm not sure,' Mallory stammered. 'I'm looking for a lady . . . a policewoman. But I don't know her name.'

'All right,' the operator said, her voice turning from crisp to kind. 'Is this an emergency?'

'No. I don't need 911. I just need to find this lady cop.'

'Well, I'll try to find her, but I'm sure another officer could help you just as well.'

'No!' Mallory cried, panic grabbing her by the throat. 'I mean, I mean, no, please. I really want to talk to this particular lady. She was on duty this past Saturday.' *Why didn't you get her name? You stupid idiot!* 'I met her at the Kroger on Glenway. She was young. And really, really tall. And African-American.'

How many tall, African-American lady cops could there be? Mallory hoped not that many.

'I don't know her personally,' the operator said, 'but I'll try to find out. Would you like her to call you back?'

Oh no. Oh no. Mallory had not thought this out. At all. How could the cop call her back?

'Oh, um . . . I don't have a phone. I'm calling from a pay phone now. Can she call me back on this phone?'

'Honey, are you all right? You don't have to give me details if someone's listening, but maybe say, "It's really hot today" if you're in trouble and need help. I can have officers there in a jif.'

Tell her. Tell. Her. But Mallory couldn't. She didn't know this lady. She wanted the lady who'd helped her. Who'd chased the man away. Who seemed to care.

'I'm fine, really,' Mallory said, injecting false warmth into her answer. 'I'm just trying to ask her some questions about being a lady cop. For a school project.'

Yeah. That's good. It's for school.

'A school project?' the operator asked carefully. 'But school hasn't started yet.'

Busted. Oh God. 'Summer school. I failed my class last year.'

'Okay,' the operator said. 'I'll try to find out. How about you call me back at this number? Ask for Lilith. That's my name. I'll find out and hold the information for you.'

Mallory's knees went weak. 'Thank you,' she whispered unsteadily.

'I want to help you, honey. Please let me help you.'

'I'll call back later,' Mallory said in a panicked rush. 'Thank you.'

She hung up, still gripping the phone's handset. She held on to it, closing her eyes and breathing deeply for a long, long moment before she felt steady enough to let go. To straighten up. To go into the store and buy his steak and his goddamn strawberries.

Cincinnati, Ohio,
Thursday 13 August, 1.30 P.M.

Kate closed the door to Decker's room and let out a breath. He'd heard her calling out to Jack in her sleep. And he'd remembered it. She wondered what else she'd said when he was in the coma. She wondered if he really was an Eagle Scout. And she wondered if she'd been wrong to lead him on by sitting at his bedside, talking to him, touching his face for the past week. *It's only leading him on if you don't intend to pursue him.*

Do you intend to pursue him? Well, do you? Yeah, she did. Because she *liked* him, more every moment she spent in his company. He was funny and irreverent and quick-witted.

Of course, she liked him in other ways, too. It had been a long time since her heart had beat that fast. At least when she wasn't on the clock, chasing killers.

He's probably in there looking me up right now. I would be if the situation were reversed.

'Agent Coppola?'

Kate started. She'd been wool-gathering, having forgotten all about the agent standing guard. She looked sideways, then way up, her eyes growing wide. Why he'd been chosen to be Decker's guard was immediately obvious. The man was huge. Had to be six-six or six-seven and he was built like a brick shithouse, as her father used to say.

Hell, he'd make Decker look downright average. *Well, a little above average*, she allowed.

The man would have been terrifyingly intimidating, with his shiny bald head and double-breasted black suit, had it not been for the fact that he was beautiful. Like model beautiful, with his dark brown skin, even darker eyes, eyelashes that should be illegal, and a winning smile. It took her a second to get her voice back and his smile became self-conscious, an aw-shucks kind of grin. Like he knew the effect he had on people but was a little too polite to openly enjoy it.

'Yes, I'm Coppola. You're Agent Triplett, Davenport's guard?'

He stuck out his hand. 'Jefferson Triplett. Nice to meet you. Welcome to Cincinnati.'

She smiled up at him as she shook his hand. 'Thank you. I kind of jumped in with both feet as soon as my plane landed last week. I think you're the first person to actually welcome me.'

He was young and earnest, somewhere in his mid-twenties, and his pretty eyes and open smile held none of the shadows that she and her teammates all seemed to share. Someday he'd have those shadows too, and that made her more than a little sad.

'I've got the day shift here. Please let me know if you or Agent Davenport need anything.'

'I'm going to run down to the cafeteria. He didn't get lunch and I barely got breakfast.'

'That'll be a safer place to get his food,' Triplett agreed. 'Well, from a tainting standpoint anyway. I can't speak to the risk of indigestion.'

Kate chuckled. 'Especially given the list of food he asked me to bring back. Man's got to have an iron gut. While I'm gone, please do not let anyone in the room unless you're with them. No one is to give him any food or medicine, or even change his IV. His nurse might only be as tall as your kneecaps, but don't underestimate her. She's a pistol.'

'No, ma'am. My mother's only five foot, but she's big on the inside.'

'And she taught you to say ma'am.' Kate sighed. 'God, I'm old.'

'No, ma'am, you're nowhere close to old,' he said with that aw-shucks grin. 'I heard about that shot you made. We're all talking about it.'

'Really? And what are you all saying?'

'Half of us don't believe it. The other half want you to teach us how to shoot like that.'

Her lips twitched. 'Which half are you, Agent Triplett?'

'Solidly in the second half, ma'am. I'd be grateful for some training.'

'We'll do that,' Kate said with a hard nod.

'Excellent. So, what about her?' He pointed to the opposite wall, where a woman waited, tapping her foot nervously. It was the nurse's assistant who'd dropped the tray.

'Oh shit,' Kate muttered. *I forgot about her.*

'She hasn't moved from that spot,' he said. 'She said that you told her to wait.'

'That I did. Thanks, Agent Triplett.' She turned to the waiting woman. 'Miss? Would you come with me, please?'

She led the woman to the same waiting room where she and Troy had talked to Zimmerman earlier. The nurse's assistant said nothing, wringing her hands and staring at her shoes as she walked. She looked damn guilty, but Kate knew better than to trust appearances.

126

'Let's have a seat,' Kate said and glanced at the woman's badge. Teresa Robbey, CNA. Certified Nurse's Assistant. 'Miss Robbey, thank you for waiting.'

Robbey looked up, eyes narrowed. 'You really didn't give me any choice. I hope I don't lose my job because of this. They had to have someone take over my shift. I'm hourly. My pay is gonna get docked and I got groceries to buy and rent to pay.'

Kate sighed. 'I'll see if I can do something about that, okay? Can you walk me through your morning – where you got the meals you were serving, who prepared them?'

'I thought you knew who did it,' Robbey said suspiciously. 'Eileen Wilkins.'

'Perhaps. Until we have proof, we need to make sure we've asked all the appropriate questions. So . . . where did you pick up the meals?'

'Same place I always do. Down in the kitchen. The ladies down there fill the trays according to the prescribed meal. They load the carts. I just go and pick up the ones I'm supposed to deliver.'

'So whoever loads the carts knows the room each tray is going to?'

'Yes. I suppose they have to.'

'Do you know who loaded up your cart?'

'Probably Jessie. She usually does it. But I didn't see her do it, if that's what you're asking. I got down there and the cart was loaded up, waiting.'

'Okay. Did you see anyone down there who didn't belong?'

'Like Eileen? No, she wasn't down there. Just the normal crew.'

'Do you know Eileen Wilkins personally?'

'Yeah.' And Miss Robbey didn't seem too pleased about that. 'I don't like her.'

Kate arched her brows. 'Because?'

Robbey hesitated. 'Look, there's a tight-knit organization here. The RNs like me and that makes my job easier. I don't wanna be telling no tales here.'

'If I can possibly help it, I won't pass on to any of the staff here what you tell me.'

Robbey sighed heavily. 'Whatever. Eileen Wilkins is a user.'

Kate waited for more, but Robbey had tightened her lips. *Not making it any easier for me, are you?* 'A user like she'd take advantage of you, or a drug user?'

'Both.'

It was Kate's turn to sigh, and she did so impatiently. 'I'm trying to be nice, Miss Robbey, since I made you wait for me.'

'And you scared me shitless!'

'That too. But you need to be more detailed in your answers. Do not make me pull it out of you a word at a time. That would make me irritated and I don't think either of us would like that. Now, Eileen Wilkins. Does she use drugs on the job?'

'Yes. Dilaudid. It's what they give folks who are allergic to morphine.'

'Have you seen her using?'

'Yeah, but she don't know it. For a long time she was dropping the leftover vials in her pocket then taking them home. I guess she'd had a hard day, because she was in the restroom, and . . .' She rolled her eyes. 'This is gonna make me sound like a pervert, but I was really just making sure whoever was in the stall was okay. I heard huffing and puffing going on, like someone was having some kind of an attack. I called out first, asked if she was all right. I didn't know it was Eileen at the time. She made a funny sound, like a groan, then she said she was fine. But she didn't sound fine. She sounded hyped up. So I peeked through the crack. Saw her sitting on the toilet lid, a needle in her arm and a vial in her hand.'

'And you're sure the vial said Dilaudid?'

'Yeah. I'm studying for my nursing diploma. I pay attention to everything. I don't want to be a CNA for the rest of my life. I got kids to put through college.'

'All right then, do you know how long she's been using?'

'A year. Maybe more. Started not too long after she met the guy she's dating.'

'Tell me about him.'

'He's built like the agent in the bed. Davenport. Big guy. Brawny. But dumb as an ox. Has a temper, too. She brought him to the

ICU Christmas party this past year.' The look she gave Kate was defensive to the point of being almost hostile. 'I tend bar at night to earn extra money. I got hired to work all the department parties.'

'Seems like they should have invited you,' Kate said quietly, and Robbey smiled bitterly.

'Not likely. They like me, but not enough to join in their reindeer games.'

Kate's lips twitched. 'Sorry. I'm seeing Nurse Choi head-butting all the other nurses like the deer do when they get their antlers tangled up.'

Robbey's lips twitched too. 'Yeah. She's fierce, all right. But she's one of the good ones. You're lucky she didn't tear you a new one today. Choi takes care of her patients.'

'Does Eileen?' she asked, and Robbey scoffed.

'No. Half the time they're not getting the painkillers they're supposed to because she needs a fix and keeps back a lot more than she gives. She skims and her patients suffer.'

Kate wondered if any of Johnnie's nurses had done that to him, and what she would have done had she caught them. Especially toward the end, when he'd really needed them. *Any nurse that cruel would have needed painkillers when I'd gotten done with her.* 'I'm curious, Miss Robbey, not judging – honest – but did you try to tell anyone? Report her?'

'No.' And she looked ashamed as she admitted it. 'The last CNA who reported a nurse ended up getting all kinds of anonymous complaints against her later. She was really good at her job, but she ended up getting fired. I couldn't get fired.'

'That sucks,' Kate said quietly. 'But you've got kids to feed. I understand. Really.' She rubbed her forehead, weary again. 'Tell me more about Eileen. If she did this thing to Agent Davenport, there has to be a reason. He'd never met her before, so she couldn't have had her own beef with him. Did she need cash?'

'Sure. Everybody does. Her kid's older than mine and she's single like me. He's got special needs, too, so I'm sure she needs money.'

'You said she had a boyfriend, that she brought him to the holiday party. What happened?'

129

'He was a jerk. He's a lot younger, and I mean a *lot* younger. She thought she was hot stuff, struttin' around, dancing with him, but the other nurses were laughing at her. Called her a cougar. Made comments about the size of his . . . you know.' She held her thumb and forefinger about an inch apart. 'All quiet-like, behind their hands.'

Kate blinked. 'They laughed because her boyfriend wasn't well endowed?'

'Yeah. Because of the steroids. Nobody gets *that* buff without them. Except for your guy in the bed there. Davenport.' She looked upward, like she was embarrassed. 'I may have looked at his tox results. No steroids.'

'Good to know,' Kate said wryly, earning her a small grin from Teresa Robbey.

'Anyway, Eileen's boyfriend was a jerk that night at the party. Drank too much, talked too loudly, even got slapped by one of the nurses because he grabbed her ass. Let's just say I was busy that night, because *everybody* drank a lot. Those nurses can put it away. Like they got hollow legs or something.'

'What was the boyfriend's name?'

She bit her lip. 'Ray? Roy?' She nodded decisively. 'Roy. I remember the nurses called him Boy-Toy Roy. But I don't know his last name.'

'That's okay. What did he do when the nurse slapped him?'

'He hauled back, ready to slap her too, but Eileen dragged him out. She wasn't so proud of him at the end. And the next time I saw her, she was wearing a hella lot of eye makeup.'

'He hit her?'

'Somebody did.'

'Did he say or do anything to make you think he was using drugs other than steroids?'

'Asked me if he could buy a couple of dime bags, like I was a dealer or something. Said he was buying for him and his "old lady" but that he'd share his with me if I'd meet him after the party – which I of course did not. Does that count?'

Kate sat back in her chair. *Shit.* 'You know you could have led with *that*.'

Robbey shrugged. 'Hell, a couple of the nurses asked me where they could get hooked up, and at least that many spouses or boyfriends. Eileen's boy toy wasn't alone there. I don't think any of them remember asking me. They were all pretty toasted by then.'

'What does Mr Boy-Toy Roy look like?'

'Tall, blond, good-looking. He may be twenty-two. Not much older. He hangs around the college kids, but he mostly just hangs out at the gym. I see him sometimes when I'm on campus for my night classes. He's got a good thing with Eileen. He lives with her for free and does what he wants while she takes extra shifts to make ends meet. But I guess that's the going rate for arm candy these days.'

'I guess so. Anything else about Eileen or Mr Boy Toy?'

Robbey gave it some thought. 'She's seemed tense the last couple of days. Maybe a week.'

'When did you see her shooting up in the restroom?'

'About . . . it was four days ago.' Another shrug. 'I dunno. I mean, I don't like her, and she does hurt the patients by stealing their painkillers, but I can't see her purposely killing anyone. That's kind of a big jump – don't you think?'

Maybe. Maybe not. If Eileen needed money . . . or if she was being blackmailed. Kate had seen it before.

'I guess we'll find out once we track her down. Thank you, Miss Robbey. You've been very helpful. What would you like to do – have me try to get you back on your shift or just go home?'

'Shift. I've got groceries to buy.'

'Got it. Who does the schedule?'

'Downstairs. Name is Lacey.' Robbey looked suspicious. 'You're really going to try?'

'Yes. It's the least I can do. I'll have her contact you directly either way, okay?'

'Okay.'

Kate stood up. 'I'm sorry I frightened you. Agent Davenport's been through a lot. When I thought he might be in danger . . . I panicked, and you were in the path of the shockwave.'

Robbey stood as well. 'I guess you had good reason, seeing as how his IV had been tampered with. And his lips *were* blue. I'd only just noticed it myself when you came in like a house on fire. I was about to ring for Choi.'

'Thank you. I appreciate that. Good luck with the nursing diploma.' Kate gave her a smile, then turned for the elevator. She'd talk to Lacey about Teresa Robbey's shift, then she'd get Decker's food. *Hell, I might even have to borrow a cart to bring it all back.*

Cincinnati, Ohio,
Thursday 13 August, 2.05 P.M.

Three years. Decker stared at the photo on Kate's tablet screen. John Fitzgerald Morrow had died three years ago. Survived by his wife of one year, Katherine A. Coppola, and his brother, Jack R. Morrow. John had been only thirty-three years old. Brain cancer.

That had to have sucked royally. For John and for Kate.

The information had been easy to find. John's obituary had popped up on Decker's first search. The online guestbook set up by the funeral home was still active. John Morrow had been well loved by many people. Lots of good memories and good wishes on that guestbook.

Decker wondered if Kate had read them. If they'd given her any comfort at all.

And then he wondered if there would have been a funeral or an online guestbook for him had he died the week before or the year before or the decade before. No, he had to concede. There wouldn't have been, because he'd been a shadow for too many years. No one really knew him. Not anymore. No one he'd ever cared for was still alive. No one had survived him to log a memory online or anywhere else.

Kate would have. Of that he had no doubt. But she'd known him for, what? A week? And all but a few hours of that he'd spent in a fucking coma.

Irrationally angry, he started to close the browser page, but . . . didn't. He kept staring at John Morrow's photograph. He'd been a handsome man. A happy man. A productive man. A man who'd inspired loyalty and respect and affection from everyone who'd known him. Everyone who'd signed the guestbook, anyway.

He'd been a high school history teacher, and apparently his students had felt comfortable enough to confide the deepest secrets of their teenage angst. They all remembered him fondly. Some had assured him that they'd grown up to be okay. And every single one of them had included the words *Seize the day and make your lives extraordinary*.

It was a line from a movie. Decker knew that much. He had a vague recollection of watching it with Mama D and Griff on DVD. He remembered Mama D crying her eyes out into her drying towel. And he remembered Robin Williams standing on a desk, but not much else.

Decker had only been fifteen then. If a movie didn't have any explosions, it was just an excuse to sit next to Mama D and be fussed over, or to play-battle with Griff for the bucket of kettlecorn. Although he did remember wishing he'd had a teacher like Robin Williams. One who didn't see the big, brutish-looking boy who didn't know all the cultural stuff he should have known by high school. One who saw him inside and would tell him that he was worth saving.

He'd gotten that teacher the following year, and between his foster folks and Dr Hearle, they'd all but dragged him to a good path. The right path. The path that had made Mama D proud.

It appeared that John Morrow had been that teacher for his students. Hell, it appeared that John Morrow had been one hell of a guy all the way around and a damn hard act to follow. *No pressure, Decker. No pressure at all.*

Jack Morrow, on the other hand, had been troubled. So troubled that six months ago he'd put a gun in his mouth and pulled the trigger. There had been no online guestbook. No fond memories that would live on in the Internet forever. Just a small entry in the *Des Moines Register* saying that he'd committed suicide after losing his job as the assistant coach of the football team of his own high school alma mater.

And that his body had been found in the Washington, DC

apartment of his sister-in-law, Special Agent Katherine Coppola, a graduate of the same high school.

God, Kate. That she'd come home to find him there . . . Decker had seen the results of suicides who'd chosen that way to go. He'd cleaned up the mess they'd left behind. He still had nightmares, and those victims had been strangers. Not family.

I'm sorry, Jack. Why? Why was Kate sorry?

I'll ask her. But not today.

Decker didn't think he could stand seeing that shattered look in her eyes again anytime soon. He closed the browser window, then deleted the search history. If she asked him directly if he'd looked, he'd be honest. Otherwise, this was knowledge he'd keep to himself until the time was right. Or until she offered it up on her own.

He stared down at the tablet screen, deflated. He'd been so intent on getting online, but now he couldn't think why. He'd wanted to know how his case had turned out, but Kate had given him all the salient details. Richard Symmes, dead. Bad guys – including Alice – all dead. *Anyone left living knows nothing that'll help land McCord's partner.*

He narrowed his eyes. *McCord.* Decker remembered how angry Alice and her father had been when Marcus O'Bannion had exposed McCord's perversions in the *Ledger* – they'd said so in the same conversation in which they'd discussed McCord's mystery partner.

But how had O'Bannion known about McCord in the first place? And why had a bunch of bloodthirsty, soulless traffickers been so utterly terrified of him?

There was a knock at his door a second before a red head peeked in. 'It's me,' Kate said. 'I have food.'

'Come on in,' he said, scowling at the questions buzzing in his head.

Kate stopped short. 'What's wrong? Did something happen?'

I know you endured a nightmare six months ago was the first thought that popped into his head, but he shoved it away. 'O'Bannion.'

'He was here?' She approached carrying a tray filled with everything he'd asked for. Except that instead of two cheeseburgers, there was only one, plus an empty plate with crumbs and some drips of ketchup and mustard.

'No. But I have a question about him and McCord. Did you eat my other burger?'

She slid the tray onto the swing table. 'You should be nicer to me. Bringing you food nearly got me reamed inside out by Nurse Choi. She was in the elevator when I was coming back up.'

'So you lied and said this was all for you and ate my burger as a cover?'

She laughed. 'No. I told the truth. And Choi said you could have it, but only one cheeseburger. So I ate the other one. I was starving.'

'Thank you.' He grinned at the tray. 'You got the M&Ms.'

'Those I lied about. I told her they were for me, and I didn't even eat one.' She dropped into the chair next to his bed. 'Although I wouldn't turn a few down if they were offered.'

He tossed her the small bag. 'Half.'

'More than fair.' She popped a few candies in her mouth, then kicked off her shoes and propped her feet up on the edge of his mattress. She had pretty feet, with painted toenails. Barely visible through her black stockings, they were pink with …

He squinted, then laughed. 'You have Captain America shields painted on your toenails.'

'It's called nail art,' she said loftily, then winked at him. 'It's one of the only ways I can accessorize and still meet dress code.' She tilted her left foot so that he could see. 'Captain America shields, Hawkeye bows, Hulk fists, *and* Thor hammers.'

'So you're a fan, I take it?'

'Deacon is. He got me hooked on the superhero movies. And Thor's so pretty.' She laughed when he rolled his eyes. Then sobered, back to business. 'So, O'Bannion. What's your question?'

He averted his eyes from her feet, because now he was wondering if the stockings went all the way up. And what it would take for her to let him pull them off. He cleared his throat and focused. 'How did he know about McCord?'

She nodded in approval. '*That* is a good question. One that Scarlett Bishop is supposed to answer for us very soon. I was going to go over to the *Ledger* after I was done working with you, but then you had your little bout of excitement.'

'Sorry.' He took a bite of the cheeseburger and grimaced. 'Oh, man. I thought I'd be hungry enough that wallpaper paste would be appetizing, but I was wrong.'

She chuckled. 'At least it's safe. I ate one and I'm okay. So far anyway.'

He frowned at her. 'Not funny, Kate.' Not when Alice was dead.

She shrugged. 'It was a little bit funny, but fine. I take it back.'

'Did Agent Troy find the nurse yet?'

'No, not yet. He's still downstairs with hospital security, looking at tapes, trying to figure out which door Eileen Wilkins used when she left today. He's also still working on getting you a secure place to recuperate. I got the doctor lined up. Dani Novak will be here soon to meet you and consult with your doctor.'

'Anybody giving you problems over this?'

She shrugged. 'The hospital doesn't like that we're working around them and the Bureau doesn't like the cost, but you could have died this morning, so . . . so what?'

'When are you going to have this meeting with Marcus O'Bannion and his people?'

'I'm still planning to go to the *Ledger*'s offices as soon as I can. You have a guard outside to make sure nobody bothers you while I'm gone.'

'I know. Agent Triplett came in to introduce himself, and he checks on me to make sure I don't have any new symptoms. Every five minutes. You could set your clock by it.'

She smiled. 'He's cute.'

Decker snorted. 'He's a goddamn behemoth.'

'So says the Sherman tank.' She put the half-bag of candy on his tray and snagged an apple, polishing it on the sleeve of her jacket. 'I think he's a nice young man.'

'So says the young woman. You're not old, Kate.'

She sighed. 'Could have fooled me,' she murmured. 'But back to how Marcus knew about McCord. Apparently Marcus and his *Ledger* team have employed questionable techniques to get info about private citizens, including McCord, so they could then expose them in the paper. Deacon told me that O'Bannion's targets were scumbags who slipped through the official net somehow.'

'I thought Agent Novak went to the jail to check out Alice's death.'

'He did. He's still there, trying to cut through bureaucratic BS, but, see, I have this thing called a cell phone. I use it to talk to people who aren't in the same room with me.'

He bit back a smile and finished off the M&Ms. 'Smartass. So Novak's not coming here?'

'No. I'm supposed to meet him at the morgue, actually, but I'm waiting for his sister to get here before I go. Deacon said she was on her way. We'll all be able to focus better if we're not worried that someone's going to come in here and poison you through your IV.'

'That'd suck,' he agreed dryly. 'So here's another question. O'Bannion had the traffickers scared shitless. They hated him because he took down McCord. But why – if his investigatory skills are so amazing that they scare hardened criminals – *why* didn't he expose McCord's partner at the same time? They were partners, presumably working together.'

She chuckled ruefully. 'I told Zimmerman that it might be a while before your brain was clicking along on all cylinders again because of the anesthesia, but I stand utterly corrected. That is another good question. I hadn't thought of that.'

'You've been a little busy,' he said quietly, holding on to her praise deep down where he hoped it didn't show.

'A little,' she allowed. 'Still, it's a damn good question. Maybe there's a reason that the partner wasn't obviously clear to O'Bannion's people. Maybe they were working on different things, or only sharing distribution channels or servers, that kind of thing.'

'Maybe. It would be helpful to know what kinds of things McCord was caught with.'

'CPD raided his house and removed his computer. It was filled to capacity with photos.' She drew a breath. 'Of kids.'

Decker pushed the tray away, no longer hungry. 'I knew that

part, about it being kids,' he said quietly. 'I meant what format – photos, videos, what?'

'I don't know exactly. One of our other team members, Adam Kimble, is with ICAC right now, going through the files that were taken into evidence. It could take them a while.'

Decker was quiet for a long, long moment. Thinking. Remembering the time that he was Decker McGee. The time before Mama D and Griff had taken him in. When he hadn't known how to fight for what was right, but had still known that he was surrounded with wrong.

Before he'd remade himself into someone worth saving.

'Where did you just go?' Kate asked softly.

Decker sighed. 'I was a foster kid. In and out of the system,' he said, and immediately she stiffened, something akin to horror flickering across her face. 'No,' he said firmly. 'Whatever you just assumed, it didn't happen.' He swallowed hard. 'But only because I could run really fast and was bigger than most of the men my mother brought home.'

'Decker,' she whispered, her sorrow on her face, in her voice. Bare for him to see.

'I ended up fine. But I knew . . . people . . . kids . . . who didn't.' Including the girl who'd had eyes just like his. 'What your colleague is having to look at right now. Man, I have to say I'm not envying him. That shit, it kills you a little more every time you see it. It kills you a little more every time you hear about a person being sold – for whatever purpose. Being made to be a *thing*. A possession, less than human. The labor trafficking is bad enough, but . . .'

'The sex trafficking rips you up inside,' she said sadly. 'And if you're not careful – or if you care too damn much – it can drain your soul, leaving you nothing but a twisted husk.'

'Did it drain yours?' he asked, totally serious.

'No. Not all the way. But then I haven't been working this area all that long. I got moved to the DC task force shortly after we helped the Minneapolis field office bring down some kiddie pornographers. I was working a double homicide and the only witness was the victims' six-year-old daughter. The murderers wanted the mother's jewelry, but they'd also planned to sell the girl to one of the Minneapolis kiddie porn guys. Kiddie porn guys went to prison. The one who wanted to buy little Lana was killed within a month. Shiv in the shower.'

'Good. One less piece of scum on the earth. What happened to the girl?' Because he needed to know. He needed to know that *some* of the kids got saved. He was relieved when Kate smiled.

'Lana and her little sister are back in Russia where they were born, living with their aunt. I got a Christmas card from the aunt with a picture of the two girls. They looked happy. Safe.'

'Those good pictures have to balance out the bad ones.'

'Except that they don't,' she said. 'Not by a long shot. But they do help to keep us from becoming dried-up husks as quickly as we might otherwise.' She went quiet then, watching him for so long that he started to feel self-conscious.

'What?' he asked warily.

'I was debating asking you who you lost.'

He flinched, then his eyes narrowed. 'What makes you think I lost anyone?'

Her mouth curved wryly. 'Maybe the anesthesia left you a little off your game, because it's written all over your face.'

Suddenly tired, he scrubbed his palms over said face. 'Anesthesia. I'll go with that.'

Kate straightened abruptly, sliding her feet off the bed and into her shoes before getting up to throw away the apple core. 'I'm sorry,' she said as she cleaned the trash from his tray. 'I shouldn't have pried. I don't like people doing that to me. Rest now. I'll stay as long as I can.'

He felt a pang of guilt that he'd pried into her husband's death, but shoved it aside. That had been necessary. *And you are a jerk, Decker. Quid pro quo her, at least. Give her something.*

No, not just *something*. He'd taken information from her when he shouldn't have. He really shouldn't have. He couldn't just give her *something*. He needed to answer her damn question.

Which meant he needed to give her *the* thing. The thing he'd kept hidden for so long. The thing that had fueled his resolve, keeping him going for the past three years.

He closed his eyes, summoning the name he hadn't spoken aloud for twenty years. He hadn't even told Griff or Mama D. Because they'd asked. *Are there others like you at home? We'll take them too. They'll be safe with us. We promise.* But Decker had shaken his head, because there hadn't been anyone. Not anymore.

He opened his eyes and found Kate checking email on her phone, thinking him asleep. 'Her name was Shelby Lynne,' he heard himself say in a voice he hadn't heard in nearly as long. He'd buried that accent the day he'd buried her. Ruthlessly he buried it again.

Kate lowered her phone to her lap slowly, lifting her gaze to lock with his. 'Who was she?'

'My sister,' he said, not in the voice he'd worked so hard to cultivate, but still infinitely more cultured than the one he'd had back then.

Her mouth opened, then closed on a quiet sigh. 'Is she dead?'

He nodded. 'Yeah. Twenty years ago. She was eleven.'

Her eyes closed. 'I'm so sorry.'

I'm sorry, Jack. I'm so sorry. Kate's life hadn't been all roses either. Maybe that gave Decker the courage to keep going. Or maybe he just wanted someone to know. If he'd died the week before – or any of the other times he'd gotten too close to a bullet or a knife – then no one would have known the truth about Shelby Lynne McGee. Someone needed to know about her.

Someone needs to remember her. Someone besides me. 'She deserves that,' he murmured.

Kate's eyes flew open. 'Who deserves what?'

'Shelby Lynne deserves to be remembered.'

Kate's smile was both sweet and sad. 'So tell me about her, and she will be.'

Seven

Kate held herself very still, afraid to even breathe, afraid the slightest movement would break the moment and give Decker an excuse not to say what he was so clearly struggling to get out. She hadn't lied. The emotion, the devastating loss, had been all over his face – the face of a man who'd maintained a successful cover for three long years.

He'd shocked her when he'd said his sister's name the first time. Not the name itself, but the accent. The tone. It was like he'd been dubbed by a very young man from the Deep South. *Shalby Lee-yun.*

The second time he'd said it, he'd sounded like himself. Like the voice she'd heard the first time she'd laid eyes on him in the traffickers' compound. A little rough, with just a hint of the South.

She had found no record of a sister, living or dead. So she sat there, statue still, waiting.

'My name isn't Griffin Davenport,' he said, and she merely blinked. That seemed to amuse him. 'No gasp of surprise, Agent Coppola?'

'Not really. I wanted to find someone who'd come to sit with you if I got called away. Someone who was family.'

'Someone who wasn't dead, like Agent Symmes.'

She nodded. 'I dug a little, called in a favor or two. Got a friend to check your file for any past emergency contacts.' She shrugged when his brows lifted. 'My friend didn't just give me the list. I had to be specific, like "Is a person named Davenport listed as next of kin?" She told me that at one time your contact information had included Griffin Davenport IV, of Biloxi, Mississippi, and his wife, Ramona. Both died during your first tour, only a few months apart.'

His throat worked as he struggled to swallow. 'I'd been in for two years. Only earned one pass home. Mama D didn't tell me she was sick during that trip home, that the doctor had told her to stay off her feet. She had a weak heart, but she stood in that kitchen over a hot stove, making all my favorite foods, while I sat at the table telling her about the desert and all the things I'd seen. She always wanted to travel, but never did. Turned out that her heart was why. She'd needed to stay close to the doctors her whole life. It was also the reason there'd never been a Griffin Davenport V. I didn't know that until I was standing at her grave with Griff. That was my second pass home.'

'For her funeral?'

'Yes. Griff died soon after. I didn't get home to put flowers on his grave for another year after that.'

'You changed your name to his. To Griffin Davenport's.'

He nodded. 'A name is important. Griffin Davenport's name was respected everywhere he went. If Griff said it, that was like currency. You could depend on his word. I didn't want to be known by the name I was born with, so I copied his.'

'He knew?'

A nod. 'He went with me to the courthouse to fill out the paperwork on my eighteenth birthday. Never asked me why I wanted to change it. I always figured that he knew. But the fact that I took his name meant something to him, I could tell that. I never knew they'd wanted kids so desperately, not until after Mama D had died.'

'What was the name you were born with?' she asked, and his expression became rigid. Reluctant. And embarrassed.

'Barron. Barron Robert McGee.'

Kate hesitated, not sure how to answer. 'Barron's not a terrible name. It's different.'

He rolled his eyes. 'It wasn't the first name. It was the last one. And the fact that everybody knew my daddy had been Duke McGee – and yes, Duke was his given name. His brother was Earl. My mother told me once that she wanted to name me Prince, but my father didn't want his son outranking him.'

Kate opened her mouth, then closed it again. 'I don't know what to say to that.'

He laughed, shaking his head. 'You and me both.' Then he sobered. 'I don't know what your house was like growing up, but living with Duke and Lizzie McGee was no bed of roses. Duke was always in trouble, always in debt to the wrong people, was always getting into fights and drinking away what little paycheck he got. Finally he fought with the wrong guy and got his head smashed in with a whiskey bottle. They don't break in real life like they do in the movies.'

He was trying to lighten his tone, but she could see the tightness around his mouth. 'No, they don't,' she murmured. 'How old were you when he died?'

'Ten. Shelby Lynne was seven. Things were pretty rough, though, even before Duke died. Children's Services took me away from them because of his violence – once before Shelby was born and twice after. One of the times we were placed together and one of the times we were in separate fosters. Both times my mother managed to get us back. Then he died and she went wild. They'd dabbled in coke and weed together, but when he died, she went over the edge.'

'Grief will do that to a person,' she said quietly, thinking of Jack.

He gave her an odd look. 'No, she didn't grieve. She was loving being single again. She was free of him. The drug use got worse and worse until she started having to turn tricks for her next hit. She'd bring men home and . . . well, some of them liked kids. I was old enough to run by then, but I stayed because of Shelby Lynne.'

'You had to take care of her.'

Another nod. 'I'd take her with me and we'd hide all night in a pup tent, then when the coast was clear, I'd take her home and get her ready for school. I did this for . . . for a long time. Months. Lizzie would get so angry – she could get better money if we cooperated.'

Kate drew in a breath, clenching her teeth against the need to say something foul.

'To make a long story short, one night she was prepared. She put something in my food, and next thing I knew I was waking up, tied to the kitchen chair.' He closed his eyes. 'Shelby Lynne was small for her age. Brittle bones. Bad nutrition, you know.'

Kate shuddered out the breath she'd been holding, her eyes filling with hot, angry tears. *God, Decker.* 'You don't have to tell me any more.' *Please don't tell me any more.*

He licked his lips. Swallowed hard. 'Yeah, I do,' he whispered. 'Because I *need* to work this case with you, to find this partner of McCord's, as soon as my legs will hold me up. HR is going to want to put me on medical leave, but I'm not going to cooperate. And I want you to understand why. And find a way to get me in.'

Shit. She understood. She really did. She also understood that under all that muscle and bone, he was frail. He needed to rest. But deep in her heart, she knew that in his place she'd need to see it through. *Dammit, Decker. Why do you need to be a goddamn hero?*

Same reason I do. She sighed. *Shit.*

'I'm listening,' she said quietly. *Not making any promises, but listening.*

He drew a breath of his own, opening his eyes to hold her gaze once again. She thought she'd see sorrow and devastation and mind-numbing rage, but she saw absolutely nothing at all. Not a flicker of emotion in his blue eyes. His face might have been a stone.

'When I woke up, I could hear everything. Shelby was screaming. I think that's what woke me. I broke the chair to get free. Lizzie was passed out on her bedroom floor, a needle still in her arm. Shelby was hysterical. Bleeding. Everywhere. The guy grabbed his clothes and ran. I called 911. Cops took one look at the place and knew what had happened.'

Kate shuddered another breath that hurt her chest. 'Please say they didn't blame you.'

'No,' he said, still in frightening control. 'They knew I'd kept her away from the house. And why. They'd seen my tent. It was a small, small town, barely a dot on a map. The cops knew. Everybody knew. But everybody said it wasn't their business.'

She wanted to lay waste to that town and to every other town

144

where people knew and did nothing. She wanted to vent her rage somehow. But he was holding on to his control, so she would too. 'What happened to Shelby Lynne?'

'I sat with her in that hospital room for three days. She was catatonic when she was conscious. Most of the time she wasn't, which was . . . merciful.' His chest rose. Fell. 'She died.'

She died. How did a person contain that much pain in two little words? 'And Lizzie?'

'Died later the night it happened. OD'd.'

'And the guy? Did the police catch him?'

'No.' It was unyieldingly stated.

'Was he a stranger?' she asked softly, suspecting that there was a great deal behind that *no.*

'No. He was quite well known in town.'

'Is he still alive?' she asked, keeping her tone oh-so-casual.

Decker met her gaze head-on. 'No.'

She nodded, tilting her head and narrowing her eyes so that he could not mistake her meaning. 'Good. I hope, however he died, that it really hurt.'

One side of his mouth lifted in a grim smile. 'The cops said that it most definitely did. That's what I read in the newspaper, anyway. He disappeared the night Shelby Lynne died. Must have gotten drunk and fallen in the river. Lots of underwater debris in that river. His body was pretty banged up when it washed up on shore outside of Natchez.'

'And Barron Robert McGee? Where did he disappear to?'

Another twitch in his taut cheek. 'He got placed in foster care because he was only fourteen and not capable of taking care of himself, according to the suits at Children's Services.'

'Except that he'd been taking care of himself and his sister for years.'

A careless shrug. 'The first two foster homes were run by nice people, but Barron was itchin' for a fight. Which worked out just fine because the assholes in the school he attended were itchin' to give him one. The third home . . . well, that one wasn't so great. Foster dad liked blond boys. So I ran away. Hitchhiked my way to New

Orleans on a semi, luckily with a nice guy. The next ride liked blonds, too, so I bailed and walked until I was so tired and hungry that I thought I'd pass out. And I was cold. I'd never been so cold. It was January and it can get down into the forties even that far south. I didn't have a coat, so I found a barn and went to sleep. Woke up with a shotgun in my face.' Both corners of his mouth lifted that time, surprising her.

'That was good?' she asked.

'Yeah. Really good. Mama D didn't like "tramps, hobos, or ne'er-do-wells", but she had a soft spot for hungry boys with dirty faces. She marched me into the kitchen, her gun in my back, me with my hands up and everything. I thought about Mama D the night you dropped out of that tree and put your rifle in my back. I almost smiled at you, but you were armed, so I figured I wouldn't antagonize you unnecessarily. Just like I didn't antagonize Mama D.'

'She was good to you?'

'Oh, yes. They both were. Best day of my life, waking up in that pile of hay.' He looked away. 'I've never told anyone about Shelby Lynne and that night. When I got the opportunity to go undercover, I figured I'd put some drug traffickers out of business, and maybe reduce the number of Lizzies out there that might sell their children for a hit. When I found out about the human trafficking . . . it was a chance to make things right by Shelby.'

'You didn't do anything wrong that you have to make right, Decker.'

He shook his head. Hesitated, then drew another breath. 'You didn't ask me if I gave the police a description of the man who raped my sister.'

No, she hadn't. Her gut had told her not to. 'I figured if you hadn't, there was a reason.'

Emotion flickered in his eyes. 'You honor me. Maybe too much.'

'I don't think so. Was he a cop?'

He looked surprised that she'd ask. 'No. But he was respected in the town and I was just Duke and Lizzie McGee's white-trash kid.' He started to say something, then closed his mouth.

Oh God. There's more. Kate braced herself. 'Go ahead.'

146

Decker met her eyes and Kate physically flinched. His expression was now as far from stone as anyone could get. *This* was the pain she'd expected to see.

'He took pictures,' he said hoarsely. 'Of my sister. Uploaded them. The Internet was new then, but kiddie porn lovers had already made it their own. Once it's there, it's there forever. You might get it taken down, but you can't erase it. It sits there, saved on hard drives like McCord's, for perverts to view whenever they want. Some of the kids in the foster homes ... they'd seen the pictures and recognized her. They made fun of her.'

Kate found herself reining in her rage once more. 'You stopped them?'

'Beat the shit out of them,' he admitted.

Reining in her rage made her stomach hurt and her head ache. 'Good. But it's still there, on the Internet. You know it's there and ... that hurts. It's gotta hurt, Decker.'

'Only when I think about it.'

'So, like all the time,' she said gently.

'Pretty much. These pictures ... they spread out, get shared, and everyone says it's a victimless crime. Tell that to the kids in the pictures,' he said bitterly. 'Trying to contain it's like trying to contain a gas with your hands. It spreads like cancer, available to every pervert in every dark corner on the face of the earth. And there isn't anything you can do about it except go after the bastards that make the shit, one at a fucking time.'

His cheeks were wet with tears and Kate wasn't sure he even knew he was crying. She got a towel from the bathroom, wet it with warm water, then carefully washed his face.

He turned into her touch, his shoulders sagging. 'So now you understand.'

'Yeah. I understand.' She brushed his hair off his forehead. 'You're really tired, Decker,' she said soothingly. 'You need to sleep.'

One side of his mouth lifted. 'These aren't the droids you're looking for?'

She chuckled thinly. 'I guess the force isn't so strong in me. But I'm wiped from hearing this, so you've got to be wiped from telling it. Go to sleep. When you wake up, Dani Novak will be here. If I'm not here too, it's because I'm working. But I will come back, I promise.'

'Then we can do the ledgers,' he whispered, giving in to the exhaustion.

'You bet.'

She hung the wet towel on the bed rail and took his hand. With her other hand, she stroked his face until his breathing evened out and a light snore rumbled out of his mouth.

She heard the door open behind her, followed by a whisper. 'Kate.'

She stepped away from the bed and turned to find Dani Novak watching her with a soft expression. 'He's asleep now,' Kate whispered.

'I see that.'

'You on board for this private room gig?'

'I am. Deacon and Adam have a place lined up. I've already consulted with Agent Davenport's doctor. We're planning to move him in an hour or so.'

Kate was surprised. 'So soon? I thought the hospital hierarchy would give us at least a little hell about moving him.'

'They did. They tried, anyway, but your boss let them have it. One of his agents was nearly killed here. Zimmerman was not kind to the hospital powers-that-be. One of the department heads suggested the FBI should have had security at his door. That's actually when Zimmerman kind of exploded at them. His security would never have known to stop the nurse this morning, and the hospital can't promise it won't happen again. That's when the powers-that-be beat a dignified retreat.' She looked at Decker. 'I'll stay with him until he's ready to be moved.'

Kate checked her phone when it buzzed with a text from Deacon telling her to meet him at the morgue. Appeared the ME had news. 'An hour should be just enough time to find out what the ME wants to tell us about Alice.' She gathered her things. 'Thank you, Dani. All of us appreciate it.'

Dani's eyes, one blue and one brown, twinkled merrily. 'I suspect some of us might appreciate it more than others.'

Kate opened her mouth to deny it, but couldn't make the words come out. It would have been a lie anyway. She shouldered her laptop case and her yarn bag. 'I'll see you soon.'

Cincinnati, Ohio,
Thursday 13 August, 2.45 P.M.

He had to laugh when the nurse drove up. He'd gotten there first because the coordinates he'd given her required that she travel down the same isolated road that Roy had used earlier. That route allowed him to see her as she approached, just to make sure she hadn't brought anyone with her.

He'd wanted Roy to see him there, so he'd been waiting out in the open. He didn't, however, want Eileen to see him, so he'd come from another direction and parked out of sight.

She'd come alone, unless she had someone hiding in her trunk, which he sincerely doubted. But she was clearly expecting an ambush. She got out of her car, a tactical helmet on her head and her torso covered in a bulletproof vest with *SWAT* printed on the back in faded ink. The vest was old, wherever she'd gotten it. But at least she wasn't completely stupid. Which would make his task a bit more of a challenge.

He found himself smiling. He hadn't had a good challenge in a long time.

He reached for the rifle under his seat and got out of his car, careful to step lightly. Eileen was looking around as if expecting him to pop out from behind a tree. Not likely. He didn't plan to let her see him until it was far too late for her to do anything about it.

He holstered his handgun and shouldered the rifle. She'd have to bend down when she retrieved the vials and wouldn't be looking around. That was when he'd fire the first shot.

He waited until she'd approached Roy's car and gingerly reached through the open window. She wore latex gloves so as not to leave prints, but was still careful not to touch anything but Roy's shirt. Very smart.

He aimed at the bare skin of her arm and gently squeezed the trigger.

Her scream reached his ears as she spun around to face his direction, her arm drawn tight against her body. He centered his sight on the hollow of her throat and pulled the trigger again before she'd finished her spin.

Yes. Blood spurted from her throat and her eyes darted around frantically for a second before going still and lifeless.

He lowered his rifle and sighed a little. As challenges went, he'd give this one a six out of ten. Mostly because she had a scrawny neck and hitting it just right while she was still moving hadn't been a no-brainer. Still, two shots – *pop pop* – and he was done.

He picked up his spent casings, then walked up to Roy's muscle car, took the empty Dilaudid vials from Roy's shirt pocket and slipped them in the pocket of the dead nurse's bulletproof vest. He then took the cell phone from her pants pocket – another phone requiring a fingerprint ID. Carefully he peeled off her glove and pressed the pad of her index finger against the screen.

Presto. He checked to be sure she hadn't contacted anyone by text, email or direct call since they'd spoken. She had not. Good enough. He reset the phone, popped out the SIM card, then took it all back to his car. He wiped the phone of prints and did a factory reset before driving away from the scene. He'd passed a construction site on the way into the park and stopped there on his way out. The site itself was deserted, but they did have a Porta-Potty. Eileen's phone went down the toilet.

The SIM card he'd hold until he got back to the city, where he'd dispose of it down a storm sewer, as he had Sidney Siler's. He checked his watch. He was running a little late.

He had appointments this afternoon, but he should be able to get there on time. And by the time he finished for the day, the Rawlings kid would be hanging with the teens at their favorite haunt, a basketball court in the park behind the CVS drugstore.

Kids today have way too much time on their hands, he thought, then laughed out loud, only mildly horrified to realize that was something his old man would have said.

His old man had never beaten them. He'd always provided food and shelter. Had never done drugs or slept around.

He'd been an academic. A thinking man. He never needed to use his fists. Why sweat when you can flay a kid's confidence with a single spoken word? A gesture, even. He'd been an asshole of the first water, a greedy bastard who doled out financial – and emotional – support on his own terms. *Which never coincided with mine.* But Pop's assholery had pushed him to get creative about making money, and *voilà*. A drug empire was born.

He only wished his father could see him now. The videos? His father would shit kittens. Which made it that much more fun.

His stomach growled then, reminding him he hadn't had lunch. He speed-dialed his sister. 'Nell, it's me.'

'I was just about to call you. Your three-thirty appointment is here. Gina Fuentes.'

'She's early,' he said, annoyed.

Nell heaved her big-sister sigh. 'And you're late?'

'Just a little. I was calling to ask you to have a sandwich delivered. Will you?'

'Sure,' she said, always eager to ensure he ate well. 'Turkey and Swiss on rye?'

'With one of the potato pancakes.'

'Remy, those things'll kill you! They're pure fat.'

She was the only one he allowed to call him Remy. Anyone else who tried would regret it. But Nell had been his mother after their actual mother decided downing a bottleful of pills was far preferable to living with their father, so he let her have this one thing. He turned on his baby brother charm. 'Please? Potato pancakes taste so good. And can you stall my early three thirty?'

'I'll try. She said she has a job interview at four on campus and has to be out the door by quarter to, which is why she came early.'

'I might make it back in time. Depends on what she's in for.'

'MMR and MCV4. She's an incoming freshman.'

He stepped on the gas pedal, careful not to exceed the speed limit. Not with a recently fired rifle under his seat and an unregistered handgun in his pocket.

'That shouldn't be a problem. And if I'm really late, you can take care of it without me.' His sister carried most of his load and they both liked it that way.

'I already offered that,' Nell said tightly. 'Miss Fuentes doesn't want a PA. She's insisting on a real doctor.'

He eased off the gas, slowing to ten miles below the limit. Miss Fuentes had insulted his sister and that simply would not do. 'Then I guess she'll have to wait for me.'

Cincinnati, Ohio,
Thursday 13 August, 3.00 P.M.

Meredith blew her hair off her forehead. She was sticky and sweaty and feeling damn nasty from the heat – and it had all been for nothing. 'They're not going to talk to us, are they?'

Wendi Cullen took a pack of wet wipes from her purse and offered Meredith one before swabbing the back of her own neck. 'Nope.'

They stood on a street corner that, by the time the sun set, would become hooker central. For now, they were surrounded by humanity, people streaming all around them, going about their lives. But the two of them were very much alone. No one made eye contact, giving them a wide berth.

It had been like that for most of the day, ever since it became known that they were searching for anyone who might have information on a . . . well, basically a porn king.

It gave Meredith renewed respect for what her friend did every single day. Meredith's clients came to her office, referred either by the police, Children's Services, or other satisfied clients. Wendi walked this beat several times a week and usually at night, the women she sought needing a direct invitation to avail themselves of the help she provided.

'You told me they wouldn't talk to me,' Meredith said with a sigh.

Wendi gave her arm a squeeze. 'I also remember saying that we needed to try. We haven't done any harm here, Mer. Word will get out and we might get some nibbles or some whispers in the next few days. You can't rush these things.'

'I know. The team feels an urgency now, though. Who knows when another case will pop up and divert their attention?'

'I do get it – striking while the iron's hot – but if you push now, you're just gonna get brittle metal.' Wendi's brow wrinkled. 'That's a thing, right? Brittle metal, from rushing . . . whatever metal makers do?'

Meredith chuckled. 'I think they're called blacksmiths. Got no clue about the brittle thing, but given that it's a hundred and fifty degrees out here and I'm melting, I'm willing to say "Sure."'

'It's only a hundred and two. Where's your sense of adventure?'

'It melted,' Meredith said dourly. 'Let's call it a day. We've passed out all the business cards both of us brought and drunk all the water you hauled around in your purse.' She gave Wendi's huge purse a hopeful look. 'Unless you can magically make it produce another bottle or two.' The purse held a surprising amount of stuff, all of which they'd needed that afternoon.

'Nope.' Wendi grinned. 'Mary Poppins's bag is hot and tired too. Let's go to my car and I'll drive you to yours.' Because Wendi had simply laughed at the idea of Meredith parking her cute convertible in the neighborhood. 'I'll call you as soon as I get a nibble.'

'Okay. Thank you, Wendi,' Meredith said as they started for Wendi's ancient Dodge. 'I know you had other things to do today.'

'Yeah, but they'll keep. This . . . Mer, this is important. You can get the women – and men – off the street, but it's like that big snake thing. You cut off a head and two more pop up. Unless we get the perps making the porn and profiting from the prostitution, there are always more women and men to take their place.'

'And kids,' Meredith added, swallowing hard.

'And kids,' Wendi echoed.

They walked a block in silence, then Meredith said, 'Hydra. That's the snake thing.'

'Hm. Some days I wish I'd gone to college,' Wendi said lightly.

Meredith laughed. 'You did.'

Wendi's smile faltered. 'Not exactly. I mean, I took the classes I needed to get certified to open my shelter. But I really wanted to study other things. Before.'

Meredith sobered. Wendi had been assaulted and victimized when she was only fourteen, her abuse filmed and shared online. Her life had been irrevocably changed. 'What did you want to study before?'

'English. I used to love English – the stories. The grammar not so much. But the stories . . .' She shrugged. 'Remembering the stories I'd read my whole life was what got me through all those bad years. I'd play the story in my mind like a movie and hide there. So I wasn't really there during the abuse. When I finally got out of the life, it seemed like a frivolous thing to study. I needed to make a living. Pay the bills. And then I started the shelter and, well, there was no time then.'

'They stole your dreams,' Meredith said sadly.

'Yes. Yes, they did. That's something nobody wants to talk about. Yes, the victims are abused, and yes, there is therapy after for the ones who manage to dig their way out.'

'Or who are lucky enough to have a lifeline extended to them by people like you.'

Wendi smiled. 'That too. But what's taken . . . it can never be replaced. Lost years. Lost innocence. Lost self-esteem. And lost dreams.'

Meredith had to blink back tears. 'We have to find you a new house. We can't let your program die, Wendi. I'll give you my own house before I let that happen.'

Wendi patted her arm. 'You've offered before and I told you already – thank you, but your house is way too teeny. It might do as a stopgap, but my girls need stability. They need to know they have a place to lay their head at night that's safe. I can't be bopping them from house to house, sleeping on floors because we don't have enough beds.'

They got to Wendi's car and she let them in. 'What about Faith?' Wendi asked. 'I didn't want to gush too much this morning when she said she might have an idea, but I've honestly thought of nothing else since she said it.'

'If she said it, it's more a done deal than not. Faith wouldn't let someone down on purpose and she's very conservative about what she promises.' Meredith hesitated. 'I think I know the house she's talking about, and you're going to have some decision-making to do.'

Wendi started the engine, sighing happily when cool air came out of the vents. 'What kind of decisions?'

'You know that Faith came here because she was running from a stalker in Miami, right?'

'Yes. They caught the guy who was after her.' Wendi shuddered. 'And found a bunch of bodies in that creepy old . . .' Her eyes widened. 'That's the house?'

'I think so.'

'But . . . but people . . . people died in that house, Meredith. Women. Victims.'

'I know.' A lot of women, all innocent of any crime. All dead because they'd satisfied a serial killer's profile. 'But it's a big house, Wendi. And sturdy. And out of the way on a pretty plot of land – at least twenty acres.'

'That's a lot of land. Enough for gardens and animals.'

Meredith nodded, glad that Wendi could at least see some benefit to the plan. 'Faith had fifty acres, but she had to sell some of it to cover the taxes. She told me a while back that she's got enough to pay the taxes and maintenance on that old place for at least ten years. She was trying to figure out what to do with it.'

'She wants me to move there? With my victims of sex abuse? Really, Mer?'

Meredith caught her gaze and held it firmly. Soberly. 'Really, Wendi. And if you think about it, *really* think about it, what better way to honor all those victims than to use the place they died to give hope to a whole new generation of women?'

Wendi's mouth fell open and Meredith reached a teasing finger under her chin to close it. 'You're letting all the bugs in,' she said with a gentle smile.

Wendi blinked, stunned. 'She'd just . . . give it away?'

'Or lease it to a foundation,' Meredith said. 'She's told me that she's considered it. Not for your girls specifically, but for someone. She said that she hated for a house that had endured so much for so many years to stand idle and empty. That it deserved to shelter survivors.'

Wendi drew a deep breath. 'My God, Meredith. I don't even know what to think.'

'Well, she hasn't offered it yet. She may not. But I think that's the most likely scenario here. I've known Faith for nine months now. She's a good person, Wendi. If she does offer and you choose to decline, do it kindly. Don't hurt her.'

'I won't. I . . . I won't.' Still rattled, Wendi pulled away from the curb. 'I'll take you back to your car. You have time to get home and cleaned up before Kendra shows up on your doorstep for free therapy.'

Meredith pursed her lips, neither confirming or denying. Even though Wendi and Kendra were sisters, any communication between Meredith and Kendra was confidential. She took confidentiality very seriously.

Wendi's lips twitched. 'I'm not fishing for information. I told her to ask you for help, y'doofus.' She sobered with a sigh. 'She's been so intense lately. She's starting to scare herself, which is scaring the hell out of me.'

'You know what she needs to tell me then?'

'Yes.' Wendi slanted her a look. 'Confidentiality is important to me, too.'

Meredith had to laugh. 'Touché. I know it is. I couldn't respect you if it weren't. And speaking of respect, I need to call SAC Zimmerman and tell him that I'm alive and that he can call off his growly bear.' Zimmerman had assigned her a guard – a bulky, angry-faced man named Agent Colby, who looked like he ate nails for breakfast.

She and Wendi hadn't even been able to get anyone to take their business cards with him as their shadow. So she'd told Zimmerman to yank him back. After that, Agent Colby had trailed them by a full half-block, which had annoyed both him and Zimmerman, prompting Meredith to agree to call both men every thirty minutes to let them know that she was still alive.

'Oh, I don't know,' Wendi said. 'I think Agent Growly Bear is kind of cute. There he is.' She gave the man a finger wave, slowing when he gestured her to park behind his car. She complied, rolling her window as far down as it would go – which was only four inches.

'We're done, Agent Colby,' Meredith said. 'Wendi's going to drive me to my car now.'

He bent over so that his face was level with the window gap. He was most assuredly not cute, Meredith thought. He had a hard look that made him appear years older than he probably was. 'Can you roll your window down the rest of the way?' he demanded, exasperated.

'Sorry,' Wendi said. 'It only goes down that far. It's a junker, but it runs and it's paid for.'

He frowned at that. 'That's a safety hazard, ma'am.'

Wendi shrugged. 'Runs and paid for.'

'I'll follow you out. Did you find anyone that knew about our suspect?'

'No,' Meredith admitted. 'They wouldn't talk to us whether you were there or not.'

'But they at least took our cards once you fell back, so it's okay,' Wendi said firmly. 'Are we doing this tomorrow?'

'I'll find out,' Meredith said. 'Thank you for watching over us, Agent Colby.'

He rolled his eyes. 'I don't think you needed any watching over, Dr Fallon. This one here is armed to the damned teeth.'

Wendi smiled sunnily. Her huge purse held pepper spray, a can of mace, and a fully operational Taser. She carried a switchblade on her belt that was probably illegal, but Colby had not said a word. 'Thank you,' she said. 'That's a nice compliment.'

His sigh was weary, as if he'd dealt with a passel of toddlers all day long. 'It wasn't meant as one. Be careful, ma'am. Both of you.'

Wendi finger-waved again. 'Like I said,' she said as she drove away. 'Kind of cute.'

Meredith laughed. 'Not my type, I'm afraid.'

Wendi shot her a considering glance. 'Who is?'

Adam Kimble. His face came to her mind, unbidden. As it had so many times since she'd met him nine months before. He was attracted to her, too. He hadn't tried to hide it.

But Adam was . . . damaged. She'd tried to help him all those months ago, and had been marginally successful, but that help had changed the balance of their relationship before it even had a chance to truly begin. She could never have been his therapist back then anyway – she'd known it the moment she'd laid eyes on him. It had been attraction at first sight, for both of them.

But she sure as hell could never be his therapist now. She wasn't even sure she could be his friend. So much water had rushed under that bridge that the bridge was washed away. 'Right now, nobody.'

'You're lying. I can always tell. But you'll tell me eventually. You always do.'

Not this time, Meredith thought sadly. It hurt too much to think about him – so close, yet so unattainable. There was no way she'd be able to dish the way Wendi wanted her to. The man had such a good heart and it was being shredded at this very moment. Zimmerman had other people he could have sent to view those photographs. He shouldn't have sent Adam. But tackling the task had been Adam's decision and he'd made it.

Meredith had meant what she'd said when she'd offered him her aid. She'd help him. And then she'd cry herself to sleep, just like she'd done before.

She started when Wendi reached over and took her hand, giving it a squeeze. 'If you never tell me,' Wendi whispered, 'it's okay. I'll still come to your house and we can watch movies and drink chocolate martinis.'

Meredith's exhale was shaky. 'It's a date.'

Eight

Cincinnati, Ohio,
Thursday 13 August, 3.20 P.M.

Kate found Deacon checking his email as he waited for her outside the morgue so they could meet with the coroner about her autopsy of Alice Newman's body. 'Hey,' he said, barely looking up. 'Did Dani get to Davenport's room okay?'

'She did. Thank you for helping to work that out.'

He shrugged. 'It was mostly Zimmerman and Troy. Adam found the place – I used it when we needed a safe house for Faith, so I know the layout. We'll be able to protect him there until he's back on his feet.'

'Which will probably be sooner than he should be, but that would be true for any of us. What are you looking at that has you so absorbed?'

He glanced up. 'The list of people who visited Alice while she was in custody. It's a fairly long list. A lot of reporters. A few lawyers. She went through lawyers like water because none of them would agree to trying to get her immunity.'

'We need to check them, though. Send me the list and we'll split it up after we're done.'

Deacon tapped a few buttons on his phone, then nodded. 'It's sent. It's the names from the sign-in sheet, plus copies of each visitor's ID.'

Kate opened the file as soon as it dropped into her inbox and let it begin its download. It was slow going as the morgue's Wi-Fi signal was weak. 'Do you know what the ME has for us?'

'No. She'd already taken the body to the morgue by the time I got to the jail.'

'Really? Does she normally do that before you've examined the scene?'

'No, and I'm dying to find out why.'

'No puns,' Kate groaned, biting back a smile. 'Please.'

'But you smiled. Admit it. Let's go find out what's going on.'

They put on masks, gloves, and cover-ups, then Kate sucked in one last breath of fresh air before following Deacon through the morgue's main door.

'Carrie—' Deacon stumbled to a stop, nearly causing Kate to plow him over.

'What the hell, D?' Kate muttered, regaining her balance without actually touching anything. Because touching stuff in a morgue was just . . . nasty. Not that she'd ever admit that out loud, of course.

She looked around Deacon and saw what had stopped him short. A tall woman, gowned head to toe in white, was standing by the morgue refrigerator, leaning over a victim's body as it lay on a tray that had been partially pulled out. From this angle, it looked like the woman's face was buried in the corpse's neck.

'Carrie?' Deacon said uncertainly, and the woman straightened.

She wore goggles and a mask, but she'd pulled the mask just below her nose, the white of the mask stark against her dark skin. She pulled it all the way down and motioned them over. 'Deacon. I'm glad you're finally here.' She tilted her head and studied Kate. 'I'm Dr Washington. You must be Agent Coppola.'

'I am. Um, not to be rude or anything, but what were you *doing*?'

Washington's eyebrows arched. 'Not to be rude or anything,' she said dryly.

Deacon shook his head. 'Nah, Kate's right. It was damn creepy, Carrie, and I don't freak easily. I thought you'd have blood all over your mask when you straightened up.'

Carrie grinned abruptly. 'Now *that* would be a funny prank.' She sobered just as abruptly. 'But no. *So* not gonna happen.' She motioned them over. 'This is Alice.'

'Holy shit,' Deacon muttered.

Kate grimaced. 'Wow.' She hadn't recognized the body. 'She's not so pretty anymore, is she?' Alice, who'd been very pretty at the time of her arrest, was now battered and bruised, her skin a rosy, almost shiny red. She had a black eye that covered half her face, her upper lip was split, and there was a deep cut in her cheek. 'What happened to her?'

'Well,' Carrie said, 'quite a few things, actually. It seems that she had a little altercation in the exercise yard yesterday.'

'I thought she was separated from the gen pop,' Kate said, frowning.

'At meals,' Deacon said. 'The warden said that she took her meals alone, but that she was permitted time in the exercise yard with a few of the minimum security prisoners. The assault happened yesterday early evening. The woman who hit her claimed that Alice had pushed her and grabbed her breasts, and several prisoners backed up her story. They'd surrounded Alice, though, so the cameras didn't get a good view of what really happened. The woman has since been separated from her cell block. But the report made it sound like Alice had a few bruises. Nothing like this. Not that I'm feeling sorry for her or anything.'

Kate agreed. 'That goes without saying.'

'Alice spent yesterday evening in the infirmary,' Carrie said. 'Apparently she had severe nausea and diarrhea on top of the cuts and bruises.'

Deacon made a face. 'Lovely. But if anyone had to get diarrhea, I'm glad it was her.'

'Alice was a lawyer with a snooty, better-than-you attitude,' Kate said. 'Based on the one time I interviewed her, the breast grabbing doesn't sound very likely.'

'What's more likely,' Carrie said, 'was that the assault was a set-up because somebody wanted Alice in the prison infirmary last night. She was exposed to some kind of toxin. I won't know exactly when and what until we finish running a battery of tests.'

'Wait.' Deacon frowned. 'I thought she was poisoned through her breakfast.'

'She was,' Carrie said. 'She was poisoned twice, with different toxins.'

Kate and Deacon shared a look of foreboding. 'By the same person?' Kate asked.

'Which two toxins?' Deacon asked at the same time.

'Whether it was the same person is impossible to say at this point because the mode of delivery was different. The first exposure was through lacerations on her skin.' Carrie pulled the tray all the way out and pointed to cuts on Alice's arms and face, then drew the sheet from Alice's feet to above her knees to show more cuts on her thighs and the back of her calves.

'All the cuts look shallow,' Kate said.

'They are. Deep enough to draw blood, but not enough to need stitches. Look at the skin around them.'

Deacon shook his head. 'The skin is red. What am I looking for?'

'A rash beneath the red. The rash is red too, so it makes it harder to see.' She handed Deacon an 8x10 photograph. 'That's this laceration, here on the left thigh. I adjusted the color contrast so that the rash showed up better.'

Kate looked over Deacon's shoulder and barely made out a rash pattern beneath the darker red. 'I see it, but it's faint.' She glanced up at the ME. They'd said she was good and they'd been right. 'You have a sharp eye.'

Carrie gave her a nod of appreciation. 'I also saw her about ninety minutes after she died. The overall redness of her skin was a little lighter then. I'm pretty sure that the rash is a result of the first exposure. The red skin came with the second exposure – ingested with her breakfast this morning – which was probably the fatal one.'

Kate ran her mind through the facts – red skin, death within an hour . . . the doctor bending over the victim, sniffing. 'Cyanide. You were sniffing her for the almond smell?'

Another nod, this one accompanied by a slight smile. 'Yes, but either I can't smell it or her body didn't produce it. There isn't always an almond smell. But her blood tested positive for cyanide, so that's a definitive cause of death.'

'Why were you smelling her, then?' Deacon asked. 'You already had the test results.'

Carrie shrugged. 'I was curious. I've never had a victim of cyanide poisoning before. It's really, really rare. Less than ten cases a year, nationally. This is going to get some press.'

'So you're going to be a celebrity ME,' Deacon said dryly. 'Will you still have time for us lowly peasants?'

Her lips twitched. 'For you, Agent Novak? Always.' She got back to business, pointing to the rash that ringed the laceration on Alice's leg. 'This is not cyanide. I'm running a series of tests but I won't know anything with certainty until I open her up.'

'But you're sure that the toxin was introduced through the wounds?' Kate asked.

Carrie's brows lifted. 'What's your question, Agent Coppola?'

'Well . . . how exactly was it introduced? I mean, Alice was a vicious, cold-hearted bitch, capable of torturing someone with a smile on her face. I can't see her just sitting there while poison was slathered all over her open cuts.'

Carrie's smile was grimly satisfied. 'I can see that in my mind. It's a good image.' Her glance swept over the other drawers. 'I have autopsied too many bodies this past week, most of which can be traced back to this . . . creature. I have no sympathy for her whatsoever. I will treat her body with respect and I'll search for the cause of death with the zeal that I have for every other body that comes through my morgue. But I'd be dishonest if I denied that I wish she'd suffered more. Had the cyanide not been administered, I think she would have. Unfortunately, her death was too quick.'

'Amen,' Deacon muttered.

'Preaching to the choir,' Kate said. 'But back to the poison – if it wasn't slathered on, then how did it get into her wounds? Was it introduced by someone in the exercise yard? Or via contaminated medical instruments once she got to the infirmary? Combined with a salve so that it looked like medicine? Sprinkled on the bandages?'

'Good questions,' Carrie said. 'I think it was at the infirmary, because they dressed her wounds. If it had been introduced in the exercise yard, it would have been washed off the skin when they cleaned her up, and if the damage had already been done, it would have been noted.' She hesitated. 'Plus, she was ill that night and into the morning. If I'd done this, I'd want to be sure she didn't attract any attention moaning in her cell. I'd want to keep her close and watch.'

'Somebody might check her out,' Deacon said. 'Somebody other than whoever did it.'

Carrie nodded. 'Exactly. Alice was still sick when she got back to her cell. I was actually surprised she ate anything this morning based on the records. I'll do an analysis of her stomach contents to tell which thing had the cyanide in it. Anyway, I got a roster of all the staff on duty in the infirmary for the time Alice was there and the shifts before and after. This took planning, especially if the ointments or bandages were poisoned.'

'Agreed,' Deacon said and blew out a breath. 'We'll question the infirmary staff and any other inmates who were patients at the time. The woman who beat her up in the exercise yard was given very specific directions as to how badly to hurt her. The wounds are too uniform in their depth to be random strikes. We need to know if she was in on the planning, or just a tool.'

Kate pulled up the email he'd sent her with the list of people who'd visited Alice. 'I'm wondering if Alice was being threatened by anyone. I can't see her keeping something like that to herself. She would have told her lawyer at least.' She scanned the list. 'Here. She spoke with her attorney's assistant yesterday. Keisha Findlay.'

'Then we move Findlay to the top of our list,' Deacon said. 'I'd like to know what Alice said before we interview anyone else.'

Kate nodded. 'I agree. Dr Washington, when do you expect to have the results of that battery of tests you mentioned – the one that will tell you what the first poison was?'

Carrie looked at the clock on the wall. 'Some of the tests may be finished. I sent them through the gas chromatograph, in order of my best guess. Let me go check. I'll be right b—'

The doors opened behind them and an assistant wheeled in another gurney bearing a sheet-covered body. 'Dr Washington, the OD case is prepared. Where do you want her?'

Carrie sighed. 'Excuse me,' she said to Kate and Deacon. 'Put her in the freezer, Toby. The poisoning is my priority. One of us will get to the OD as soon as possible.' She disappeared into the office for a half-minute, returning as the assistant was sliding the new body onto the drawer tray next to Alice. Setting the printouts in her hand aside for a moment, Carrie gently lifted the sheet to look at the face of the deceased, a young African-American woman. The expression on the ME's face was one of sorrow and regret, quite unlike the look of contempt she'd worn for Alice.

Carrie looked up to see Kate watching her and lowered the sheet as gently as she'd lifted it. 'She was a grad student with her whole life ahead of her. I hate to see these kids throwing their lives away for a damn high, especially kids who've pulled themselves out of the projects like this girl did. There are so few black women in academia, and she wanted to be a professor. Now we're one fewer.'

Kate wasn't sure what to say, so she asked a question, keeping her voice respectful. 'Do you know the history of all the deceased?'

Carrie shook her head sadly as she closed the drawer. 'No. I heard about this one on the news this morning. Her body was found at King's College on the edge of the campus.' She picked up the printouts she'd set aside and rifled through them. 'I was right.' She looked up. 'Deacon?'

Deacon had stepped closer to the swinging doors, but quickly rejoined them. 'I was downloading my mail. It's slow down here.'

'It's a dead zone,' Carrie quipped, and both Kate and Deacon groaned. 'Oh, come on,' Carrie said with a smile. 'Don't tell me you never thought it yourselves.'

'I can honestly say I didn't,' Kate said. 'What were you right about?'

Carrie sobered. 'The first poison Alice was exposed to was ricin.'

Kate and Deacon stared at each other. 'Ricin?' Deacon asked. 'Are you kidding?'

'Nope. The symptoms pointed to something in that family, and we have been getting an increasing number of deaths by either ricin or a variant. Thank you, *Breaking Bad*,' she added sarcastically. 'Walter White made a couple of batches and all of a sudden recipes for ricin are popping up all over the Internet. So now it's one of the tests I run when I see this rash combined with gastrointestinal distress prior to death.'

'Ricin,' Deacon muttered. 'I'm thinking KGB umbrellas with secret dosing needles.'

'But,' Kate said, 'if my memory is accurate, ricin would have taken a while to kill her.'

'Thirty-six hours to a few days,' Carrie confirmed.

'Then why fool with the cyanide?' Kate frowned. 'It was either two different perps or . . . maybe they were nervous that she hadn't gotten enough in her system and they finished the job?'

'Sounds like you two are going to be busy finding out,' Carrie said.

'Yeah,' Kate said grimly. 'Thank you, Dr Washington. It was nice to meet you.'

'Next time just call me Carrie, how's that?'

'If you'll call me Kate.' She shook the woman's hand, then she and Deacon left the morgue, stopping in the hallway to strip off the paper gowns and masks. 'What first?'

'I'll take the infirmary staff,' Deacon said. 'You take the visitor list, starting with the lawyer's assistant, then, when we've got a little more information, we'll both interview the woman who threw the punches. We call each other when either of us gets something.'

'Sounds good.' Following him to the elevator, Kate pulled up the form that the lawyer's assistant had filled out at the desk of the jail. Keisha Findlay worked for Heath, Gill, and Schwartz, Attorneys at Law. Their offices were downtown, so it wouldn't take too long to get there. She scrolled down to the copy of the woman's photo ID.

And then froze just as the elevator dinged and the doors slid open. 'Oh fucking hell.'

Deacon frowned at her. 'What?'

Goddammit. 'We gotta go back.' She turned and ran back to the morgue, stopping long enough to shove her phone in her pocket and grab a pair of gloves and a face mask before pushing through the doors and heading to the wall of drawers.

'No,' Deacon was saying behind her. 'Tell me you are not serious.'

'I wish I could,' Kate said grimly, snapping on the gloves. The assistant who'd delivered the body was standing in front of a desk, typing into a computer. 'Excuse me. Toby, was it?'

He turned, one brow lifted. 'Yes. How can I help you?'

She pointed at the drawer next to Alice's. 'Can you open this one, please? All the way so that I can check the toe tag?'

Toby complied, holding the tag so that Kate could read the name. *Sidney Siler.*

'No,' Deacon said again, but much more wearily than before. 'No fucking way.'

Kate pulled the sheet away from the dead grad student and held her phone next to the woman's face. 'Yes, fucking way. Meet Sidney Siler, aka, Keisha Findlay the lawyer's assistant, aka the last person to visit Alice before she went into the exercise yard.'

Deacon's shoulders sagged. 'Fucking hell.'

Cincinnati, Ohio,
Thursday 13 August, 4.00 P.M.

'Agent Davenport, wake up.'

The voice was soft, feminine. But not Kate. *Where is Kate?*

'Agent Davenport.' The voice became sharper. 'I need you to wake up *now.*'

Decker came awake in a rush, lurching to sit up. And then wishing he hadn't. He blinked hard when the room spun, but it wasn't as bad as it had been before. He blinked again, then found himself looking into a pair of mismatched eyes – one blue and one brown. Another blink allowed him to focus on the woman's face, framed with streaks of bright white hair on either side. The rest of her hair was jet black. She was most definitely Deacon Novak's kin. They looked like male and female sides of the same coin.

'You would be Dr Novak,' Decker said, his throat dry and raspy.

'You would be correct.' She handed him a cup with a straw. 'Drink.'

He eyed it suspiciously. 'What is it?'

She looked amused. 'Gin and tonic, what do you think? It's water. Just drink it.'

He took several long pulls on the straw and felt immediately better. Less like something the cat had dragged in, anyway. 'Kate trusts you.'

'She should.' Novak's mismatched eyes twinkled. 'I'm an awesome doctor.'

'I'm sure that's true, but she trusts you not to murder me in my sleep, and that's better.'

She looked aggravated. 'I'm sorry that happened to you, Agent Davenport. I'll make sure you stay safe, to the best of my ability.'

'I appreciate it.' Now that he'd had a nap, he felt restless. 'Can I walk?'

'To the toilet and back. For now.' She put down the rail, arranged the IV bag on a stand with wheels, then rolled a walker to the side of the bed. 'Try your legs. See how it feels.'

He swung his legs over the side of the bed, determined he was going to walk soon and often and as many steps as he possibly could. Because he had to get back into the game.

He had to find McCord's partner. For . . .

He faltered, gripping the edge of the thin mattress. *Holy God.* Had he really told Kate about Shelby, or had he dreamed it? He thought hard for a second or two. No, he'd really told her. He'd told her everything. He'd all but confessed to murdering the bastard who'd violated his sister. *Hell.*

And he'd cried, too, on top of it all. He couldn't stop his wince. *Way to impress her, genius.* But Kate hadn't judged. She'd shown him compassion but not pity. She'd called him a good man. She'd been glad the bastard had suffered. And she'd cried, too. *For both Shelby Lynne and me*, he thought.

But she hadn't agreed to let him back in the game. That detail had not escaped his attention. He'd have to make his own way. Which started with a round trip to the toilet.

He glanced up at Dr Novak. She was waiting patiently, watching him. 'I'm going to assume,' she said, 'that you're not a coward and that if you need help you will ask for it.'

Dr Novak knew the buttons to push. 'And she bypasses the triple dog dare, going straight to the cowardice card,' he murmured, and she laughed, making him grin. 'Yes, ma'am. If I need help I am not too proud – or cowardly – to ask.'

'You're not as big a pain in the derrière as my brother led me to believe,' she said.

He grinned wider. 'Sure I am. Just give me a chance.' He gripped the walker with both hands, ignoring the discomfort in his IV hand, then hefted himself to his feet and stood there for a moment, letting his legs steady out.

It took him twenty times longer than he thought it should have, but he made it to the toilet and back, barely getting his ass into bed before the door opened and Agent Troy entered, closing the door behind him.

Dr Novak moved in front of Decker, which made Decker smile. 'And you are?' she asked in a tone that would make any sane man think twice before crossing her.

'Special Agent Troy. We spoke on the phone.' He showed her his badge.

'He's legit, Doc. I met him this morning. Did you find her?' Decker asked Troy when Dr Novak had moved out of the way. 'Nurse Evil?'

Troy shook his head. 'Not yet. She slipped in and out one of the staff doors behind another nurse. She didn't use her ID, so she's not on file as having entered or exited. If you hadn't seen her, we might not have known to look for her. There isn't a camera in this room, and the cameras in the hall didn't catch her face. She kept her head down. She didn't use the elevator either – she came up the stairs – so we can't prove she was here unless someone saw her. Which no one did.'

'Or will admit to,' Dr Novak said quietly. 'This is a good hospital, don't get me wrong, but the staff are human, just like everywhere else. Some will give the shirt off their back to help you without even being asked, but others . . .' She shrugged. 'Especially if they want to stay under the radar themselves because they're using, like Eileen Wilkins. I think the public would be shocked if they knew how many medical professionals – doctors and nurses – have substance abuse issues. We work crazy hours, we need to be alert, and the stuff is everywhere.'

'And too easy to steal,' Troy said grimly. 'Which is what it appears Wilkins had been doing. None of the other nurses on her shift suspected her, but I don't know that they were telling me the truth. We've got a BOLO out on Wilkins and we have undercover agents at the school her son attends. If she tries to pick him up, we'll pick her up. Apparently she also had a boyfriend – a much younger guy who got her hooked to start with.'

Dr Novak shook her head. 'Unless he held her down and injected her, kicking and screaming, he did not "get her hooked". She made bad choices. Let's call it straight.'

'Here, here,' Decker said.

Troy looked annoyed. 'I was trying to be considerate,' he said, his jaw taut.

'Don't,' Dr Novak said. 'Not on my account.' She smiled to soften her words. 'I do appreciate your attempt to spare my tender sensibilities, but I've seen too many patients put at risk because a doctor or nurse is using. I don't have many tender sensibilities left. And this one,' she pointed to Decker with her thumb, 'well, according to my brother he has a tougher hide than a rhinoceros.'

Keeping it light, Decker snorted. 'I wish. I've had too many bullets pierce my hide and I've got the scars to prove it. Twelve of them, not that I was counting.'

Dr Novak turned to him, her eyes filled with horror. 'You've been shot *twelve times*?'

Decker started to give her a flip reply then remembered her brother was a federal agent and she probably lived with the fear that he'd be shot at some point in his career. 'Only twice since I joined the Bureau,' he said, and watched her tension ease. 'And one of those was planned.'

She stared at him. 'You let yourself get shot on purpose?'

He grimaced. 'It seemed like a good idea at the time. I needed to get into the accounting books of the traffickers, but I was a good bodyguard and they didn't want to move me. My handler and I decided that if I got hurt protecting my boss there was a better chance of me getting a desk job for a while. My handler was supposed to nick me on the leg, just enough to need a stitch or two. He missed, but it was a through and through. Hardly bled at all.'

'You realize now how patently stupid that plan was?' she said tartly.

Well, sure. Now. 'Hey, it worked. Got me into the accounting department. Most of the other bullets I took in Afghanistan, but that was a war, so they were to be expected.'

'Most of the others?' she pressed.

He shrugged. 'I had an eventful adolescence,' he said, and left it at that.

Decker was grateful when Troy stepped in to change the subject. 'I've got an orderly out in the hall with a wheelchair. We're going to transfer you to a safe house.'

Decker's eyes widened. 'Already? Damn, you guys are good.'

'Yes, we are.' Troy handed him a plain black backpack. 'A change of clothing.'

Decker unzipped the backpack with trepidation. Not many places had his size, and he really didn't want to have to wiggle into something that was too tight. To his surprise, the clothes were too big. 'Wow. This never happens. These'll swallow me whole.'

Troy smiled. 'Agent Triplett donated some of his clothing to the cause. None of the rest of us could have. It's a button-up shirt and a pair of shorts. We didn't want to paint a target on your head by wheeling you out in a hospital gown. Just in case Ms Wilkins or whoever secured her cooperation is waiting for you downstairs with a scope.'

'That would suck,' Decker said. Especially if they hit a civilian. Like Dr Novak.

Dr Novak shook her head. 'Are all you guys masters of under-statement?' She started taking clothes out of the backpack and handed him a pair of boxers.

'I'm more of a boxer-brief guy myself,' Decker said. 'Ma'am, could you wait outside?'

She looked up at him. 'I'm a doctor. You got that, right?'

Decker gave her a direct look. 'Yes, ma'am. And if I need examining, I'll be as cooperative as any patient you've ever had. But this is different and I'd really prefer my privacy.'

She stepped back immediately. 'Of course. Just don't yank out your IV.'

'Yes, ma'am.' Once she was gone, Decker turned to Troy, who looked puzzled at his modesty. 'Are we putting her in danger by asking her to babysit me while I heal up?'

The wrinkles in Troy's brow smoothed out. 'No. If we were, Zimmerman never would have approved it. The safe house is the penthouse floor of an exclusive condo in Eden Park. There is only one elevator that goes to that level and it requires a key card to get past the floor below it. The stairwell doors are also secure. CPD has used this apartment in the past. The windows are bullet-resistant and the doors are solid. There is no access from the roof and the angle makes it unlikely that a potential attacker could rappel down. You'll have coverage, either via CPD or the Bureau. She's much safer with you than at the free clinic at the Meadow where she'll be working next week. That's in a bad part of town.'

'The Meadow?' Decker asked. 'You mean that shelter? She's working there? Why?'

Troy pulled the rest of the clothes from the backpack. 'She resigned from the hospital yesterday.'

'Yeah, I remember that. She came to talk to Kate when I was trying to wake up. Kate was worried about her. Asked if she had a job to go to. Why did she resign?'

'It wasn't because of malpractice or incompetence, that's all I know.' Troy held out the shirt. 'I'll help you get your arms in the sleeves.'

He proceeded to dress Decker with a quick competence that indicated he'd done this before, especially when it came to taking care with the IV needle. Pulling on a pair of gloves, he disconnected the IV then reattached it like he was tying his own shoes.

'Who did you take care of?' Decker asked him as Troy was buttoning him up.

Troy's hands faltered for a split second before resuming his task.

'My partner,' he said. Hesitantly. As if he were expecting a reproof. He'd get none from Decker.

'I'm sorry,' Decker said, because Troy was clearly still grieving. 'How long ago?'

'Five years. He was in an accident and ended up in a wheelchair. Paraplegic. He got pneumonia and . . . yeah.' Troy handed him the boxers. 'Do you need help with these?'

'Maybe.' Decker got his feet in and managed to pull them up a little at a time, finally getting them on. He had to rest afterwards, though. 'I have to get my strength back.'

'You just woke up this morning,' Troy said mildly. 'Here, let me get the shorts.'

They were exercise shorts, with *Crimson Tide* printed on the leg. 'For heaven's sake,' Decker grumbled. 'The kid went to 'Bama? Now we're going to have to hate each other.'

Troy laughed as he grabbed the shoes at the bottom of the pile. 'You went to Ole Miss?'

'No, Southern Miss, but I have to hate 'Bama on principle. Thank you,' he added when Troy crouched to slip the shoes on Decker's feet, tying them tight.

'They're not as big as I thought they'd be, but you're still going to have to be careful walking in them. Most of the time you'll be in a wheelchair, so it'll be— Hold on. I just got a text.' Rising, he scanned his phone's screen, then sighed. 'Fuck it.'

Decker's smile slid away. 'What? Please,' he added when Troy looked like he wasn't going to say. 'Is Kate okay?'

'Yes. She's at the morgue with Deacon. They just discovered that a young woman who OD'd last night was the last person to visit Alice yesterday. Kate's going to get us more details as she has them.' He frowned. 'Shit, I forgot.' He pulled a second phone from his pocket. 'Zimmerman told me to give you this. It's a loaner until you can get one from the department. Evidently Coppola texted you too.'

Decker felt better about that. She was okay and she was communicating with him. But when he read the text, his gut twisted. 'Cyanide? *And* ricin? Hell, somebody wanted to make sure that

Alice didn't talk. I guess I'm glad I just got hit with an opioid.'

'Dead is dead,' Troy muttered. 'However you get there.'

Decker agreed with that. 'I don't want Dr Novak in the vehicle with me. Bring her in separately. I don't want someone taking a shot at me and hitting her by mistake.'

'I was thinking the same thing. She won't like it, but she's going to have to deal.'

Someone knocked on the door. 'It's Triplett. You ready to roll?'

'Yes,' Decker called. 'Come on in.'

The door opened and Triplett filled the space. 'There's a hat, too, Agent Troy,' he said. 'Front pouch of the backpack.'

Chuckling wickedly, Troy found the Crimson Tide ball cap and Decker sighed.

'Insult to frickin' injury,' he grumbled as he put the cap on his head. 'You *had* to go to Alabama, Triplett?'

'If I wanted to stay part of my family, I did. My dad went there. Played football.' His eyes narrowed. 'Ole Miss?'

'No, but he has to hate you on principle,' Troy said. 'Can we get this moving, people?'

Triplett grinned at Decker. 'Sorry.'

'No you're not,' Decker said.

Triplett's grin grew wider. 'No, I'm not. You ready for the wheelchair?'

'Hell, yeah. The sooner I get out of here, the better.' He made sure Kate's tablet was in the backpack. 'When I get to the safe house, I have to work.'

Dr Novak nudged Triplett aside so that she could push the wheelchair into the room. 'When you get there, you will rest.'

Decker noticed that both Troy and Triplett were looking anywhere but at Dr Novak. 'Cowards,' he muttered as he moved his body from the bed to the chair.

'Just choosing the important battles,' Troy corrected. 'Like telling Dr Novak that she needs to ride in a separate vehicle because you have a target painted on your ass that can be seen from space.'

Dr Novak stared at Troy. 'Excuse me?'

'Yes, ma'am. You'll be a few cars behind.'

'But—' she started to protest.

Troy cut her off. 'But if you're hurt, we won't have anyone to take care of him. It's not far. Fifteen minutes, tops.'

She pursed her lips. 'Can I drive my own car?'

'We'd prefer that you didn't,' Troy said. 'It's for your own protection. If you have to leave for any reason, we'll take you to your car or wherever you need to go. Whoever is snipping loose ends is doing it very religiously. We won't risk your life.'

'All right. Let's go, then.' She gestured to the orderly, who wheeled Decker out of the room. She pushed the IV stand alongside him, and with Troy out in front and Triplett behind, they made their way to the elevator without incident, except for the scowl from a waiting nurse when she was told she'd have to wait for the next one.

Once the elevator doors were closed, Troy seemed to relax. 'We'll take the express route,' he said, producing a master key. Sure enough, they made no stops all the way down to the basement. A windowless van was waiting at an underground loading area with none other than Special Agent in Charge Zimmerman at the wheel. A ramp allowed the orderly to load Decker directly in the back, wheelchair and all. Troy joined him, sitting on a side bench.

'I'll drive you, Dr Novak,' Triplett said. 'We'll meet you guys there.' He shut the doors and Zimmerman started the engine.

'I didn't expect to see you, sir,' Decker said.

Zimmerman glanced up into the rear-view mirror. 'We've kept this operation small and need-to-know only. Besides, I wanted to see how you were doing myself, now that you're awake.'

'Not bad. I can breathe on my own and I got to eat real food this afternoon. On the other hand, I'm wearing rival school colors, but I can't complain too much because I'm not dead.'

Zimmerman chuckled. 'Let's keep it that way, shall we?'

'Amen,' Troy said quietly, picking up the rifle that lay at his feet and checking that it was loaded. He did the same with a handgun he took from a case under his seat, then handed it to Decker. 'Just in case.'

'Thank you,' Decker said soberly. 'I felt a little naked before.'

'You'll feel less naked in a minute,' Troy said. He opened a large plastic tub and pulled out a Kevlar vest, open at the sides. 'This will go over your head without disturbing your IV. And you can wear this instead of the cap.' He gave Decker a tactical helmet. 'We have an unmarked following us and one waiting for us at the safe house to provide cover if necessary.' He finished attaching the vest and Decker traded the helmet for the cap. 'Any questions? Concerns?'

'No.' Just when he'd see Kate again, but he kept that one to himself. 'I'm good.'

Cincinnati, Ohio,
Thursday 13 August, 4.25 P.M.

'This is bad, guys,' Carrie Washington said, coming through the door of her office.

Kate and Deacon looked up from their phones. They were sitting in the ME's office, planning out their next steps and waiting for the results of the quick preliminary test Carrie had done on the body of Sidney Siler, the King's College grad student.

'Bad like you found something?' Deacon asked. 'Or bad that you didn't?'

'Door number one. There's cyanide in her system. I might have missed it because she also has cocaine. And ketamine. Her skin tone hid some of the redness that would have alerted me to cyanide.'

'So . . .' Kate said, wishing she hadn't left her yarn in the car, because she was very tense and her mind was whirling too fast to make much sense. She reached into the printer, took out a few sheets of paper, and began folding them into familiar origami patterns. 'Same killer, different MO's. Why?'

'Or two different killers working together,' Deacon said. 'Although it seems like a big risk that we'd connect the two victims, seeing as how they were killed on the same day and would end up in the morgue at the same time. How was the cyanide delivered to the grad student, Carrie?'

'I won't know until I open her up and check the contents of her stomach. She snorted the cocaine-ketamine mix, though. There are remnants inside her nostrils. She'd been using coke for some time. Her nasal membranes show signs of long-term substance abuse.'

Kate set a paper boat aside and began folding a helicopter. 'Maybe they thought we'd be so busy with Alice and Decker – because he was supposed to have been dead – that we wouldn't pay attention to a grad student who'd OD'd. But why not just give her too much cocaine and ket? Why make himself conspicuous with the cyanide?'

'He may have wanted a quick death, but one I might not check for,' Carrie said. 'Cyanide deaths have gone undetected in the past. Who knows how many have slipped through?'

'What we do know,' Kate said, 'is that she spoke with Alice, posing as an attorney's assistant. I called the firm and they have no one there named Keisha Findlay. She had a letter of intro on the firm's letterhead and the font looks identical to that used on the firm's website.'

'Why did she pick that firm?' Deacon asked.

'Because they were assigned by the court to represent Alice,' Kate said. 'She went through three more firms before she ended up in the infirmary last night. She fired all of them because they wouldn't try to get her total immunity. But the first attorney was still on record as being assigned by the court.'

'We need to find out what Alice told those attorneys,' Deacon said.

Kate scoffed. 'Good luck with that. They'll hide behind privilege.' She set the helicopter aside and started folding a dog. 'We also know that this killer – be he McCord's partner or not – sends someone else in to do his dirty work. Eileen with Decker and now Sidney with Alice. Maybe he doesn't want to be caught on camera meeting them.'

'Sidney was a coke user,' Deacon said thoughtfully. 'Carrie, will you be able to test the residue in her nose? I'm wondering if we can trace it to her dealer.'

'I'll do the best I can.'

Kate finished the dog and stared at the next sheet of paper, her brain finally starting to cooperate. 'Both Eileen Wilkins and Sidney

Siler were cocaine users. The nurse's assistant who was in Decker's room when I got there . . .' She turned to Carrie. 'You heard that one of our agents was given an intentional overdose of an opioid this morning while he was in the hospital, right?'

Carrie's eyes widened. 'No. Is he okay?'

Kate nodded. 'Yes, but only because you were so quick to identify Alice's cause of death as poison. She died a few hours after Agent Davenport woke up and started talking about a huge loose end in the case he'd been working last week. The one that filled all your drawers. I ran to his room just as the drug was kicking in. The attending doctor gave him an antidote quickly.'

'Narcan,' she murmured. 'It's substantially cut the number of heroin ODs I see.'

'It was a nurse who'd drugged him,' Kate said, starting to fold a new sheet of paper, but with less urgency than she'd had before. She'd blown off the worst of the pressure in her mind and she could think again. 'Somewhere, at some point, Eileen Wilkins crossed paths with whoever killed Sidney Siler. Eileen got coke from her boyfriend – a much younger guy named Roy, according to the assistant I spoke to. Roy hangs out at King's College, takes a class a semester, but mainly he dabbles and goes to the gym. Sidney Siler went to King's College too. It's possible they share a dealer.'

'If you can find any of that nurse's stash,' Carrie said, 'I might be able to match it to the residue in Sidney's nasal cavities.'

'That's really good, Kate,' Deacon said, giving her an oddly assessing look. 'I'm gonna have to start folding paper if it lets me make those quick connections.'

Kate knew what the look meant and knew he'd ask her about it later. She hadn't needed to fold paper or knit or anything when she'd worked with him in Baltimore. She'd managed the stress in other ways and on her own time. Now it seemed like she couldn't escape the noise in her head.

'It was a hurricane in there,' she admitted quietly, tapping her temple. 'Cat 5. Now it's a Cat 2. I can think through a Cat 2. Agent Troy may have tracked Roy down already,' she went on, needing to turn the attention away from herself, 'because he was looking for

Eileen. Troy found out that Eileen has a son who's fifteen. The son should just be getting out of school – it's a special needs program he goes to during the summer. Troy's got plain-clothes agents waiting to follow whoever picks him up. Or to follow him home if he takes himself. Troy's also got Wilkins's house under surveillance. He should have a search warrant by now. I'll let him know he should set aside whatever drugs they find for testing.' She started to text on her phone, but Deacon stopped her.

'I'll text Zimmerman and Troy. You keep folding paper and thinking.'

Kate did as he asked, a more complex figure taking form as she folded. 'The ricin. Like you said, Carrie, recipes all over the damn Internet. A nineteen-year-old at Georgetown University recently made some in his dorm bedroom with materials he got at Home Depot – enough to kill a lot of people. All someone needs is access to the materials, a basic knowledge of high school chemistry and some low-tech lab equipment.'

Deacon blew out a breath. 'McCord was a high school teacher. Maybe his partner is too. McCord, at least, would have access to a lab. Gimme some of that paper, Coppola.'

She flashed him a grin. 'You got the witchy eyes that scare people into confessing. Leave me a superpower of my own.' She made the last fold and examined the origami figure with a critical eye. 'Not bad.'

Carrie leaned in curiously. 'What is it? An eagle or a hawk?'

'Something like that,' she evaded, then glanced at Deacon, who was rolling his eyes.

'It's a gryphon,' Deacon said flatly, sucking in one cheek. 'Mythical creature. Half eagle, half lion. *Not real*,' he added meaningfully.

'Still very cool,' Carrie said, missing the undercurrent.

'We'll just leave you to start your autopsies.' Kate swept her little paper figures into her hand. 'Where's the garbage can?'

Carrie held out her own hand. 'Leave them. I've got a five-year-old godson who will take these apart to figure out how you folded them. He's a budding engineer.'

Kate and Deacon gathered their things and left the morgue, their silence awkward until Deacon got a text while they waited for the elevator.

'It's from Scarlett,' he said. 'From fifteen minutes ago, dammit. It really is a dead zone in there. She and Marcus have been waiting at the *Ledger* building for one of us to come down and review their investigation into Woody McCord.'

'Shit, I forgot.' Kate checked her own phone, which was buzzing as several new texts downloaded. 'I have a bunch of messages from Troy. Decker's been moved to the safe house with no issues. Your sister is with them. Troy and Zimmerman are debriefing Decker now. Scarlett contacted Zimmerman first, apparently. He told her to come to the safe house since he and Troy would be there a while. Zimmerman wants us all to sit down together and listen to what Marcus O'Bannion has to say about McCord.'

'Davenport too?' Deacon asked with a frown.

'Yes,' Kate said, not hiding her impatience. 'Decker might have heard something at the traffickers' compound that he didn't know was important. I think he needs to hear what Marcus has to say. Plus, he did risk his life to make sure we knew that McCord had a partner. You'd want to know in his place.'

'Yeah, I would,' Deacon admitted. 'I'll tell Scarlett we're on our way.' He sent the text, then sighed. 'Be careful about Davenport. I don't like the way that man looks at you.'

That man looks at me like I'm his salvation, she thought, but would never utter those words aloud. Nor would she share any of what Decker had confided that morning. Those secrets were his to share, not hers.

'Why?' she asked instead. 'Why don't you like him?'

'Because he looks at you like he's been on a desert island with no women for way too long,' Deacon said bluntly. 'And because he managed to stay undercover for three years. Who knows what he had to do during those years, or what kind of man he is? I've known undercover guys in the past. They're good at undercover because they don't form attachments. And they don't make commitments. Not ones they keep, anyway.'

Ah. Kate understood his concern now, even though she didn't believe it applied to Decker. At least she didn't want it to.

'I'm a big girl, Deacon. I can take care of myself.' She smiled at him so that he would know her words were sincere. 'But thank you for caring.'

The elevator doors opened and Kate was grateful for the distraction. And the fresher air when they stepped out upstairs. 'I really hate the smell of the morgue,' she said, sniffing her suit jacket. 'Now I smell bad. This is why I don't take my yarn bag in there. My projects suck in the stink.'

Deacon slid on his wraparound shades. 'There are three showers in the safe house,' he said. 'Feel free to use any of them.'

'I've got a change of clothes in my car. I may take you up on it.'

They'd parked next to each other, so they walked out of the building together, cringing simultaneously when the heat of the day smacked them hard. Still, it was better than the morgue.

Kate was about to get into her car when Deacon stopped her.

'Kate, wait.' He hesitated. 'The hurricanes in your head . . . they seem worse than they did before I left DC. You didn't *need* to knit then. This morning, you kind of reminded me of an addict jonesing for a fix. Just now, with the paper, it was the same way. Are you okay?'

'Yeah. Mostly.'

'What changed?'

'Some of it's hormones. I'm getting older.' She wished she could see his eyes, to know if he'd bought her excuse. But he had been her rock and he deserved more than a half-truth. 'Mostly it was Jack.'

'Oh.' His face twisted. 'I should have known that. I'm sorry, Kate.'

'Why?' She patted his cheek sweetly. 'You've got your life, Deacon, and I am thrilled for you. I'm finding my way. I'm just glad I'm here. Knowing you have my back is enough.'

'I do. You know that.'

'Yeah. That's why I let you rag on Decker. But cut him a little slack, at least until you get to know him. If you still distrust him, I promise you that I'll listen.'

'Okay.' He checked his phone. 'Text from Scar. They have Stone with them too. That's Marcus's brother. He insisted on being a part of this.' He glanced up, his expression tense. 'Stone's not supposed to be moving around. We should take this to him.'

'Decker's not supposed to be moving around either,' she said quietly. 'This is as important to him as it is to Stone. Besides, they're on their way already. At least this way Stone will have your sister nearby if he needs medical attention.'

'True.'

'What about Kimble?' Kate asked. 'Should he hear this too?'

'Yes. I'll text him and meet you there.'

Nine

Dani Novak was worse than his very worst drill sergeant, Decker thought as he looked down at the tray of food on his lap. It was chicken – boiled and bland – and unseasoned green beans from a can. At least the carrots were fresh. He bit into one, harder than he needed to.

'Kate brought me wings,' he said. 'And a cheeseburger. And M&Ms.'

'Kate is not your doctor,' Dani said sharply. 'I am. And don't whine. It's not becoming.'

'I don't care,' he snapped. 'I'm hungry.'

She sat in the chair next to his bed with her own tray. 'Then eat what I gave you and stop behaving like a three-year-old who missed his nap.'

From his post beside the door, Agent Triplett made a strangled noise, like he was trying not to laugh. Decker glared at him. 'You shut up.'

Triplett held his hands up, palms out. 'Hey, man, I didn't say a word.'

Decker sighed grumpily. 'Whatever.' He turned away from both of them and looked out through the wall of windows at the city and the river below. They'd set up his hospital bed in the living room of what was the most luxurious apartment he'd ever seen, much less stayed in, and the view was breathtaking. 'How did you guys get access to this place?'

183

'Through Adam,' Dani said. 'Adam Kimble,' she added when he looked at her blankly.

'Oh, right. Kate told me about him. He's the team member working with ICAC right now.' The one looking at the photos taken from McCord's computer.

Shadows flickered in Dani's mismatched eyes. 'Yes. I hope that works out.'

She was angry, Decker realized. Furious, actually. 'What do you mean?'

She bit her lip, then shrugged. 'It's not like everyone doesn't know. Adam got transferred to Personal Crimes about a year ago.'

'Oh.' Personal Crimes was a CPD euphemism for sex crimes. 'That's a hard gig.'

She nodded. 'He lasted about three months, but during that time he changed. Drastically. He used to be happy and optimistic and patient, but he turned all dark and scary, even.'

'He's a personal friend of yours, then?'

'He's my cousin. Well, *our* cousin – mine and Deacon's. We grew up together.'

'Oh. Wow. I had no idea all the relationships were so . . . intricate.' Decker glanced over at Triplett, who also looked intrigued, then back to Dani. 'You said that Adam lasted three months. So what happened?'

'I don't know. He hasn't told me. Or Deacon, for that matter. It had to have been something pretty bad, though, because he ended up taking a leave of absence. When he came back, he went back to reporting to the boss he'd had before Personal Crimes. That's Lieutenant Isenberg, who now heads up the joint task force between CPD and the FBI. She's Deacon and Scarlett's boss.'

'Why would they send him to look at . . . well, to look at material that would drive most decent people crazy?' Decker asked.

'Good question,' she said grimly. 'I helped pick up the pieces the first time. I don't want to think about having to do that again.' She looked down at her plate with a sigh. 'Anyway, this place belongs to a man whose child was kidnapped several years ago. Adam was instrumental in the child's safe return and the man was beyond grateful. He had this place built to be intruder-proof afterward. He's a local marketing guru and took a four-year assignment in Asia, and he gave Adam permission to use this place as a safe house. It's got excellent security and is easily defendable.'

'I'm grateful,' Decker said quietly. 'I'm sorry I snapped. I'm just really hungry and this did not fill me up.'

'Me either,' Dani admitted, 'but this was what Agent Troy had in his own fridge. He knew the food was safe. It'll feed you until one of us can stock the pantry.'

'He eats this?' Decker asked, truly horrified. Glancing at the closed door to the little office where Troy and Zimmerman had gone to work, he lowered his voice. 'Voluntarily?'

'He has an ulcer,' Triplett volunteered. 'He has to eat bland foods.'

'Oh.' Dani worried her lower lip. 'We'll work on that. You Feds, with your hours and the stress and your eating habits. It's a wonder any of you have any functional GI tracts.'

'And you medical professionals are any different?' Decker challenged. 'You keep the same hours and stress. And those of you who don't abuse drugs have other vices, just like we do.'

'Touché.' She tilted her head. 'What's your vice, Decker?'

He thought about it for a minute. 'Not drugs. Or sex, or even rock 'n' roll,' he added with a self-deprecating shake of his head. 'I rarely drink.' Because in his mind he'd always see his parents, drunk as skunks, every time he took a sip of anything alcoholic. 'Probably the work itself. Hi, I'm Griffin Davenport, and I'm a workaholic.'

'Hi, Griffin,' Triplett said from his position at the door. 'I'm Jefferson Triplett, and I run.'

'Exercise is healthy,' Dani said, but she was studying Triplett with a clinical expression.

'Not the way I do it,' Triplett said sadly. 'I've ripped up my knees and my back and I still run. I have to or I can't sleep at night. And I've only been on the job a year.'

Oh, kid, Decker thought with pity. *The Bureau's gonna chew you up and spit you out.*

'We're a pathetic lot,' Dani said. 'I'm a workaholic too, and it's not good for me either. I can't drink and I take way too many drugs as it is.' She pushed her plate away. 'Look, since we're all maudlin, I need to tell you both something so you'll know what to do if there's an emergency. What precautions to take. Or so that you, Decker, can decide if you want me to continue as your doctor. I'm HIV positive. My counts are good, my viral loads undetectable. I can be your doctor without putting you at risk. But if anything happens and blood spills . . .'

Decker blinked at her. 'That is the last thing I expected you to say. But, for the record, I'm totally okay with you continuing to be my doctor. Whether Triplett stays or not is up to him.'

'I'm not going anywhere,' Triplett said steadily. 'I guess we should make sure you don't bleed then, huh, Doc?'

Dani's shoulders visibly relaxed. 'That's always a good plan. Thank you.'

'No thanks necessary,' Decker said. 'I'm familiar with the risks and how you contract it and how you don't. I do have a question and you don't have to answer it, but . . . is that why you quit your job? One of the ICU nurses said that the hospital had treated you poorly.'

'It became an issue,' Dani allowed. 'But you need to know that I took every precaution and followed every rule and policy.'

'Then they were dicks,' Triplett said matter-of-factly.

Decker snorted a surprised laugh. 'The kid nailed it,' he said, and Dani's grin broke through.

Decker took a moment to appreciate the view. She was very pretty, but when she smiled, she lit up like an incandescent bulb. She didn't move him, though. Not the way a certain redhead did.

And speak of the devil. His phone picked that moment to buzz with an incoming text from a certain redhead who was on her way to him now. Decker read her message with satisfaction. 'Seems like we're about to have company. Kate, your brother, your cousin and some folks from the *Ledger* will be here in—'

Triplett pulled his phone from his pocket and answered it, the device looking like a child's toy in his huge hand. 'Send them up. I'll be waiting.' He hung up. 'Detective Bishop is on her way up with the *Ledger* guys. One's in a wheelchair, so we need to clear a path.'

Dani had already begun clearing away the dishes from lunch, but she stopped and stared at Triplett. 'They're bringing *Stone*? Are they in*sane*?'

'Who's Stone?' Decker asked.

Dani huffed, irritated. 'Marcus's brother. He was shot last week. Multiple times.'

Something clicked. 'Stone O'Bannion? The reporter? Was he embedded with the troops a few years back?'

'He was,' Dani confirmed. 'Did you meet him over there?'

'No, but I read a few of his reports. Most of us hated reporters, but he'd served a tour or two himself. He was one of us, so we trusted him.' One report in particular was seared in Decker's memory forever. 'He wrote a damn nice tribute to a group of medics who were fired on despite displaying the red cross.'

'Did you lose friends in that attack?' Triplett asked. 'Sorry, didn't mean to pry. You just looked really . . . intense there for a second.'

'Yeah, I did,' Decker said, pushing the memory aside. He'd already cried over Shelby Lynne today. He didn't want to risk getting all emotional about Beth, which might happen if he let himself think about her. 'Some very good friends.'

Dani was frowning. 'I'm glad Stone wrote a nice tribute. But it doesn't change the fact that he should be at home. Resting.'

'He can have the bed,' Decker said. 'Seriously. I do not want to be in this bed while everyone else is here. Trip, can you give me a hand into the wheelchair?'

Triplett hustled over to help him, both of them ignoring Dani giving them the evil eye

'This counts against the time you're allowed out of bed today,' she said, but she didn't argue with him and for that Decker was grateful.

'I have out-of-bed time limits?' he whined – on purpose this time. 'Gosh darn it, Ma.'

Dani snickered and swept up the remnants of their meal. 'Hush or I'll take your electronics.'

'What*ever*.' Decker settled into the wheelchair just as the doorbell rang. Triplett opened it after checking the security camera. Scarlett Bishop was the first to enter.

'Wow,' she said, looking around. 'I forgot how nice this place is.'

'I like your house better.' That came from Marcus O'Bannion, who was pushing a wheelchair. He eased it over the threshold as if it were a stroller carrying a sleeping baby.

The man sitting in the chair rolled his eyes. 'I'm not made of glass, Marcus.'

'No, but your head is filled with rocks, *Stone*,' Marcus replied. 'You shouldn't be here.'

'Amen,' Dani muttered. 'You men don't have the sense God gave a turnip.'

Stone smiled up at her, unperturbed. 'I didn't know you were going to be here, Dr Dani.'

Decker watched the exchange, trying to figure out how Stone knew Dani Novak. These people had a tangled relationship tree, what with cousins and boyfriends and fiancées. Most likely through Deacon Novak. The man seemed to be everywhere.

'I'm tending *him*. And his head's harder than yours.' Dani jerked her shoulder toward Decker, but her body stilled as the last person in the group filed in, closing the door behind him.

The last guy could be Triplett's twin, except he was Caucasian and covered with tattoos. And he seemed . . . dangerous when Triplett was just huge.

Okay, Decker amended, *they have nothing in common except their size*. And their bald heads, shaved and shiny. Decker hoped no one shined a light at the pair, because the rest of them would be blinded by the reflections.

The new guy didn't crack a smile, his eyes doing a sweep of the place as if scanning for traps and attackers was second nature. *Military*, Decker thought. *Clearly*. But the moment the guy saw Dani Novak, he went as still as she had.

Their stillness was different. Dani's was a tread-carefully-so-as-not-to-spook-the-scary-fucker kind of stillness. The man's stillness . . . it was the kind that made you look for the nearest exit in case he blew sky high. He was *that* tense, and in that moment everyone in the room seemed to be holding their collective breath.

Dani broke the silence. 'Coach Diesel,' she said softly. 'It's good to see you again.'

The man jerked a nod, but said nothing.

Stone sighed softly. 'Dr Dani? The lab coat. Can you lose it?'

Her eyes widened. 'Oh, of course. Excuse me.' She disappeared into the bedroom she'd claimed as her own, returning without the coat. She aimed a winsome smile at the tattooed mountain. 'Better?'

The tattooed mountain blushed. He actually blushed. Decker stared, fascinated, then glanced around to see if anyone else was watching, but almost everyone else was pretending to be busy. Marcus pushed his brother's wheelchair close to Decker's, then walked with Scarlett to the window to stare at the view. Stone was studying Decker, which was a little weird.

Only Triplett was also watching Dani and the mountain, but his stare was one of threat assessment. He must have been satisfied, because he stepped forward, hand out. 'Jeff Triplett.'

'Diesel Kennedy,' the mountain rumbled, his voice like an idling Harley-Davidson. 'I work for Marcus at the *Ledger*.'

'Come on in, Coach,' Dani said, still gentling the big man. 'Go meet Agent Davenport.'

Diesel swallowed hard. Leaving Dani standing by the door, he took a seat next to Stone's wheelchair and gave Stone a glare that dared him to say a word.

With a roll of his eyes, Stone turned to Decker. 'So, you up for a wheelchair race?'

Decker barked out a laugh, then winced. 'Ow. That still hurts. No, I think Dr Novak would be most displeased if I tried that. I'm hoping to get some pizza later if I'm well behaved.'

Stone sighed. 'I'd say you were whipped, but pizza sounds amazing. I'm still eating soft foods.' His eyes sharpened. 'How long were you undercover with the traffickers?'

'I am not giving an interview, Mr O'Bannion.' Decker softened his refusal with a smile. He hadn't even been fully debriefed yet, although he had managed to share quite a bit with Zimmerman after they'd arrived here. Enough that Zimmerman now had a long list of follow-up items and had excused himself to the apartment's home office to assign tasks to his staff. Unfortunately, none of what he'd remembered so far had anything to do with McCord's partner.

Stone sighed again. 'I didn't think you would, but it was worth a try.'

'So I know you're a reporter,' Decker said to Stone, then turned to Diesel, 'but why did Dr Novak call you Coach?'

Diesel blushed again, although it seemed that once he was no longer in direct proximity to Dani Novak, he could actually speak. 'I coach pee wee soccer. One of my players got hurt and was treated by Dr Novak at the free clinic. She volunteers there.'

'She's going to work there starting next week,' Decker said.

Diesel's eyes narrowed. 'Full-time? That place is dangerous.' He twisted around in the chair to glare silently at Dani, who was oblivious to his ire.

'There's never been an incident involving free-clinic staff,' Stone told him. 'She'll be fine. A couple of the cops volunteer there too. They're good security.'

Diesel twisted back to glare at Stone. 'How do you know that?'

'She told me about the job when she stopped by to check on me after dinner last night. I figured you'd be worried, so I asked.'

Diesel scowled. 'It's her business.'

Stone rolled his eyes again. 'Yes, it is, Diesel. Unless you want to make it yours, too. If not, then you're not allowed to complain about it.' He turned to Decker, leaving Diesel sputtering. 'What do we call you, Agent Davenport? Griffin? Griff?'

'Decker is fine.'

Diesel humphed. 'I'm not sure if Decker is better than Mr Surfer USA or not.'

Decker's brows shot up. 'Excuse me?'

Diesel shrugged. 'I was there last week at the traffickers' compound. I was the one who drove Agent Novak out there to help save your ass.'

Decker pursed his lips. That Deacon Novak had stopped the bleeding after he'd been shot was a sore point. 'I suppose I should say thank you. But that doesn't explain the surfer thing.'

'I saw you and Agent Coppola talking and I asked Marcus who Mr Surfer USA was, because you have that beach bum vibe going on, but he said you were the undercover guy.'

Decker wondered how a civilian had known that an undercover guy existed, but he filed the question away for later. 'I've been called many things in my life, but never Mr Surfer USA.'

'Not that you know of,' Diesel said wryly.

'True. But I don't remember you, and I know I would have for the tats alone.'

'I didn't stick around. Too many cops.' Diesel feigned a shudder. 'Gives me hives.'

'Me too,' Stone said, glancing over at Scarlett and his brother, who were standing next to the window, arms around each other's waists. 'Now I have to be nice to that one.'

'I heard that!' Scarlett called, not turning around.

'I know!' Stone replied, grinning when Scarlett flipped him the bird behind her back.

Diesel shook his head. 'Stop picking at her, Stone.'

'Hey, I can't go back to work for a few weeks and I'm having to give up sports for a few months. Picking at her is the only fun thing I have left to do. Hell, Decker here is in better shape and he just woke up from a fucking coma.'

Decker certainly hoped he looked better than Stone O'Bannion did. The man was tall and broad, but he seemed fragile. His skin was deathly pale, his cheeks sunken. His five o'clock shadow made his face look pasty and haggard. He'd been shot the week before when one of the traffickers came into the *Ledger* building looking for Marcus. When he didn't find Marcus, the man had opened fire, killing several people and critically wounding Stone. But Stone had saved the lives of several others in the process, so, fragile as he seemed, he was a bona fide hero.

And, of course, both Stone and Kennedy had had something to do with exposing Woody McCord, which made them heroes already. They may have gone about it in a way that was a little less than legal, but Decker wasn't going to hold them at fault.

Not after some of the things he'd had to do.

He shifted his gaze to the front door, where Triplett was letting Kate through. Sitting up a little straighter in the chair, he waited for her to see him, childishly pleased when she flashed him a smile.

Behind her was a dark-haired man in a conservative suit who looked pale and . . . shaken. He stepped through the door and was greeted by Dani, who wrapped him in her arms and rocked him where they stood. Comfort, Decker understood. This would be Detective Adam Kimble, her cousin.

'What's with Kimble?' Diesel asked under his breath. 'He looks like his dog just died.'

'He just came from ICAC,' Decker whispered. 'Reviewing McCord's hard drive.'

This statement was met with utter and complete silence – until Deacon Novak entered and closed the door behind him.

Stone huffed in disgust. 'Terrific. His royal freaky-eyed assness is here too.'

Shocked, Decker nearly choked on a laugh. 'What?'

'Novak,' Diesel explained. 'Stone wants to hate him too.'

'But I can't,' Stone said morosely. 'He's marrying my cousin, Faith. We did so well avoiding cops, and now we have two to worry about. Christmas will never be the same.'

'Ah,' Decker said. 'That's the connection. I was wondering how you knew Dani.'

'All one big happy family,' Stone said sarcastically. 'Everybody's happy but me and Diesel here. We're about to get our asses reamed out by CPD and the FBI and we probably won't even be able to use it in a story, so it's a lose-lose deal.'

Diesel sighed. 'Don't let him fool you,' he murmured. 'We didn't know there was a partner. We've been racking our brains all day and we can't figure out how we missed that. And if he's been hurting kids all this time . . . Goddammit.' The big man closed his eyes miserably and Decker's heart squeezed in sympathy.

'If you'd known, you'd have turned him in too, right?' Decker murmured back.

Diesel's eyes popped open to stare at him indignantly. 'Of course!'

'Then you shouldn't feel guilty,' Decker said simply.

'Easier said than done,' Stone said flatly, and Decker realized that the man had been putting up a sarcastic front to cover his anxiety. And his guilt. 'It's time to face the music.'

Cincinnati, Ohio,
Thursday 13 August, 5.05 P.M.

The safe house was very nice, Kate thought, glad that Decker would be able to convalesce here instead of in the hospital. The dining room table sat ten comfortably, which was a good thing, because once Troy and Zimmerman had joined them, ten was how many they had.

Dani had excused herself to her bedroom to work on reviewing patient files from the shelter's free clinic in preparation for her transition from volunteer to full-time staff doctor. Triplett stood at the door to ensure no one came close enough to bother them.

Not that anyone could. Zimmerman had stationed agents at every entrance downstairs and they had been thorough, checking everyone's ID against the list they'd been provided with.

Everyone took a seat, with the two wheelchairs at either end of the table. They'd lined up, Kate noted with a silent sigh, in teams. She sat closest to Decker, with Troy, Zimmerman, and Adam Kimble on her side of the table. Diesel Kennedy sat closest to Stone, with Marcus on Diesel's other side. That Scarlett put herself next to Marcus was not a surprise. That Scarlett gave Kate a thinly veiled look of warning wasn't either, based on the detective's reluctance to share her new beau's secrets that morning. They'd been through a lot, Scarlett had said. Kate saw the *don't hurt them* in the other woman's dark eyes. That Scarlett Bishop cared about protecting children had never been in doubt. But she was there to protect Marcus, Stone, and Diesel, too, and she wanted Kate to know it.

Deacon sat next to Scarlett, putting him on the other side of Decker, directly across from Kate. He considered himself the bridge, Kate thought. But then he and Scarlett shared a grim look that made Kate wonder how much her former partner really knew.

193

For a long moment nobody said anything, as everyone sized everyone else up warily. Kate decided to try breaking the ice and hoped her levity didn't blow up in her face.

'If I'd known we were going to do this meeting,' she said wryly, 'I'd have ordered T-shirts. You know, "Team: Cop" and "Team: *Ledger*".' There were some rueful smiles and a few chuckles, giving her the confidence to continue. 'Or maybe just one shirt – "Team: Let's Get McCord's Fucking Partner and Put Him Away Forever".'

Marcus's laugh was low and rumbly and . . . melodious. The man had a voice that could both soothe and charm, and that was exactly what he proceeded to do. 'That's a little long, Kate, but it's a shirt I'd wear.' He looked over at Diesel and his brother, and sobered. 'I want it known that what they did, they did at my direction. I am solely responsible.'

'Bull*shit*,' Diesel snapped. 'What we did, we did on our own.'

'And we'd do it again,' Stone added quietly. 'But we'd do it better, because we obviously missed something fucking important.'

Deacon was right, Kate thought. *Stone should not have come.* He was clearly drained, just from sitting in his wheelchair. But some things had to be faced, and she had a great deal of respect for Stone O'Bannion being brave enough to face this head on.

'Maybe we should start at the beginning,' Kate said softly. 'I figure you all at the *Ledger* were the ones to "anonymously" report McCord to the authorities. I also figure if you knew what was on his hard drive, you managed to sneak in somehow and peek.'

Marcus nodded. 'That's correct.' He hesitated, then looked up at the ceiling. 'There are some very bad people who manage to slip through the justice net. We see it every day. We report on it. It sickens us.'

'So you fixed what you could,' Decker said, his tone straight-forward. Uncondemning.

Marcus's mouth curved. 'Yeah. It was that or go quietly insane.'

'Not so quietly,' Stone said dryly, his jaw taut. 'We picked people who'd done terrible things. Not jaywalking or shoplifting. We picked people who'd hurt kids and who thought they'd gotten away with it, whether it be through slimy lawyers, incompetent cops or social workers, or simply the ability to frighten and cow their victims into silence.'

'How did you pick your targets?' Troy asked. 'How did you pick McCord?'

'Our tips came from various sources,' Marcus said evasively. 'And I'm not going to tell you exactly who those sources are, so please don't ask me.'

'We'll get back to that,' Zimmerman stated firmly, implacably.

Marcus smiled at him thinly. 'No, sir, we won't. If you want to know how we got McCord, you'll have to let us tell our story the best way we know how. This meeting is about McCord only. I will tell you how we learned about him, but the other targets we've exposed over the years are not on the table. I can tell you that none of our sources on those other cases broke any laws. Some of them might have breached confidentiality a time or two. Lawyers' assistants who were good people who saw bad things happening. A social worker here or there. A schoolteacher who'd reported an abused student, only to have the situation continue unchanged. Things they might be fired for telling us, but not things you could ever arrest them for. I hope that eases your concerns.'

Zimmerman looked at Deacon. 'Well? Should it ease my concerns?'

'I think you need to let him tell it his way,' Deacon said without hesitation.

Zimmerman sighed. 'Fine. Proceed, please, Mr O'Bannion.'

Marcus nodded. 'Okay. McCord was made known to me personally. I'm a volunteer coach on one of the junior varsity football teams. The *Ledger* sponsors youth sports. It's part of our community service. It also keeps us connected in the community itself. And it fosters an environment where kids are free to talk.'

Decker leaned forward. 'Is that why you coach pee wee soccer, Diesel?'

The big man's face flushed uncomfortably. 'One of the reasons, yes. Most of these kids grow up in homes without any male role models. I did, too.' He shrugged. 'I want better for them, that's all. No big deal.'

'It's a very big deal,' Decker said kindly. 'Because I was one of those kids too, and I would have benefitted from anyone who cared. I'm sorry, Marcus, I didn't mean to interrupt. Please continue.'

Moved, Kate wanted to reach for Decker's hand at that moment, but she couldn't. Not with all the eyes watching. *Later*, she thought, swallowing the lump in her throat as she wondered how in hell a man with his compassion had survived three years in the vile belly of the beast.

Marcus gave Decker a grateful look, because Diesel's expression had lost a fraction of its misery. 'I started hearing about McCord from some of the kids on the JV team, students in his class. I know these kids and they trust me. I won't betray that trust by just giving you their names, but I will ask them to come forward and tell you what they know. None of them said that McCord did anything more than show them too much attention. I asked. None admitted that they were photographed or abused in any way.'

Zimmerman's displeasure was clear. 'Will they come forward?'

Marcus shrugged. 'McCord's dead. He can't hurt them anymore. But you can never tell which way kids are gonna go. They might feel like a hero because they helped bring him down, in which case they'll cooperate. But they might not want anyone to think they were abused – especially the boys. It's a difficult age. It could make them a target for some of the predator kids if they admit they were touched by McCord in any way. It tends to diminish their status in the pack.'

'If they agree to talk to us, we should have Meredith Fallon present,' Kate said to Zimmerman. 'They should have had counseling over this anyway.'

Zimmerman nodded. 'Agreed. So McCord was their teacher, Marcus?'

'Yes. He taught freshman science and tended to lean in a little too close for the kids' comfort when he was checking over their lab experiments. That was the extent of their exposure to him. He didn't sponsor any clubs or after-school programs.'

Kate's gaze swung to meet Deacon's. 'Science teacher,' she murmured.

Deacon's mouth tilted up. 'Go ahead, oh origami queen. It's yours to tell.'

So Kate did, sharing what they'd learned at the morgue about the ricin. 'We wondered if McCord's partner was a fellow teacher. It makes even more sense if he's a science teacher.'

Marcus frowned, thinking. 'It's possible. I don't remember any of the other teachers' names coming up from the kids, though. And I asked. It was McCord alone who was giving them the creeps.'

'It's still good information, Kate,' Troy said. She'd called him from her car as she'd driven over from the morgue. As her partner, he'd deserved the update before everyone else and he'd been both appreciative and supportive. 'Maybe he teaches at a different school. I compiled a list of the science teachers in the county after we talked. There aren't that many, especially given that Alice called him "he" on Decker's recording.'

Zimmerman frowned. 'I would hope that if he is a teacher, any students he'd victimized would have come forward after McCord's arrest, once they'd seen that abusers do get punished.'

Stone shook his head. 'Too many victimized kids don't talk. It's not that they won't, but they *can't*. It's like . . . there's a wall inside and they can't breach it. I wouldn't depend on the partner's victims coming forward. Too much stigma and too much to lose.'

Kate noticed the pain flickering in Marcus's eyes as his brother talked so factually, so dispassionately. As if he was reciting the words from a book. It made Kate wonder exactly how much Stone knew from experience, but that wasn't her business.

'So how did you get McCord?' she asked Marcus.

'I did,' Diesel said flatly. 'I'm decent with computers.'

Stone snorted. 'And Rembrandt dabbled in paint. Diesel's an artist. His medium is hacking.'

'Jesus, Stone,' Diesel grumbled. 'It's not like we're talking to the FBI or anything.'

Stone rolled his eyes. 'You would have tap-danced around it for days and I don't have enough energy for that.' He met Zimmerman's gaze straight on. 'Diesel hacked into McCord's home Wi-Fi network.

Took him a couple of days. The bastard had *layers* of network security.'

'It was surprisingly well protected,' Diesel admitted. 'That's when I knew we were on the right track. Normally it takes me a few hours at the most. Most people never even change their router's default password. Then again, most people don't have a hard drive full of kiddie porn either,' he added bitterly. He swallowed hard, dropping his gaze to the tabletop. 'Really vile shit,' he whispered.

'I know,' Adam said quietly.

Diesel lifted his devastated gaze to Adam's. 'I am so sorry you had to see that, man.'

Adam's smile was sad. Haunted. 'Me too.'

'So, Diesel, you broke in,' Kate said gently. 'Then what?'

'I backed right out,' Diesel said with a shudder. 'Actually, I threw up, then I backed out. I . . . wasn't expecting what I found. Normally I make a copy of whatever I find on a person's hard drive, but not that time. I couldn't. I wouldn't. I copied the document files, that's all. No pictures. No videos. Then I backed out, called Stone, and we told Marcus, who called CPD and ICAC. Anonymously. The next thing I knew, they'd raided McCord's house and taken his computer.'

'They got a warrant based on your tip,' Adam said, but he was frowning. 'I had a printout of McCord's file directory, and there were no document files. Just picture files.'

Diesel leaned back in his chair, eyes narrowed. 'What? That's not possible.'

'We had the document files that Diesel copied in our possession,' Scarlett said. 'I turned them over to ICAC as part of the evidence on this case. I turned them over *personally*. I walked in with the hard drive in my hand and I got a receipt, so I know that they have them.'

'Did you tell ICAC that they belonged to McCord?' Adam asked.

'Of course.' But then Scarlett faltered. 'I'm pretty sure I did. I must have.'

'They gave me access to everything that had McCord's name on it,' Adam said. 'There was nothing there other than the computer they took from his home nine months ago.'

'Maybe they hadn't catalogued it yet,' Deacon offered. 'Those guys are always behind because they're not staffed for the job.' He grimaced. 'They could have every man and woman in CPD working ICAC and it wouldn't be enough staff for the job.'

'That's the truth,' Adam muttered. 'Give me a second.' He typed a text into his phone. 'I just asked the detective at ICAC to check any evidence that's waiting to be filed.'

Scarlett rubbed her eyes in a gesture of frustration. 'I took it to them the day after everything went down last week. Stone was in the hospital and so was Agent Davenport, and we'd lost so many people . . . I took it over there and I walked it in. I didn't want us to keep it any longer than we needed to. God, what if I didn't log it in properly?'

But Diesel was shaking his head. 'It shouldn't matter, Scarlett. What you did or didn't give them last week was evidence they already had. They've had it for nine months. The only thing on that drive I gave you last week was stuff that was on McCord's home computer nine months ago.'

Scarlett nodded, visibly calming herself. 'Thanks, Diesel. I couldn't stand it knowing I'd let a monster roam for even another week.'

'But that's what I'm trying to say, Scarlett,' Adam said. 'There weren't any document files on the drive that they took from McCord's house.' He lifted his computer bag from beneath his chair to the table and withdrew a thin stack of papers with rows and rows of text. 'This is a printout of all the file names on McCord's computer. No dot-docs. No videos.'

Deacon half stood, reaching across the table for the papers. 'Let me see those.' His white brows crunched as he set the papers down on the table and together he and Scarlett went through each page. He looked up after the last one. 'This isn't right. Or something isn't right. I saw the contents of the drive. There were *only* document files.'

Zimmerman drew a breath. 'You didn't mention that you'd seen it too, Deacon.'

'I never told Deacon where I'd gotten the drive,' Scarlett inserted before Deacon could say anything. 'He didn't know.'

'Like hell I didn't.' Deacon's jaw cocked in irritation. 'I'm not stupid, Scar. Diesel has mad computer skills. I put two and two together and got four.' He turned to Zimmerman. 'We thought there might be something on it to lead us to the traffickers' compound. There wasn't.'

'Were you planning to tell me?' Zimmerman asked.

'No,' Deacon said curtly. 'McCord was dead. ICAC had his files. We brought down the bad guys. We thought we were done. Frankly I didn't see the point.'

Zimmerman was clearly unhappy. 'We'll talk about that later. For now, let's figure out how Diesel got a copy of something that apparently does not exist.' He turned to Diesel. 'How much time elapsed between the major points on the timeline? Be as specific as you can.'

Diesel ran his palm over his shaved head. 'I broke through McCord's network security at about ten at night. This was way back before Christmas, so I may not be exact.'

'Do the best you can,' Zimmerman said.

'No pressure,' he muttered. 'Do you remember, Stone? I called you right after I found it.'

'It was about a quarter till eleven, because *Criminal Minds* was on. I had to DVR the episode to see how it ended because I dropped everything and met you at the office. You showed me what you'd found and we called Marcus.'

'It was eleven thirty when they called me. And I wasn't watching TV. I just remember it because Diesel was panicking, and he doesn't panic easily. Unless hospitals or doctors are involved, but that's another issue.'

'Thanks a lot, Marcus,' Diesel muttered. 'You wanna skywrite it next time?'

'We kind of figured that out ourselves,' Decker offered dryly, shaking his head when Diesel crossed his arms over his chest in a huff. 'Marcus, when did you call ICAC, and from where?'

'From a burner phone, sitting in my car, right outside their offices. With what Diesel had discovered, I didn't want any chance that my call could be traced to me or to my residence or my office. It took me about fifteen minutes to get to ICAC, so eleven forty-five. They raided McCord's house at six the next morning. They drove up just as he was walking outside for his newspaper.' He shrugged. 'I was there with my camera. That's the picture we put on the front page of the *Ledger* – McCord being arrested in his bathrobe.' He held up his hand when Zimmerman started to ask a question. 'I got a tip on my personal cell phone. I don't know who it was. I don't know if they knew it was me that sent them the information. I've wondered if it wasn't a quid pro quo. But I don't know for sure and that's the truth.'

'Did you try to trace the number that called you?' Decker asked.

'Of course I did. It was a burner, just like mine.'

'So there's a leak in ICAC,' Zimmerman said coldly.

Marcus shrugged. 'Or maybe someone who's just fed up with child abusers getting off with a slap on the wrist. McCord ended up tried in the court of public opinion. That photo I took of him in his bathrobe made every major newspaper in the country.' His voice went cold as well, and sharp as a blade. 'He was completely and utterly humiliated. His life as he knew it was ruined. Just like he'd ruined the lives of every child in every one of those pictures.'

Zimmerman held his stare. 'And you consider that justice, Mr O'Bannion?'

'No,' Marcus said levelly. 'But murder was against the law, last time I checked.'

Wincing, Kate prepared to jump in and steer the conversation to more neutral waters, because Zimmerman's eyes had narrowed and he seemed to be re-evaluating his opinion of Marcus O'Bannion. But Decker beat her to it.

'Well said,' he cut in, not flinching when Zimmerman turned his cold expression on him. 'If I learned anything in the three years I was under, it was that these criminals are driven by money, power, and ego. McCord lost all three, spectacularly. His death in jail wasn't justice either. It was far too quick and far too painless, but it did save the cost of a public trial, and – more importantly – it saved his victims from having to testify against him. However,' he barreled on before Zimmerman had a chance to respond, 'I think the idea of a leak at ICAC is the one we should be focusing on, sir. Something happened in those six hours between Marcus's anonymous call and the raid on McCord's home, because somehow, files disappeared – and McCord himself wasn't warned. If he'd been warned, he would have wiped his hard drive and the raiding police would have found nothing.'

He kept his voice pleasant through it all, non-threatening and very polite, letting a little more of his accent emerge. It made him sound folksy and sincere.

Zimmerman wasn't buying it. 'Don't think you've distracted me, Agent Davenport.'

'Of course not, sir,' Decker said mildly. 'Wouldn't dream of it.'

'But your point is well taken,' Zimmerman admitted. 'Assuming McCord's hard drive was manipulated.'

'Wouldn't ICAC have found evidence of that?' Troy asked. 'Some indication that files had been deleted?'

'If they'd looked,' Decker said. 'Why would they look, though? They hit the mother lode with what they did find. They caught him with enough porn to arrest him and have bail denied.'

There's something here, Kate thought, frustrated. Something they were missing. She bowed her head, closed her eyes. Tried to think. 'What was in the document files?' she asked.

Silence was her answer, and she looked up to find everyone on the *Ledger* side of the table looking at each other in question. 'Nobody opened them?' she asked incredulously.

Heads shook. All except the bright white one sitting directly across from her.

Deacon sighed. 'We briefly looked at each one because we were looking for clues as to the traffickers' whereabouts. They were stories.' He swallowed hard. 'Dialog.'

'Scripts?' Decker asked hesitantly.

'Maybe.' Deacon looked ill. 'I don't know.'

Kate felt just as ill as she thought about McCord and his partner casually abusing children as though it was their right. Thinking they'd never be caught, that they could get away with it. Her anxiety began to build, the static in her mind thickening like a blizzard.

Not now. Her hands were reaching under her chair for her yarn bag before she knew it, so she went with it, clutching her knitting needles so tightly that it was a wonder they didn't snap.

'But why?' Scarlett asked. 'Why would someone remove scripts and leave actual photos?'

'They removed videos, too,' Diesel said. 'There *were* videos. Long ones. Some were more than sixty minutes long. How did they do that? Did they hack in like I did? Did they break into his house? And how did they know? We didn't tell them – Stone, Marcus, and I were the only ones who knew that night. Did someone in ICAC tip them off?'

No one said anything for a long moment.

'They had to have,' Decker said heavily. 'The traffickers – Alice especially – blamed Marcus and Marcus alone. You were supposed to die, Marcus, nine months ago when McCord first landed in jail.' He massaged his brow bone with his non-IV'd hand, so hard he left the skin rough and red. 'I'm trying to remember . . . It was a conversation I overheard when I was still a bodyguard – before I got myself moved into the accounting department.'

By allowing himself to be shot, Kate thought with a sudden burst of blinding fury. Troy had passed on that little tidbit as she'd driven from the morgue. Twelve times, Troy had told her. Twelve times Decker had been shot, and once had been on purpose.

Not now. She could be angry again later. Now, Decker was speaking in fits and spurts, trying to dig up a memory, and she had to focus. She relaxed her hands, because they'd tensed, her needles frozen mid-stitch. A few deep breaths and she was once again engaged in the here and now, her hands moving fluidly, keeping the anxious side of her mind too occupied to implode. Like a hamster in a wheel, she had to keep it busy.

Run, little hamster, run.

Dammit, Kate. Listen.

A sudden rumble that vibrated the table provided the distraction she needed to rein in her racing brain, forcing herself to focus, because Adam Kimble was staring at his phone.

'Shit,' he muttered, then looked up. 'ICAC is not behind in filing evidence. The detective found a record of you dropping off a hard drive, Scarlett, but the drive is not there. The storage slot where it's supposed to be is empty. The record shows it was checked out.'

'By whom?' Zimmerman asked, as though he really didn't want to know the answer.

'By Detective Scarlett Bishop,' Adam said grimly.

Ten

Bloody hell, Decker thought wearily, because (a) they not only had a leak in ICAC, they had an actual traitor, and (b) Scarlett Bishop had grown pale with either anger or shock. He figured it was both, with a healthy dose of panic thrown in there because the woman was imagining her career going up in flames before her very eyes.

'But I didn't,' she said, her voice gone quiet.

'Of course you didn't,' stated Kate, who had seemed to miraculously find her calm place in the last minute. Before that, she'd been ready to climb out of her own skin – he'd felt her anxiety coming off her in waves. Now her knitting needles were clacking rhythmically. 'They picked you because you brought it in, and if it disappeared, you were going to have to come clean about where you got it in the first place if you wanted to make an issue of it.'

No one disputed this and Decker found himself relaxing along with Scarlett and Marcus, who'd taken Scarlett's hand and was squeezing it hard. 'So now what?' Marcus asked.

Kate smiled encouragingly at the newspaperman, who'd clearly been shaken by the attempt to discredit Scarlett. 'Nothing different than we were doing five minutes ago,' she said. 'We find McCord's fucking partner and put him away forever. Knowing there's a dirty cop in play simply gives us another avenue to pursue.'

'They overplayed their hand, Scarlett,' Decker said, admiring the way Kate hadn't let them get distracted. 'They didn't think you'd willingly admit to working with hackers. Now they've given us a way to connect them to McCord's fucking partner.'

Kate gave him a wink before dropping her gaze to the knitting in her lap, but Decker wasn't fooled. She was completely aware of what was happening all around the table.

'This is also what happens when you're square with your bosses,' Zimmerman added to Scarlett and Deacon. 'You give these people nothing with which to blackmail you. I assume you've told your lieutenant, Detective Bishop?'

'Before I came here,' Scarlett confirmed. 'Chain of command. Plus, just the right thing.'

'I agree,' Zimmerman said with a nod. He turned to Decker. 'You were saying something about a conversation you overheard.'

Decker nodded. The distraction had given him a chance to pull his thoughts together – a real challenge the longer he remained awake. He didn't want to admit that Dani Novak was right, but she was *so* right. He needed to rest. 'It was early November, right after Halloween. Alice and her father were talking with her father's friend.' He grimaced, the thought leaving a bad taste in his mouth. 'They were angry at McCord for not keeping his hands to himself and at Marcus for being a . . . a blood-sucking media leech.' He paused, glancing at Marcus. 'Sorry.'

'I've been called worse,' Marcus assured him.

'They were arguing about what to do with you, Marcus. Alice was matter-of-fact. You had to go. They'd already taken care of McCord. Except they didn't use his name or yours. They just called him "Idiot". You were "Leech". Alice's father said . . .' Decker rubbed his head again, blinking hard, and nobody moved, allowing him to think, which he appreciated. 'He wanted you dead too. It was the friend that insisted they wait. You were in the hospital at the time. They said that you'd poked the wrong snake and it'd bitten you in the ass.'

Scarlett raised her brows. 'Well that's one way of putting it. Marcus saved a young woman's life and got a bullet from a killer in the process.'

'I know the story now.' Decker gave the *Ledger* side of the table a rueful smile. 'I read about it in your newspaper afterwards, but I didn't know who they were talking about at the time.' He knew that Marcus and Stone had lost their younger brother to that same killer, that the bullet Marcus had taken had nearly killed him too. 'Anyway, being in the hospital at that point saved your life, Marcus. They figured you were out of commission and unable to do any more digging on the teacher, but that they'd watch you while you recovered to see if you intended to pursue it further. Alice said they shouldn't worry, that she'd take care of it, and that if you did revisit the matter, she had a well-placed friend who'd let her know. Her father asked if the friend was discreet and trustworthy and Alice said . . .' He frowned, trying to remember the exact words, because this was important. 'Something like "How do you think we knew to wipe his desktop? He saved our bacon." Her father asked what this friend wanted in return. Alice didn't say anything but both the men groaned and her father said, "I don't want to know. Do not say another word." I took that to mean she'd given the man sexual favors for his information.'

Zimmerman grimaced. 'God, he must have been desperate. She was pretty enough, I guess, but talk about a praying mantis. I'm surprised she let him live afterward.'

Marcus shuddered. 'I don't even want to think about it.'

'I think we have to,' Kate said without looking up from her knitting. 'We really know very little about Alice other than that she was a colossal bitch.'

'You got that right,' Scarlett muttered. 'And that she was a gym rat. That's how she kept an eye on Marcus.'

Decker raised his brows. He hadn't known this.

Kate glanced up at him, gave him a nod. 'Alice stalked him. Pretended she had a kid brother who'd been friends with the youngest O'Bannion brother.'

'The one who was killed?' Decker murmured, and she nodded before addressing the group.

'We also know that she joined the gym when Marcus returned after recovering from his bullet wound. She used a fake ID and gave an address that doesn't exist. We don't know where she actually lived.'

'At the compound with her father,' Decker said, then shook his head, his memory stuttering. 'No, that's not right. She lived there at the end, but not at the beginning.' He rubbed his temple. 'I drove her home several times.'

Kate's needles stopped clacking. 'Really?'

He pointed at her knitting. 'Do that, please. The sound helps me think. I think I latched onto it when I was trying to wake up the last few days in the hospital.'

She looked surprised, but complied. 'Where did you drive her? If she kept a place of her own, perhaps we can find a lead to the men she gave favors to.'

He shook his head. 'She never trusted me. I'd have to drop her off at different places, but if you give me a map, I can mark off the ones I remember. It was somewhere around Hyde Park, because that's where she went when it was really cold. I figured she wouldn't want to walk as far when it was cold.'

'You may not have to do that,' Novak said slowly. 'Hold on.' He got his laptop out of its case and started it up. 'Listen to this – it's part of that same recording we heard this morning, right before they talk about McCord and his partner. It's still Alice and her father.'

'*Demetrius acts like a big stud with all his love of torture and beating people up, but he's a whiny baby when it comes to pain. He acts like a paper cut is a double amputation.*' It was Alice's father who had spoken, and Decker had to swallow hard against a wave of nausea, because he knew what was coming next. '*I'll get what I need out of him after Decker makes sure he's not going to bleed to death.*'

'*Nice.*' That was Alice.

They had gotten what they'd needed, Decker thought. But he hadn't been able to stop the man from bleeding to death. He propped his elbow on the arm of the wheelchair and let it take the weight of his body as he pressed his fist against his lips, remembering all the blood that had followed this conversation. And the body parts Decker had cleaned up.

On the recording there was a pause. *'You knew about the tracking?'* Alice's father asked.

'Yeah,' Alice said. *'For several months now. You stopped asking me where I was when I went on dates. Sean too.'*

'That's why I didn't know about you and DJ,' he said.

Novak paused the clip. 'Sean was their IT guy. He died with the man who shot you, Decker. Kate took them out.'

'I know.' Decker didn't look at Kate. He simply focused on keeping Troy's bland chicken in his stomach. 'She told me.'

'DJ is the son of Demetrius,' Novak continued, 'the man who procured their "assets".' He turned his freaky eyes on Decker, his expression unreadable. 'We found Demetrius's body behind the compound. I'm guessing you weren't able to stop him from bleeding to death.'

'No,' Decker said quietly. 'I tried. I wanted him to testify.'

'It was a grisly death,' Novak said, sounding troubled. 'Demetrius suffered.'

Yes, he had. 'Is there a question in there, Agent Novak?' Decker asked, hearing his own voice slur a little. He was quickly running out of steam.

'Deacon,' Zimmerman admonished. 'Where are you going with this?'

Novak frowned. 'I know an agent undercover has to do things they don't always want to do, and I know that Agent Davenport helped save people when he could, but he also watched a lot of people being murdered. I'm just wondering . . . Would he have let Marcus die too, if they'd decided to take him out?'

Decker met Novak's eyes, and told him the truth. 'I didn't know who they were talking about in November, but I knew last week. I would have stopped it if it was humanly possible. However, if you're asking if I would have jeopardized my cover, the answer is no. Too many other lives depended on it. Does that satisfy you, Agent Novak?'

'No, not really,' Novak said, although much of his hostility receded. 'But I suppose there weren't many good choices. I apologize for asking the question, but I needed to know.'

'Well now you do,' Kate snapped. 'Play the rest of the clip so he can get out of that chair and go back to bed where he belongs. Stone, too.' She looked to the other end of the table and sighed. Stone had gone to sleep in his wheelchair and was snoring softly. 'Finish the tape so we can figure out what to do about this and Marcus and Diesel can take Stone home.'

Decker almost smiled. That she was concerned for him was sweet, but unnecessary. 'I'm okay, Kate.'

'Bullshit,' she muttered. 'Play the fucking clip, Deacon.'

Novak looked regretful. 'I did apologize, Kate.' She gestured toward his laptop, without another word. Novak hit play and Alice's father began to speak once again.

'*It doesn't . . . bother you? That I was tracking you?*'

'*Yeah.*' Alice sounded annoyed. '*But we knew you were worried about your leadership team, so we just left our phones behind when we didn't want you to know where we were.*'

'*How did you know for sure?*' he asked.

'*Sean hacked your phone. Took him a minute and a half.*'

Novak turned off the recording. 'We have their phones – Alice's and her father's. If Alice's father tracked her phone online, we may be able to access that information from his cell phone. If Sean hacked it in a minute and a half, maybe we can too.'

'Haven't you tried to crack their phones?' Scarlett asked, looking skeptical.

Novak nodded. 'Yes, of course. But we were looking for evidence of deals and contact information – their suppliers and customers. Not the existence of tracking software.'

Decker thought it would be easier to try to triangulate an approximate location by mapping it out, and had started to say so when Agent Troy slid an old-fashioned city map in front of him.

Decker ignored Novak's scowl to give Troy a nod of appreciation. 'Thank y—'

'Wait.' Diesel abruptly reached around Marcus to the print-outs of McCord's directory that Adam had provided. 'Let me see those.'

His movement jostled Stone, who woke up sputtering and

disoriented. 'What the hell, Diesel?' he demanded. He gave his head a hard shake, then winced. 'What are you doing?'

'Looking at something,' Diesel muttered as he scanned each of the printout pages, then glanced at Adam. 'Where was McCord's computer found?'

Adam took another stack of papers from his briefcase and began flipping through them. 'This is the police report. "One laptop, found in the suspect's bedroom closet, locked in lead-lined fire safe." Why?'

Diesel pointed at the list of files from the hard drive directory. 'Because look at the dates.'

'They're all within a year of McCord's arrest,' Scarlett said.

Diesel shook his head. 'No. This column lists the dates the files were accessed. These are the dates the files were created. Every file was created before 2010.'

'They're not new victims,' Adam said, frowning. 'The photos I saw today . . .' He hesitated. 'They didn't have a lot of clues as to time period. You know, clothing and such.' He flipped through a few more pages and sighed. 'The laptop didn't even have Wi-Fi capability. Its card had been removed.'

Diesel leaned back in his chair. 'This was likely McCord's personal collection then. And nobody could have wiped the document files from that laptop unless they'd physically gone into his house and put their hands on it. I couldn't have accessed that laptop, for that matter. Did he have another computer?'

'Yes. Nothing was found on it, so it wasn't turned over to ICAC. It's sitting in the CPD evidence locker. According to the report, there was no evidence of tampering, though.'

Diesel scoffed. 'Please. I never leave evidence of tampering.'

Marcus winced. 'Um, Diesel? FBI? You don't have to sound quite so proud.'

Diesel shrugged. 'It's not like I have many secrets left. Plus, it's true. And it'll probably be just as true if it is the same hard drive I saw and someone else did go in and wipe away any evidence of current crimes.'

'Will you be able to tell?' Kate asked. 'I mean, can you tell if it's the same hard drive you saw when you hacked that night?'

'Yes, I'll be able to tell. There was other stuff on it – normal stuff like tax forms and McCord's lesson plans. Your IT specialists should be able to find evidence that something had been there, even if they can't tell what it was. Just because the files were deleted doesn't mean they're completely erased, although it sounds like whoever did it might have been sophisticated enough to pull it off.'

Decker looked up from the map he was marking. 'If it was Alice's half-brother, Sean, he was sophisticated enough. He was a frickin' computer genius. And Alice told her father that Sean helped McCord's partner set up proxies and offshore servers after McCord's arrest and murder. Sean could have jumped in and taken care of anything incriminating that night.'

Diesel's shoulders slumped. 'Then it could be gone.'

Decker felt his frustration. 'Possibly, but their servers would have been moved offshore by now anyway, so you wouldn't have an electronic trail to follow. I'm wondering if Alice and the others thought they'd fixed it by wiping the evidence from McCord's Wi-Fi-enabled computer.'

Kate drew in a breath. 'Oh. You mean they either didn't know about the laptop in the fire safe and were shocked when he got arrested, or they *did* know and used it to set McCord up? As a sacrificial lamb of sorts.'

Decker nodded. 'Exactly. But I'd bet on the first one. I don't think they knew.'

'I've been wondering why they'd leave evidence like that behind,' Zimmerman admitted. 'It doesn't make sense, especially since McCord seemed to be a weak link. He was about to turn state's evidence and expose them all when they killed him.'

Scarlett was nodding. 'And if McCord's cronies didn't know about the laptop in the closet before the raid, it also explains why they were so scared of Marcus. They figured someone would see that the files on McCord's laptop were all old and—'

'And that the damn laptop wasn't hackable,' Diesel interrupted, 'so how would Marcus have even seen anything to report to them . . . anonymously.'

'And that whoever invited me to a curbside viewing of McCord's

212

arrest might tell me and I'd dig some more.' Marcus seemed to relax. 'Whoever tipped me off was probably not the same person who tipped off Alice. That makes me feel a bit better, actually.'

'Okay,' Kate said, still knitting. 'We have two leaks in ICAC and/or CPD. One is benevolent to us – or to Marcus, anyway – and the other is on Team Evil with McCord's partner. We can look at who was on duty that night when Marcus made his anonymous call, or who was called in to plan the raid. They would have had time to tip off Alice. We know that Alice was engaged in some sort of sexual relationship with this Team Evil leak. There may or may not have been financial payoff as well. We need to investigate Alice's personal life – which necessitates finding her apartment – to hopefully find some link to this dirty cop.' She grabbed both needles in one hand to dig in her bag. 'I need a pen so I can write this down.'

'Novak's taking notes on his computer,' Zimmerman said. 'He'll email them to you.'

'So keep knitting,' Novak added with unmistakable fondness.

Her grin was quick, then gone as her hands resumed their task. 'Alice, dirty cop . . .' she muttered. 'Oh, right. Alice's killer and ricin. We need to investigate McCord's associates to find out who has the knowledge to make ricin in a home lab or possibly even one at school. We can start with Troy's list of science teachers.'

'Although the partner doesn't have to be local,' Troy said. 'He could be anywhere.'

'He's close enough to recruit Sidney Siler and Eileen Wilkins,' Kate replied, not missing a stitch. 'Recruit them, sell to them, extort them – at least in the case of Nurse Wilkins.'

'And then kill Sidney,' Novak added.

Kate went still, then looked up, her expression sad. 'She had friends, Sidney did. She was popular at King's College. Somebody – even one person – had to know she was using. We have to find that person. We need to find her dealer.'

'We also have Eileen Wilkins's boyfriend,' Novak said. 'If he shares a dealer, that's another avenue.'

'What about a boyfriend?' Decker asked, feeling irritated that

Novak knew information that he didn't. He was annoyed with himself for it, but he couldn't deny the reaction.

'The nurse who tried to kill you?' Kate said. 'Her boy toy hangs around King's College and uses coke, just like Sidney Siler. He most likely uses steroids too. Guy's supposed to be all buff and burly and . . . you know, *grrrr*,' she growled, making Decker's lips twitch. 'Boy toy – his name is Roy – hangs at the gym near the college. Takes a class or two, but mostly hangs at the gym getting buffer and burlier while Eileen supports him.'

Kate leaned forward to look at Zimmerman a few chairs down. 'Since the victims on McCord's laptop are not recent and probably not associated with McCord's partner, are we still reviewing them?' she asked carefully.

Zimmerman drew a long breath, then let it out. 'God, I've been dreading this question. We can't ignore them, but at this point it would be very difficult to tell where they came from. We'd make better use of our resources to search out current victims.'

'The documents on McCord's computer before they were wiped were most likely scripts,' Novak said. 'For films. Meredith Fallon was going to talk to the young women in the halfway house to see if any of them were familiar with film-makers here in the city.'

'She was at it all morning,' Zimmerman confirmed, 'texting me every half-hour so that I knew she was okay.' He lifted his brows and shook his head. 'Because she ditched the agent I sent to protect her.'

'What!' Adam demanded.

'She said nobody would talk to her with "Agent Tall, Dark, and Scary" following her around.' He shook his head again. 'Agent Colby.'

Novak looked pissed off. 'He is scary. I can't believe he's still on the job.'

Zimmerman sighed. 'We've been over this, Deacon. He did the required counseling. Faith's forgiven him.'

Novak glared. 'Yeah, well she's nicer than I am.' He glanced at Decker. 'Colby went off on my fiancée when his partner got killed, and grabbed Faith by the throat. He and his partner were supposed to be guarding her. I don't think he's stable, but the department shrink disagrees.' He rolled his shoulders, trying to throw off his anger. 'But this is about Meredith. We can't let her put herself in danger like that.'

'That's why she texted me every thirty minutes,' Zimmerman said evenly. 'She had a friend with her. Wendi Cullen.'

Adam snorted. 'Wendi Cullen is five-feet-nothing and a strong breeze would blow her away. She's not exactly protection.'

'Don't let Wendi hear you say that,' Scarlett cautioned. 'She'll take you out.'

'As entertaining as that would be,' Zimmerman said dryly, 'there is no need. Agent Colby stayed a block back so that he didn't scare away the women she was trying to talk to. Marcus, Diesel, and Stone, thank you for coming. You've helped us clear up some critical items. But you need to get Stone home where he can properly rest. I'm sure we'll be in touch with you as more questions arise.'

'Thank God,' Stone said. 'I was about to cry uncle and ask to be excused.'

'I'll be going too,' Scarlett said.

Decker frowned. 'Why?'

'I've recused myself,' Scarlett said. 'Too much conflict of interest. But if any of you need anything, you call, okay? It was good to see you again, Decker.' Her lips turned up. 'We're all really glad that you're not dead.'

'So am I,' Decker said. He watched Diesel push Stone's wheelchair to the door. Hopefully everyone would leave soon and he could go to bed too. He was barely holding himself up. Marcus and Scarlett followed them out, then Zimmerman rubbed his eyes wearily.

'Okay,' he said. 'Assignments. Deacon, find Alice's apartment. Work with IT to crack into that cell phone that belonged to Alice's father so you get that tracking info. And while they're doing that, take the map Decker marked up and triangulate a position.'

Novak nodded his head. 'Once I've narrowed it down, I'll get some uniforms to canvass the neighborhood with a picture of Alice while I view the CCTV tapes, run them through facial recognition software. If we're lucky, a camera somewhere got a shot of her face.

If we're really lucky, we'll be able to use that tracking info, because even with facial recognition software, going through the tapes will take a long time.'

'Then you'd best get busy,' Zimmerman said grimly. 'Troy, same assignment as this morning. Dig into Alice's background. Check the gym. I want a profile on the woman. Kate, you take the Siler woman – find her dealer and whoever she was meeting last night.'

Kate nodded. 'What about Eileen, her boy-toy boyfriend, and his dealer?'

'The nurse is still missing. Her son will need to be taken by Children's Services. Adam, you take her house and interview her kid. Get Meredith involved when you do the interview. Find out who their dealer is.'

'Got it,' Adam said, looking relieved.

'What about the jail?' Novak asked. 'We need to chat with the infirmary staff and the woman who attacked Alice in the exercise yard yesterday evening.'

'I'll take that,' Zimmerman said. 'I need to make my presence known to the warden over there. If he didn't direct the cover-up, he let it happen. I'm going to give the dirty cop to your lieutenant, since it's really a CPD issue.'

'She's gonna love that,' Novak said grimly.

'I can—' Decker started, but he was quickly shot down.

'Sleep,' Zimmerman said.

'Sleep!' Kate said at the same time. 'And then start writing down the ledger details you can recall.'

'Okay, okay,' Decker muttered, peeved and relieved at the same time.

'The next meeting will be in my office,' Zimmerman said. 'Tomorrow morning, oh nine hundred hours.'

'I'll be there too,' Decker said, and Zimmerman gave him an impatient look.

'We'll see what Dr Novak says.'

The woman herself came out of the bedroom, looking annoyed with them. 'I'm this far from giving you all a piece of my mind for keeping him in that chair so long.'

'I've been a recipient of a piece of her mind, and it ain't fun, so I'm gone.' Novak gathered his things. 'Be safe, all of you.'

Adam, Troy, and Zimmerman took their leave, and then it was only himself, Kate, Dani, and Triplett. Kate put her knitting into her yarn bag while Triplett helped Decker back into the hospital bed.

As soon as he was prone, Decker groaned quietly. 'God, I'm tired. I just sat in a chair.'

'You'll be stronger tomorrow,' Dani promised. 'Now go to sleep. Kate, you're great and all, but you need to get your ass out of here.'

Kate laughed. 'Give me a minute to speak with Agent Davenport, then I will.'

His eyes were closed when she came to stand next to his bed, but she brushed her fingers over his face, and he sighed because it felt so nice. He'd craved this while he'd been sitting next to her, unable to touch her. 'Be careful out there, Kate. Promise me.'

'I will. I'm thinking that this place is more comfortable than my hotel room. If Dani's okay with it, I'll come back here to sleep tonight. That'll be another gun watching over you.'

'Wake me when you get here.'

'I will. Sleep now, Decker. It'll all be here when you wake up.'

He knew she was right. It was on that damn depressing point that he went to sleep.

Cincinnati, Ohio,
Thursday 13 August, 6.15 P.M.

He sank into the chair behind his desk, rubbing the back of his neck. 'I'm too young to feel this damn old.'

Nell mirrored his movement, taking the more comfortable of the chairs on the other side of the desk. 'Tomorrow will be better,' she said quietly.

He let go of his neck to smile at her. 'Today wasn't so bad,' he said. 'I'm just whining.'

She pointed to the uneaten half-sandwich on his desk. 'You never even finished your lunch. You should eat it now.'

He grimaced. 'I don't think so. Food poisoning is not on my list

217

of favorite things to do. Besides, Mallory's making steaks for dinner.'

She lifted her brows to study him over the wide expanse of desk that had once belonged to their father. 'What is?'

He frowned at her. 'What is what?'

'What is on your list of favorite things to do?' She shrugged. 'I mean, being here isn't one of them. You hate this.'

His frown deepened. 'I hate what?'

She gestured grandly. 'All this. The office, the patients, the responsibility of it all. Be honest with me. You hate it.'

'No, I don't hate it. Not exactly.' But there were *so* many other things he preferred doing. Working in his basement, for one. Developing his special blends always made him happy. And rich. He made far more selling chemical enhancements to high school and college students with way too much disposable income than he did giving shots and physicals to those same kids.

They liked him more as the Professor, too. Which wasn't a huge shock. Who wouldn't prefer the cool guy selling them top-notch chemicals over the guy telling them to stay away from drugs and observe safe sex? *Boring*.

But the practice was a practical necessity. It gave him respectability and a legitimate source of reportable income, so the government stayed off his back. It also gave him the inside scoop as to which of his patients would make the best customers of the Professor's wares.

So he didn't actually *hate* it.

Nell shook her head. 'You could have fooled me. Look, Remy, this practice isn't your dream. It was Dad's. He built it, nurtured it. Made it grow.' She smiled sadly. 'You haven't grown it a bit. We're still the same size we were the day Dad died. No offense.'

'None taken. You're the heart and soul of this place and I'm good with that.' He had no vested pride in the family business. It was simply a means to an end. And it allowed Nell the opportunity to become what their father had always denied her. She should have been the one to go to med school, but dear old Dad had been an old-fashioned guy. Only his son needed college. His two daughters needed husbands so that they could produce grandchildren.

The fact that neither of them had done so had been revenge enough. Nell had never been so inclined, choosing instead to live on her own, working her way through school. Becoming a physician's assistant had taken her far longer than it had taken him to become a doctor. But she'd done it and now she saw most of the patients. He was here to sign papers, supervise, and put in the requisite few hours a week so that he could get a paycheck.

That Nell was the one who kept their father's practice alive seemed fitting. And, when combined with the fact that the college degree his father had subsidized was being used to make very high-quality, very illegal drugs, he and Nell had each achieved the final fuck-you to their father, who had to be spinning in his grave like a rotisserie chicken.

Their little sister Gemma had been the only one to want kids, but she couldn't have them. She'd tried to adopt via legit agencies, but had never passed the psych test. Which was both a surprise and a shame, because she passed so well for sane on a day-to-day basis. He'd honestly thought she'd have been able to fool the testers, but she hadn't, so he'd stepped in to the rescue, brokering a private adoption.

He'd won the eternal gratitude of his sister, but more importantly, that of her husband as well. It was a debt his brother-in-law had repaid a thousand times over. It made good business sense to do favors for people who could do the same in return.

It had been his first deal with a crack mama. Her toddler for a week's worth of hits. He'd gotten Macy that way – and the surprise bonus of Macy's big sister, Mallory, who'd been only twelve at the time. And so damn pretty. A natural for the camera.

'So?' Nell asked. 'What is your dream? What's making you smile right now?'

'I hadn't realized I was,' he said, but he wasn't surprised. He'd always thought that mixing chemicals for fun and profit was the thing that made him happiest – until the first time he'd turned the camera on pretty little Mallory.

Sunshine Suzie had been born, and she'd been more profitable than even his very best special blend. He'd retired her a few years ago, but Sunshine Suzie was a gift that kept on giving, her videos still downloaded by thousands of fans every year. He'd made hundreds of videos in the last few years, but not one had made as much money as even the least successful Suzie vid. All because of Mallory.

And she's mine. Still mine. Because of Macy. Mallory behaved herself because she knew he'd make Macy his next star if she didn't. Of course, he fully intended to do so anyway, when Macy was old enough. Just a few more years.

Nell made a grumpy sound and he realized she was frowning at him.

'What?' he asked, genuinely puzzled.

'I hate when you do that. When you get all up inside your head. If you don't want to tell me what's making you so happy, then don't. But just say so instead of going off to la-la land.'

'I'm sorry,' he said, and he was. Nell had been there for him when they were growing up. He owed her much. 'I was thinking about how mad Dad would be if he could see us now.'

Her lips twitched. 'Really?'

No, not really, but he wasn't about to tell his big sister that the brother she thought hung the moon was smiling about making kiddie porn. She would not approve. He didn't want to hurt her, but neither did he need her approval.

'Yeah, really,' he said, knowing she would never suspect him of telling the smallest untruth. He was far too good a liar, knowing exactly how to blend the lie with a truth to make something that anyone would believe. 'He would've shit a brick if he'd known you were running the place while I went out and did charitable work.' Which he also did from time to time. It opened doors, exposing him to contacts that he'd never otherwise have known. Charity work was how he'd met Mallory and Macy's mother, piece of work that she'd been.

Charity had helped make him a very rich man.

'Yes, he would have,' Nell said fondly. She'd loved the old ass, even though he'd made her life a living hell. That was the difference between him and Nell. *I don't love anyone.*

Not even Nell. He cared about her, but he'd walk away from this place in an instant if it suited him. So far, it hadn't suited him.

He straightened in his chair, stretching his neck until he felt it pop. 'Unless you have anything else for me to do, I think I'm going to call it a day.' Because Mallory was making steaks for dinner and strawberry shortcake for dessert.

And because he still had to take care of Rawlings, the prison guard.

And then he'd talk with his newest customer and share the plans he had for his latest group of initiates. His customer was very, very interested. And very, very rich. There would be no profits from future downloads, because his customer would buy the assets along with the film for his own private use, but the upfront money was more than enough to make up for it.

'No, you're done.' Nell patted the stack of file folders she'd brought in with her. 'I've got a few hours of paperwork yet to do, though.'

'We could hire a receptionist.'

She rolled her eyes. 'We did. Her name is Gemma. She comes in when she feels like it. Today she didn't feel like it because she had to shop for Macy. Back-to-school clothes, you know. Even though Macy's home-schooled.'

Their sister was completely unreliable, doing a piss-poor job when she actually did show up. 'You know you can fire her. I've told you that before.'

Nell's face twisted in a pained grimace. 'I tried. She cried.'

He frowned, annoyed with both of his sisters. 'She cries because you let her. Fire her ass, Nell. Hire a competent assistant.'

'What about Mallory? She's eighteen now, right?'

No. No, no, no. Letting Mallory go to the grocery store was one thing, especially when he could track her every movement. He knew where she'd gone, how long she'd been gone, and what route she'd taken – and that she'd made no stops. Letting her sit in an office, with a computer? No fucking way in hell.

He kept his expression bland. 'She's doing some charity work for Roxy and me.'

A slight frown of concern wrinkled Nell's forehead. 'How is Roxy doing?'

'She's a raging alcoholic, Nell,' he said sharply. 'Just like she was the last time you asked.' Which was just the way he liked it. His wife was the equalizing presence – no one questioned that he had Mallory living with him as long as Roxy lived with him too. No one knew that ninety percent of the time Roxy was sleeping off a drunken binge. Not even Nell knew how bad it really was. Because before her liver had gone on strike, Roxy had been a totally functional drunk. Now that Mallory was eighteen, Roxy had become less important to the equation. Which was convenient timing, because Roxy was dying.

Nell looked hurt. 'I worry about Roxy, Remy. She's my sister-in-law. She needs help.'

Of course Roxy needed help. But she'd never get it, not as long as he drew breath. He liked things just the way they were, thank you very much. 'You're trying to divert attention from the fact that you could hire a perfectly good admin assistant if you fired the one you've got.'

Nell sighed. 'All right. I'll try.'

And she'd fail. So he wasn't going to feel guilty that she'd be here late doing the work she should have hired someone else to do a long time ago. He stood up, clearing the trash from his desk and tossing it in the wastebasket. 'What are those, anyway?' he asked as she pushed the stack of files to the cleared space on his side of the desk. She'd take the chair when he was gone, but while he was here in the office, she'd never dare. She deferred to him out of habit, and he let her. It kept their relationship neat and tidy.

'Files of patients who either graduated last year or . . .' She sighed. 'Or who died.' She patted the top folder.

Sidney Siler. 'Oh, right,' he said quietly, his face twisting in sham sympathy. 'Poor kid.'

Nell's eyes hardened. 'She was using for a long time, Remy. She made bad choices.'

'I can still be sorry she's gone,' he said mournfully, while inwardly he rolled his eyes. Nell could be hard on a coke addict, but she let her own baby sister run roughshod all over her.

'Yeah, I guess so. Well, I'll see you tomorrow, Remy. Have a good evening.'

He dropped a kiss on her upturned cheek. 'You too.'

He paused outside the office door to call Mallory and tell her that he was on his way home so she could put the steaks on, then he went to his car and put the top down, forgetting about Nell, the practice, and even Sidney Siler as soon as he felt the wind on his face.

Eleven

Cincinnati, Ohio,
Thursday 13 August, 6.50 P.M.

Kate knocked on the door of Sidney Siler's apartment a third time, listening for any indication of activity inside, but heard nothing. Sidney had shared the small efficiency with Chelsea Emory, another King's College grad student. If Chelsea was inside, she wasn't making any noise. And she wasn't coming to the door.

She glanced at the uniformed CPD officer that Deacon and Scarlett's lieutenant had assigned to guard duty. 'Nobody's come in or out?' she asked.

'Not since I got here at four fifteen. A few other residents have come and gone. I noted a description of each one, the apartment they came in or out of, and the time.'

'Did any of them approach you?'

'No, ma'am. They avoided me like the plague.'

'Okay, thanks.' That Chelsea had not returned to her apartment was worrisome. Sidney was – presumably – killed because she knew something that her killer didn't want known. If she had confided in Chelsea, the roommate could be in danger as well. And if Chelsea believed that Sidney had died of an overdose, she'd be vulnerable. Unable to take the most basic of precautions. Hopefully Chelsea wasn't dead, too.

It could be more simple than that, though, and Kate hoped it was. Maybe Chelsea wasn't home because she'd sought solace with other friends or family. Sidney and Chelsea had been friends before they became roommates, according to the police report.

Chelsea had ID'd Sidney's body at the scene early that morning, providing the first responders the contact information for Sidney's parents, who lived in Houston and who were now on their way to claim their daughter's body. They were expected to arrive sometime this evening and, according to Carrie Washington, had not yet been to the morgue. Which was good, because they didn't know their daughter had been murdered any more than Chelsea did.

Damn. The parents would have to be told, and Kate would be the one to tell them.

Since no one was answering the door, Kate went to the next apartment. It was university housing, so the women's neighbors would be fellow students. She needed to know who Sidney hung with, specifically anyone who knew about her drug use and the identity of her dealer. If no one was home, she'd hit the eateries around campus next since it was supper time.

She'd raised her fist to knock on the next door when she heard voices coming around the corner from the elevator. One young-sounding female and an older male. A third person – most likely a woman – was sobbing.

'Are you sure, Ruth?' the female was asking. 'You don't have to do this today. You can rest tonight and do it in the morning. I can find you a hotel room and—'

'Yes, I do,' the sobbing woman insisted. 'I need to do it tonight. *Tonight.*'

'We'd like to get it over with,' the male said hoarsely. 'I won't be able to rest until this is done. Until . . .' His voice broke. 'Until I see her with my own eyes.'

The trio rounded the corner, a female who was grad-student-aged with her arm around a sobbing older woman who appeared to be in her fifties. The man's red eyes were evidence that he'd been crying too. The three stumbled to a stop when they saw Kate standing at the neighbor's door.

'They're not home,' the young woman told her.

'Are you Chelsea Emory?' Kate asked, and the young woman's eyes narrowed.

'Yes. Who are you? And why is there a cop standing outside my door?'

Kate held out her shield. 'I'm Special Agent Coppola, FBI. I'd like to talk to you.'

'This is *not* a good time,' Chelsea said impatiently, but fear flickered in her eyes.

'I know,' Kate said gently. 'There's never a good time for this. May I come in?'

'This isn't my apartment. That is. And why is there a goddamned cop standing there?'

Ignoring Chelsea's repeated question about the officer, Kate turned to the older couple. 'You're Alan and Ruth Siler?'

Mr Siler jerked a nod. 'What's this about?'

Kate could tell that the man knew something was wrong. More wrong. 'I don't want to do this in the hall.' She walked to Chelsea's door and waited. 'Please.'

Chelsea looked uncertainly at Mr Siler. 'Go ahead,' he said. 'Let's get this over with too.'

Kate waited until they were all in the little apartment and had pulled the door shut. It was a tight fit – the place was even smaller than Kate's college apartment had been. Chelsea started to move things, a nervous attempt at tidying, and Kate stopped her.

'Please don't. Don't touch anything yet.' She pulled two desk chairs over to an ugly orange futon. 'Mr and Mrs Siler? You might be more comfortable using the chairs.'

Silent, hostile, they sat. Kate perched on a wooden bar stool that had seen better days and Chelsea sank down onto the futon.

Kate drew a breath. 'First, I'm sorry for your loss.'

Mrs Siler glared at her. 'Just get to the point, Agent Whatever-your-name-is.'

'Ruth,' Mr Siler murmured, still holding her hand. He met Kate's gaze head on. 'We came here to see what's left of our daughter's life before we identify her body in the morgue, Agent Coppola. Please make this brief.'

'All right. Your daughter, Sidney, didn't die of an overdose. She was murdered.'

Three gasps sliced through the air. Three pairs of shocked eyes stared at her.

Chelsea was the first to speak. '*No.* The EMT said it was dirty coke.'

Carrie had tested the residue she'd found in Sidney's nostrils and had also determined that the cyanide had been delivered in a capsule that Sidney had crushed in her teeth – there was still residue of both the cyanide and the gelatin used as the capsule wall between her molars.

'Yes, she did take cocaine. It was mixed with ketamine, in a dose high enough to temporarily paralyze her. But before the ketamine kicked in, she was given poison.'

Mr Siler shook his head, as if trying to comprehend another language. 'The cocaine was . . . *is* poison. So many kids snorting their lives away. We'd thought she'd escaped it.'

Kate addressed Mr Siler, but from the corner of her eye she was watching for Chelsea's reaction. 'Your daughter seemed to have been using cocaine for some time. But last night she was also given cyanide.'

Mrs Siler began to hyperventilate. 'Wha— What? How? Why?'

Chelsea's mouth fell open in what seemed once again to be genuine shock. Either that, or the girl was a damn fine actress.

'You're saying our daughter was *murdered*?' Mr Siler demanded.

'Yes, sir,' Kate said calmly. She'd said it before and it hadn't sunk in. It seemed to be sinking in now. 'We believe the cocaine was supposed to cover the real cause of death, which was cyanide poisoning. We're not entirely sure why yet. Or who.'

'Oh my Lord.' Mrs Siler began to cry anew, rocking back and forth, her hand tightly clamped over her mouth to stifle her keening sobs.

'We're looking for her dealer,' Kate said bluntly. 'Chelsea, can you help me?'

'No,' Chelsea whispered. 'I don't know who she bought from. I . . . don't do that. I begged her to stop, but I don't know who her dealer was.'

Now the girl was lying. A simple test would show if she'd snorted any coke recently.

'I see,' Kate said quietly, and Chelsea flinched, but offered nothing more. Kate decided she'd table the drugs for now. Chelsea might be more willing to talk when not in the presence of Sidney's parents. 'Sidney made a trip to the jail yesterday to visit an inmate.'

The parents looked tormented. Chelsea, however, frowned.

'That damn paper of hers,' Mr Siler spat. 'Interviewing deviants and sociopaths. I bet one of them targeted her.'

Mrs Siler wrung her hands. 'I told her no good would come of that. But she didn't listen. And now she's dead! My baby is dead,' she added in a mournful wail.

Kate said nothing, waiting for Chelsea to speak. Finally Chelsea nodded, but slowly, like she wasn't sure what to say but wasn't trying to hide anything. 'She'd done that a few times. For her research. She was a clinical psych grad student, working on her dissertation.'

'Did you know she was going yesterday?'

'No, but I knew something was up because she was so . . . excited. I thought she'd snorted some coke but she said it was a natural high. That she was gonna get published in all the psych journals.' Her eyes filled with tears. 'She always wanted to get published. Now she never will.'

'Did she keep notes?'

'Yes. Yes, of course.' Chelsea went to one of the two desks in the room.

Kate followed, pulling on a pair of gloves. 'Just point, Chelsea. Don't touch.'

'That one.' Chelsea indicated a generic notebook, one that could be bought in any drugstore in the country. 'That's her current volume. The drawer has all of her older notes.'

Kate flipped to the last entry. 'These are dated several months ago.'

Chelsea looked over Kate's arm to study the page. 'Yes. That was her last interview, up in Chillicothe Prison. She went with her grad advisor. They're writing an article together.'

'Why is this important, Agent Coppola?' Mr Siler asked fretfully.

Alice's death was already on the news. The Silers might even have seen the reports on the TVs in the airport that morning. If they hadn't, they'd soon put two and two together. 'The inmate she went to see was killed this morning,' Kate told them. 'She was poisoned.'

Mrs Siler's sobs had quieted. Now she just rocked and Mr Siler pulled her into his arms. 'Dear God,' he whispered. 'Dear God. What did you do, Sidney? What did you do?'

Chelsea closed her eyes. 'Did you find her pen with her things?'

Kate stilled. *That's an odd question.* 'I don't know. Why?'

'She had a fancy recorder pen. A spy pen,' Chelsea said, her mouth twisting bitterly. 'She thought she was hot stuff because she'd sneaked it through the jails several times. She recorded every word when she went on these interviews. Her grad advisor thought she had a genius memory. Sid said it was her ace in the hole.'

'Give me a moment.' Kate opened the apartment's front door and motioned the officer to stand inside. 'I'll just be a moment. Can you make sure no one leaves the room?'

Mr Siler gasped in outrage. 'Are we suspects?' he thundered.

'No, sir,' Kate said kindly, then looked directly at Chelsea. 'Not you and Mrs Siler.'

Chelsea paled and Mr Siler lurched to his feet, dragging his wife with him, still awkwardly patting her shoulder. 'Are you accusing Chelsea of killing Sidney? That is crazy talk. Just crazy! They were like sisters!'

Kate kept her gaze on Chelsea's pale face. 'We'll search the apartment, Chelsea. We'll find your stash too. I need to make a phone call, and then I'm going to ask you about Sidney's dealer again. You need to be thinking about your answer. A little hint? "I don't know" is not the answer I'm looking for.' She looked at the officer. 'No phone calls, nobody touches anything. She stays in this room. All three of them stay. For their own protection, if nothing else. Okay?'

The officer nodded once. 'Yes, ma'am.'

Kate called Zimmerman, Deacon, and Troy, conferencing the three of them together. 'Do we know where Sidney Siler's effects are located at this moment?' she asked them. 'Specifically her backpack.'

'It's either with the morgue or with Forensics,' Deacon answered. 'Give me a minute and I'll call Tanaka in CSU.'

'What's this about, Kate?' Zimmerman asked when Deacon had put them on hold.

'Possibly the motive for Sidney's murder,' Kate said. 'Let's wait for Deacon and I'll tell you all together.'

Deacon was back in less than a minute. 'Vince Tanaka said that her backpack isn't with CSU. It must still be at the morgue.'

'Okay. We need someone we trust to get over there and search it. I need to finish this interview.' She gave them a brief update. 'So we're looking for a spy pen,' she finished.

'Sidney recorded her conversation with Alice,' Zimmerman said with satisfaction. 'I'll go over there myself and supervise the search.'

'You can trust Tanaka to do that,' Deacon said with conviction. 'And Carrie Washington, too. But just to protect everyone, please record the search on video.'

'And then upload the contents to the evidence server right away,' Kate added. 'And send us copies.'

'Will do,' Zimmerman said. 'I'm leaving the jail now.'

'Thanks,' Kate said. 'I'm going to try again for the dealer's name. Wish me luck.'

Cincinnati, Ohio,
Thursday 13 August, 7.05 P.M.

He pulled into his driveway, satisfied when he smelled barbecuing steak on the air. Mallory had become a very competent cook and housekeeper, timing their meals just right, especially when he remembered to call her on his way home.

But his satisfaction took a sharp nosedive when the back door opened and JJ came out to stand on the back porch, a frown on her face. She crossed her arms over her chest as she waited for him to put the top up on his car.

He took his time, knowing she was growing more impatient by the second. *Which serves her right. She shouldn't be here.* He hadn't invited her, and the fact that she'd just shown up made him angry. But he schooled his features to be blandly confused as he turned to look up at her.

'JJ? What's wrong?'

'That girl,' JJ said stonily. 'She won't let me in the kitchen.'

Propping his foot on the bottom step, he studied JJ's face. 'I wasn't expecting you tonight.'

JJ's mouth tightened. 'I brought ingredients to make you dinner. I thought after today . . . well, maybe you'd need something special.'

After today. She'd done him a favor by telling him that Davenport had survived so that he could take care of Eileen Wilkins, and now she expected him to take their relationship to the next level. She'd never made such a presumption before.

Then again, she'd never given him information before that led directly to the death of another human being. And once Eileen's body was found, she'd demand even more because she'd have something real on him then. *I don't think so.*

He injected a chill into his tone. 'I did want something special. The steak that Mallory's making for me.'

JJ's eyes grew abruptly shiny, something else that was new. She wasn't a crier. Never had been before, anyway. So either something had changed or she was attempting to manipulate him. Her lips twisted into something between a pout and a sneer. 'If you had a *real* wife, you wouldn't need *Mallory* anymore.'

Mallory's presence drove JJ crazy, because JJ had wanted to be his number one woman from the start. She wanted Mallory gone. She'd never actually come out and said it, but recently she'd been hinting heavily.

Which meant that JJ was coming close to her expiration date as a lover. But not today. Not so soon after Eileen's very obvious execution. He'd string her along a little longer, making her think she was getting what she wanted. Then he'd end her.

He frowned at her, projecting confusion. 'I'm married, JJ. I've never made a secret of that.'

She rolled her eyes dismissively. 'Roxy is a joke. You could divorce her like that' – she snapped her fingers – 'and no court would even blink. You probably wouldn't even owe any alimony.'

He would not have divorced Roxy even if she hadn't been dying. Roxy had been incredibly useful in her role as his wife, doing as she was told, asking no questions.

He morphed his feigned confusion into quiet outrage. 'She is my *wife*, JJ. I won't be divorcing her. Not when she needs me most. She's *dying*.'

JJ flinched, then blinked, sending several tears down her cheeks. 'You said you loved me.'

No, he hadn't. He hadn't even said he wanted her. He'd said he needed her, which was true. And he needed her to hang with him for a few more days before she disappeared. Just until Eileen and poor Roy became old news.

'And I meant every word I said,' he told her soothingly. 'But what kind of man would I be if I put poor Roxy out with nowhere to go? Who would take care of her?' He watched uncertainty flicker in her eyes. Good. He'd hit a nerve. But it wasn't *that* big an accomplishment. Using the concept of 'care' to reach a nurse was pretty basic stuff. 'Mallory is here to see to her needs. There's no need to be jealous of the girl.'

More uncertainty played across JJ's face. 'But why? Why keep Roxy here? She could be getting help in a rehab center. They're trained for such things.'

Because Roxy was *way* too far gone for that. 'Because the last time I tried, she had a nervous breakdown.' So totally a lie. He'd never tried. There was nothing in it for him. 'She's not going to get better. The best I can do is keep her comfortable until she's . . . gone.'

JJ pulled her arms tighter across her chest and looked away. 'How am I supposed to be angry at that?' she asked softly but bitterly.

'It's my life, hon,' he said with a sigh. 'I told you that from the beginning.'

'Yeah, you did.' Her throat worked as she tried to swallow what looked like more tears. 'What about dinner? I was going to cook for you.'

'I can see if Mallory can throw another steak on the grill.'

Her jaw tightened, and she muttered under her breath, 'She'll probably spit on my food.'

He pretended not to hear, leaning forward, his ear tilted toward her. 'What was that?' he asked, biting back a snort of laughter. Mallory just might, because the girl didn't like JJ either.

'Nothing.' JJ stood still for the better part of a minute, then turned back to face him, eyes wounded. 'If Mallory makes dinner tonight, will you come to my place tomorrow and let me cook the meal I planned for you?'

It was a fair request, and the best way to handle her at the moment was to let her have her way. 'Of course. I'll bring the wine.' He climbed the stairs and gently pushed by her, quelling the desire to grab her by the throat and squeeze until she was no longer a distraction. Or a threat.

Mallory was standing at the sink washing strawberries. She glanced over her shoulder when he came in. 'I can put another steak on,' she said, her tone flat. 'And I won't spit in her food.'

Chuckling, he closed the back door, effectively shutting JJ out of the conversation. Through the window he could see the nurse's back go ramrod straight and knew he'd angered her again. But she'd behave. For now.

He went to the sink and slid his arms around Mallory's waist, the stiffening of her back a clear sign that she abhorred his touch. Which of course made her that much more enticing. 'You can spit in her food if you want to,' he murmured. 'She won't bother you, I promise.'

Mallory's hands stilled. She had such pretty hands. Long and elegant. They looked so good touching him. He loved to make her touch him. Loved that she hated it. Loved that she didn't have any choice – and that she knew it.

'That's okay,' she murmured. 'She hates me enough already. I think I'll pass.'

There was something in her voice that made him frown. He'd find out what was wrong in a minute. After he found out how JJ had gotten in the house to begin with. He leaned in, his lips nuzzling her neck, bared by her ponytail. 'Why did you let her in?'

She resumed washing the strawberries. 'I didn't,' she said tersely. 'She had a key.'

He froze. 'What?'

'She. Had. A. Key,' Mallory enunciated, even more tersely.

He straightened abruptly. 'Where the hell did she get a key?'

'I don't know. I didn't ask. She wouldn't have told me anyway.'

There was a great deal more. He could see it in the taut line of Mallory's jaw. 'What aren't you telling me?' He closed a hand over her throat and squeezed, just enough to show her that he meant business. 'What happened?'

Mallory's hands stilled again, her eyes lifting to stare sightlessly at the wall above the sink. 'I was upstairs, changing Roxy's sheets,' she said, her voice devoid of any emotion whatsoever. 'I came downstairs and saw JJ trying to get into the basement.'

He released her throat and drew a deep breath, counting to ten to control the surge of fury. 'Why didn't you tell me?'

'You were already on your way home. Plus I was a little busy.'

'Doing?' he prompted.

She pointed to a raw steak on the countertop. 'Putting that on my face.'

He twisted to see the other side of her face. 'Fucking bitch,' he hissed. It was already swollen, turning black and blue. 'She did that to you?'

'She did,' Mallory said flatly. 'When I told her to leave or I'd call you. Now if you'll excuse me, I need to get your steak off the grill or it will burn.' She pushed against his chest with her shoulders and he took a step back, silently giving way. She grabbed the steak she'd used on her face and put it on a plate before closing the kitchen door behind her.

Through the window he saw her move past JJ without a look or a word. Then he realized that Mallory was going to cook the used steak for JJ's dinner. It was funny – unless she'd ever done the same thing to him. But she wouldn't dare. Mallory knew her place. JJ obviously did not.

So JJ has a key to my house. He wondered where she'd gotten it. Wondered who else had one. It didn't really matter, because he'd re-key the locks himself and reset all his alarm codes. JJ wouldn't be able to get in ever again anyway, because she wasn't leaving here alive.

He'd just changed his mind about keeping her around for another few days. She'd tried to get into the basement. She knew that was where he kept his stash. She knew he sold drugs and she'd been okay with it because he'd supplied her in exchange for information. Especially for information on ODs that came through County's ER. Some of which would need *not* to survive. Just in case they were persuaded to roll on their dealer.

So she knew he sold. She didn't know he was the Professor. *Or does she?* He was positive she didn't know about the porn, because she'd have turned him in already.

JJ was an addict, but she had her standards, and kiddie porn was not okay in her book. But if she knew that he was the Professor? That would be bad. However, he wasn't going to borrow trouble. It was entirely possible that she just wanted more of the drugs he supplied for her services. It was possible she felt he owed her an extra hit for the info she'd provided today. It was also possible that she felt she was entitled, since she was moving herself up from lover to potential new wife – not that that was going to happen, ever.

He'd get the truth out of her, one way or another. He opened the back door, found her still standing where he'd left her on the stoop, back turned and arms crossed. 'JJ,' he said, making his tone apologetic, 'come inside and have a drink. Let Mallory wait on you tonight. You've earned it.'

She turned and looked at him, narrowing her eyes. 'She tried to hit me earlier.'

He frowned, once again feigning confusion. 'That doesn't sound like Mallory. Are you sure?'

JJ's spine straightened, outrage on her face. 'Yes, I'm sure. I knocked on the door with my hands filled with grocery bags and she was rude. Didn't offer to help me with the bags or anything. Told me I wasn't allowed in. She tried to shove me out, so I pushed past her and she slapped me.' She let out a breath. 'I slapped her back. I won't stay if she's here.'

She was lying. He could see it in her eyes. *Bitch.* 'I'll send her to her room then,' he promised. 'It'll be just the two of us. I'll open a bottle of wine, the kind you like.'

She looked like she was debating whether to come back inside or not. He hoped she didn't turn for her car, because he'd have to drag her back and he didn't want to get all hot and sweaty. It would be a lot easier to drag her through an air-conditioned house.

'Please?' he added in a gentle tone. When she finally nodded and came inside, he pointed to the living room. 'Go and put your feet up,' he said. 'You've had a hard day.'

She paused, her lips bent in a frown. 'You'll punish her for being rude to me?'

He wanted to roll his eyes, but refrained. 'Absolutely,' he promised. He watched her take a seat, stiffly. 'I'll be just a minute. Let me get a bottle of wine from the cellar for dinner.'

He made a show of unlocking the door to the basement, purposely leaving it open and the key in the lock to see what she'd do. He went down the stairs, bypassing his lab and going on to the wine cellar. Quickly choosing a bottle of wine, he waited at the base of the stairs, listening for the jingle of keys.

He heard it – but just barely. JJ was good. Very light-fingered. Too bad he had to kill her. She was probably making a clay impression of his key. He'd find out soon enough.

She'd be busy for at least another minute, so he let himself into his lab, locking the door behind him, and took a single dose of GHB from his storeroom. Locking everything up again, he went back to the stairs and made a noise as he started up, giving her time to return to her chair.

Cincinnati, Ohio,
Thursday 13 August, 7.25 P.M.

Kate had to fight the compulsion to run down to the morgue so that she could supervise the search of Sidney's knapsack for the victim's magic spy pen. It was silly, of course. Vince Tanaka, the CSI guy, was perfectly capable of searching a knapsack, documenting as he went.

Plus Zimmerman would be there and Kate trusted him. She did. Mostly. She didn't distrust him. But in reality, she only really trusted herself. And Deacon Novak.

And Decker, of course. The very certainty of the thought made her pause, her hand on the doorknob to Sidney Siler's apartment, where the victim's devastated parents and terrified roommate were waiting for her to return. *Of course?* It shouldn't be an 'of course'. Not yet. But it was.

She poked at it a little in her mind, turning it over and examining the thought from all angles, and came out in the same place. *Yes. I trust Decker too.* Why she did, she wasn't entirely sure. There was . . . something. Something about him.

Maybe it was his eyes. Or the way he'd bared his soul sharing about his sister.

Or maybe it was just him.

Oh. She had to draw a deep breath and consciously hold herself rigidly upright because her knees had just seriously wobbled. She'd felt this way once before, and while it hadn't scared her then, it sure as hell scared her now. She'd trusted Johnnie the first time she'd met his eyes. The first time he'd smiled at her. She'd trusted him with her life. Her heart.

But Johnnie was gone, and he wasn't ever coming back. *And now there's Decker.* That she trusted him this fast might be a problem.

Or it could be a gift. The whisper in her mind was deep and sweet and made her heart hurt. Johnnie hadn't wanted her to be alone. He hadn't wanted her to be afraid. He hadn't wanted her to stop living just because he no longer did.

He wouldn't have wanted Jack to do what he'd done either, but that was water under the bridge now. And a nightmare that didn't want to fade.

A gift, Kate. This time the whisper in her mind made her smile. *Okay. I'll think about it.*

Later. She'd have time to explore the trust – and the attraction – after they closed this case. Which was waiting on the other side of the door. She pushed away the sentimentality and girded herself in the psychological armor that had earned her the nickname of the Kate-inator during her army tours. Or the Frigidaire or Ice Queen. Or the Bitch. It was all the same, really.

She opened the door and gave the officer a nod. 'Thank you,' she said.

'I'll be outside if you need me,' he said and closed the door behind him.

Chelsea stood, pale and trembling, in the exact spot in which Kate had left her. 'Please remain where you are, Miss Emory.' She met the ravaged faces of Sidney's parents. 'Some of what I need to ask Chelsea will be hard for you to listen to. I can get you an escort to the morgue if you'd like. Or you can wait for me, and I'll take you myself.'

Mr Siler nodded heavily. 'We'll wait. We need to know.'

'All right.' Kate pulled two chairs over to where Chelsea stood. 'Have a seat.'

Visibly shaking, the young woman obeyed.

'Okay,' Kate said after she'd sat down too. 'We were talking about Sidney's dealer. Allow me to connect some dots for you. Sidney went to the jail to interview an accused human trafficker, posing as a lawyer's assistant, using a fake name and a fake ID.' She heard the parents gasp and flicked a glance their way. Both were shocked, their expressions a twin study of desperate disbelief. But they didn't say a word. Chelsea, on the other hand, looked ill, but there was not a trace of skepticism in her eyes. 'You're not surprised, Chelsea.'

'No. Sid was single-minded in her focus. "Publish or perish".' She used air quotes. 'She wanted her name in print. She was willing to break rules to get that or whatever she wanted. I've known Sid since we were freshmen. She didn't blink at using a fake ID to drink before she was twenty-one. I'm sorry,' she said to Sidney's parents. 'I know that's not what you wanted to hear.'

Mrs Siler's sigh was one of the heaviest Kate had ever heard. 'If only that were the worst of her problems. But I know drinking was the least of it. We saw a change in Sidney after her first semester away from home. I tried to tell myself it was part of growing up, but on some level I knew she was using. I didn't want to admit it.'

Mr Siler stared at his wife in wounded shock. 'Ruth?'

Mrs Siler squeezed her husband's hand, suddenly the strong one. 'Please, Agent Coppola. Go on. We want whoever murdered our daughter to be punished. Just because she used drugs didn't mean she should have been killed.'

'I agree,' Kate said quietly and turned back to Chelsea. 'So Sidney left the jail and only a few hours later she's dead. Poisoned. And not even twelve hours after that, the trafficker she spoke to is dead. Poisoned with the same stuff. Now, Chelsea, where were you last night?'

Chelsea's eyes popped open. 'Me? I was in the library with my study group. At least four other people were with me and I'm sure I'm on the cameras somewhere.'

Kate gave the girl her notepad and a pen. 'Write the names down. I'll talk with them to confirm your alibi.' She waited until Chelsea had done so, then continued. 'You were on the scene this morning when the first responders showed up.'

Chelsea nodded unsteadily. 'Yeah. I got back from the library after midnight and Sid wasn't here, but that wasn't unusual. Sometimes she'd come in at three, four o'clock in the morning. Especially when she'd been partying. But I woke up at six this morning and she still wasn't back. I called her cell, but there wasn't any answer.'

'Did it ring?' Kate asked gently. 'Or go straight to voicemail?'

'Straight to voicemail,' Chelsea whispered, then cleared her throat. 'I texted, but nothing, so I was worried. I went to the lane and—'

'What lane?' Kate interrupted.

Chelsea rolled her eyes. 'Lovers' Lane. It's where you go to get screwed or high.'

'And the college allows this?' Mrs Siler asked, horrified.

'No, not on paper, anyway,' Chelsea said. 'But they don't patrol there, especially during the summer break, and the cameras are always broken. After those two girls were kidnapped off the campus last year, they fixed all the cameras, but students just broke them again. The school gave up after a few repairs and things went back to the way they were.'

'How did you get to the lane?' Kate asked her.

'I have a car. When I got there, I saw Sid's bike. Her motorbike. And then I saw Sid.' Her voice broke and tears began to run down her face unchecked. 'I ran over to her, tried to wake her up, but she was cold. So cold.' She wrapped her arms around herself and rocked. 'I tried to find a pulse, but there wasn't one. I . . . I called 911. I didn't know what else to do. I should have gone down there last night. I should have looked for her when she wasn't back by midnight. Dammit,' she cursed hoarsely. 'Why didn't I go to check?'

'Because she'd always come home before,' Kate said gently. 'And she was probably dead by midnight, so there wouldn't have been anything you could do. But now you can. You can tell me who sold her the drugs.'

Chelsea's wet eyes widened. 'You think her dealer killed her? That doesn't make any sense. He wouldn't kill a customer. He wouldn't kill his income. He's not a stupid man.'

'So you do know him?' Kate murmured.

Chelsea jerked a nod. 'You're going to find my stuff. It's not a lot. I didn't use like Sid did. I couldn't afford it, but mostly I didn't need it. I used when I had finals. When I needed to stay awake and alert. But I hadn't used in a while because that's how Sid started too, and she'd gone out of control. I kept begging her to go to the clinic, but she kept saying no. That she'd quit when she got her degree. When she got *published*,' she spat. 'Goddamn that advisor, always pushing her to publish, publish, publish. "Publish or perish." Such a fucking joke. Sid perished anyway.'

'What's her advisor's name?' Kate asked.

'Dr Sanderson. She's relentless.'

'She called us,' Mr Siler said dully. 'She sounded ripped up.'

'Sidney said she liked her,' Mrs Siler added. 'Was she lying about that too?'

'I'll check it out as soon as we're done here,' Kate told her, as kindly as possible, then turned back to Chelsea, firming her voice. 'Now for the tough questions. Who was her dealer?'

Chelsea closed her eyes. 'I want to tell you. God, I want to tell you! But if the others find out, I'll be . . . I don't know what I'll be, but it won't be good.'

'You're worried about being shunned?' Kate asked, eyebrows lifted.

'No. I'm worried about being beaten up. Or worse. If I tell you, he'll go under. If he goes under, the supply disappears and then the low-ends move back in. Everyone will be mad.'

Kate didn't doubt that Chelsea believed it. 'Well, I can tell you that if you keep your silence, the "or worse" will happen anyway. Whoever killed Sidney is snipping off loose ends. You are her roommate. You've now been seen in the company of a federal agent. How long do you think it'll take before word gets back to him? He'll come after you next.'

Chelsea paled. 'But I don't know anything!'

'You knew where she was going,' Kate said calmly. 'You knew where to find her.'

'Because her kit wasn't here! I figured she'd gone out to score. I swear it!'

'And *I* might even believe you. But Sidney's killer won't.'

'But . . . but . . .' Chelsea sputtered, terror in her eyes. 'This isn't fair!'

'Neither is your friend lying in a drawer in the morgue!' Kate snapped. 'You're wasting my time, Chelsea.' She stood up, took the cuffs from her belt. 'On your feet.'

'You're *arresting* me?' Chelsea hit a note that made Kate wince.

'Damn straight. Either way you're going into custody. If you tell me, it'll be protective custody. If you don't, gen pop. That's general population, you know.'

'My roommate had a thing for sociopaths on death row,' Chelsea snarled, still sitting down. 'I know what gen pop means. Fuck you and the horse you rode in on, Agent Coppola. I haven't done anything wrong.'

'Except buy drugs, however intermittently. And the intermittent nature of your usage is all according to you. Once I search the place, I might find that you're lying about that.'

Chelsea flinched and Kate knew she'd scored a direct hit. 'So stand up, Miss Emory.' She grabbed Chelsea's collar, pulled her to her feet, and snapped the cuff on one arm. 'Last chance.'

'Fuck you,' Chelsea growled. 'It's the Professor. He calls himself the Professor. I don't know his real name or what he looks like. He wears a fucking disguise.'

Kate nudged her back into the chair. She didn't take the cuff off, though. 'This is a good start. What's his disguise?'

'He makes himself up to look older. I don't think most people notice it, but then most people aren't looking at his face. Most people just want his product. It's the best around.'

'Which I'm sure we'll be able to verify in the lab when we find your stash.'

'I want a deal,' Chelsea said, her chin jutting out stubbornly.

'I can talk to the DA for you. I can't make a deal myself.'

'Of course you can't,' Chelsea muttered.

'I really can't. That whole law and order thing. I'm the order, not the law. Okay, if no one knows he has a disguise, how did you know?'

'I'm into theater. I do the backstage stuff. One of the times I bought from him, it was hot and his appliances had slipped. I don't think Sid even noticed. I truly don't buy from him often, because I can't afford it.'

'How did Sidney?' Mr Siler asked. 'We could barely send her any money at all.'

Chelsea closed her eyes on a sigh. 'Sid likes . . . *liked* to live large. Clothes, jewelry, shoes, vacations. She did what she thought she had to so that she could afford it. She . . . recruited for the Professor. Brought him new clients. Sometimes she bought for them. Kept a little for herself.'

'She was a dealer, too?' Mrs Siler whispered, her pain as clear as day.

'Sometimes. And sometimes she'd barter . . . things to be able to afford what she wanted.'

Kate glanced at the parents from the corner of her eye, then met Chelsea's gaze squarely, unwilling to add to the Silers' pain by asking the question aloud. The younger woman nodded at her silent question.

'With the Professor?' Kate murmured.

'No. He didn't go with anyone. Not that I heard, anyway. At least no one from the college. I imagine he's doing it with someone. Most people are.'

Not everybody, Kate thought, suddenly realizing it had been more than three long years since she'd done anything with anyone. Cursing at herself, she dragged her thoughts back on track. 'So how old do you think he really is?'

'Late thirties, early forties maybe. No older than fifty for sure. He moves young.'

I get that, Kate thought, barely remembering what it was like to move young. 'Could you tell what he looked like under the appliances?'

'He has blond hair. Dark blond. He wears a wig that's gray, but his hair is light. His jaw is sharp. Angular. It was the jaw piece that had slipped and exposed his hairline. Just a few millimeters, but enough to see if you were looking. I didn't want him to know I was looking. If he gets mad, he stops selling for a while.'

'Is that what you meant by him going under?'

'Yeah. Sometimes he'll go away for a few weeks or longer. Once he disappeared for three months and the cokeheads were walking around campus moaning like zombies. The other dealers' stuff wasn't nearly as good.'

'Can you remember when that was?'

'Not if you take me in,' Chelsea said, acting tough, but it was an act. Kate could see it. The girl was so scared she was shaking.

'I tell you what,' Kate offered. 'You promise to tell me what I want to know, and when we leave here I'll make it known that you held out on me. That you didn't tell me anything. I'll make sure your fellow students hear me. The grapevine will do the rest. Do we have a deal?'

Chelsea hesitated for only a second or two. 'Yes.'

'But if you screw me, you will be so damn sorry,' Kate said seriously.

'I won't,' Chelsea insisted. 'Are we almost done?'

'Yeah.' Kate turned the facts over in her mind and remembered one other thing she needed to know. 'Do you go to a gym?'

'Yeah. The one on campus. It's cheap for students.'

'What about the one just off campus?'

'That's where all the bodybuilders go.' Chelsea's brows shot up. 'Yes, he dealt there, if that's what you want to know. I had a friend who worked there, a few years ago now. He said the Professor sold the best, purest 'roids anywhere.'

'Did you ever know a guy named Roy?'

Chelsea shook her head. 'Like I said, I don't go for the body-builders.'

'Who do you go for?'

Chelsea swallowed hard, and for the first time Kate thought she was seeing the real woman behind the facade. There was a blistering, searing pain in Chelsea's eyes, such that Kate knew what her answer would be before she said it. 'Sid.'

'Oh,' Kate said quietly. 'You were lovers?'

'Yeah.' New tears filled her eyes and she let them fall. 'I didn't want her folks to find out this way,' she said, as if the Silers weren't sitting in the same room. 'She was going to tell them. But she kept putting it off until the time was right. But that time never came.'

Kate exhaled, feeling the exhaustion that weighted her down. 'So the advisor . . . ?'

Chelsea's chin dropped to her chest and her shoulders shook with sobs. 'I hate that woman. And I hated Sid for selling out. For selling herself. But I still loved her. Pretty stupid, huh?'

'No,' Kate said quietly. 'Pretty human.' She sighed. 'I'll have the officer take you in, and you'll be put in protective custody. I'll make sure your neighbors hear me tell the officer to throw you in a cell and let you rot with the hookers. Okay? I'm going to put the cuffs on, but gently. Just for show.'

Chelsea nodded, still sobbing. 'Okay. Okay.' She lifted her eyes to the shocked faces of Sidney's parents. 'I'm sorry. I should have checked on her. I should have stopped her. I should have dragged her to rehab. I'm so sorry.'

The Silers nodded, saying nothing while Kate carefully cuffed

Chelsea's hands in front of her and pushed a few tissues into one clenched fist. She brought the officer into the room and gave him instructions just as she'd promised Chelsea, then called for backup to guard the apartment until CSU could arrive.

She followed Chelsea and the officer into the hall, noting the other doors on the hall easing open. She cocked her jaw, like she was angry. 'Maybe a night in a cell will change her mind. Make sure she's not alone. I want her to have the full experience. Put her in with the hookers and maybe she'll be more willing to talk tomorrow. If not, I can make it even more fun.'

The officer gave her a brisk nod of full understanding. 'I'll make sure it happens.'

Kate held the pose until Chelsea and the officer disappeared around the corner, then went back into the apartment and closed the door. She leaned back against it, closing her eyes for a fast few seconds. When she opened them, the Silers were staring at her, worry on their faces.

'Are *you* all right, Agent Coppola?' Mr Siler asked quietly.

Kate wanted to be ashamed that she'd allowed the victim's family to see her fatigue, but she was too tired to care. *I need to sleep. I need to see Decker.*

The thought that this Professor had been operating in the city, selling to the college kids for God knew how long without ever being caught, and that he had contacts inside the hospital, the jail and CPD itself was sobering. And frightening. Because that same clever craftiness had nearly ended Decker's life today. So no, Kate was not all right.

But she nodded anyway. 'Yes, sir, but thank you for asking. I normally would have had that conversation in an interview room at the field office, but Chelsea seemed ready to talk. I didn't want to give her any time to shore up her defenses.'

'I'm glad we heard it,' Mr Siler said, infinitely more weary than Kate could ever have been. 'That their child is using drugs is not what any parent wants to hear, but Sidney was our daughter and we loved her. We would have welcomed Chelsea into our family. We still will.'

'She was always like a daughter to us,' Mrs Siler said faintly. 'Now, more so. She's all we have left of Sidney.' She broke down then, crying in her husband's arms.

'Would you like to see Sidney tonight?' Kate asked. 'Or we can wait until tomorrow.'

'Tonight,' Mr Siler managed. 'Then we can grieve in peace.'

'All right. As soon as another officer comes to guard the door, I'll drive you to see your daughter, and then I'll find you a place to stay.'

Twelve

Cincinnati, Ohio,
Thursday 13 August, 7.30 P.M.

Bottle of wine in hand, he locked the basement door and retrieved his keys. He entered the living room with the bottle angled so that JJ could see the label. 'One of my best.'

She was sitting where he'd left her, in exactly the same position, the same expression on her face. If he hadn't heard her messing with his keys, he never would have suspected. 'I like that one,' she said with an approving nod. 'It'll go well with the steak.'

He sighed loudly as he went behind the bar and bent down to search for a corkscrew. And to slip the GHB into her glass. He filled the glasses with rich red wine. 'I was thinking,' he said.

'About?' she prompted when he didn't go on.

He swirled the wine, making sure the powder in her glass was dissolved. 'You shouldn't have to deal with Mallory's insolence. I'm sorry, JJ.'

She smiled at him when he offered her the glass and sat down beside her. 'As long as she's taught how to behave, I'm sure I'll live.'

No, you really won't. He gently clinked their glasses together. 'Thank you for the heads-up today. I appreciate you telling me about Davenport. I suppose I'll have to find another way.'

She sipped her wine. 'That's going to be tough. I found out that he's left the hospital.'

He sucked in a sharp breath. 'Why didn't you tell me?'

She frowned at him. 'I was *going* to. That's the other reason I came over. But then Mallory picked a fight.' JJ's lip poked out in a slight pout, not an attractive look for a woman of her age. 'He left the hospital around four o'clock. I found out from the charge nurse who came on duty second shift while I was driving over here with our dinner. That we're not going to eat tonight.'

Fuck the damn dinner. 'Did the charge nurse know where he went?'

'No, but she told me who he left with.'

He waited for a split second, then made an impatient sound. 'JJ?'

'Will you fire Mallory?'

Oh, you are gonna suffer, he thought furiously, but kept his expression impatient. 'I said I'd punish her. If I fire her, who's going to clean up after Roxy? Who's going to change her sheets when she vomits and pisses all over herself? You?'

'Hell no,' JJ said with a grimace. 'I get enough vomit and pee at work, thank you very much. Will you at least look for a replacement?'

No way, he thought, wishing he could kill JJ now. But he had too many questions and he didn't think she'd be terribly forthcoming without incentive, and incentive took time. He had too many things to do tonight to work her over now. He'd dope her up and put her on ice till later.

'I will do that,' he said. 'Who did Davenport leave with?'

'Dani Novak,' she said, then made a face, gulping a big mouthful of wine as if the woman's name tasted bad. 'She quit, y'know. She never should have been working in a hospital to begin with.' Disgust twisted her mouth. 'Exposing everyone in the ER to HIV.'

His eyes widened, his surprise genuine. He knew Dani Novak, but hadn't expected her to be taking care of Davenport. He supposed he should have. Dani's brother was FBI too. It would make sense that they'd be concerned about Davenport after his near miss that morning. 'Selfish,' he agreed. 'Did you get re-tested?'

'I did.' JJ shuddered. 'If she'd given me HIV, I'd've killed her myself.'

'I know Dr Novak. She took care of one of my patients when he broke his arm ice-skating last winter. But I had no idea she was HIV positive.'

248

He had, of course. Everyone in the city's medical community did. But that wasn't important now. He could use Dr Novak to get to Davenport. Things were looking up.

'She has been since she finished her residency,' JJ said with a sneer. 'God only knows how she picked it up.'

'Well, that's not my biggest concern right now,' he said honestly. 'I'm more interested in finding Griffin Davenport. Do you have any idea where they took him?'

'Not a clue.' She took a larger sip, tilting her head, puzzled. Then frowned, her eyes going wide with alarm as she realized what was happening. 'You sonofabish,' she slurred.

He snagged her glass so that she didn't spill red wine all over his upholstery. 'Yep. That's me.' He dumped both glasses of wine down the sink and hefted her to her feet. She wasn't that large, but she was sturdy, and moving her was harder than he'd thought it would be. He led her staggering body to the guest room on the first floor, lowered her to the bed and removed her shoes. Those he'd take with him. It was harder to run in bare feet.

He tied her hands behind her, then bound her feet and hogtied the rope. Into her mouth he shoved a handkerchief to keep her quiet. He pulled the cover over her, arranging her so that she merely appeared asleep to anyone glancing in the room.

'I'll be back,' he promised, in case she was still conscious. 'We have things to discuss.'

He locked the door from the outside. He didn't want JJ waking up and making enough noise to draw Mallory's attention. This was regrettable. JJ had been an amazing asset while she'd lasted. It was starting to look like he'd have to take a small hiatus and rebuild his networks. He was losing operatives all over the damn place.

'Droppin' like fuckin' flies,' he muttered as he returned to the kitchen, where Mallory had the mixer going. She was whipping cream for his strawberry shortcake, but there was a frown on her face as she stared into the bowl. 'What's wrong?' he asked.

'It's not whipping. It's just . . . flat.'

He leaned over her shoulder to look. Then he sniffed it and grimaced. 'It's spoiled.'

'I just bought it.' She looked up, fear in her eyes, as if she was afraid he'd strike her. A legitimate fear, because he had hit her for making mistakes in the kitchen. 'I swear.'

He checked the carton. 'It's curdled. But you're right, it's new. It shouldn't be spoiled.' He watched her shoulders sag, relief replacing the fear. 'Do you have more?'

'No. I'm sorry.'

'Well, we're not having strawberry shortcake tonight,' he said grumpily. 'It's not the same without the whipped cream.'

'I can go to the store and get some more,' she offered.

He sighed again, feeling petulant. 'No, don't bother. I have things to do tonight and I don't have time to wait around. Go get it tomorrow. Is the steak ready, at least?'

'It is. I put it in the warmer. The table is set. Where is Miss JJ?'

'She had to take a nap,' he said. 'She had a little too much wine and got tipsy. Leave her alone and let her sleep it off.'

'Should I wrap up her dinner for her to eat later?'

'Nah. Eat it yourself.'

'What should I do with the food she brought?'

He checked out the grocery bags on the countertop. They held a rotisserie chicken and deli containers filled with potato salad and the like. *So much for* cooking *dinner*, he thought, rolling his eyes. He pried the lid off one of the packages of potato salad, noticing the deli tape was torn. Someone had already opened the package.

Someone had already opened all of the packages.

He looked at Mallory sharply. 'Did you touch any of this stuff?'

She shook her head warily. 'I put the bags on the counter after I caught her trying to get into the basement and she wouldn't leave. She yelled at me when I tried to put the cartons away in the refrigerator. She didn't want me touching her stuff. That's when I told her that if she didn't leave, I'd call you.' She pressed her fingertips to her swollen face tentatively. 'That's when she hit me.'

'I see.' He was afraid that he did. He opened one of the packages and gave it a sniff, but smelled nothing. Which meant nothing. 'I'll need to test this. Don't eat any of it.'

He didn't want Mallory dying. Not until he was finished with her, anyway. Her little sister still had a little more growing up to do before she could be a viable replacement.

Mallory's eyes widened. 'What should I do with it? Is it safe to put down the disposal?'

'I'll handle it.' He took the food JJ had brought and reached for the carton of cream at the same time that Mallory did. The carton tipped over, spilling curdled cream all over the cabinets and the floor. He glared at Mallory, who backed up a step, looking suitably frightened.

'I'm sorry,' she whispered. 'I was trying to help.'

'Well *don't*,' he snapped. 'Clean this mess up. I'll be downstairs.'

She nodded. 'What about your dinner?'

'I've lost my appetite right now. I'll eat while I'm out.'

Cincinnati, Ohio,
Thursday 13 August, 7.50 P.M.

Mallory watched him go, gripping the countertop for support when her knees threatened to buckle. *Oh God. That was close.* She drew a breath through her nose, trying to slow her racing heart. *I did it. He believed me.*

The black eye she'd surely sport tomorrow was worth it. So worth it. She'd been racking her brain all afternoon, trying to figure out how to get out of the house tomorrow, needing an excuse to go back to the grocery store so that she could call that lady from the police and get the name of the cop who'd helped her.

She sank to her knees and cleaned the mess with paper towels. Paper towels could be ground up in the garbage disposal, all the evidence of her lie washed down the drain.

It wouldn't take him long to realize that the curdled cream was only the result of added lemon juice. She hadn't thought far enough ahead to consider that he'd want to test the cream along with JJ's food, so spilling it had been a reflex action. *Hurry. Get rid of the mess, before he figures it out.*

251

She'd come up with the idea of intentionally spoiling the cream as she'd driven back from the store, but fear had her dismissing it before she'd pulled into the driveway. If he caught her, he'd kill her. Then he'd take Macy and . . .

No. Not going to think about that. She was going to think positively. She'd contact that lady cop and somebody would believe her this time. *Please let someone believe me this time.*

She'd thought about her options all afternoon while doing her chores and taking care of Roxy, who *really* needed to be in the hospital. Roxy's usefulness as a prop wife was over. She'd never go to another party. Never lie for him again. Soon she would be found dead in her bed, or she'd simply disappear. *And only I'll know who really killed her.*

He'd find someone else to take to parties. To smile at the parents of his teenaged victims so that they believed this was a normal house with a normal, childless couple who just wanted to help poor, disadvantaged kids. He'd find someone else to lie for him when the need arose. *Maybe even me.* The thought made her want to throw up. She'd become used to being his sexual outlet over the years, but lying for him . . . luring other kids into this hell . . . *I can't.*

Don't think about that now. She made herself think instead about JJ, who was in for some serious torture. Because JJ really had broken in and really had been trying to get into the basement. Mallory had discovered her while coming down the stairs with a basket full of Roxy's soiled bedding. JJ had been trying to unlock the basement door with a key that didn't fit, much to her ire. Then the woman had pulled out a set of lock-picking tools.

Mallory had made herself as still as a mouse, backing up on the landing to stay unseen. JJ had known what was in the basement. Mallory had never liked the woman and the feeling was intensely mutual. She'd known JJ was an addict, but hadn't thought her desperate enough – or stupid enough – to risk breaking into his stash.

Finally JJ had given up and gone into the kitchen. Mallory had sneaked down the stairs and peeked around the corner, stunned to see JJ adding white powder to all the deli containers and stirring them well.

Poison? Or maybe drugs. JJ was a nurse, after all. She'd have the same access to drugs that he did. Maybe more, because she was a nurse in a hospital.

He's going to find out and then blame me had been Mallory's first terrified thought. And then she realized she could use this. Make it work for her. If she spoiled the whipping cream, maybe he'd believe JJ had done it all. But only if she could find a way to pin it on JJ.

Then JJ had turned around, seen her spying, and hit her so hard that she'd gone down like a rock, dropping the basket of soiled sheets. It had hurt like hell, but it had been the break she'd been looking for. Sitting on the floor, covered by Roxy's vomit-and-pee-soaked sheets, Mallory had figured out how she could use this to hide her own actions.

And it had worked. She lifted her eyes skyward. *If you can hear me, thank you.*

She grabbed a bottle of bleach, dropping to her knees to scrub the kitchen floor, to clean everywhere the cream had spilled, ensuring that there was nothing left of her deception.

She'd go to the store again tomorrow for more cream. She'd call the police. She'd get the name of the lady cop and tell her everything. Including the name of the man he wanted to kill.

Griffin Davenport. She'd heard him say the name to JJ.

The police could protect Davenport and the lady who was taking care of him – Dani Novak. Surely the fact that she knew the names would be enough to make them believe her. She lifted her eyes skyward once more. *Please let them believe me this time. And don't let him hurt Macy. Please keep Macy safe.*

And please let Macy love me? Just a little. But even if Macy thought she was a monster forever, Mallory could accept it if only her sister was safe.

Cincinnati, Ohio,
Thursday 13 August, 8.00 P.M.

Meredith had just put the kettle on to boil when her doorbell rang. Kendra stood on the stoop, looking like she wanted to run away. 'Are you coming or going?' Meredith asked.

Kendra grimaced. 'I hate talking about my feelings.'

Meredith opened the door wider. 'Then come in for tea. I just put on the kettle.'

Kendra held out two bags, one from Skyline and one from Kroger. 'I brought dinner and dessert. Ice cream.'

Meredith took the bags, opened the one from Skyline and sniffed appreciatively. 'Five-ways? My favorite.' She peeked in the grocery bag. 'Ooh. Graeter's. Ah. Black Raspberry Chip. Have you been talking to Faith?'

'Yep. She said that you two hit the Skyline once a week.'

'And we keep the freezer in the office stocked with this exact ice cream for the days when we've listened to too many victims telling us brutal stories that make us homicidal. Then we hit the treadmill hard for a week after,' she added ruefully. 'Come on in. Stay a while.'

Kendra followed her in, looking around her living room with a small smile. 'Your house is always so cozy. And quiet.'

'Right now. This time tomorrow, I'll be up to my eyeballs in nine-year-olds. Bailey's bringing Hope because Ryan's got some man's night thing going on. They're going to play poker and watch baseball, so the girls are coming over here for pizza and a *Princess Diaries* marathon.'

'How does one nine-year-old equate to "up to your eyeballs"?'

'Because Hope asked if she could invite a friend. One friend became two. Then six. And then it became a slumber party. So I stocked up on glitter nail polish and junk food.'

Kendra snorted. 'You just can't say no. That's your problem.'

Meredith sighed, but it was largely for show. She loved having company in her little house. Because sometimes quiet was overrated. The kettle began to whistle, underscoring the thought. She used a teakettle to heat water instead of the microwave – she loved the cheerful little whistle. 'Have a seat. I'll bring the tea. We can eat after we've talked.'

When she came back with the tea tray, she found Kendra standing at her bookshelves, stooping over to examine the bottles of nail polish she'd bought that day and arranged on the shelf at nine-year-old level, salon-style, because choosing the right color was half the fun.

Meredith set the tray on the coffee table and poured her own cup before curling up in the corner of the sofa. 'If you want, we can paint each other's nails instead of talking.'

Straightening to her full impressive height, Kendra turned with a grin that didn't come close to reaching her eyes. 'The Cherry Pop is real pretty. Too bad my nails are wrecked.'

'Because you bite them,' Meredith said. 'Why?'

'Nerves. Habit.' Kendra shrugged and sat stiffly in the other corner of the sofa. Then smiled a little when she saw that Meredith had put a peppermint tea bag next to her cup. 'You always remember what I like.'

'Only because you told me why you drink it.'

Kendra dropped the bag in the cup and poured water with hands that trembled. 'Because you can't over-steep it. I always forget. I'm not allowed to make microwave popcorn either because I get distracted and it burns.'

Meredith sipped her tea. 'Me too. Seems like I always overestimate what I can do in the two minutes I'm waiting for the kernels to stop popping.'

Kendra shot her a grateful look. 'You're letting me ramble.'

Meredith's lips curved. 'But I'm withholding dinner until you get to the point. I'll get you started. You said you're having violent fantasies with respect to perpetrators of sexual crimes.'

Kendra nodded. 'Yeah. But I'm not sure where to start.'

'How about with how long you've had these fantasies?'

'Years. I just never did anything about them until now.'

Meredith lifted her brows, concerned. 'What have you done now?' she asked carefully.

Kendra stared into her cup. 'I stopped a potential assault on Saturday.'

Meredith frowned. 'But that's good, right?'

'Yeah, but the intended vic has been on my mind for days. I was on my break, actually, and had run into Kroger on Glenway for a salad. I saw this girl, maybe eighteen, shopping with a really scared expression. She was trying to go for adult and blasé, but she wasn't cuttin' it. A man followed her all the way through the store and out to the parking lot. He was late twenties, former football jock type. He kind of trapped her between himself and the back of her car – he was talking to a pal on FaceTime and held up his phone so that the other guy could see this girl.'

'So you broke it up? Sent him packing?'

'Yeah, but when I gave her the opportunity to tell me what had happened, she denied that anything had. Then she got in her car and drove away like a bat outta hell. I tried to follow her, but by the time I got to my cruiser, she was long gone. I'd snapped a pic of her license plates, so I ran them. They came up as stolen and not matching the car she was driving.'

Meredith's frown deepened. 'Okay, that's bad. All of that sounds bad, actually. But how can *I* help, Kenny? So far everything you've said has been cop stuff, not therapist stuff.'

'I'm trying to get there. The guy called her Sunshine Suzie. I looked it up after my shift.' Kendra closed her eyes and shook her head. 'The hits that came up . . .' She swallowed hard. 'She was an Internet porn sensation up until about three years ago. Meredith . . . she was abused on camera for *years*.' Her voice broke. 'I gave the information to ICAC. They said they'd follow up, but that they're overloaded and she's not a minor anymore. They've got a list of kids they have to focus on first. Fucking budget cuts.'

'Frustrating, but true,' Meredith murmured, her mind already racing. The Internet Crimes Against Children task force faced a never-ending challenge, and the problem was huge. There simply were not enough resources. But now there was a task force focusing on finding a local pornographer. And this girl shopped at a local supermarket.

This could be important. This girl could be important for reasons bigger than herself. But for now, Meredith's focus was on Kendra, who was crying quietly and without drama.

Kendra quickly swiped her knuckles under her eyes. 'I mean, I know lots of girls who've been abused, who've been forced to be prostitutes. Hell, Wendi and I have a house full of them.'

Meredith passed her a box of tissues. 'But?'

'I can't get *this* girl's face out of my head. I can't forget any of their faces, but this girl . . . There was something about her. Something about seeing her pursued like that. In a grocery store. In the middle of the day. In *public*. It made me sick.' She dried her eyes. 'Of course Wendi said that if we find her, she'll be welcome at the house.'

'*If* you find her.'

Closing her eyes, Kendra nodded miserably. 'Big fucking "if". But that's not why I wanted to talk to you. See, when I realized she was long gone out of the parking lot, I waited at the exit for the asshole ex-jock to drive by and snapped a photo of his plates too. So I'd have an ID just in case he harassed her again.' When she opened her eyes, they were tortured. 'I know his address now and his name. And . . . I'm so goddamn angry, Mer,' she whispered.

'You should be,' Meredith said quietly.

Kendra shook her head. 'No. Not like this. I kept thinking of what that bastard boyfriend of Wendi's mama did to Wendi when she was a kid. I kept remembering the nightmares she used to have when we were fosters. We shared a room, y'know.'

'No, I didn't know that. I didn't know she'd had nightmares, either, but I'm not surprised.'

'She doesn't talk about them. But *I* remember. Sometimes I still have nightmares about her nightmares. She used to make this . . . this *sound* while she was asleep . . . like an animal with its leg stuck in a trap.' Kendra shuddered. 'She used to cry because she knew people were still looking at her pictures, that she'd never get them back.'

'Once on the Net, forever on the Net,' Meredith said sadly.

Kendra's lip curled in helpless fury. 'Yeah. But in my mind, the people looking at her were these creepy, slimy, bug-eyed men who live in their mothers' basements.'

'Easily detected in a crowd.'

'If they ever left their mother's basement.' Kendra sighed. 'It's stupid. I mean, I'm a cop. I *know* that the bad guys sometimes look pretty, but seeing this grown man harassing this girl like he *owned* her. Right there in the grocery store. He wasn't ashamed and he wasn't bug-eyed. He looked handsome and healthy and fit and . . .'

'Normal?'

'Yeah.' A shaky nod was followed by an embarrassed grimace. 'So . . . to my point. I've driven by his house six times since Saturday. I . . .' A deep breath. 'I fantasize about . . . well, about things I have no business fantasizing about.'

Oh dear. This was more serious than she'd thought. 'What do you want to do to this man?'

Kendra exhaled quietly. 'What I say won't leave this room?'

'Never. Not unless you follow through, but we're not going to let that happen.'

'Okay.' She squared her shoulders. 'I want him to suffer and I want him to pay. I want him to be afraid, so afraid that he begs for mercy, and then I don't want to give him any. I want to march up to his front door and tell his wife what he's been up to. I want to arrest him for viewing child porn. I want Marcus O'Bannion to put him on the front page so everyone will know what a fucking pervert he is. And when he goes to jail, I want him to be victimized every damn day of every damn year. And I want it to *hurt*.'

Meredith waited, sipping her tea. There had to be more. None of those things Kendra had listed were bad enough to make her ask for help. But Kendra said nothing, just sat there absently dunking the tea bag in her cup, then lifting it and watching the tea drip.

'Do you have a specific plan, Kenny? Because otherwise your fantasies aren't all that violent. In fact, I'd say they're a good bit more vanilla than mine.'

A full minute ticked by. Then two. Finally Kendra spoke. 'I want to kill him,' she whispered. 'I want to wait for him to come out of his house and I want to put a gun to his head. I want to force him into my car and I want to take him somewhere quiet. Where no one can hear him scream.' She drew a breath. 'I know a place.'

'Where?'

Kendra darted her a sideways glance. 'Faith's house. That big place way out in the country. Nobody around for miles. Another killer got away with it for years. Why not me?'

All right. Now we're getting somewhere. 'How would you do it?'

Kendra blinked. 'What?'

'How would you kill him?'

Kendra's mouth opened, then closed. 'I don't know. I could shoot him, but that's kind of anticlimactic.'

Meredith sipped her tea. 'Indeed.'

'I suppose I could slice him to bits,' Kendra said thoughtfully. 'Cut off important appendages first.'

'You could. He'd scream.'

'Good,' Kendra said coldly.

'He might even beg.'

Her jaw tightened. 'I hope he would.'

Would, Meredith thought. Not *will.* Kendra hadn't really planned out any of this. She just wanted to be able to. 'There is the problem of his victims, of course.'

Kendra frowned. 'What d'ya mean?'

'Well, you get all the fun. What about them?'

Kendra hesitated. 'I don't know. I suppose they could help, if they wanted to.'

'You'd make them murderers too?' Meredith asked softly.

Kendra flinched. 'Goddammit, Meredith.' She pulled the tea bag from the water and set it aside, then took an angry gulp. She hissed in displeasure. 'That's hot.'

'It's hot tea. You gulp it, you're gonna get burned. There are consequences to everything we do, even if it's accidental. Or even well-intentioned.'

Kendra's eyes narrowed. 'Goddamn, woman, you're really good.'

Meredith grinned. 'I know.'

'Did you just think of that? On the fly?'

'I'm really good at improv,' Meredith said smugly, then sobered. 'See, here's the thing, Kenny. It's one thing to want to kill someone who deserves it. It's quite another to actually do it. That's a line that most of us never cross. Most of us just talk about it. We might even create a nebulous plan. But to actually *do* it . . . That's different. To follow through with it requires a personality trait that most of us don't have. We might kill to protect ourselves or to protect another. We might even kill to keep a person from hurting someone again. But to kill in premeditated cold blood . . . That's not something that most of us can do. Or should do, even if we can.'

'Just because we can, doesn't mean we should,' Kendra said quietly.

'Exactly. You're *going* to want to kill them. That's just human nature. You might even fantasize a very loosely structured plan. But Kendra, you *knew* that driving by the man's house was bad for you. That's why you're here, honey. What's more, you know what you need to do. It was one of the first things you said.'

'Arrest him for child porn and let his fellow prisoners whoop his ass?'

'Bingo to the arrest. And a less enthusiastic yes to the penal ass-whooping.'

Kendra's lips twitched. 'Penal? Really? Are you twelve?'

Meredith grinned again. 'Nah. But I work with kids. "Penal" is one of those words that sounds way dirtier than it really is. And it made you smile. Almost.'

Kendra's almost-smile became a frown. 'Okay, I'll bite. Why less enthusiastic? Don't you want them to hurt?'

'*Hell*, yeah. But to make them hurt, someone else has to do the hurting. Someone else has to live with the consequences of that action. And violence is cumulative. It desensitizes us. Every time we do it, see it, it takes something from us. Even from those scary mofos in lockup.'

'It pushes us further away from the light.'

'Yes. Let's go back to the positive. How can you make that arrest for child porn happen?'

'I reported it to ICAC.'

'That's a good start.'

Kendra frowned. 'But nobody called me back and it's been days.'

'That's . . . troubling. But they're so busy, maybe they're just behind.' *No one should be that behind.* This had been a hot, live tip. *ICAC should have been on that like white on rice.* 'But we're in luck. You know that text Scarlett got at breakfast this morning? She was called to a meeting at the FBI field office. I was invited to the same meeting. We're looking for a kiddie porn kingpin, right here in Cinci. I think they'll be interested in finding this girl if for no other reason than to see what she knows about the sex trade here in the city.'

Kendra nodded hard. 'Good. And the asshole who stalked her in the Kroger?'

'Him too, especially since he's unlikely to have made this girl his sole viewing. He'll have more kiddie porn on his computer or he'll have access to it. The team has a meeting scheduled for tomorrow morning. I'll bring it up then.'

'But what about the girl?' Kendra asked, troubled. 'She went back to someone or something illegal. The plates on her car were stolen.'

'Did you take a photo of the girl as well as her plates?'

'No, but . . .' Kendra swallowed. 'There was a photo of her on Google. I . . . cropped it so that it was just her face. I did it on the computer at the precinct and I made a notation of why because just opening the file should have raised a whole lot of red flags.' Her eyes grew shiny once again. 'It was a horrible picture, Mer. And when I looked at her, I saw Wendi when she was the same age. And I wasn't sure if I was angry for the girl or for my sister.'

'Does it matter? You saw something wrong and you sought to fix it. That's doing your job, Kenny. That's what law enforcement is all about – protecting the innocent.'

'I really do want to kill him, Meredith,' she confessed quietly.

'I know, honey. So do I.' Meredith unwound herself from the sofa and stood, reaching for the ceiling. 'So tonight we learn basic breathing techniques. Stand up. I'm gonna teach you some ways to deal.' She met Kendra's eyes. 'Because if you don't deal, you're going to crash and burn, and Wendi and I'll be picking up the pieces.

Your career will be over because you'll be all broken and used up. But I don't want your career to be over. I want you to be a cop for a long, long time.'

'Why?' Kendra asked hoarsely.

'Because you *care*. Because you *would* kill him if you had to, but you came here so that you didn't have to. I'm proud of you, Grasshopper.'

Kendra's snorted laugh was part sob. 'You're so full of shit.' But she stood up and reached for the ceiling. 'But teach me anyway. And then we can have five-ways.'

'Mmm.' Chili on noodles with cheese, onions, and beans. 'And then ice cream.'

Kendra's smile bloomed slowly, rising to fill her eyes. 'Hell, yeah.'

Cincinnati, Ohio,
Thursday 13 August, 8.45 P.M.

Well, fuck. He drove away from the park behind the CVS drugstore, frustrated as hell. It had taken him more time than he'd expected to re-key his locks and to run all the tests on JJ's food. So, while his locks were secure and he'd proven that JJ had dumped digitalis into his dinner, he'd missed his opportunity to hit Rawlings where it really hurt.

Rawlings's kid wasn't there. None of the kids were there. It had started to rain, with thunder and lightning even. Damn teenagers were pussies. Getting a little wet sent them scurrying home to Mommy and Daddy, who gave them way too much money and free time. Little bastards.

Now he'd have to come back tomorrow. He'd been all ready to teach Rawlings Senior that it was a mistake to threaten the Professor. Instead he'd have to deliver the promised drugs and be content with playing the guard's game. He'd have to say that he'd written Rawlings's name down in the event he got killed. He'd also be able to threaten Rawlings with the combined ire of all of his customers who'd no longer be able to access his superlative products.

But he didn't want to simply match the man. He wanted to *best* him. To grind him into the dirt. To teach him who was boss and who was the peon who simply followed orders.

He wanted to break him. See him utterly destroyed. *So that he never considers threatening me again as long as he lives.*

Tomorrow. He'd have to do that tomorrow, because it was almost time for his scheduled call with his client. He pulled away from the CVS and into the parking lot of a Wal-Mart store. There were plenty of cars still parked, so him sitting here while he talked on the phone would draw no curious stares or unwanted attention.

At the top of the hour, he placed the call.

'Hello?' came the cautious greeting, delivered in heavily accented English. 'Who is this?'

'Buzz.' Because Woody McCord had been his partner, of course. 'I wanted to know if you'd had a chance to check out the stills I sent you.'

Pictures he'd taken of the kids he'd invited to his home the Saturday before. They'd all been so happy and goofy. *Give a hungry kid a burger and some ice cream and they smile like the sun.*

'I did. They will suffice.'

He frowned, recognizing the ploy. His customer was about to try negotiating a lower price. 'If they'll only suffice, I'm sure I can find another buyer. I wouldn't want to disappoint you. Maybe we can do business at another time. Have a good day.' He checked his watch. It was still day over there, wasn't it? 'See you around.'

'Wait.' It was a disgruntled mutter. 'They're dirty.'

'They'll wash. I guarantee it.'

'They're pure?'

'They are now. They won't be when you get them, of course.'

'Good. They must know what to expect. Trained. Willing.'

'I agree. I sent you my contract. I haven't received it back with your signature.'

'Why a contract? It's not enforceable. It's ludicrous.'

'It's to protect you, actually. I want to be sure you are comfortable with everything I'm sending you. It's not like I can take it back to where I got it. Once I've taken payment, then made my delivery, I don't make exchanges. Just check the boxes that say you approve my proposed delivery. That's all I need. I do not want there to be any misunderstandings between us.'

'All right. But it's not like I'll sign my real name.'

'Doesn't matter. You'll send me my money first. I'm the vulnerable one here. You know where I can be found. I only know where you want your purchases delivered to.'

'To where you want your purchases delivered.'

Condescending sonofabitch. He made himself smile so that his voice remained rock solid. 'Sorry. I slept through English class.'

'Just like an American. I speak five languages fluently.'

Of course you do, asshole. 'Look. Do you want the delivery or not?'

'I do. Proceed with your preparation. I will do the same so that my new guests will be comfortable here.'

'Good. I'm sure they'll be pleased when they arrive.'

He hung up and rolled his eyes. The number of zeros on the bank deposit required him to be nice to the fucking clients, but he didn't have to enjoy it.

Now he had to get to the meet with Rawlings. He checked under his seat to be sure he still had all the tools he needed. 'Product, check.' It had started out as quality product, but he'd purposely cut it with all kinds of things that humans shouldn't be putting in their bodies. *Shouldn't have threatened me, asshole. For that, you'll pay.* When Rawlings tried to sell it, he'd find himself on the bad side of some very scary inmates. *And I'll keep my hands clean.* 'Nine mil in my holster, check. Rifle under the seat, check. And dart gun, check.' He placed the dart gun in the center console so that he could reach it quickly, then set out to begin the payback.

He wasn't happy that Rawlings had used the cyanide pill on Alice, since she and Sidney had entered the morgue on the same day. The cyanide pill was supposed to be used only as a last resort, if the ricin hadn't worked and it looked like Alice was about to talk. And Rawlings was supposed to have cleared its use first. Hopefully Sidney's skin color would hide any side effects from the MEs, or they might make uncomfortable connections.

Tonight Rawlings would believe he had the Professor's nuts in a vise, but tomorrow he'd be sorry he ever tried to use their transaction to blackmail him. He'd be broken. He'd be malleable. He'd be perfect.

Cincinnati, Ohio,
Thursday 13 August, 9.25 P.M.

Meredith walked Kendra to the door and gave her a hug. 'Call if you need me,' she ordered. 'And thank you for dinner and the dessert.' Together, she and Kendra had annihilated that pint of ice cream perfection. 'Wendi and I walked around the city this afternoon for hours. I think I only have to do twenty hours on the treadmill tomorrow instead of twenty-four.'

Kendra hugged her. 'Thanks. Call me when your team finds out something about the girl.'

They'd both agreed that 'the girl' was a far better name than 'Sunshine Suzie'. Using her porn name was adding insult to injury. She'd already been victimized enough.

'You bet, but don't forget to send me the photo.' Meredith lightened her tone. 'You sure you don't want to come to the slumber party tomorrow? Even if you've bitten off your fingernails, the girls can paint your toenails. It'll be fun!'

'A barrel of laughs on which I shall still pass,' Kendra said dryly, then stopped on the porch, going quietly watchful. 'Mer, you might have a problem.'

'What?' Meredith poked her head around Kendra's shoulder because she wasn't tall enough to see over it. It had started to rain while they'd been eating Skyline and ice cream, but she saw the problem before Kendra even pointed.

'That old Jeep across the street. It was there when I drove up. It drove away, but I got the feeling the driver was watching your house. Now it's back.'

Meredith sighed. 'It's a problem all right, but not the one you're thinking of.'

'You know the driver?'

And how. 'Yeah. It's all right. It's Dani's cousin, Adam.'

265

The car door opened and Adam got out and stood next to the Jeep. Waiting. Without an umbrella. *He's getting drenched. And you're a fool to care.*

Kendra hesitated. 'You sure? I've heard stories about him. He took a mental health break, you know. But when he came back he wasn't . . . Well, he's still not okay.'

No, Adam most definitely was not okay, but it wasn't any of Kendra's business. 'He won't hurt me. I can promise you that.' Not physically. Her heart . . . not so much.

That train had left the station nine months ago.

'Did Dani introduce you two?'

'No. Adam and I met in the hospital. He was working an attempted homicide last fall – one of the girls who was kidnapped from the college. I was called in because the girl was a minor and a ward of the state.'

However, her friend didn't look inclined to leave, staring at Adam as he folded his arms across his chest, unmovable in the pouring rain. Meredith sighed again. 'Look, I can tell you this much. You know how you felt after looking at one picture of the girl?'

'Yeah.'

'Imagine looking at hundreds of those pictures. Every day. For weeks.'

Kendra shuddered. 'Understood.'

'Good. Now go home and run on the treadmill, like we discussed. If you want to run with me, I'm out at five every morning. Except not Saturday because, you know, slumber party.'

Kendra shuddered again, this time in jest. 'I am so out of here.'

'Chicken!' Meredith called after her as she ran down the steps to her car. Adam continued to stand there, getting wet. *Watching me.*

Meredith wanted to shut the door. Wanted to tell him no. But knew she wouldn't. He carried more guilt than just about anyone she'd ever met. But giving him comfort came at a high price.

Too high. So high that she wasn't sure if it was the right thing to do or not.

But he continued to stand in the rain, watching her. So she waved him to come. He moved slowly, deliberately. Putting one foot in front of the other like he was walking through molasses. Or to his final meal.

Because we're just that irresistible, aren't we, Mer? she thought bitterly.

You're talking to yourself again. Using the royal we, no less. Stop that.

She wanted to tell herself to shut the hell up, but was suddenly too tired to do so. She leaned against the door, waiting until he was standing before her, dripping wet from the rain.

And still the most beautiful man she'd ever seen in her life.

But so not okay. He looked down at her, his dark eyes hooded. Wary. Tentative. As if he was afraid she'd toss him out onto the street.

As if she could. 'Come on in,' she murmured and watched his shoulders sag in mute relief. 'Stay a while.' She moved away from the door without waiting for his answer, unsurprised when he closed, then locked the door – both deadbolts. She busied herself in the kitchen, loading the dishwasher. 'If I'd known you were coming tonight, I'd have asked Kendra to bring more food.'

She looked over her shoulder. He was in the kitchen, but just barely. Dripping wet. He'd taken off his suit coat, and his soaked dress shirt was plastered to his chest, revealing every ripple of muscle. His shoulder holster only amplified the effect.

Meredith closed her eyes, a shiver running over her skin. Adam Kimble was everything she'd always wanted. So close, yet so unattainable. Because he was definitely *not* okay.

'I'll go down to the laundry room and get you some towels,' she finally said when he remained silent. 'I might have some clothes in the guest room that will fit you from the last time Daniel came to visit. Just give me a minute to finish cleaning up here and I'll check.'

He moved so quickly, so quietly that one second he wasn't there and then he was, standing behind her, inches between them. His body was throwing off heat like a furnace.

'Who the hell,' he asked in a deep, rasping voice, 'is Daniel?'

Meredith forced herself to turn in the small space he'd left her, to meet and hold his gaze. To not back away. To not let her voice tremble. He would not respect a weak woman, not as a partner or a therapist. Or a lover. Though none of those things were ever going to happen. *Not again, anyway.*

'Daniel Vartanian, my cousin Alex's husband. They came for Christmas.'

He jerked a nod, some of the starch melting away. 'Thank you.'

She lifted her brows. 'For what? Not lying to you? I already told you, Adam, I'm not going to lie to you. I won't tell you only what you want to hear.'

Liar, liar. Because she hadn't told him how she really felt. How much he'd hurt her. Nine months ago he'd come to her, needing someone to talk to because the images in his mind were wreaking havoc with his emotions until he was too shredded to stand alone. But there'd been a spark from the moment they'd met and she'd allowed that spark to ignite, against her better judgment, which turned out to be right, because she'd gone to sleep that night with him in her bed, his arms wrapped around her like he'd never let go, and woken the next morning alone.

Not even a note. *Because I'm just that stupid.*

He closed his eyes. 'I'm sorry, Meredith.'

'For what?' she asked again.

'For not being the man you need me to be. And for needing you too much to stay away.'

She swallowed hard, her heart aching at the pain in his voice. And at her own need to make his pain go away. 'What happened today, Adam?'

He leaned forward, dropping his chin until their foreheads were touching. The simple contact had her grateful for the countertop at her back, because her knees had just turned to rubber. She clenched her fists at her sides to keep herself from touching him anywhere else.

'I saw you again,' he said quietly. 'But I wasn't going to come here. I promised myself I wouldn't.'

'Yet here you are.'

'Yes.' His swallow was audible. 'I won't do what I did last time. I promise.'

Her eyes burned. 'Which thing, Adam? Coming to me for

support? Because you're already here. Maybe you mean sleeping with me? Or maybe leaving without a note or a phone call or even a text? For nine fucking months?'

He stiffened, then straightened, making her lift her chin to see his face. His eyes opened, his jaw tightening until a muscle ticked in his cheek.

She tightened her fists, determined that she would not touch him.

'I hurt you,' he said woodenly.

'Y'think?' she snapped.

'I'm . . . sorry. I'll go.' He turned on his heel and she stared at his back. For all of a second.

'Wait,' she said sharply, and he stopped dead but didn't look back. 'You're here. Just . . .' *Damn this. Damn him. Damn me.* 'Just wait. I'll get you some dry things. You can tell me what happened today so that you don't implode. The team needs you sharp.'

He turned his head, bringing his profile into view. 'The team,' he said bitterly.

'What else is there? You don't want me. If you did, you would have come back. Unless you expected me to chase after you and beg? I won't do that.' She softened her tone, because he looked like he was preparing himself for a flogging. 'But I will listen. If it will help you, I will listen.'

His lips twisted. 'For the team?'

'Yes, but also for you. And for me. I don't want to be this bitter, angry person, Adam. You never made me any promises, so I don't have any right to be bitter and angry. That's why I offered this morning. I will listen. If you want that, stay here while I get you some towels and dry clothes from the basement. If you don't want that, then go. Just close the door on your way out.'

Leaving him standing there, she took the basement stairs at a snail's crawl, giving him enough time to make up his mind. She had towels in the linen closet upstairs, but she'd left Daniel's clothes in the guest bedroom she gave to visiting couples. It was far enough away that she didn't have to hear any . . . night sounds.

Her cousin Alex tended to make a lot of night sounds with her husband. As they should. It was still hard to hear after so many years of being alone.

Towels and dry clothes in hand, she climbed the stairs as slowly as she'd descended, fully expecting to find nothing in the kitchen but a puddle of water. Sucking in a breath, she opened the door and . . . her gut settled.

He was still here. And looking painfully uncertain.

Join the club, buster. 'You can change in the bathroom downstairs and put your wet things in the dryer while we talk. Then you can leave with dry clothes.'

Without a word he took the bundle from her arms. But he was staring at her hard, too many questions in his dark eyes. Too many questions and too much hurt.

She put the kettle back on and wished that Kendra had brought more of the ice cream. She had the feeling she'd be needing dairy courage before the evening was over.

Thirteen

'You'd better not hurt yourself,' Triplett grunted.

Decker gave the big man his best sneer, even though every bone in his body ached. He'd walked too much for his first time up and he knew it. But he needed to get better. Stronger. He needed to be able to walk beside Kate as she investigated the case *he'd* started – and intended to finish.

He'd been walking laps around the interior of the safe house for thirty minutes, which had become painful about twenty-eight minutes before. 'You're just scared of Dani,' he mocked.

'Hell, yeah,' Trip said without shame. 'Aren't you?'

'Yeah,' he admitted, making the other man chuckle. 'Help me to the kitchen table, if you would.'

Trip did, and Decker sank onto the chair with a grimace.

'There is the smallest of chances that I might have overdone it.'

'No,' Trip deadpanned. 'You're lyin'.'

Decker grinned despite his fatigue. 'Fuck off, Trip,' he said congenially. He leaned sideways, trying to reach the fridge door, and nearly fell out of the chair.

Trip smirked. 'Something you want, farm boy?'

'Telling you I grew up on a farm was a mistake, wasn't it?' But Trip had asked where he'd come from, and Griffin and Mama D's farm *was* home. Even though it didn't exist any longer.

'Hell, yeah.' But Trip opened the refrigerator for him. 'What do you want?'

271

Anything with flavor, he wanted to say, but he didn't want word to get back to Agent Troy, who really had been kind. Troy's food was one step up from cardboard, but he'd shared what he'd had. So Decker wasn't going to diss him. 'What's in that blue carton?'

Trip waggled his brows. 'Barbecue and slaw. Jalepeño cornbread. Shrimp and grits.'

'Oh God.' Decker was practically drooling. 'Where did it come from?'

'I went out to get it while you were sleeping. You should have slept longer, by the way. Dani's gonna be pissed.'

'Not if you don't tell her. So shut up, kid, and gimme some of that barbecue.'

Trip grinned at him. 'You sure you can take extra spicy?'

'No, but I'm willing to die trying. I am so damn hungry.'

'I figured you would be. Like a bear coming out of hibernation. Disposition of one, too.' But he dished up the food and Decker tucked in with relish, his mouth on fire but happily so.

Trip stilled and tapped his earpiece. 'Send her in.' He tapped again. 'Kate's back. I'll let her in.'

Decker pushed himself to his feet and shuffled to the kitchen doorway. He could see the front door from here. He wanted to see her as soon as she came in. Because . . . well, just because. He wanted to. But standing on his own two feet.

Trip let her in and she smiled up at him wearily. 'I thought you'd be home asleep by now, Agent Triplett.'

'I took a double shift. Agent Davenport wanted to walk and I'm the only one big enough to scoop his ass off the floor if he falls down.'

She grinned. 'Don't let him hear you say that.'

'Too late,' Decker said dryly, then everything in him settled when she met his eyes. She was back and okay. Physically. Her eyes were shadowed by exhaustion and something else. *Sadness.*

'I know,' Trip said, just as dryly. 'I heard you shuffling like an old man in a retirement home. If you slept more, you might not shuffle.'

'*You* are a pain in the ass.' Decker leaned against the wall, his head a little light. 'Or maybe you're just sucking up to Dani.'

'Guilty as charged – of both. Doesn't change the truth.' Trip shook his head and Decker figured the kid might just be sincerely concerned. But Kate was smiling at him and he instantly forgot about Trip and his mother hen clucking.

'You don't have the IV anymore,' she said, giving him a visual once-over that felt more like a medical exam than anything remotely sensual.

He shrugged. 'I'm eating real food now, so the doc took it out.' He didn't want a medical exam, not from Kate. Because he had slept. And he'd dreamed of her, waking up with a tent in his shorts, the sheet poking up embarrassingly. But while his cock's activity continued to be a relief that all the important stuff still worked, he didn't want the whole place to know. And until he was in a regular bed rather than a hospital bed in the middle of the living room, everyone *would* know.

But now that she was here, he found himself in the same aroused state. *Shit.* He shoved his frustration down, because she'd come back, like she'd promised. Dragging two large suitcases.

Trip was eyeing the luggage curiously. 'You planning to stay a month, Agent Coppola?'

She chuckled. 'I figured I'd stay a night or two. It's more comfortable than my hotel, so I packed my stuff and checked out. Then I went by the grocery store and picked up a few things so I could cook a real meal. I haven't had one of those since I left DC.'

Trip gathered the grocery bags she'd hooked over the suitcase handles. 'I'll take these to the kitchen, then I'll put your suitcases in the empty room. You put your feet up. You're looking ragged around the edges, if you don't mind my saying so.'

Kate followed Trip to the kitchen, but stopped where Decker leaned against the doorway and offered him her arm. 'Let's sit down,' she said. 'Triplett's right. I'm beat.'

He looked at her arm. 'If I fall, I'll pull you down.'

'No you won't. I've done this before.'

With Johnnie, he thought. *Her husband.* The guy had been Decker's size before the cancer, so Decker took her at her word and leaned on her. She led him to the kitchen table, easing him into a chair. Then lowered herself into the chair across from him, closing her eyes as she did so.

'Thank you, Agent Triplett,' she said, because he'd put the groceries away.

'No problem. I'll leave your suitcases in your room, then head out. Agent Daily is on duty for the night. I'll be back in the morning.' He backed out of the kitchen, leaving them alone.

'What happened tonight?' Decker asked softly.

She opened her eyes to stare at his half-eaten plate. 'That looks amazing. I'm starving.'

He pushed the plate to the middle of the table. 'Forks are in that drawer. I'd get you one but I think I might just keel over and put your care-giver skills to the test.'

She got up long enough to get a fork and one of the sodas that Trip had put in the fridge. 'I shouldn't have caffeine so late, but I still have to write a report before I go to bed, and I'm so tired I thought I'd fall asleep behind the wheel. It was all I could do to stay awake enough to make sure I wasn't followed.' She devoured the barbecue in silence, then sat back in her chair. 'We have a motive for Sidney Siler's death.'

'What did she know that her killer didn't want her to tell?'

'She'd been to see Alice, right? It wasn't the first time she'd interviewed accused murderers, because she was working on her doctorate on deviants and sociopaths. It *was* the first time she'd used a fake ID to get an interview, but not the first time she'd broken some rules. She carried a recording pen to all her interviews. Her roommate alerted us to it and it was found with Sidney's things. CPD's CSI guy found it, with Zimmerman and the ME as witnesses. They taped the search and uploaded it to the evidence database. Everyone kept copies of the tape.'

'Your idea?' Of course it was. His Kate was thorough.

'Mine and Deacon's. We wanted to make sure that no more evidence conveniently disappeared. Anyway, we have the recorded interview in its entirety. Alice said a lot of shit. But she did say one thing worth dying for – that there were no written records of her transactions. It was all in her head. A few hours later she was beaten in the exercise yard and by morning she was dead.'

'So there are no records left that incriminate McCord's missing partner. He could kill her and that was the end of any damning evidence.'

'Right. We also learned who Sidney's dealer was. Some guy named the Professor.'

Decker frowned. 'I've heard that name before. My bosses did not like him. They bought from him for distribution up and down I-75, but they didn't like him. He also dealt straight from his own stash, and that was competition the traffickers didn't want. But then sometimes he'd just disappear from the scene and Alice's father would be happy again because profits were better.'

'How do you know that he'd disappear?'

He frowned harder, trying to remember, but there was still some fog in his mind. 'I might have heard it on the tapes, but I think it came directly from Alice's father. He was cursing the Professor because the man had upped his prices. He said that even when the Professor wasn't dealing directly, he was still making a profit from the local trafficking rings. His product was high quality and in demand. So the Professor is the connection between Eileen Wilkins, Sidney Siler, and Alice?'

'Looks like it.'

Decker studied her face. Her mouth drooped, her eyes were still sad. 'What else happened?'

'I met Sidney's parents. They were there when I interviewed her roommate, Chelsea. Who was also Sidney's lover.'

'Heartbreak all around then,' he said quietly.

'Exactly. Anyway, I put the roomie in protective custody and let everyone believe she hadn't told me jack shit, because she was afraid of what would happen if people found out she'd narked on the Professor. He has quite the fan club.'

'I knew that. Like I said, he made good-quality drugs. Users would buy directly from him when he was selling.'

'Oh, and he wore a disguise. The roomie saw it peeling from his face while making a buy.'

His brows jumped up. 'That I didn't know.'

'The roomie said most people didn't. They were too busy buying to examine him closely.'

'So . . . back to the parents,' he said gently. 'I'm guessing they took it hard.'

'Very. After I sent the roomie into protective custody, I took the parents to the morgue.'

'That was kind of you.'

She shrugged. 'They loved her. It was really hard for them, especially after learning that their daughter was an addict who sold her body for pocket money and dealt for the Professor.'

Decker winced. 'Hell.'

'I know. I tried to help them find a hotel, but it was late and they didn't have a lot of cash. I was planning to come here anyway, so I gathered up my stuff and let them have my room. It's paid for through Tuesday. Someone should get to use it.'

Decker's heart squeezed. 'You're a nice woman, Kate. But I won't tell anyone.'

Her lips curved. 'Thank you.' She rolled her neck and Decker could hear it crack from across the small table. 'I was going to go see Sidney's advisor, but I decided it would have to wait until tomorrow. I won't be able to pay proper attention until after I get some sleep.'

'Come here,' he said, patting the chair next to him.

Her eyes narrowed. 'Why?'

'Just come here. Please.'

She was still suspicious, but she complied. 'Why?'

'You're not supposed to crack your neck like that. Here. Let me.' He twisted in his chair so that he could put his hands on her shoulders. He started massaging, using his thumbs to work the kinks from her neck. She moaned, the sound going straight to his groin.

'That feels so good. Where did you learn to do that?'

'Army. I had a friend who was a medic. She had good hands.'

Her shoulders stiffened. 'Who was she to you?'

That she'd guessed wasn't a huge surprise. She had a way of

reading between the lines that gave her an edge at her job. 'We dated for a while. About a year.'

She drew a breath, let it out. 'Did you love her?'

'I could have, if we'd had more time,' he answered honestly. 'I did a little.'

'What happened to her?'

He swallowed hard, but kept up the massage. Somehow it was easier to talk about Beth when his hands were on Kate's warm skin. 'She died. IED hit her Humvee.'

'I'm sorry.'

'Me too. She was a nice woman. She didn't deserve to die, much less that way.' His voice had wobbled a little on the last few words.

Kate looked over her shoulder, her brown eyes sober and sympathetic. 'What way?'

He couldn't look away. Didn't want to. But he didn't want to answer her question either. Not completely. It was still too painful to actively recall. His flashbacks were bad enough, thank you very much. 'She was . . . closest to the IED. There wasn't much of her left.'

Her eyes narrowed slightly, but thoughtfully, as if she was trying to see inside his skin. 'How do you know that?' she asked, so gently that he wondered if she already knew the answer.

'I was cleanup crew.'

Her eyes slid closed, her head bowing respectfully. 'I'm so sorry.'

She *had* known. 'How did you know?' he asked.

She met his eyes again. 'After this morning, Zimmerman bumped up the number of agents listening to your tapes. They've been transcribing all day, focusing on any conversation that included Alice. Zimmerman sent the files they'd finished to the team to read. I got stuck in the longest line at the grocery, so I read a few conversations. There was one among all the traffickers that included you. Alice's father was angry because one of his people had instructed you to dispose of a witness. An innocent bystander, basically. You said you'd done it and gotten rid of her body already.'

The conversation returned to him in a rush. 'I didn't, by the way.'

'I know. I interviewed the woman myself later. You posed as a federal agent and told her to go into hiding for a few days.'

He huffed a mirthless chuckle. 'Yeah. I was a federal agent posing as a human trafficker's gun-for-hire, posing as a federal agent.'

Her lips quirked up. 'Hell of an identity crisis.'

'You have no idea.'

She sobered. 'No, I don't. I can't imagine being under for so long, cut off from everyone you knew. Having to keep all of the lies straight. I guess it helped to use a few truths.'

He nodded. 'I needed them to think I didn't mind taking care of the grislier details. They used . . .' It was his turn to close his eyes, his stomach doing a nasty roll in his gut. 'They used a chipper-shredder to dispose of the bodies. But you know that. You had to have found it.'

'Yep,' she said ruefully. 'It was kind of hard to miss. The stench alone was awesome.'

He opened his eyes in time to see hers roll. 'I know. They just mixed up all the victims and left them to compost. And even with as much as I'd seen in the desert, it really freaked me out. Couldn't let them see that. So I told them about being on the cleanup crew.'

'You sounded perfectly convincing.' She was clearly impressed and it was all he could do not to preen. He *had* been perfectly convincing.

'I wouldn't have survived too long if I hadn't been. Alice was a vicious shark. She was born and raised by a whole flock of soulless vultures and looked for deception everywhere. So, yes, it helped to throw in truth when I could. Made living the lie a little easier.'

'And it let you retain some of Griffin Davenport. You, I mean. Although I suppose remembering your foster dad helped. Gave you a tether so you didn't get too lost in the charade.'

She got it. She got *him*. 'It made having to be an utter asshole a little more bearable. That was the worst part. People were dying all around me for three years, and I couldn't stop it. I did what I could, but it was a piss-poor minimum.'

Her brows rose. 'Did you enjoy it? Did you enjoy being an utter asshole?'

He recoiled. 'No. Hell, no.'

'My point exactly. You did things you didn't want to do. You were cleanup crew to those GIs in the desert. You picked up the pieces and helped sort them as best you could. You put them in coffins so that their families would have something to bury. That was a good thing, a human thing. And that one of those GIs was someone you cared for . . . that was a *super*human thing. So was spending three years as an utter asshole and not losing the real Griffin Davenport.'

His cheeks heated. 'We all have to do things we don't want to do.' His hands had stilled at some point during her speech, but he kept his thumbs resting against her skin. 'You did, too.' He drew a fortifying breath and confessed. 'I looked you up. You and Jack and Johnnie.'

One side of her mouth curled up. 'I figured you did. I wouldn't have been able to resist doing the same thing in your place.' Her mouth lost the little curve and went back to being sad. 'I had cleanup duty when Jack did . . . what he did.'

He jerked, stunned. 'Why? Why didn't you hire someone to do that? I didn't have a choice. I was the cleanup crew. But you could have hired a service.'

She seemed to deflate before his eyes. 'Because it was the least I could do.'

He opened his mouth, then closed it, regarding her carefully. There was something here. Something important. *Guilt*, he realized. *I'm sorry, Jack. I'm so sorry.*

'Why?' he asked again, gentling his voice. 'Why was it the least you could do?'

Her throat worked as she tried to swallow. 'Because it was my fault,' she whispered.

Cincinnati, Ohio,
Thursday 13 August, 10.20 P.M.

Meredith sat at her kitchen table, sipping tea as she contemplated the box of colored pencils. 'Purple,' she murmured and began coloring the feather that belonged to what would become a magnificent peacock when she was finished.

'You're coloring.'

Meredith didn't have to look up to know that Adam Kimble was standing in her kitchen doorway. He'd taken so long to shower and change that she'd been ready to call his cousin Deacon to come over and check on him. But she'd heard the shower shut off and had known the exact moment he'd filled the doorway. He'd been standing there for at least five minutes, just watching her while she colored.

'Yes, I'm coloring. It's very relaxing. You should try it.'

'I don't . . . I'm not . . .' He hmphed. 'Coloring books are for kids.'

'That's where you're wrong.' She looked up then, having fortified herself. Damn, he was a pretty man. Dark hair, dark eyes. All that stubble. Made him look like a pirate. 'Coloring is one of the ways I've done therapy for years. It works better with kids because they're less resistant to the idea, but adults are starting to glom on to it. Coloring books are the new best-seller.'

'You're kidding me.'

'I don't kid about coloring, Adam. It's important. I've got a few designs here you might like.' She spread out the pages she'd printed while he'd been in the shower. 'Stained glass. A dinosaur. A babbling brook. And this one is just . . . shapes. Give it a try. I won't tell anyone.'

'No,' he murmured. 'You wouldn't, would you? Thank you for that.'

'You're welcome. But if you really want to thank me, stop looming and color with me.'

He pulled out a chair on the opposite side of the table, as far away from her as he could sit. He hesitated, then planted his butt in the chair and stared at the pages she'd pushed his way. 'I feel ridiculous,' he muttered, but he took the page with the stained glass and chose a red pencil.

'Just color, Adam,' she said quietly. 'It's all you have to do.'

'Okay.'

Ten minutes later, he was still coloring with the red pencil. Every single panel was red. He was meticulously staying in the lines, but every piece of the stained glass was red. *Don't have to be a shrink to figure that one out*, she thought sadly, remembering the night he'd reached out to her, nine long months ago.

Red was his nightmare. *So much blood*. He'd said it over and over as he'd fallen apart in her arms. He'd said it over and over in his sleep as he'd dreamed. Nightmares. She didn't have to wonder if he still had them. It was written all over his face. And on the solid red page.

Gently she reached across the table and tried to pull the red pencil from his hand so that she could replace it with a blue one. His hand tightened on it, refusing to give it up.

He looked up at her then, eyes shiny with tears he refused to shed. Because men didn't cry.

Bullshit! She wanted to scream it, but she didn't. She took a tissue and dabbed his eyes with all the gentleness she could muster, controlling the shaking of her hands through sheer will. She wouldn't fall apart. Not in front of him. She'd wait until he was gone and then she'd make a late-night run to the grocery store for more ice cream and ibuprofen, because she was sure to have one helluva headache tomorrow morning after crying herself to sleep tonight.

She tried to change the red pencil for blue again, but he held on to the red, not wanting to give it up. 'I'm not finished,' he said, his voice a hoarse rasp.

Blue wasn't going to cut it, she realized. Not tonight. 'Then I'll sharpen this one for you,' she murmured. He'd colored the red pencil down until the point was flat.

He nodded numbly, waiting until she'd done so, then took the red pencil back and continued coloring his stained-glass window solid red. Meredith got up to put the kettle on, waiting next to the stove until it whistled, letting the whistle stretch on a few more seconds than she needed to because it was so damn quiet in her kitchen. It was making her even more nervous than she'd already been. She finally made them both a cup of tea and set his at his elbow. He didn't lift his eyes from the orderly mass of red, but his pencil did still.

'Adam?' she asked quietly.

He looked up, his eyes raw. 'What?'

'You're not going back to ICAC again tomorrow, are you?' *Please say you're not.*

The sound of his swallow seemed to echo in her quiet kitchen. 'No. It was a bad lead. All the pictures were at least ten years old.'

'But you looked at them anyway?'

He put the pencil down and picked up the mug, cradling it in his hands like he was cold. 'I didn't know then. I didn't know until we had our afternoon debrief. Diesel figured it out.'

'Diesel? The guy who works for Marcus?'

'Yeah. Big, hulking Brutus, covered in tattoos. He was the one who found the files on McCord's computer, but he wasn't able to look at the pictures at the time. He . . . I think he identified with the victims too closely.'

'Oh.' She leaned her hip against the table edge. 'So many hurt people trying to make things right,' she murmured.

'Yeah.' He gulped a swallow of tea, then winced when it burned his mouth, but he didn't complain. 'Anyway, he realized that the files he'd found were different from the ones the police confiscated. Two separate computers. The pictures I looked at today weren't of recent victims. They probably weren't made by either McCord or the guy we're looking for.'

'So you looked at them for nothing?'

He nodded grimly. 'Pretty much.'

'Your contact at ICAC didn't know they were old?'

'He hadn't looked at them either. I guess he hadn't looked at the dates on the files.'

Checking a file's date is a damn basic thing, Meredith thought, annoyed. They'd put Adam through hell for nothing. 'Fuck that.'

Surprisingly, he smiled. 'It's okay. I'm okay.'

'No you're not,' she whispered.

'Then let me pretend,' he whispered back. 'I need to believe it.'

She looked at the solid red sheet. 'Okay, for now. But you are going to have to address that.'

He drew a breath, his shoulders sagging. 'Not tonight.'

'Okay. For now.' She folded her arms across her chest. 'Who was your contact at ICAC?'

'Wyatt Hanson, but don't be going all ballistic on his ass. Wyatt's not a bad guy, just overworked and overwhelmed.' One side of his mouth quirked up. 'Maybe he should color, too.'

'Maybe he should. Maybe you all should. Too much damn stress in you cops.' She'd discuss it with Zimmerman. 'If I can't go all ballistic on Wyatt Hanson's ass, then what can I do to help you with this case?'

Another half-smile, but this one was brittle. 'You don't have to phrase things so carefully. I'm not going to ask you for any help other than on the case. And maybe for the sharpener so that I can fix the pencil again.'

She returned to her chair with her own teacup and tossed him the sharpener. 'Knock yourself out.'

He focused on the pencil, sharpening it with the attention to detail he seemed to give everything. 'I will need your help in the morning. My assignment tonight was to find a possible suspect and her son. We had a uniform waiting outside his school – it's a special needs summer program – but the kid is sharp and managed to give our guy the slip. The suspect, an ICU nurse at County, didn't come home tonight, but the kid finally did when the rain started. I got him into emergency foster care, but we need to interview him in the morning. He's not going to be cooperative. Zimmerman asked that you be there for the interview.'

'What's his special need?'

'Emotional. He was . . . fragile. On the edge of a major meltdown.'

'Okay. Why won't he be cooperative?'

'His mother is the nurse that tried to kill Agent Davenport today. You heard about that, right?'

'Yes. Zimmerman told me this afternoon when I called him to fire Agent Colby.'

Adam frowned. 'I heard about that. Not smart, Meredith. We've got witnesses dropping all over the damn place. This mystery partner almost killed a federal agent in a hospital.'

'I'm being careful. But thank you for your concern.'

He scowled at her. 'I *hate* that prissy tone of yours. It's just a ladylike way of telling me to fuck myself.'

Her lips twitched. *Busted*. 'So, the kid. Mom's a possible killer – will he try to protect her?'

'Maybe. Mom's an addict – coke and stolen hospital opioids. Her boyfriend, who's not much older than her son, is an addict. Steroids and coke. Boyfriend got the mom addicted to coke, then leeched off her to feed his own habit. Kid's been sneaking their leftovers.'

Meredith sighed. 'That makes me want to slap the parents until they bleed.'

'Me too. So kid's lost his supply source and he's gonna be needing a hit. I'm trying to get him a slot in rehab.' He took another drink of the tea, giving the cup a considering look. 'That's not bad when it's not scalding the taste buds off my tongue.'

She rolled her eyes. 'It's *hot* tea. How many people do I have to tell this to? Kendra said the same thing.'

'That was Kendra? I thought she was Wendi Cullen's sister.'

'Fosters.'

'Oh. Well.' He went back to his coloring. 'Why was Kendra here?'

Same reason as you, she thought sadly. 'We had dinner.'

'Then you did yoga?' He shrugged when she stared at him. 'I could see right through your front window. You need better drapes. Any creeper could be watching you.'

She shuddered. 'I'll pull the shades.'

'Thank you,' he said, then regarded his stained-glass picture. 'I'm done.'

She gave him a dry smile to try to hide how sad she felt at seeing all that red. 'Should we put it on my fridge?'

He slid it across the table to her. 'Sure.'

Her brows lifted, but she did as he indicated, making sure the page was hung squarely, the magnet properly centered. 'There you go.'

He looked at the red pencil in his hand, shorter now by half than when he'd started. 'I'll get you another red pencil. I almost used this one up.'

'If you want to, but you don't have to.'

He looked at the stack of pages on her side of the table. 'What are those?'

'*My Little Pony*, Elsa from *Frozen*, and horses. My niece is coming tomorrow with a horde of her nine-year-old friends.'

He smiled then, so sweetly that she stared. 'You girls have a good time.' He stood up and pushed his chair in. 'I won't bother you again, but thank you for letting me sit here tonight. I'll see you in the morning at Zimmerman's.' He turned for the door, then looked back over his shoulder to where she still sat, stunned and staring. 'Lock up after me. And get some drapes.'

Meredith followed him to the door, still unable to think. His smile, his real smile, had short-circuited her brain. 'Good night,' she managed. 'Be careful.'

He hesitated in the open doorway, then stroked her cheek once, his touch feather-light. 'Good night. Lock up.'

She closed the door and locked it, then stood at her big window watching him cross the street and get into his car. He sat there for at least a minute, maybe longer, then cranked the ignition and drove away. It was then that she realized he'd left his clothes in her dryer.

No worry there. He'd be back eventually, if for no other reason to color in a room where he wasn't alone. She'd keep his clothes until then.

Cincinnati, Ohio,
Thursday 13 August, 10.50 P.M.

Decker stared at Kate in the quiet of the safe house kitchen, her confession hanging between them. *Because it was my fault.*

Bullshit, Decker thought viciously. Kate's brother-in-law had shot himself in the head in her apartment. How that possibly could have been her fault was beyond him, but he didn't try to dissuade her, because she clearly believed what she'd said. 'How?' he asked quietly.

'I . . . We pushed him into doing something that he didn't want to do. Johnnie and I.'

He opened his mouth again and it hung that way as images of

threesomes flitted across the big screen in his mind.

Her eyes widened. '*No*,' she said quickly, obviously reading him accurately. 'Not like that. Not . . . sexual.' She grimaced. 'Holy God. The very thought.' She shook her head hard. 'I'm by no means a prude, Decker, but um . . . I keep it to two. *Two*.'

He let out a relieved breath. 'Good to know.'

Her lips twitched, surprising him again. 'Oh my God. The look on your face . . .' Her shoulders shook with silent laughter. 'It was almost worth the embarrassment just now.'

'I'm a country boy, Kate,' he said wryly. 'I like things basic. Two people. I don't care how they mix it up gender-wise, but I'm not . . . I can't imagine more than two. I mean, I know other people get into the kinkier things, because I saw it. Furloughs, you know.'

'Oh, I know.' Her eyes still twinkled.

'You're having entirely too much fun at my expense,' he grumbled, but he didn't mean it. She was smiling again and he'd needed to see that. Needed it like he needed food. And air. He drew a breath that felt easier. Freer.

'I'm sorry,' she said.

'No you're not, but it's okay.' He lifted a hand to her face, tentatively stroking her cheek with his thumb, gratified when she leaned into his touch. She hadn't really answered his question about why she thought her brother-in-law's suicide was her fault, but he'd let it go for now because she was smiling again. 'So . . . not a prude?'

Her cheeks flamed, but she didn't look away, and that sent his respect for her up several more notches. 'No.'

'Good to know,' he said again, continuing to stroke her face, enjoying the feel of her skin.

She closed her eyes on a sigh as if she'd needed this too. 'What's going on, Decker?'

'I don't know. But I like it. It's been a long time since I've . . . well, not been a prude.'

She didn't open her eyes. 'How long?' she asked reluctantly.

'Well, it wasn't going to happen while I was undercover, that's for damn sure. God. I wouldn't have let my guard down for a split second around any of those vipers.'

She did open her eyes then, skewering him. 'How long, Decker?'

He was tempted to make a joke, to laugh it off, but the seriousness in her wide brown eyes wouldn't let him. 'Four years,' he answered quietly. 'The night before Beth got into that Humvee. After that . . . I couldn't. Not with just anyone.'

Something shifted in her eyes. 'There's no shame in that,' she murmured.

His throat grew tight, his skin too warm. 'How long for you?'

'Almost the same. Johnnie's been gone three years, but he was too sick for months before that. Chemo leveled him. It was . . . difficult to watch.'

'You took care of him.' It wasn't a question. That she'd care for her dying husband was as sure as anything he'd ever believed.

'Until he drew his final breath.'

'Where was this?'

'Chicago. It was my assignment before Baltimore.'

'Baltimore was where you met Deacon.'

She nodded, nuzzling her cheek into his hand. 'He was my friend when I desperately needed one. That's why I came to Cincinnati. Because I desperately needed a friend again.'

'Because of Jack.'

She pursed her lips, but nodded. 'I know I didn't answer your question before. But I can't. Not right now.'

'Then it'll keep,' he murmured softly.

'Thank you. I . . . I came here tonight because I was hoping for this.'

'Barbecue?' he asked lightly and was gratified to see her smile again, albeit a sad one.

'Yeah. Barbecue. And this.' Another nuzzle of her cheek into his hand. 'I watched Sidney's parents grieve, Decker. I watched Chelsea grieve. And . . . I needed something.'

'Human contact. Don't,' he said sharply when she started to pull away. 'I need it too. I've been alone for a long time, Kate. And then one night I got a rifle poked in my back and some broad was ordering me to get down on the ground with my hands visible.'

Her lips curved. 'What a mean bitch that broad was, to do that to you.'

'It was hotter than hell,' he confessed. 'Especially when I looked up and saw you. And then everything went to shit and it was dark and . . . and then I heard you talking to me. Felt you touching me. You stroked my hair. Why?'

Her swallow was audible in the quiet of the kitchen. 'Because I needed to. I needed to do something for you. You were alone and so was I.'

'You weren't alone. You had friends.'

'Yes. But time marches on and people change. Deacon was my best friend, but now he has other friends. His family is here. He has a life. I'm not jealous, really I'm not. I'm so damn happy for him. But I guess maybe I'm feeling a little displaced.'

'I get that. I felt that way when I came home from Afghanistan. Nobody was waiting for me here. Nobody was waiting for me there. Everyone was dead. It's unsettling.'

'We need tethers.' She looked at him, troubled now. 'Is that all this is?'

'No, I don't think so. Richard Symmes was a friend, a tether if you will. But while I'll grieve him and miss him like hell, I sure didn't feel like *this* about him.'

'Like what?' It was almost a purr and made him catch his breath. Made him want. He wanted everything and he wanted it *now*. He held himself back, because once he got started, he wasn't sure he'd be able to stop. He exhaled quietly. 'I think this could be a bad idea.'

She jerked back out of his reach, looking away. 'I'm sorry.'

'And I'm a clumsy bastard. I didn't mean what you think I meant.' He turned her chair so that they were facing each other and spread his thighs, pulling her chair between them. Slowly he reached out and touched her face, giving her time to tell him no. But he got no protest, so he wiggled his fingers up into the rich red hair she'd pinned to the back of her head in a pretty twist. He massaged her scalp and she melted like butter, moaning softly once again.

'What did you mean then?' It was a breathy, husky murmur that made him harder when he hadn't thought it possible.

'I meant that it's been four years since I touched a woman and if I start something it'll be a breaking dam. It won't be pretty.'

'Mmmm, I see. Exploding concrete and rushing water. The valley will become a lake. Townsfolk in jeopardy. Crowds of people rushing to escape, trampling each other like stampeding wildebeests. I get it.'

Stampeding wildebeests? His lips twitched. 'I'm serious, Kate. I won't be able to stop.'

She drew a very deep breath, then leaned closer. 'Maybe I wouldn't want you to,' she whispered. 'Besides, you just got out of a coma. How much punch can you possibly pack?'

It was a dare, silkily delivered, sending a shiver racing over his skin. 'I don't know.'

'Then maybe we should find out.' She leaned in until her lips brushed his, her eyes so close that he could see golden flecks that weren't visible from further away. 'And if I want you to stop, I'll stop you. That's a promise.'

His heart was pounding like a jackhammer inside of his chest. 'I don't want to hurt you. I got a lotta need stored up.' He heard his drawl emerge and he didn't even care.

Her chuckle vibrated against his lips. 'Shut up and kiss me, Decker.' Then she grabbed his shirt and kissed him first.

He sucked in a gasp. It wasn't sweet and it wasn't tentative. It was hot and hard and hungry.

God, she was hungry. *Just like me.*

His fingers tightened in her hair and he jerked her closer. And the fucking dam broke. He kissed her greedily, starving for the feel of her on his lips, in his hands. He tugged and she fell into him, her hands on his shoulders. She was touching him. Not just a stroke of his hair or holding his hand, but really touching him.

It wasn't enough. He'd known it wouldn't be enough. He ripped his mouth away, his breath coming in pants. But hers was too, so he felt no shame. He pulled one hand from her hair to grab the hand that clutched his shirt, splaying it flat against the skin at his open collar, a jolt of electricity his reward. 'Please,' he whispered, not caring that he was begging. 'It's been too long.'

Too long since he'd been simply touched. Although there was nothing simple about what she was doing to him. Holding his gaze, she unbuttoned the top three buttons of his shirt and slid her hands under the fabric, spreading her fingers wide, and he groaned softly. He hadn't known how much he needed this.

She slid her palms slowly over his skin, inching her way across his pecs to his shoulders. 'I don't want to go near your bandage.' She scooted to the edge of her chair, running one hand over his shoulder under his shirt to cup the back of his neck. Then she pulled him in for another kiss, softer this time.

Sweeter. Slower. Sumptuous. Like a rich dark chocolate meant to be savored. He hummed his appreciation and she sucked his lower lip into her mouth for a little tug before releasing him.

'How's the dam?' she asked against his lips, making him smile.

'The valley is an ocean, but the townsfolk are evacuating in an orderly fashion.'

She giggled, sounding, for that moment, so very young and carefree. It made him proud, because he didn't think she was carefree very often. 'So they're safe?' she asked.

'For now. I make no promises, though. Their situation could change on a dime.'

'I thought they'd be okay. Your dam didn't break. It just needed to vent a little steam.'

He brushed his lips over hers, enjoying the texture. 'You're mixing metaphors.'

'So sue me.'

'I'd rather hold you.' He ran his hands down her sides, biting the inside of his lip to keep from touching her breasts, gripping the curve of her waist instead. He pulled her closer. 'Come here.' He patted his thigh.

She shook her head with a frown. 'I'll hurt you.'

He parroted her words back to her. 'If I want you to stop, I'll stop you. That's a promise.'

'No fair, using my words against me,' she muttered, her eyes lit up, all trace of sadness gone. She straddled his thighs and lowered herself to his lap, resting her arms on his shoulders, her hands clasped loosely at the back of his neck. 'If Dani catches me, she'll throw me out.'

She was holding herself rigid, feet planted on the floor, supporting her own weight. He pulled her down so that she put all her weight on him. *Ah. Better.* He bracketed her thighs with his arms, palming the round cheeks of the butt he'd admired that morning. He grinned when she frowned at him, but she made no effort to move.

'It'll be like being a teenager again,' he said lightly. 'Necking on the front porch in the dark and listening for your folks with half an ear so your dad doesn't chase me away with a shotgun.'

The light in her eyes abruptly extinguished, and he could see her tongue rubbing her front tooth. He stilled, studying her face. He'd been teasing, but her reaction was troubled. Almost haunted. 'What's up with the tooth?' he asked casually.

She froze, her tongue sliding back into her mouth, and he wanted to follow it with his own, but he held back. He nudged her by jiggling his thigh. 'Kate?' Gently he pushed her upper lip up, focusing on the tooth. It was two-toned, but only if you looked closely. At some point it had been broken and she'd had it fixed.

Sudden understanding made him angry. 'Who hit you?' he asked, very softly.

She pushed off his lap and he wanted to pull her back, but he let her go. She washed her hands, then began searching the cupboards for mixing bowls, measuring cups, and the baking ingredients she'd brought from the grocery store.

He sat there, watching her. Her hands never stopped and he remembered the knitting from that afternoon. She kept her hands busy when she was stressed. 'I didn't mean to open an old wound,' he murmured.

'You didn't. It's never closed.'

'Then why are you baking?'

'Because I enjoy it. It's a de-stresser and I've had a rather stressful day.'

'How much did you knit today?'

She gave him a sideways glance. 'Counting the hours you were asleep? Several inches.'

'What's it going to be?'

She smiled as she measured out flour into the bowl. 'This or the knitting?'

'Either. Both.'

'I'm knitting a blanket for a vet in the VA hospital. Any soldier who needs it. This,' she said, measuring out the sugar, 'will be the best brownies you have ever put in your mouth.'

He was touched, but not surprised. Of course she'd be thinking of the vets. The brownies were a surprise, but a very pleasant one, especially as he'd just been thinking about dark chocolate. 'I dunno. Mama D was a very good cook and she taught me what she knew. She made a mean peach pie, and if you're a good girl, I'll make it for you.'

She gave him a naughty look that had him shifting in his chair. 'What if I'm a bad girl?'

'Then I'll give you Mama D's secret recipe.'

'Mmm. I'll give it some serious thought, then.'

He was quiet for a few minutes, watching. She handled the ingredients like a pro, working from memory. He waited until she'd poured the batter into the pan. 'Who hit you, Kate?'

She let out a breath, then turned away to slide the pan into the oven. Straightening, she began to clean up. She was silent for so long that he didn't think she'd answer, but she finally sighed and said, 'My father. I was not what you'd call a biddable child.'

'If you're going to say you deserved it, you need to be prepared for me to yell at you.'

'No need for that. I didn't deserve any of the beatings he gave me. Neither did my brothers, but we thought we did at the time. Usually he hit where the bruises wouldn't show. One particular day, he was too angry to aim and I was too slow to duck.'

'So he broke your tooth.'

'Yep.'

He drew a breath and let it out. 'Did anyone call the cops?'

She smiled bitterly. 'He was a cop. Still is. He's the captain now. Small-town police force in Iowa. Very small town. Nearest city is Des Moines, a couple of hours away.'

Fury had him literally seeing red, but he forced himself to calm down. 'What happened that *particular* day?'

'He'd been suspended for using undue force to subdue a teenager who weighed a hundred pounds soaking wet. The kid was gay and a friend of mine. I had the bad judgment to tell my father that I agreed with the suspension, that he'd behaved like a bully and a thug.'

'So to show you that he wasn't a bully and a thug, he hit you . . . like a bully and a thug.'

Her lips curved. 'Essentially.'

'Where was your mother during all this?'

'Standing at his side.' She'd put all the bowls in the dishwasher and was now scrubbing the countertop with more force than necessary. 'When I picked myself up off the floor, she slapped me back down. Said that I had to apologize or find another place to live when I turned eighteen.'

Decker's jaw hurt from clenching it so hard. 'When would you have been eighteen?'

'Another eight months. I figured my life would be shit until then, but I wouldn't apologize – I was far too stubborn.'

'No,' he drawled. 'Say it ain't so.'

She grinned tightly. ''Fraid so.'

'What did you do when you turned eighteen?'

'It turned out I didn't have to wait that long. I went to school the next day with a swollen lip and a broken tooth. My mother had tried to keep me home, but I snuck out the window. I had an English test that I didn't want to miss. Besides, I figured I could hurt my father more by showing my face all banged up than by defying him under his own roof.'

'And did you? Hurt him more?'

'Not like I'd hoped. My English teacher took one look at me and called Children's Services. They listened to what I had to say and said they'd investigate, but I'd overplayed my hand. I thought I'd go to foster care, but nobody wanted to make my father mad. Still, it wasn't anything compared to what you went through. Your mother was an addict who sold her own child.'

'Abuse is abuse,' he said sharply, then rubbed the back of his trembling hand over his mouth. 'I'm sorry. I shouldn't have used that tone. What did happen?'

'My last class that day was chemistry. My lab partner – who was one of my best friends – realized what had happened and marched me to his mother, who was the school's drama teacher. She took me home with her and I never went back to my father's house. She sent her husband to collect my clothes. He was the wrestling coach and nobody fucked with him. Not even my dad.' She shrugged. 'Wrestling is big in Iowa and we had a championship team.'

'That was kind of them. I'm glad you had someone on your side.'

She nodded, but didn't look at him. She was staring at the countertop like it held the secret of life. 'My friend's name was Jack Morrow.'

'Oh,' he breathed.

'Yeah. His mom became like my mom. Then Thanksgiving rolled around and her older son came home from college for the long weekend.'

Jealousy welled to take the place of the rage and wasn't as easy to shove aside. 'Johnnie.'

'Yes. I was too young the first time I saw him, but it didn't change the fact that I fell hard. So did he. Christmas was a real temptation, but Johnnie wasn't going to touch me until I was eighteen.' Her lips curved, a true smile. 'I made it difficult for him, though. I was a brat.'

The thought of Kate at seventeen made him pity Johnnie and respect the man's self-control. But mostly pity him, especially because John Morrow hadn't been allowed to grow old with her. *I can be magnanimous in this case. Maybe.* 'Again, say it ain't so.'

Her smile broadened. 'Even I am not capable of telling such a whopper. I turned eighteen about a month after I graduated from high school.'

'Did your parents come to your graduation?'

'No. Neither did any of my brothers, but that was okay. The Morrows were all there, including Johnnie. I didn't have any money, so I joined the army to pay my way through college. Johnnie was so angry that I signed up without telling him.'

Decker's brows rose. 'I would've been angry too.'

'The Morrows had planned to pay for me to go to college, but I wasn't going to let them. They were barely making ends meet as it was, and they did suffer for taking me in. They kept their jobs, but they were shunned. They said they didn't care, but I know they did. They had deep roots in the community, but it was a fickle place. And nobody wanted to get on my father's bad side.'

'So you joined up.'

'Yeah. Served in the Gulf, two tours. I was an MP.'

'Why?'

'I wanted to be a cop. I wanted to be more than my father. So I put in for an MP track.'

'And Johnnie forgave you for joining up?'

'Eventually. But even though he was mad, he wrote me letters. Every month, without fail. I was just a kid in lust before, but I fell in love with him through his letters. He was a good man.'

'I know. I read his obituary and all the tributes. "*Seize the day . . .*"'

'"*. . . and make your lives extraordinary*".' She finished the quote softly. 'Those students loved him. He loved them.'

Decker thought about the timeline. 'You two dated a long time.'

'We did. When I came home, I went to college on the east coast and he was teaching in Iowa, so we did the long-distance thing a few years more. He wanted to give me the time to be sure that he was the one. Like I needed it. It was always him. But it did light a fire under my butt so that I finished my degree a year early and got accepted to the FBI academy, and we got engaged. We didn't want to get married until I'd graduated from Quantico and worked for a few years, because we were saving to buy a house. My first posting was Chicago, so he left his teaching position in Iowa and got a job on the South Side, which I was *so* against. I thought he'd get hit by a stray bullet, but . . .'

'But he got cancer instead.'

'Yes. Our plans changed, because he got sick so fast. I pushed up the wedding so that I could take leave and care for him. The family leave act only covers husbands, not fiancés. And then . . .' She closed her eyes.

'And then he died,' Decker supplied quietly. 'I'm so sorry.' And he was.

Her smile was sad. 'Thank you. I went back to work afterward. I got posted in Baltimore. Worked my ass off, and now I'm here.'

She hadn't mentioned Jack's suicide or why she felt she was to blame. He wasn't going to push it for now. 'I'm sorry for all the things that brought you here, but I am very glad you're here.'

She draped the scrub rag over the sink faucet and came back to straddle his lap. 'Thank you. I'm glad I'm here too. I'm glad I jumped out of that tree and shoved a rifle in your back.'

He wrapped his arms around her waist. 'Best introduction ever.'

'I have to agree, Agent Davenport.' She rested her forehead against his. 'You've been sitting here a while. You should go to bed.'

He gritted his teeth when his cock rose at the mention of bed. Her eyes widened in surprise. 'O-kay,' she said with a blink. 'Hello there to you too.'

He had to laugh. 'I want to wait for the brownies.'

'If you let me walk you to bed and tuck you in, I will bring you a plate as soon as I take them out of the oven.' She slid off his lap and helped him to his feet, shoring him up when he swayed a little. 'Take it slower tomorrow, okay? I want you healthy.'

'I want to get out of here,' he muttered, sweat breaking out on his brow. He was far more tired than he'd thought.

'I know. But this Professor asshole tried to kill you today. If you cross paths again, I want you strong enough to return the favor.'

Damn. He bit his lip as his body responded yet again. Bloodthirsty, a crack shot, a kind heart, and she could bake. He could definitely fall for this woman. 'Yes, ma'am.'

Cincinnati, Ohio,
Thursday 13 August, 11.15 P.M.

Dammit. He'd arrived at the meeting place forty-five minutes early, but Rawlings was already there, the asshole. It made him squirrelly when he didn't have time to get his zen on. *Bastard.* He couldn't get into position this way, but he'd made a plan B. He always had a plan B.

Which did not allow the prison guard to see him until he was ready. He brought his dart gun out from under his seat and made sure it was set up and that the dome light wouldn't go on when he opened his car door. Sliding out of the car, he wriggled on his stomach across the wet ground until he had a clear line of sight, silently cursing the rain the whole time. The range of the dart gun was only a hundred feet, so he had to get closer than he liked. He needed Rawlings out of the car, too. And if he missed, the man would be really pissed. So he drew his pistol from his holster and put it on the ground beside him. Just in case.

Taking his cell phone from his pocket, he turned it on, covering the screen with his hand so that it wouldn't give his position away. *I'm here*, he typed. *Want to see ur hands. Pls get out of ur car. Want no surprises while I deliver ur payment.* He hit SEND and waited.

It took Rawlings less than thirty seconds to respond. *Not getting out. Not stupid.*

Neither am I. Shld I drop your payment off w/ur boss @ the jail?

Fuck you.

No thx. Ur not my type. U want the stuff or not?

Fuck you, came the repeated reply, but Rawlings got out of his car.

Hunkering down into the slimy grass, he lined up his shot and gently squeezed the trigger. Then held his breath until . . . *Yes.*

Rawlings slapped his neck like he was going after a mosquito, then pulled the dart from his skin with a scowl. With a glare, the prison guard began to charge in his direction. But he'd expected that, so he had his next shot lined up. The dart hit Rawlings's shoulder. The man kept running, but then he stumbled, then staggered, then went down to his knees. He crawled another few feet, then fell face down in the dirt.

The sedative wouldn't last long, so he gathered both his weapons, got up and jogged to Rawlings's car. He dropped the package on the driver's seat, then jogged back to his own car and drove a safe distance away before pulling off the road into a darkened parking lot.

He sent one more text. *Paid in full. Sorry for the nap. I couldn't trust that you'd keep your word.* He hit SEND and pulled out of the lot and back into traffic.

He hadn't even considered dragging Rawlings back to his car. The man was a bodybuilder with solid muscles that had to weigh a ton. No, definitely not his type. His son, now? Totally different matter. Not for his own pleasure, of course, but Rawlings's son was a real cute boy. He'd look good on camera. If it came to that, it was one way to keep Rawlings in check.

Fucker. Put my *name on his list of favors? Threaten to turn me in?*

After tonight, Rawlings would be a little less cocky. And if not . . . then filming his son would be the next step. It was a mighty hammer.

Turn me in, will you? Then your kid will be a star. Forever. Because once on the Net, always on the Net. Forever. *Just ask Mallory. She'll tell you.*

Fourteen

He pulled into his driveway and parked behind the house in his customary spot next to the car he'd procured for Mallory to drive. A car that he'd fitted with two separate tracking devices. Just in case she decided to get brave and take one off. She never had, but he would continue to be careful with her. He was always careful with his best toys.

He got out of the car, still soggy from his commando crawl through the mud. The rain had stopped, but the air was heavy with humidity. Felt like breathing goddamn water.

He had his hand on the doorknob when he realized that he couldn't see JJ's car. Momentary panic speared him. *She's gone. How can she be gone?*

Mallory. Fury rose to supplant the panic. She'd helped JJ escape. *Hold on. Just wait.*

In return for what? Not out of the goodness of her heart – Mallory hated JJ as much as JJ hated her. So Mallory helping JJ escape didn't make sense.

He calmed himself and realized he didn't remember seeing JJ's car when he got home earlier. He'd been so surprised to see her here that he hadn't even thought about it.

Now he was thinking about it. *The bitch.* She'd hidden her car. Where, he could easily determine. He'd slipped a tracker under its frame the first time they'd fucked. It was a trick he'd learned from Alice, because she'd done the same the first time she'd taken him to

299

her bed. He'd found the tracker and confronted her, but Alice had been unrepentant. She liked to know where her customers – and lovers – were at all times.

And so do I. He'd find JJ's car, then send it and its owner's body far away from here. He didn't want anyone to miss her so soon after Eileen Wilkins's death. Two nurses killed on the same day would raise a lot of questions that he didn't want asked or answered.

Calm and composed, he entered the house and walked up the stairs to Mallory's room. She was in bed, already asleep. He crossed the bedroom and shook her.

'Mallory. Wake up,' he commanded.

She rolled over sleepily, her eyes widening when she saw his clothes. 'You're muddy.'

He ignored her statement of the obvious. 'How is JJ?'

'Loud. She woke up a little while ago. I came up here so that I couldn't hear her.'

He frowned. He'd left JJ gagged. She shouldn't have been loud at all. 'Did you go in there?' But she couldn't have – he'd locked the door and only he had the key.

'No. You told me not to. Should I prepare her dinner? She never did get to eat.'

'Was there any food left from what she brought? Other than what you gave me?' Because if there was, he'd make JJ eat it. *Try to poison me with digitalis. Bitch.*

'No. That was all of it.'

'Then no. She won't be needing any dinner.'

A quiet nod. 'Roxy is due for her evening meds. Should I give them to her?'

'Yes. I don't know when I'll be back.' He slid into the bed beside her, drawing her to him so that he could nuzzle her neck, smiling when she went stiff. It was necessary, showing her who was the boss. It was also fun. She lay there, frozen as an ice sculpture, her breathing even. He tipped her chin up so that he could see her face and scowled. She'd wiped her expression clean. Other than stiff shoulders, she showed no reaction whatsoever.

Suddenly annoyed, he shoved her away. It was no fun when they didn't show they were scared. Maybe Mallory was nearing her expiration date earlier than he'd anticipated.

Still scowling, he went back downstairs to the guest room, briefly detouring to retrieve his scalpel set, but his good humor was restored when JJ met him with a glare. She'd managed to spit out the gag and roll over so that she was facing the door, but she was still hogtied firmly.

'What the fuck, Brandon? What kind of sick kink is this?'

'No sick kink.' He smiled at her pleasantly. 'I'm going to kill you.'

She went instantly pale. 'What? Why?'

'Because you tried to poison me.'

She shook her head hard. 'No. I didn't. I wouldn't. It was the girl. The girl did it.'

'No, she didn't, because Mallory knows what would happen to her if anything happened to me.' Mallory had been told over and over that if she tried to escape or told anyone, her little sister would suffer. And that if anything happened to him, his partner would take over – and that his partner wouldn't wait until little Macy was of age.

Mallory had tried to get away one time. Only once. He'd shown her how easily he could make good on his threat. He'd been pleased to see that she was smart enough to learn from her mistakes. He'd also been very careful not to let her know that his partner had died in jail. In Mallory's mind, the threat was still very real. He had no worry that she would poison him.

JJ was trembling. 'But she did it. I swear she did.'

'You can swear all you like. I've got security tapes of everything that goes on in my house.'

She went even paler, so much so that he thought she'd pass out. 'You're lying.'

'Why would I do that?' He wasn't lying. He did have video cameras everywhere, but he hadn't yet checked the tapes. He didn't have to, because JJ clearly *was* lying. 'You know, you get this little line right here when you lie.' He pointed to his forehead. 'It's an easy tell.'

She lifted her chin and stared daggers. 'I told people I was coming here. They'll be coming here to find me if I don't call in.'

He regarded her evenly. She was still lying. Ignoring her, he accessed the tracking software on his phone. Her car was less than a mile away, parked in the lot of a motel.

'Did you hear me?' she screeched. 'People know I'm here!'

'Which people?' he asked calmly.

'I'm not telling you. You'll kill them.'

'Of course I will. Tell me who. I want names.'

'No. I won't.'

He smiled then. *A challenge.* 'Yes you will. Although it doesn't really matter. When they come to save you, I'll be waiting.'

'They'll bring the cops.'

'Oh, I don't think they'll do that either, because that means they'd have to explain why you were in danger in the first place. Unless they tell the police that it was an affair gone wrong, and in that case, I'll write up some notes that make you look like a deranged, drug-addicted spurned lover and sign your name. The police won't believe a deranged woman over me.'

'I hate you.'

'Feeling's mutual, sweetheart. I don't like being double-crossed and I don't like being poisoned. It makes me cranky.'

'I didn't drive myself. My friend drove me.' She gave a little nod, pleased with herself. 'That's how he'll know where to look for me.'

'You realize I have cameras around the exterior of the house too, right?' he said, playing along on the off chance she had told someone. 'If he dropped you off, I'll have a photo ID of him and a picture of his license plate. I'll find him. And I'll kill him.'

She opened her mouth, then closed it. 'He didn't drive me here directly.' She licked her lips, her desperation plain. Her pupils were dilated, her eyes wild. She was experiencing withdrawal. He'd be able to use that. 'He dropped me off at the end of the road. I walked.'

That was close to the truth. She had walked. But from the motel parking lot where she'd left her car. She didn't have a partner after all.

'Look, JJ, we had some fun in bed. You were useful to me and in exchange you got some high-quality blow for free. But you got greedy and tried to double-cross me and I caught you in the act. Surely you knew there would be risks. You came into my house and tried to poison me and steal from me. You must have considered the consequences.'

Her eyes filled with tears. *Crocodile tears.* 'I didn't do it. It was the girl. I swear it.'

'I left you alone for hours. I would have hoped you'd have used that time to come up with a better lie.' He arranged his scalpels on the nightstand, enjoying the mindless panic that filled her eyes.

'What are you doing?' she whispered, horrified.

'Making an example out of you, my dear. Just in case my next mistress gets any ideas about putting digitalis in my food.' He chose his first tool with deliberate care. 'Let's see how loudly you can scream.'

Cincinnati, Ohio,
Friday 14 August, 2.05 A.M.

Hurry, hurry, hurry. Kate ran up the apartment stairs two at a time, her heart thundering, her eyes already burning with tears. Hurry or you'll be too late.

She fumbled her keys in the front door, but the lock turned and she shoved the door open. Jack sat there in her easy chair, waiting, a mocking sneer on his face.

'Stop,' Kate pleaded. 'Don't do this.'

He shoved the barrel of the gun under his chin. 'Now you tell me not to do it? Make up your mind, Kate. Kill or don't kill? You can't have it both ways.'

She took a step toward the chair, which he'd covered with her afghan. The one Gran had made her. 'Don't kill, Jack. Don't.' She got close enough to reach for him, to grab the gun, but he just laughed and pulled the trigger, and she screamed. And screamed and screamed.

'Kate. *Kate.*' Big hands on her shoulders, squeezing tight. *No. No.* She fought them off, but she was trapped. '*Kate!*'

She sucked in a breath and opened her eyes. And saw blue. Familiar blue. Like the sky.

Decker. She shuddered, trying to breathe, panting hard. She was wrapped in a blanket. Like a straitjacket. His arms wrapped around her over the blanket. 'Let me go. Please.'

'Look at me, Kate.' He shook her a little, not hard enough to hurt. 'I need you to breathe.'

She tried, but the air was sawing in and out of her lungs and she felt light-headed.

'What happened?' A female voice. Dani.

'Nightmare,' Decker said curtly. 'Get me a bag or something for her to breathe into. Sshh.' The soothing shushing was next to her ear. 'You're okay, Kate. You're okay.'

No I'm not. I'll never be okay again. But she nodded. 'Yeah. I'm okay.'

Her body was moving. Rocking. Decker was rocking her and shushing in her ear. 'You're in the safe house. In Cincinnati. *Safe. House,*' he reiterated.

She nodded, too exhausted to fight anymore. Closing her eyes, she dropped her head to rest on his chest. 'What time is it?'

'A little after two,' he murmured, then turned his head. 'Leave it on the nightstand. She's okay for now.'

There was a rustle of paper, then Dani's voice again. 'The guard wants to come in and check on you both.'

No! Kate didn't want anyone else to see her this way, wild and insane-looking. It was bad enough that Decker had seen her like this. *Fucking hell.*

'No,' Decker said firmly. 'Tell him it was a nightmare. Hell, tell him *I* was screaming if you have to. Just don't let him in here.'

A hand ghosted over her hair. 'You okay, Kate?' Dani asked softly.

Kate didn't open her eyes, unwilling to see the pity in Dani's. 'I will be, thanks.'

The door closed, and Decker whispered, 'It's just me now. I'm going to let you go.'

Kate pressed her face harder into his chest when his arms loosened. 'No. Not yet.'

He tightened his hold. 'Okay. We'll just sit here then.'

He twisted a little, grunting as he moved his body, taking her with him. He settled against the headboard, hitching her up so that she sat in his lap, all wrapped up like a burrito. Her mind prickled with memory. *He's hurt. He should be in bed, not me.*

'You can let me go now. I'm too heavy.'

'Pfft,' he scoffed. 'Don't be insulting, Agent Coppola.'

His drawl was thick tonight. His guard was down. 'Did I wake you up?'

'Nah. That shitty excuse for a hospital bed woke me up. Thing's as hard as a rock, and I should know, because I've slept on rocks.'

Her lips curved, because she had too. 'Rocks and sand and sand and sand.'

He exaggerated a shudder. 'I hated that damn sand.'

'Me too.' She let out a little sigh when he rested his cheek on top of her head, just holding her. 'I'm sorry if I scared you.'

'Well, I did get a cardio workout when you screamed. I was glad I had that walker or I'd have fallen on my ass trying to get to you. You have one hell of a set of lungs, lady.'

'I wouldn't know,' she said archly. 'I didn't hear me because I was asleep.'

He huffed a chuckle. 'Let's just say it would have curled my hair if I didn't keep it so short.' His hand, strong and heavy, stroked her hair. 'It's beautiful, by the way. Your hair. Like a sunset.'

Her heart settled into an easy rhythm. 'Yours is too. It looks like spun gold.' He made a strangled sound that had her grinning. 'Like Thor and Cap all rolled into one.'

He groaned. 'You're going to give me indigestion.'

She laughed softly. 'Right. Like you don't know that your face makes women sigh.'

'It's a face, Kate,' he said gruffly. 'Kind of banged up at that.'

'I like it. It's a nice face.'

'Hmm. Back atcha,' he muttered, making her grin again.

She tried to move and he tightened his arms. 'Just a little longer,' he murmured.

'I'm going to hurt you.'

'Not like this. I was more worried when you were still asleep. You kind of . . . flailed.'

Horrified, she pulled away far enough to see his nice face. 'Did I hurt you?'

He met her eyes squarely. 'I've had a lot worse.'

'Not from me!'

He palmed the back of her head and urged her back to his chest. 'Don't worry about it. Let me hold you for a little while.'

There was something in his voice that made her comply. He needed this too. 'Can you at least let me get my hands free?' He loosened the blanket until her arms were outside the burrito. She let herself relax against him, drawing a deep breath. He smelled good. Like soap and . . . chocolate. 'Have you been in the brownies?' she asked accusingly.

'Yep,' he said, unrepentant. 'They were a*maz*ing.'

'Were? Did you save any for Triplett and the others?'

'Maybe. One or two. Really small ones.'

She sputtered. 'I can't believe you ate them all by yourself!'

'Not *all* by myself. I did give a few to the night guard. I needed someone to stand outside the shower in case I fell on my ass. He agreed not to wake you or the doc if I shared the brownies. So I didn't eat them all. Just most of them.'

'Do I need to make another batch?'

'Might not be a bad idea,' he said cagily. 'Chocolate helps me think.'

She pulled back again, this time to smile up at him. 'Helps you think, huh?'

'Hell, yeah. I was sitting at the kitchen table writing down all the ledger entries I saw just before Alice got herself arrested. That's about the time her dad went batshit insane and everything fell apart. I didn't get to see most of the ledgers. Whipple, the head accountant, he kept them locked up pretty tight. But one of the final days, I was in the head office helping Sean, the IT guy, with a few things and he had a copy.' He paused and frowned. 'Wait. He shouldn't have had a copy, now that I think about it. I think I realized that then, too. The leadership team was careful not to keep anything electronic, at least nothing that could be accessed online. Everyone kept their own records, so that if one of them went down, the others would be protected. But Sean had all of the records.'

'But now he's dead.' Because she'd shot the getaway car and wrecked it. Two of the three passengers had been killed and the one who'd lived was worthless.

'Not your fault,' Decker said firmly. 'I'm sure you all looked, but I gotta ask anyway. Did you find anything on him? Files or flash drives or anything like that?'

'Nothing like that, and Forensics went over that car with a pair of tweezers. There was nothing in the car or on the passengers. Or *in* them, even. We X-rayed them and everything, to make sure they hadn't swallowed anything. Could Sean have stashed the ledgers somewhere?'

'Maybe. More likely he uploaded them to a server that only he knew about. He was kind of sneaky that way. Everyone thought he was this clueless, dorky geek when in reality he was planning a coup. Which he almost pulled off.' He was quiet again, and she studied his face until he met her eyes. 'What?'

'I'm wondering where you just went. Your eyes kind of glazed over.'

'I was looking at the computer screens in my mind. I'd sneak looks over Sean's shoulder. Joel Whipple's, too. They'd always change the screen really fast to something innocuous, but sometimes I got in a good peek or two.'

'Zimmerman said you have an eidetic memory.'

'Not entirely, but I do remember computer screens and pieces of paper. Faces to a much smaller extent.'

'Let's go to Vegas,' Kate said lightly.

'Right. They'd make you in a minute. You scream "Fed!" in blinking neon lights.'

'Gee, thanks.'

'Have you ever gone undercover?'

'No,' she admitted grumpily. 'Change the subject.'

He chuckled, then sighed. 'We need to find Sean's files. Even if they have no link to this kiddie pornographer, they'll tell us about their other customers and suppliers.'

'Won't the ledgers tell us that, too?'

'Maybe, but I only caught glimpses. A page here and there. Plus the names on the accounts were all in code.'

'I'm good at code.' Code was just math.

'So am I, but I don't think I got enough for us to work with. You can try if you want to, but I think we'd do better to find Sean's files.'

'Where would we start?'

'I'd say with Alice, because they were half-siblings, but she's dead. Sean was a loner, really. I think he cared about Alice, but he didn't really socialize with people. Not that anyone knew of, anyway. It's like he lived at the office.'

'Which we checked thoroughly as well,' Kate said. They'd left no stone unturned.

'Then I'll think on it some more.' He went back to stroking her hair. 'I like it down. Your hair. I didn't know it was so long. Halfway down your back.'

'I usually braid it up so that it can't get tangled while I sleep, but I think I fell asleep before I could do that.' She snuggled against him, more content than she'd been in a long time. It had been so long since anyone had stroked her hair. 'That feels nice.'

'Good.' His hand stilled after a few more strokes. 'Kate, what were you dreaming about?'

She closed her eyes, the contentment vanishing like mist. 'Jack.'

'I thought so. Was that because I asked you about it tonight?'

He sounded like he felt guilty, and she couldn't have that. 'No. I had the dream most nights after he . . . you know.'

'Killed himself.'

'Yes. But it had calmed down recently, until I came here. I shot the guys in that getaway car and the dream started back. I think it might have been the gunshots that triggered it.'

'No pun intended.' He kissed her temple. 'Have you talked to anyone?'

'No,' she said, more sharply than she'd intended. 'Did you see a shrink after you lost Beth?'

'No,' he said, but kindly, making her feel like shit.

'I'm sorry. I just don't want to go there. Ever. With anyone.'

He drew a breath that expanded his chest, and her head rode the swell. 'Got it.'

'Decker, I . . . It's . . . I can't.'

'Kate, I said I got it,' he said mildly.

'I really don't think you do. It's nothing to do with you.'

'That's what they all say,' he said wryly.

'But it's true. If I tell a shrink, I could . . .' *I could lose my job. I could go to prison. And Decker would not look at me the way he has today.* 'It wouldn't be nice, that's all.'

'Kate, I said I got it. You don't have to explain.'

But she did. She would. Someday. If they went any further. She owed any man the courtesy of deciding whether or not he could live with what she'd done. Jack sure as hell hadn't been able to. But she'd do it again. In a heartbeat.

Decker made a grumpy sound. 'Dammit, woman, you're thinking too loud. Swallow or spit it out, but don't chew it to death.'

She stared up at him. 'That's revolting.'

He smiled smugly. 'But you aren't thinking about what you were thinking about anymore.'

'You give me a headache, Decker.'

'Then I'll rub it away.' He pulled her close to him again, one hand massaging the back of her head, making her moan. 'Hush that moaning or the doc will think we're hanky-pankying and she'll come back to investigate.'

She laughed quietly. 'Yes, sir.'

'That's better,' he said, humor in his voice. 'Sshh now. Get some sleep while you can.'

She rubbed her cheek against his chest. 'You too.'

'Not in that torture device. I'll sleep on the couch.'

'Or . . . you could stay here,' she offered tentatively.

He immediately slid down so that his head was on the pillow. 'Thought you'd never ask.' He fixed her blanket burrito so that she lay chastely at his side and closed his eyes. 'Go to sleep. No loud thinking.'

'Yes, sir.' She slid her hand under his shirt, which was another button-up style. Except that he hadn't buttoned it up. It hung open, displaying every ridge and ripple of muscle, including a six-pack that was as close to heaven as a woman could hope for. Avoiding the bandage that covered his healing wounds, she caressed his smooth chest, petting him, feeling his rumble of approval tickling her palm. 'Decker? The light's still on.'

Eyes closed, he fumbled for the switch at the base of the lamp on the nightstand. A second later, the room was plunged into darkness, the only illumination the red glow of the digital clock. Carefully she pushed up on her elbow so that she could look at him. The clock's glow reflected off the gold of his hair, giving it a strawberry tinge. His face was in shadow, but she could still see the strong jaw, the sharp cheekbones, and the nose that was slightly less than straight – and covered by a surprising smattering of freckles. He looked rugged and boyish all at once.

Her gaze dropped to his mouth. Firm and soft. His mouth had been soft. She still couldn't believe she'd kissed him like that. She wasn't sure what had come over her.

But she was glad she'd taken the initiative. She'd needed to know. Now she did.

He'd rocked her with a single kiss, just like Johnnie had. Did people get second chances like this? Really? It seemed too good to be true. *I guess time will tell.* For now, she planned to enjoy the anticipation. Because Decker made her want things she hadn't wanted in so very long. Things she'd thought she'd never want again after telling Johnnie goodbye. But now she wanted.

She wanted those big hands on her skin. All of her skin. And that piece he'd been packing ... *Mother Mary.* He'd been so damned hard when she'd sat on his lap that she'd needed to get up to keep from grinding against him, from putting that iron ridge to good use.

Her gaze dropped lower and her breath caught. He'd changed out of the khaki shorts he'd been wearing into a loose-fitting pair of sweats. *Thank you, God.*

Because he was hard again and the sweats did nothing to disguise the fact. *That* was what she'd felt in the kitchen earlier. *That's for me.*

Because of me. Face growing hot, she winced at a little throb in her lip. She'd been biting it as she stared.

Her fingers flexed once before she tightened them into a fist. How would he feel in her hand? Her mouth? Her body? She shivered at the thought. He'd be gentle sometimes, but he'd also be rough. Either way, he'd be amazing. She just knew it.

She sucked in a breath when the object of her fascination suddenly bobbed, accompanied by a harsh, shuddering exhale next to her ear.

Her face, already flushed, now flamed. *Busted.* Slowly she dragged her gaze up his body to meet blue eyes that . . . smoldered. Without saying a word, he shoved his fingers into her hair, grabbing a handful and pulling her into a kiss so hot she thought she'd combust. She gripped the back of his head, following his lead when he used her hair to angle her head, perfecting the fit of her lips over his. He licked at her lips and she opened for him without a second thought. He licked up into her mouth, tasting her. Claiming her. Making her whimper.

So much need, all bottled up. *Mine. His. I could have it. I could have all that energy focused only on me.* And she wanted it. She wanted it so much that when he let go of her hair to grab her hand, she didn't question. She just let him. Let him tangle his fingers with hers. Let him drag her hand down his body, to that iron ridge that strained against the soft fabric of his sweats.

He let go of her hand, releasing her a scant inch away from his erection. His hips surged, but he left the decision up to her.

Breathing hard, she lifted her head enough to see his face. His eyes were clenched shut, his jaw taut. His lips moved, but no sound emerged. *Please. Touch me.*

He hadn't needed to beg. She took her hand down the rest of the way, closing around him, only the thin layer of fabric between her palm and his throbbing cock. She squeezed experimentally, and he arched his back, groaning his pleasure.

'God. Kate.'

'Sshh.' She kissed him again to quiet him down. All they needed was for the night guard to investigate. Or, even worse, Dani. *This is probably not on her list of recovery strategies.* But Kate didn't care.

Couldn't care. Because Decker was rolling his hips, thrusting into her hand, growling deep in his throat.

He was . . . *God.* She shuddered when he groaned again. He was better than she'd imagined. She stroked him firmly, wishing she could feel his skin. Wishing she'd been braver. *Should have snuck under the sweats.* Because she'd missed this. Missed the feel of hot, silky skin sliding over iron.

'I'm . . . God, it's been too long. I'm not gonna . . . Fuck it.' He grimaced, grinding his teeth. Trying to keep from coming too soon.

Fuck it, she echoed, letting him go long enough to yank the sweats past his hips. He growled because she'd let him go, but the growl deepened when she touched his bare skin.

'Kate.' He arched his back again, digging elbows and heels into the mattress, driving into her fist with a hard, steady rhythm that showed her in no uncertain terms what he'd be like if he was inside her right now. And God, she wished he was, because it would feel so, so good.

Next time, she told herself, even though her body was screaming *Now!* This time was for him, but she wanted to give him more than simple release. Wanted him to remember this moment for a long, long time. Wanted him to remember her.

Releasing his cock, she flattened her palm on his stomach, feeling his muscles clenching hard. His eyes flew open, wild with arousal. 'No,' he rasped. 'Don't stop now.'

'Sshh.' Pressing her palm against his stomach, she leaned in to kiss his mouth, gentling him. 'Relax. It's not a race.' She kissed him again, licking into his mouth, swallowing another guttural groan she could feel vibrating against her palm. 'Let me take care of you.'

His swallow was loud in the quiet of the room. 'You're gonna kill me.'

She smiled against his lips. 'But what a way to go.'

He laughed, the sound making her glad that she was still wrapped in the blanket, because if she'd been free, she'd be jumping his bones right now. Drawing a breath that expanded his chest, he kicked off the sweatpants, leaving him bare except for the unbuttoned shirt.

She took a moment to look, then knew she'd never have her fill, because just looking left her breathless. He was truly beautiful, from his broad smooth chest to his long, long legs, bent at the knees, spread wide in invitation. He had scars on his chest, some new, most old. Some straight, some jagged. His legs bore the evidence of war, too, another scar that cut across his left thigh diagonally. And those were only the ones she could see. He had more, she knew. On his back. In his heart. But he was still beautiful. Inside and out.

He exhaled on a ragged sigh. 'Not a race,' he repeated.

'Nope,' she whispered. 'Let me.' Holding his gaze, she swept her hand down his chest, trailing her fingers downward, making sure she avoided his bandages. With one finger she lightly followed the narrow trail of hair down his stomach, down his groin, up his length, smiling at the shudder he couldn't suppress.

'Let me make you feel good,' she said, and he nodded, his eyes closed in concentration, his hands gripping the sheets, his mouth open as he tried to control his breathing. Closing her fist around him again, she began stroking, first long and slow, then fast and hard, intermittently sweeping her thumb over the crown, already wet with the release his body couldn't hold in.

Shuddering violently, he groaned once more, softly this time. 'Kate, please.'

She kissed him again and he let go of his grip on the sheet and grabbed the back of her neck, pulling her in to him, mindlessly kissing her back in a clash of tongues and teeth as his hips began to thrust again. He was close, but she wasn't finished. She needed to make it last as long as she could, needed to give him all the pleasure he'd been missing for four long years.

Well, no, she allowed. Not *all* the pleasure. *All* would include swinging her leg over his hips, mounting him, taking that big, gorgeous erection deep inside her and riding him until they both exploded. And if she got the chance again, she'd jump him in a heartbeat. But not tonight. She wouldn't hurt him for the world, and she didn't have any condoms. So no riding. No exploding. She nearly moaned at the loss, but touch would have to be enough for tonight. From the look on his face, he was more than making do.

313

Touch me, he'd all but begged. No one had done so in such a long time. Too long. No one had touched her either, and God, she'd missed it too. Her body clenched, throbbed, needed. *More.* She needed so much more. She wriggled her hips, trying to get close enough to rub against him, but the damn blanket was in the way. Cursing, she let go of his cock to pry his hand from the back of her neck and splay it over her breast, pressing it hard against her nipple. The blanket was still between them, but the pressure felt good. So good. She heard herself whimper as the contact sent a zing between her thighs and—

She felt the exact moment that Decker's control snapped. Growling deep in his throat, he twisted his hand to get control of hers and dragged it back to his erection. He folded her fingers around him, then gripped her neck and yanked her back down for a kiss that bordered on brutal, unleashing all the ferocity he'd been keeping restrained.

It was rough, but Kate liked rough, and right now, she needed rough. She kissed him back, squeezing her fist when he bucked his hips, holding back the release he sought. He let go of her neck and grabbed the blanket, wrenching it down then pulling desperately at her T-shirt until he reached the bare skin of her stomach. His palm splayed wide for a second before he slid it up to cup her breast, flicking her nipple with his thumb.

Oh God. More. More. More. The plea pounded in her mind, in sync with the pounding of her heart. Her hand stroked him harder, faster, and he pulled away from the kiss, throwing his head back on the pillow.

Watch. She dragged her gaze from her hand on his cock to his clenching abs, then up to his face, sharp and feral as his release barreled through him.

See. Remember. A low groan ripped from his throat as he came, long and hard.

Beautiful. He was so damn beautiful.

He collapsed back, panting, eyes still closed. 'My God,' he breathed. 'Oh my God. Kate.' He shuddered, trembling, his body jerking with aftershocks. 'Thank you.'

She kissed him, gently this time, first on the lips, then on his temple, trying to bring him back down. 'Sshh,' she soothed. 'Let me take care of you.'

He huffed a choked laugh. 'Isn't that what you just did?'

'Mmm. Yes. And it was . . . remarkable. You are a beautiful man, Griffin Davenport.'

He grimaced again, embarrassed now. 'You didn't come.'

'Not this time.' Almost. She almost had, just by watching him. She really wanted to now, but she'd taxed his healing body enough for one night. 'So now you owe me.'

His teeth gleamed in the darkness as he flashed a predatory grin. 'I like that kind of debt.'

'I thought you might.' She struggled out of the blanket and crawled off the bed, but he caught her around the waist with surprising strength, considering he'd just come enough for three men. He pulled her to sit on the narrow strip of mattress between him and the edge of the bed.

'Don't go,' he whispered. 'Stay. Please.'

'I'll be back. I'll get something to . . . you know.' She waved her hand toward his chest, now shiny with his ejaculate.

He smirked at her. 'I thought you weren't a prude.'

She lifted her chin. 'I'm not. I got you off, didn't I?'

He grinned again, slow and sexy. 'I'd have to say that's a definite yes.'

She nodded crisply. 'All right then. So stay here. I'll be right back.'

Her bedroom had an en suite bath, so at least there was no danger of running into Dani or the night guard. Because there was no way in hell she'd be able to swallow the Cheshire Cat grin that had taken over her face.

But she was wrong. The grin faded as she wet a cloth with warm water. The last time she'd done this had been for Johnnie, a few short months before he died. He'd been too weak to make love to her, so she'd loved him as best she could.

She looked in the mirror and wanted to sigh. She looked . . . tired. *Because I am tired.* But there was more in the glass than a tired woman,

315

and that little bit extra made her lean a little closer. Studying her reflection, she glimpsed the ember that flared in her eyes.

She hadn't had any kind of fire in three long years. Until tonight. Until the man who waited for her in the bed they'd share for at least tonight. She wrung out the cloth in the sink, hoping that this lasted for more than one night. She'd missed her own fire.

Decker's eyes were closed when she started to wash his stomach, but they snapped open. He hadn't been asleep. In fact, he was very much awake, his eyes sharp. 'My debt's starting to accrue interest,' he said quietly, sending a shiver down her back.

'At an alarming rate.' She finished the cleanup, then tossed the cloth into a hamper. 'You should arrest me for usury,' she said lightly, but it sounded forced. Because he was ready again. Very ready. She swallowed hard. She wanted it, wanted *him*, but not tonight.

She turned to find his sweatpants, but he grabbed a handful of her T-shirt and held her in place. 'What do you want, Kate?' he asked in a low rumble that melted her from the inside out.

She tried to smile. 'Nothing that we can do tonight. Not gonna risk your stitches.'

He tightened his hold when she tried to pull away. He gripped more of her shirt, reeling her closer, then rolled to his side and up on one elbow, so that his face was level with what had become a bona fide, completely visible wet spot on her sleep shorts. He raised his eyes to hers, then, gazes still locked, drew a deep breath, making it clear that he was scenting her arousal.

Oh God. Her knees went weak.

'What do you want, Kate?' he whispered.

Her cheeks heated. Hell, all of her heated. Her eyes darted to his erection. 'You,' she said honestly. 'I want you. Inside me. But I won't hurt you. I can wait.'

'I can't.' He tugged her shirt hard, catching her when she fell across him. He lifted her easily, arranging her so that she straddled his chest, then gripped the hem of her shirt. 'If this isn't what you want, tell me now.'

His blue eyes were hot and fierce, his lips still swollen from their

316

kisses. And Kate still ached. Deliberately she pulled his hands from her shirt and placed them on her thighs, then pulled the shirt off herself.

He stared up at her, hungry, his fingers clenching convulsively on her thighs. He was breathing hard again, his chest rising and falling. His fingers clenched once more before skimming up her body and closing over her breasts.

She closed her eyes and simply enjoyed as he fondled and teased, rolling her nipples between thumb and forefinger, gasping when he pinched lightly. 'You like that?' he whispered, and she nodded, unable to say a word because her throat had thickened.

It felt so good she wanted to cry.

It had been so long since anyone had touched her. Like she was beautiful and vital and necessary. The warmth of his hands left her breasts and slid up her back, pressing her forward. She let herself fall, grabbing onto the edges of his pillow, gasping again when the tip of his tongue teased one taut nipple before sucking it into his mouth.

He let her go long enough to push her hair out of the way so that he could see her face. 'Open your eyes, Kate. Watch me.'

She opened her eyes as he slowly closed his lips over her breast, the sight blurry until she blinked. He thumbed her cheeks, wiping them dry. 'What's this? Why the tears?'

'It's . . . it's been so long. It's overwhelming. But don't stop.'

His smile was sharp and dark and full of understanding. 'Then keep your eyes open.' He sucked her in again, hard, tonguing her nipple with enough force that she shuddered before releasing her to do the same to the other breast. His hands dropped to her thighs, gliding up and down, going higher each time, brushing up under the hem of her shorts, teasing the elastic of her panties, but never touching where she really wanted him.

By the time he dropped his head back to the pillow, she was shaking, she wanted him so badly. Her cheeks were wet but her panties were wetter.

He'd held her eyes the whole time and now he smiled again, looking like a blue-eyed wolf on the prowl. At some point she'd started rocking her hips, trying to relieve the pressure between her legs, but she couldn't get the angle right. He gripped her butt, holding her still, making her whimper in frustration.

'I'm going to taste you now,' he said, and she shuddered hard, her body jerking involuntarily. 'Don't worry. I won't leave you like this. Okay?' She nodded unsteadily. 'Good,' he murmured soothingly. 'Now sit back. I won't let you fall.'

She leaned back to find that he'd bent his knees, making his body into a chair.

'Lift up,' he ordered softly, and she did, sucking in a breath when he pulled her shorts and panties down to her knees. He bent one of her legs, then the other, pulling her shorts completely off, leaving her naked and . . . so damn horny. She reached behind her, knowing he was fully erect and probably throbbing, but he grabbed her wrist, still gentle with her. 'Don't touch me. I won't be able to stop myself.' He lifted a brow. 'And you'll have to explain any blown stitches to Dani.'

She blushed, making him chuckle. Then he sobered, his eyes taking a slow, thorough journey over her body. His throat worked as he tried to swallow. 'You're perfect.'

She started to deny it, but stopped herself. He looked perfect to her, scars and all. Denying him the same would cheapen the moment. For both of them. 'Thank you.'

His hands burned a path up the inside of her thighs, stopping millimeters short of what should have been his goal. She hissed a warning and he chuckled again, darkly this time.

He cupped her ass and, lifting her, hauled her to the top of his chest, where he draped her thighs over his shoulders and tilted her forward so that she straddled his face. And then he ripped a strangled cry from her throat because *finally* he was touching her.

God. He was touching her. Licking her. Tasting her. Driving her insane. She drove her fingers into his hair and held on, pulling him closer.

He pulled back, his eyes hot, his lips shiny. 'I want to fuck you so bad,' he whispered hoarsely. 'Next time, Kate. Okay? We'll get condoms and . . . next time. Okay?'

She nodded breathlessly. 'Yes.' Her voice cracked and she didn't care. 'Fine. Just . . . don't stop. *Please.*'

'Yes, ma'am.'

She leaned her head back and let her eyes close and . . . *felt.* She felt beautiful and desirable and sexual. *Finally.* After so long, she *felt* again.

He seemed to know what she needed and gave it to her. And gave and gave some more. He sucked and licked, parting her with his fingers so that he could get closer still. He stabbed her with his tongue and reached up and fondled her breasts, and she was so close. So close.

And then he coordinated his attack, nipping her with his teeth while he pinched her nipples, sending her over the edge into freefall. She was flying, weightless, surrounded by light, the pleasure almost too big to contain. And then it *was* too big. It was too much. She was crashing into the sea, where a giant wave pulled her under and all the light turned dark.

And then she was in his arms, shaking. Crying. Clutching him like he was a life preserver.

'Sshh.' He was rocking her, soothing her, stroking her hair. 'It's okay. It's okay.'

She drew a shaky breath, swiping at her wet face. 'Oh God. Oh my God. What was that?'

'Breaking dam,' he said dryly. 'Terrified townsfolk. Stampeding wildebeests, even.' He kissed the top of her head. 'Otherwise known as an orgasm that was long overdue.'

'Holy shit,' she whispered. 'The first part was amazing. But then . . .'

'It was too much,' he said quietly. 'I guess we'll have to make sure you don't go too long before the next one. Wouldn't want you to get all built up like that again.'

Her lips curved. 'You're so altruistic.'

'Aren't I though?' He yawned so wide that his jaw cracked, then he slipped from the bed. 'I'll be back. I have to clean myself up. You weren't the only one who came just now,' he added with a jaunty grin. 'If you hear a thud, come help me up. Otherwise, just stay here.'

She heard the shower running and briefly contemplated joining him, but decided against it when her body would not move. She'd almost fallen asleep on top of the blanket, stark naked, when he came back and carefully lifted her and tucked her under the cover.

'Sleep with me?' she asked drowsily.

'Absolutely,' he said softly, getting in beside her, spooning behind her.

Fifteen

Mallory made her way clumsily down the stairs to the kitchen to make a pot of coffee before taking on her morning Roxy chores. She hadn't slept well last night.

She still couldn't get the sound of JJ's screams out of her mind. He'd tortured her for the better part of three hours. Which Mallory figured he'd done partly to make sure that Mallory knew he could and would. He'd been intimate with JJ. She'd fed him information about his drug customers who'd shown up in the ER because they'd OD'd. JJ had made sure that those customers had not survived to tell anyone who'd sold them the drugs. *JJ had been useful.*

Mallory had no idea how many people JJ had killed for him. But he'd forgotten all of that at the end, judging by the way the woman had screamed.

And screamed and screamed. Either she'd finally passed out or he'd gotten what he wanted and finished her off, because the screaming had stopped at about three a.m.

It had been a warning. *Cross me and this can happen to you too.* Hands shaking, Mallory spooned coffee into the filter and started the machine. Could he know what she was planning? How could he know?

Would it stop her if he did?

She hung her head, shoulders bowing as she drew a deep breath. Mallory had been through hell, but the agony that he'd visited on JJ for hours? She wasn't sure if she could endure that.

She sent a silent prayer upward. *Give me courage.*

Although prayers hadn't helped JJ last night. Nor any amount of begging and pleading.

Mallory straightened resolutely and turned to get a coffee cup from the cabinet. And that was when she saw them, lined up by the back door.

Three suitcases. Hard-shell plastic. Black. One large, one small, and one medium. She'd never seen them before, but instinctively she knew what they were. She clenched her teeth, trying to forget the sounds that had followed JJ's final silence.

An electric saw. High-pitched and whining. She'd tried to tell herself that it wasn't a saw. That it was a vacuum cleaner or a carpet cleaner or anything but what she'd known it really was.

'No.' It was a whimper and it had come from her lips. Because she knew she was looking at what was left of JJ. It was another warning.

Knees wobbling, she staggered to the trash in time to throw up. *Cross me and this can happen to you.* 'God. Oh God.'

Clutching the sides of the trashcan, she pushed to her feet and made her way to the sink, where she washed out her mouth and splashed water on her face. It was then that she saw the note, taped to the window overlooking the backyard. Printed on a printer. He rarely wrote notes by hand. Just in case, he'd always say with a laugh that wasn't funny at all. *Evil.* It was evil.

And now he wanted Mallory to be evil too. *Again.* Her hands were shaking so badly that she had to try twice to grab the paper. When she finally did, she put the note on the table and sank into a chair to read it, trying not to look at those suitcases.

Good morning, Mallory! :-) I hope you slept well, my dear. I have an errand for you this morning, so get to it as quickly as possible. Take the three suitcases by the door, put them in the trunk of your car (which has been lined with a plastic tarp, just in case!), and drive them to the parking lot of the motel by the highway. The one with the tacky gorilla on its roof. I'm sure you know the one I mean. Look for a blue Honda Civic and use the key tied to the handle of the smallest suitcase to open its trunk. Transfer the contents of your trunk to the Honda's trunk, then close it up tight. Leave the key in the Honda's ignition. Leave all the doors unlocked and the driver's-side window open. Then return home.

Later, when you go to the grocery store for the cream, also pick up the following items: hot dogs, hamburgers, buns, large Vidalia onions – so that you can make those onion rings you do so well – frozen French fries, ice cream, and all the toppings. You know what to do. Oh, and get a box of microwave popcorn – my guests and I will be watching movies tomorrow.

xoxoxo

Mallory swallowed hard as her eyes fell to the bottom of the page. The printer had reproduced a photograph of a child in black and white, purposely blurred so that no one would recognize the face. No one but the sister who still loved her. Her throat thick, Mallory traced the photo of Macy with a trembling finger. Her baby sister was nine. Old enough soon.

Too soon. And his guests . . . They would be the kids who'd come here last Saturday. He was showing them movies already. He wasn't supposed to do that for another few weeks. This group was being herded through his grooming program faster than the others had been.

All the others. I can't let it happen. Not again. But . . .

She slapped her hands to her ears so that she didn't hear JJ's screams, but it was no use. They were in her head. Forever. *I can't do it. I can't. I can't.*

She would die. She would end up like JJ. Boxed in suitcases and left in the sun to rot.

But only if you get caught. So don't get caught.

Again she read the list of items she was to buy at the grocery store, then stared at the blurry photo and knew that she couldn't let that group of kids become the next Sunshine Suzies. She knew she had to protect Macy. Even if it meant ending up in a cheap set of hard plastic luggage.

So don't get caught.

Cincinnati, Ohio,
Friday 14 August, 7.05 A.M.

Kate jogged across the field, still wet from the rain they'd had the night before, which, dammit, would have probably washed away a lot of usable evidence. She joined the two men already at the scene, both crouched next to a body slumped against a car, their heads nearly touching. Two cousins, one dark, one bright white. Both starkly handsome.

But all she could think about was the golden man she'd left in her borrowed bed. Decker had roused slightly when her phone had rung, summoning her to the crime scene, but she'd kissed him, covered him up and ordered him back to sleep. That he'd obeyed was a sign of how much he'd exhausted himself the night before.

But boy, was she glad he had. The sight of him at the height of his pleasure would be an image she'd keep forever, even if they never had another stolen interlude. But she sure hoped they did. Just the thought of all that energy – and that beautiful body – made her shiver. And want. God, did she want.

But work came before play, especially since the man who was responsible for this scene had nearly killed Decker and was unlikely to give up. She stopped next to the two men, who were visually examining the body of a Caucasian woman in her early forties. 'Eileen Wilkins?' she asked.

Crouching near the body, Deacon looked up with a short nod and a vaguely uncomfortable squint. He wasn't wearing his shades and the sun was starting to peek over the horizon. Kate crouched so that they were at eye level and caught the quick smile of appreciation.

'In the flesh,' Adam Kimble said grimly. He thumbed over his shoulder to the car. 'And her boy toy Roy.'

'Ah, shit,' she muttered. 'Roy too?'

'Roy first,' Deacon said.

Kate rose to look into the car's open window. The seat was reclined all the way, making the victim appear asleep. He was a giant of a man, broader and more muscular than Decker, even. Had to weigh two-thirty, two-fifty, easily.

324

Steroids, check, she thought. His face was still caught in a grimace, but his massive shoulders had relaxed. 'He's been dead a while.'

'I figure at least eighteen hours,' Deacon said. 'Rigor's fading. His fingers are still stiff, but the arm and leg muscles are pliant.'

Because the larger muscles stiffened first, then relaxed first after full rigor had been achieved. She dropped back into a crouch to look at Eileen. The woman had a bullet wound to the arm and another in her throat. She was wearing a bulletproof vest and a tactical helmet. 'She's still stiff as a board,' Kate noted.

Adam nodded. 'So, maybe twelve, fifteen hours?'

Kate did the math. 'The attempt on Decker's life was at noon. Roy would have been dead.'

'So this was what forced Eileen to drug Davenport?' Deacon asked with a frown.

'I don't know.' Kate worried her lower lip with her teeth. 'According to the nurse's assistant I talked to, Eileen really didn't like Roy any more. I got the impression that getting rid of him would be a blessing, not something she'd risk her career to stop. Which makes me wonder why she's here at all. If she cared about him, I can see her coming to check on him if she was told he was here. But she didn't care about him.'

'She expected trouble, for sure.' Deacon pointed at the helmet and vest. 'But she still came.'

'Maybe there was something else that she wanted enough to risk her life?' Kate mused.

'I doubt we'll find it, whatever it was,' Adam said. 'She was lured here with the promise of it, so I doubt he left it here.'

'Dammit,' Kate muttered. 'I haven't had enough coffee for this. How did you find the scene?'

'Roy's car had a theft recovery system installed,' Adam said. 'I put in the request yesterday for Eileen's car, but didn't think about Roy's until I talked to some of his friends at the gym this morning.'

Kate's brows lifted. 'What time were you at Roy's gym this morning?'

'Five a.m., give or take a few minutes.'

Deacon regarded his cousin with concern. 'Did you sleep at all?'

325

'Yeah,' Adam said shortly. 'Stop,' he added when Deacon looked like he was going to push. 'I'm not going to implode on you again, okay? I'm dealing.'

Deacon frowned like he wanted to say more, but he nodded anyway. 'Okay. What did Roy's buddies tell you?'

'That this car was his prized possession. And that he was getting plenty of sex on the side. Eileen was his meal ticket only. His buddies were worried about him, that she'd done something to him. The guy at the front desk this morning called the guy on duty last night to see if Roy had shown up, but he hadn't. Apparently his car was his god and the gym was his church.'

'That *she'd* done something to *him*?' Kate shook her head. 'He's twice her size.'

'But "he had to sleep sometime" was what his friends said.' Adam shrugged. 'And that she was supplying him with opioids.'

'That's what she used to drug Decker,' Kate said. 'Did you find any in her house?'

'Oh yeah. Lots of needles, too.' Adam scowled. 'In her kid's room as well. He'd been filching from her stash and from Roy's. Eileen had a dozen little vials, some nearly full, some with just a few drops.' He took out his phone and looked through his photos. 'Here.' He showed Kate and Deacon the photo of a vial labeled 'Dilaudid'. 'I submitted everything to the lab. They're checking it against what was in Davenport's IV bag from yesterday. This stuff is powerful. Four times stronger than morphine. Davenport was lucky you got there when you did.'

Kate drew a breath, not wanting to consider the alternative. *Shit.*

'He's okay,' Deacon said quietly, soothing her as he'd always been able to do. 'Right?'

Her mouth curved before she could stop it, and Deacon gave her a look of disbelief. 'You've got to be kidding, Kate. Really?'

Adam scoffed. 'Like you weren't on Faith like white on rice minutes after meeting her.'

Kate pursed her lips, trying not to smile. 'Oh my God, Adam. He is actually blushing.'

'Ah, that's nothin',' Adam said. 'I got stories that'll—'

'Let's get back to the Eileen and Roy Show, shall we?' Deacon interrupted, disgruntled.

The three of them sobered. 'Right,' Kate said with a nod. 'So Roy gets here first. Lured by, I assume, this Professor character. Did you see the memo on that? Zimmerman sent it out after we met at the morgue last night.'

Both men nodded. 'The Professor sold coke to Sidney Siler,' Deacon said. 'And steroids to Roy as well, apparently. Finding Sidney's spy pen was good work, by the way. At least we know why she was killed.'

'Even if it means that we got nothing of Alice's to go on now,' Adam said glumly. 'I hate it when the bad guys don't keep written records.'

He sounded so put-upon that Kate nearly smiled. 'Decker had heard of the Professor,' she said. 'Sometimes he dealt directly and sometimes he sold to other dealers, like Alice and her father. Alice and her father didn't like him because he cut into their profits when he sold direct.'

'Why would they tolerate that?' Kimble asked. 'They killed a lot of people for a lot less.'

'Decker said it was because the Professor's product was so good that it was requested by name. If they killed him, they'd lose a valuable supply source. I imagine they also put up with him because they couldn't find him to kill him,' she added dryly. 'On account of the disguise.'

'Which means he's going to be harder for us to find,' Deacon said with a sigh. 'Especially now that he knows we're connecting dots.'

'He goes under from time to time, according to Sidney's roommate. Months can go by when he doesn't sell anything.'

'Which means he either invests his drug money well,' Adam said, 'or he has another source of income.'

Kate considered it. 'Entirely possible. Goes along with our teacher or chemist theory. He had to have crossed paths with McCord at some point, because they partnered up. We need to figure out where.' She stood up and studied the dead Roy. 'He's a huge man.'

'A gorilla,' Adam agreed with a grunt as he came to his feet. 'Must've taken an elephant dose to down him.'

'Exactly what I was thinking.' Kate unclipped her flashlight. 'Carrie Washington will be able to confirm it, but I'm thinking he died right here in this seat. I wouldn't want to drag him here after he was dead.' Leaning inside the open window, she flashed her light at Roy's nostrils and saw the reflection off a few crystals that remained on the inside of his nose. 'He'd snorted something right before he died. Just like Sidney. I wonder if this Professor made him take cyanide or ricin, like Sidney and Alice.' Or . . . She shone the light on his exposed arms. 'Oh yeah. There we go.' She backed out of the window and handed the light to Deacon. 'Take a look at his arm, right above the bend of his elbow. You see the little prick?'

Deacon gave her a wry glance over his shoulder. 'I thought I was looking at his arm.'

Kate rolled her eyes. 'Why did I miss you again?'

Deacon flashed her a grin. 'Because I'm awesome,' he said smugly, then handed the light to Adam. 'And so are you, Kate. He was injected right as he died. The blood is caked around the needle mark.'

Kate smiled at the compliment. She *had* missed him. 'Carrie will have to run blood tests, but I'm thinking . . . It could have been his steroids, but why inject him with that? An overdose of steroids wouldn't be likely to kill him. So he was probably injected with something else. Something stronger. Maybe like Dilaudid – just like they used trying to kill Decker. And we know that Eileen was stealing Dilaudid. What if the Professor knew that too? What if that's what he used to lure her here?'

'Vials of the same drug she'd stolen?' Adam asked. 'Possible.'

'The serial numbers would match up with the hospital's records,' Kate said, sure of it now. 'That would be enough to get her to come here – and it would explain why she expected to be shot at.'

Deacon had dropped back into a crouch and was lightly patting the pockets of Eileen's bulletproof vest. 'Bingo. There's vials in this one. Two from the feel of it.' He peeled the pocket flap back, giving the Velcro a tug.

'Careful,' Adam cautioned. 'Carrie'll have your head if you disturb the body.'

'I know, I know,' Deacon muttered. He slid one of the vials from the pocket with the skill of a professional pickpocket. 'Yep. Dilaudid. Eileen came to get the vials back, so that she couldn't be linked to Roy's death, not so that she could help him. Cold.'

'Doesn't sound like there was a great deal of love lost between them.' Kate picked her way around Roy's car slowly, so as not to contaminate the scene. 'So how did this happen? Roy meets the Professor here and buys some coke to snort. How does this Professor guy get the Dilaudid? Did Roy bring it? Did he have any of those vials in his room?'

Adam shook his head. 'Just coke and 'roids, but he could have taken them from Eileen. She didn't have them locked up.'

'Which is how her son got them,' Kate said, disgusted. 'God, it's not fair that some people get to be parents. So either Roy brought them or the Professor had access to her home and stole them. More likely Roy brought them, since he came here voluntarily by all accounts.'

'He's a big guy,' Adam said doubtfully. 'He wouldn't have just agreed to be injected and I don't see any evidence that he was restrained.'

'Sidney took a mixture of coke and ket,' Deacon said. 'Ket would have immobilized her while the cyanide did its job. Roy snorted something, just like Sidney did. We'll have Carrie check for coke, ket, any of the big hitters. Hell, I would have immobilized him before touching him at all. Next question, why not cyanide here? Or why not use Dilaudid on Sidney?'

'We almost missed the cyanide in Sidney,' Kate said. 'If we hadn't had the photo from the jail's visitors' file, we wouldn't have recognized her.'

'*You* wouldn't have,' Deacon corrected. '*I* would have missed it entirely. I'd already looked at that file before I met you at the morgue and I didn't recognize Sidney as the woman who'd last visited Alice in jail.'

Kate shrugged away the praise. 'My point was that we would

have missed the cyanide and Carrie might have as well. The red skin side effect was masked by Sidney's natural skin tone. Maybe he chose the cyanide because we wouldn't notice. Or because he happened to have some left over after having Alice killed. He didn't use the Dilaudid on Sidney because she didn't have track marks. It would have looked fake. He wanted it to look like she'd OD'd on coke.'

'He knew Eileen and Roy would be found,' Adam said quietly. 'Why wouldn't he try to hide them?'

'Eileen's is a punishment killing,' Kate said. 'Which means he knew that she'd failed. When did the attack hit the media?'

'Hospital security kept it out of the press through the end of the shift,' Deacon said. 'Eileen was probably dead by then. Which means the Professor has another source of information in the hospital.'

Kate frowned. 'Trouble is, hospital grapevines are frickin' notorious. It wouldn't have taken long for the news to spread, especially since Decker had been a topic of conversation all along. We don't know who would have told this Professor person that Decker didn't die. Terrific. We have another crazy-assed medical professional on the loose.'

'I'm glad Dani is out of that place,' Adam said. 'I didn't like them because they treated her like shit, but now I'm glad because it could have become dangerous for her.'

Deacon scowled. 'She's going to work at the clinic at the Meadows. That's not exactly safe.'

Kate snapped her fingers. 'Roy and Eileen Show, guys.' She picked her way around Roy's car, careful not to disturb anything. 'So Roy shows up to meet the Professor of his own free will, vials in hand. Why? Was he going to sell them? Trade them?'

'Possible,' Adam said again. 'He was killed in his seat, so does that mean the Professor came to sit in his car?'

Kate peered in the closed window. 'Maybe. If he did, and if he left anything behind, CSU will find it.' She did a slow three-sixty, looking around. 'Why here? I mean, I know why not his usual haunt, because it's a crime scene now. But why here? How did he know about it? It's part of the state park.'

Adam and Deacon shared a look and Adam shrugged. 'Possible.'

'What?' Kate asked.

'State parks in Kentucky and this part of Ohio?' Adam said. 'Especially in the corners where no one goes? Big for pot. Climate's perfect.'

'We'll get some drug-sniffing dogs back here,' Deacon said. 'It would be nice to get a sample of his weed for comparison if we find a pot plot.'

'We have a sample,' Kate said with satisfaction. 'Chelsea – Sidney's roommate – bought weed from him. I found it when I searched her apartment last night after I was finished with Sidney's folks at the morgue.' And before she'd gone grocery shopping for Decker. And before all the stuff that followed.

Focus, Kate. Her mind snapped back. 'But we're not going to catch him here now. I wouldn't come back here if I were a bad guy, even for the best pot plot ever. Not with cops crawling all over the place.'

'Maybe not,' Deacon allowed. 'But we're creating a profile here. And if we're able to figure out how old his plants are, we'll know how long he's been growing. Another detail.'

She smiled at him. 'You're good with those.' Suddenly impatient, she picked her way back to Eileen's body. 'He's a fucking good shot,' she commented, looking at Eileen's mutilated throat. 'She drove here, got out, saw Roy was dead, then came over to get the vials.'

Adam crouched by the body. 'She was facing the car when she was hit by the first shot. It was a through-and-through, because the bullet got embedded in the door.' He pointed at the empty hole. 'Paint's been chipped away. He pried the bullet out.'

'So Eileen is shot facing the car,' Kate continued. 'She spins around, maybe planning to run, but the second bullet hits her in the throat before she can.'

'That's a through-and-through too,' Adam said. 'The exit hole is at the back of her neck. But she was standing up at the time, because there are no other bullet holes in the car.' He backed away to stand behind Roy's car, drawing a trajectory in the air with his finger. 'Bullet should have hit the ground. If we're lucky, he didn't find it.'

'Where did it come from?' Deacon asked, looking around. 'Where was he standing?'

Kate pointed to the treeline. 'If it'd been me, I would have stood there, in those trees. Eileen came anticipating trouble, so she made it harder for him. Like I said, he's a good shot to get her in the throat like that, especially if she was intending to make a break for her car. He had it timed just right.'

Deacon slid on his wraparound shades, the sun now over the horizon. 'So we know he's a good shot, that we need to search for a spent rifle cartridge somewhere over there,' he pointed beyond Roy's car, 'and that he probably has at least one more mole inside the hospital. Have we talked to the son yet?'

'Not yet,' Adam said. 'The uniforms I put outside his house found him last night trying to sneak in. He was wet and shaky and jonesin', so I called for the medics. They took him to Children's and I put a guard outside his door. I'm trying to find him a room in juvie rehab and Meredith is going to be present later this morning when I interview him. Hopefully Children's will have gotten him stable – at least enough so that he can answer some questions.'

'Good that Meredith will be there,' Kate said, feeling sympathy for a kid whose mother had let him down so terribly. 'He's going to need therapy when he finds out his mother is dead. We need to be getting to Zimmerman's office. It's nearly time for his morning meeting.'

'I'll stay here until the ME and CSU show up,' Adam said. 'Meet you two there.'

'I'll get some decent coffee,' Deacon offered. 'You caffeinating this morning, Kate?'

'Sure. I got some sleep last night, so a small cup of coffee won't send me over the edge. Just no espresso, okay? That stuff makes my heart go into overdrive.'

Deacon walked her to her car. 'So you got sleep last night?' he asked, too casually.

She frowned at him. 'What?'

He shrugged. 'Nothing. Just thinking that you look a little more rested. It's good.' He slipped off his shades to meet her eyes squarely. 'For now, it's good. Just be careful, okay?'

Kate's cheeks heated. 'How do you always know stuff about me?'

He flashed a quick grin. 'I told you – I'm awesome. And I looked the same way after I met Faith.' His grin faded. 'Adam didn't like her and Scarlett didn't quite trust her. But I knew. As soon as I saw her, I knew she was mine.'

She wanted to say, *Me too. That's how I felt when I first laid eyes on Decker.* But she didn't, because Deacon was giving her a steady, worried look that managed to make her . . . unsure. 'I'm glad for you two,' she said instead, meaning every word. 'Really, really glad.'

'I know you are. But I also know that your heart isn't as ironclad as you'd have everyone believe. You're in a vulnerable place right now. If Davenport can calm you, that's good. Just understand that these guys who go undercover . . . they're good at disengaging. You might think you've got your course set for happily ever after, when he'll suddenly exit stage right without a second thought. I'll pick up the pieces if I have to, but I'd really rather not have to.'

With that he slid his shades back on, got into his SUV, and drove away. Kate followed in her own car more slowly, wondering if he could be right. Her gut told her no, that Decker seemed to want roots. But maybe it was because she wanted them so badly herself.

She missed having roots. She missed having someone to come home to.

And she was being ridiculous. She'd known the man a day, really, because the time in the coma simply didn't count. *I'm going to slow this down. I'm going to see what happens.*

I am such a damn liar. Because even as she made the vows, she was counting the minutes before she saw him again. *Shit.*

Cincinnati, Ohio,
Friday 14 August, 8.45 A.M.

Decker was pretty proud of himself. He'd showered all by himself, shaved, eaten every bite of breakfast the doc had put on his plate and still had time to work out some of the coded entries in the ledgers he'd reproduced.

And he'd managed to get to Zimmerman's conference room, thanks to Agents Troy and Triplett. The two men had come to his assistance that morning, badgering Dani about allowing him to attend the meeting, until she'd thrown up her hands in surrender. They'd also made sure he'd arrived at the field office safe and sound.

When he'd thanked them, they'd been pragmatic. He had information they needed to bring in the last of the traffickers – one who peddled kids. Catching McCord's mystery partner was a high priority for them all.

'What. The. Hell?' Zimmerman came into the conference room and stared. 'What are you doing here, Griff?'

'Working,' Decker said evenly. 'The doc said it was okay.'

'No she didn't,' Dani said sourly from the other end of the table. 'The doc was steamrolled. The doc said you needed to stay in bed one more day. So don't you go putting words in the doc's mouth, Agent Davenport. Got it?'

'Yeah,' Decker grumbled. 'I got it. Okay, the doc graciously allowed me to leave the safe house as long as I stay in the wheelchair and don't overdo it. Better?'

Dani scowled at him. 'What*ever*. I don't know why you even need me. You're obviously healed,' she said sarcastically. 'It's a miracle!'

'I don't think Dr Novak is happy with you this morning, Griffin,' Zimmerman said mildly.

'You will be, though,' Decker said. He held up the notepad he'd filled with the traffickers' code, but Zimmerman ignored it, taking the seat next to his wheelchair.

'You really shouldn't be here, son.'

Decker tightened his jaw. He wasn't Zimmerman's son. Even

though he understood the man was trying to help, his attitude was patronizing, and Decker didn't do patronizing well.

'I really need to get back to work, sir. With all due respect, you don't know my body.' Only Kate did, but Decker shoved that thought back down to where it wouldn't show. He hoped. He got hard every time he thought about those few minutes of searing pleasure the night before. He was sure that going without for four years had played a part in the intensity of his orgasm, but that it was Kate's hand touching him . . .

Focus, Davenport. For God's sake, you're not a goddamn teenager.

'Which is why we brought in a *doctor* to evaluate you,' Zimmerman said, still patronizing.

Dani sighed. 'I can observe him as well here as in the condo. And if we weren't here, he'd be up walking laps like he did most of the night. He was even talking about using the treadmill.'

'I thought walking was good,' Zimmerman said, as if Decker weren't sitting next to him.

'It is, but not if he overdoes it. He can't do that here, so it's not a bad idea to let him sit still for a bit. He can walk when he gets back.'

'His wounds?' Zimmerman asked.

'Healing nicely. Staying in the coma a few extra days did him some good.' Her lips curved, but it was not a nice smile. 'It might have been the only way to keep him compliant.'

Decker glared at her. 'I *am* here, you know. Right. Here.'

'Yes, I know,' Dani said. 'So maybe you're getting an idea of what it's like to be ignored.'

Decker winced. 'I'm sorry. I will be the best patient you could ever ask for after this meeting is over.'

Dani rolled her eyes. 'You said that yesterday, so forgive me if I don't believe you today.' She turned to Zimmerman. 'Bottom line, he probably would have been discharged from the hospital after the weekend. Having him up and around most likely won't do him any harm. Either way, he doesn't need me watching him 24/7. If it's okay, I'd like to use an empty office while you have your meeting.' She patted the messenger bag she'd slung over her shoulder. 'I got a few files in my email this morning. One patient I saw last week is having complications and it's pretty serious. I might need to go into the clinic for a few hours, but I'll make sure Agent Davenport is provided coverage. Meredith Fallon's cousin is a nurse. Her name is Bailey Beardsley and she works with Wendi Cullen. I've known Bailey for several years. She's good people. You won't have to worry. She also has a current background check and fingerprints on file because she's a drug rehab counselor.'

'She sounds like a fine substitute,' Zimmerman said. 'I'll have my assistant show you to an office.' He looked down at the notepad that Decker was tapping impatiently. 'What's all this?'

'I've been writing down what I remember of the traffickers' ledgers. All the customers and suppliers are written in code. I didn't think I had enough entries to wrap my brain around the code last night, but a few hours' sleep seems to have made a difference.' Actually, he thought the orgasm had done more to renew him than the sleep, but he wasn't going to say that out loud. 'If I can get access to decrypting software, I might be able to give you some actual names.'

Zimmerman looked pleased. 'I'll set you up with access after the meeting. I was able to connect to the server remotely from the safe house yesterday, so you shouldn't have any trouble.'

The door from the hallway opened just then, and Zimmerman's people filed in. Decker watched their faces until he saw the one he'd been waiting for. But Kate wasn't any more pleased to see him than Zimmerman had been at first.

'What are you doing here?' she demanded, then turned to Dani. 'He should be resting at least another day!'

Dani put her hands out like a traffic cop. 'Yell at him and his two stooges.' She pointed to Trip and Troy, who both blinked innocently. 'I'm going to another office to work.'

'He looked fine to us,' Troy said when Dani had left the room. 'Chill, Kate. He's a grown man. He's been wounded before. How many times, Decker?'

'An even dozen,' Decker replied. 'I know my limits. Besides, Eileen is dead, right? So she's not coming for me again.'

Kate dropped into a chair and rubbed her face. 'Yeah, but this

Professor asshole isn't likely to give up. You're by no means home free.'

'All the more reason for me to pitch in,' he said quietly.

She looked at his notepad. 'You're cracking the code,' she said, sounding impressed.

At least he'd done something right. 'Workin' on it.'

She glanced up at him apologetically. 'I'm sorry I growled. I was surprised to see you here. I still think you should rest, but I'd be chomping at the bit in your place.'

That made him want to growl right back – the thought of Kate in his place. He had to remind himself that the woman was a better shot than he was. Some men might have found that off-putting, but Decker was relieved. She could take care of herself.

Zimmerman tapped the table. 'Let's get this done, people. We have work to do today.'

Everyone had taken a seat and there wasn't anyone here that Decker didn't know, although he had expected there to be one woman he hadn't met yet. The child psychologist, Meredith Fallon.

Zimmerman realized it at the same moment. 'Where's Meredith?'

Adam Kimble frowned. 'She was right behind us.'

The door to the conference room opened and another redhead hurried in, talking on her cell phone. *This must be Meredith Fallon.* She crossed the room gracefully on four-inch heels that made her as tall as Kate, but that was where the similarity ended. Meredith's hair was a darker red, almost auburn, and her skin was pure peaches and cream.

Kate was much prettier, Decker thought, her features sharper. Her hair every shade of the sunset. Her body was rangier. More athletic. She was exactly the kind of woman he liked. *Lucky for me, then.*

'I'll get the number here,' Meredith said into her cell phone, speaking urgently. 'I want you to call the conference room phone so that I can put you on speaker. I'll get the number and text it to you. Just . . . sit tight.' She hung up.

Zimmerman tore a sheet from Decker's notepad, wrote down a number and gave it to her. 'Who was that?' Zimmerman asked.

'Officer Kendra Cullen.' Meredith texted the phone number as she spoke. 'She's CPD, assigned to patrol. She has a lead I want you all to hear at the same time.'

Both Decker and Troy looked at Kate, who shrugged. 'I don't know what she's talking about,' Kate said as the phone on the table rang.

Zimmerman put it on speaker. 'Officer Cullen? This is Special Agent Zimmerman. I understand you have a lead for us.'

'I think so.' The woman had a deep, husky voice. 'Should I just start talking, or do you have a meeting agenda you need to cover first?'

'Start talking,' Meredith said. She looked at Zimmerman. 'That's okay, yes?'

'You have the floor,' Zimmerman said.

'Thank you. Kendra, this is the meeting of the task force I told you about. In the room are Agents Zimmerman, Novak, Coppola, Troy, Triplett and . . .' Meredith lifted her brows. 'You're Davenport, right?'

'Yes, ma'am,' Decker said politely, and her lips quirked up.

'And Agent Davenport,' Meredith said. 'We also have Detective Kimble from CPD.'

'Is Scarlett not there?' Kendra asked.

'No, she had personal ties to this case, so she's recused herself. Folks, last Saturday Officer Cullen stopped a possible assault in the parking lot of the Glenway Kroger. The victim will be of interest to this group. Kendra, go ahead.'

'I was on break last Saturday and had gone into the Kroger for my lunch. I saw a man of about thirty following and harassing a young woman who was about eighteen. I followed them out to the parking lot where the man had the girl trapped against the trunk of her car, a rusted-out Chevy Impala, back bumper covered with primer. I asked the girl if she needed help, but she said no, that it was a misunderstanding. I got photos of her license plate and that of the man, just in case she filed a complaint later. He called her Sunshine Suzie.'

Adam sucked in a shocked breath. '*What?* Sorry, this is Adam Kimble. What did you say her name was?'

'He called her Sunshine Suzie,' Kendra repeated. 'You know her?'

Adam exhaled, the vein in his temple working overtime. 'I know *of* her. She's famous in kiddie porn circles. She was one of the stars of the child circuit,' he added bitterly. 'She was filmed for about three years, from age twelve to fifteen.'

The atmosphere in the room had grown thick with tension. 'Twelve,' Kate whispered. 'God. What happened when she turned fifteen, Adam?'

Adam shrugged. 'She disappeared. No more movies. At least that's the report I read when I was working Personal Crimes. No one in ICAC realized she was local.'

'She's at least local right now,' Kendra said. 'On Saturday I tried to follow her, but she exited the parking lot before I got to my car. She was fast. I ran both sets of plates – hers and the man's. Hers were stolen and didn't match the car she was driving. His were registered to a Corey Addison. He's also local, lives off of East Galbraith and works downtown. I've already sent his home address to Dr Fallon.'

'So all this happened last Saturday?' Troy asked. 'What happened this morning that prompted your call?'

'She called me,' Kendra said urgently. 'But she didn't know my name. She called the central number yesterday afternoon from a payphone outside of the Kroger in Price Hill. She told the operator that she was doing a project for school and wanted to talk to me – the African-American lady cop who was on duty near Glenway on Saturday. The operator knew something was hinky, so she tried to get more information, but she said the girl was terrified and wouldn't say any more. The operator tracked me down through my duty schedule and left me a message. It was sitting in my mailbox this morning. I called back right away to ask how to reach the girl, but the girl had told the operator that she didn't have a phone. She's supposed to call back from the pay phone as soon as she can. The operator gave the young woman her name, to make sure they connected again and that the girl didn't get someone else.'

Meredith studied the group. 'So, what do we do next?'

'We let her call,' Zimmerman said. 'And we put a plain-clothes cop in the parking lot to watch for her.' He grimaced. 'I assume we can get a photo of her, but God, I don't want to visit that site. I don't want any of us to have to do it.'

'I'll do it,' Adam said quietly.

Meredith shook her head. 'You don't have to. Kendra got a photo and cropped it to show only her face.'

Adam's shoulders sagged, his relief unmistakable. 'Thank you, Kendra.'

'You're welcome,' Kendra said gruffly. 'It wasn't pleasant. I did it on one of the precinct's computers,' she added hesitantly. 'I told my CO why I'd accessed the site. I didn't want to get written up or investigated by Internal Affairs.'

Zimmerman frowned. 'Who's your CO?'

'Captain Berry.'

'Have you told him about the girl trying to reach you yesterday?'

'No, sir. Not yet. I was about to, but Meredith had mentioned there was a task force working on kiddie pornographers, so I called her first.'

'Don't tell your captain just yet,' Zimmerman told her. 'We may have a leak and I want to guard this information. I'll tell Detective Kimble's lieutenant so you're covered.'

'Okay,' Kendra said warily. 'So what else should I do?'

'Go about your duties as you normally do,' Zimmerman said. 'If we need you to do anything differently, the order will come directly from Lieutenant Isenberg.'

'Okay,' she said again, her doubt clear. 'I don't want to lose my job, Agent Zimmerman.'

'You won't. Hopefully we won't need this veil of secrecy for long. This was nice work, Officer. Thank you.'

'You're welcome, sir. Is there anything else you need from me?'

'No. You're dismissed. I'm going to have Dr Fallon text you some more telephone numbers – my direct line as well as those of Isenberg, Kimble, Novak, Troy, and Coppola. If you run into any issues, call one of us as soon as you can.'

'Yes, sir. Thank you.'

'One more thing. If this woman manages to call in from a number other than the Kroger pay phone, does the operator have a way to reach you?'

'Yes, sir. I gave her my cell phone number already.'

'Good. Then have a good day, Officer. Be careful.'

'I always am.' The phone went dead and Meredith leaned back with a sigh.

'I was going to tell you about this young woman this morning, but when I heard she'd called asking for Kenny . . . It seemed important enough to shanghai your meeting.'

Zimmerman smiled at her in a fatherly way. 'You did the right thing. Give me a few minutes to set up surveillance at the Kroger.'

'You need to make it a woman, Agent Zimmerman,' Meredith cautioned. 'This young woman will run from a man.'

'I figured that out for myself,' Zimmerman said, then looked at Kate. 'Do I know everything you're going to discuss?'

Kate nodded. 'You do.'

'Then you go first. I'll be back as soon as I can.'

Sixteen

Cincinnati, Ohio,
Friday 14 August, 8.55 A.M.

'That should do it,' he murmured to himself, looking at the neatly stacked piles on his kitchen table. *DVDs, check.* He'd chosen mostly PG-13 titles, but there were a few R and one NC-17 in the mix. He'd leave them in the stack and let his guests choose. If they chose the R or NC-17 DVDs, it showed that they were willing to break a few rules if given the space.

Nearly every kid he'd ever groomed chose an R or NC-17. They were curious. Sexuality was a natural, human thing to be curious about.

Assuming these four would be equally curious, he'd already replaced one of the R movies with a triple-X. He'd introduce that one into their stack while they were taking a break from the movies to have their lunch outside by the pool. Tomorrow was going to be another scorcher and he'd make sure he kept them out in the sun long enough to get good and hot. Then he'd suggest they take a dip.

Swimsuits, check. He never told the kids to bring one, but always planned for pool play. The suits were a little racy. Just enough to make the girls look sexy and for the boys to notice.

Like any self-respecting adolescent male needed help with that, he thought with an eye roll.

If they weren't aroused after pool play, they would be after having a light snack – which he'd supplement with the party drugs that were *the* reason the kids kept coming back. And also the reason they'd do anything he asked of them, until they were in too deep and wanted out. That was when they disappeared, resurfacing as the property of a collector who wanted his own little porn star. Or *her* own, because a surprising number of his customers were women.

Or if he had no buyers, the quitters were found dead on the street, just another unfortunate overdose case. Either way, they'd live forever on DVD and streaming video.

He tipped an imaginary hat. Many thanks to Alice's brother Sean for helping him set up the e-commerce and video streaming on servers located all over the world. *Where no one can find me.*

It really was the perfect setup.

This group tomorrow, however, would be a little trickier. He'd never worked with so many kids at one time before. Always just one or two. But his client had requested a foursome, so that was what he'd deliver. He'd have to watch the kids carefully and see if any of them were uncomfortable to the point of telling their parents.

Or, more correctly, their *parent*. Not one of the kids came from a normal home, whatever the hell that was anymore. That one parent, or sister, or grandmother, was the reason they were his to begin with. They had granted him access to the kids in return for drugs. They didn't know what he wanted access for, of course. He usually convinced them that he was only interested in helping their kids. In opening the doors that would give them better lives.

He appealed to the parents' greed, their addictions, or even to their pathetic belief that they just needed to get through a rough spot at work, or with their abusive boyfriend, or whatever the newest chaos in their lives happened to be. He told them that he'd fill in, providing a strong role model for their kids while they worked out their own life messes.

He'd do whatever he needed to do, say whatever they needed to hear, so that he could get his hands on their fresh-faced adolescents. Because fresh-faced always brought in more cash. Most of his clients didn't want to see used, old-before-their-time teenagers on film. They wanted it fresh, fun, spirited. They wanted to believe the kids wanted it too. They wanted the fantasy.

And so that's what I give them.

Unfortunately, this time he'd had to cobble together a foursome that was less polished than usual. School was out and people were on vacation, so the soccer moms from the 'burbs with their secret addictions weren't around in their normal droves. In another few weeks, he'd have had the pick of the litter. This job had a time limit, though, with a shortened delivery deadline.

He'd had to pick this foursome from a lower class of addicts and users, harder to do when they'd grown up in trailer parks and projects. But possible. Thanks to the Professor, he knew the addicts who'd sell their kids in a heartbeat for another hit. He'd picked the most functional ones, the ones who still had some semblance of a soul, of optimism for the future of the kids for whom they were responsible. These kids still had a spark of hope. But he had work to do to get them prettied up.

So . . . *Lotions, check. Shampoo, check. Salon stylist . . . not so much.* He glanced up at the ceiling. Roxy's bedroom was just above his head. Roxy had been so good at that, once upon a time. But not anymore.

He needed to find a new stylist who'd come and go without asking questions. Maybe Mallory could be trained. It was something to consider. But that would take time, and he needed this group shiny. Not necessarily today, but within two weeks. He had two weeks to work a miracle, because his client was only going to be in the country for a short time and wanted to leave with his new acquisitions in hand. And he wanted them enthusiastic.

No pressure. It just meant he had to work fast. Speed up the timeline.

And if any of the kids looked like they'd spill the beans about things they'd seen and the 'funny feeling' they'd gotten after eating his 'supplemented snacks'? Well, terrible accidents sometimes happened.

Not here. Not in my house or on my property. But they happened elsewhere. Car crashes were the most effective, especially when their parent or sister or grandmother was driving under the influence. It was pitifully easy to make this happen with the suburban soccer moms who did *all* their activities under the influence. Usually cocaine, although meth was shockingly popular. Too many activities, too little time. Oh, and husbands who wanted them to look like they did on their wedding day. Busy soccer moms were the Professor's bread and butter.

However, the guardians of his newest foursome weren't sub-urban soccer moms. They were simply your garden-variety addicts and would be so much easier to eliminate. It was a wonder they'd lived as long as they had. All he had to do was give the parent, sister, or grandmother a concentrated dose and they'd snort it or shoot it into their veins without his help. He'd make sure the kid took the same drug, even if he had to hold them down to make it happen. Then he'd leave kid and parent in a heap for someone else to find.

The media might notice and they'd wag their heads sadly. *Another overdose. Such a shame. Inner-city issues. Such a shame. So how about those Kardashians?*

And life would go on as if the kid and their parent or sister or grandmother had never existed to begin with. Then he'd choose a new asset. And he would continue making films and fulfilling orders for special clients while he waited for Mallory's little sister to grow old enough to pick up where Mallory had left off. When she did, he'd be making movie magic once again.

He'd taken video of her for years, at birthday parties, holidays. Macy had the same sparkle that Mallory had had, and the camera loved her face. She was genuine and beautiful, exactly how Mallory had been at the same age. She'd grow up to look just like Mallory.

Just like Sunshine Suzie. Nobody had ever sold videos the way Suzie had. Soon he'd be selling like he had before. He'd call Macy 'Suzie' and no one would question him. Relieved that Suzie was back, they'd just download and download and download.

And I'll make lots of money. But that was still at least three years away. Macy was only nine. *Almost ten*, he realized, brightening. Her birthday was in a few weeks.

'Mallory!' he called, smiling when she stumbled into the kitchen, still pale from her morning surprise – the three suitcases that had become JJ's final resting place. He sometimes needed to remind Mallory who was boss. She couldn't be allowed to play games with him like she'd done the night before. Couldn't be allowed to escape into her mind, leaving her body colder than a dead fish.

That was why she was so successful as Sunshine Suzie. I was able to make her enjoy it. Mallory had simply sparkled. And her fans had seen that joy, that *life*, and they'd watched and watched and watched her. It was too bad that Mallory had grown too old.

He studied her face carefully. Her downcast eyes were developing bags. He'd have to give her a Botox injection, stat. She was really aging fast. He found himself hoping that Macy stayed younger-looking longer than her sister had.

'Yes?' Mallory finally asked. He'd been standing there watching her, waiting for her to meet his eyes.

'Have you gone to the store yet?'

She swallowed hard. 'No, not yet.'

'Are you feeling all right, my dear?' he asked with a mocking smirk.

Her eyes flickered, but it was enough of a reaction for now. 'I'm fine. I'll go to the store after I've given Roxy her lunch.'

'Is she going to be up to greeting my guests tomorrow?'

Mallory gave him a look of shocked disbelief, quickly extinguished. 'No,' she said carefully. 'She's really sick. Maybe you should check on her.'

He grimaced. Roxy's room always smelled like a nursing home. 'Maybe we should just plan on telling my guests that my wife is visiting her mother.'

Mallory nodded, her expression flat once again. 'If that's what you think we should do.'

Damn, she was getting good at hiding from him in plain sight. Unacceptable. 'Did you find my list?'

'Yes, I did.'

'And the picture at the bottom?'

'It was blurry. Hard to tell who it was.'

He smiled at her. She was lying. 'Well maybe that's because little Macy is growing up so fast.' Mallory blanched and his smile widened. *Yes.* 'In fact, she has a birthday coming up, so I'd like you to add a few things to the list.'

Mallory's jaw clenched. 'All right. Like what?'

'Makings for a cake. Maybe some pretty bottles of bubble bath, although they wouldn't have those at the grocery store. I'll have to order online. Or better yet, the Kroger out in East Gate is across from one of those home stores. If you go there, you can get the bubble bath afterward. And definitely get a birthday card. I want one that says "For my darling niece".'

It had been a stroke of luck, really, that Mallory's mother had had two daughters. He'd wanted Mallory on sight, but Macy represented power over her. Macy was the one thing on this earth that Mallory loved. A threat to Macy got her immediate attention. And as Macy's dear uncle and godfather, no one would question him assuming custody of the child if anything ever happened to his sister and brother-in-law.

He'd made sure that Mallory understood this. Often.

Mallory's eyes had narrowed, her nostrils flaring as she breathed much faster. Much harder. 'All right,' she said, her voice strained. 'I'll get a card.'

'Oh, and better pick up some more bleach for the guest bath,' he said, and had the satisfaction of watching her purse her lips against nausea. 'I may have left a bit of a mess and I wouldn't want my guests to see it tomorrow.'

A nod. She'd gone a little green.

'And while you're at the home store? Pick up another matched set of hard plastic luggage. Get black. It hides *all* the worst stains.' He leaned into her, pecking her cheek. Enjoying the feel of cold marble under his lips. She was terrified now. *Good.* She'd carry out his bidding exactly. 'Hurry back. We'll have a nice dinner and watch a movie. Together.'

Mallory backed out of the room and ran up the stairs like her clothes were on fire. *Perfect.*

Cincinnati, Ohio,
Friday 14 August, 9.10 A.M.

'Wow,' Decker murmured, still stunned by Kendra's story. Sunshine Suzie popping up now – and at the Glenway Kroger, no less. A glance around the table showed that he was not alone.

'This is unexpected,' Kate said. 'And something of a coincidence.'

Novak nodded. 'I thought the same thing. Why is she coming forward now?'

Decker turned it over in his mind, considering it in context with everything that had happened that week. 'Maybe because of the media coverage of the traffickers' arrests. If the Professor is snipping loose ends for McCord's partner – or if he *is* McCord's partner – he's got to be getting nervous. Maybe she's coming forward because she feels like someone is going to do something about it. Like when one victim accuses her rapist, other past victims add their voice.'

'That could very well be,' Meredith said thoughtfully. 'Or it could be that she's eighteen now and feels like she's emancipated from him.'

'Maybe,' Kate said. She chewed on her lower lip. 'But I wouldn't imagine he'd just cut her loose. If this guy is the Professor, he plans. He's meticulous. His product is the best in the city.'

Meredith frowned. 'Is this the place where you tell us what you know?'

'Zimmerman sent most of what I know out in a memo to the team last night,' Kate said. 'You should have received it too, but for now I'll give you the CliffsNotes version.' She brought the psychologist up to speed with the discovery of the Professor as well as the spy pen in Sidney's backpack that had given them his motive for Alice's death. 'I don't think he'd just give this young woman her freedom. Either she's escaped and has been hiding, or he knows where she is and has secured her silence, probably with a threat. Otherwise he would have killed her.'

'But either scenario explains her need for secrecy,' Troy agreed. 'If I had to bet, I'd say that he's threatened her and she believes he's watching her, whether he is or not. Otherwise she wouldn't have used the pay phone.'

'You're right,' Meredith said with a nod. 'I hope she calls back. Otherwise I'm not sure how we can help her. If we do a BOLO, she'll get scared and run.'

'We aren't doing an official BOLO,' Zimmerman said, returning to the table. 'I don't want that information leaked. I have no doubt that she'd run at the first hint that we're after her. So Kate's shared what she learned last night. Deacon? You were going to find Alice's apartment.'

'I haven't yet. I gathered surveillance and security videos from the city along with those of storeowners in the area Davenport identified yesterday. I was going to start reviewing the tapes today.'

Zimmerman shook his head. 'I need you at the jail. I didn't get far with the staff last night before I left to witness the search of the Siler woman's bag. Find out who put the cyanide in Alice's food and the ricin in her bandages. I'll give the tapes from her neighborhood to a clerk.'

'Give them to me,' Decker said. 'I dropped Alice off several times. Maybe I'll see something that jogs my memory. At a minimum, I can narrow it down to an area to canvass to see if anyone recognizes her.'

'Can we put out a request for information through the media?' Deacon asked. 'Maybe give Alice's photo to the TV news and newspapers to see if we get any hits? I know Marcus will help us out and keep back whatever details we don't want shared.'

'Let me consider that,' Zimmerman said. 'I'd like to not broadcast our interest, at least until we find out who in the prison participated in her murder. Let's try to find her apartment ourselves first.'

'And when we find it, we might also find a lead to where the IT guy kept his files,' Kate added.

Decker nodded. 'Alice's half-brother, Sean, was the IT guy. He had ledgers and other financial information on his computer screen because I saw them there.' He frowned, another thought coming to mind. 'Sean also knew the access information for his father's offshore accounts and his false ID. I overheard them arguing, minutes before your people stormed the compound,' he said to Zimmerman. 'Sean knew his father's fake name and where he was planning to hide from the police. He had transferred all the money from his father's offshore account to his own account. He knew all kinds of things he shouldn't have known. If he recorded it anywhere, we'll have access to the inner workings of the traffickers. He might also even have known Alice's business – including the identity of the kiddie pornographer.'

'Okay, Griff,' Zimmerman said with a sigh that said he was agreeing against his best judgment. 'I know you should be resting, but I need your eyes. The CCTV tapes are yours.'

Decker's pulse did a little dance. He was back in the game, even if he was on the bench. Next stop: the field. 'Thank you.'

'Don't overdo it or Dani will make us pay.'

Novak was unsuccessful at biting back a grin. 'You're scared of my sister, sir?'

Zimmerman pinned him with a glance. 'Aren't you?'

Novak made a face. 'Good point.'

'I thought so.' Zimmerman turned to Troy. 'Any progress on Alice's profile?'

'The gym where she stalked Marcus O'Bannion didn't know her as Alice,' Troy said. 'She used an alias. Allison Bassett. The gym personnel were pretty useless, actually. Either the dumb jock stereotype is true, or these guys were really good at acting empty-brained. I'm surprised they remembered their *own* names, much less anything about Alice.'

'Was it the gym near King's College?' Kate asked.

Troy shook his head. 'No, near Marcus O'Bannion's old apartment in Hyde Park. Why? You were thinking this Professor might have dealt steroids at Alice's gym?'

Kate's forehead bunched as she frowned. 'Maybe.' She waved her hands vaguely. 'Let me think on it.'

Novak reached into his computer bag and pulled out a stack of printer paper. 'Fold.'

She smiled at her old partner. 'You brought paper just for me?'

'Anything that helps you,' Novak said.

Kate gave him a sober nod. 'Thank you.' She started folding a sheet of paper and it quickly took on the shape of a dog.

It was the equivalent of her knitting and baking, Decker realized. She needed to keep her hands busy to concentrate. *That's why Novak called her the origami queen yesterday.*

'I'm wondering about the gym,' she said, 'specifically the Professor's clients. Everyone knows about him, apparently. He'd hold court at Lovers' Lane at King's College, for example, and everyone came to him. But we don't know how he was supplying the steroids to the gym rats. We also don't know how he chose them. He had to be careful. He's been selling for at least a few years without getting caught. He chooses his customers well. He may have been supplying to multiple gyms all over the city.'

'That might be a better tactic,' Troy said. 'Finding out how he chooses his clients – does he have a certain type? Do they come to him through word of mouth? And he disappears from time to time. Maybe those absences follow some kind of a pattern. I think that would be a better use of my time than trying to build a profile on Alice.'

'Agreed,' Zimmerman said. 'Proceed. Adam, you found the bodies of the nurse and her boyfriend. That was good work. Have you questioned her son?'

'Not yet. Meredith and I were going to see him after we're done here. He was admitted to the hospital last night for withdrawal.'

'Addicted to his mother's drugs,' Meredith said with disgust.

'Poor kid,' Decker murmured. *That could have so easily been me.*

'I know what I want to do,' Kate said, her jaw cocked aggressively. She was folding her third animal, which looked like a seal or a walrus. 'I want to arrest Mr Corey Addison for possession of child pornography. With Kendra's report and the way he harassed that poor girl, we should be able to get a warrant to search his home and office, shouldn't we, boss?'

'We should,' Zimmerman said firmly. 'I'll have it drawn up and signed. When we're done here, you go arrest him, Kate. Make sure there are lots of witnesses when you drag his ass in. And be as loud as you possibly can be.'

'Oh, I will,' Kate said grimly. 'Fucking turd.' She winced. 'Sorry, sir.'

'No apologies required,' Zimmerman said. 'I couldn't have said it better myself.'

Kate flashed him a small grin, then bent back down to start folding another sheet of paper. 'I'd like to take Officer Cullen with me when I make the arrest. She can provide a positive ID and,' a small shrug, 'she did all the legwork. She should be in on the collar.'

'I'll call Isenberg and see if we can clear it with her CO,' Zimmerman promised. 'But only if she's positioned to get to that Kroger quickly if she's contacted by the young woman. In fact, Meredith, I'd like you to be on call as well. The young woman will trust Officer Cullen because she tried to help her on Saturday, but . . .' He frowned. 'She's going to need so much therapy after this. I can't even fathom it.'

Meredith nodded, her mouth drooping sadly. 'I think the only person I know who *can* fathom it is Kendra Cullen's sister, Wendi, because she's been there. Once we've made sure that this young lady is safe from her abusers – or whoever has her so scared – she'll be welcomed into Wendi's program. That is, if that's what she wants. She's eighteen, so she can choose not to live at Mariposa House if she doesn't want to, but I hope she'll want to.'

'So do I.' Zimmerman looked around the table. 'Anyone have anything else? No? Then we all have assignments. Go. Be careful. Griffin, go back to the safe house and rest. Look at the videos, but sleep some too. I want you field-ready as soon as possible. Everyone back here at seventeen hundred, and keep each other in the loop.'

Cincinnati, Ohio,
Friday 14 August, 9.10 A.M.

Mallory had barely gotten to her room and closed the door when her knees gave out. She crawled to her bed and buried her face in the mattress. She knew he was probably watching. He loved to watch.

Loved to bait her until she lost a little more of her mind and then he'd watch her fall apart. And he'd laugh.

Sick, twisted, perverted sonofabitch, she thought. Because thinking was the only thing she could do. Her mind was the only place he couldn't see. So she escaped inside her mind and cowered there, shaking like a leaf on the outside, crying on the inside.

He knows. But how could he? She hadn't said a word. No, it was the way she'd spurned him last night, going into her mind when he started to touch her. Everything he'd done this morning – the list, the picture of Macy, the matched luggage that was heavy and made squishy noises? That was him playing head games. He was trying to make her lose her mind, because he could.

She drew a measured breath, held it for several seconds, then let it out, then did it again and again until her lungs weren't working double overtime. She imagined a pretty meadow with a little creek that made sweet noises as it washed over rocks and sticks. She imagined a deer, calmly eating grass. She imagined a field of flowers, swaying in the breeze.

Until she was calm on the inside too. Until she could think.

He was going to show them films tomorrow. He'd sped up his normal timetable. She'd thought she'd have weeks and weeks. But not if he'd moved them to films already. She knew he planned pool play. She'd washed and folded the swimsuits herself.

She needed to contact that operator at the police station. Lilith had been her name. She said she'd find the lady cop who'd saved Mallory from the man last Saturday.

But he'd stymied her plans. There was no pay phone at the Kroger across from the Home Store on Eastgate. She knew this for a fact. *What am I going to do?*

She honestly didn't know. *So figure it out.* Maybe she could ask someone to borrow their phone. *Because that ended so well last time, didn't it?*

Shut up. Sarcasm is not helping. But it was true. It had been five years ago, but she remembered it like it was yesterday. He'd broken her that day. He'd let her know there was nowhere to turn.

The woman whose phone she'd borrowed had listened as she'd

called the police, as she'd reported him. The woman's face had been both compassionate and horrified. *She believed me. For a little while someone believed me.* Someone had believed that she lived with a monster who made her do . . . things. Sexual things that she didn't want to do.

The police had actually shown up at his old house. The one he'd later sold because they knew his address. They'd come to the old house and questioned him.

And he'd been so mad. So very mad. Not to the police. Oh no. To the police he showed his pretty face. His worried face. His compassionate, aren't-I-a-nice-guy face. And then he'd shown them her medical records – all fabricated by him. He showed them pictures of her looking crazy and strung out – stills from the video he'd made of her portraying that same character: a crazy, strung-out addict. All makeup. All disguises. All lies.

But so damn believable. He looked so sincere. He talked so intelligently. He helped so many people. Everyone who knew him loved him. She didn't even blame the police for backing away, begging his pardon for bothering him.

She'd been ready to die that day. The only thing that stopped him from beating her was the fact that he'd already sold a video of her that he hadn't yet made. He didn't want marks or bruises to show up in the cut. Instead, he'd doped her up and then he'd done what he'd threatened from the very first day.

He'd gone after Macy. He'd sent one of his addicts to his sister and brother-in-law's home, had him wave a gun in their faces. The addict had even shot at Macy's mother before Macy's father had shot the addict dead.

So close, he'd crooned in Mallory's ear later. Macy had come so close to being an orphan, and who would get custody? Him. So Mallory better not tell anyone ever again. And she hadn't. She'd toed the line.

Until today. Because he was going to do to those kids what he'd done to her. He was going to steal their childhoods. Suck out their souls. Leave them used and empty and hurting and hating life. And then he'd sell them. Or maybe kill them. *I can't let that happen.*

All right. So now she knew what she was going to do. She was going to find a way to call that lady cop. She was going to tell her everything.

Now she just had to figure out *how*.

Cincinnati, Ohio,
Friday 14 August, 9.10 A.M.

Cup of coffee in hand, he went to his home office, sitting down in front of the giant computer monitor that displayed all the cameras in his properties. It allowed him to monitor security at this house, the office downtown, the house where he and McCord had located their studio, as well as his sisters' homes. Neither of them knew he was watching them and he didn't intrude on their privacy often, but he kept watch over Macy because . . . well, there was a reason his younger sister, Gemma, had not been able to adopt through traditional means. She was batshit crazy.

He didn't want Macy harmed. Gemma wasn't violent, but she was incredibly self-centered and sometimes left Macy by herself for 'just a few minutes' while she had her hair or nails done.

It wouldn't do for Macy to tell anyone about her mother's neglect. The state would take the child away, for one, and he was waiting for her to grow up a little more. They'd also investigate her parents, and there would be media because his brother-in-law had progressed nicely through the ranks of CPD over the years. He wanted his brother-in-law to stay put. He was valuable exactly where he was. *He's scratched my back, I've scratched his.*

But the main concern if the state took Macy away would be their investigation into her adoption and their discovery that it wasn't quite cricket. *Which would lead them straight to me.*

So he protected Macy as best he could by watching her. It was no hardship. She was a beautiful child. Maybe even more beautiful than Mallory.

Who was walking into her bedroom at the moment on shaky legs that collapsed as soon as she got to her bed, a frilly, lacy concoction that any little girl would absolutely love. As Mallory had. At first.

But lately . . . the girl's behavior was starting to worry him. He'd allowed her too much freedom, he decided. He'd shaken her up today, though. He sipped his coffee with a smile, watching her slump to the floor, defeated.

He was so happy Mallory's mother had had two daughters. Macy was Mallory's kryptonite.

Mallory rested her cheek on her bed, her expression devastated. He waited for the tears. She didn't always cry, but when she did, her emotions were really spectacular to watch.

But the tears didn't come. Instead, she went very still. Too still.

She's thinking. Again. Dammit. It was time to rein the girl in. He picked up his phone and dialed his younger sister's number. It went to voicemail.

Like she's too busy to answer, he thought with a mental snort. Gemma was a professional loafer. He tapped a few keys on his keyboard to bring up the cameras in her house, tabbing from room to room until he found her in the guest bathroom, peering at her reflection in the mirror, stretching the skin on her face so that her wrinkles disappeared.

His baby sister had wrinkles. *We're getting old.*

It was a jolting notion. He didn't feel old. As the Professor, he looked old and his customers treated him with deferential respect. But that was mostly because he sold them primo shit, not because they respected their elders. But as himself? As Brandon? He wasn't old. Not yet.

Still, he barely stopped himself from touching his own face to feel if he had wrinkles. He knew he did not, because he took care of himself. Exercised. Ate right. Flossed.

Hell, he was in his prime. Master of his destiny. Master of all he surveyed.

And right now he was surveying a split monitor, one side showing Mallory sitting too still on the floor next to her bed. *Planning something.* On the other side of the screen, his sister paused, cocked her head as if listening for something, then slowly went down on one knee and pulled a bag of feminine hygiene products from the vanity under the bathroom sink.

If Gemma hadn't been moving with such quiet deliberation, he'd be turning the camera off now, because watching his sisters with feminine hygiene products was too gross, even for him. But Gemma was up to something, so he kept watching. She rooted inside the plastic bag of pads, finally pulling out a much smaller bag with a designer logo. Again she cocked her head to listen, then she smiled and took out a mirror and a third, even smaller bag – filled with white powder.

Fuck. Gemma was using. As if that was going to make her any saner. *Not.* He called her cell phone again, satisfied when she jumped at the ringtone, dropping her mirror into the sink with a clatter. It didn't break, but she shoved everything back into the designer bag and then back into the bag of pads before answering the phone.

'Brandon!' she answered with false brightness. Into the mirror she scowled and mouthed *fucker*. 'What can I do for you?'

'It's about Mallory,' he said, using his most serious voice. 'I'm worried about her.'

His sister rolled her eyes and made a face in the mirror, but when she spoke, she oozed sincere concern. 'Oh no. What's happened?'

'Nothing's happened yet, but I'm worried that something will. I'm worried that she's . . . well, that she's gotten involved in something over her head.'

Gemma sighed. 'A mud puddle is over her head, Brandon. I don't know why you bother with her. She should be in juvie or a home for girls. She should be locked up.'

A valid opinion based on everything he'd told her about Mallory for the last six years. Most of it was lies, of course, but with enough of a kernel of truth so that Mallory's behavior made sense to the people he allowed to know about her. 'We've been over this before, Gemma. She's my daughter. Just like Macy is yours. How is Macy, by the way?'

'Oh, she's fine. Watching TV. Educational, of course.'

Half of that was true, at least. He'd seen Macy parked in front of the television when he'd been searching for Gemma. But she was watching reruns of *Family Feud*, which was not educational in anyone's book. 'Good. Good to hear. Like I said, though, I'm worried about Mallory. I think . . . I think she might be using drugs.'

Gemma gasped. 'No.' She eyed her bag longingly. 'What makes you say that?'

'Her behavior lately. She's moody, temperamental. Flashes of anger. Just edgy in general.'

'Well . . . some of that could just be, y'know, monthly stuff. PMS.'

Exactly what he'd hoped she'd say. 'I thought that as well. I was wondering if you'd have a chat with her. Maybe get a feel for her state of mind.'

In the mirror she rolled her eyes again. 'I'd be happy to,' she said sweetly, 'but Nell might be a better choice. Since she's a nurse and all.'

'True, but she's so much older than Mallory. You're much closer to her age.'

It was his turn to roll his eyes, because his sister preened. *So damn predictable.* Appealing to her vanity had always been the key that turned her lock. 'True. I *am* closer to her age. Do you want me to come over there?'

'No, that's not necessary. It's so out of your way. But she'll be at the Home Store and the Kroger on East Gate this afternoon, buying some party supplies for Macy's birthday.'

In the mirror Gemma grimaced and mouthed *fuck*. She'd forgotten. He could tell. She'd forgotten her own daughter's birthday. 'But that's not for a few weeks.'

'Next week,' he said, keeping his voice as light as hers. 'Time flies by so fast, doesn't it?'

'It does,' she agreed. 'Sure, I'll go to the store to check on Mallory. I need to pick up a few last-minute things for Macy anyway, so it'll be a win-win. I'll let you know what I find out, k-k?'

'K-k,' he repeated merrily, then hung up and stuck out his tongue. 'Gag me,' he muttered. But at least Gemma had put her drugs away. Her hands didn't shake, so she wasn't in deep. Yet.

He wondered where she'd gotten her product. It wasn't going to be as good as what he sold, but it wasn't like he was going to tell her that. He flicked off the camera to her house and stared at

Mallory. Her jaw had clenched and he didn't think she was even aware of it.

Yes, she was planning something all right. He had appointments this afternoon or he'd watch her himself. Maybe he should call in sick and have Nell cancel whatever appointments she couldn't handle herself. None of the patients on this afternoon's roster were potential clients, so it wasn't like he'd lose real business.

On camera, Mallory shook herself and pushed to her feet, her expression grimly determined.

Damn. He picked up the phone and dialed his older sister. He coughed hard, making his voice momentarily hoarse. 'Nell?' he asked, feigning a stuffy nose while he was at it.

'Oh Lord,' Nell said with a sigh. 'You're sick? Dammit, Remy. You have to take better care of yourself.'

'I'm sorry,' he said forlornly. 'I feel awful. Leaving you in the lurch, too.'

She sighed again. 'I'll figure it out. Just get some rest. I need you better by Monday.'

'What happens Monday?' he asked, manufacturing a sniffle.

'We start interviewing receptionists. I thought about what you said and I placed an ad in today's paper.'

'Good idea. I like it.' And he had several candidates in mind, specifically nurses who needed the extra cash. Better a devil he knew behind the office desk than an angel he didn't. 'Maybe consider another nurse so you have backup?'

'I thought about that, too. If we hire another nurse we can take more patients. That'll help us defray the cost of her salary, plus pay our fixed costs like the utility bill.'

'Whatever you think is best,' he said, then coughed.

'Go to bed, Remy. We can talk more over the weekend when you feel better.'

'Okay.' He hung up, cleared his throat. Now that that was done, he could tackle the next item on his list – how to handle the prison guard Rawlings via his kid. He didn't want to hurt the kid, and he certainly didn't want to kill him. But he did want to send a message to the kid's dad: *Don't fuck with me. Do not think about threatening me with your little list of favors. My reach is longer than yours and I'll hurt the things you love the most.*

Cincinnati, Ohio,
Friday 14 August, 9.45 A.M.

The group pushed away from the table, a flurry of side conversations immediately upping the volume, but Decker ignored them, his eyes on Kate, who also remained seated. *Next to me.*

But not looking at me. Her gaze was fixed on the little animals she'd folded out of paper, her mouth turned down in a troubled frown.

Decker leaned in close to her, propping his elbow on the wheelchair's armrest, drawing in the scent of her hair, once again in its tidy twist. But he'd seen it long, had stroked it, had felt it glide over his bare skin. He shifted in the wheelchair, covering his lap with his notepad. 'I like the origami,' he murmured in her ear.

She drew a breath. 'Thank you.'

'But?'

Her shrug was oddly childish and endearing. And vulnerable. 'I hate that I've become dependent on it.' She dropped her eyes to fiddle with the paper figures. 'Makes me look crazy.'

'No,' he said softly. 'It makes you look intense.' *And hot.* 'I've seen crazy. You ain't that, trust me.'

She looked up, brows crunched. 'I do. And that bothers me, too.'

He leaned in until their heads were nearly touching. 'What, that you trust me so quickly?' he murmured, and she nodded. 'I'm the same, but it doesn't bother me. Trusting someone quickly isn't necessarily a bad thing. I won't hurt you, Kate.'

'I know that. Not on purpose, anyway.'

He was about to reassure her when a dark duffle bag was dropped on the table in front of them, making both of them jump. Novak was looking down at him with a now-familiar scowl.

'The CCTV and neighborhood surveillance video,' Novak said, his bi-colored gaze darting a worried glance toward Kate before returning to meet Decker's eyes squarely.

'Thank you,' Decker said formally. 'Are these copies or will we be returning them?'

'They're yours.' One white brow lifted. 'Knock yourself out. I gotta go to jail.'

Kate looked up at Novak, her mouth curving upward, although the smile didn't reach her eyes. 'I am editing myself so much right now,' she said lightly.

'Don't on my behalf,' Novak told her. 'Hit me with your best shot.'

She shook her head. 'I don't even know where to start.'

'Maybe here.' Novak slid a business card under one of her origami animals. 'Just give it a chance,' he said quietly, then walked away as she pushed the folded paper aside.

She stared at the card with a weary sigh. 'Goddammit, Novak,' she whispered.

'What is it?' Decker asked.

'A PTSD specialist.'

Decker looked across the conference room at Novak with a new respect. The guy really cared for Kate, that was clear. Novak was on his way out the door, but he paused to give Decker a nod, his white head tilting almost quizzically as he did so. Then he was gone.

Decker turned back to Kate, who was frowning at the card. 'You said the dreams started again after you fired those shots last week,' he said. 'Novak could be right. It could be that PTSD is exacerbating your existing ADHD.'

Kate's eyes widened. 'Wait. Are you *agreeing* with Deacon Novak?'

Decker's lips twitched. 'Just this once. Maybe. But don't tell him.'

She tucked the card in her pocket. 'Your secret's safe with me.' She gave him a meaningful look. 'All of them.'

'I know. Same goes.' Even though he hadn't even scratched the surface of her secrets.

A little nod. 'I need to go. I still have to get a work address for Mr Corey Addison. Kendra said he works downtown. I hope it's somewhere very public. I want as many people as possible to see him utterly and completely humiliated.' She stood up and gathered her folded paper animals. 'Where's the trashcan?'

'Wait!' Meredith Fallon hurried over to them. 'Don't throw them away. Can I have them?'

Kate blinked. 'Why does everyone want my folded paper?'

"Cause they're cool,' Decker said.

'They are,' Meredith agreed. 'Do you have the pattern?'

'No, I just . . . do it.'

'Ah.' Meredith smiled. 'One of those artistic types. I do play and art therapy with kids. This kind of thing is perfect for them. I'll take them apart and figure it out. Maybe you can make me more?'

Kate looked bemused. 'Sure?' she said slowly.

Meredith took the little paper animals, then hesitated. 'I have to confess. I do want these, but that's not why I came over here. It's about Kendra Cullen. Thank you for including her in this arrest. This case . . . it means something to her.'

Kate tilted her head much like Novak had just done. 'Because of her sister. Her sister endured the same kind of abuse.'

'Yes. But.' Meredith bit her lower lip. 'Just . . . keep an eye out for her, okay?'

Kate's brows scrunched and Decker could practically hear the wheels turning in her brain. 'Oh,' she said softly, her expression changing from confusion to realization and compassion. 'She had the addresses and she came to you. She's pissed off, isn't she?'

Meredith lifted her eyes to the ceiling. 'Just . . . keep an eye out for her, okay?' she repeated.

'Should I not ask her to join me?' Kate asked, and Meredith shook her head.

'No. It'll be good for her to go. This will be one of her first big arrests. It's important to her.'

'Got it. I'll watch out for her, and if she starts to get too angry, I'll have her take a powder. How's that?'

'Perfect. Thank you for understanding. And for the origami, too. Corinne – that's my intern – will love these. She's always looking for new art projects to do with the kids. I'm going to suggest fiber crafts to her as well. Our youngest kids don't have the dexterity for knitting yet, but the older ones will enjoy the challenge. Or maybe crocheting would be better,' she added to herself. 'They'll have sword fights with knitting needles. They might even stab each other.'

'They make blunter, shorter needles for kids to avoid the bloodshed,' Kate said, then pulled the PTSD specialist's card from her pocket and gave it a sniff. 'You gave this to Deacon?'

Meredith winced a little. 'Busted. Yes. He wanted to help. Don't be too mad at him.'

'Oh, I'm not mad,' Kate assured her. 'I was just curious. I figured Deacon had gotten the card from Faith, but it smells like your perfume.'

'I keep forgetting I'm working with detectives,' Meredith said lightly, but her expression was serious. 'Dr Lane is good. She's got lots of experience and she's very discreet. For what it's worth, she'll probably tell you that your knitting and paper-folding are good coping mechanisms. There's nothing wrong with it.'

'Except everyone knows I'm about to lose my mind.'

Decker grabbed her hand and squeezed it hard, but let it go before anyone other than Meredith noticed. 'You do what you need to do, Kate. Because it's working. You're productive. Nobody here gives a rat's ass if you knit or fold or whatever.'

'Listen to the man,' Meredith said quietly. 'Dr Lane may have a few other suggestions that are less noticeable. Give her a try. Worst that can happen is you waste an hour or two.'

Kate studied the card for a long moment. 'I'll think about it. Thank you. Now I'm going to find out where Corey Addison works.'

Once again Meredith hesitated, then leaned in close. 'He's in advertising,' she whispered. 'Smith, Addison, and Nagel, Main and Sixth. If you're lucky, you might catch him giving a presentation. He'll take a long lunch, so get there before noon.'

Kate's brows lifted. 'Wow. Kendra really did her homework.'

Meredith shrugged. 'I hear stuff from all over the place. I keep my sources very secret.'

'Speaking of sources,' Decker said thoughtfully. 'I bet you that Marcus O'Bannion would send someone with a camera to film Addison's arrest if he were given an anonymous tip.'

Meredith punched a few buttons on her phone. 'Done and done.'

'Meredith,' Adam called from the door. 'We need to roll. The social worker's at the hospital with Eileen Wilkins's son. I'll meet you at Children's in the front lobby.'

'I've been summoned.' Meredith dropped the origami animals in her purse. 'They'll get squished, but Corinne will be able to figure it out. Gotta fly. Bye.' She started to turn, but stopped herself. 'It was nice to meet you, Agent Davenport. And Kate, I run every day at five a.m. I'll send you my address. Good way to work off some of the tension.'

'Meredith!' Adam called impatiently. 'I'm leaving now.'

Meredith rolled her eyes, then spun around and walk-ran to the door in heels so high they made Decker's feet hurt just looking at them. 'I'm coming!' she called back. 'Jeez.'

'I think she's always late,' Kate said. 'Just a hunch.'

Decker laughed. 'I think you're right.' He squeezed her hand once more, quickly, happy when she squeezed back. 'Text me when you've picked up the fucking turd, okay? I need to know you're okay.'

'Will do. Have fun searching for Alice.'

Seventeen

'Posh,' Kate murmured as she walked into the building that housed the ad firm where Mr Corey Addison was a junior vice president. 'I guess these folks don't observe casual Fridays.'

Kendra Cullen snorted softly. 'This *is* casual, Agent Coppola,' she said, sounding a little nervous now that they were here and actually getting ready to arrest the sonofabitch who thought it was funny to harass a young woman who'd already been victimized.

'Head up, Officer,' Kate said softly. 'You did a damn good thing for that girl. Now you're gonna do one better by taking out one of the reasons slimebags keep making kiddie porn.'

'He's one man,' Kendra said. 'There are so many more.'

'I know. And we won't stop them all. But we'll stop this one and it might give some others pause.' Kate looked over her shoulder to where Marcus stood outside the building, a video camera on his shoulder and Scarlett at his side. 'Looks like we've got media support from the *Ledger*'s big cheese himself.'

Kendra smiled, relaxing a tiny bit. 'Marcus covered the McCord arrest too. This kind of thing, exposing the bad guys, is important to him. Scarlett says it's part of why she fell for him. That, and he's really easy on the eye.'

A young man wearing a pair of white coveralls with *FBI* printed on the back approached them from across the lobby. 'Agent Coppola? I'm Agent Quincy Taylor.'

'Nice to meet you, Quincy. I'm Kate, and this is Kendra Cullen. She did the legwork.'

Quincy gave Kendra a nod of respect. 'I heard. Nicely done.'

'Quincy's here to search Addison's office,' Kate told Kendra, 'and to take his computer. It's covered in the warrant, but I'm not expecting cooperation.'

Quincy's brows waggled a little. 'That'll make it more exciting. So, we ready?'

Kendra straightened her spine. 'Yes,' she said resolutely. 'Let's do this thing.'

Kate grinned. 'Absolutely.' She and Kendra started walking, Quincy Taylor bringing up the rear. 'And it starts . . . now.'

A security guard approached, looking none too pleased. 'Can I help you?'

'Yes.' Kate showed him her badge. 'Special Agent Coppola, FBI, along with Special Agent Taylor and Officer Cullen, CPD. I have an arrest warrant for one of the occupants of this building. Please stand aside, sir.'

An ugly expression darkened the man's face, but he stepped back to allow the three of them to pass. Then he walked behind them, following them into the elevator. Kendra went to press the button for Addison's floor, but Kate shook her head slightly and Kendra dropped her hand.

'Well?' the guard asked belligerently. 'If you're in such a hurry, press the button already.'

Kate pressed a button, but it was the one to hold the doors open. She looked into the lobby and caught the eye of one of the two detectives sent by Lieutenant Isenberg. The lieutenant had also assigned officers to cover the exits. It was largely for effect, as no one believed Addison would jump out a window or take the fire escape down, but when the arrest was made, it would make a great show of strength on camera.

Detective Muller stopped outside the open elevator doors. 'Can I help you, Agent Coppola?'

It was amazing how different the same words sounded when spoken respectfully.

'Yes. Can you escort this gentleman to the lobby and make sure he doesn't use either his radio or the cell phone in his hand?' She smiled at the guard. 'Just in case you plan to warn someone up there, you'll be staying here.'

The guard's mouth fell open. 'You have no right to bust in here like you own the place.'

'This warrant says I do. Detective Muller has a copy. I'm sure he'd be happy to let you read it. Please step outside the elevator now or we'll take you in as well.' Kate smiled at him again. 'And trust me, sir. You do not want to be associated with the man we'll be bringing out.'

The guard didn't fight when the detective lightly took his arm and guided him out of the elevator, but he did give Kate the evil eye. 'I'll be reporting this to your supervisor.'

'Please do,' Kate said with a smile. 'Coppola. Two p's, one l. Everyone always misspells it.' She released the button holding the doors open and they slid closed.

Kendra hit the button for the fifth floor. 'You think he would have warned them, really?'

'I think so,' Quincy said. 'He was texting on the phone in his pocket.'

'Huh.' Kendra shrugged. 'I wasn't expecting that from a man his age. I thought only teenagers did that when they wanted to text in class.'

'He's ex-military,' Kate said. 'This is his territory, the tenants are his people to protect. He was posturing, wanting to be the big man when we arrested Addison. He would have thrown his weight around, just to make sure everyone saw him doing his job. I met a thousand guys just like him when I was in the army. Mostly as I was processing them after an arrest.'

'You were an MP?' Kendra asked, then grinned. 'Meredith said you were a badass with a yarn bag. I guess she got the badass part right.'

Kate laughed. 'She got the yarn bag part right too. I left it in my car.' The bell dinged for the fifth floor and they got out. 'Smith, Addison, and Nagel. Corey's daddy is a partner.'

'I'm shocked,' Quincy said dryly, and Kendra's lips curved.

Kate made a note to thank Quincy later. Kendra was nervous, but Quincy Taylor had put her at ease.

The office was bustling with conversation and activity – until about five seconds after they stepped through the door. Kate led with her badge, her voice loud in the silence. *Excellent. Louder the better.* 'FBI,' she said to the receptionist, who was staring at her with eyes like saucers. 'We're here for Corey Addison. Where is he?'

The receptionist pointed to a closed door. 'But he's in with a client. You can't—'

Oh, watch me, sweetheart. 'Your diligence is noted,' Kate interrupted and led her little team through the door into a conference room with a mahogany table that must have cost the earth. Corey Addison stood at the front of the room next to an easel, pointing to a concept board. He halted mid-sentence. 'What is the meaning of this? How did you get in here? This is a private office.'

Addison looked exactly like the photo in the DMV database, down to the dimple in his chin. He'd been a football player in high school and college and looked like he kept up with his workouts. He'd be a handful if he decided to fight.

Kate glanced at Kendra, who nodded. 'Yes,' she said quietly. 'That's him.'

The table was occupied by six middle-aged men in suits and one young woman dressed conservatively in slacks and a linen jacket. *The clients*, Kate thought, smiling on the inside. They were about to get an eyeful. *Thank you, Lord.* 'Mr Addison? Corey Addison?' Not waiting for an answer, she approached him, handcuffing him before he got out another word. Because he was staring at Kendra, his jaw tight. His eyes furious.

'What is this?' he asked, enunciating every word.

Kate took him by the arm. 'Corey Addison, you're under arrest for harassment.'

'What the hell?' he exploded.

The exclamation was echoed by an older man who stood in the doorway. He looked like Addison, just aged twenty years. This would be the daddy. 'What the hell is this? I've called Security. We'll have these people escorted out.'

Kate held out a copy of the arrest warrant. 'You'll find everything in order, sir,' she said as the older man snatched the paper from her hand.

'Harassment? Who did he harass?' Addison Senior demanded. He scanned the warrant, then glared at his son. 'What have you done?'

'Nothing! She butted in on a private conversation.' He tossed his head toward Kendra. 'I did not harass anyone.'

'He harassed a young girl at the Kroger last Saturday,' Kate said, keeping an eye on Kendra, who appeared to be in control.

'That?' Cory drew a breath, releasing it on an embarrassed laugh. 'That was me trying to ask a girl out on a date. I was about to walk away. It was nothing.' He glanced at the suits around the table, who looked both horrified and fascinated. 'I swear this is all a misunderstanding.'

'I don't think so,' Kate said. 'We'll be taking your computer and all of your office files. We also have a team searching your home as we speak.'

'Looking for what?' the father sputtered.

'Child pornography,' Kate said clearly and loudly.

The suits at the table gasped. The father sagged against the door frame, all the color drained from his face. Corey Addison went still, giving Kate only a split second of warning before throwing his weight against her. Flowing with him, she used his own momentum to shove him to the floor, rolling him so that he landed on his stomach with a grunt. He bucked, trying to throw her off, so she drew her weapon and held it to his head.

'We'll be adding a resisting arrest charge,' she said levelly. She drew a breath of her own, her heart pounding. The last time she'd had a weapon in her hand, she'd killed two men. To her relief, Corey Addison seemed to settle down, although he panted like a bull ready to charge. From the corner of her eye she was unsurprised to see that Quincy and Kendra had both drawn their weapons as well. 'Officer Cullen, please cover me while I restrain his legs. Agent

Taylor, please proceed to Mr Addison's office and collect everything that's not nailed down.' She flicked a glance at the doorway, where the father still leaned, staring at his son like he was a stranger. 'And can one of you folks at the table call for an ambulance? I think the elder Mr Addison may need medical assistance.' She pulled a FlexiCuff from her pocket and quickly restrained Corey's feet before rising and holstering her weapon.

'What should we do with him?' Kendra asked.

Kate's pulse was nearly normal again, her hand steady when she ran it over her hair. *Good.* Her twist was still in place. Nothing worse than escaping tendrils of hair to make a cop look unprofessional.

'For now, he can lie there. I'm going to call the team at his house and let them know we have him in custody.' She made the call on her cell and then crouched next to the chair where Corey's father now sat, shaking. She gently pressed her fingertips to the man's wrist and took his pulse. 'Do you have a heart problem, sir?' she asked.

He nodded. 'Yeah. Under control except . . .' His lips twisted as he stared down at his son, cuffed and prone. 'Except for times of stress like this.'

The receptionist rushed in with a prescription bottle and a glass of water. 'I called 911,' she told Kate. 'An ambulance is coming.' She shook one of the pills into her palm and offered it to the elder Addison. 'Just nitro,' she murmured to Kate.

The father slipped the pill under his tongue and within a minute his pulse had steadied.

Kate rose and turned to the suits around the table. 'I'm sorry, but we're going to have to ask you to stay for just a little while. We'll need your names and addresses for the report.'

The woman at the table held up her phone. 'I got it all on video. I started recording when you came in. For my own purposes, of course. I won't sell to the media, but I'm happy to provide you with a copy if you want one.'

Kate blinked at her. 'What purposes? Why would you need a recording in the first place?'

'To protect myself.' She tossed a disgusted look at one of her colleagues. 'I *told* you he'd made an inappropriate pass at me and you didn't believe me. I asked you to remove him from our vendor list and you refused. I asked you to transfer me to another project and you suggested that would be bad for my career.'

Her colleague tugged at his tight collar uncomfortably. 'I'm sorry. I . . .' He looked around the table, but none of the others would meet his eyes. 'I shouldn't have doubted your word.'

'Thank you,' she said with dignity. 'Agent . . . I missed your name before.'

'Coppola.' Kate gave the woman her card. 'I'd appreciate the copy, but it would be more appropriate for our techs to do the transmission. Would you accompany me to the field office?'

'If I can have the afternoon off.' She aimed a look at her colleague, who nodded stiffly.

'Fine. We will give the authorities our full cooperation. Take whatever time you need.'

'Thank you.' She gave Kate her business card. 'I'm Felicia Petrie. If you need additional evidence against him, I have the names of other women he's harassed. I'm twenty-one. This is my first job out of college. And I'm downright *elderly* compared to the other women.'

Corey hadn't moved, his face turned away from the group. He was breathing, however, so Kate wasn't too worried. 'Is Mr Addison all right, Officer Cullen?' she asked, purely for form.

Kendra didn't show any emotion at all. *Good for you, kid.* 'Yes, Agent Coppola. He's . . . Well, he's weeping, ma'am.'

A guttural growl came from Corey. 'Fuck you, bitch.'

The father closed his eyes. 'Dear God. This is a nightmare.'

'You can say that again,' Felicia muttered. 'That man has been my nightmare since I started this job two months ago. I would have quit, but I would have had to pay back all my moving expenses.'

The collar-tugging colleague winced at that but said no more.

'How do you know about the other women he harassed?' Kate asked Felicia.

'Online forum,' Felicia answered. 'A place where women can report assholes who don't understand that *no* means *no*. Sometimes

371

it becomes an avenue to dump on old boyfriends, but in my case, it worked. I typed in "Corey Addison" and got a bunch of hits.'

More victims, Kate thought grimly. 'If you could email me a link to that site, I'd be grateful.'

A commotion in the hallway signaled the arrival of the paramedics, and Kate stepped back to let them work. Standing close to Kendra, she murmured, 'At ease, Officer. Holster your weapon now.' Kendra did so, her hand trembling so slightly that Kate only saw it because she'd been watching. Giving her a nod of approval, Kate said, 'Officer Cullen, please go help Agent Taylor. You've done well here. I'll need you again when we escort him out.'

Kendra looked at her then, really looked at her, and for a moment there was such turbulence in her eyes that Kate caught her breath. Satisfaction and despair, triumph and helpless rage. But mostly sweet, blessed relief. 'Yes, ma'am,' she said aloud, but those eyes said *thank you*.

Cincinnati, Ohio,
Friday 14 August, 1.00 P.M.

Decker looked away from his monitor when his cell phone buzzed, and his gut settled. A text from Kate. *Got him. All is well.*

Excellent. She had Corey Addison in custody. Decker wanted details, but that she was okay was enough for now. He turned back to his monitor, scrutinizing the neighborhood Alice had called home, specifically a row of small shops that were central to where he'd dropped her off each time he'd been her driver.

Someone cleared their throat next to him, and Decker lifted his eyes to look over the edge of his laptop screen. 'What can I do for you, Hope?'

Hope Beardsley was the daughter of Bailey Beardsley, the nurse Dani had left to monitor him when she'd been called in to the clinic. The little girl was nine, she'd informed him very politely, before asking his permission to sit at the kitchen table with him so that she could 'work'. Her mother had issued a gentle reprimand, but Decker liked kids, so he'd told Hope to stay. Turned out her work was a book she was reading for school, even though school hadn't started yet. 'Pre-reading,' she'd explained. 'I'm in the gifted program.'

Then she'd been as quiet as a mouse until the moment she'd cleared her throat.

'I was wondering if you were hungry,' she said. 'I was going to get myself a snack.'

Decker found his lips curving, because she'd said the words like she was reciting from a script. A glance at the clock on his screen said it was top of the hour, the exact time that Dani had set for him to eat. 'What kind of snack?'

Hope frowned a little. 'A healthy one,' she said, sounding disappointed.

Decker chuckled. 'Dang it. If Dr Dani was gonna make you tell me to eat, at least she could have made it tasty.'

Hope's eyes widened. 'How did you . . . ?' She pursed her lips and he laughed out loud.

'You didn't give it away, sweetheart. Dr Dani is very thorough. She wouldn't have left without making sure you and your mom had my schedule. Tell you what. If we eat some fruit, I think we should get some chocolate. For balance, you know.'

'You have some?' she asked conspiratorially, as if they were discussing illegal drugs.

'I have a stash. Agent Coppola brought me some last night. A whole pound bag of peanut M&Ms.'

'Oh, I like those,' she whispered. 'My dad always gets me some when we go out. I'm not supposed to tell, because Mom doesn't like me to eat too many sweets.'

'Lunchtime,' Bailey announced as she walked into the kitchen. 'Hope's not bothering you, is she, Agent Davenport?'

'Heavens, no,' he answered. 'She's been the perfect office mate. We're just discussing health food.' He gave Hope a wink and the little girl grinned back.

'Candy, you mean,' Bailey said knowingly, then laughed at the look of dismay on her daughter's face. 'Baby, I always know when you and Daddy have been sneaking candy. I can taste it when he kisses me.'

Dismay became mild disgust. 'Mom. I don't wanna know about that stuff.'

'So what healthy food have you two decided you want for lunch?' Bailey asked. 'Dr Dani said that Agent Davenport needs to eat bland food.'

Decker scoffed. 'Of course she did, but that was just her way of getting back at me. There's some shrimp and grits left over from last night. And Kate brought back some fried chicken from the grocery store deli. It's pretty tasty, too, but there's not much left. I got hungry during the night.' He'd been snacking on fried chicken and brownies when Kate had started screaming. He'd forgotten to put the food away so he figured Dani must have done it and seen that he wasn't following her diet. 'I think the doc was mainly *suggesting* bland foods. I don't think she really expects me to eat them. So, Hope, what'll it be? Fried chicken or shrimp and grits?'

'Both?' Hope asked, well, hopefully. Together they looked at her mother with puppy-dog eyes. 'Please, Mama?'

'I'd be obliged, ma'am,' Decker added, layering on the charm.

Bailey's lips twitched. 'Ah, a good southern boy. I can hear it in your voice.'

'Well, the southern bit is true. I grew up in Mississippi. But I don't know how good I am.' He winked at Hope again, who giggled this time, and it was like music. His sister used to giggle like that, but not too often. There hadn't been much to giggle about in their house, so when he'd heard it, he'd treasured it. He still did.

Hope slid off her chair and came to look at the papers he'd spread on his side of the table. 'I wanted to ask questions, but it was work time. Now it's lunchtime, so can I ask?'

Bailey started to tell her no, but Decker shook his head. 'Of course you can ask. I'm not looking at anything that's classified or confidential. All completely G-rated, Mom,' he added, because he figured Bailey knew who they were looking for.

'Just a few minutes, Hope,' Bailey said. 'Then let him get back to work.'

Hope nodded once, then tapped the map on his left. 'What's this for?'

'I'm trying to find out where a certain person lived. On my old job, I was supposed to take her home, but she always had me drop her off somewhere that was close to her apartment, but not the actual address. So I plotted out all the places I remember dropping her off and they make kind of a circle. See?'

'A scatter plot,' Hope pronounced, and Decker laughed in surprise.

'They teach you that kind of stuff in elementary school?'

'Yep,' Hope said. 'Honors math.'

'Private school,' Bailey explained. 'My husband teaches there.'

'He was a chaplain in the army,' Hope said, 'but he doesn't do that anymore. He's retired. But he teaches at my school and then he goes to prison.'

Bailey coughed. 'He teaches classes to inmates,' she clarified. 'One more question, Hope.'

Hope frowned. 'Okay, Mama. I need to think of one.' She pursed her lips and stared at the computer screen. 'Why are you playing a game if you're supposed to be working?'

'Hope!' Bailey blinked, her mouth working, but nothing more came out.

'It's okay. It's a good question. And a fair one.' Decker pointed to the screen. 'It's not a game, Hope. That's the street view on Google Maps of this street here.' He tapped the map he'd marked up. 'This street is in the center of the scatter plot.'

'Oh.' Hope leaned against the table, peering at his laptop screen. 'So it's like you dropped her off and she went shopping.'

'That's exactly what I was thinking,' he said, impressed with her logic. 'I was trying to remember if the woman I drove home was ever carrying any bags from these stores.'

Hope glanced up at him. 'Was she your girlfriend?'

'Hope!' Bailey shook her head. 'Sit. Now.'

Decker had already shuddered his revulsion. 'It's okay, Mom. Again, the question is not a bad one. No, Hope, she was definitely *not* my girlfriend. She was a criminal. And I was working undercover to get information.'

Hope's eyes widened almost comically. 'Really? That's what I want to do. Be a cop like my Uncle Daniel and Uncle Luke. But I wanna go undercover too.'

Bailey huffed. 'You said you wanted to be a doctor like Dani.'

Hope shrugged. 'That would be fun too.'

Decker bit his lip, holding back a laugh. 'If it's okay, Mama, I'd like to talk to Hope a little more. My brain needs a break. Can she stay?'

Hope looked at him with thankful adoration and Bailey sighed heavily. 'If you really want her to. She can be a little precocious.'

Hope frowned. 'I don't know that one.'

'It means advanced for your age,' Decker confided. 'It's usually what parents and teachers say when a kid is smart in intelligence but a little bit of a smartass – I mean smart *alec* – too.'

Hope snickered. 'My uncles say smartass. It's okay.'

'Well, not really,' Decker said. 'At least not from me, because you don't know me yet.'

Hope shrugged and leaned in to see the screen again. 'I think we've been here.'

Bailey stepped behind them to look over Decker's shoulder. 'I don't think so, baby. I don't recognize that street. I recognize the street name, though. That's Hyde Park.'

'Actually, it's Oakley,' Decker said. 'Next to but less expensive than Hyde Park.'

'How long were you undercover?' Bailey asked, surprised.

'Three years, why?'

'Because I thought you were new in town, but you know the neighborhoods better than I do and I've been here five years.'

'I guess I feel new. When you're undercover, you're not really a part of anything. You just pretend to be, but you live on the edges.'

'Always on the outside, looking in,' Bailey murmured. 'Sounds a bit lonely.'

'It was,' he admitted, suspecting where Hope's mama was taking this conversation. 'You can't make real friends because you're surrounded by really bad guys. And if you have friends in the real world, you can't even say hi to them because you might blow your cover.'

Hope looked uncertain. 'Maybe a doctor would be better than an undercover cop.'

'A lot better,' Bailey said fervently. 'Anyway, we don't live anywhere near that street on the computer screen, and those shops are still more expensive than we can afford. I'm sure we've never been there, Hope.'

'Oh, not me and you, Mama. Me and Dad. We went to one of the stores right there for your bir—' She pursed her lips again, her expression becoming glum.

'Birds?' Decker asked, trying to provide her with a distraction.

'I don't have birds,' Bailey said, ruffling Hope's hair. 'Next time you and Dad go shopping for my birthday present, tell him I'd like one. It should be yellow, okay? I like yellow.'

'Okay, Mama.' Hope mouthed a relieved *thank you* to Decker, then squinted at the screen again. 'We passed by all these places, though, and then we got an ice cream cone here. Because it was hella hot.'

Bailey opened her mouth to reprimand her daughter, then sighed, shaking her head. 'I put the chicken in the oven to warm. When the timer dings, I'll get it out. Don't touch it, Hope. You'll burn your fingers. And do not bother Agent Davenport.'

She left the kitchen and Hope made an angry face. 'She thinks I'm a baby.'

'She loves you a lot,' Decker corrected quietly. 'That makes you a very lucky girl. My mama didn't love me or my sister like that. You should count your blessings, honey.'

Hope's expression changed again, becoming sweetly compassionate. 'I'm sorry, Agent Davenport.'

'You can call me Decker if you want.'

'No, I'm not allowed to call grownups by their first names. Maybe Mr Decker?'

'That works. Tell me about the ice cream.' Because that was ringing a bell in his mind.

He listened as she chattered about ice cream and the flavors she and her dad had tried and the cones they'd finally bought and eaten while they walked to the . . . sign shop? 'Wait,' he said, because she'd whispered the word. 'You and your dad went to a sign shop?'

'No,' she whispered louder, scowling at him. 'A consignment shop. Don't say it so loud. Mama will hear!'

'Oh,' he whispered back. 'So that was the birthday present shop?'

She nodded. 'Dad got Mama a pair of glass lamps that go on the wall. Antiques. Mama loves old stuff, but only in her sewing room. She says the rest of the house should be lived in. That Dad shouldn't have to worry about where he puts his feet or that he'll knock something over and break it. Dad is kind of big. Like you. Not fat,' she said hastily. 'Neither of you are fat. And I'm sure you're not clumsy. I'm sure you wouldn't break anything!'

Decker's chest shook as he laughed silently. 'Thank you. I am a little clumsy, but thanks for saying I'm not fat, because that means I can eat fried chicken and M&Ms and brownies and not worry. At least for now.'

Hope raised a brow. 'I saw a pan in the sink with brownie crumbs in it. Are there any left?'

'Nope. Sorry, kid. But I'll ask Kate to make some more. Tell me about the antique store.' Because while he was pretty sure that Alice had gone into the ice cream shop a time or two, it was a popular enough place that she might not be remembered, and at this point he couldn't pinpoint an exact day he'd taken her there, so asking for a specific surveillance video wasn't possible. An antique store, though . . .

There was a definite memory pinging around in his mind.

'They sell old stuff,' Hope said with a shrug. 'A lot of fancy side tables and stuff from Europe. Dad bought the lamps there because they matched one that Mama already had, from her mama. Her mama died before I was born, so I never met her,' she ended sadly.

'I'm sorry,' he said. 'I never knew any of my grandparents, but I had foster parents and one of them still had a mama living. For a little while anyway. She died when I was in high school.'

'Did she let you call her Grandma?'

Decker smiled at the sweet question. 'She did. And she was awesome.'

'Good. What happened to your foster mom and dad?'

'They died when I was in the army. They were older, but it was still too soon to lose them. They were awesome, too.'

'I'm sorry for your loss,' Hope said gravely, and he wondered who she'd heard say those words. Her ex-chaplain dad maybe? Or her two cop uncles? But he didn't ask and a second later she patted his hand and turned back to the screen. 'Did the lady you're looking for go to any of these stores?'

'The ice cream store and maybe the antique store, too. I wonder if they do repairs.'

'They do. I saw the sign on the wall. They fix glass and restore paintings and clean antique furniture. Because if you don't do it right, you could lose all the value. I watch *Antiques Roadshow*,' she added. 'Religiously.'

'Religiously, huh? Well I do too.' He closed his eyes for a moment, during which Hope didn't make a sound, even to breathe. He focused on his memory of Alice, of driving her home. Of her snappishness and bad manners. Of how she'd treated him like a stupid jock. And of the one time he'd stopped in front of that same antique shop and she'd gotten out of the car with a clock in her hands. *If they fix clocks, then we might have a lead.*

He googled the shop and placed a call, crossing his fingers. Hope crossed hers too, both hands. 'Hello,' he said when the shop owner answered. 'This is Special Agent Davenport with the FBI, and I'm trying to track down a person of interest who might have shopped in your store.'

There was a moment of startled silence on the other end. 'Oh. Of course,' the woman said. 'I'm happy to cooperate. But first give me your badge number. I'd like to check your identity before I answer any questions.'

Decker was a little annoyed at the delay, but mostly impressed at the owner's caution. 'Of course.' He recited his badge number. 'The person I'm looking for is named Alice Newman. She would have been about five-seven, thin, blonde. She brought in a clock to be fixed.'

'If you can give me a date, that would help me search more quickly,' she said politely.

'I don't have a specific date, I'm sorry.' It had been cold, he remembered that. 'Perhaps late February or early March of this year?'

'That will help me considerably. Let me check your badge number with the local authorities, then I'll search. Should I call you back at the number on my caller ID?'

'Yes, please. And when you call the Cincinnati Field Office, ask for Special Agent in Charge Zimmerman. He's my boss.'

'Okay. I'll do that right now, and hopefully I'll have the information you need.'

Decker hung up and sighed. 'She's checking me out.'

'That's smart of her,' Hope said. 'My uncles say to never trust anyone who calls you on the phone unless you *know* them.'

'Your uncles sound very smart, too.'

'Oh they are. They work for the GBI. I guess that's almost like the FBI. Just one letter off.' She began to clear away her books, leaving him to puzzle that one out.

'Oh. Georgia Bureau of Investigation,' he said.

'Uh-huh,' she nodded. 'We lived in Atlanta. Mama and me. And then she met my dad. And then they got married and we moved here and lived with Aunt Meredith for a while. Now we have our own house and I have my own room.'

'I see. The GBI is state law enforcement. FBI is federal. We sometimes work with the state guys. Maybe someday I'll meet your uncles.'

'Maybe. They come up for holidays. If you don't have any family because they all died, you can have Thanksgiving and Christmas with us. My mama is a good cook.' The offer was made without an ounce of guile, and Decker found that his eyes were stinging.

'Thank you,' he said, his voice more hoarse than he'd intended.

The child looked up and met his eyes, and in hers he saw understanding and compassion. 'The timer's about to ring, so you should tidy your space. You need room for your plate.'

'I will. Thank you, Hope. You've helped me a great deal in my search.' The truth was, he would have gotten there on his own, but listening to her talk had helped jog his memory. And her offer of a shared meal on a lonely holiday . . . that was gold. Bright, shiny, and unblemished.

Her smile was brighter still. 'You're welcome, Mr Decker. I like to help people.'

Cincinnati, Ohio,
Friday 14 August, 1.15 P.M.

He'd been waiting for nearly an hour, parked behind the trees near the end of his driveway. Mallory had gotten a late start for the store, so he'd sat twiddling his thumbs, watching for her to emerge, and he was getting cranky. It was damn hot in his car, even with his A/C running non-stop. Finally he heard the smooth roar of her engine seconds before she pulled out of the driveway and started for the store.

He hit a button on his phone, dialing Gemma. 'Hi, it's me. Mallory should be on her way to the store. I wanted to remind you about talking to her.'

'I didn't forget. Where are you going? You sound like you're in the car.'

'I'm going to get some . . . personal items for Roxy,' he lied.

'So you're going to the liquor store,' Gemma said flatly. 'God, Brandon. The woman is a drunk. Toss her out on her ass.'

Roxy might be a drunk, but you're a hypocritical cokehead, Gemma. 'No, I'm going to the medical supply store. Roxy can't get out of bed any longer. I'm going to get some bedpans.' Actually, they were way past needing bedpans. He should catheterize her.

'God, Brandon,' Gemma whined. 'I hope you don't expect me to be changing bedpans.'

'Have I ever asked you to do anything for Roxy?'

'No,' came her fractious reply. 'Anyway, I thought you were sick.'

He blinked, surprised. His sisters had compared notes about him. 'I took an antihistamine so I can breathe, but I'm still not ready to tend patients.' His phone beeped in his ear. 'I'm getting another call. I gotta go.' He hung up on Gemma and accepted the next call without looking at the caller ID. 'Hello?'

'Good morning, Professor,' Rawlings said coldly.

'Good morning, Mr Rawlings,' he said cheerfully, thinking that the guard did not sound happy. He guessed a mud facial was not Rawlings's cuppa. 'How are you?'

'Lighter weight-wise than I should be. I seem to be missing the product you were supposed to deliver last night.'

What the hell was Rawlings trying to pull? 'I left it on the driver's seat of your car,' he said, matching the guard's cold tone.

'Then someone lifted it after you left me face down in the fucking mud. So you'll be replacing it. With interest. Double it.'

Like hell. I'll do no such thing. 'I'm not responsible for the product after I've made my delivery, Mr Rawlings.'

'Then maybe this will help you reconsider. I've just had a long, long talk with Special Agent Deacon Novak. He grilled me for over an hour, and I have to tell you he is one creepy fucker.'

He imagined that Rawlings was thinking this would make him nervous. 'He is a creepy fucker,' he agreed mildly.

'I didn't give you up. Yet. I can give you up in a way that doesn't reflect on me whatsoever. My record's clean. And you're a drug dealer who's connected to a lot of dead people.'

'I'm a middleman who facilitates the schemes of others,' he maintained levelly.

'Hm. So that's why Agent Novak was drilling me about the Professor? Had I ever heard of him? Did I know him?'

Fuck. Panic skittered down his spine, and that made him angry as hell. He drew a calming breath that he'd intended to be silent, but Rawlings must have heard because he chuckled like the fucking bastard he was. 'It was very hard to be blasé,' he mocked. 'It might be even harder the next time. So be smart, Professor. Be smart.'

He gritted his teeth at the guard's condescending tone, but didn't rise to the bait. *Because I am very smart. Far more so than you.* He'd always been prepared to jettison the Professor if the authorities ever got too close, and he had the perfect ace in the hole – his brother-in-law would make sure that whatever alibi he presented was rock solid. He'd planned ahead.

But the best tool in his arsenal was his own self. *I have no one whose death will utterly destroy me. Whereas you do.*

He made his voice tremble, just a touch. 'I'll . . . I'll need to think about this.'

'You do that,' Rawlings drawled, pleased. 'And don't forget my little list. It's still in play. Anything happens to me, my record of favors goes public.' The guard ended the call, seeming quite comfortable in the belief that he had the upper hand in their little game.

He turned into the first parking lot he came to and watched Mallory's vehicle disappear around the curve. Then he turned around and headed for home.

Rawlings had quite a bit to learn about the game's rules. And its penalties.

Eighteen

Decker's phone buzzed with an incoming call from Agent Triplett as he cleaned the last of the shrimp and grits off his plate. He and Hope had already demolished what had been left of the fried chicken. He wiped his fingers on a napkin and hit ACCEPT.

'Decker here. What's up, Trip?'

'I'm on duty downstairs today. You have a visitor coming up. That Diesel Kennedy guy from yesterday. He's alone this time, though.'

'Thanks. Hey, are you going out for lunch again today?'

Trip chuckled. 'I can. What do you want?'

'More of that barbecue from yesterday and anything else they have on the menu. I'll pay you back, cross my heart.' Decker eyed Hope. 'And maybe a few desserts, too. Anything they got. One of each.'

Hope grinned at him and Decker winked back.

'Holy cow, man,' Trip said. 'Your appetite came back like a hurricane.'

'Well, I *was* in a coma for a week, so I have an excuse. Besides, I have some help today. My little assistant, Hope. She likes sweets, but that's our secret.'

'Mum's the word,' Trip promised. 'I'll make a run when I get my break.'

'Thanks. Gotta go. Doorbell's ringing.' He hung up and got up, stretching his back while Hope's eyes grew huge.

'You're a lot taller than my dad. I didn't know because you were sitting down.'

'Maybe you can introduce me to him. He sounds nice.'

Dani had graduated him from a walker to a cane when he'd come back from the morning meeting, and he used it now to hobble to the door. To his amusement, Hope stayed glued to his side, holding her little hands out like she'd steady him if he started to fall.

Well, mostly amusement. He had to admit that the sight made his eyes sting again. Just a bit. 'If I fall, honey, I'll squash you like a tree squashing a bug.'

She blinked up at him. 'Well then, don't fall.'

He was laughing as the guard outside opened the front door. But his laughter was abruptly extinguished at the sight of Diesel Kennedy's face. The man was sheet white, the tattoo on his neck standing out in stark contrast.

Decker's attention was briefly diverted by Hope taking a giant sliding step to plant her body in front of his, her little arms folded across her chest, her chin lifted as she stared up at the tattooed mountain.

Decker laid his hand on top of her head. 'It's fine, honey. He's got tats, but he's a nice man. You don't need to worry about him.'

Diesel looked down, having just noticed Decker's pint-sized bodyguard. 'You Feds are hirin' 'em awful young now, aren't you?'

'I'm not an agent,' Hope informed him archly. 'Who are you, please?'

'Hope!' Bailey came in from the bedroom that Dani had slept in, her arms filled with boxes of bandages, her eyes wide and alarmed at the sight of Diesel. Decker held up his hand slightly to tell her it was all right. Bailey continued to approach, but slowly.

Hope didn't budge. 'I said "please", Mama.'

'Yes, ma'am, she did.' Diesel went down on one knee so that he could look Hope in the eye. 'My name is Diesel Kennedy. I'm a friend of Agent Davenport's. I've brought him something for his case. May I come in?' His tone was respectful and serious, as if he was speaking to a peer rather than a nine-year-old girl.

'Do you work at the FBI too?' Hope asked.

'No. I work for a newspaper, the *Ledger*.'

Hope brightened. 'Do you know Miss Scarlett? I mean Detective Bishop.'

Diesel's mouth curved. 'I call her Miss Scarlett too, sometimes. Yes. I like her. I think she likes me too.'

'Are you Marcus?'

Diesel coughed. 'No. She doesn't *like* me, like me. She just, you know, likes me.'

'So she's your friend.'

Diesel cleared his throat. 'Yes. That is correct. So you know Miss Scarlett?'

'She's friends with my mama and my aunt Meredith. This is my mama. She's a nurse.'

'I'm Bailey Beardsley,' Bailey said quietly. 'It's nice to meet you, Mr Kennedy. Hope, it's time for you to come with me and let these gentlemen speak.'

'Okay, Mama.' Hope turned to look at Decker. 'You're sure you'll be all right?'

'I'm sure,' Decker said soberly. 'But thank you.' He watched as Hope walked to the bedroom with her mother, then turned back to Diesel, who hadn't moved. He was still on one knee, frowning after the mother and daughter. 'I'd offer you a hand up,' Decker said dryly, 'but I can guarantee that will not end well.'

Diesel scrambled to his feet. 'Why do you have a nurse? Where's your doctor?' He blurted the words like an accusation.

'Dani had to go into the clinic for an emergency.'

Diesel's shoulders bowed out, his pale face flushing red with sudden anger. '*By herself*? You let her go *by herself*?'

Decker took a wobbly step back. 'One of the agents drove her to her car, but yes, I think she's working alone. I told her not to go without an escort, but she said it would be fine at the shelter. She said she'd be back later, that Bailey is her friend. Bailey's background checked out. Her kid is cute. That's all I know, man. So chill.'

'Sorry.' Diesel calmed himself. 'I brought you something.' He looked away. 'I kind of . . . didn't tell all the truth yesterday at that meeting.'

Decker lifted his brows. 'Should I sit down for this?'

'No, but I should. Where?'

'I'm set up in the kitchen.' Decker walked back to his computer and sat down, then waited for Diesel to do the same.

After staring at the chair for almost a minute, Diesel dug a flash drive from his pocket, tossed it on the table between them and dropped into the chair so hard it creaked.

'What is it?' Decker asked without picking it up, because Diesel was glaring at it like it was a cobra, coiled and ready to strike.

'The contents of McCord's hard drive. The real one that was hooked up to the Internet that night I hacked in.'

Decker stared at him. 'What the fuck, Diesel? Why didn't you mention this yesterday?'

'Because I wasn't sure if I actually had it. I didn't want to give your boss ammunition he might use against me later if the tides ever changed. Not without being sure that I actually had something to give.'

'Okay,' Decker said slowly. 'But now you're sure?'

'Yeah.' Diesel nodded grimly. 'I checked.'

Oh. That might explain the whiter-than-death face. 'So why were you not sure if you had it or not?'

Diesel dropped his chin, leaning forward, his elbows on his knees. 'When I finally cracked through all of the layers of security on McCord's computer, I realized I was under a time crunch. His network security was continually resetting itself. So I downloaded everything I could before I either got kicked out or discovered.'

'So at one point you had the entire contents of his hard drive. Not just the documents.'

'Only for a few minutes. I opened the first picture and . . .' His swallow was audible, his whisper not so much. 'I got sick. I . . . I have . . . experience with this.'

Decker's heart cracked, right in two. 'As a victim?' he asked, very gently. Diesel gave him a silent nod. 'My sister,' Decker said. 'Also.'

Another audible swallow and Diesel raised his head. 'I'm so sorry, man.'

387

Decker nodded. 'Me too,' he whispered, because his voice wasn't working. 'Her attacker killed her. He was . . . fierce.'

Diesel's eyes grew shiny and he dropped his chin again. 'Fuck. Fuck all of this. Fuck.'

'Yeah.' Decker took the flash drive in his hand, squeezed it tight in his fist. 'So after you got sick, you deleted everything you'd downloaded except for the documents?' Another silent nod. 'Where was your backup?'

'External hard drive.' The words were muffled. 'Set to auto update. I wasn't sure when it had. *If* it had. I wasn't thinking at that moment. I only wanted to get rid of those pictures.'

'I understand,' Decker said evenly. 'You'll get no judgment from me.'

A shudder shook Diesel. 'And then we had to bury Marcus's little brother, and that . . . that was hard. Kid was like my own brother too, y'know? Afterward, we were all on autopilot. This was nine months ago, and Marcus had gotten shot and almost died and we were running the *Ledger* without him and not doing any . . .' An unsteady sigh. 'Extracurricular investigating. And then it was New Year's.'

'What happened on New Year's?'

'I visit my safe deposit box the day after.'

'And?' Decker prodded gently.

Diesel's shoulders lifted with the deep, careful breath he drew, but he still didn't look up. 'Every New Year's, I take my external hard drive to the box and leave it in there and then I come home and start a new drive. Clean out everything from my laptop that I don't need anymore. New year, new start. Clean hard drive backup.'

For a moment Decker envisioned that safe deposit box, filled with hard drives and other things that Diesel Kennedy chose to leave behind when he started a new year. But he let it go, needing Diesel to focus on the mission before them and not the ghosts in his rear-view mirror. 'That's where you went today?' he asked. 'To your safe deposit box?'

'Last night. I . . . I couldn't sleep, so I went last night. Had to drive a while to get there and back. Then I had to make myself look at what was on there when I got home.'

Decker opened his palm, stared at the flash drive. 'So these are the real victims?'

Another head-down nod, so weary. 'Most of them foreign. Southeast Asian. South American. Indian – from India, I mean.'

'These were kids that McCord purchased through Alice and her father?'

'Yeah. I guess so.' Diesel had started to tremble and Decker wasn't sure what to do for him, so he went with his gut and clamped his hand over the back of Diesel's neck, holding on when those big shoulders heaved, tightening his grip when a sob barreled up from Diesel's chest.

Diesel didn't struggle as he cried, didn't say a word. He simply fell apart. So Decker kept that hand on him, hoping to hold him together just a little, so that he didn't completely lose his shit. But it was hard. So hard to watch a big man – *a man like me* – laid flat. Flayed open. There was nothing soft about Diesel Kennedy, especially not his sobs. Quietly harsh, they sounded like an animal in such great pain that it couldn't even howl.

Decker swiped at his own wet face with his shoulder as Diesel's grating sobs gouged into his chest like dulled knives. He remembered the pain from watching his sister die, but he hadn't been the one attacked. He couldn't imagine having to live with that all this time.

He heard a noise behind him and turned to find Bailey standing in the kitchen doorway looking helpless, tears on her face as well. Decker shook his head and she disappeared, giving Diesel the privacy he needed to grieve. To be angry. To just be.

When Diesel's sobs had finally quieted, Decker got up, splashed water on his own face, then wet a clean dishcloth and dangled it over Diesel's shoulder so that he could take it without turning. Then he made up an ice pack and pressed it to Diesel's face, giving him something to hide behind while they finished their conversation.

'Why me?' Decker asked quietly. 'Why trust me with this?'

Diesel shook his head. 'I don't know. I guess I just figured I could.' He shuddered out a breath, holding the ice pack against his eyes with both hands. 'I was disappointed that Dani wasn't here, but now . . . Shit, I'm glad she's not. Sucks enough that you were here.'

Decker didn't take offense. 'I won't tell her.'

'What about the nurse?'

'You knew she was there?'

Diesel lowered the ice pack enough to give him a sarcastic look. 'I was in the desert too. Rangers. I know when someone's sneaking up on me.'

Rangers? 'I guess you do. But Dani trusts her. I think we can trust her to be discreet.'

'All right.' The ice pack went back against Diesel's eyes. 'What happened to the fucker that killed your sister?'

Decker's jaw tightened. 'He's dead.'

A nod, accompanied by a grunt of approval. 'Good. Hope you made him hurt.'

'He hurt,' Decker said quietly. 'A lot.'

Diesel huffed a mirthless laugh. 'Love how you Feds answer a question without ever incriminating yourselves.'

'And you newspaper guys don't do the same? But yeah. He hurt. Best part is that he'll never do it to another girl. Or boy. Neither will McCord. Nor will his partner, because we will catch him. We won't catch them all, but we will catch this one, Diesel.'

'Thank you.' He tipped his head back, keeping the ice on his face. 'What will you tell your boss about the flash drive?'

Decker looked at the little piece of plastic and metal in his hand. 'What you told me. That your backup system made a copy that you didn't find until you went back and looked. He doesn't need to know where the drive was kept and that you have more of them.'

'You sure you're a Fed?'

'Last I checked. Thank you for this. Finding out who McCord's victims were will hopefully help us find his partner.'

'If any of those kids are still alive.'

'I pray they are, but even if they're not, we might find patterns leading us to the partner.' Decker sure hoped so. The victims of

Alice and her father's trafficking who'd been saved by Scarlett and Deacon a week ago had all been sold for labor. None had been photographed or sold into the sex trade.

Diesel stood up on legs that wobbled. 'Shit, I got a headache now. But the ice helped.'

'There's ibuprofen in that big bottle over there. Kate went a little crazy at the store last night.' *And then she went a little crazy on me.* She'd be coming back soon. *And maybe she'll do it again. Maybe even more.* And maybe he'd better stop thinking about Kate, because his sweats weren't hiding a thing. Again.

Diesel's lips twitched. 'You do realize that Deacon considers Kate to be his sister?'

'Glad to hear it.' Decker got two bottles of water from the fridge and tossed one to Diesel, mostly so that he could surreptitiously adjust himself before closing the fridge door. 'Because I do *not* consider her to be *my* sister.'

Diesel's laugh was a little bit evil. 'This is gonna be fun.'

Decker grinned, but then his cell phone rang and he sobered in a second. It was the antique store. 'Cross your fingers,' he muttered, then hit ACCEPT. 'This is Agent Davenport. Did you check me out?'

'I did,' the owner said. 'Your boss says I should give you my full cooperation. So this is what I found: a woman brought in a clock to be repaired at the end of February, but her name wasn't Alice. Our surveillance only goes back three months and then gets recorded over, so I don't know if she matches the description of the woman you're looking for.'

'She might have used an alias. Can you give me a second?' He muted the phone and snapped his fingers rhythmically, trying to remember the aliases Alice had used. 'Troy said yesterday that she used a fake name at the gym.'

'You muttering about Alice?' Diesel asked.

'Yeah. I need the name she was using.'

'Allison Bassett,' he said without blinking. 'That's the name she gave Marcus when she sat with him in the hospital, then stalked him when he got out. She wanted to make sure he wasn't reopening the McCord case, I guess. Now we know why.'

'Yeah,' Decker said grimly. He unmuted the phone. 'Was it Allison Bassett?'

'Yes,' the woman said with relief. 'I would have given it to you anyway, but I feel so much better doing it since you had the right name. She left an address so that we could deliver it when the repair was complete. Do you want it?'

Decker's smile stretched his face. 'Yes, ma'am, I certainly do.'

Cincinnati, Ohio,
Friday 14 August, 1.55 P.M.

Mallory parked the car in front of the Home Store, but didn't turn off the engine. She felt sick. *Dammit. Just do it. Get it over with.* And then?

And then accept the consequences, whatever those are. As long as Macy was okay.

I'll talk to the lady cop. I'll tell her everything. After she goes to Gemma's house and removes Macy into protective custody. The cops could do that. She'd seen it on the television once. A documentary, not one of those fictional cop shows. The man on the documentary had gotten protection for his wife and son in return for giving the cops valuable evidence.

Saving four kids from a life of making Internet porn seemed like a valuable trade.

She got out of the car, weaving slightly on her feet when the heat smacked her in the face. In the documentary, the man and his family went into the witness protection program and were given new identities and a new home. If she got to move, she'd move far away from this city with its frigid, gray winters and unbearably humid summers. Maybe Maine. Or Seattle. Or maybe somewhere in the middle of nowhere, where no one would recognize her as Sunshine Suzie.

Stop stalling, Mallory. Go into the store and ask the manager if you can use the phone. Use that phone to call the nice lady at the police station. Just do it.

She locked the car and forced her feet to move. *One foot in front of the other.* She started walking, looking over her shoulder to scan the lot. She'd felt like she was being followed for a while, but there had been no one behind her until she'd reached the highway.

You're being paranoid. But better safe than sorry. Or dead. Like JJ.

She'd slowed down as she'd passed the motel parking lot where she'd left JJ's remains early that morning. JJ's car was gone. *Just like he knew it would be. That's why he told me to leave the keys in it.* Either he'd sent someone to dispose of it – and JJ – or someone had stolen it. Either way, Mallory's fingerprints were all over it.

He'd set her up. He'd made her complicit in murder. *So?* He'd already made her complicit in child abuse. Why not murder too?

Suddenly the idea of telling the cops everything wasn't sounding as good. *If the cops find those suitcases, I'm going to jail.* She paused, half turning back to the car.

But if she said nothing, four more human beings would become Sunshine Suzies.

So she kept walking toward the store. Which had a pay phone! She'd never looked in front of this Home Store before, only in front of the grocery stores. She quickened her step, and was ten feet from the phone when she heard a voice behind her.

'Mallory! Sweetie!'

Dread mixed with anticipation in Mallory's gut. Dread because it was Gemma and nothing good ever came of being near the woman. Anticipation because Gemma would have Macy.

Mallory turned, disappointment smacking her harder than the heat had. Because there was no Macy. Gemma was alone, a too-bright smile on her face.

'Mal, how are you, girl? It's been a dog's age since I've seen you. What a coincidence.'

No, not a coincidence. It couldn't be. Gemma was looking her up and down critically.

Mallory wondered what he'd told his sister this time. 'I'm fine, Gemma,' she said politely, because if she was rude, he'd make her sorry later. 'How are you?'

'Never better!' Gemma sang.

The dread in Mallory's gut grew exponentially. Gemma's smile was too bright, her eyes too sparkly. *Oh God.* The woman taking care of Macy was high. 'Where's Macy?'

Gemma's overly bright eyes narrowed. 'She's with her daddy.' It was a warning for Mallory to stay away. But then Gemma sidled up to Mallory and put an arm around her shoulders. 'I came to pick up a few last-minute items for Macy's birthday. You have such good taste. Would you mind helping me?'

The lie was so blatant, Mallory nearly broke down there and then. *She knows. She knows I wanted to use the phone. That I wanted to tell.*

No, that was ridiculous. How could she possibly know? But it didn't matter in the end. What mattered was that Gemma was plastered to her side and looking like she didn't plan to leave. There would be no phone call today.

But the kids were coming over tomorrow. Four of them.

He won't touch them tomorrow. Tomorrow is movies and pool play. But what if he did?

I'll just have to create another reason to go to the store again tomorrow.

Cincinnati, Ohio,
Friday 14 August, 3.15 P.M.

'Kate? You called?'

Kate said a silent prayer of thanks when Adam Kimble walked in the room. She'd never been so glad to have an excuse to turn away from a computer monitor. At the same time, she'd never been so sorry to have to ask a colleague for a consult. 'Yeah.' She grabbed her water bottle and hit the monitor's off button. 'We arrested Corey Addison.'

'I heard. I also heard from Quincy Taylor that you have mad ninja skills.'

Kate's lips quirked up. 'Thank you. I'm rather proud of my ninja skills. I'm not sure where Addison thought he was going. I had him cuffed and there were all kinds of cops and Feds surrounding the building.' She smiled. 'It made for amazing TV when we dragged him out, hobbling because I had to cuff his feet too.'

'I know.' Adam's smile was just as evil as hers. 'I saw it on every news station in town and on CNN. I think we even made the BBC.'

'Huzzah!' Then Kate let out a breath. *God. I hate this so damn much.* 'Adam . . . we searched his office and his home. And we found . . . stuff.'

Adam's smile fizzled. 'I figured as much.'

'I don't want you to have to view it all, not by yourself. That's not right.'

'It's okay.' He held up a bag with the logo of a local bookstore. 'I've got coping strategies now.' He dumped the bag on the table and Kate found herself smiling again.

'Coloring books and *Origami for Dummies*? Excellent.'

'It's a start. I also need to deal with the anger.' He winced. 'I'm looking for a therapist.'

'I thought you and Meredith . . . ?'

He shook his head. 'Oh, no. No. We're friends. I can't expect her to treat me. It's not fair to her. So I need someone . . . else.'

'I get that.' The PTSD specialist's card was burning a hole in her pocket. 'I'm going to try to find someone to help me with my . . .' She exaggerated trembling hands. 'I get so wound up, I can't think. And knitting or origami will not always be appropriate.'

Adam sat down in front of the dark monitor. 'You didn't ask me here to talk about our feelings, although you're welcome to call me if you need to be talked off a ledge.'

'If you'll do the same.' She took the chair next to him when he nodded. 'Okay. We'll be therapy buddies. I never thought I'd say those words out loud, but there you are.' She took a breath, then caved and reached for the knitting she'd been doing when he came in. 'There wasn't anything on Addison's office computer. He was smart enough not to surf for porn at work, at least. But his home computer was full and he had a *lot* of DVDs. Some were professionally done – and I use that term very lightly. Others he'd recorded himself and that's a whole 'nother investigation. But relevant to this one were some old-style CDs. They were labeled with "SS" and the year and the volume. The dates started six years ago and continued for three years.'

'When Sunshine Suzie was being forced to make the films,' Adam said tightly.

'Yeah. There are several volumes for each year, especially the first. Corey Addison was a real fan. I took a look at the first CD from each of the three years, just to get an idea of the flow and if anything had changed.'

'Like the set or the props. Good thinking.'

Kate bobbed her head nervously, knitting until she hit the end of a row and realized she'd been silently bobbing her head for a long time. She looked up, embarrassed, and saw understanding in Adam's eyes.

'It sucks,' he murmured. 'And not everyone handles it the same way. I . . . self-detonated. Cut myself off from family and friends. However you deal with it is gonna be your normal.'

'That sounds like it came from a textbook or a sensei.'

'Second one. I had a mentor while I was working Personal Crimes. He was the guy I met with yesterday to review the files found on McCord's PC. Bottom line is, don't be embarrassed. And, I guess . . . don't be afraid to ask for help.'

'That's the problem,' she said miserably. 'I'm asking you for help because you'll be able to analyze this faster than the rest of us.'

'So there were changes between year one and year three?'

'Yes. The set changed. And then I went to the website that Corey Addison had bookmarked to compare the recorded ones with the Suzie videos online and most were the same, but the year one videos weren't. There were extra ones on Addison's recordings – ones that aren't available online. I couldn't find them, at least. But I haven't learned all the places to look yet.'

'None of us know that. They change daily. Somehow the perverts get the memo, though.' He took a series of deep breaths. 'I don't need to look at the online videos. I viewed them at ICAC this afternoon to refresh my memory. I figured we should know what she'd been through. Meredith will need to know, anyway, so she can properly counsel her once we find her. I didn't want Mer to have to see this.'

Kate squeezed his shoulder. 'You're a good guy, Kimble.'

He grimaced. 'I don't think so.'

She grabbed his chin and made him look at her. 'You are a good guy,' she repeated firmly. 'We all deal differently, but one of the commonalities should be that we don't diss ourselves. And we don't let friends diss themselves, either. So stop it. Got it?'

He smiled awkwardly, since she still held his chin. 'Yes, oh mighty ninja queen.'

'I like that better than origami queen,' she said loftily, then let him go. 'The video I have open is one of Corey Addison's first Suzie recordings. She's young, Adam. Really young.'

He nodded. Then hit the monitor's ON button. And his face tightened. As did his fists. 'Jesus God,' he whispered. 'Why? I mean, how could anyone be that . . .'

'Evil?' Kate supplied sadly. 'I don't know. But God, do I want to find the man who did this to her.'

'Me too.' He frowned and focused on the monitor. 'You're right. The videos were produced in two different places. The light is different for one. See how it fills the window here? But there's no actual sun stream.'

'Northern exposure,' Kate said. 'I wanted to be a tracker when I joined the army, but back then it wasn't really possible if you were a girl.'

'That's bullshit. You shoot better than just about any man I know.'

'Thank you, but that's the way it was. Regardless, I can navigate my way out of just about anywhere, cloudy day or sunny. Night or day.' She wasn't bragging. It was simply a statement of skill.

'Then maybe you can give my mom some lessons,' Adam said lightly. 'She gets lost going to the corner store.'

'Maybe she'd be better off with a GPS.' Kate went along with the levity because it seemed to be calming them both.

Adam laughed. 'Maybe.' He sighed. 'Anyway, the light is different, so it's at least a different room in the same house.' He paused the video and tilted his head. 'Nope, different house. The ceilings are higher in the newer videos.'

She leaned over to see the screen. 'Now that you point it out, I can see it, yes.'

'It could still be the same house, but the landscape is different when you look through the window. I'm not sure this matters, though. If it is a different place and he's not filming there anymore, it probably won't help us to locate it. Especially if it's been years.'

'But *why* are these older videos no longer available?' Kate pressed. 'It seems like he'd want to get all the hits he could, to make the most money.'

'True.' Adam leaned back in his chair, thinking. 'It would make sense if this first place was compromised somehow.'

'Like people he knew might identify him through the house?'

'Exactly. It would have to be people who could use it against him. Maybe blackmail him.' His dark brows shot up. 'Or arrest him.'

Kate smiled slowly. 'Like maybe the cops saw his house. If they did, they didn't realize what he was doing there, because they didn't arrest him. Or . . .' Her smile faded. 'Or they did figure it out and wanted in on the deal.'

'All maybes, but all places to start.'

'If we could figure out where this place is, Adam, we could check it against police reports. It wouldn't be old. He filmed there six years ago. By five years ago, he was somewhere else.'

'No one's been able to figure out where that place is,' Adam said. 'ICAC didn't know she was local when she first came on the scene. There weren't any cues suggesting the videos were made in the Midwest. In the US generally, yes, but that's all.'

'Cues like what? Electrical outlet configurations?'

'Yeah, that and products sitting out on kitchen counters and bathroom sinks. Wallpaper styles. Shoe styles. That kind of thing. Now the technology is so much better, they might be able to figure out where he filmed both at the beginning and then later, after he moved.' He looked at her then, his eyes intense. 'This is the first time I've felt any hope at all working these cases, Kate.'

'Good. Then I don't feel so bad calling you in.'

'You shouldn't have worried about it anyway. This is a job. My job.'

She hesitated. 'Actually, your job is the violent crime task force, isn't it? You're not going back to Personal Crimes, are you?'

'Yes to the first and no to the second. So this is my job for now.'

'That sounds better. So what next?'

'I take the CDs and run them through whoever's software is the latest and greatest. I'm betting you the Feds have better tech than ICAC does.'

'You're probably right. Troy will be able to help you with that.' She frowned. 'I wonder where he is. I haven't heard from him in hours, but I get no cell signal in here.' She was in the equivalent of a vault, the place they went to discuss or to view anything highly confidential. 'He was going to dig into the Professor.' She dialed Troy's phone from the room's landline. 'Hey,' she said when he answered. 'What's your location?'

'On my way to Alice's apartment. Decker came through in a big way.'

Kate's mouth fell open. 'What? Why didn't anyone tell me?'

'He did,' Troy said. 'He sent out a group text to you, me, and Zimmerman.'

'Dammit. I really hate when I'm disconnected like this.'

'You're in the vault?'

'Yeah. But I'll come meet you at Alice's.' She looked over at Adam. 'Is that okay with you? If I leave you with this?'

'Of course,' Adam said, 'but let me talk to Troy.'

Kate handed the phone off to him, gathering her things while he and Troy talked tech. Her phone started pinging and buzzing as soon as she was twenty feet outside of the vault. One text from Troy, responding to Decker's group text. One from Zimmerman, same.

One group text from Deacon, saying that he'd be at the jail for a while, that one of the guards was acting 'squirrelly'.

One from Meredith, thanking her for taking Kendra under her wing.

One from Felicia Petrie, with her thanks and a video attachment of Kate being attacked by Corey Addison and the resulting 'ninja action'.

And eight texts from Decker. One was the group text, saying

he'd found Alice's apartment and providing the Oakley address. Kate didn't know the city yet, but she'd Google Map it. The seven remaining texts had been sent privately, just to her.

Ate all the chicken. Sorry. Maybe we can go out later for more? I'll wear a tactical helmet. Going stir crazy just sitting here.

Yeah, right, she thought. They were not going out for chicken or anything else. She'd pick up more food on her way back. She already planned to stop for more brownie ingredients. He'd stay put in the safe house. Where it was *safe,* for heaven's sake. *God. Men.*

Rolling her eyes, she read on. The next text had been sent an hour ago.

Found Alice's place. Then, five minutes later: *Saw you on TV escorting the SOB out of his building. Leg cuffs. Nice touch.*

Fifteen minutes after that: *Yo, Kate, you there?*

And then, ten minutes later, *Helllooooo? Now you're scaring me. Call me. Need to know you're OK.*

And a few minutes after that: *Oh. Vault. Z told me you're OK. Next time, take an effing coffee break, okay? Let your phone connect with the universe.* That last one made her smile.

The smile was wiped off her face by the final text, sent fifteen minutes ago: *Meet me at Alice's. Address in group text. Back in the game! Hell yeah.*

'Hell *no,*' Kate muttered as she race-walked to her car, ignoring the heat and humidity. 'Goddamn man needs a fucking keeper.'

'They *all* do, honey,' an older lady said as she got out of the car next to Kate's.

Kate spared a second to smile at her. 'I was hoping they got smarter with age.'

The lady laughed. 'We wish.'

'Have a nice day,' Kate said, then jumped in her rental and cranked the engine. 'Decker, you have some serious explaining to do.'

Cincinnati, Ohio,
Friday 14 August, 3.20 P.M.

He watched the handoff through binoculars, a good block away. The frontman was just a kid himself, no one special. But the kid – whose name was Charlie – thought he was all that because the Professor had hand-picked him to try his newest pick-me-up. In reality he'd chosen Charlie because he was the first one who'd shown up at the basketball court behind the CVS.

Charlie probably wouldn't be feeling so great in a few minutes, but that was the way the ball rolled. *I leave no witnesses. Ever.*

Rawlings's son had shown up after his shift at the McDonald's across the street, as was his routine. All the kids were drawn to the place like homing pigeons during the school year, descending minutes after the final bell. It was the place to be seen. Boys played basketball, showing off, and girls sat in little bevies and watched, cooing their admiration. Year after year. Fashions might change, but kids in general remained pretty predictable.

During the summer, far fewer kids showed up to play, and they didn't stay long. *Because, like, heat stroke,* he thought derisively. Every summer he and Nell got at least one heat stroke victim off this very basketball court. In fact, he was pretty sure he'd treated Charlie at some time in the past. He'd definitely treated the kid for other things – colds, flu. He'd known Charlie since he was a snot-nosed fifth-grader.

He'd known Charlie's mother even longer, both as a family doctor and as the Professor. They'd gone to college together and she'd been one of the Professor's very infrequent customers, back in the days when she'd used only enough to get her through finals. To get her through the bar exam. Then to get through an especially challenging court case.

But children came along and she and her husband kept progressing in their careers, and there never seemed to be enough hours in the day to cook the food and shuttle the kids and go to softball games and be a cut-throat attorney and, oh yeah, to stay fit and slim for her husband, who liked to brag that she could still fit into her high-school cheerleading uniform. Which was simply madness, but Charlie's mom bought it, lock, stock and barrel.

And started taking more and more of the Professor's pills, because being all things to all people was hard work. Now she was one of his best customers, and perhaps a little careless, too. Because Charlie had brought him his mother's pills to trade for something that was a little more fun, not knowing that he was dealing with his mom's dealer.

And he'd certainly never tell the kid, because there was honor in the client/dealer relationship. He dealt with every customer individually. No blabbing everybody's business. Besides, he really didn't care, except about the money it brought in.

Tim Rawlings Junior and Charlie were pals. He knew this because he'd watched them play together before. The two had already sweated through their shirts, and Tim Junior had pulled his off and was mopping his face with it. Both kids were nice-looking, but Tim Junior was a little slimmer, muscles a little more defined. Probably spent more time in his dad's home gym. He'd look good on film.

If he lived, of course. *That* would depend on Rawlings Senior.

Charlie took a swig of water, then pulled out the little medicine bottle he carried and shook out a pill or two, carefully examining them before popping them in his mouth. He'd taken the correct ones. One generic meth pill plus a blue capsule. *Because you're bigger*, he'd explained to the kid when he'd given him the pills. The yellow capsule was for Tim Junior because he was lighter-weight.

In reality, Charlie's blue capsule was filled with sugar, while Junior's contained something far more deadly. Something that would give Rawlings Senior pause. Something that would make Rawlings Senior back the hell off his threats and demands. Something that would strike the fear of God into the guard's heart. *Or, better still, the fear of me.*

He watched as Charlie offered Junior his pills and earnestly explained the 'pick-me-up' concept – a way to magnify the effects of the meth safely. *Safely* yanked them in every time.

Sheep, he thought with contempt. But lucrative sheep, so he couldn't complain.

He watched as Tim Junior frowned at the pills for a minute, then looked at Charlie assessingly. Charlie had taken his pill and he was okay, therefore Tim Junior would be. He popped both pills in his mouth and downed them with a bottle of water.

He sat back in the driver's seat and let out the breath he'd been holding. That little scenario could have played out so many different ways. But it had worked.

Now all he needed to do was wait for the capsule coating to wear away in Junior's stomach. Pain would begin within a few hours. If Tim Junior went untreated, he'd be dead in three days. *Luckily I won't have to explain the dangers of ricin to Rawlings Senior.* The guard had handled the stuff himself when dealing with Alice in prison.

He waited patiently for the boys to get too hot to play anymore. Junior took off on his bike and Charlie ambled back toward where he sat parked, as was their agreement. Charlie was his frontman. His job was to get his friends to try the Professor's new pill.

In exchange for special goodies, just for him. *Sheep.*

He slid the binoculars under his seat when Charlie approached, then turned to him when the kid slid into the passenger side. 'Charlie, my man. What did you think?'

Charlie shrugged. 'Dunno. Doesn't seem that much different.'

The kid was honest, at least. 'Here. Try this one then.' He handed Charlie a pill that was pure meth, guaranteed to blow the kid's heart to smithereens. In hindsight, he should have used this on Sidney Siler, but he hadn't wanted to wait around to make sure she was dead. Cyanide was faster, and with her skin tone, any residual skin changes would have been undetectable. Plus, he'd still had it on hand after giving it to Rawlings as a last-resort pill for taking care of Alice.

Plus, cyanide was just too cool. But too much of a good thing wouldn't do, and Charlie was as pasty as Elmer's glue. If his skin turned red from cyanide, everyone would know.

'Cool. Thanks.' Within a few minutes, Charlie was jumpy. A few minutes later, he was breathing very hard. 'Wow. Professor. This feels . . . freaky.'

'Give it some time. It'll mellow out. So . . . did your pal ask where the pills came from?'

'Nah. I always get them from my ma's medicine cabinet. He knows that.' Charlie wiped his brow. 'Damn, Professor. This feels really weird.'

Fifteen minutes later, the job was done. He drove Charlie's body back to the basketball court, now completely empty, and pushed him out of the passenger seat to the ground behind the boy's car.

He'd give it an hour or two, then he'd call Rawlings Senior and tell him what he needed to do to save his son. He smiled, visualizing it.

But he couldn't crack open the bubbly just yet, because he had one more end to snip. It was time to get down to business about removing Agent Davenport from the equation. Which meant removing him from the earth.

Then he'd remove the Professor from his face and destroy the disguise.

And then *I'll crack open the bubbly, because I'll be home free.*

Nineteen

Decker knew without looking that Zimmerman had entered Alice's apartment. He could actually feel the man's scowl.

'Are you trying to put yourself back in the hospital?' Zimmerman asked impatiently.

Decker turned around in the folding chair to look over his shoulder. Zimmerman stood in the doorway of Alice's bedroom, arms crossed tight and looking generally pissed.

'No, sir. But I asked Dr Novak and she didn't say no.'

'Did she say yes?' Zimmerman demanded.

'Not exactly. Truthfully, she didn't say anything at all. She never returned my text. I figured she's pissed off with me, so I'll buy her some pretty flowers and apologize later.'

Zimmerman rolled his eyes. 'Who drove you here?'

'Trip. But he was following a direct order from me, so please don't penalize him. Look, we have good security here and I'm feeling strong.'

'Until your adrenaline crashes,' Zimmerman said with a shake of his head, but he walked to the large square hole in the wall, standing next to Decker's chair. 'Well, you're here. We'll deal with the fact that you aren't cleared for duty later. What did you find?'

Decker pointed to the growing stack of DVDs on the floor. 'Video. Lots and lots of video.'

Zimmerman frowned. 'Alice kept the child porn here too?'

'No, sir. Not child porn. These all seem to be sex tapes of adults.

405

Specifically Alice and . . . well, lots of guys. Not at the same time,' he added when Zimmerman looked rather scandalized. 'But she seemed to be remarkably . . . active.'

'God. How many have you found?'

'About twenty-five so far.' Decker pointed at the hole in the wall, then at the set of bookshelves about three feet away. 'She used the bookshelves to hide the hole.'

'How did you find it?'

'Tracks in the carpet, and the paint on the wall was scraped. She must have pushed it back and forth frequently.'

'Good work, but please don't do this again. Wait until Dr Novak clears you fully.'

Decker nodded dutifully. 'Yes, sir.'

Zimmerman rolled his eyes again. 'You lie like a rug, son. One big question. Did you tell Kate that you're here? Because I don't want to be around when she finds out.'

The front door opened, setting off blinking lights overhead – a silent warning system Alice had set up. The warning this time was accompanied by a familiar voice demanding to know where Agent Davenport was. 'I asked her to meet me here, yes. I imagine she's not too pleased.'

Zimmerman shook his head. 'I imagine you're right.'

Seconds later, Kate strode in, her expression dark and forbidding. God, she was gorgeous. Decker was instantly hard. 'Agent Coppola,' he said pleasantly. 'Glad you could join us.'

Kate stopped next to Zimmerman, not looking at Decker. 'Please tell me you didn't condone this, sir.'

'I did not,' Zimmerman said. 'Apparently Agent Davenport recruited a little help from Triplett and Troy. I don't think they knew that Dr Novak hadn't cleared him.'

'It wouldn't have mattered if they had,' she muttered, ignoring Decker completely. 'Agent Davenport could charm a snake out of its skin.'

Zimmerman grunted in agreement. 'Then I suppose it's a good thing that he uses his snake-charming powers for good and not evil.'

'His charm isn't going to help him if he puts himself back in the hospital.'

'That's what I tried to tell him,' Zimmerman said with a nod.

'I'm right here,' Decker said mildly.

'Oh, of that I am well aware.' Kate drew a breath and let it out.

Decker held up his hand, hoping to ward off a tirade. 'I know you're upset—' he started.

'Yes, I am,' she interrupted. 'I'm *upset* that you care so little for your own recovery. The doctors saved your life once. How many times do you expect them to be able to do that? Hell, I killed two men to save your life. Two bad men, sure, but *I killed two men*. And then you do *this*? How many more do I need to kill to save you? Just tell me so that I can prepare myself. Two more? Ten more?'

Decker winced. 'Good one, Kate. Direct hit.'

Zimmerman backed away, the coward. 'I'm going to check on Agent Taylor's progress.'

'I hit where I aim,' she said when the boss was gone. 'I meant it to get your attention.'

Decker pinched the bridge of his nose. Technically, she hadn't killed two men to save his life. They'd already shot him and were escaping. She'd shot at their car to stop them. But he decided not to belabor that point, because at the end of the day, she had killed two men. He wouldn't have felt one iota of guilt, but he wasn't Kate.

Kate was the woman who listened to Disney music when she was sad, but only in secret because she wanted people to believe she was an iron lady. She was the woman who'd given Sidney Siler's grieving parents her own hotel room because they couldn't afford one of their own, and who'd cared for her dying husband until he'd drawn his last breath.

She was the woman who'd sat by his side for a week because he'd had no one else. It had been her voice that he'd listened for when he'd been in the dark, when he'd been disoriented and . . . yes, afraid. Her touch that had grounded him when he'd gone so long without.

So she *had* saved him, just not in the way she was thinking, and he wasn't going to insult her by minimizing her guilt or her gift. But nor would he allow her to treat him like a stray puppy she'd taken in and needed to coddle.

'I'm not going to apologize for doing my job. I'm wearing Kevlar. We have personnel all over the damn place. My nurse came with me. She's the nice lady sitting in the living room. Her name is Bailey. She said it would be good for me to walk. To get some fresh air. To work off some of the tension that had my blood pressure creeping up. Her husband had already picked up their daughter from the safe house, so I asked her to join us because I knew you'd be more comfortable if I had medical coverage nearby.'

Kate's eyes blazed. '*I'd* be more comfortable? What about the fact that you just got out of the hospital yesterday, Decker? Out of a fucking coma?'

'Medically induced,' he said stubbornly, hearing the defensiveness in his own voice. 'And I'm walking today. I'm *working* today. I figured out where Alice lived today.'

'And you figured it was only fair that you got to be here for the search,' Kate said quietly, and he couldn't decide if she was for or against that statement. He couldn't let himself care.

'Look. You can be angry with me all you want. It's not going to change reality. You say you killed two men to save my life. *I* say that you killed two men, saved my life, and now I should *do* something with the life you saved. That won't happen if I'm cooped up in a fancy-ass kitchen in a safe house, staring at a computer monitor. And whether you'll admit it or not, you'd be doing the same thing as me if *I'd* killed two people for *you.*'

'Are you done?' Kate asked, her expression not giving an inch.

Decker sighed. 'Guess so.'

'Then show me what you've found. Please.'

'Okay,' he said warily. 'This hole appears to have been the only secret hiding place in the house, but CSU is bringing in some wall X-ray equipment to make sure Alice didn't stash stuff all over the place. The hiding place was filled with DVDs that she made using that camera, right there.' He pointed to the wall opposite the bed. 'It was camouflaged by some pictures she'd hung around it. The camera was focused on the bed. From the few DVDs we've looked at so far, it seems she taped herself having sex with several partners. One at a time. So far. Quincy Taylor is cataloging them now, getting stills of their faces so we can put them through facial recognition software. I just finished digging out the last of the DVDs right there.' He pointed at the stack.

'Why would she tape them?'

'Maybe just her kink. She wrote the date, a set of initials, and a rating on each jacket.'

'Rating as in R, X, or triple X?'

'No.' Decker could feel his cheeks heating. 'As in six out of ten, seven out of ten, nine point five out of ten. A . . . performance measure.' He cleared his throat. 'One of the first ones we checked featured the son of one of the other traffickers, the one you interviewed in the jail. We're hoping that her other partners were also involved in the traffickers' ring. Then we get her business contacts.'

'Makes sense, actually,' Kate said thoughtfully. 'Alice had to keep her identity secret to outsiders, so she spent her free time with insiders.'

'It's also possible she was using the DVDs as leverage. Maybe some of the men were married. Or, like I said before, it could just be a kink. Or a way to feel powerful. Her dad kept her on a pretty short leash.'

'That I actually understand,' she said, rubbing her tongue over her broken tooth in that subconscious gesture. 'Did you find any ledgers or any record of her business dealings inside the wall? Contracts or invoices?'

Decker had to push away his anger at the man who'd broken her tooth so that he could focus on her questions. 'Not yet, but I may have another lead on customers and suppliers. I was given a flash drive with the contents of McCord's *real* computer – the one hooked up to the Net.'

Her eyes narrowed and sparkled simultaneously. 'Diesel came through. He had a backup.'

'I got it from a source who's worried the FBI could make his life miserable and put his friends in jail,' he averred, for form only. 'I promised anonymity.'

Kate smiled for the first time since entering like a hurricane. 'Diesel came through,' she said again.

'I don't reveal my sources,' Decker said, but nodded. 'He'd looked over the files before he gave them to me, to make sure they were what we were looking for. He was in bad shape.'

Kate's smile vanished. 'Poor guy.'

'You have no idea.' Decker grabbed her hand, relieved when she didn't pull away. He held on, needing her. 'He didn't realize there was a backup. He checked to see, then brought the evidence straight to me. I checked some of the picture files myself after he left, while we were waiting on the search warrant for this place.' He closed his eyes, shaking his head. 'It was what you'd expect. Just vile.'

Kate squeezed his hand. 'I reviewed some of the Sunshine Suzie films today,' she whispered. 'She was only twelve. So I know what you mean.'

'I had to get out of the apartment, Kate.' His voice sounded bleak to his own ears. 'After looking at McCord's picture files . . . I had to *do* something.'

She crouched beside him. 'I get it, Decker. I do. But until you can run and jump and dodge bullets, you are a danger to yourself. I don't want to watch you bleeding on the ground again, or sit with you for another week because you're in a coma.' Her voice broke a little and he was rocked to see tears in her eyes. 'Please don't make me do that.'

He exhaled heavily. 'Okay. I'll . . . respect my recovery, because it hurts you if I don't.'

She pressed her forehead against their joined hands. 'Thank you.'

'But if there's adequate security, I will work. I won't be coddled. You wouldn't be if our situations were reversed. You said that yourself.'

She looked up, her eyes damp but clear, and he suspected her dark slacks had absorbed a tear or two that she'd let fall. 'I did say that. And I'll help you go through the files from McCord's computer. I don't think we should involve anyone else until we're sure there's no leak.'

'I agree. Are we okay now?'

'Can I coddle you, just a little?'

'If it involves baking, that's a yes. If it involves . . . other things, that's a yes, too. If it involves wrapping me in bubble wrap, that would be a no.'

'I love that bubble stuff,' she said wistfully. 'Pops like a gun, but nobody gets hurt.'

He smiled, delighted with her. 'I really like you, Kate.'

'Good. Same goes.' She released his hand and pivoted, landing on her knees next to the hole in the wall. 'I think Alice forfeited her security deposit.'

Decker chuckled. 'I'd have to say she did.'

Kate pulled her flashlight from her belt and shined it down into the black space. 'It's clean at least. No mice or snakes. So their skins are safe from charmers.'

'Ha ha,' he said flatly. 'Everyone's a comedian.'

She switched off her light and came to her feet. 'Nothing more in there. If this had been a real hidey-hole, she would have had other stuff, like a fake passport, or ledgers. Maybe ammunition and firearms. I imagine the important papers are in a safe or maybe a safe deposit box somewhere. She was a good shot, so she should have a rifle hidden away. But there isn't one here. The hidey-hole was for her DVDs and was easily accessible. Alice liked to watch.'

'I don't want to watch her,' Decker said wearily. 'I've seen too many things today that my brain can't unsee.'

'Me too. But we'll have to help. There are too many for a single person to process quickly.'

'I know. But I can still not want to. When do you want to start?'

'Well, I think we need to be sure we've searched every nook and cranny. You said CSU is coming in with X-ray machines to check the rest of the walls. When is that?'

'Tomorrow at the earliest, I think. They're going to focus on searching what's out in the open first. Drawers and closets and such.'

'Then while they're doing that, we can work on the videos. But

411

first, I think I could use some supper and maybe a short nap. I'm running on fumes.'

'A nap sounds good to me.' His cell phone buzzed and so did Kate's. 'Diesel,' he said when he saw caller ID.

'Mine's from Deacon,' she said, a worried frown tilting her mouth down. She took a few steps back so that they didn't talk over each other's conversation.

'Diesel, what's up?' Decker said when he answered. 'Everything okay?'

'No.' The man sounded downright frantic. 'It's not okay. It's not fucking okay.'

Oh shit. 'Slow down,' he said steadily. 'What's happened?'

'It's Dani. She's hurt. She was stabbed. I'm taking her to the ER. Can you tell Kate?'

A few feet away, Kate's face had drained of color.

'I think Deacon's telling her right now,' Decker murmured.

'Yeah. I called him first.'

'Which hospital are you taking her to?' Decker asked, trying to stay calm for Diesel's sake. And Kate's too. He gripped her hand hard and she held on like he was a lifeline. 'County?'

'When hell freezes over,' Diesel snapped. 'Besides, I'm closest to Christ.'

Decker was mostly relieved. County had bullied Dani into resigning and was where he'd been drugged. He didn't trust them to keep Dani safe. But while Christ Hospital was only a five-minute drive from the clinic, it was at least fifteen minutes from Alice's apartment with rush-hour traffic. 'We'll be there as soon as we can,' Decker said, daring Kate to challenge him about going. He was relieved when she nodded.

She ended her call with Deacon. 'Ask Diesel where the attack happened.'

'I heard her,' Diesel said sharply. 'At that damned clinic. I was right to be worried.'

'We'll have some uniforms get over there to protect the crime scene,' Decker told him. 'You focus on getting her to the hospital in one piece. Hear me, Diesel?'

'Yeah,' Diesel's tone was grimly determined. 'I heard. Gotta go.'

The call ended and Decker stood up, folded his chair and tucked it under his arm. 'Let's go. Christ Hospital. You can drive.'

Cincinnati, Ohio,
Friday 14 August, 5.20 P.M.

'I should have stopped her,' Decker said, so quietly that Kate almost didn't hear him.

She'd just pulled up to the ER door to let Decker out when he'd spoken – his first words since they'd left Alice's apartment. 'And exactly how would you have done that, Decker? Dani doesn't take orders any better than her brother does. Or than you do. Or me.' She smiled at him, hoping to lighten his dark mood. 'We're like herding cats.'

He didn't smile back. 'I didn't listen to her when she said she didn't know why I'd even asked for a doctor. I thought she was just ranting.'

'Maybe she was. She was forced to quit a job she worked hard to earn, and she was pissed in general. She'll make the best of her new position at the free clinic because that's what we all do. We survive and we do our best to make things better. But I don't think she would have said no to an emergency at the clinic even if you'd been an obedient little couch potato. Do you?'

He shook his head. 'No, not really.'

'And truthfully? You probably didn't need a doctor once you were awake and breathing on your own. Dani told me that herself when she agreed to tend you. She'd talked first with your doctor and he told her that you'd healed a lot while you were in that coma, which was the whole point of inducing it, I suppose. You just needed rest, *appropriate* exercise, and time to rebuild your strength.'

'And a health care professional who wasn't going to kill me,' he added with a grimace.

'Mostly that,' she agreed with a nod. 'If we'd had more time, we probably would have hired a nurse. But Dani was available and she said it made her feel . . . useful.'

He winced. 'Now I feel even worse.'

'You shouldn't. It wasn't your responsibility to make her feel useful. It's your responsibility to recuperate as quickly as you can so that you can do what you've actually been doing all day – your job. Making Dani feel useful was merely a bonus.'

He frowned at her suspiciously. 'Who are you and what have you done with the real Kate?'

She shrugged. 'The real Kate thought about what you said. About how you needed to *do* something with your life, since it *had* been saved, after all. And you were right. About that and about how I'd be doing the same thing as you if our situations were reversed. It doesn't mean that I'm okay with you pushing yourself like you're doing. But I get why you are. It's because this is who you are. And you shouldn't change, not for Dani and not for me, no matter how much I want to wrap you in bubble wrap and keep you healthy.'

The suspicion in his eyes softened to a gratitude so raw and so . . . *vulnerable* that it made her eyes sting. 'So,' she finished before he could say anything that would turn that stinging into an instant waterfall, 'you couldn't have stopped her, because Dani is who she is too. Now put on your game face and get in there. Deacon's going to need us strong, because he was falling apart on the phone.'

Decker's throat worked as he tried to swallow. 'So was Diesel.'

'He cares for her. Diesel, I mean.'

'He followed her around with his eyes yesterday when he thought no one was looking.'

He was stalling, Kate realized. But why? Was he afraid that the others would blame him for not stopping a headstrong doctor from responding to a call? *Yeah*, she thought. That was exactly it. New friends. Finally a circle he belonged to after being alone for so long. Kate wouldn't want to risk it either in his place.

'They won't blame you,' she murmured, and he did smile then, ruefully.

'How did you know?'

'Because I'd feel the same way. Diesel called you, Decker. He brought that file to you. He obviously trusts you. So go in there and be a friend.' She hooked her hand around the back of his neck and

414

pulled him in for a kiss that she'd intended to be a peck. But he deepened it, made it tender. Then touched his forehead to hers.

'Thank you,' he whispered, and it was her turn to try to swallow.

'Just walk fast. If this was a way to lure us all here, he couldn't have done much better.'

'I thought of that too.'

She grabbed the front of his shirt, pulling it far enough from his body to see that he was wearing a Kevlar vest. 'Just making sure you're all suited up. Go on in. I'll be right behind you as soon as I park the car.'

He did what she asked, leaning on his cane as he closed the distance between the car and the ER's double doors at a half-jog that made her sorry she'd been such a bitch to him earlier. He really was feeling better, and he did know his own body.

But dammit, she wanted a chance to get to know it too, and him landing himself back in the hospital would put a severe cramp in her plans. Because she had plans.

She found a parking place at the far end of the lot, recognizing a few of the vehicles as she ran past them. Deacon's SUV, of course. Marcus O'Bannion's Subaru. He would have brought Scarlett, who'd be here for Deacon too. And Adam's beat-up Jeep. She'd seen it that morning when he'd called her and Deacon to Eileen Wilkins's murder scene. Of course Adam would have rushed here. He and Deacon and Dani had grown up together. Cousins. *Family.*

A part of Kate's heart hoped that they'd be her family if she ever ended up here in the ER. That she wouldn't be like Decker and have no one. *At least Decker has people now, too.*

She ran a little faster as she approached the door. She wasn't going to make herself an easy target if this was a trap. Because McCord's partner had to know by now that they were searching. He'd killed four people – that they knew of. He was going to show up on law enforcement's radar sooner or later.

The ER waiting room was already halfway full. Closest to the door, Meredith sat next to Adam, her normally serene expression full of trepidation.

Oh God. This was bad.

415

Deacon sat hunched over, elbows on his thighs, his white head hanging low. Faith had her hand on his back, rubbing big comforting circles.

Diesel Kennedy stood near the window, staring out at nothing. Decker had planted himself next to the tattooed man, leaning up against the wall. Saying nothing. Just being a friend.

Kate straightened her spine and walked up to Deacon, crouching in front of him so that she could see his downturned face. 'What happened? Have you heard anything?'

A wag of that white head. 'No, not yet.'

'She was stabbed in the abdomen,' Faith murmured. 'And hit on the head, hard enough to knock her out for a few minutes.'

Not good. Kate squeezed Deacon's knee. 'Was she conscious when Diesel brought her in?'

'He said so. But the doctors took her straight into surgery. I didn't see her.'

'Diesel was with her when she was attacked?'

'Yes.' He swallowed hard. 'I worried she'd get the flu or some weird disease working in the ER.' He looked up, his bi-colored eyes devastated and wet. 'She can't get sick. She thinks she's superwoman, but even a cold could make her dead.'

Kate took Deacon's hands in hers. 'She's strong, yes?'

Deacon nodded grimly. 'Too damn strong.'

'She *is* your sister,' Kate said lightly. 'If there's a way for her to be fine, she'll make that happen. And we'll help her. Got it?'

'Yeah.' One side of his mouth lifted sadly. 'But you of all people know it doesn't work out sometimes.'

Kate's throat thickened. 'I know. But Dani getting stabbed isn't the same thing as Johnnie dying from a brain tumor, and you know it. You need to get hold of yourself. She's going to need you strong when she wakes up, so you make sure you're strong by then. *Capisce?*'

Faith kissed his shoulder. 'I couldn't have said that better myself.'

'Thank you. All right now.' She crisped her voice. 'Special Agent Novak, I need you to put on your cop hat for a minute. I contacted your lieutenant and she's gone to supervise the scene herself. Just in case this wasn't a routine mugging gone wrong. Do you know of anyone who'd want to hurt your sister?'

Deacon closed his eyes. 'She had hate mail, all sent to County. People who didn't want her spreading "her AIDS". A few threatened to sue. None of the mail went to her apartment.'

'Actually . . .' Faith bit her lip. 'It did. She didn't want to worry you.'

Deacon's head whipped up to stare at his fiancée, his expression going from numb to furious in a heartbeat. 'What in the *hell*, Faith?'

Faith pressed her fingertips to his mouth to halt what would have been very angry words. 'I heard about it just yesterday morning at our breakfast at Bailey's house. I told her that she had two choices – to either let us hire security or to move back in with us. Either way, I told her she had to tell you by tonight or I was telling you myself. I figured I could give her a few days to do it herself, since she was at the safe house. Caring for Decker was supposed to be a two-fer. She got some supplemental pay and free bodyguards. I should have known she'd leave if she got a call.'

Deacon pulled Faith's hand from his mouth and kissed her palm. 'I'm sorry. I should have trusted you before I got mad.'

'Yeah, you should have,' Faith said, 'but I'll cut you some slack since you're upset.'

'I wouldn't have cut him any slack,' Kate inserted, and Deacon huffed a laugh.

'Yeah, you would have. You've already cut that big lug over there too much.' He jerked his head in Decker's direction.

Kate lifted her brows. 'Pot. Kettle. So shut up. I'll get the threatening emails or letters from County. I'm sure they kept them to cover their cowardly asses.' She patted Deacon's knee. 'I'm going to talk to Diesel now. I don't want you to follow me. You're too invested.'

He narrowed his eyes at her. 'God, I forgot how bossy you are.'

She winked at him, then smiled at Faith. 'I was just tenderizing him for you, Faith.'

'Appreciated.' Faith stood up when Kate rose from her crouch, pulling her into a hard hug. 'He's going to try anyway,' she

417

whispered in Kate's ear. 'Don't let him investigate Dani's case, please. It'll destroy him. Especially if . . .' Her voice broke. 'You know.'

If Dani dies. Maybe not from blood loss or the stab wound, but from an infection later. It wouldn't matter. She'd still be gone.

Kate patted Faith's back, feeling the other woman draw a deep breath as she struggled not to cry. 'I know,' she whispered back. 'He was my partner. I know he's got a fucking hard head.'

Faith stepped back, wiping her eyes. 'I'm really glad you're here.'

'Me too.' Kate looked up at Faith, then over at Meredith. 'Although I think if we bring in one more redhead, we'll set the whole place on fire,' she added dryly.

Meredith lifted her chin. 'Mine is auburn.'

'So, like, *red*?' Kate put her hand on Deacon's shoulder without even looking at him, pushing him back in his chair when he moved to stand. 'God, were you always this predictable? I said stay the hell here, Novak. I meant it. You trust me, right?'

Deacon scowled. 'Yeah. But I'm not liking you much right now.'

'I can live with that. Stay. Here.' She rolled her eyes. 'Stubborn men. They all need goddamn keepers.'

'Hear, hear,' Faith said.

'No argument from me,' Meredith added.

'Hey,' Adam said defensively. 'I didn't do anything.'

Just friends, my ass, Kate thought. Adam was a goner and she wondered why he was fighting it so hard.

'Yet,' said Meredith. 'Kate, I'm available if you need me.'

'Because Diesel is barely keeping it together?' Kate murmured. It was true. The man was holding himself so tight, so still, that he looked as if he was about to break. 'I can see that. I'll ask if I need you.' She looked around the room. 'Where are Scarlett and Marcus? I saw Marcus's car in the parking lot.'

'None of us got lunch, and it's likely to be a long wait, so they went to get coffee and some food,' Adam answered. 'From someplace that's not a hospital. Just in case the asshole who tried to kill Decker has minions here too.'

'Makes sense,' Kate said, 'although it's batshit crazy that we have to even think it. Adam? You're on Deacon duty until Scarlett gets back, okay? Do not let him leave this hospital, even if you have to tie him to the chair.'

Adam gave her a little salute, but the gesture was a sad one. 'Yes, ma'am.'

Deacon leveled her a glare and Kate shrugged it away. 'You were planning your escape,' she said. 'Don't even try to deny it.'

'Your aunt and uncle are going to need you,' Faith said softly. 'And your little brother most of all. Greg doesn't need a big bad cop right now. He needs his brother. So let Kate do her job. Please.'

He closed his eyes, shoulders sagging in defeat and despair. 'Okay. I'll stay.'

Kate squeezed his arm. 'Thank you.' She went over to Diesel. 'I need to ask you a few questions,' she said softly. 'Can you come with me? We'll find a quiet room. Decker can join us if it makes you more comfortable.'

Diesel looked over at her, his dark eyes steely and cold. 'You don't have to be gentle with me, Agent Coppola. I don't freeze up with cops. Doctors, yes. Cops, I just don't like.'

Kate smiled at him. 'Sometimes I don't either. But I promise you that I'll do everything in my power to make this right.'

He faltered then, some of his control crumbling. 'For Deacon.'

'And for you. But especially for Dani.' She put her hand on his tattooed forearm and gave it a light squeeze. 'Come on. Let's see if we can find some coffee, and you can tell me a story.'

Twenty

Decker followed Kate into an empty family conference room, making sure he stayed one step behind Diesel Kennedy, because the man looked like he would bolt any second. He shut the door and sat next to Diesel, bumping his shoulder as a show of support. Diesel had been deathly white when he'd shown up at the door to the safe house, but now he was almost gray. Sweat covered his forehead and he was trembling.

He wore a T-shirt with the *Ledger*'s name on the back and the name of a kiddie tee-ball team on the front. Decker remembered that Diesel coached kids in his spare time, because sometimes kids just needed attention from an adult who genuinely cared. But it was a different shirt than he'd been wearing a few hours earlier, and Decker wondered if he'd changed because he'd been covered in Dani's blood.

Dani's HIV-positive blood. Decker could hear Dani's voice in his mind, not quite steady as she'd informed them of her risk. Then Trip's voice, gentle and modulated. *I guess we should make sure you don't bleed then, huh, Doc?*

Decker could only pray that she'd be okay, for the sake of the mental health of everyone on the team. But right now, he focused on Diesel's mental health. And it was not looking good.

'Give me a minute,' Decker murmured, and left the room, leaning heavily on his cane. His energy was draining. He needed to eat. He'd do that after they got Diesel squared away. He flagged down a

420

nurse and got a stack of paper barf bags. They would do.

When he got back to the room, Diesel was panting. Kate had pulled her knitting from her bag, as well as the slim stack of paper that Deacon had given her during their morning meeting. She was calm and collected and Decker found himself fucking proud of her.

'Here.' He gave Diesel one of the bags. 'Breathe.'

With a nod of thanks, Diesel obeyed. Decker eased his body into a chair while Kate knitted away. 'Can you teach me to do that?' Decker asked her.

'Of course. I have extra needles and yarn back in my luggage. You'll be knitting in no time.' She paused long enough to push the stack of paper in front of Diesel. 'I don't care if you make lousy paper airplanes, but you need to fold a lot more than I do right now.'

No longer panting, Diesel put the bag aside and sat back in his chair, eyes closed. 'I hate hospitals.'

'We noticed,' Kate said dryly. 'You're gonna need a spare shirt if you keep sweating.'

'This *was* my spare,' Diesel said heavily. 'The ER nurse took the one I was wearing. Said it was a fucking biohazard. Dammit.'

'Did you know about Dani's status?' Decker asked.

Diesel shook his head. 'We've never had an actual conversation.' He glared at Decker. 'How did *you* know? You've known her less time than I have.'

'She told me when she arrived at the safe house yesterday. Told Trip, too. She figured we needed to know so that we could protect ourselves if something happened. She even gave us the option of firing her. Which was ridiculous, of course.'

Diesel's nod was shaky. 'I carried her in and she was bleeding.' He looked down at his huge hands. 'All over me. All over the floor. She kept trying to talk while I was driving her here. I kept telling her to save her breath for staying the fuck alive. She was trying to tell me about the blood. The ER docs recognized her right away, of course. Y'know, the hair.'

'It is unusual,' Decker agreed. 'Black with the white streaks in front. Like Rogue from *X-Men*.'

421

Diesel grunted. 'Prettier,' he whispered, then shook himself back to attention. 'They told me to stop. I didn't know why. They double-gloved up and put her on a stretcher. Took her to a little room and took me to wash up. Examined me for open wounds. Asked if we'd been . . . intimate.' He looked away, flushing bright red. 'God.'

'They were trying to protect you,' Decker said quietly. 'But it couldn't have felt that way.'

'It did not. They put my clothes in one of those red biohazard bags. Gave me scrubs to wear.' He gripped his thighs so hard his knuckles went white. 'Hell of a way to find out.'

'She was managing it,' Kate said, her needles clacking in the rhythm Decker had found so soothing when he'd been struggling to regain consciousness. He still found it soothing. 'But it does complicate things for her surgery and recovery. She'll need help. Deacon will, too.'

Diesel nodded, steadier now. 'Help afterward I can do. It's hospitals that make me insane.'

'Me too,' Kate said, in a way that made Decker realize exactly what it had cost her to sit by his side for a week. 'So tell us what happened, Diesel.'

Diesel closed his eyes again, hands still gripping his thighs. 'I was at the safe house, giving Decker something, when I heard that Dani had gone to the clinic by herself. Fool woman.'

'No argument from me,' Kate said mildly. 'But then Decker left the safe house to go to the apartment of a woman who was a known killer.' She shrugged. 'Whatcha gonna do?'

'I'd say tie 'em up for their own good, but that's probably illegal,' Diesel said bitterly.

'Only if they don't consent,' Kate replied very dryly, and Diesel's eyes flew open.

Stunned, he stared at her for a moment, then barked out a laugh. 'I pity you, Decker. She'll keep you on your toes.'

'Hopin' so,' Decker drawled, then sobered. 'You need to tell us what happened,' he said, because Diesel was stalling. 'We need to find whoever did this.'

'Why are you guys involved in this anyway?' Diesel asked.

'I thought CPD would be doing the questioning.'

'They might still,' Kate said. 'But when I called Lieutenant Isenberg to get uniforms sent over to the clinic, she asked us to take your statement. If this is a simple mugging, then we'll hand it off to CPD.'

Diesel went very still. 'You don't think it was a mugging, do you?'

Kate shrugged, her needles continuing their rhythmic clacking. 'Don't know. Won't know till we get more information. The sooner you start talking, the sooner we'll know.'

Diesel drew a breath, squared his shoulders. And then started folding the paper Kate had given him into airplanes. But really cool airplanes. *Huh*, Decker thought. *Who knew?*

'I left the safe house and I was . . . not myself. But not out of control,' Diesel added hastily, then looked helplessly to Decker.

'He'd viewed the files we discussed,' Decker told Kate. 'He was shaken. As was I when I viewed them later.'

Kate nodded. 'As was I when I viewed similar files taken from a pedophile's computer this afternoon. Nobody's going to judge you, Diesel. Not here.'

Decker noticed that Diesel had begun to sway – minute movements, but in sync with Kate's clacking. 'Where did you go when you left the safe house?' Decker asked.

'To the shelter. I just needed to see her. To be sure she was okay.' He looked up from the airplane he'd made and frowned at Kate. 'I'm not a stalker.'

'Of course you're not,' she said firmly. 'You were concerned. So was I when I heard she'd gone out on her own. Did you go into the clinic?'

'No. I . . . I couldn't. Too many doctors.' He swallowed hard. 'And the smell. I hate the smell.'

'You and me both,' Kate said, then glanced up. Diesel's hands had stilled and he was staring numbly into space. She paused her knitting and rapped hard on the table, making him jump. 'Don't go there,' she ordered. 'Wherever you just went, do *not* go there. It's a bad place.'

423

Diesel glared. 'How would *you* know?' he asked scathingly. 'You don't know jack.'

Uh-oh, Decker thought. *Wrong question and* really *wrong use of jack.*

Kate's expression went cold. Ruthless. This was the woman who'd held a rifle to his back. 'Because I sometimes go to my own bad place and I get stuck there. And the tape plays in my head over and over. I don't know what your tapes look like. But mine are . . . disturbing. And they change with my mood or the situation or whatever has triggered them. Lately I keep seeing my brother-in-law's brains spewing all over my living room because he ate my fucking gun.'

Oh God. Decker hadn't known it was her own gun. He wanted to comfort her, because there was pain in her eyes. Pain and guilt. But also fury, which she was currently unloading on Diesel.

She leaned forward, pinning Diesel with her glare. 'So don't you *tell* me what I don't know. Your tapes might be leftovers from the army. Yes, I know you served,' she snapped when Diesel's eyes widened, 'and yes, I know you were a Ranger. And yes, I know you're one fucked-up pup. I pay attention, Mr Kennedy, and I know how to do research. As soon as I knew you were a key player in that whole McCord mess, I looked you up. Maybe you see explosions and people getting blown up, or maybe somebody you couldn't save. But you do *not* tell me that I don't know. Don't you even imply it. You do *not* have that right.'

She was breathing hard now, her eyes shooting daggers. Slowly she resumed her knitting. 'And this is why I knit,' she said quietly. 'Because I open my mouth and words come out. Sometimes not nice words. Sometimes words I have to apologize for.'

Diesel was regarding her with respect, his demeanor calmer. 'Are you apologizing?'

She made a sound of scorn. 'Fuck, no. Are you?'

'Yes,' Diesel said. 'I am. I respectfully apologize, Special Agent Coppola, because you're right. I don't know what you've seen any more than you know what I've seen. But I was wrong to assume that you've had an easier life simply because you have your shit together.'

Kate's mouth fell open. 'What the ever-*lovin'* hell? Do you *see* this knitting, Diesel? This is compulsion. A crutch. This is not the behavior of a woman who has it together.' She looked away. 'And for the record, I've never had it together. I'm just really good at faking it.'

Decker's brows shot up and Diesel was unsuccessful in biting back a grin. Kate frowned for a second, then realized what she'd said and rolled her eyes at the two of them. 'Oh, for the love of God. I didn't mean faking *that*. Are you guys *twelve*?'

'You sound like Marcus,' Diesel said. 'He's always asking me and Stone if we're twelve.'

Kate looked him in the eye. 'And what is your reply?'

'Not yet!' His grin faded, leaving him looking sad. 'We were both stunted back at six.'

Decker and Kate shared a glance, a line of communication opening between them.

Is he saying what I think he's saying? she asked with a slight narrowing of her eyes.

Yes, he told her. Diesel had admitted to having experience with the acts he'd forced himself to see when he'd reviewed McCord's hard drive. He had definitely suffered abuse, something that had made him take up hacking to expose men like McCord, risking future censure by the FBI by admitting to possessing a cache of stored files that he'd stolen over the years. Stolen from perverts who molested kids, true, but still stolen. It didn't take a certified therapist to guess what had happened to the man. *Be gentle with him.*

Don't worry. I will.

Kate's needles began clacking once again. 'So, Diesel, you went to the shelter, but you didn't go inside. Did Dani know you were there?'

'No. I don't think anyone did. I can stay hidden when I need to. Even though I'm big.'

'I believe you,' Kate said. 'I assume you could see Dani, even if she didn't see you?'

'Of course. It's why I went there to begin with.'

425

She nodded. 'Fair enough. Was anyone hanging around her? Bothering her?'

'No. She was upset, though. She'd been called in to see a patient who'd had trouble last week and who'd relapsed when Dani was still in the safe house. The woman apparently told the nurse on duty that she'd only see Dani and she'd be back later. But she never showed. Dani was worried that she'd become too sick to return. The nurse said she'd call the woman's house, but an hour passed and she didn't make the call. I knew the sick woman too, and I was worried. She didn't look good last week, or the week before that.'

Kate looked up, brows raised. 'Where exactly were you hiding?'

'Around the back of the building, watching her through one of the windows – it looks out onto an alley.'

'Why would someone put a window looking onto an alley?' Decker asked.

Diesel shrugged. 'It's an old building. There probably wasn't anything next to it when it was built. Anyway, it's a good hiding place. You can see the whole waiting area through that window. I couldn't see into the patient rooms, but mostly she was seeing older people and little kids, so I didn't worry too much.'

Kate nodded. 'So I get how you saw everything, but how did you hear all of that?'

Diesel looked embarrassed. 'I have a kit. Kind of a . . . spy kit. It has a listening device. We all had them, all of us on Marcus's team at the *Ledger*. Never knew when we'd need to hear what was going on inside a house.'

Kate sighed. 'If you tapped phones, I do not want to know. So what was the nurse's name? The one who was supposed to call the patient's house?'

'Belinda. I didn't hear a last name. People just called her Nurse Belinda.'

Kate put her knitting aside and took a notebook from her bag. 'Can you describe her?'

'She was much shorter than Dani. Maybe five-two? Dark hair. Really tired face, even though she didn't seem tired. I think she was new. She didn't know where things were supposed to go. She might have been a volunteer. She kept thanking Dani for coming in, saying that she hadn't figured it all out yet.'

Kate looked up from the notes she was taking. 'How did you know the patient?'

'Her grandson is on my pee wee soccer team. I had his home number in my phone, so I called. Grandma answered and said she was fine. That it must have been a misunderstanding, that she'd been feeling much better and hadn't come to the clinic today. That got me more worried.'

'Me too,' Kate murmured.

Agitated, Diesel thrust his fingers against his scalp like he still had hair, then flinched when he remembered he didn't. 'Fuck,' he muttered and started to fold another paper airplane. 'This shit is addictive, y'know?'

'Yes, I know,' Kate said wryly. 'Go on. Please.'

'I'd hung up from talking to Grandma and was about to go inside and tell Dani, but then she said to hell with waiting for the woman to come in and she was going to pay a house call. I ran around to the side of the building where she'd parked her car to stop her, but . . . he was already on her.' His hands clenched, crunching the paper he was folding. 'Five-ten. Dressed in black. Gloves. Ski mask.' He scrubbed his palms over his face. 'I don't know where he came from. He was just all of a sudden *there*, grabbing her.'

'Dani was stabbed,' Kate said, her tone matter-of-fact. 'Did you see a knife?'

Diesel nodded, his body beginning to tremble again. 'In his hand. He was holding it to her throat. He had his other hand in her hair, pulling it so hard she was walking on her toes. He was trying to force her into a car. Crappy old sedan. Chevy Impala. Lots of rust.'

Kate looked up abruptly. 'With a primer-painted back bumper?'

Decker's mind searched frantically for the connection, nodding when he found it. *The girl's car.* The one Officer Kendra Cullen had seen in the Kroger parking lot the Saturday before.

Shit. It was what he had feared. This wasn't a mugging. This was a failed abduction – and an attempted murder. And the only reason anyone could want to abduct Dani . . . He closed his eyes. *Is me.*

To get to me. Goddamn this all to fucking hell.

Diesel had sucked in a breath. 'You know who did this?'

Decker opened his eyes to find Kate waiting for him to look at her. Again the unspoken link between them flared to life.

Not your fault, she told him.

Yes. Decker swallowed hard. *Yes, it is.*

You could not have stopped her from going to the clinic. Remember that. Kate turned to Diesel. 'I know of the car,' she said levelly, then tilted her head. 'Does the nickname "the Professor" ring any bells for you?'

Diesel's chest expanded and froze there for long seconds before he let the breath out slowly. 'I know the name. I've never done business with him personally. What would a drug dealer want with Dani? She's not a user. Was he trying to steal drugs from the clinic?'

'We think the owner of that car is tied to the computer files you found,' Kate said.

Diesel shook his head. 'But why hurt Dani? She isn't involved in this. She's a doctor, for God's sake. Not a cop. She didn't know anything. She never hurt anyone.'

'She knew where I was,' Decker said quietly.

Diesel's mouth fell open. 'Then the grandmother emergency really *was* just a lure.'

'Very likely,' Kate said. 'Okay, he had a knife to her throat. He was forcing her toward a car. Was the car's engine running?'

Diesel's brow furrowed. 'No. I heard it start after I chased him away from her.'

'All right.' Kate's voice was calm and the clacking of her needles soothed once more. 'How did you chase him away?'

'I didn't see the knife at first. His back was to me. I could just see him forcing her to the car. So I yelled her name.' Diesel scrubbed his palms down his face again. 'I startled him, because he whipped around, eyes wide.'

'What color were his eyes?'

'Blue,' he said quickly. 'His eyes were blue.'

'Like Decker's?'

Decker turned to Diesel, opening his eyes wide. Diesel stared a moment, then shook his head. 'More gray. But I only saw them for a second. Because Dani was bleeding already. He'd cut her. When he spun around to face me, he'd cut her. Here.' He pointed to his collarbone.

'Could have been worse,' Kate said brusquely. 'He could have slit her throat. Then there would have been nothing that any of us could have done.'

Strangely enough, this seemed to settle Diesel, who nodded. 'True. That's true. He looked at me and said, "Fuck!" and then he did try to slit her throat. But I had a knife too,' he said grimly. 'I always have a knife. I practice throwing it. And I'm damn good.'

Of that Decker had no doubt. 'Where'd you hit him?' he asked.

'His knife arm. He dropped her. His arm just went limp.'

Kate's brows lifted slightly. 'You didn't worry you'd hit Dani?'

Diesel made a scoffing noise. 'I hit where I aim.'

'Good to know,' Kate said simply. 'So then?'

'He pulled my knife out of his arm . . .' Diesel's eyes screwed shut. 'He stabbed her again with it. In the gut. Then he took his knife, left mine in Dani, and ran. By then, I was on my knees next to Dani and he was in his car. The engine started and he drove away.'

'How did the engine sound?' Decker asked him. 'Rusty or smooth?'

'Smooth,' Diesel answered automatically. 'Powerful. That car looked like a piece of shit, but it'd had some serious work done under its hood. Maybe a V8.'

'Good,' Kate said, approval in her voice. 'Did Dani say anything to you?'

'No. She couldn't speak. She just gasped. So I picked her up and ran with her into the clinic. The nurse was there and she went white when she saw Dani bleeding. She said she wasn't a doctor, that she couldn't sew her up, but she'd call 911. I figured I could get her there faster than waiting for the medics, so I put her in my car and brought her here, to the ER. I . . . I left the knife in her. I was afraid to take it out. They said it was good I didn't take it out, because she might have bled out before I got her here.'

'Did you tell the nurse at the clinic what you'd heard?' Decker asked.

'No. I was too . . . All I could think of was getting Dani help. That nurse – if she was one at all – didn't even try to help her,' he added bitterly.

'Would you remember the way the man sounded if you heard him say "Fuck" again?' Kate asked, and Diesel bared his teeth.

'Hell, yeah. You find him. I'll know.' Diesel stood up, his chair scraping the floor. 'Am I done now? Can I go back to the waiting room?'

Kate stopped knitting and locked her gaze on his. 'In a minute. How do you know of the Professor? I need names. I need people to tell me everything they know about him.'

Diesel hesitated and Kate's eyes flashed. 'For God's sake, Kennedy! This is not the time to be protecting anyone. Whose secrets are worth letting this fucker get away?'

Diesel drew a breath. 'Stone's,' he said on a harsh exhale. 'Stone O'Bannion's.'

Cincinnati, Ohio,
Friday 14 August, 5.50 P.M.

He closed himself in his office, his body trembling. His arm was burning like fire. But that was better than being ice cold, which it had been when he'd first pulled that fucker's knife out. Goddammit. Where had that tattooed asshole come from?

He'd been afraid that Dani Novak would never come out of that damn clinic, but she finally had. He'd been waiting for over an hour and roasting in the heat, dressed in black as he was. He'd been vacillating about putting on the fucking ski mask because he thought he might pass out from heat stroke, but now he was glad he had. He'd considered going mask-free, figuring that if anyone had seen him dragging Dr Novak to her car, they'd describe the Professor, who he planned to retire anyway. But it had still been full daylight, and it was better that everyone think the good doc was being mugged. It was believable. Bad part of town, pretty doc who might be carrying drugs with a street value? Nobody would be surprised about a mugging.

He sat down heavily behind his desk and took a look at his arm. He'd stopped the bleeding, thankfully, and hadn't left a drop at the scene, other than what had been on the knife, which he'd left in the doctor's gut. If he'd had one more second – and the use of his good arm, dammit – he would have slit her fucking throat.

But that tattooed nightmare had charged him like a rabid bull, and he'd done the only thing he could do – he'd gutted the doc and run like hell.

God, I hope the bitch dies. She hadn't told him what he wanted to know when he'd held the knife at her throat. Hadn't spilled Davenport's location when he'd forced her toward his car. He should have figured her for a tougher cookie than she looked. He knew what she'd been through in recent months. *Dammit.*

She'd bled on him, that first, accidental slice across her collarbone when that asshole had burst from behind him, roaring her name. *Scared the shit out of me.* And he did not scare that easily.

But HIV? Hell, yeah, that scared him too. Because that asshole had thrown a knife at his goddamn arm, opening him up like a can of tuna. He examined his shirt carefully. Dani Novak's blood had spattered on one side of it, opposite the arm that hurt like a motherfucker. But at least it didn't appear to have commingled with his own.

He'd have to go on a preventative cocktail, just to make sure. And wouldn't that be fun? His system didn't do well with drugs of any kind. *So . . . no. Not gonna be fun at all.*

And there was still the issue of the doctor herself. If she lived, she'd tell them he was asking about Davenport. She was another loose end. And he *still* didn't know where Davenport was.

'*Goddammit.*' He glanced at the door, double-checking that he'd locked it. Nell was gone for the day, but she sometimes left for dinner then came back to do paperwork. He hoped she'd be lazy tonight. Or have a date or something. He didn't want to have to explain this to her. She'd call the cops on his behalf, and that would not do at all.

He assembled all the materials he needed to stitch himself up, something he hadn't needed to do in years, not since his early dealing days. The Professor had attained a kind of rock-star status and normally nobody gave him any shit.

Gritting his teeth, he cleaned and stitched the wound, relieved to find it was a smooth cut and not a jagged one. Smooth cuts were so much faster to stitch. He ground his teeth harder, until the pain in his jaw distracted him from the pain in his arm. That had been one hell of a sharp knife, and this wound was fucking deep. And he'd never achieved ambidexterity, so his fingers kept fumbling the needle.

Finally he was done, and he sat back and let himself pant it out. Sweat drenched him and he smelled absolutely horrible. Emptying his pockets, he stripped off his clothes and bagged them. He'd burn them later. Standing still for a moment, he lifted his face to the A/C duct and let the cold air cool his heated skin, before going to the sink and washing up as best he could. He'd shower later, in the privacy of his own bathroom. He might even risk one of the painkillers he made such a fortune selling. Which he was now going to have to find a different way to sell.

He hated to get rid of the Professor. He'd become . . . a friend. A very useful friend.

He tossed back a handful of ibuprofen. OTC would have to do for now. He dressed in the spare clothes he kept in his desk drawer, still feeling like shit, but a little closer to human at least.

I need food, or that ibuprofen is gonna rip up my gut. But all he could find in the drawers were granola bars and the lollipops they gave kids after shots, even the high school and college kids. They were bigger babies than the real babies. Lollipops to make the owie feel better.

He wolfed down a granola bar, popped a lollipop in his mouth, then smiled. He knew exactly what would make *his* owie feel better now. Pulling a packet of gauze from the drawer, he accessed a spoofing site and dialed 911 using poor Charlie's number.

'This is 911. What is the nature of your emergency?'

He covered the phone's mic with the gauze and altered his voice, making it higher – like a teenager's. 'My friend took something. He needs help.' He gave Rawlings's address, and hung up before the operator could ask anything more.

Then he dialed Rawlings and sat back to savor.

'What do you want?' Rawlings barked into his phone. 'I'm a little busy right now.'

He smiled at the sounds of moaning and retching. Tim Junior had a quick metabolism. 'I'm sorry to bother you at such an inopportune moment. Is your son feeling poorly?'

There was a long silence. 'What have you done to him?' Rawlings hissed.

'Well, technically I didn't do anything directly. Your son did it to himself.'

Heavy, angry breathing assaulted his ears. 'What *the fuck* have you done to my son?'

'You should probably take him to the ER, stat. I wouldn't delay. Have them pump his stomach, maybe give him some activated charcoal. Check for liver, kidney damage.'

'You *poisoned* him?' Rawlings whispered. 'With what?'

'Same stuff you used on Alice.'

'Oh my God,' he moaned. '*Why?* He's just a boy.'

'Because I can. Because you threatened me.'

'I will tell them everything,' Rawlings said hoarsely.

'No, I really don't think so. Because they're going to want to know why someone poisoned your son with ricin. You said Agent Novak was already pressing you with questions. This isn't going to look good for you.'

'I'll tell them you hired me. That you threatened me. That you forced me.'

'I don't think you'll do that either. Because you still have two other children, don't you? I can get to them too, Rawlings. Any time. Any place. So . . . let's be friends, not enemies. You tear up your little list and we'll have no more issues between us.'

An audible swallow, a shuddering exhale. Then a cagily asked question. 'How will you know I tore up the list?'

Some people simply do not learn. 'I won't. Hopefully you won't die.

433

And if anyone comes sniffing after the Professor, I'll know to come after you. Or your family.'

'You're a monster.'

He laughed. 'Like you didn't know that already? I'd tend to your son now, Rawlings. Every minute that shit stays in his stomach is another minute that it's starving his body of protein. Internal organs really don't like being starved of protein. Look, I could have done worse. I could have had him inhale it. Death would have been inevitable then. At least with ingestion, you have a chance of saving him if you pump it out of his stomach soon.'

'When he wakes up, the cops will want to know who gave it to him,' Rawlings said desperately. 'I don't want him in danger because he could expose you.'

'He can't. He'll say he got the pills from a buddy. And the buddy won't be saying a word.'

A shocked moment of silence. 'You killed his friend? My God. You really are a monster.'

'My God,' he mocked in reply. 'Jesus, Rawlings. I gave you a little more credit.' The sound of sirens in the background made him grin. 'I think you're about to have company.'

A gasp. 'What did you do?'

'Saved your son's life. I'm going to go now.' He hung up and nodded once. 'Better than any painkiller ever.'

He gathered together his dirty clothes and the bloody gauze pads he'd used to clean his wound. He'd get a proper meal, a proper shower, then figure out what to do about Davenport.

And Dani Novak, if she managed to survive.

Cincinnati, Ohio,
Friday 14 August, 5.50 P.M.

Decker let out a breath, staring at Diesel Kennedy. 'Stone O'Bannion knows the Professor?'

Kate had blinked once, her surprise hidden in an instant. 'The same Stone O'Bannion who sat at the table with us yesterday? Marcus's brother?'

Diesel nodded woodenly. 'He won't want to tell you anything. He's ashamed.'

'Does his brother know?' Decker asked quietly.

'No. Stone never wanted him to.' A muscle in his jaw twitched. 'And now Marcus will know because I opened my big fucking mouth.'

'For Dani,' Decker told him. 'Does Stone still use?'

'No.' Diesel shook his head hard. 'Hell, no. It was when he came home from the Gulf. He's been clean for a few years now.'

'Lots of guys turned to chemical help when they came home,' Decker said levelly. 'I know I was tempted, so I'm not gonna judge.'

'You might be the only one,' Diesel snapped. 'Can I fucking *go* now?'

Kate's nod was weary. 'Yes. You can go. Thank you.'

Diesel closed the door behind him hard, making her wince.

Decker sighed. 'Shit. What a mess.'

'Yes. It is.' Kate shook her head slightly, her focus dropping back to her knitting. 'Dammit, I dropped a stitch when he said Stone's name.' She fixed her stitch, then looked back up at him, her expression pained. 'Stone has been through the wringer. I do not want to ask him about this.'

'But you will. You have to. He's a reporter, Kate. He would have noticed little things about this Professor asshole that his other customers might not have.'

'I know.' She shoved her knitting back in the bag. 'This all sucks, Decker. Dani in surgery, four people in the morgue, and the girl never called back either.' She pressed trembling fingers to her temples. 'I hope he hasn't killed her too. I hope that by arresting Corey Addison so publicly I didn't paint a target on the girl. She's already suffered so much. Why did I do that? It wasn't worth the risk to her to parade Addison around like that.'

Part of Decker wanted to soothe her by telling her that it would be okay, that the girl was probably okay, but because he respected her, he didn't. Because there was a better-than-decent chance that the girl had been targeted as well, especially if the man who'd forced her into porn knew she'd contacted the police. Which also was possible, because the bastard seemed to have eyes and ears everywhere.

So rather than insult her with platitudes, he pulled her hands from her temples and kissed her fingertips, his heart squeezing when her eyes got glassy with unshed tears. 'This isn't about one girl, Kate. It never was. It's about all the kids out there who're being abused on camera and off, right now. By showing that viewers of child porn get caught, you might make potential customers think twice before they download that video. Before that kid who was filmed is watched again. Victimized again. Besides, you never mentioned Sunshine Suzie on the broadcast.'

She was unconvinced. 'Tell me that again if we find her body, okay?' she said, her sarcasm brutally cutting. 'I'll need to hear that lie once more.'

He swallowed a sigh and tried a different approach. 'Then you can remind me that it's not my fault if Dani dies. I'll need to hear that lie too.'

She blinked, sending the tears down her cheeks. 'It's not the same.' She tried to tug her hands free, but he held on, wiping her wet cheeks with his thumbs. 'It's *not* your fault that Dani was stabbed.'

'Then how can it be your fault if the girl is killed by the same man?' he asked softly.

'No fair using logic,' she whispered.

His mouth curved. 'Did it work?'

She shook her head, new tears filling her eyes. 'Not really. Dammit. I hate doing this.' Again she tugged her hands free, and this time he let her go. She swiped her eyes with the heels of her hands.

'Hate what?' he asked. 'Being human?'

'Crying like this. It's stupid and weak and useless and I can't *do* this now. I don't have *time* for this now. Dammit to hell.' Because the tears continued to flow and she held her breath against a sob.

Decker couldn't watch her beat herself up any longer. Pulling her into his arms, he settled her in his lap, her head against his shoulder. 'Cry it out,' he murmured. 'I've got you.'

Her sob busted free, muffled against his shirt, the sound making his chest hurt. But her crying jag was short as she pulled her grief back into herself with what felt like sheer will, and that made his chest hurt even more. She drew a deep breath, her sobs completely stilled.

'Sorry,' she whispered. 'This is the second time I've cried all over you.'

'I don't mind, and I won't tell anyone. You're safe with me, Kate. You can let it out.'

'I know. But if I let it out, my face will be all puffy, and people will know I'm upset, which will suck if I have to be an utter asshole. Maybe I can take a rain check? Let it out later?' She asked the question hesitantly, as if she wasn't sure what his answer would be.

'I insist you do,' he said lightly, and she instantly relaxed, melting against him. He relaxed as well, because it seemed he'd said the right thing in the right way. 'As I recall, the first time you cried all over me ended pretty damn well. For both of us.'

She *mmmed* softly. 'That it did.'

She made no move to leave, so he began rubbing her back. 'In fact,' he said, 'I've read that tears and sex both produce endorphins, so crying it out followed by . . . y'know, ending it pretty damn well? Just know that I'm *here* for you,' he said with mock sobriety. 'Whatever you need.'

She chuckled. 'You're so altruistic. Or a master of bullshit, I'm not sure which.'

'Maybe a little of both,' he allowed, smiling because he'd succeeded in lightening her mood. He hugged her hard, gratified when she wrapped her arms around his middle and hugged him back. 'Mostly I just want you,' he whispered in her ear, and her rough shiver did not hurt his ego at all. 'So I'll use whatever excuse works.'

'I think "I want you" works really, really well. Thank you, Decker,' she added softly. 'I needed that re-set. If I let myself start crying about the victims, I'll never stop.'

'You're not the only one,' he said with total seriousness this time. 'None of this is easy.'

She nuzzled her cheek against his chest before sliding off his lap. 'I need to call Lieutenant Isenberg and tell her about Nurse Belinda so she can be brought in for questioning.'

'If Belinda's still at the clinic. I know I wouldn't be.'

'Yeah, but she doesn't know that Diesel heard her telling Dani about the patient. Even if Dani survives to tell, she'll think she can say Dani was mistaken.'

'I still would be running for the hills. If she even worked there legitimately to begin with.'

'Good point.' She made the call to Isenberg, giving her the details of Diesel's account, including the make and model of the masked man's getaway car. 'But that car had stolen plates last time, so don't hold your breath for an ID,' she added. 'Okay, I'll wait.' She looked up at Decker. 'She's going to find the nurse.'

Decker waited patiently, but Kate paced, her steps growing quicker and more agitated as the seconds ticked by. Finally he took the phone from her hand and put it on speaker, gestured to her chair, then put her knitting in her hands once she'd sat down.

'I wish I didn't need to do this,' she muttered. 'But thank you.'

He leaned in and kissed her forehead. 'You're welcome.'

'Coppola?' Isenberg's voice came from the cell phone's speaker. 'I'm here with Agent Davenport. Did you find her?'

'No,' Isenberg said crisply. 'She's gone.'

Kate's shoulders slumped and she gave Decker a you-were-right look. 'Do we have an address where we can start searching for her?'

'Yes. I've sent one of my detectives out to her house to bring her in for questioning. Her full name is Belinda Boyette and she lives in Madeira. One of the pricier parts.'

'On a nurse's salary?' Decker asked. 'Does she have a spouse who earns a bigger salary?'

A slight pause. 'Why do you ask, Agent Davenport?'

'Because she seemed determined to get Dani Novak out of the clinic and over to that patient's house. Her reaction to seeing Dani stabbed and bleeding indicates that she didn't know what was going to happen.'

'You mean she was a stooge,' Isenberg said.

'That's my assumption, given that this perp's already used staff at County to drug me and at the jail's infirmary to kill Alice. If Belinda was being coerced into lying to Dani – like Eileen Wilkins was coerced into trying to kill me – maybe she's also being blackmailed. I assume she's using. If her husband makes enough for a pricey house, maybe he makes enough for her to fund her side habit and she buys her drugs from the Professor, versus stealing them like Eileen did.'

'Makes sense,' Isenberg said, sounding reluctantly impressed. 'It appears that Belinda cut out shortly after Mr Kennedy brought Dr Novak in here. One of the patients reported seeing her turn white as a ghost, then she grabbed her purse and ran. A volunteer in the shelter saw her leaving, got the scoop about Dr Novak from the patients, called 911 first, then the director of the clinic. He arrived a short while ago and has been very helpful.'

'That's good at least,' Kate said. 'You'll call us with any news?'

'Right away. If there's nothing else?'

'No, Lieutenant,' Kate answered, surprising Decker.

He waited until she'd hung up. 'You didn't tell her about Stone's connection to the Professor.'

'No, I didn't. Not yet. Not until after we talk to Stone.'

Decker raised his brows. 'Who is we?'

'You and/or me. I'm not sure if he'll be more comfortable talking to me or to you.'

'We'll both go,' Decker said, intensely satisfied that she'd included him so easily. 'If he only wants one of us, the other can stand guard. But let's check on Dani before we go.' He stood when she did and lifted her chin with his finger, turning her head one way then the other. 'Not too much damage from crying, but if you want to fix your face, I'll wait.'

'I don't carry makeup in my bag. Just a tablet, extra ammo and my knitting.' She peeked in the bag. 'A couple FlexiCuffs, a few protein bars, a bottle of water, and a book.'

He smiled. 'In case you get bored.'

'Nah. The book's a ruse.' She winked at him. 'It's for if I want to spy on people in the vicinity without them noticing me.'

439

His smile broadened, because she was so damn cute. 'Does that ever work?'

She held up the book and his eyes popped at the title. 'It's one of those uber-hot erotica books,' she said.

He cleared his throat, all the blood in his head threatening to go south at the thought of what she'd read. 'I, um, see.'

Her grin was small and brief, but wicked. 'It makes me invisible because most people won't make eye contact with me when I'm reading it. So yeah, it works.' She returned the book to the bag and he wanted to whimper. 'I got paper for folding. Some Kleenex. But no makeup. Sorry.' She made a face. 'What you see is what you get.'

He grabbed the back of her neck and hauled her in for a kiss that he'd intended to be hot and hard and horny, but quickly changed to long and lush and tender. He framed her face with his hands, enjoying the way her whole body softened for him. He ended the kiss with a little bite to her lower lip, making her smile. 'That's better,' he whispered against her mouth. 'I am very happy that what I see is what I get, because I like what I see.'

She was breathing hard, her eyes wide. 'Good to know.'

He stepped back, his hands dropping to his sides. 'Come on. Let's go see Stone.'

Twenty-one

Cincinnati, Ohio,
Friday 14 August, 6.30 P.M.

The ER waiting room was a lot more crowded when Kate returned, Decker at her side. He was hobbling more slowly, leaning more heavily on his cane, but he was moving under his own power and she bit back the impulse to nag him to sit.

'Wow,' Decker murmured. 'This is one hell of a crowd.'

'Dani knows a lot of people,' she murmured back. 'Lots of people love her.'

Their eyes met for just a moment, but long enough that she saw the wistfulness in his and figured he'd seen the same in hers. 'They'd be here for you too,' he said quietly. 'The core group at least. You've got family here, Kate.'

'Thanks to Deacon, I do. Stick around for a while, Davenport. They'll suck you in too.'

His mouth curved. 'I think I'd like that,' he said. He turned back to the standing-room-only waiting room. 'So who are all these people?'

Kate pointed at an older couple sitting between Deacon and Adam. 'That's Adam's mom and dad. They raised Deacon and Dani after their parents died. The teenager sitting between Deacon and Faith is his brother Greg. Nice kid.'

'He's terrified.' Decker's observation was softened by compassion he didn't try to hide.

'Yeah, he is. Dani's been like his mom all these years.' She moved on before the thickness in her throat became more tears. 'That group of women over there? I only recognize a few of them. Of course, Bailey you know.' The nurse had followed them from Alice's apartment to the ER in her own car and now gave Decker a completely clinical assessment. Whatever she saw must have satisfied her, because she returned her focus to the baby blanket she was crocheting. Kindred spirit, Kate thought. 'The tall African-American woman next to her is Kendra Cullen.'

'I know. I saw her on TV when the two of you escorted Addison from his office.'

Kate's worry over the lack of contact from the girl who'd sought Kendra's help surged again in a wave, but a knowing look from Decker helped her push it back. Still, it couldn't hurt to pray. *Please let her be alive. Please.*

'I think the short woman next to Kendra is her sister, Wendi,' she went on. 'And the young woman with the cane? That's Corinne Longstreet. I've never met her, but I read the news clips about her. Got abducted nine months ago and was held captive, but she managed to escape and save a little girl's life in the process. She works for Meredith now.'

'The intern who does art therapy,' Decker remembered.

'I guess so. And the little woman at the end is Delores. She was also nearly killed by the same man who abducted Corinne. Who also killed Stone and Marcus's youngest brother, Mikhail, and nearly killed Marcus. Mikhail was only seventeen at the time.'

'Fuck,' Decker breathed. 'And now Stone's recuperating from nearly being killed himself? Now I know what you mean about him having been through the wringer.'

'And that's only the tip of the iceberg,' Kate muttered, remembering the other articles she'd read. 'Stone's got childhood issues out the yin-yang. I'll fill you in on the way up to see him.'

'Which is why you don't want to push him on the Professor,' Decker said softly.

She nodded. 'I'm stunned that he's not still a junkie. I don't want to drive him back to using.'

'If he starts using again, it won't be because of you. Sounds like he's got a million other reasons to use even if you don't say a word.

Still, we may want to give someone the heads-up so that he can get the support he needs afterward. Maybe his brother?'

'We'll have to play it by ear. Diesel said Marcus doesn't know, so I'm thinking that's a secret I don't want to be responsible for cracking open.' She scanned the faces thoughtfully. 'Delores, I think. She visited him in the hospital last week. Wouldn't leave his side.'

'What does Delores do?'

Kate chuckled. 'She runs a shelter for dogs. Nearly everyone in this group has adopted one of her animals, including Deacon, whose shoes will never be the same. Puppy teeth.'

Decker's wistful look returned. 'I was just thinking yesterday that I'd love to get a dog. Now that I'm not under anymore.'

'Then Delores is your woman.'

He leaned sideways on his cane so that his mouth brushed her ear. 'I'd rather that be you, actually.' Then he leaned back in one fluid motion, straightening as if he hadn't said a word. But his mouth quirked up slyly. 'You're blushing, Kate.'

'I wonder why.' Pulling her hormones back under control, she found Scarlett Bishop in the group. 'I'm going to see if there's any news on Dani, then we can go.' She started toward the woman with the black braid, but didn't make it two steps before Scarlett headed her way.

'I've been waiting for you,' Scarlett said urgently, then gave Decker a critical look. 'Weren't you just in a wheelchair, Davenport?'

'Old news, Bishop,' Decker said lightly. 'Try to keep up.'

Kate shook her head. 'Don't even try,' she said to Scarlett. 'He's got a mind of his own. I think it's in his ass, which is why he's not sitting on it right now.'

Scarlett snickered and Decker growled. 'Kate,' he said warningly.

'Decker.' Kate echoed his tone, then looked back at Scarlett, who was pursing her lips hard to keep from smiling. 'How's Dani?'

Scarlett abruptly sobered. 'We haven't heard yet. But at least we know the team that's in there with her now. The surgeon is a friend of Carrie Washington's and Carrie vouches for her.'

'Carrie is the ME,' Kate told Decker.

'So Dani is in good hands,' Decker said. 'That's a relief.'

'Every little bit helps,' Scarlett allowed. 'But that's not why I came over. Do you see that guy over there?' She pointed to a middle-aged man pacing the hallway, arms crossed tightly over his chest. He looked over his shoulder, saw them watching him, and sent them a look so vicious that Kate blinked.

'You mean Mr Psycho?'

'Yeah. You missed some fireworks. Ah, dammit.' Scarlett sighed when Deacon got up from his seat and joined them. 'I told you to stay out of this.'

'I am,' Deacon said levelly. 'I haven't killed him. Yet.'

'And you won't,' Scarlett said firmly. 'Dammit, D, I just broke you in. I don't want a new partner because you got yourself thrown in jail.'

Kate and Decker shared a glance. 'O-kay,' Kate said. 'So who is he?'

'Tim Rawlings,' Deacon said and swallowed. He was furious. 'Guard at the jail.'

'The squirrelly one?' Kate asked, all kinds of bells going off in her mind. 'The one who was Alice's guard?'

Deacon nodded once. 'The very one.'

Decker pivoted, using his cane for balance, watching the man glare at them. 'Who'd he bring in? Wife or kid?'

'Kid,' Deacon confirmed. 'Son, aged sixteen. Convulsions, vomiting, diarrhea.'

'Kid's still alive, right?' Decker said. 'Because he's still here pacing. So it wasn't cyanide.' He turned back to them, blond brows lifted. 'But ricin'll do that to you, if ingested.'

Deacon gave him a measuring, almost approving look. 'That it will.'

Scarlett rolled her eyes. 'They're bonding,' she said to Kate in a stage whisper, earning them both disgruntled glares from the men. 'Diesel told us about your theory that Dani's attacker was really after you, Davenport, so I gathered a few facts.' She gave Deacon the eye. 'Because now that Dani's involved, Deacon and Adam should be recusing themselves from this case too.'

'Jesus,' Kate muttered. 'We're dropping like flies.'

'Which might be part of his strategy,' Decker murmured.

Deacon made a scary noise in his throat. 'Fucker.'

Scarlett squeezed Deacon's arm in sympathy. 'An opinion shared by all of us. Probably even by our pacing guard. His son is Tim Junior. The paramedics and a pair of uniformed cops responded to a 911 call received from a cell phone registered to Charlie Chalmers, also aged sixteen. The caller said his friend had taken something. Responders arrived at the address provided by the caller and found Tim Junior in serious distress, but still communicative. He told them he'd taken some uppers plus "something special", but he didn't know what. He was given the drugs by his friend Charlie after they'd finished playing basketball at the park.'

'Excellent,' Kate said, excitement buzzing down her spine. 'So we can talk to this Charlie and get him . . .' She trailed off at the look on Scarlett's face. 'Charlie's dead, isn't he?'

Scarlett nodded sadly. 'That's how we got all the phone info so quickly. The medics got the kid loaded up and the uniforms went to the park to see if Charlie was also sick like Tim Junior. Kid wasn't breathing and they couldn't find a pulse. They followed procedure, called it in as an OD, and another pair of medics packed Charlie up. He was DOA. His body's in one of the bays back there. Such a waste.' She sighed. 'Anyway, one of the medics saw me in the waiting room with all these people after he'd dropped Tim Junior off. The medic pulled me aside, told me that the dad was acting weird. They were zoned to go to County, but the father protested so vehemently, they brought him here. He said the father had been yelling about killer nurses in the Professor's pocket, that his kid wasn't safe at County. The medic had heard that one of the County nurses had been found dead after trying to kill a federal agent, so he thought I should know.'

'So this was a warning to the dad,' Kate said quietly. 'Don't spill the beans.'

'I wonder why the Professor didn't just kill the dad directly,' Decker added. 'He killed Sidney after she'd served her purpose, and then Eileen after she'd botched hers. Why not kill the guard who, if he didn't poison Alice directly, probably knew who did?'

'That is a damn good question,' Deacon said, jaw still clenched.

'Rawlings was so glib this afternoon when I interviewed him. Such a smug bastard. He's not so smug now.'

Decker pivoted to study the man once again, being obvious about it. Rawlings turned his back and stared at the doors leading into the ER. 'No, now he's terrified and furious.'

'The furious is my doing,' Scarlett admitted. 'The medic and I were still talking when the uniforms radioed him that the second boy was dead at the scene. I called Carrie right away, asked her to come and supervise the contents of Tim Junior's stomach after it was pumped. She's on her way. I called Isenberg and she gave the order not to allow the father back there, in case he tried to silence his son somehow.' She nodded toward two uniformed officers, one standing against the wall closest to where Rawlings paced, the other by the exit. 'They're here to watch him. He's not under arrest – yet – but we're not letting him leave either. If he tries to leave, they're under orders to cuff him.'

'Did he try to silence his son when the medics were working on him?' Decker asked.

'I asked and the medic said no. He was quiet when they got to the house. Just let them in and pointed to his son.'

'Like he was expecting them,' Decker said. 'Even though he hadn't made the 911 call.'

Kate followed his thought. 'Because he had already been informed. I'm betting Charlie Chalmers didn't make that 911 call either. He was probably already dead. Where are his effects? I'd like to look at his cell phone.'

'With his body,' Scarlett said. 'I've got a uniform back there too. He's watching both boys, making sure nobody removes any evidence.'

'Where is Mrs Rawlings?' Decker asked. 'I'd have thought she'd be here.'

'Another good question,' Scarlett said. 'She wasn't answering her phone, so I sent a unit to their house. Neighbor said the wife and two kids tore out of there with suitcases.'

'She's on the run,' Kate said. 'Trying to protect the kids she has left.'

446

'Have Charlie's parents been notified?' Decker asked and Scarlett nodded.

'The ER called them when Charlie arrived. They got the number out of his phone. They didn't tell them that he'd died, only that he was here. Both parents are on their way.'

Kate sighed. 'I'll do the notification. Hopefully by then we'll know if Rawlings's son will live, because I want to haul the man's ass into an interview room and ask him a few questions.'

'There are rooms here,' Deacon said, menace dripping from every word. His eyes locked on Rawlings, who still stood with his back to them, arms crossed. 'I'd like to talk to him myself.'

Kate was trying to think of how to defuse the ticking bomb that was her former partner, but fortunately Faith picked that moment to join them, sliding her arm around Deacon's waist.

'I need you,' Faith said quietly. 'Please come back with me. Please trust Kate. *Please*.'

It was the final *please* that did it. Deacon shuddered, his gaze dropping to his clenched fists. 'I want to beat it out of him, Faith. He knows who did this. He knows how to contact him.'

'I know, baby,' she whispered. 'And Kate and Decker will get it out of him. Now come sit with me and the others. Greg needs you. *I* need you.'

He nodded, allowing his fiancée to guide him back to their chairs, where he dropped into the same miserable position, back bowed, head down.

The moment Deacon was sitting, Rawlings turned to face them, mocking triumph in his eyes. And Kate's temper snapped. She wanted to throttle the guard until he turned purple. But that wasn't going to solve anything. So instead she leaned close to Scarlett. 'Can you alert the uniforms that Rawlings might try to make a break for it?' she whispered.

'Gladly.' Scarlett went off to do as Kate asked.

'Decker, can you do me a favor?'

'Depends. You're not planning to ditch me, are you? This is just starting to get interesting.'

She spared a second to smile up at him. 'No, but I need to make sure I have the proper information before I peel that man's skin off his bones.' From the corner of her eye she saw that Rawlings had turned his mocking smirk on her. *Good. He's listening.* 'Can you get any notes that Agent Novak took while at the jail today? I'm specifically interested in anything he learned from the young woman who started the fight with Alice. I'd like a full background check on her – her family, friends, former employers, cellmates past and present. Anyone who could have been used to coerce her behavior. Especially children – her own, or her brothers' or sisters'.'

Decker nodded soberly. 'The threat against one's child can be a powerful motivator.'

Rawlings's smirk had faltered, becoming an angry scowl.

Kate smiled up at Decker again. He knew where she was going and was playing along. 'Exactly. Also, find out if Agent Novak spoke with anyone in the jail infirmary. Same questions. Oh, and one more thing.' She crooked her finger, asking him to stoop a little so that she could whisper in his ear. 'Be ready with your phone to snap a photo.'

Decker turned his head so that his eyes were only inches from hers. He lifted his brows in question, but he nodded. *He's baiting you,* he said with his eyes.

I know. Don't worry. Kate had a firm grip on her temper, mainly because she didn't want the guy to walk and he might if she did what she really wanted to. *Well, he wouldn't walk because his legs would be broken. Maybe he'd crawl.* But he'd be free, and that was not okay.

She approached Rawlings slowly. 'What does your wife do for a living, Mr Rawlings?'

He blinked, not anticipating that question. 'She's a teacher.'

'Oh. She has good benefits, then. That's good for your son, assuming he lives.'

He narrowed his eyes. 'What is *that* supposed to mean?'

'They did tell you the long-term effects of ricin exposure, didn't they? Liver failure, kidneys . . . Your son could be looking at a long recovery. Assuming he lives.'

Rawlings's nostrils flared. 'If you want to arrest me, then arrest me. Otherwise, leave me the hell alone. Don't try to make me so angry that I confess. I haven't done anything wrong.'

'I understand,' Kate said, then sighed. 'Those crime shows on TV make getting a confession look so simple. Unfortunately the smart criminals won't fall for it and the stupid criminals leave so much incriminating evidence that we don't need to resort to such trickery.'

'Is there a question in there, Detective . . . whoever you are?'

'Oh, my bad. I'm Special Agent Coppola, FBI. I'll be the one taking over Agent Novak's role in the investigation. You know,' she said in a conspiratorial voice, 'talking to the ladies in the jail. Woman's touch and all that.'

He looked at her with contempt. 'They won't tell you anything. There isn't anything to tell.'

'They may not have been willing to talk to Agent Novak, but they may be a lot more willing to talk to me. Especially once I tell them that you're in custody.'

'You can't arrest me. I haven't done anything.'

'Yes, I heard you the first time. I don't actually have to arrest you. I just have to tell them that I did. Although I suspect I'll have enough to arrest you once we get back the lab results on your son's stomach contents and compare them to Alice's. If the ricin is a chemical match, then you're the common denominator. That will be enough for a warrant. Once I spread the word that you've been detained for questioning and likely won't return to your job, anyone who owes you a favor will know you won't pay it back, and anyone you're extorting will know you no longer have leverage against them. They'll spill their secrets fast enough. No loyalty.'

He smiled pleasantly. 'You're full of hot air, Agent Coppola.'

She gave him a brilliant smile, grabbing his hand and shaking it. 'Thank you. Thank you.'

'What the fuck?' He yanked his hand back. 'Don't touch me.'

Kate looked over at Decker, pleased to see him holding his phone in front of his eye. 'Did you get it?'

Decker lowered his phone. 'I did.' He walked up to her, showing his phone's screen. It was exactly as she'd hoped – a friendly exchange with Kate looking grateful.

Rawlings's mouth fell open. 'You can't do that. It looks like I cooperated.'

Kate shrugged. 'I can do pretty much what I want. Unless you tell me what I want to know.'

Rawlings went pale. 'He'll kill me. He'll kill my family.'

Kate regarded the guard coldly. 'He tried to kill Agent Novak's sister. He killed your son's best friend and at least four other people that we know of. They had families who are grieving them. He tried to kill *your son*. You'd let him get away with that?' She gave him a few seconds to answer, but realized he wasn't going to. 'Tell me what I want to know, or I'll make copies of that photo and distribute them to every goddamn cell in that jail. And then I'll send you back to work with a smile and all my thanks. I'll make an announcement over the PA about how glad we at the FBI are to have a willing, cooperative, *talkative* public servant like you.'

Rawlings was breathing hard. 'You'd sentence the rest of my family to death?'

Kate shrugged. 'No. You will. Either way you go with this, I'll make sure he thinks you cooperated, so you might as well tell me what I want to know.'

She expected him to lunge, but was a bit surprised when he actually did, because he didn't attempt to escape. Instead he kicked at Decker's cane, knocking him down and snatching the phone from his hand. Without breaking stride, Rawlings threw the phone against the wall as hard as he could. It splintered, raining to the floor in shards.

The two uniforms charged him, cuffing his hands behind him and pushing him to his knees. Decker sat on the floor looking annoyed but unhurt.

'I'm fine,' he snapped before Kate could ask. 'Just my pride and my ass. In that order.'

Rawlings looked grimly satisfied. 'Now that photo goes nowhere.'

Decker snorted. 'Except to the cloud. I sent it to my email at work. Yours too, Kate.'

'You gotta love technology,' Kate said lightly, allowing herself to breathe. She'd had a moment of panic on seeing her leverage smashed to smithereens. She pulled her own phone from her pocket and checked her email. 'Here it is. Let's add another one to it.' She handed the phone to one of the officers as she took her place next to the kneeling Rawlings. 'Make sure you get our faces and the cuffs in the frame.'

'Yes, ma'am.' The officer snapped the picture. 'I can take another if you need me to.'

She checked the photo. 'It's good. Very good.' Borrowing from Decker's manual, she sent the photo to her work email before showing it to Rawlings. 'You look a little pale, but that's probably because you are. Which will just make the photo that much more effective when I distribute it.' She set up her phone to record video, then handed it back to the same cop. 'Hit the red button, please, and tell me when to start.' She waited for the officer's signal. 'Tim Rawlings, you're under arrest for assault on a federal agent and the destruction of government property.' She recited the Miranda, then nodded at the officer, who stopped the recording and handed her back her phone. 'This will convince them if the photos don't.'

Rawlings looked up at her with hate in his eyes. 'My family's blood is on your hands.'

'I'll put your wife and kids in protective custody if we can find them,' Kate said. 'You just worry about you, Mr Rawlings. And your son in there.'

She looked over at Deacon, who'd surged to his feet when Rawlings had gone after Decker, but was now smiling at her. Grimly, but it was a smile.

He walked back over to them long enough to pull Decker to his feet. 'You two make a good team,' was all he said before sitting back down between Faith and his brother to wait for news.

She met Decker's eyes and smiled, and he smiled back. They did make a damn good team.

'What do we do with him, Agent Coppola?' the officer asked.

'Search him,' she said. 'Make sure he's not armed with anything.' She patted down his pockets until she found his phone. Two phones actually, which was no shock. One was probably a burner. She put

451

them in evidence bags and sealed them. 'I'll call Agent Troy to take him in. Let him sit in a chair until then. I don't want any accusations of mistreatment.'

She heard raised voices behind her and saw a man and woman dressed in suits, the woman in hysterics. Both were demanding to see their son, Charlie Chalmers. Kate's shoulders sagged.

'I can do it,' Decker offered quietly.

'I'm tempted to let you. Let's do it together.'

Cincinnati, Ohio,
Friday 14 August, 6.45 P.M.

It's like a cop buffet. He parked his car at the far end of the ER parking lot after driving up one aisle and down the other, studying the cars as he passed. Both Dani Novak and Tim Rawlings Junior had been brought to this ER versus County's.

Not that he could blame their people at all. Bad things had happened at County. *All directed by me, true, but still.*

He didn't have his own people inside this hospital. Not yet. But he was all right for now. Dani Novak had been taken to surgery, so she wouldn't be talking for a while. He had time to deal with her. In the meantime, everyone and his brother had flocked to this ER. Cops and Feds and reporters . . .

It was truly a fucking buffet. There was Deacon Novak's SUV, Marcus O'Bannion's Subaru, Adam Kimble's Jeep, and Kate Coppola's rented Toyota. There was no telling when they'd all come out of the ER, but when they did, he'd be able to follow them. Or one of them, anyway. He'd removed the tracker from JJ's car before having Mallory store her body in the trunk, so he had one in his pocket.

The choice was pretty straightforward. Kate Coppola seemed to have adopted Griffin Davenport. The woman had spent days by his side in ICU and had run the hallways like an obstacle course to save his life at County yesterday. If anyone knew the location of Davenport's safe house, it would be Coppola.

So of all the vehicles on the buffet, Coppola's was the one to watch. He put on a cap, pulled the brim over his face, snapped on a pair of gloves, then strolled past the cars, stopping to pretend to tie his shoe when he reached the rental Toyota.

He slipped the tracker under the car, then strolled back. If he was going to go head-to-head with Coppola to get to Davenport, he needed to be better prepared. The woman had quickly built a reputation as a crack shot. He looked at his arm with disgust. *And at the moment, I am not.*

Give it up. Davenport's already told them everything he knows.

He shook his head. Trouble was, he didn't know what Davenport knew. The Fed had been undercover, spying on Alice and her father, for three years. A man could hear a lot in three years. And what if Alice had lied about not leaving a paper trail? The woman had lied easier than she breathed.

No, Davenport was still a threat. Besides, now it was a matter of professional pride. If he didn't snip that thread, it would gnaw at him forever. He'd always be looking over his shoulder, wondering if they'd learned something new.

I won't be able to get back to business until he's dead.

And to make sure that happened, he had to go through Coppola. Until his arm healed, it would be smarter to deal with her remotely, where he was nowhere near her line of sight. Luckily he had just the thing back in his storeroom.

Cincinnati, Ohio,
Friday 14 August, 8.10 P.M.

'Decker. Decker, wake up. We're here.'

Decker blinked awake slowly, turning his head to find Kate leaning over the console between their seats, her hand on his shoulder, her face inches away from his. Big brown eyes and soft lips that tempted. He grabbed her by the back of the neck, pulled her closer, and kissed her, feeling her stiffen at first but quickly go pliant under his hand.

She pulled away reluctantly, licking her lips in a way that made him want to go back for seconds. She smiled ruefully. 'At least you're awake.'

453

He blinked again and realized a few things. First, he hadn't woken that peacefully, that smoothly, in more years than he could recall. He'd been dreaming of her and then she was there. No jolting awake. No gasping for air. No clenching of fists or grabbing for an M16 that no longer stood ready by his cot. Just a lovely waking. Like a normal person. He'd have to think on that more later.

Because he also realized they were in her car. In a driveway. In front of a massive house that might even be a mansion.

'Holy shit,' he whispered. 'This is where Stone O'Bannion lives?'

'His dad does,' Kate answered. 'Stone's recuperating here. I got the impression that staying with his mother wasn't the best option.'

Decker tilted his head, waiting for more explanation, and Kate sighed. 'She drinks,' she said. 'A lot. I met her last week and she was barely functional. She's lost two sons, both to violence, and her two surviving sons were both nearly killed in the last nine months.'

'You said that Stone and Marcus's brother was murdered nine months ago.'

Kate nodded. 'Mikhail, who was Faith's cousin, so she and Deacon have been helping the family heal. But the mother lost another son to kidnappers when he was only a toddler. Stone and Marcus were also abducted. Marcus was eight, Stone six. I've only read the newspaper clippings, but I can't see how anyone could emerge from that unaffected.'

Decker digested that. 'That's what Diesel meant when he said he and Stone were both stuck at age six. And another reason you didn't judge Stone for getting . . . well, stoned. I figured it was because of all the shit he reported on during the war. I know what he saw, because I saw some of it too, and it would have been enough reason to get sucked into using.'

'Lots of my friends did,' Kate murmured. 'We MPs didn't see combat so much as the after-effects. The fights, the drinking. The violence. We were all changed when we got back.'

He swept his thumb across her cheek in a caress. 'Do you knit them camo yarn blankets?'

She rolled her eyes a little in embarrassment. 'Yeah. Why, do you want one too?'

'Only if you're under it.'

She cleared her throat. 'I think we need to go inside and work. They're probably watching us right now.' She pointed at a camera hung from the eaves of the garage. 'Not so subtle.'

'Then we should go for broke, Special Agent Coppola, and give them a real show.'

She eased away from him and gathered her bag. 'As tempting as that is, I think it's a very bad plan, Special Agent Davenport.' She checked her eyes in the visor mirror and sighed. 'Still red. I hate notifications, especially when it's kids.'

She'd informed Mr and Mrs Chalmers that their son Charlie was dead with compassion and respect. Then she'd come out to the car with Decker and cried as she drove them out of the parking lot. All he could do was hold her hand. Once again, she hadn't let herself cry for long, done by the time they'd hit the interstate. She'd pulled herself back together and gone on to the next task, because she had a job to do.

'Maybe I *should* start carrying makeup,' she murmured, then snapped the visor shut with a sigh. 'Did you hear me on the phone when you were asleep?'

'No. I was out like a light.' As soon as she'd stopped crying. He couldn't sleep while she grieved.

'You should be in bed right now,' she said with a small frown. 'Resting. *Alone*,' she stressed when he perked up. 'Anyway, I got a call from Deacon. Dani's out of surgery. They closed up the wound and she's in Recovery. She'll be in ICU tonight. We have a guard inside her room, and Carrie and her surgeon friend have hand-picked the nursing staff, every one of whom submitted to a drug screen. Hopefully the Professor hasn't sunk his hooks into any more nurses.'

'More?' he asked, completely serious now.

'Troy called me too. There may have been another nurse being controlled by the Professor, other than Eileen Wilkins. Troy had just gotten Mr Rawlings settled in a holding cell when he heard from his security contact at County Hospital. He worked with them to track Eileen's movements through the hospital after she tried to drug you yesterday. He'd asked the security guy to keep an eye on the cameras and the computer entry logs, to let him know if anyone used their badge to get in who wasn't on duty or if any of the staff didn't show up for work. One of the ER nurses did both – used her badge yesterday when she wasn't on duty, and didn't show up for her scheduled shift today. Janet Jungers. The security guy had been watching footage from the floor where you were drugged and noticed Miss Jungers hanging out. In fact, she was one of the nurses I passed when I was running to get to you yesterday.'

'When you cleared staff like hurdles,' he murmured. 'Do you have a photo of her?'

Kate produced her phone. 'Troy said he'd email it. Yep, here it is.' She downloaded the photo and leaned over the console again so that Decker could see her screen too.

Damn, she smelled good. *Focus, Davenport.* He blinked hard, then studied the photo and compared it to the pictures his mind had cataloged from the day before. Usually the pictures were sharp and clear, but yesterday's pictures were spotty and sketchy. He hated the after-effects of anesthesia. He'd be fuzzy for days. 'I don't remember . . . Oh, wait. Maybe . . .' The picture in his mind fell into place. 'The elevator. She was waiting for the elevator when Dani, Troy, and Trip took me downstairs. They told her she'd have to wait for the next one.'

Kate looked impressed. 'Damn, Decker. That's really good. Troy only remembered her after the hospital security guy told him that the camera had picked her up in the elevator area. So now he's looking for her. He put a BOLO out on her and her vehicle and he's running backgrounds. So you're up to speed now. Let's go talk to Stone.'

'Do you think they have a butler? Even the traffickers didn't have a butler.'

She grinned at him as he'd hoped she would. 'I don't know. Let's find out.'

He got his cane and followed her up the well-tended walk. 'What does Stone's dad do?' Whatever it was, the man was loaded.

'Jeremy O'Bannion's a teaching doctor, because he was in a car accident that burned his hand. He was a surgeon before that. He lives with his husband, Keith.' She lowered her voice so that he had to lean in to hear. 'Deacon and Faith really like Jeremy. Keith can apparently be . . . abrasive. Deacon doesn't dislike the man, but says he's hard to get to know. Now you know everything I do about this family.'

The door was opened before Kate was able to knock by a forty-something man wearing a lightweight gray suit, a tie, and black leather gloves. 'Agent Coppola?'

'Dr O'Bannion,' Kate responded politely. 'This is Special Agent Davenport. I hope we're not calling at a bad time.'

Decker studied the man carefully and did the math in his head. Stone had to be thirty, at least. Marcus was even older. This guy didn't look more than forty-five. Stepfather, then?

'No, of course not,' Jeremy was saying. 'Please come—'

'Jeremy! Goddammit!' There was a thumping sound from behind the door seconds before a bulky man appeared, positioning himself in front of Jeremy. Dressed far more casually in jeans and a polo, the man also had a gun holstered on his belt. He leaned heavily on a walking stick that looked hand-carved out of very heavy wood. It also sported a shiny brass grip – perfect for whacking the hell out of someone. *I need to get me one of those*, Decker thought.

'I told you to let me get the damn door,' the man said, glaring at them.

Ah. The abrasive Keith.

'I knew who it was,' Jeremy said very mildly, as if this was an argument they had often. 'Can you invite our guests in, please?' The two men stepped back, then Jeremy drew a sharp breath as he got a good look at Kate's face in the light of a crystal chandelier that probably cost Decker's salary for a year. 'You've been crying. Is Dani . . .'

Kate shook her head quickly. 'No, sir. Dani's out of surgery and she's going to be okay.'

He was clearly relieved. 'Good. I know the surgeon who worked on her. She's one of my former students. Straight A's. Talented hands.'

Kate's mouth curved. 'The grapevine's been working overtime.'

'Marcus called me. He knew I'd be worried about Dani. I've only met her a few times, through Deacon and Faith, but she's an extraordinary woman. Please come in.' He led them into an honest-to-God parlor with a silver tea service on the coffee table. 'Can I offer you tea?'

'No thank you,' Kate said politely, taking the chair Keith indicated with a grunt. Decker eased himself into the chair beside her while Jeremy and Keith sat on the sofa opposite them. 'We're actually here to see Stone. We won't stay long, I promise.'

Jeremy gave her a sharp look before glancing at Decker. 'You're up and about, Agent Davenport. From what I read in the *Ledger*, you should still be in bed.'

Kate snorted softly. 'Sayin',' she muttered, and Jeremy's lips twitched.

'Keith didn't want to rest and recover either.' He gave his husband a look that was both fond and scolding and some of Keith's anger visibly melted away. 'But what can you do?'

'Nothing,' Kate said, resigned. 'Is Stone here?'

'Yes,' Jeremy said, then hesitated.

Keith rolled his eyes. 'Stone said he'll talk to Davenport but not you, Agent Coppola. Jeremy doesn't want to hurt your feelings.'

Decker and Kate exchanged a glance, in sync again. *Diesel warned him*, Decker said.

Go on. It's okay. 'Tell him I understand,' Kate added aloud, very evenly. 'I think I will have a cup of tea, Dr O'Bannion, if that's okay.'

'Of course,' Jeremy said. 'Keith, will you take Agent Davenport to Stone?'

Keith pushed to his feet and jerked his head toward the door. 'This way.'

Decker looked over his shoulder as he followed the gruff man. Kate and Jeremy were smiling as Jeremy poured tea. 'They're going to talk about us,' Decker complained.

Keith shrugged. 'They worry about us, I guess.'

'I guess. So, what's your story?' Decker pointed to the walking stick.

'Knee replacements. Got popped nine months ago.' He crooked his hand like a gun and pointed at each knee. 'Bang, bang.'

Decker winced. 'Ouch.'

'You got no idea.'

'Not exactly, but I've taken a bullet or two. Or twelve.'

Keith gave him another considering look. 'Army?'

'Two tours. Afghanistan.' Decker was quiet for a moment, but curiosity got the better of him. 'Lotsa stuff happened nine months ago.'

'Very little of it good,' Keith said darkly. 'Except for meeting Faith. She's a sweet kid. I like her. Deacon, too, even though he thinks I'm abrasive.'

Decker's cheeks heated. 'Busted. I wondered if you had the cameras wired for sound.'

'I take my duties seriously. I take care of my family.' It was meant to be a warning, and Decker took it as such.

'I hear and understand.' They hobbled along together for another few seconds. 'I like your walking stick, by the way. Can I ask where you got it? My cane came from the hospital and it sucks ass.'

Keith grunted what could have been a chuckle. 'I've got a spare. I can loan it to you.'

'Does it have the brass knuckle equivalent on the end? Because I want me one of those.'

Keith smiled then, an actual smile. 'Got a spare one of those too. Had 'em made special.'

'I'd appreciate it. Hopefully I won't need it for long. No offense, but I'm hoping I'm back to snuff pretty damn quick, because I'm at a disadvantage like this. I can't keep up with Kate if she needs to run. I can still shoot, but she does that better than I do too.'

A grunt. 'She made that shot last week. When you were hit. Read about it in the paper.'

'She's deceptively deadly,' Decker said, and he heard the pride in his voice and didn't care.

Keith grunted again and Decker decided it was a chuckle. 'I think you've got secret weapons of your own, Davenport. Don't think I don't know when I'm being charmed.'

Decker grinned. 'Damn. Busted again.' Then he drew a breath, sobering. 'So, cards on the table. Stone knew we were coming?'

'Yes. Diesel called him. Don't know why you're here. Don't want to know. Just . . . if it's going to impact Jeremy, I need to know. Cards on the table.'

'I think we can keep it from coming to that,' Decker said quietly.

'Thank you.' They stopped at a set of dark wooden doors, pulled closed. 'He's in here.' Keith hit the door once with the head of his stick. 'Stone!' he barked. 'Davenport's here.'

'Well let him in,' Stone barked back. 'I'm ready for him.'

Keith opened the doors, revealing a library that soared three stories, packed with books. Dark wood everywhere. A giant circular window let in the dimming evening light, casting shadows. 'Holy fuck,' Decker breathed, then shook himself. 'Sorry. I was . . . well, it's an impressive sight. Thanks for seeing me, Stone.'

Stone sat in his wheelchair next to a hospital bed, his dark hair combed but still wet. He'd just shaved, too, his cheekbones stark and prominent in a face that was far thinner than it should have been. His eyes were dark, his mouth tight with pain.

'Sure,' he said wearily. 'Come on in.'

'Can I get you anything, Stone?' Keith asked, surprisingly gentle.

'No, but thanks. Davenport? You hungry?'

Decker hesitated, then figured what the hell. 'Famished. Kate stopped at a drive-thru when we left the hospital, but it wasn't nearly enough.'

'I'll bring something. Go sit with him.' Keith closed the doors and it was quiet.

Decker pulled a chair from a reading table carved from the same dark wood as the walls. 'Goddamn,' he muttered as he sat down, because it felt far too good to sit. 'Hate this recovery shit. Hated it every time I've done it.'

'Better than the alternative,' Stone said with a shrug. 'Besides, you just woke up yesterday and look at you. Running all over the damn place. I'm . . .' He shook his head wearily. 'I feel eighty years old.'

'You were shot how many times, Stone?' Decker asked. 'Four? Five?'

'More.' Stone said nothing else and Decker sighed.

'You know why I'm here, right?'

'Yes. But before we get to that, I need to know why Coppola was crying.' He pointed to his laptop, on the hospital bed. On the screen was the view from the camera mounted on the garage. 'I saw her get out of the car. Her eyes were all swollen. Is Dani really okay? Marcus said so, but sometimes he sugar-coats when he thinks it's going to hurt us.'

'Kate said Deacon said she'd be okay. Kate was crying because she had to notify two parents that their sixteen-year-old son was dead. OD'd. Courtesy of the Professor.'

Stone closed his eyes, paling. 'I haven't seen or talked to him in four years.'

'Diesel didn't want to tell us. Kate guilted him into it. The bastard was the one who stabbed Dani. The Professor, I mean. Not Diesel.'

Stone huffed a chuckle. 'Diesel's a bastard too, but a good-hearted one.' He looked away, shame on his face. 'I didn't tell anyone about the drugs. Not even Diesel. He dropped by my apartment one morning unannounced and found me high as a fucking kite. He'd suspected something was wrong and wanted to catch me in the act. I agreed to go to rehab if he didn't tell Marcus. To my knowledge, he never did.'

'He said Marcus doesn't know. How did Diesel know about the Professor?'

Stone's lips twisted bitterly. 'Apparently I'm chatty when I'm stoned out of my mind.'

'Why didn't you turn the guy in when you were clean and sober? Why didn't Diesel?' Decker's temper was heating. 'Dammit, Stone, he was selling to *kids*.'

Stone grew even more drawn and suddenly he really did look eighty years old. 'I know he was selling to kids,' he said almost in a whisper. 'Because I was one of them.'

Twenty-two

Cincinnati, Ohio,
Friday 14 August, 8.30 P.M.

Decker blinked at the man slumped in the wheelchair. Stone O'Bannion had been buying drugs from the Professor since he was a child? *Shit*. He remembered what Kate had told him about Stone and Marcus being kidnapped. Their baby brother's death. 'Dammit, Stone.'

Stone made a sound that was not a growl, not a sob. It was pure pain. 'I'll tell you what I know. Arrest me if you have to. But let me tell my dad first, okay? He doesn't know.'

'All right,' Decker said quietly. 'But if I can possibly not arrest you, I won't. And if I can help you maintain your privacy, I will.'

Stone's startled gaze snapped up to meet his. 'Why in the *fuck* would you do that? My silence, my *pride*, just caused a sixteen-year-old kid to *die*.'

Decker swallowed hard, because his sympathy for this man made his chest hurt. 'For the record, I know you were kidnapped as a kid. I know your brother was killed when you were a kid yourself. I know you've served your country with distinction and I know you've been through hell during the last nine months because you lost another brother and you nearly lost Marcus and you nearly died yourself. And I know you're hurting right now because I can see it on your face. Did they give you pain meds?'

'Yeah. I flush them. I'm an addict. I can't take them.'

'You can take something. Let's find someone who can help you with the pain, okay?'

462

Sharp dark eyes considered him. 'You didn't answer my question, Davenport. Why would you help me? You're one of the good guys. Golden. Why would you risk your career to help an addict who let kids die? Why?'

'Because you're not the only one who's done things he's not proud of.' He let that statement float between them. 'I will probably spend the rest of my life making amends for the sister I couldn't save and for how I dealt with the bastard who did it. If you want to make amends, start by telling me what you know of this asshole Professor.'

Stone nodded unsteadily. 'I was already going to do that.'

'Then let's start with the most recent information. You said you hadn't spoken to him in four years. How did you contact him, what did you buy, and where did you buy it? I'll assume you paid with cash.'

'Of course. He contacted me, actually. Used my cell phone. I'd just come back from my second tour. I'd signed up for classes at King's College.'

Decker perked up at that. 'One victim was a student at King's. Another took a class or two there, but hung at the gym. These last two were in high school. He's going after students.'

'Two?' Stone recoiled. 'I thought you said one kid died.'

'One died. The other's getting his stomach pumped. The kid who lived was the actual target, or rather his father was. The kid who died . . . He may have been collateral damage.'

Stone hung his head. 'Fuck this shit.' He drew a breath, squared his shoulders, still broad even with the weight he'd lost. 'The Professor had a wide user base and he recruited carefully. Some of us had been customers since middle school. He sold high-quality stuff. Nobody wanted to turn him in. Nobody even discussed him with anyone else. You wanted to stay on his good side or he'd cut you off cold. He called me when I got home from the Gulf to say I was looking good. Buff. That the army had worked off all my baby fat. He asked if I wanted to be even stronger. Offered me steroids.' A shrug. 'I took them for a little while. But my poison was usually pills. I just wanted to be happy or sleep. Or forget. Whatever made my brain stop thinking.'

Decker figured they'd get to the pills in a minute, but he needed to understand something else first. 'Baby fat?'

Stone shrugged. 'I was a real chunky kid. Never met a donut I didn't like. I started to slim down when I took the uppers the Professor was selling around the school. Private school, lots of kids with disposable income. Me included. I took uppers to lose weight, feel happier. I took downers to sleep at night. Because . . . well, you obviously know about the abduction.'

'Just that it happened. So this man drew you in at the beginning by exploiting your vulnerability. He hit on the thing that made you the most self-conscious. The guy is a royal sonofabitch, preying on children.'

'And college students and anyone who had cash, including middle-aged women. One time I met up with him, I was just a kid, maybe fourteen? I'd paid him and he was handing me my stuff when this woman came running. He looked surprised that she'd approach him. He dealt with everyone one-on-one for the most part. He had his favorites and they'd be his middlemen. I'd take the cash from my friends, make the buy for all of us, because he liked me. Anyway, this woman came up to him, begging for a fix. He told her to call him later, in a real mean voice, and she got desperate. Ripped her blouse open. Said she'd do him right there if he'd give her just enough to get her through until her husband got paid and she could take cash from his wallet.'

Decker's eyes widened. 'Whoa. Can you describe the woman?'

Stone gave him a look. 'Dude, I was fourteen and she was flashing her breasts. I was not looking at her face.'

'Fair enough.'

Stone frowned thoughtfully. 'But she did pull his shirt out of his pants. He . . . he had a tattoo. I don't know what it was, and that's the truth. I only saw the top edge of it. It was on his ass. Made me want one too. I'd forgotten about that.'

'What did he do about the woman?'

'He slapped her, knocked her down. I can remember being really shocked. She just . . . crumpled on the ground, sobbing. He told her to go to her car and he'd meet her there.'

'Where did you meet him?'

'In the park.' Stone frowned. 'East Fork. Rumor had it that he had a pot patch there.'

'That's where we found the body of the nurse who drugged me.'

Stone blinked. 'You'd think after twenty years that he'd have moved to a different place.'

Twenty years? 'So how old were you when you started buying from him?'

'Thirteen.' Stone shook his head bitterly. 'We thought he was a god, man. He had a face that got the chicks, a muscle car that purred like a tiger, and he wore really nice clothes. Now I know he got the chicks by selling them blow.'

'Describe him for me.'

'Five-ten, average build, brown hair. Green eyes. Or maybe blue. I can't remember.'

'And when you saw him again after coming home from the Gulf?'

'Same, just older. Some gray in his hair. A few wrinkles.'

'Huh.' Decker was reluctantly impressed. 'His disguise ages.'

Stone stared. 'He wears a disguise? How the hell do you know that?'

'One of our witnesses saw a buckle in the seam of his facial appliance one day when it got hot.'

Stone sat back in the wheelchair, stunned. 'Holy shit. I never would have suspected that. Hell of a reporter I am.'

'He's survived twenty years without getting caught,' Decker said dryly. 'He's good.'

Stone scowled. 'I'm supposed to be better.'

'You were mired in your own shit, Stone,' Decker snapped. 'Cut yourself some slack, will you?' He rubbed his temples. 'Sorry. I'm tired and hungry.' He looked away, then froze when his eyes focused on the laptop on Stone's bed. 'What the fuck?' He lurched from the chair. A man was creeping up to Kate's car.

'Oh hell,' Stone said, dialing his cell. 'Keith. Someone's in the driveway.'

Decker grabbed the grips on Stone's wheelchair. 'Hang on.'

Pausing long enough to open the double doors, he gripped the chair again and began running down the long hallway, using the chair for balance. He got to the front of the house to find the parlor deserted, empty teacups the only sign that someone had been there.

And then his heart stopped. Rifle fire. Outside. 'Stay here,' he barked to Stone, drawing his service weapon and limping to the front door.

'Keith's walking sticks.' Stone pointed to the doorway. 'Tall can by the door.'

Decker picked one with a brass grip, just in case.

Cincinnati, Ohio,
Friday 14 August, 8.40 P.M.

Kate was having a very nice chat with Jeremy O'Bannion. She could see why Deacon liked him so much. The man was obviously brilliant, but self-effacing, and he loved his children. He just glowed with pride – and worry – when he talked about Marcus, Stone, and Audrey, who Kate hadn't met yet. She had been keeping him entertained with stories of the cases she and Deacon had worked in Baltimore when he'd shocked her by re-asking the question she thought she'd dodged.

'Why were you crying, Kate?'

A glance told her that he wouldn't allow her to evade the question a second time. 'I had to do a death notification right before we came. The boy was sixteen. His parents . . . they fell apart.'

Jeremy seemed to sag where he sat. 'I know what that feels like.'

'I just never know what to say. I can't make it feel . . . better.'

He surprised her by reaching across the table and covering her hand with his, still wearing the black glove. 'The fact that you wish you could? That comes through. The bereaved parents will feel it. Maybe not when you're telling them, because there's just a mental wall, a fog. You can't hear anything except that your child is dead. Afterwards, though, you remember.'

'Thank you.' Kate's eyes stung and she really didn't want to cry anymore, so she reached for the teapot to refill her cup, nearly spilling it when Jeremy surprised her again.

'Are you planning to arrest Stone?'

Kate bobbled the pot, splashing tea onto the silver tray. She met his eyes. 'No. I'm not. But I don't think he'll be a happy man.'

Jeremy nudged her hands aside, taking over the task of cleaning the spilt tea. 'Stone has never been happy. I've seen him content. I've seen him impassioned over a cause, but I've never seen him happy, and that is a hard truth for any parent to bear.'

'You're very . . . young-looking. Are you his stepfather?'

Jeremy's lips curved. 'I guess I should be flattered that I'm still considered "young-looking".' He chuckled when Kate winced. 'It's okay. I married their mother when I was only twenty-one. Marcus was ten and Stone was eight.' He sighed. 'And broken already. He learned to pretend to be fixed, but he's still broken. What has he done, Agent Coppola?'

'I think you should ask him that, sir. I don't want to make things worse for any of you.'

'See? Good heart. I hope you and that very handsome man of yours find happiness.'

'Thank you.' She smiled slyly. 'He *is* very handsome, isn't he?'

'He reminds me of Thor in the movie,' Jeremy confided.

'I thought the same thing.' She settled back in her chair with her tea, but quickly came to attention when Keith thundered in from the kitchen, his walking stick thumping so hard the floor shook. He looked grim and urgent. And held a rifle in his hand.

'Coppola, someone's tampering with your car.'

She set the cup down and jumped to her feet. 'You stay here and call 911,' she said to Jeremy, drawing her weapon from its holster. 'Where's the side door? I don't want to go out the front.'

'Follow me.' Keith led her to the garage and pointed at a door, then held out the rifle. 'Here. Use this if you need it. You got Kevlar?'

'Under my blouse.' She holstered her handgun and took the rifle. 'Please stay here.'

He pulled his gun from its holster. 'This is my home. I will defend it if need be.'

467

She rolled her eyes. 'Fine. Can you see the camera feed from in here?'

'On my phone.' He held it out, her car at the center of the screen, a shadow to the left of the vehicle, low to the ground. 'He's putting something under your car.'

She frowned. 'There's a camera there. Why is he taking that risk?'

'You can only see the camera from a certain angle, like from the front seat of your car. Otherwise it's hidden by the eaves.'

'Makes sense.' She slipped out of the side door, keeping close to the house. She'd gotten to the end of the wall when she heard a noise. Raising the rifle to her shoulder, she edged around the corner. And found herself staring at the man Sidney Siler's roommate had described. *The Professor.*

He was standing behind her car, his own weapon drawn and pointing straight at her.

'Put the gun down,' she commanded.

He smiled at her.

And fired.

She grunted with the impact of the bullet against her Kevlar, then fired back with the rifle. But he'd already dropped behind her car, out of sight. She didn't fire again. He was still there. *Waiting for me to come out so he can shoot me again. Asshole. I can wait too.*

A noise caught her attention and she glanced down and cursed. A small canister had rolled to her feet. *Grenade* was her first thought, and she reflexively sprinted away, toward the door through which she'd come. Away from the car where he was hiding.

Fucker. Where did he get a goddamned grenade? But it didn't blow. It slowly began spraying smoke, the wind carrying it away from her, thank God. She ran into the house, slamming the door behind her. 'Let's go! Get away from this room!' She swore again when she saw Decker jogging from the garage into the house, using one of Keith's walking sticks to propel himself forward. She followed, making sure Keith was behind her.

'He's running,' Decker called over his shoulder. 'What was it he threw?'

'We saw him on the camera,' Keith said.

'A gas canister,' Kate said and ran after Decker. 'Get everyone to the opposite side of the house. If you have surgical masks, use them.'

'What kind of gas?' Keith called after her.

'Maybe smoke. But maybe ricin.' *Shit.* She needed to take precautions. 'I'll need a change of clothes and a plastic garbage bag. And a shower.'

'I'll take care of it. He's gone, Agent Coppola. Stay here and take care of yourself.'

'I'll be right back,' she promised. 'The wind carried it away, so I didn't get hit with it.' And even if she had, she had to find Decker. *He's gone after him. Unprotected.*

Decker was standing at the front window. 'He's gone. He ran down the street wearing a gas mask, then drove by again in a dark green Mercedes.' His expression turned grave. 'You should have waited for me. What were you thinking, going after him without backup?'

She stared at him, gaping, and her temper boiled over. 'Oh I don't know! Maybe that you were in a fucking *coma* two days ago? *Goddammit*, Decker!'

He didn't raise his voice. 'I could have covered you. You should have waited.'

She opened her mouth to argue, then realized . . . *He's right. He could have covered me.* She sighed. 'You're right. I'm sorry. I keep doing that. Forgetting that you're . . .'

'Capable?' he said, his jaw taut.

'Shit. No. I didn't mean . . .' She sighed. 'I should have waited for backup. I keep seeing you . . . hurt. I don't want you to be hurt.'

'And I want *you* to be?' He shook his head. 'Just go, Kate. I'll call this in. You go take care of your clothes and shower off. You could be contaminated.'

'The wind changed. I'm probably fine.'

'And if you're not?' he asked sharply. 'Rawlings's kid swallowed it and he might die. But if you breathed it in? You're dead already.'

He was right again. *Dammit. Damn me.* She'd behaved impulsively, going after the intruder alone. She drew a deep breath that made her wince. 'Ouch,' she muttered.

469

She'd been shot. Luckily in the chest. If he'd aimed for her head, she'd be dead.

'I heard two shots,' he said, his eyes cold for the first time. 'One his, one yours?'

Her heart sank. She'd wounded Decker. Wounded his pride. *We can't work together like this. Emotions are involved. His. Mine.* 'Yes. Got me in the Kevlar. Knocked the breath out of me.'

A muscle twitched in his jaw. 'Which is why you missed your shot.'

She nodded. 'Yeah.' She closed her eyes. 'I fucked up.'

'Yeah, you did.' He drew a breath and she waited for him to say more. To be angry. To tell her she was no good. That she'd lost them their only chance to catch the bastard who'd killed so many people. But he said nothing, and she opened her eyes to find him looking at her with such sadness it made them sting yet again.

'We'll talk more about this later,' he said quietly. So very gently. 'In private. Okay?'

She swallowed hard and nodded. 'I told Jeremy to call 911.'

'He did. They're on their way,' Stone said, and they both turned to see him in his wheelchair, watching them. 'You two okay?'

Kate blew out a breath. 'Yeah. I think.' She risked a glance up at Decker. 'You?'

But Decker was staring at her chest, his throat working. 'There's a bullet hole in your shirt,' he said, his voice hoarse. 'Over your heart.'

'Yes, I know.' She frowned. 'He was aiming for my heart. Why?'

Decker's reply held an edge of panic, like it was finally sinking in. 'To fucking *kill* you?'

'Well, yeah, but why my heart? He was fifteen feet away. He shot Eileen Wilkins dead center of her throat from across a meadow. Couple hundred feet, easy. He's a crack shot. He had to have known I'd be wearing some protection. Why not aim for my head?'

Decker closed his eyes, breathing hard. 'I can't do this. I cannot do this.'

'I'm okay. I'm not hurt.'

'You could have been.'

'But. I'm. Not.'

'It's because Diesel hit his arm with a knife,' Stone said from his chair.

Decker's chest expanded as he drew a deep breath, and when he spoke, he was calm again. 'True. Hit his right arm. He was holding the gun in his left hand just now, but he held the knife in his right when he went after Dani. I bet he's right-handed and didn't have the accuracy with his left. He went for the broadest target.'

'But he came prepared,' Kate said. 'I need to make sure that canister is safe and that no one goes near it, then call in the bomb squad. They'll have the equipment to properly contain it so that it can be tested.' She tilted her head. 'Cover me?'

Decker's laugh was strangled. 'Jesus, Kate. Why the hell not? Throw the dog a bone.'

She frowned, troubled by the blatant sarcasm in his voice, but Keith came out of the kitchen before she could address it. He was carrying a large pot in one hand, a man's shirt and sweatpants folded over his arm. He gave her the pot. 'You can use this to cover it. There are gloves and two gas masks inside. Like I said, I take my duties seriously.' He glanced at Decker. 'You're looking a bit green, Davenport. Maybe you should sit down.'

'I'm fine,' Decker insisted.

Kate handed Decker the rifle and one of the masks, so that he could cover her, then she put on the other mask and went out the front door, carrying the pot in hands that trembled. *Later*, she told herself. *Fall apart later.* And if Decker stayed angry with her?

Later. Think about that later.

She upended the pot over the canister, which lay inert on the grass where the Professor had tossed it. *Asshole.* She was walking around her car, giving it an extra wide berth in case he'd put something even worse under it, when an old car rattled to a stop in the street. A tiny blonde popped out of the driver's side and whistled for an enormous dog, which followed her up the driveway, sticking to her side even though she used no leash.

Delores stopped in her tracks at the sight of Kate wearing the mask. Kate gestured to her to quickly move into the house. Decker waited on the front walk until everyone was inside, then followed them in and closed the door. He set the rifle by the door and took off his mask, and waited for Kate to do the same. 'Zimmerman's sending a bomb squad and HazMat.'

Jeremy hurried to join them. 'Everyone, come in. Please. Away from the windows.' The huge dog bounded up to Stone, tail wagging. Stone leaned down and the dog licked his face. Then he looked up and smiled at Delores. 'Hi.'

'Hi yourself,' Delores said, then looked at the tense faces around her. 'What happened?'

'Intruder,' Kate said. 'He got away.'

Delores's eyes widened. 'Mercedes? Dark green?'

'Yes,' Decker said. 'Did you see him?'

'He nearly ran me off the road!' Delores exclaimed. 'I thought he was rude, but . . .' She trailed off, her eyes growing even wider as she stared at Kate. 'You have a bullet hole in your shirt. He shot you.'

'Kevlar,' Kate muttered, not wanting to set Decker off again.

Delores let out a breath. 'Holy shit. I need to sit down.' She sat on the sofa, still staring at Kate's shirt. 'I . . . I followed him.'

'You *what*?' Stone exploded, then winced when Delores flinched. 'I'm sorry,' he said, gentling his tone. 'Why did you do that?'

'Because I wanted to get his license plate. He was a bad driver. He could have killed me! But I didn't know he had a gun. He really could have killed me!'

Stone wheeled his chair to the sofa and took her hand. 'Did you get the plate?'

'Yes.' Delores held out her arm, which was covered in scribble with a black marker. She was visibly shaking. 'I wrote it down.'

Kate copied the information into her notebook. It was unlikely that he'd use his own car or his own plates, but if he'd been desperate enough to come that close to her car, he might be making more mistakes. 'I'll run the plates. Thank you, Delores.'

Delores nodded numbly. 'I came to see you, Stone. Diesel said you might need me.' Then she grimaced. 'Darn it. I wasn't supposed to say that.' She peered up at him through her bangs. 'We can just forget I said that, right?'

Stone laughed and suddenly looked years younger. 'Yes,' he said. 'We can forget it. I'm just happy you're here and okay.'

Jeremy was looking at Stone, his expression one of wonder tinged with hope. Because Stone really did look happy.

Then Keith turned from the front window, where he'd been standing, watching out front. 'Cops are outside,' he said. 'I'll show them in.'

Smile disappearing, Stone turned to Decker. 'Give me a minute to talk to my dad, okay?'

Decker seemed to understand. 'Take all the time you need. Kate, go shower and change your clothes. I'll handle things until you come back.'

Cincinnati, Ohio,
Friday 14 August, 10.15 P.M.

'Mallory! *Mallory!*'

Oh wonderful. He's home. And he sounded angry.

Mallory backed away from Roxy's bedside, ashamed to be grateful for the temporary reprieve. Because the sheets needed changing. Again. And it made Mallory gag every time. *I am so not a nurse.* She had the feeling she was hurting Roxy every time she touched her, and Roxy had always been nice to her, so she hated hurting her.

Mallory backed as far as the doorway, her hands still gloved up from washing the poor woman's bedsores. 'Yes?' she called down.

'Don't yes me! Get your fucking ass down here now!'

'I'm coming,' she called. Then softly added to the woman in the bed, 'I'll be back when I can. I'm sorry.' She carefully peeled off the gloves, folding them so that the outside was tucked against itself. She'd dispose of them downstairs.

She hurried down the stairs, wishing she had the courage to simply put a pillow over Roxy's face and end her suffering. *But I'm a coward. I can't do that.* At least it wouldn't be long now. Mallory didn't know how she knew that. She'd never been around anyone sick before.

She walked into the kitchen and stopped short. He was sitting at the table, struggling with his shirt. His right arm was bandaged, and blood had soaked through the gauze. 'I'm here,' she said quietly, knowing better than to ask what had happened. 'How should I help you?'

He glared up at her. 'Get some scissors, two pairs. Disinfect them with alcohol. And get the first aid kit. Hurry.'

She scrambled to obey, running back upstairs for the kit, then back down to where he sat muttering to himself. 'Fucking bitch. Come at me with a fucking rifle. Goddammit.'

She went to the sink and put the two pairs of scissors on the counter, then opened the alcohol and poured it liberally over them. 'What next?'

'Cut this shirt off my arm. And if you cut *me*, I will kill you.'

She didn't doubt him. 'If you shout at me, my hands will shake. So please don't shout until I'm finished,' she requested, keeping her tone respectful.

He stared at her, then huffed a laugh. 'Fine. Just hurry.'

She obeyed, gently sliding the shirt away. It was dirty and smelled like sweat. Sour sweat.

'Now,' he said, 'wash your hands *well*. Put on a pair of gloves, take the other scissors and cut the bandage off. Carefully.'

'Yes, sir.' Again she obeyed, willing her hands not to shake as she worked. Trying not to grimace at the sight of his cut. It was long and deep. Someone had sewn it up clumsily. The stitches were uneven, the edges of his skin puffy and red.

He'd probably stitched himself. If Nell had done it, the stitches would be perfect. Mallory should know. Nell had patched her up a few times when he'd hit her a little too hard, telling his sister that Mallory had been falling-down drunk or in a rage, so far gone she'd hurt herself.

'What should I do with the bandages?'

'Put them in a trash bag. I've got some other items to burn later too. Now, take the bottle of antiseptic wash out of the kit and spray it on the cut. Then there should be a tube in there, silver gel. Do you see it? Spread a little of it on the gauze and lay that on the cut. Then wrap it with the rolled gauze. Can you remember that?'

She nodded and set about doing his bidding, thinking while she worked. He'd need her to change the bandage tomorrow. She had plenty of supplies, so that wouldn't be a problem. Unless she were to run out of something on purpose. The tube of silver ointment was nearly full, but the bottle of antiseptic wash was about two-thirds empty.

If he got a little more infected, and the bottle was empty, he'd need her to go to the store. *And then I can call the woman at the police station. Ask for the lady cop.*

It could work. She looked at the gloves on her hands and thought of the pair in her pocket. The ones she'd used on Roxy. Wouldn't it be fitting if his cut got infected from his wife's sores? If he were humane, Roxy would have gone to a hospital long ago. He could even have killed her himself, but Mallory had realized long ago that the man enjoyed seeing people suffer.

Because he could. She looked over her shoulder. His back was to her, so she pulled the gloves out of her pocket and turned them so that the surface that had touched Roxy's skin was exposed. She rubbed the gauze quickly over the glove, then squirted the ointment on. It might not affect him at all. The ointment might kill all the germs before she laid it on his skin.

How am I supposed to know? I'm no doctor. Her hands surprisingly steady, she turned back to him and finished dressing the wound, winding the gauze around his arm as he directed.

'Good enough. Clean everything up and put it in a bag. Leave it next to the back door. I'll burn it all tomorrow. I'm going to bed now. Do not wake me up.'

'Yes, sir.' She waited until she heard his door close, then gave the top of the spray a quick twist, opening the bottle and dumping all but a squirt or two down the drain. She put the supplies back in the first aid kit and cleaned everything else. Just as he'd instructed.

Then she went back upstairs to change Roxy's sheets.

And hoped that by this time tomorrow everything would be

different. Better. For all of them. *Me, Macy, those four kids. And even Roxy. Please.*

Cincinnati, Ohio,
Saturday 15 August, 1.20 A.M.

'You know you were lucky,' Zimmerman said for what seemed like the hundredth time.

Decker wanted to smack him, because every time he said it, Kate seemed to shrink a little more. 'Yes.' She nodded dutifully. 'I know.'

She *had* been lucky. They'd known that the moment the doctor had pronounced her free of contamination, largely thanks to Kate's quick reflexes and a cooperative wind. The bastard Professor, whoever he was, had used ricin in that canister – a very finely milled powder he'd aerosolized and released using a jerry-rigged flea bomb. It wouldn't have had much of a range even in a closed room, but unlike ingested ricin, inhaled ricin was a death sentence. Had she not moved upwind, she might have breathed it in and died.

If the shot to her chest hadn't killed her first. So yes, she'd been lucky.

Decker had known that even before the bomb squad had found the crude but effective explosive device under Kate's car. Even before Zimmerman had charged into the O'Bannion home.

Their boss had been angry. They'd had their suspect in their hands and they'd allowed him to escape.

Allowed nothing. The bastard had come prepared, willing to kill more innocent people.

Decker wondered if he'd planned to fling the ricin gas into the house once he'd finished planting the small but powerful home-made bomb under Kate's car. Because Stone was a former client who might have told them everything.

Which Stone had done, and Decker had been incredibly proud of him.

'We'd like to sleep now, sir,' Decker said respectfully. He was holding the door of the safe house apartment, where Zimmerman had been standing for the last few minutes. A few minutes during

476

which he'd managed to tell Kate she'd been lucky no fewer than five more times. 'I think Agent Coppola realizes how lucky she was,' he added with a look of reproach.

Zimmerman blinked, realization dawning in his eyes. 'I said that already, didn't I?'

'Several times, sir,' Decker said levelly. 'And I could really use the rest.'

'You slept two whole hours in the van,' Troy said with his trademark sarcasm. 'Wasn't that enough, farm boy?'

Decker's lips twitched despite his exhaustion. He had slept like the dead the entire drive to the safe house, which Troy, Zimmerman, and Trip had somehow managed to stretch from forty-five minutes to a few hours, changing vehicles several times in case they were being followed. For once Decker hadn't complained about being in the wheelchair. He'd been snoring too loudly.

'Hell, yeah,' Decker said sarcastically. 'I'm raring to go. Let's go for a ten-mile run.'

'They're fine, boss,' Troy said to Zimmerman. 'I'm in here tonight. Trip's outside. You've got two more men downstairs. We're all fine. Go home.'

Zimmerman nodded, giving Kate one last look over his shoulder, apology in his eyes. 'I don't truthfully know what I would have done differently. We'll start again tomorrow. Good night, everyone.'

Decker shut the door and walked to the sofa, where he sank into the cushion next to Kate. 'I thought he'd never leave.'

Troy had been standing next to Kate the whole time, as if he was her personal sentry. Now he patted her on the shoulder kindly. 'Z cares too much and he's already lost too many agents on this case. For the record, I wouldn't have done anything differently either. I'm going to sleep in the room Dani used. I am a very light sleeper. I would appreciate discretion on your part.'

Kate looked up at him, eyes narrowed. 'I beg your pardon?'

'Oh.' Troy rolled his eyes. 'She's polite *now*. Not so much last night when you made the night guard listen to you two . . . you know. Gettin' it on, doing the horizontal mambo.'

'She wasn't horizontal, as I recall,' Decker said smugly.

Both Kate and Troy stared at him, Kate in horror and Troy in momentary shock. Then Troy threw back his head and laughed until tears ran down his face.

'Oh my God,' he gasped when he could speak. 'Kate, you're going to have to duct-tape his mouth shut when this is all over and you date like normal people.' He sobered on a sigh. 'Because when this is over – and you are both still standing because you *will* be more careful . . .' His expression softened into something wistful. 'You have the chance for something real. Don't fuck it up by getting killed. Now Uncle Luther is going to sleep. *Please* do not wake me up.'

Kate's mouth had fallen open and remained so as she watched him walk to the bedroom. She kept staring after he had closed the door.

Decker curled his finger under her chin, closing her mouth. 'He cares too.'

She exhaled helplessly. 'I'm . . . God, Decker. I don't know what I am. I thought for a few minutes that Zimmerman was going to fire me, and if he hadn't, that Deacon would skin me.'

Deacon and Faith had shown up with Scarlett and Marcus soon after Zimmerman had stormed in like a hurricane, and for a little while there had been mass pandemonium, with everyone talking at once, until little Delores Kaminsky had stood on the sofa and whistled so sharply they'd all fallen silent. 'Delores saved you,' Decker said fondly.

Kate's lips curved. 'She wasn't going to let them upset Stone. I was just lucky to be covered by that wave.' Her smile faltered. 'God, Decker. Stone . . . I never would have dreamed he'd suffered so much. And to go through rehab all alone like that . . . Diesel helped him, sure, but keeping his family in the dark? God, how incredibly lonely he must have been.'

'I know.' Because Stone had realized as soon as the shots were fired that the police would come, and he'd known the big question would be why two agents had come to visit him. He'd come clean about everything. In front of his family, friends, Delores . . . 'He was so afraid that Marcus and his dad would be hurt. Or not respect him.'

Another smile bloomed on her face. 'But they stood up for him. I have to say, for a minute there I wanted to beg Jeremy O'Bannion to adopt me.'

'Me too. So now we know that Stone has a support system, and we know valuable things about the Professor.'

'Twenty years,' Kate said, shaking her head. 'How could he go twenty years and not be caught, Decker? He's got to have friends in CPD. He's got to.'

'I agree. Somebody would have had to say something along the way. File a report . . . something.' He reached out his arm in invitation, content when she scooted over to lay her head on his shoulder. He wrapped his arm around her and pulled her close and for several quiet heartbeats just let them be.

Then she sighed. 'I'm sorry, Decker. I'm sorry I excluded you this evening. I rushed into that situation without thinking. And things could have been so different. I'm bossy and I'm clumsy. With feelings.'

'No you're not. You're just too used to being alone. What did you think I'd say, standing there in Jeremy's foyer?' When she'd closed her eyes and waited, like she was ready to take a hit. Verbal or physical. It had nearly broken him.

'That I deserved what was coming to me. That I was bossy and a bitch and ran roughshod over people to get what I wanted.' She swallowed hard. 'That you were done with me before we even got started. Because you looked so devastated. Like I'd ripped your heart out.'

'I thought as much. Not all the things you just said, but I figured you were thinking like that. But I didn't think any of those things. I only wondered who'd said them to you. Then I figured it was your dad and your brothers. I just hoped it wasn't Johnnie.'

She pulled away enough to see his face, her eyes filled with a relief so profound it shook him. 'I'm almost more relieved to hear that than that I was ricin-free.'

He frowned at her. 'Now that's just stupid, Kate.'

'I said almost.' She relaxed into him, sighing wearily. 'Not Johnnie. Never Johnnie. My dad, yes. Mom, yes. Brothers, hell yes. And even Jack, there at the end. But not Johnnie.'

'Good.' He pushed away the tinge of envy that wormed its way into his mind. 'I'm glad.'

'Johnnie is dead, Decker. You're not. And because – according to Zimmerman – I'm the luckiest special agent on the frickin' planet, neither am I.'

He kissed the top of her head. 'Are we good now?'

'Yes. Until I rush into something again and have to apologize.'

He squeezed her shoulders, making her flinch. Immediately he let her go. He was so relieved about the ricin exposure that he kept forgetting she had a bruise on her chest from the fucking Professor's fucking bullet.

She stiffened a little in surprise. 'Did you just growl, Decker?'

'Yes. Bastard, shooting you in the chest. I owe Diesel Kennedy dinner for life for maiming that fucker's arm. Otherwise we wouldn't have had to worry about the ricin. You'd have been dead either way.'

'Or in a medically induced coma for a week so my wound could heal,' she said tartly.

That took the starch out of his sails. 'Oh. Right. I kind of forgot.'

She snickered. 'Holy shit, Decker, we're a pair.'

He had to laugh. 'Peas in a pod.'

Her snicker turned into silent laughter that shook her shoulders. 'We both need a keeper.'

He tilted her chin up, so damn happy to see her laughing. So damn happy, period. He kept staring, drinking her in, committing the image of her laughing face to memory. She stopped laughing, gazing up at him, and the moment abruptly changed, the relief in her eyes now hunger.

And that fast, he was hungry too. He stood up, took her hand. Pulled her to her feet.

Then took her mouth, possessiveness overwhelming him like a dark flood. *You're mine.* She'd been his since she'd dropped out of that tree and shoved a rifle in his back.

Making a low noise in the back of her throat, she wrapped her arms around his neck, kissing him back with a desperation he needed to quell.

'Sshh,' he whispered. 'I'm right here. It's not a race. And I'm not going anywhere.'

Her arms relaxed a fraction and she licked her lips, then licked his. 'I really think we'd better go somewhere. Because we're not doing any horizontal mamboing out here.'

He grinned and kissed her again, this one lush and far less desperate. She hummed in her throat and melted into him, pressing her breasts into his chest. He slipped his hands under the hem of the heavy shirt she wore, brushing his fingers over the silky skin of her lower back before venturing higher, massaging where a bra would have been, had she been wearing one.

She'd shucked off all her clothes before showering, including her bra. And being a houseful of men, nobody had an extra one for her to borrow. She'd worn a button-up shirt over the T-shirt Keith had loaned her, so she looked perfectly modest. But Decker had known.

'Drove me crazy, knowing you were naked under this shirt.' He started walking toward the bedroom and she stuck with him, moving backwards with grace. And trust. Like she knew he wouldn't let her get hurt.

She smiled. 'Yeah?'

'Yeah. I kept remembering what you looked like. And felt like. And tasted like.' He whispered the words, nuzzling her neck, finally making it to the bedroom. He closed the door quietly. 'I want you.'

She licked his lower lip again, little flicks of her tongue. 'Then take what you want, Decker. And I'll take what I want.'

'What do you want?' he asked, then slowly pulled the T-shirt over her head, leaving her bared to the waist and so beautiful. All soft skin and curves. So many curves. And one nasty bruise. He bent down to kiss it, not realizing his muscles had gone rigid until she ran her hands over his shoulders, kneading them gently before giving them a soft rub and a shove.

'I want you to look at me, not the bruises.' She petted his chest through his shirt, gentling him. 'Because I'm always going to have bruises, Decker. It's part of who I am.'

She was right. He knew that. So he licked a path from the bruise to her throat, letting his palms roam up her sides, cupping her breasts. Feeling her shiver.

'Slow?' he asked. 'Or fast?' He flicked her nipples with his thumbs. 'Sweet or dirty? Tell me.'

Her head dropped back, leaving her throat exposed. 'I don't know. I can't think when you do that. Just don't stop.'

Chuckling, he kissed the curve of her throat. 'Slow, then.'

She hummed, the vibration tickling his lips. 'I like slow. Sometimes. But not tonight. Not right now. Right now I want to take a shower. I smell like hospital soap.'

He brushed his lips over her ear, pinching her nipples lightly because it had driven her crazy the night before, and she shivered again, harder. 'I don't care,' he whispered.

She rolled her shoulders, straightening in his arms. Gently pulling his hands off her breasts. 'I do.'

'Then I'll join you.'

She hesitated. 'We need to cover your bandages with something to keep them dry.'

'No need. The bandage where they took out the chest tube is gone. I had the doctor look at it at the hospital when you were being decontaminated. I'm cleared for full shower activities.'

'Good to know.' She grabbed a handful of his shirt and turned for the bathroom, pulling him along with her. 'Come with me.'

He didn't argue, just toed off his shoes, letting her lead. For now. She turned on the water and began unbuttoning his shirt, pushing it off his shoulders, then tugged at the Velcro tab on the Kevlar vest he wore beneath. He took it off and hung it on a hook on the door. Because he'd need it tomorrow, and wrinkled Kevlar itched like a bitch.

Then her hands were on him, fanning over his skin, and he forgot about Kevlar and he forgot tomorrow. He closed his eyes and simply . . . felt. 'I went without touch for so long,' he whispered, the words coming out gravelly. 'I'm gonna really need it for a while.'

She didn't say a word. Just kissed the hollow of his throat tenderly while her busy fingers unbuckled his belt and pulled it from his pants. The belt clattered when it hit the tile floor, but the sound barely registered because she was undoing the button of his pants, sliding down the zipper, then pushing them off, pants and shorts together. She followed them down, ending in a crouch, looking up at him with a wicked gleam in her eyes that had his cock jumping while she watched.

She kissed the skin above his knee, then feathered more kisses over his thighs, up to his hip, and it took a minute for him to realize that her lips were brushing over his scars. Then he didn't think at all because her mouth was on him, hot and wet, and a groan rattled out of his chest.

She pulled away, that wicked gleam unabated. 'You have to be quiet or I won't do this.'

He clamped his jaws closed, pursing his lips, and she laughed softly. 'I thought so,' she said, then took him deep again and he thought he'd lose his mind. His head fell back, his hands splaying flat on the wall behind him as she worked him, sucking and licking until he couldn't stand it any longer. He grabbed her shoulders and yanked her to her feet, taking her mouth with a ferocity that should have given him pause, but she met him with equal force, gripping his head, her fingers raking through his hair, her nails scraping his scalp as she pulled him into her, giving as good as she got.

He tore his mouth away, panting. 'I'm one breath away from dragging you to the bed and fucking you blind. So if you don't want to smell like hospital soap, you'd better hurry.'

She pulled him down for another kiss, ending it with a teasing nip to his lip. 'I'm still half dressed, Agent Davenport.'

He growled at her then, dragging her borrowed sweatpants down her body, tossing them aside before she could protest – not that she'd planned to – then grabbed her lace panties and tore them in his haste. On one knee, he looked up, found her staring at him, her cheeks flushed with arousal. 'All night I've been picturing you commando under Keith's sweats,' he said, his voice husky. 'Where did these come from?'

'Jeremy's daughter left them at his house. They were still in the package,' she said breathlessly. 'Never been worn. Never will again now.'

'I'd apologize, but I'm not sorry.' He pressed an open-mouthed kiss on the inside of her thigh, drawing in the luscious scent of her need. 'But I will replace them.'

Her laugh was half moan. 'It's all right. I've never had my panties torn off me before. That was really hot, Decker.' She backed into the shower and crooked her finger. 'Are you coming?'

He closed his eyes for a second. 'You could have just said you didn't want slow.'

She laughed then, low and sultry, and he damn near came right where he knelt. 'I said I liked slow sometimes.' She held out her hand. 'Just not tonight.'

He rose on his own power, then followed her into the shower and flattened her against the wall, thrusting against her and making her moan. 'Hurry. I need to be inside you.'

He took the soap from her hands and lathered her up quickly. Too quickly, but he needed her too much. That he'd thought he could actually go slow . . . *Ludicrous*. He lathered himself, conscious of her eyes on his chest, following his hands down as he washed lower.

He threw the soap into the dish, rinsed, turned off the water and grabbed the towel to do a cursory job of drying them off. Then he pulled her out of the shower, slowing only enough to take a condom from the pocket of his pants before dragging her to the bed and following her down, covering her with his body and thrusting against her, nearly coming again from the friction alone.

She pushed at his shoulders, turning him on his back, and snagged the condom out of his grip. She straddled him as she had done the night before, but this time she rolled the condom over him with quick, efficient fingers. 'Okay?'

His gaze bounced from her hand on his cock to her breasts and finally her face. 'Huh? Is what okay?'

She grinned down at him. 'This way. With me . . . you know.'

He closed his eyes, tried to find a sliver of sanity. She was protecting him again, giving him time to heal before expecting him to be on top. He dug his fingers into her hips, flexing restlessly. 'Kate, I swear t'God, as long as I get inside you in the next five seconds, I don't care if you're hanging from a fucking trapeze.'

'Now that . . .' She kissed him softly, drawing a groan from his throat that sounded more like a whine. 'That sounds very interesting.'

'Kate.'

'Sshh.' She lifted her hips . . . and took him deep. *Finally*. He groaned again, but she'd covered his mouth with hers, swallowing the sound. Then she started to move, and he could swear he'd died and gone to heaven she felt so good.

He exhaled raggedly. 'Faster. Please.'

She pushed up so that she sat upright, taking him even deeper, then let her head fall back and rode him hard and fast and dirty, her breasts in constant motion. He wanted to watch her body, wanted to see her face, but his vision blurred and his hips jerked up, trying to get more of her. Needing to fill her, to take her . . . to possess her so fully that nobody else, past, present or future, would ever matter again.

He blinked hard, needing to see, something inside him relaxing when she met his gaze, never pausing as she rode him, the only sounds in the room the slapping of flesh and the harsh breaths sawing in and out of their lungs. He planted one foot on the mattress so that he could thrust higher, and she made a keening sound, her back arching like a bow.

She covered her mouth with her hand, muffling her cry as she came, her orgasm triggering his. He pulled her down, kissed her hard, rolled them so that she was on her back. Closing his eyes, he snapped his hips, driving into her, matching the rhythm that pounded in his head.

And when he came . . . it was electric, little lights sparking behind his eyelids. It was a deluge, sweeping away everything in its path. And then it was . . . quiet.

Peace. He carefully lowered himself to his elbows, burying his face in the curve of her shoulder, shivering at the feel of her hand lightly stroking his back, setting a new, slower, richer rhythm.

Peace, he thought again. He shuddered, pressing his lips to the side of her neck, rousing himself enough to kiss her temple, then her forehead. Then he opened his eyes and found her smiling at him.

This. This was what he wanted. What he'd hoped for all those nights he'd spent alone. Her, smiling up at him. He wanted to see her smiling like this every day for the rest of his life.

'You are incredibly beautiful,' she whispered.

His lips curved. 'I thought that was my line. Except it wouldn't be. A line. You know.'

She touched his face with a quiet reverence. 'I know.'

He didn't want to leave her, never wanted to pull out of the warmth of her body, but he had to take care of things. He was gone only long enough to deal with the condom, but when he came back, her eyes had drifted closed.

He slid his arm around her, lifting her so that he could pull the covers down. Then he settled her on the pillow, pulling the pins from her hair and arranging it around her shoulders, giving himself a pretty picture to dream of when he went to sleep.

Twenty-three

Cincinnati, Ohio,
Saturday 15 August, 4.45 A.M.

'Are you actually human, Davenport?'

Decker looked up from his computer screen to see Troy stumbling into the kitchen wearing boxer shorts and rubbing his eyes. 'Last I checked, yes,' he said mildly.

'I don't believe you. Why aren't you dead from lack of sleep?'

Because sex had him all juiced up, but he wasn't going to say that to Troy. 'I slept for a frickin' week in the hospital. I'm good for a few days. Why are *you* awake?'

'Goddamn ulcer,' Troy muttered. He turned on the electric kettle and opened cabinets until he found a mug. 'Tea. Chamomile. It helps.' He pressed a palm to his stomach with a grimace. 'Dinner would also have helped. I forgot to eat.'

'There's food in the fridge. Keith O'Bannion sent it with us. He's an awesome cook.'

Troy scowled. 'Can't eat awesome stuff. If it tastes good, I gotta spit it out.'

'Maybe not. I told him that we had an agent with an ulcer, and it turns out Jeremy has one too, so he's used to cooking ulcer-friendly food. It's in the fridge, labeled *UFF*.'

Troy looked surprised. 'That was nice of you, Davenport. And nice of O'Bannion.' He found the bowls in the fridge, filled a plate, and put it in the microwave. 'What are you doing?'

'Going through the files Diesel brought me this afternoon. Well, yesterday now.'

Troy grimaced again, this time in sympathy. 'More photos?'

'Yeah, but I had a thought. I kept wondering when—' He cut himself off as Kate walked in, thankfully dressed in her T-shirt and sleep shorts. She had her yarn bag over her shoulder. 'Why are you awake?' he asked.

'I heard voices and didn't want to miss out on all the fun,' she said lightly, but Decker wasn't fooled. She had that haunted look in her eyes.

You had the nightmare again? he asked with his eyes, and she nodded wearily.

'What did you just do there?' Troy asked suspiciously.

'Private talk, Uncle Luther,' Kate said. 'Cute shorts, by the way. Glad you're a Cap fan or I might have to ask for a *new* new partner.'

Troy blushed. His boxers were covered with Captain America shields. 'I'll go change. I thought I was the only one awake.'

Kate waved her hand and sat down at the table. 'I was raised with four brothers, and those are the most modest shorts I've ever seen. I'm okay if you are.'

'I'm not,' Troy said. 'Some lines should not be crossed.' He disappeared into his room and returned less than a minute later wearing sweats and an FBI T-shirt. 'I'm heating some food. You two hungry?'

Kate tilted her head. 'Yeah, I am. I didn't eat dinner at Keith's . . . not like *some* people.' She eyed Decker.

'Hey, I slept for a week and starved for a week. I'm starving again.' Decker nodded at Troy. 'So please and thank you.'

Troy busied himself with plates and silverware. 'What were you doing again, Davenport?'

Decker returned his attention to his computer screen. It was covered with photos, but not the kind that would give him nightmares. 'I was thinking about something that Stone said tonight – that he started buying from the Professor when he was in middle school. It pissed me off so much when he said it that I didn't think about anything other than the Professor being a predatory asshole. Then I calmed down and could think. Now we know how the Professor recruited his kids – he crossed their paths when they were young through the schools, or gyms and college campuses when they were older.'

'I still have that list of male teachers in the entire Tri-State area,' Troy said. 'I can go back to sifting the records to match height and body type.'

'Please do,' Decker said, 'but I also wondered again how he crossed paths with McCord.'

Kate bit at her lip. 'We lost that thread somewhere, didn't we? So our dealer is connected with school-aged kids, selling them drugs, and McCord is connected with kids as their teacher. But he was buying kids for his porn through Alice and her father.' She lifted her brows. 'Were *all* of McCord's victims purchased? That seems very expensive. How would he have turned a profit?'

'Good point,' Decker murmured, noting it down. 'I hadn't gotten to the profit aspect. I may have to turn in my CPA card.'

'Or tell us what you were thinking instead,' Kate said, subdued. 'Sorry, didn't mean to derail your train of thought.'

He gave her a look of reproach. 'You don't have to walk on eggshells around me, Kate. Profit is a good point. Following the money is always relevant.' He pointed to the flash drive plugged into his computer. 'But back to this. I gave a copy of this drive to Zimmerman when we met up at Alice's apartment yesterday, and he's got national task force members checking photos, comparing them to known victims . . . all the stuff they do as part of a routine investigation. But I'm still wondering where McCord and our dealer crossed paths. Even if both were teachers, it's not like you just walk up to a colleague one day and say, 'You like baseball? I like baseball. You make kiddie porn? Me too. Let's go into business together.' That's just not going to happen.'

Troy put hot plates of Keith's warm-ups on the table and sat down. 'Too much risk. There has to be another connection. So speak while I eat,' he said and started shoveling food into his mouth. 'Oh, wow.' He closed his eyes in bliss. 'This is really good. And it won't kill me?'

Decker grinned at him. 'I sure hope not, but if it does, you'll go out happy.'

Troy pointed his fork at him, his scowl now all show. 'Talk. How do they cross paths?'

'Well, going back to Kate's point, that McCord didn't always use victims purchased from Alice and her father. His files start about ten years ago, about the same time the files on that PC in the closet end. I only scanned them,' Decker admitted. 'I . . . I couldn't make myself study each one.' Kate squeezed his arm encouragingly. 'They're . . . American-looking kids at the beginning. Not so many as I feared. Most had the appearance of a lower socioeconomic level. Used clothes, hungry faces, and just a defeated look, if you know what I mean.'

'McCord taught at a school in the inner city,' Troy said, straightening in his chair. 'Former students maybe?'

Decker nodded. 'That's what I was doing when you two came in. Going through yearbook photos, seeing if I recognized any of the kids. So far, I've matched one.' Kate and Troy started to speak, but Decker raised his hand. 'He's dead,' he added, and both Kate and Troy slumped.

'How?' Kate asked.

'Suicide. OD'd on pills.'

They all got quiet. Troy pushed his plate away. 'Dammit.'

Kate sighed. 'Maybe we can talk to his family. Find some connection there. When did he commit suicide?'

'Five years ago. That's also when McCord started using teens he'd purchased from Alice. His victims go from poor American-looking kids to poor Southeast Asian kids. Thai and Vietnamese. Also Filipino and a few from India. Stills and videos.'

Kate swallowed hard. 'Where are they? Where are these kids?'

Decker rubbed the back of his neck, where pain had suddenly spiked. 'I don't know. No children were found in McCord's house after he died, and there are no other properties associated with his name.' He cleared his throat. 'I'm assuming he either resold them or killed them. If he resold them, Alice and her father would have known. All their victims wore ankle trackers, which were recorded in a notebook kept by Alice's father, locked in his desk drawer in his home office. I saw the book once.'

'It wasn't in the desk when we searched it,' Kate said. 'Or in his briefcase.'

'Sean – Alice's brother – might have taken it. But we don't know where he's hidden his files. I know you guys searched the traffickers' compound, but if it wasn't in the car when he died, it has to still be somewhere in that compound. We need to search it again.'

'We also haven't finished searching Alice's apartment yet,' Troy said. 'We bring in the X-ray machines for the walls today. Maybe the files are hidden there.'

'I hope you're right,' Decker said fervently. 'I didn't count all the kids in the photos, but he bought at least ten over those five years. Maybe more.'

'We'll keep searching,' Kate said firmly. 'In the meantime, five years ago the Sunshine Suzie films changed location. Five years ago McCord switched to foreign kids. Five years ago a former victim committed suicide. Coincidence?'

'I'm gonna say no,' Troy said. 'The young woman that Corey Addison called Suzie was seen in the same car that was later used in the attack on Dani. It's all connected. What if we assume that McCord formed a partnership with the Professor five years ago? What does that contradict?'

'Nothing so far.' Kate pulled her knitting from her yarn bag and her needles began their soft clacking. 'The Suzie films went on for two more years, but with a different look. Different studio. I assumed there was something identifiable in the first location, because those films aren't available online any longer.'

'You could still be right.' Troy got up, refilled his mug, the scent of chamomile mixing with the aroma of the food still on their plates. 'McCord and the Professor have separate businesses until something drives them to work together. McCord's student that he victimized kills himself. Suzie's abuser – who I think we all believe is the Professor or someone associated with him – changes his studio and yanks a year's worth of popular videos, denying himself the sales. But they still have to come across each other. The Professor is local – or at least local enough to be selling drugs to local kids for twenty years. McCord lived in the same town where he grew up. They had to have met here in Cincinnati.'

Decker finished the food on his plate. He was heartsick over the victims but still hungry as hell, and had been raised to never waste food. Wordlessly Kate pushed her half-eaten plate in front of him. 'Thank you,' he told her. 'So what makes a person start making kiddie porn? I mean, I guess some might do it for money, but it's a dangerous thing to get involved with when an Internet search can flag you to the Feds. Seems like the urge to see it, make it, has to be worth the risk. Seems like the Professor – and McCord too – were probably fans before they started making their own.'

'Makes sense,' Troy said, blowing on his tea to cool it. 'And? Go on.'

Kate took up Decker's line of reasoning, allowing him to eat. 'What if,' she said slowly, knitting all the while, 'the Professor's watching one day and recognizes a kid he already knows, because he's sold him drugs? He's making the Suzie films, but has to change locations for whatever reason. The early Suzie films have an amateur look to them. What if he got scared that his place would be identified and wanted a partner with more experience? He approaches the kid he's recognized from the films and gets hooked up with McCord.'

'That works,' Troy said, 'except the Professor was selling to rich kids.'

'That Stone knew of,' Decker said. 'Stone was a rich kid himself. He probably wouldn't have had any contact with poor kids. Doesn't mean the Professor wasn't selling to them. Stone said he was selling to middle-aged women, too.'

'Ah, yes.' Troy grimaced. 'Where's he meeting the women?'

'Don't know,' Decker said. 'But the woman Stone saw wasn't poor either. Stone remembers she said that her husband would be home soon and she'd take the cash from his wallet to pay for the drugs. If he had enough cash for her to sneak for her drugs, he wasn't poor.'

'The Professor's also connected to nurses,' Kate mused. 'He met Eileen Wilkins through her boyfriend, who was a customer via the college gym. Eileen was using opioids she stole from the hospital, part of a national epidemic of nurses who have substance abuse issues. Another group who have substance abuse issues are . . .' She looked up. 'Middle-aged soccer moms. Career women with kids in general. Too much to do, too little time. They need a pick-me-up, and an afternoon latte from Starbucks just won't cut it anymore. Or they get sucked in via prescription painkillers, then switch to heroin. How would he recruit these mothers?'

'Schools?' Troy shrugged. 'PTA. Grocery store. Zumba at the gym, hanging in the bleachers. Too many places.'

'But some of these soccer-mom addicts have to have gotten clean,' Decker said. 'Stone went through rehab and only Diesel knew. But what if we talked to someone who works at a rehab center – like Bailey Beardsley. She's not going to tell us about current clients, but what about successful ones?'

Troy looked doubtful. 'If they were going to talk to us, they've had twenty years.'

'Maybe they're afraid,' Kate said softly. 'We learned tonight that this guy isn't above using a child to get to a parent, or taking out an innocent kid like Charlie Chalmers. If they believe their family's in danger, they're not going to talk. But it certainly can't hurt to ask. Maybe if we ask, someone will have the courage to answer us.'

His stomach finally full, Decker was swamped by a wave of exhaustion. 'I'll talk to Bailey in the morning.' He yawned so widely that he heard his jaw crack. 'I think I just hit the wall.'

'Thank God,' Troy said fervently. 'I was about to cry uncle, trying to stay awake with you. We've got a few hours till morning meeting. Let's get some more sleep.' He put his dishes in the sink and went back to his room.

Decker stood up, grateful for the walking stick he'd borrowed from Keith O'Bannion, because the room had gone all wavy. 'Shit. I really did hit the wall. You coming?'

Kate put her knitting back in the yarn bag. 'Sure, but if I can't sleep, I'll come back out here and work so that I don't disturb you.'

There was an odd reluctance to her movements as she walked to the bedroom and climbed into bed. Decker thought he knew why – or at least part of why. But he needed to know more so that he could help her. He got comfortable beside her, drawing her to his side, her head pillowed on his chest, before turning out the light.

Then into the darkness he murmured, 'You had another nightmare.'

She went still against him. 'Yes.'

'Are you going to tell me why?'

A long, long moment of hesitation. 'Yes.'

After an even longer moment of silence, he brushed a kiss over her hair. 'I can't help you if I'm flying blind.'

'I don't think you can help me at all, Decker. There's nothing to help. I did what I did. I can't undo it. And I wouldn't if I could.'

'But you're not dreaming about what you did, are you? You're dreaming about what Jack did.' He felt the warm puff of her sigh on his bare chest. 'Do you think I'll think less of you?'

'I don't know. But if you did . . .' Her voice trembled. 'I'm not sure I could stand it.'

He wanted her to trust him. But after such a short time, that wasn't really reasonable to expect. Not unless he made it reasonable. He drew a breath, then quickly spoke the words he'd never uttered aloud before he could lose his nerve. 'I killed the man who killed my sister.'

She petted his chest with her fingertips. 'I know. I figured it out for myself.'

But he hadn't said it out loud. Ever. 'I hit him on the head with a baseball bat. Hard. I heard his skull crack. Then I pushed him in the river. He was still alive at the time. He drowned without regaining consciousness, according to the coroner's report.'

Her voice hardened. 'He got off easy, then.'

'Probably so. I thought I'd be okay with it, but even though I would do it again, I . . . I wasn't okay with it. I'm still not.'

She sighed. 'Decker, if that was a test to see if it would make me bail . . . it won't. If it was to make me more comfortable spilling to you, I appreciate it. I really do.'

'But?'

'No buts. I owe you the truth. It's just hard to say. Hard to remember. Impossible to forget.'

494

'Just tell it like a story, then. Once there was a woman named Kate who loved her husband.'

Her swallow was audible. 'But he got brain cancer and it wasn't operable. So he had the hard talk with the people who loved him the most – his fiancée and his brother. He decided he didn't want to do chemo because he wanted to enjoy the time he had left, and he asked them to respect his decision and not to try to get him to change his mind. It was hard, but they agreed. He was supposed to have a whole year. So he made a bucket list. He and his fiancée went sky-diving and Rocky Mountain climbing. And . . .' Her voice wobbled. Broke.

Cracking a piece of his heart right along with it. 'And two point seven seconds on a bull named Fu Manchu?' he asked, getting the song reference.

'No. He was too sick by then and he didn't want to hurt a bull anyway. So his fiancée found a mechanical bull and rode it for . . . well, not quite two point seven seconds. But long enough to make him smile. And then she photoshopped a Fu Manchu mustache on the mechanical bull in a photo that he took while she was hanging on for dear life.'

He kissed her forehead, then leaned back into the pillow. 'I hope you still have those photos. I'd like to see that someday.'

'They're on the iPad I loaned you. All the photos are.'

He was so glad now that he hadn't sneaked a peek at them when he'd had the chance in the hospital. 'You can show them to me when you're ready. So . . . he got worse.'

'Yes. And he had to quit his job that he loved. His students cried. He cried. His fiancée . . . didn't. Because she was strong for him. But then she cried later, when she was alone, because nobody's that strong, you know?'

'Yeah. I know.'

'They'd planned their wedding for June, on his parents' anniversary, because they'd died in a car wreck and both he and his fiancée had loved them and had wanted to honor them. But his fiancée found out that she couldn't take leave under the family leave act for a fiancée, only for a husband, so they got married at the courthouse with his brother as their witness. They figured they could always have a wedding in June for their friends. But he got much sicker really fast and they didn't make it to June.'

'I'm sorry.'

'Me too.' He felt the warm wetness of her tears on his chest. 'Anyway, he was fading so fast. And one of the things we'd discussed in that hard conversation when he was first diagnosed was that he wanted to die at home and on his terms. The doctors told him that at the end he'd forget us. That he'd be in pain.' Her chuckle was watery. 'Johnnie didn't like pain. He was a big wuss. Got hysterical over a paper cut.' She cleared her throat. 'He didn't want to die a shell of himself, a man we no longer knew. So he made us promise . . .'

The wetness on his chest spread and her shoulders shook, and Decker was helpless to do anything but hold her.

'He made us promise that when he had his first episode of forgetting us, if he came back to himself, we'd let him go. He made us promise that we'd leave his pain pills out for him and let him end it on his own terms. I didn't want to promise that and Jack really didn't want to promise, but Johnnie . . . he could charm the skin off a snake too, and he talked us into it. And then the day came. In March. It was cold and snowing and he woke up one morning screaming. He didn't know where he was, who he was, who I was, and he was afraid. I gave him something to help him sleep. Just a little. And I called Jack, who came as quickly as he could. He was in Iowa, because he coached at the same high school we'd all graduated from. He drove through a blizzard and got there just as Johnnie was waking up. I thought Johnnie might not remember his episode, but he did. And he reminded us of our promise.'

'Did Jack try to change his mind?'

'No. He tried to get *me* to change Johnnie's mind, but I wouldn't, and he was so angry with me. But we'd promised, and Johnnie was in pain. The thing was, we couldn't figure out who would actually leave the bottle out. It's not as easy to do as you'd think.'

'How did you decide?'

She huffed a sad, sad laugh. 'Rock, paper, scissors. I could always kick Jack's ass in that. I almost let him win. If I could change anything, that would be it. I'd have let him win and I would have been the one to leave the bottle out for Johnnie. But I played it straight and Jack lost. He put the bottle out, kissed Johnnie on the forehead, then ran out of the house like a bat out of hell. Found himself a bar and got rip-roaring drunk.'

'Leaving you to watch Johnnie die alone?'

'Yes. I'd always known Jack couldn't do that. So . . . I climbed into bed with Johnnie and held him, and we watched his favorite movie, and by the final credits, he was gone.'

Decker blinked hard, his own tears running down his temples. 'I'm so sorry.'

'I'm not. Like I said, I'd do it again. It was against the law and it shouldn't have been. It was his right to die the way he wanted. When the coroner came to take him away, he asked me how Johnnie had gotten the pills, and I lied. I said we'd kept them in the bathroom and that he'd managed to get in there himself. That I'd fallen asleep and by the time I woke up, he was gone. But Johnnie hadn't been able to walk on his own for a few weeks at that point. And I think the coroner knew that. But he didn't press. I got the death certificates and everything said "cancer". Not suicide. Certainly not assisted suicide. I would have been charged.'

'Because you wouldn't have implicated Jack.'

'I couldn't. He hadn't wanted to do it. He barely made it through the memorial service, he was so drunk. But he was out of his mind with grief, so nobody knew. Johnnie's students came to the service and they sang . . .' She exhaled raggedly and sniffled. 'They sang "Wish You Were Here". That part about two lost souls swimming in a fishbowl, year after year . . . It always rips my heart out, because after Johnnie died, Jack and I were the lost souls.'

'That explains a lot,' Decker whispered. 'I heard you singing it the night I woke up. I heard you crying. I wanted to help you, but I didn't know how. I still don't know how.'

'You're here. You're listening. You haven't called me a murdering bitch who was too selfish to take care of a dying man for a few more days. That's helping.'

He caught his breath. 'Jack said that to you?'

497

'Oh yeah. That and a lot more. I chalked it up to grief. Figured he'd work his way through it, but he never did. He kept drinking and drinking. He took pills to stay awake long enough to get through the school day, and pills to sleep, and it's a wonder he didn't kill himself that way, because he never stopped drinking. He actually managed to stay functional for more than two full school years, but finally he lost his job and things really got bad. He'd call me at all hours, threatening to tell. So that I'd lose *my* job. Because I'd loved my job more than I loved Johnnie. He said that Johnnie would have lived months more if I hadn't pushed Jack to kill him. That I'd just wanted to get back to my job. Of course none of that was true. Jack was unraveling and there wasn't a damn thing I could do. I tried to get him into rehab, but he fought me.'

She sighed. 'I should have insisted. I knew that if I forced it, he'd tell what we did, but by the end, I was ready to do that. At least I hope I was. I never got a chance to find out. Jack disappeared. Nobody could find him. He'd been gone for nearly a month when I came back to my apartment from a case in another town. I'd been in DC for three years by then. My apartment was a third-floor walk-up. I came home with my suitcase and climbed the stairs like always, but my door was open. Just a crack.'

Oh God, Decker thought. *This is it*. He could hear the grim finality in her voice.

'I thought I had an intruder. I actually started to call 911 from the landing outside my front door, but then I heard his voice. Jack's voice. Turns out he'd made a key at some point. So I hung up before I dialed the final 1, and opened the door, and there he was. Sitting in my easy chair with my gun in his mouth. Not my service revolver, but one of my other guns. He'd figured out the combination to my gun safe. Not too hard. It was my wedding date. Although they found another gun on him later, so he'd come prepared either way. He'd thought it out, down to taking the afghan off my bed and draping it over the recliner. My grandmother had made me that afghan. It was the only thing I took from home when I left after my dad hit me.'

'Which Jack knew because he was your best friend back then.'

'Yes. I tried to talk him out of it. I begged him not to kill himself and he laughed at me. Told me that I needed to make up my mind. Either he should kill or not kill. Then he pulled the trigger.'

Decker flinched. 'He wanted you to see.'

'Yes. And he wanted me to *know*. So he left me a recording. He'd made it sitting right there in my living room. Said he'd been there for two days, waiting for me to come home. He was so angry. Told me that I'd made him hate himself. That he wasn't sure if he'd killed his brother out of mercy, cowardice, or selfishness. It was a rant. It made no sense, except to show how much pain he was in. That's what I dream, over and over. I run up the stairs and he's always in my chair. He always laughs. And he always shoots himself. And I'm always . . . helpless.'

That, he thought, was the key. In that moment right before Jack had pulled the trigger, she'd been helpless. It was probably her worst fear. 'Who did you call to help you?' he asked softly.

'My boss, Joseph Carter, and his wife, Daphne. Daphne had become a friend to both Deacon and me when we worked for Joseph. She tried so hard to make me feel better. I think Joseph knew there was more to Jack's suicide than simple grief, but he never pressed. And when I asked for a transfer, he helped make it happen.'

'Then I'm glad you had them,' Decker said simply.

She rolled up on her elbow to study his face. 'You're not upset?'

'Of course I am, but only because it hurt you. Kate . . . I saw men in pain when I was in Afghanistan. Picked up the pieces, sometimes when there wasn't much of them left, but they were still alive and they were suffering. You helped the man you loved die with dignity. I think that makes you . . . strong.'

She swallowed hard. 'Thank you. But I don't feel strong most of the time.'

He smiled at her. 'You fake it well, though. Sometimes that's all you can do.'

He could see the shine of her eyes even in the darkness, so he was unsurprised when tears streaked down her face. 'I'm *so* glad I dropped out of that tree behind you,' she whispered.

He pulled her down for a kiss, as sweet and tender as he could make it. 'Me too. Let's sleep now. You have to keep up your strength to keep faking it as well as you do.'

She snuggled into him, her head on his shoulder, her arm around his waist. 'Okay.'

Cincinnati, Ohio,
Saturday 15 August, 8.45 A.M.

Mallory's hands shook as she poured his coffee. He'd woken angry and in pain this morning, and so far nothing she'd done was right. His eggs were too runny, the house was too hot, she'd bought the wrong brands of treats for his young guests, who'd be arriving soon.

At least Gemma had given him a good report, because he hadn't mentioned it. Unless he was saving his accusations for another time.

She hoped she'd done the right thing by emptying the antiseptic spray bottle last night. If nothing else, it would give her a reason to go to the drugstore. She'd find someone there to call the police and pray that they believed her enough to put Macy under protection until he was arrested and unable to make good on his threats.

Although that was still going to be a nearly impossible sell. Nobody was going to believe Macy was in danger. Not until it was too late. Macy's adoptive father was a cop, for God's sake.

Years ago, Mallory had tried to tell Macy's father what his brother-in-law was forcing her to do. He'd backhanded her into a wall and threatened to have her put in a home so far away that she'd never see Macy again. And then he'd told his wife, and Gemma had told her brother.

Who'd locked Mallory in a dark closet for three days. When he'd finally let her out, he'd had a little surprise for her – a new studio. A new partner. Woody McCord.

Mallory shuddered at the memory of McCord's hands on her. He was the one reason she hadn't killed the doctor years ago. If something happened to the doctor, McCord would take over, and he liked girls Macy's age.

That could never happen. *I'll kill them both first.* Although . . . She frowned. McCord hadn't been around in a long time – nearly a year. Something might have happened to him.

She felt a spurt of hope that allowed her to steady her hands enough to place the coffee cup on the table without spilling any.

He looked up from the slice of ham he was struggling to cut, his mouth curled into a snarl. 'Cut this,' he snapped, shoving the plate towards her.

Obediently she sliced the meat into small pieces, wishing she had the courage to stab him with the knife. But it wasn't a big knife, and it wasn't very sharp. Which was why he was having such trouble cutting his meat with it, but there was no way she was saying that out loud.

'I need you to change my bandages before my guests arrive,' he said, unbuttoning his cuff. 'Go get the first aid kit.'

She focused on breathing normally. *This is it.* 'Yes, sir.' She went to get it from the closet and heard his vile curse. When she went back into the kitchen, she couldn't control her gasp. 'Oh God.' His arm was dark red, the cut angry-looking. Infected. Oozing pus. *Gross.*

He glared at her. 'What the *fuck* did you do to me last night?'

Panic stole her breath. 'Nothing. I . . . I did what you said. Exactly what you said.'

'Fuck.' He pinched the bridge of his nose with his good hand. 'I need an antibiotic.'

'Do . . . do you want me to get your bag for you?' she asked in a small voice.

He lifted his gaze to her, so cold it froze her on the spot. 'No. I will tell you what I want you to do.' He looked down at his arm. 'Drugs out the shitter and not one antibiotic,' he muttered. 'All right. Clean it, dress it, then I'll send you to the pharmacy with a script.'

Her hands trembled as she opened the first aid box. 'I don't want to hurt you,' she said to cover her nerves, but it was a lie. She'd like nothing better than to make him howl with pain.

He huffed impatiently, grabbing the box from her. He found the bottle of antiseptic spray and shook it, then gave her another vicious glare. 'This is almost empty.'

'I . . . I used a lot last night. The cut was . . . dirty. I tried to clean it.' She stiffened, preparing herself for a slap, but none came.

He exhaled slowly. 'I'm not going to hit you. I don't want you any more bruised than JJ already made you. People will talk.' He got up, went to his office and came back with his prescription pad, tearing the top page off. 'Here's the script for an antibiotic. Pick up more antiseptic, too. Just go to the drugstore. Don't drive all the way to the grocery.'

'Bu—' The word started to slip out, but she caught it in time. She nodded, hoping he hadn't noticed her lapse. 'Be right back.'

'Do not dawdle. I want this tended before I have to go into the city to pick up my guests.'

The script was written for Roxy, as was his habit. Mallory wondered what he'd do when Roxy died, because she had looked terrible that morning. But Mallory didn't say a word, not wanting to jinx her luck. She was going out again. She dropped her gaze as she backed away, so he wouldn't see her look of relieved triumph. 'I'll hurry.'

Cincinnati, Ohio,
Saturday 15 August, 10.30 A.M.

'Where's Kate?'

Decker looked up from his laptop screen. Deacon Novak had taken the seat across from him at Zimmerman's conference room table. 'She and Troy got called to a crime scene this morning. They should be here any minute.'

Adam took the chair next to Novak, both men frowning. 'Crime scene?' he asked wearily. 'What's happened now?'

'Did you know about the ER nurse who went missing from County?' Decker asked. 'Troy heard about it last night from his security contact there,' he explained when both men looked blank. 'It would have been when Dani was either still in surgery or in recovery, so he may not have wanted to saddle you with it then.'

'I knew he'd asked the security guys at the hospital to keep an eye out for anyone coming in when it wasn't their shift, or not showing,' Novak said. 'So we have another one?'

'Janet Jungers. She was lurking on my floor day before yesterday when I got drugged.'

'And now she's dead?' Adam asked.

'Oh yeah,' Kate said as she came in with Troy and Zimmerman, all three carrying cups of coffee. She sat next to Decker and sniffed the sleeve of her blouse. 'She is very dead.'

Troy sat down with a grimace. 'I'm always amazed that a body can smell that bad that fast.'

'A day in the trunk of her car in the August sun will do it,' Zimmerman said grimly.

'The body was found by teenagers,' Troy said. 'They found Miss Jungers's car parked in front of a 7-Eleven, the keys in it and the motor running, so they took it for a joyride. When they stopped for gas about four hours later, they smelled something "funky", opened the trunk, retched, and took off running. The gas station owner chased them because they didn't pay. Luckily the kids kept stopping to hurl. The owner was able to catch them. He dragged them back and called the cops, who recognized the license plate from the BOLO and called me. CPD had already taken the teenagers to their precinct for booking and I had the car towed to the garage here. The ME's office came to get the body and Quincy Taylor is going over the car itself now.'

'How do you know the kids were telling the truth about finding the car with the motor running?' Decker asked.

Kate rolled her eyes. 'Because we also interviewed the geniuses who left the car outside the 7-Eleven. They're in CPD's holding cell too. They left the motor running because they were actually *robbing* the 7-Eleven, and the car was supposed to be their getaway vehicle. Except the other punks took it, leaving them high and dry. The guy behind the counter was armed and held them until the cops showed up.'

Adam snorted. 'You can't make this shit up.'

Kate shook her head. 'I know. The would-be robbers claim they found the car parked in the lot of a Holiday Inn yesterday morning. They were hitchhiking and thought it was karma or kismet or a gift from God. They say the keys were in it. They claimed they didn't look in the trunk. They just took the car.'

'Cause of death?' Novak asked.

'Not sure yet,' Kate said. She swallowed a gulp of coffee. 'But she was stored in three suitcases in the trunk.'

'Oh God,' Adam said with disgust. 'I hate those.'

'Yeah, well, I'm not keen on them either,' Kate said and drank more coffee. 'Takes forever to get that taste out of your mouth. Anyway, the suitcases are nothing special. Probably bought at Wal-Mart or Target, one of those sets of three with different sizes. Carrie will have to let us know if there's any forensic evidence, although I'm doubting it. He left her for us to find just like he left Eileen Wilkins, and the only reason I can see is that they're supposed to be a warning to any other minions he has lurking that they'd better not fuck with him.'

'Just as he warned Rawlings with the attack on his kid,' Decker said. 'He thinks he's safe because he's disguised as the Professor when he does these things.'

'What about Janet Jungers?' Novak asked. 'Do we know anything about her?'

'She'd been an ER nurse for fifteen years,' Troy said. 'We haven't had a chance to talk to anyone in her department yet, but the security guys who called me last night said she rarely missed a shift. Her personnel file lists her as unmarried.'

'I had surveillance put on her house as soon as we heard she was missing last night,' Zimmerman said. 'Nobody's gone in or come out. We'll need to search the place when we're done here.' He looked over at Novak. 'How's Dani?'

Novak sighed. 'Alive, but still in ICU. It's nerve-racking not knowing who we can trust. Bailey's with her now, but even she won't know if an IV bag's been tampered with. We're hand-picking her nurses based on background checks and personal relationships with people we trust, like Carrie Washington. And, of course, they're watching her for infection. That's going to be the hard part.'

Kate reached across the table and squeezed his hand. 'We can take shifts. Watch over her.'

His smile was grateful. 'Thank you. Good news is that her counts were good before the attack, so she was healthy going in. Diesel saved her life.'

'And hasn't left the hospital,' Adam said quietly. 'That's a big deal for him. He has major PTSD when it comes to hospitals.'

'Has she been able to talk about the attack?' Decker asked. 'Did the assailant say anything to her?'

Novak shook his head. 'She hasn't woken up quite enough to answer questions. She knows we're there, and the few words she's said have been to comfort us.' His throat worked and his jaw tightened. 'Idiot woman. Going in to the clinic to begin with.'

Adam clasped Novak's shoulder and gave it an almost brutal squeeze. 'She's tough,' he said to the rest of them. 'She'll be okay.'

Decker closed his eyes, fresh guilt hitting him hard. Then a fist hit him harder, right in the shoulder, and his eyes popped open. Kate was shaking out her hand. 'You hit me,' he said, stunned.

Kate looked at Novak and Adam. 'He's sitting here feeling guilty because he thinks he could have stopped Dani from going into the clinic.'

Novak actually grinned. 'Then he's the idiot.'

Adam was shaking his head, chuckling. 'Nobody makes Dani do anything and nobody can stop her when she's made up her mind. That's why she's gonna be fine.'

Novak's grin faded into a genuine smile. 'But thank you,' he said to Decker, 'for wishing that you could have stopped her.' He opened his notebook then, pen in hand, his expression suddenly brusque. 'So what do we do next? Because I really want this bastard.'

A knock on the door had them all turning. The door opened and Meredith peeked in. 'I've got Wendi Cullen with me. Can she join us?'

'Of course,' Zimmerman said, motioning them in.

Meredith was followed in by a woman Decker remembered seeing from the ER waiting room the night before. Bringing up the rear was an agent Decker hadn't yet met. That the man was an FBI agent was unarguable, though. He was spit right out of the stereotypical mold.

Ah. Right. Decker remembered now. Meredith and Wendi Cullen had gone hunting for possible victims, using Wendi's contacts in the neighborhood where she ran her halfway house for women and girls who'd come out of lives of prostitution. Adam had been worried, but Zimmerman had told him one of their agents was guarding them. Meredith had ditched the guy because his presence was scaring people away.

Decker could easily see why.

'Meredith, Miss Cullen,' Zimmerman said, 'please have a seat. You too, Agent Colby. We have plenty of chairs.'

Colby obeyed stiffly, saying nothing at all.

Wendi gave Zimmerman a warm smile after he'd introduced everyone at the table. 'I do appreciate the extra coverage,' she said, 'but I really don't need a chaperone. Surely the taxpayers' money can be better spent. Like maybe on a donation to my halfway house.'

Zimmerman looked surprised, but a stern look from Colby had the boss's eyes widening even more. 'Um, well,' Zimmerman stammered, then cleared his throat. 'You and Meredith may have attracted our suspect's attention by asking around about anyone who had been approached for the porn industry. After Dr Novak's attack, we're being careful.'

Wendi sat back in her chair, eyes narrowing. 'Are you sure you're a real FBI agent, sir? Because you don't lie very well. Agent Colby is shadowing me on his own time, isn't he?'

Colby scowled and said nothing.

Zimmerman laughed. 'Well, I used to be a better liar. I've been behind a desk too long.' He sobered with a sigh. 'But it is true that we have to be more careful. I didn't expect our suspect to come after Dani Novak that way.'

Wendi glanced up at the silent agent sitting beside her. 'Thank you,' she said softly, and Colby flushed a dark red. 'I accept your protection for me and my girls.' She squared her shoulders and addressed the table. 'I've had several responses to the inquiries Meredith and I made two days ago. Word's gotten out in the neighborhood that we have a predator, and people are talking, watching out for each other. I'm not so worried about myself, but if the man who attacked Dani comes after the girls under my protection . . . I'm not sure what I'd do.'

She pulled a thick manila envelope from her handbag, along with a flash drive. 'I've heard from four people so far, mothers and grandmothers who are the heads of their families. They stopped by to bring me food, but it was a cover so that they could talk to me. Each one had lost a child. Three are simply gone. Disappeared. One killed himself. OD'd on pills.'

Decker stilled, the hairs rising on the back of his neck.

'Each one,' Wendi went on, 'said their teenager had changed abruptly. Become secretive. Moody in the extreme. Each one said a search of the teen's room turned up drugs. Coke, pills, and weed. They all said that when they confronted their child, the child was too terrified to tell the truth, but these moms were relentless and nagged until their children admitted they'd been sexually molested. That the drugs had been the lure and that they were hooked now. That someone had taken pictures of them and put them on the Internet in exchange for more drugs. And that if they told who'd done it, they'd be killed along with everyone in their household.'

Decker didn't have to check his notes. He'd found two more kids in the yearbook photos from McCord's school that matched faces he'd seen in the files Diesel had given him. 'Was Wesley Young one of them? The one who OD'd?'

Wendi turned to him, shocked. 'Yes. How did you know?'

Zimmerman looked stunned as well. 'Yes, Agent Davenport, how *did* you know?'

Decker brought them up to speed, telling them about the flash drive without mentioning Diesel's name, calling him his 'confidential informant'. He could see that Novak and Adam realized who his informant was, and that Meredith and Wendi did not. Zimmerman, of course, had known about the files' existence as well, even before Decker had given him a copy the previous day. But he hadn't had the chance to tell his boss about the work he'd done overnight.

Decker explained his search and the theories he, Kate, and Troy had posited the night before. 'McCord and this Professor crossed paths somewhere. Stone was recruited out of middle school, so I figured McCord's school was a good place to start.'

'When did you do all of this?' Zimmerman asked, visibly impressed.

Decker felt a flush climbing up the back of his neck. 'Last night and this morning.'

'Because he doesn't require sleep,' Troy complained. 'I still don't think he's human.'

'I slept for a fu ... reaking week,' Decker protested, editing himself mid-curse.

'I'm not a doctor, but I'm pretty sure comas don't count as sleep, Davenport,' Adam said, looking impressed as well. 'That's really good work.'

'I'm going to have to agree,' Novak added with what Decker hoped was mock reluctance. 'I guess you might be okay after all.'

'Thank you,' Decker said dryly. 'So happy to finally pass muster.' He looked at Kate and Troy with a sigh. 'I found two more this morning after you left to work the nurse's murder. Lashonda Hubbell and Trina Pasco.'

Wendi had been studying him soberly since he'd mentioned the drive he'd received from his confidential informant and he figured she'd press for more information, but instead she emptied the contents of the manila envelope on to the table. 'Lashonda was one of the ones who disappeared. I have two more you haven't found yet. These are photographs and descriptions of the missing kids, along with the pertinent dates – when their behavior changed, when they disappeared, et cetera.' Her lips trembled and she firmed them. 'But it sounds like this guy is not afraid to end lives to tie off his loose ends, so I imagine he's killed them too.'

The table went utterly silent for a long moment. Then Zimmerman spoke. 'How many of these teens are we talking about, Decker?'

'I didn't look at every file,' Decker said, wishing now that he'd found the courage to force himself to do so, but Kate derailed that with a soft nudge of her foot against his calf.

'Stop it,' she murmured. 'You can't do it all.'

'Pot, kettle,' he muttered under his breath, then answered

Zimmerman's question. 'Of the McCord files I did examine, I found ten. Half were African-American, the other half were Caucasian. Eight were girls, two boys. All looked to be about thirteen to fifteen. All were photographed multiple times between five and ten years ago. I made notes of the file names so that ICAC can review them.'

'Ten,' Wendi said dully. 'Plus the two others whose mothers came to me. And that's just the ones we know of.'

'What about Trina Pasco?' Decker asked her. 'She graduated a year after Lashonda – I've got her senior yearbook photo on my laptop.' He woke it up, found the right picture and turned his screen around.

Wendi shook her head at first, then stood up and leaned over the table to get a closer look. 'Yeah. I've seen her. She doesn't look like this anymore and she doesn't go by Trina, either.' She looked up, her jaw hard, but her eyes soft and . . . hurt. 'I haven't seen her in a year or two at least, but last time I did, she was turning tricks. She'd been doing meth. Looked sixty instead of twenty. I'd be shocked if she's still alive, but we can ask around. Send me the other photos, the ones you haven't identified yet. I'll see if I know them.'

Decker hesitated. 'They're graphic. I can edit them so only their faces show.'

Wendi sat back down, her mouth curved bitterly. 'Agent Davenport, I know what those photos look like. There are plenty of them out there of me, too. But, please, crop them back so that I can show them around, if that's okay with you, Agent Zimmerman.'

Zimmerman glanced at the still-silent Agent Colby, who nodded once. 'I'm okay with it if you allow Agent Colby to go with you.'

Wendi looked up at Colby with a sigh. 'Can you look . . . regular? Like . . . not a Fed?'

Colby finally spoke. 'Probably not. But I'll try.'

'I suppose that's all I can ask.' Wendi passed one of her business cards to Decker. 'My email. Can you send me the photos as soon as possible? And at some point I will need to know where these files came from. Someone collected them . . .' Her eyes flashed. 'You can't shield that person from punishment by calling him your confidential informant.'

Decker now understood her probing stare. 'It wasn't like that. I can't say any more except that the . . . the finding of these photos hurt my informant deeply.'

Wendi turned that probing stare onto Novak. 'Do you agree with that statement?'

Novak nodded. 'Yes. Absolutely, yes. The person who found these wasn't looking for them. They came across them while doing a good deed of another sort. You can trust that.'

'All right. Because I trust Dani and I know she trusts you.' Wendi touched Meredith's shoulder. 'You'll make sure Kendra isn't caught up in any of this dangerous stuff?'

Meredith's smile was wry. 'Kenny's a cop, Wen. She can take care of herself. But because I know you worry, sure. I'll watch out for her.' She gestured to the table. 'They all will.'

Meredith's wry smile remained in place until Wendi had left, accompanied by Agent Colby. Then her face fell. 'Kendra is not okay.'

Twenty-four

Cincinnati, Ohio,
Saturday 15 August, 10.35 A.M.

Mallory parked the car in front of the drugstore and tried not to cry. There was no pay phone here and the pharmacist on duty knew who she lived with and believed she was a dangerous, moody juvenile delinquent who'd been sent away for trying to kill someone when she'd had a nervous breakdown. If she asked to use a phone inside . . .

He'd find out. She wasn't ready for that to happen yet. Not until she got some promises from a police officer she could trust. Not until she was sure Macy would be safe.

He'd always had a tracker on the car. She'd known it since the day he gave her the keys and a shopping list, wearing a sly grin that taunted. It was the only way he'd give her even that much freedom. Still, she'd stolen a quick look under the car when she'd arrived at the store that very first day she'd driven herself. The tracker was clearly visible and would have been easily removable – which told her that he'd hidden a second one in a position that wasn't so visible. It had been a test. She'd known it then.

He'd confirmed it with another sly grin when she'd returned. *Smart girl*, he'd said, patting her on the head. So she never deviated. Never disobeyed.

Because he'd know. He always knew.

She closed her eyes, trying to think of what she could do. She had ten dollars in quarters. That wouldn't buy anything. Except . . . She sat up straighter and looked over her shoulder at the bus stop

511

on the corner. It might buy a ride on a bus.

She caught her breath when a taxi pulled into the parking lot one drive down. It was an attorney's office. They knew him in there too, so their phone was also off limits. Everyone in this little shopping center knew him. And they knew Mallory – or believed they did.

But a taxi . . . Surely the driver would be safe. *It's not like everyone knows him.*

Move, Mallory. But what if she didn't have enough money? *You won't know until you ask. Go now, before he drives away.*

Swallowing hard, she got out of the car and locked it, pocketing the key, then walked to the cab, waiting while the woman in the back got out. The woman went into the attorney's office and, heart beating in her throat, Mallory leaned down to look at the driver through the passenger's window. He was an older man with a beard. He wore a turban. And he smiled at her.

A nice smile. Not a leer.

'Can I help you?' he asked, his accent heavy.

She opened her mouth, but no words came out. *Stop this. Speak.* 'I need to go to the Kroger on Enright in Price Hill.' It was closer than the one she'd used before and the only other one she knew that had a pay phone. 'How much does it cost?'

'At least twenty dollars, miss.'

Her heart sank. 'Oh. Thank you anyway.' She backed away from the window.

'Wait!' he said, and got out of the car, studying her over the cab's roof. 'How much do you have, child?'

'Ten dollars, but I need fifty cents of it.'

His eyes softened. 'I will take you for nine dollars and fifty cents. Get in.'

She hesitated, not trusting at the last moment. 'Why?'

'Because you look scared and my granddaughter is your age. I hope someone would help her if she had only nine dollars and fifty cents. Sit in the back. You will be safe in my cab.'

Mallory choked on a sob. 'Okay. Thank you.' She got in, every muscle tensed, ready to flee the moment he looked at her with evil intent. Because Mallory knew what that looked like.

512

He got in the car and met her eyes in the rear-view mirror. 'How will you get from the grocery store to your home?'

'I'm meeting someone there.' *The nice lady cop will come if I call. I hope. She'll take me somewhere safe. I hope.* And if not, the woman would at least take her back to her car. She hoped. She'd pick up his prescription and the first aid stuff just in case. If she ended up going home, it would be bad enough that she'd be seriously late. To walk back in empty-handed would be just plain stupid.

His gaze became grave. 'All right. I will ask you this next question only once and will respect your answer. Do you need a police officer?'

She swallowed hard and the truth spilled out. 'Yes, but that's why I need to go to the Kroger. I'm meeting her there.'

He nodded. 'Very well.'

Cincinnati, Ohio,
Saturday 15 August, 10.50 A.M.

'Why is Kendra not okay?' Decker asked Meredith.

Meredith glanced at the door once again, as if she expected Wendi Cullen to pop back in, then sighed. 'Because she's spent every hour that she wasn't with us in the ER driving from one Kroger to another. She's focusing on the stores with pay phones. She's . . . obsessing over this girl and I'm worried.' She shrugged. 'I'm worried about Kendra and I'm worried about the girl herself. As Wendi pointed out, he's not averse to taking lives to snip loose ends.'

Kate looked away, the guilt clear on her face. 'I keep thinking we shouldn't have arrested Corey Addison so publicly. It's like we threw down a gauntlet.'

Annoyed, Decker flicked her arm with his finger. 'Stop it. You didn't even mention Sunshine Suzie when you were taking him out of the building. And yes, you should have arrested him so publicly. Addison's arrest wasn't about taunting the Professor. It was sending a clear message of our own to child predators: "Do it and you'll get caught." So stop.'

'You're right,' Kate muttered.

'Of course I am,' he said, then gave Meredith an apologetic smile because they'd derailed her concern. 'I think we've all obsessed over a case at least once. Unless you think Kendra's going to cause harm, will it hurt her to look?'

Meredith shook her head. 'I guess not. And it makes her feel like she's doing something productive. I shouldn't have said anything. I just hate not being able to fix things for people.'

'Join the club,' Kate said sourly. 'I think our best hope in finding the girl, at this point, is to find the Professor. What are our leads?'

'We still have Rawlings in custody,' Novak said. 'He knows how to contact the man.'

'We examined Rawlings's phone,' Troy said. 'Found the number in his call log that is probably the Professor's, but guys like that know how to cover their tracks. He'll have several numbers. And either he's turned his phone off or he's blocked Rawlings, because when we called from Rawlings's phone, we got voice-mail every time. We talked last night about finding more adults who're now clean and sober and asking them about their history with the Professor. If we can find just one, we can make contact using that person's name, pretend he's fallen off the wagon, and set up a meet.'

'I don't feel comfortable using civilians as bait,' Zimmerman said. 'Even if we're doing the calling, he could come back and kill their families.'

Adam frowned thoughtfully. 'What if that person was a cop?'

Everyone turned to him in surprise, Meredith most of all. 'Adam?' she said, stunned.

'Oh no,' he said, shaking his head. 'Not me. I haven't bought from him, but there have to be cops who have or he wouldn't have been able to operate without impunity for twenty fucking years. We know we have someone leaking information to him about the McCord files – we still don't know who really signed out the hard drive that was removed from McCord's house, but we know it wasn't Scarlett. What if the cop who's feeding him information is also buying drugs from him?'

'Good point,' Zimmerman said. 'But we still don't know who our leak is.'

'Maybe we set a trap,' Kate said quietly. 'Provide information they can't resist taking to the Professor.'

Zimmerman considered, then nodded. 'Let's do it. I'll take point on this. I've already broached the subject of police involvement to the captain. I need to brush up on my lying skills anyway.'

Kate's lips curved. 'I'm sure you can be a first-class liar, sir.'

'Suck-up,' Novak said with a snort. 'Back to Rawlings. He knows more than he's letting on. And we still don't know how he killed Alice. He had help, either willing or unwilling. I'm not the right one to go back to the jail, but someone should. Someone who's a real sweet talker.'

Kate smiled at Decker. 'A snake charmer.'

'I hate being called that,' Decker said. 'I hate snakes.'

Zimmerman's lips were twitching. 'Fine. You two go to the jail. Use those photos you took last night to make the inmates think he's turned evidence.'

'Or that he's defeated and no longer a threat,' Kate said. 'You know, ding dong, the witch is dead. We'll play it by ear.'

'I could use a break from looking at the kids' photos,' Decker admitted.

'It's not easy,' Adam said quietly. 'But speaking of photos, I've been looking at the bedroom window in the Suzie videos. Most of the filming was done at night and you can see star patterns outside the window. I don't know if I can do anything with that or not, but it's a detail that can help us pinpoint location at least in a general sense. We're still assuming he's local because he sells drugs here. But we know he goes for blocks of time without selling to anyone, so maybe he's filming then. And maybe he's not filming here in Ohio. I don't want to be looking locally for a studio that's not here.'

'Another good point,' Zimmerman murmured.

'Also, the last Suzie video was uploaded three years ago. He's been filming more recently with McCord. If he used the same set, the same location, we should be able to match it to videos on the drive that Decker's informant gave him. I've got access to some of your best Fed software now, too, so let me keep looking for the studio.'

'Okay.' Zimmerman consulted his own list. 'I have a few items. Carrie Washington tested the stomach contents of Rawlings's son – the ricin is similar in purity to what was used on Alice, and in the gas bomb he threw at you, Kate. It's another dotted i, not that we needed it. Everything we have points to the same guy.' He flipped a page. 'Oh. This one is very interesting, and before I read it, let me remind you that we will not use civilians in our effort to arrest this dealer. Okay? Okay. I got an email from Lieutenant Isenberg this morning. You remember Mrs Chalmers? Charlie's mother?'

'Yes,' Kate said. 'I couldn't get her out of my mind last night. Is she all right? She didn't . . . do anything to herself, did she?'

'Not suicide, if that's what you mean,' Zimmerman said. 'This happened after you and Decker left the ER last night. Mrs Chalmers became so hysterical she had to be sedated. She almost coded. Turned out she was already high when she got to the ER. Methamphetamine. She had a whole bottle of pills in her purse. She's been a user for some time. And guess who she was buying from?'

'Professor Asshole,' Novak said bitterly.

Decker looked at Kate, impressed, but also distressed. 'You were right. Soccer moms and career women. Charlie's mom was right under our noses.'

Kate drew a breath. 'Sir, I respectfully disagree with not using civilians to catch this man. He killed her son. I can't imagine he can do much worse at this point. If she wanted to help us, I'd say we let her.'

'Disagreement noted,' Zimmerman said. 'The answer is still no. Besides, the woman is in no mental state to accept the consequences of helping us. She almost died last night. They had to use the paddles to bring her back. And even if she were competent to agree, Professor Asshole wouldn't buy it.' Zimmerman's jaw was hard and his eyes were shadowed. 'He knows that she knows he killed her son. He won't believe that any overtures she makes are not revenge-motivated.'

She nodded miserably. 'You're right. I know you are. But . . . dammit.' Her eyes grew bright and she drew a steadying breath. 'Dammit.'

'I know, Kate,' Zimmerman said gently. 'I do know. But we'll have to find another way.'

'We still have Alice's videos to analyze,' Troy said. 'I'll watch amateur porn for the team.'

Kate hiccupped a laugh. 'Dammit, Troy. You—'

'Hey, you're the one who said we needed to laugh, remember.'

She smiled at him. 'Yeah. You're a good new partner.'

Troy preened for her benefit. 'I know.' Then he sighed. 'But seriously, I do dread those movies. Alice is . . . was . . . vocal.' He shuddered. '"Do me, baby, do me",' he added in a falsetto. 'I have to fast-forward through those parts. But the pillow talk afterward . . . we might actually get some information we can use. For now I'm focusing on her partners' faces. All of them. And by "all", I mean a hella lot.'

Zimmerman cleared his throat. 'And on that note, you're dismissed.'

Everyone got up, shaking their heads over Troy's really tasteless – but incredibly necessary – sense of humor, then froze when the phone in the middle of the table rang.

'I told my assistant to only forward critical calls,' Zimmerman said, picking up the receiver. 'This is Zimmerman.' He listened for a moment. 'Which one?' Then he nodded at Meredith, who looked up from reading a message on her cell phone. 'Stay where you are, Officer. Don't approach her yet. I'm sending backup.' He hung up. 'Kendra texted you?'

Meredith nodded. 'Her obsession paid off. She just saw the girl get out of a cab, make a call at the pay phone, and go into the Kroger on Enright. I need to get there fast. Who can drive me with lights flashing? Kate?'

'Kate goes, but you both have backup.' Zimmerman pointed at Adam. 'You go with Meredith. Stay out of sight. I don't want to spook this kid into running. Kate, you go with Troy. Decker, Deacon, you have your assignments. Go.'

Kate squeezed Decker's knee under the table. 'I'll be safe. Don't worry.'

But of course Decker did. He didn't move, staying at the table while everyone rushed out, including Zimmerman, who would coordinate backup. 'Kate's idea of "safe" is not my idea of safe,' he murmured.

Novak hadn't moved either. 'Oh, I know,' he murmured back. 'You know, I didn't actually get an assignment.'

'I think Zimmerman intended you to go back to the hospital to be with Dani.'

'And I think he intended you to go back to the safe house and rest.'

'Not gonna happen.'

Novak raised a white brow. 'Which won't happen? Your assignment or mine?'

'Either. Both. You got a car?'

'I do. And I really want to catch this bastard.'

They looked at each other for a moment, assessing the situation and each other. 'I call shotgun,' Decker said.

Novak nodded once. 'Let's go.'

Cincinnati, Ohio,
Saturday 15 August, 11.00 A.M.

Where the hell was she? He looked out the back window for the tenth time, knowing Mallory would not be coming up the driveway because she was still at the damned drugstore. Once again he debated the wisdom of not giving her a cell phone, then decided that he'd been right not to. Cell phones were freedom. He'd given her enough freedom with the car. Which he would change as soon as she came home. No longer would she be able to take herself to the store if she couldn't get there and back in a reasonable period of time.

He rolled his shoulder, wincing at the pain. It was well and truly infected. Mallory needed to get her ass home where she belonged.

'Excuse me, sir?'

He pasted a smile on his face and turned to the oldest of the four he'd chosen. 'Yes, Seth?'

'We were wondering if we can have pop in the living room.'

'Of course!' He opened the fridge door wide. 'We have Coke, Sprite, and root beer, plus a few diet drinks.'

The boy made a face. 'Not diet. That stuff is full of chemicals.'

So is Coke, he thought. *Both kinds.* Soon he'd find out how much experience these kids had with the illegal type. 'Then choose whatever you'd like.'

The boy grabbed four Cokes. 'Thank you. We're going to watch *Eyes Wide Shut*,' he added, just a hair of hesitation in his voice.

One of the racier R-rated movies. 'I like that one. I'll be in to watch with you in a little while. I have a few things to do for work first. There's ice cream and snacks if you get hungry.'

'Thank you,' the boy said, so polite, but there was a gleam in his eyes that said he'd found a sucker and would push as far as he could.

Excellent. Just the kind of leader he needed to fast-track these kids.

He went to his office and popped a handful of ibuprofen, hoping it would cut through some of the pain, because he did not want to take anything stronger. He needed to be alert. Ready.

His cell buzzed and he frowned. *Better not be Rawlings again.* The ass had called him ten times after being taken into custody. But it wasn't Rawlings, he saw when he looked at the caller ID. This just might be worse. 'Yes?'

'You need to watch your step.'

He frowned again. 'What's happened?'

'Some guy was arrested yesterday. Corey Addison. Did you catch the news?'

'No, I was busy.' *Getting stabbed and missing Griffin Davenport again.*

'Addison was arrested for possession of kiddie porn.'

He was glad he was sitting down. 'Oh?'

'He was taken away from his office by Special Agent Kate Coppola.'

519

He swallowed the growl that rose in his throat. He should have killed her when he'd had the chance. *Fucking Kevlar. Fucking bum arm. Fucking tattooed bastard who'd thrown that fucking knife.* 'So?' he asked, managing to keep his tone light.

'So, she was accompanied by Officer Kendra Cullen. They made the six o'clock and eleven o'clock news as well as every damn Internet news source.'

Get to the goddamn point. 'Again . . . so?' he asked, making himself sound bored.

'So . . . Cullen is a brand-new cop. Less than two years out of the Academy.'

Oh. 'Why does a brand-new cop accompany a seasoned FBI agent on a high-profile bust?'

'Exactly. I did a little digging and found that Cullen filed a report a week ago. She got between Corey Addison and a young woman he was harassing. He called her Sunshine Suzie.'

Fuck, fuck, fuck. He drew in an unsteady breath. 'And?'

'And Sunshine Suzie just called the central operator, who passed on a message to Officer Kendra Cullen asking to meet her at the Enright Kroger.'

'Impossible. Mallory's at the drugstore.'

'You sure? Sounds like she's at the Kroger.'

He was only sure that the *car* was at the drugstore. Suddenly everything made sense. She'd been angling to get to the grocery store for days. She hadn't wanted to go to a different store yesterday. He'd been right. She *was* planning something. *Goddammit to hell.*

'Thank you.'

'No problem. Usual payment.'

'Sure. Later.' He hung up and dropped his head into his good hand. *Think. Think, dammit.* She wouldn't talk. Nobody would believe her.

That might have been true last week. Depending on what she knew . . .

Fuck. He grabbed his keys and ran into the living room. Four sets of eyes looked up at him. He made himself smile. 'Guys, I have a little family emergency I have to deal with. Can I trust you to stay here and stay out of trouble?'

Seth nodded. 'I'll make sure everyone behaves.'

'Pffft.' The older girl pulled a face. 'More like we girls will keep you boys in line.' She smiled up at him. 'We'll be fine, sir. I hope everything's okay.'

'It'll be fine,' he said with a fake smile. He walked at a normal pace to the door, but once he was outside, he ran to the Mercedes.

Cincinnati, Ohio,
Saturday 15 August, 11.50 A.M.

'There.' Kate pointed to Kendra, who was leaning against a car parked in the handicapped space. The car had a handicapped sticker, so it wasn't Kendra's. The officer's eyes were pinned to the front door of the Kroger. Troy stopped behind the car and Kate rolled down her window. 'She still in there?' she asked.

Kendra nodded. 'Yes. My partner is behind the store with our squad car, in case she spooks and runs. He's got a photo of me to show her to calm her down if she does go out that way.'

'You said she got dropped off by a cab?' Troy asked.

Kendra nodded. 'I would have missed her if I hadn't been looking right at the pay phone at the time. I'd been watching for that beat-up car of hers.'

'I don't know that we'll see that again,' Kate said quietly. 'It was used in Dani's attack.'

Kendra's eyes widened, but she didn't look away from the storefront. 'I didn't hear that.'

The girl is not getting away if Kendra can help it, Kate thought. 'We're keeping some of the details from the media. Oh, there's Meredith.' Adam had stopped in front of the store to let her out. 'She and I are going in the store. We'll shop.'

Kendra frowned. 'No offense, Agent Coppola, but you look like a cop. Meredith doesn't. You might scare the girl away.'

Kate sighed. 'I know. I've been told this.' She glared at Troy, whose lips twitched but who wisely said nothing. 'But I've got to cover Meredith. Adam looks more like a cop than I do, and he'll hover.' She rolled up her window and murmured to Troy, 'Watch out for Kendra?'

Troy nodded. 'She's an earnest one, isn't she?'

'A kinder term for obsessed,' she muttered, then joined Meredith at the store's entrance. 'I'll follow you, but at a distance. You're wearing a vest, right?'

'Yes, and it itches like hell.'

'I was glad for mine last night.'

Meredith lifted her brows. 'So I heard. We'll talk later about the risks you take, Kate.' She got a cart and entered the store.

Kate picked up a basket and filled it with canned goods from the first display she saw. They'd make a handy rolling mess if she needed a non-ballistic diversion. *So many shoppers. Noon on a Saturday? Suzie couldn't have picked a worse time for this.*

But the girl had been determined to get here. *A cab. Wow.*

Kate followed Meredith, watching her from the endcaps. They both spotted the girl at the same time. She was at the cash register, buying first aid supplies. She looked just like the photo that Kendra had downloaded from the web, barely any older at all. She appeared nervous, but determined. She also looked banged up. A fading bruise was still visible on her cheek, and her lip was split. *But she's alive.*

Meredith abandoned her cart and made her way casually around the cash registers, and Kate followed, dialing Troy on her cell. 'She's coming out,' she murmured and disconnected.

The girl waited at the curb, looking anxiously one way, then the other. When she saw Kendra straighten and raise her hand in greeting, a look of profound relief took over the girl's face. She started to push her cart across the street.

And all hell broke loose. Kate saw the dark green Mercedes from the corner of her eye as its engine revved, loud enough to overwhelm the background noise of carts and shoppers. It roared then, speeding through the loading lane, headed straight for the girl. Drawing her weapon, Kate ran for the girl, but not fast enough to beat the car.

People screamed and Kate aimed. She had one shot that was

clear of shoppers, so she took it. More screams filled her head, but her focus was the car's back window, which pebbled on the bullet's impact, but didn't shatter. With a squeal of tires, the car took off through the crowded parking lot, forcing shoppers to leap out of its way. The crash of metal followed by a scream twisted her gut. An elderly woman hadn't been able to get out of the way fast enough.

The revving of another car followed. A big black SUV, Deacon behind the wheel and Decker riding shotgun. They'd taken off after the Mercedes, but had slowed when the old woman went down.

Kate evaluated the scene in a glance. Suzie was lying in the street, eyes closed, completely still, her leg bent at an impossible angle. Her head was bleeding, but Meredith was crouching over her and Adam Kimble and Kendra had their weapons drawn, providing cover.

Kate ran toward the elderly victim, waving at Deacon to keep driving. The SUV revved again and took off after the Mercedes.

The entire course of events had taken less than thirty seconds. Kate knelt by the old woman, who was moaning pitifully. Kate could see Adam on his phone, sure he was getting help. 'I'm Special Agent Coppola. We've called for an ambulance. Try to hold still.'

When Adam finished his call, she dialed his number. 'I have another victim. She's hurt, but conscious.'

'I saw her. I called for two ambulances,' Adam said. 'That green Mercedes . . . ?'

'It matches the one that Delores saw last night. Is the girl . . . ?'

'Alive. Not conscious.'

Kate's heart sank, but her phone beeped, keeping her focused. 'Got a call coming in.' She tapped her screen and heard Decker's voice, strong, but pissed.

'He's gone. He ditched the Mercedes behind the store, but first he plowed it into a row of parked cars. We're checking now to see if anyone was in the cars, but it looks like they were all unoccupied. Probably belong to folks on shift in the store. Deacon and I didn't get a good look at him, did you?'

'No. The vehicle had tinted windows.'

'We don't even know who we're looking for, Kate.'

'I know.' The man used disguises. 'He could be anyone. Contact Adam, let him know.'

'Where's our CPD backup?'

Lieutenant Isenberg had sent four unmarked cars. 'Blocking the exits and controlling the crowd. I can see two of them.' She waved one of the cars over to wait with the elderly lady until the ambulance arrived. 'I'm going to do a walkaround in the front parking lot.'

Hanging up, she walked through the crowd, searching for the eyes that had stared at her the night before, just before shooting her in the chest, but she saw none that were even close. She spotted Troy establishing a perimeter and jogged over to help him. 'Nothing,' she said shortly.

Troy shrugged. 'I didn't think so. He could be anywhere.'

She was spared having to reply by the ringing of her cell phone. Decker again. 'Yeah?'

'Was Kendra here with her partner?' Decker asked. 'Caucasian male, about forty?'

Kate's shoulders sagged. 'She said he was watching the back. He was in his squad car.'

'That's what we were afraid of. We know how the Professor got away.'

'He stole the squad car,' she murmured. 'Is her partner alive?' she asked, and beside her, Troy sighed.

Decker's hesitation answered the question even before he spoke. 'No. He was shot twice. Once in the temple and once in the back of the head. His gun belt and service weapon are gone. So are his shirt and hat. Buttons everywhere. His shirt was literally torn off him. There appear to be silencer marks on his skin. It was quick. Took only a minute or two tops. This guy is fast, Kate. He thinks on his feet. We actually saw the cruiser drive by. We thought it was backup, so we let it go. It exited to the access road behind the store. We were ten feet away from him, dammit,' he finished bitterly. 'Novak's calling in the BOLO now. We almost had him. Goddammit.'

'Great,' Kate said, suddenly so tired she wanted to cry. 'Just fucking great.'

Troy nudged her. 'Kate. Adam's waving at us to come over

there.'

'I'll call you back,' she said to Decker, and she and Troy jogged over to where Adam crouched on the girl's left side. Meredith knelt on her right, holding her hand. Kendra stood sentry, silently watching.

The girl's eyes were closed, her respiration unsteady. Her leg was broken, the bone visible where it poked through the skin. Kate could look at a body that had been cut up and stored in a set of matched luggage, but that bone made her queasy. *The pain must be excruciating.*

Kate tore her eyes away from the girl's broken leg and looked at Kendra. *She doesn't know yet,* Kate thought. *I get to tell her. Fabulous.*

'Kendra,' Kate said carefully. 'Did you drive here today with your partner?'

'No. I called him when I saw her get out of the cab. He met me here. Why?' But something on Kate's face must have told her, because Kendra's eyes widened in horror. 'No. *No.*'

Kate put her hand on the younger woman's arm. 'I . . .' She had no idea what to say.

Troy took over. 'Come with me, Officer Cullen,' he said gently. 'We'll wait in my car.'

Numbly Kendra let herself be led away.

Adam looked up at Kate grimly. 'The partner's dead?'

Kate nodded. 'And the squad car is gone.'

Meredith closed her eyes. 'This is a nightmare.'

'Come down here,' Adam said. 'I don't want to shout.'

Kate immediately dropped into a crouch, putting her ear close to Adam's mouth so that he could whisper in her ear. 'She opened her eyes for about a minute. Said her name is Mallory. Said we have to save the kids at his house. And also we have to save Macy.'

Kate frowned. 'Who is Macy?' she whispered back.

Meredith stroked the girl's hair from her face. 'We don't know. Except that she's worth Mallory risking her life to save.'

525

Twenty-five

Cincinnati, Ohio,
Saturday 15 August, 12.45 P.M.

Breathe. Just breathe. He drew air through his nose, trying to slow his pulse. *This is not the time to panic. This is the time for clear, logical thinking.* He'd get out of this. He would.

Mallory had called the police. He still couldn't believe it. *I should have killed the bitch a long time ago.*

How? How had this happened? *Too much freedom.* He'd allowed her too much freedom.

But that didn't matter now. He needed to tie off loose ends, but every time he turned around, he had even more loose ends to tie off.

At least they still don't know who I am. He'd listened to the police radio the whole time he'd driven the stolen cruiser. There was not one BOLO issued for him. *The Professor, yes, but not for me.* No one knew what his real face looked like. Yet.

Which meant Mallory hadn't yet talked, probably because, according to the police radio, she was unconscious. If she did talk once she regained consciousness, they would know way too much. *Should have killed the fucking bitch this morning.*

But he hadn't, and so now here he was, standing on Gemma's back doorstep, shaking like a damn leaf. He hadn't rung the bell. He didn't want her to know he was here.

Plus, he had a key. He got it out now, managing to turn the lock and push the back door open. He snagged a set of keys to Gemma's minivan from the pegboard by the back door. He'd dropped the stolen cruiser off in the parking lot of a crowded shopping center about a quarter-mile away. He'd taken with him the bag with his tools – he'd had the presence of mind to remove it from the Mercedes before abandoning it – and walked the remaining distance to Gemma's house, discarding the dead officer's torn shirt and hat in a dumpster along the way.

He crept through the house, listening. His brother-in-law was at work, but Gemma was here somewhere. Probably getting high again. He could hear the TV in Macy's bedroom. Sounded like cartoons. He went to the closet and disabled the security system. His cameras ran off a different system and had been hidden so well, Gemma and her husband had never known they were there. Which was how he wanted to keep it.

He'd need to keep a watch on Gemma after she learned her child had been stolen, to make sure she didn't go off the deep end or that her cop husband didn't put two and two together and actually get four for the first time in his life.

He planned to simply take Macy and keep her hidden until it was time to film her. In the meantime, he'd publicly grieve her abduction like the good uncle and godfather he was.

The fact that he had Macy would keep Mallory quiet for the time being, at least until he was able to get close enough to finish what he'd tried to do in the parking lot. *End her. Hopefully painfully*.

He rooted around the closet for something he could use to hide his face. He didn't expect Gemma would have a ski mask, but an old ski cap would do. He found one with the winter wear and pulled it all the way down so that it covered his eyes and nose, leaving only his lips visible.

Just in case they had cameras he didn't know about. It was possible. He took the cap off long enough to use his blade to cut holes for his eyes, then pulled it back on. It wasn't ideal, but it would do in a pinch.

He opened his bag and found the ether he'd brought. He'd intended to use it on Mallory when she emerged from the grocery store. But the cops had beaten him there. They'd been waiting for her, surrounding her.

If he'd had full use of his right hand, he would have shot her between the eyes. But he knew he'd never hit a moving target with his left hand, not from that distance. So he'd done the only thing he could think of and used the Mercedes itself as a weapon.

He poured just enough ether on a rag to knock Macy out, then crept through the hallway to her bedroom. She was sitting at her desk, reading, ignoring the blaring TV next to her bed. She had earbuds in her ears, listening to music on her phone. Which was ridiculous – giving a child her age a phone. Macy's was pink, the case decorated with sparkles and decals of the Powerpuff Girls. At least the earbuds would keep her from hearing him approach. *Bonus.*

He was within reaching distance when she looked up and saw his reflection in the window over her desk.

She got off a shriek before he slammed the rag over her mouth. He grunted, because the kid was surprisingly strong for an almost-ten-year-old. She struggled, knocking into his injured arm with her elbow, and he almost moaned out loud.

Then she kicked over her chair with a final burst of panicked desperation, and his heart stopped. He froze, listening.

'Macy?'

Fuck. It was Gemma. He put the now-sleeping Macy on her bed and waited behind the bedroom door. He had enough ether left in the bottle to knock Gemma out as well. He'd tie her up and leave her here and she'd be none the wiser. She'd report a masked intruder. He held his breath, preparing himself, then grabbed her as soon as she came through the door.

'Ma—'

He covered her mouth and growled a warning. 'Don't struggle and nobody gets hurt.'

But she did struggle, and she was so much stronger than he'd expected. She fought like a wildcat, clawing at the skin at his wrists, trying to force his hand from her mouth, trying to scream. Then she slumped against him and he slumped back against the wall, breathing hard. His arm throbbed and dark spots floated in front of his eyes. He was hyperventilating. He'd never done that in his life.

Dammit. When had she gotten so strong? *Since she started using coke*, he thought, heaving air into his lungs. He let his right arm go lax—

And then she shocked the hell out of him by springing from his grasp and grabbing the pretty pink lamp from the nightstand, spinning and hefting it into the air. She hadn't been unconscious. She'd been faking it. Playing possum. He straightened abruptly, reluctantly impressed. He'd underestimated his baby sister.

She swung the lamp toward his head and he blocked it with his left arm. He knocked it aside easily and grabbed her arm, twisting it behind her back.

He was pushing her toward the bed when she shocked him again – and sealed her own fate. Reaching back with her free hand, she grabbed the hat from his head and pulled, looking over her shoulder as she bared his face.

She froze, her eyes wide on his face. *Fuck, Gemma. Why'd you have to go and do that?*

She squinted up at him, confused. 'Brandon? What are you doing here?'

He didn't say a word, but he did grab that free hand and hold both of her hands with his strong left. Gritting his teeth, he forced her to the bed, using his full weight to hold her down. He pulled his switchblade from his pocket, flicked the release, and slid the blade along the bedspread, under her throat. Then he gave a mighty yank, pulling the blade across her throat.

Her eyes were wide with terror as blood spurted out, soaking her daughter's mattress. And then her eyes were . . . nothing. Dim. Her life drained along with her blood. He rolled her over, pulled his gun with the silencer from his bag, put it to the center of her forehead, and fired. Then he checked her eyes, her pulse, just to be sure she really was down this time.

She was. She was permanently down. He'd killed her.

And I'd do it again. She'd brought it on herself. He pulled the hat back onto his head, squatted next to the bed and hoisted Macy to his shoulder, then stood up. His arm hurt like fucking fire, and by the time he got the child into the garage and hidden in the back of Gemma's minivan, he felt like vomiting.

But that would be a mistake. He wouldn't leave DNA for the cops to find.

He leaned against the minivan and breathed until the nausea passed. Then he tied Macy's hands and feet, put duct tape over her mouth, and took out his phone and snapped a photo of her so that he could—

'Shit,' he whispered. Major flaw in his hastily concocted plan. How was he supposed to show it to Mallory? She was surrounded by cops in the ER. She didn't have a sparkly pink cell phone, so he couldn't send it to her, and it wasn't like he could just waltz in there and . . .

Then again . . . *Hide in plain sight.* He'd been doing it for twenty years.

He went back in the house, into the closet next to Gemma's. This was her husband's closet and it was filled with uniforms. He was a little taller than his brother-in-law, but leaner, because his brother-in-law liked beer and donuts. One of the shirts would fit him. Not perfectly, but well enough for what he needed to do.

He dressed himself and then went back into Macy's room and picked up her pink sparkly phone. Back at the minivan, he took a photo of Macy, then he covered her with a blanket, closed the minivan's hatch and drove to the hospital.

He'd hide in plain sight, waltz into the hospital and make sure that Mallory knew Macy was in trouble. The girl wouldn't say a word. *She'll be too scared.* And as soon as he was able to get Mallory alone, he'd kill her too.

Cincinnati, Ohio,
Saturday 15 August, 2.05 P.M.

She was cold. Really cold. And . . .

Ohmygod. It hurt. Her leg really hurt. She heard a whimper. *That was me,* she thought, everything floaty. Panicked, she tried to move, but she couldn't. Another whimper came out of her.

'Hi, honey. Don't be scared.'

She knew the voice. She'd heard it already. Where? *Where?*

530

'My name is Meredith. I came in with you on the ambulance. You got hit by a car in front of the grocery store. You have a broken leg. I know it must hurt. It was a bad break.'

Mallory's teeth chattered and someone covered her with a blanket. 'Where . . . where is the lady cop?'

'She's not here,' Meredith said. 'But we're friends, she and I. We've been hoping you'd call back so we could help you.'

So cold. And she wanted the lady cop. *I remember. She was there.*

Mallory opened her eyes to see a very pretty lady smiling back at her. But not the lady cop. The lady cop had smiled too. *She was waiting for me outside Kroger.* She'd smiled and waved.

And then . . . the car. His car. His green Mercedes. *He'd known. He'd known.*

How? She whimpered again, hating the sound. Unable to stop herself from doing it.

How had he found her? She'd left the car at the drugstore. She'd taken a cab. The nice man hadn't charged her anything. He'd let her keep all nine dollars and fifty cents. Just in case no one came to take her home.

Maybe the man had told. *But how?* She hadn't given her name.

Tears filled her eyes and she blinked, sending them down her face. They were warm at least. A soft tissue dried her cheeks.

'Don't cry, Mallory,' Meredith said.

Mallory hunched back into the pillow. 'How do you know me?'

'You told me. You said you were Mallory and we needed to save the kids. And Macy.'

It was a lie. Mallory didn't remember any of that. She wouldn't have told a stranger about Macy. But the lady cop had been there. *Maybe I told her.* 'I want the lady cop,' she said, her voice hoarse. Meredith put a straw in her mouth, let her sip some water. It felt good.

'Maybe we can get Kendra in here,' another voice said. Another lady.

Mallory looked to her right, slowly, because her head hurt. Meredith wore a pretty green shirt and khaki pants. She had a pretty

531

necklace, too. But the other lady wore all black. Pants, jacket. Her shirt was white . . . but it had blood on it.

And she had a gun. But she smiled, and then she didn't look so mean.

'Kendra?' Mallory asked.

'The lady cop's name is Kendra Cullen,' the lady in black said. 'I'm a lady cop too, if that helps. My name is Special Agent Coppola. I'm with the FBI. You can call me Kate if you want. Yesterday Kendra and I arrested the man who harassed you last week.'

Mallory frowned. *What? Oh.* She remembered now. 'Football guy,' she murmured.

'Yes. His name is Corey Addison,' Kate said. 'He's in jail. He can't hurt you again.'

'Thank you,' Mallory said politely. 'I still want the lady cop. Kendra.'

The two women glanced at each other over her bed. 'I'll try,' Meredith said, 'but she's upset.'

'Why?' Mallory asked.

Meredith sighed again. 'Her partner was waiting outside the grocery store, in the back, in case you got scared and tried to run. The man who hurt you, he . . . killed Kendra's partner.'

Mallory stared at her, not understanding the words at first. Then she did. *My fault*, she thought. *My fault. Oh God. It's my fault.*

'We were hoping you could tell us where we could find that man,' Kate said softly.

Mallory's eyes whipped to the right to see Kate. And that was when she saw it. A pink sparkly phone. It was Macy's phone. She'd gotten it from her mom at Christmas. The phone sat on the little table next to Mallory's bed.

Mallory began to breathe harder. As she reached tentatively for the phone, she became aware of the silence in the little room.

'Where did that come from?' Meredith asked in an odd voice.

Kate shrugged. 'I thought you kept it for her while they set her leg. You didn't?'

'No. And I know it wasn't here fifteen minutes ago. The nurse moved the tray out the way when she set up the IV.'

Kate reached for the phone, her movement abrupt. Mallory grabbed it and turned it on.

And stared. And stared. And heard the whimpering again. Coming from her own throat.

Kate moved more slowly, and now she had gloves on. Carefully she turned the phone to see the screen, then she exhaled like she was mad.

Good. Be mad. Somebody should be mad. He had Macy. *He tied her up. He put her in a car. He put tape on her mouth. He's going to hurt her. He's going to turn her into me.*

Meredith leaned over the bed to see. 'Oh God,' she breathed. 'Mallory, is this Macy?'

Mallory closed her eyes and pursed her lips. *Say nothing. He's here. Somewhere. He has Macy and he's here. He can see you. He can hear you. He's here.* Her hands went limp and Kate pulled the phone away from her gently.

'It's not Macy?' Meredith asked.

'It is,' Kate said, and she sounded grim. 'It says "Macy" on the back in sparkles.'

'Mallory,' Meredith murmured. 'Who is Macy?'

Mallory pursed her lips harder. Say nothing.

'My guess?' Kate said. 'Her sister. The two look so much alike.'

'Is Macy your sister, Mallory?' Meredith asked, still gently.

Mallory trembled. *Don't say yes. Don't say anything. He's here.*

'This photo wasn't texted from someone,' Kate said. 'It was taken using this phone. Someone left it here to frighten Mallory.'

'Goddamn, I hate this guy,' Meredith said softly.

Tears fell from Mallory's eyes. *Me too. Me too.*

'He threatened Macy?' Kate said. 'Is that how he got you to be silent all this time?'

Say nothing. Say nothing. Say nothing.

'Mallory,' Kate tried again. 'We need your help. You asked us to save the kids. You need to tell us where they are.'

Kids? Oh God. The kids. She wanted to tell. She wanted so badly to tell.

'We know about the videos,' Meredith said. 'We want to help

533

you.' But then she sighed. 'She's terrified, Kate. And in pain. I don't think she's going to talk right now.'

There was a soft sound. Kate rubbing her face. 'I really hate this guy too. We get close and then he messes with us.' She was quiet a minute, and then she leaned close. 'Mallory, I'm going to go now, but I'll be back. I'll try to bring Kendra. But you need to understand something, honey. You are our best lead so far to finding the man who hurt you and who took your sister. I need your help, and I'm not lying. So rest. I'll be back soon.'

Say nothing, because he's here.

A hand softly stroked her hair. 'Just rest,' Meredith said. 'I won't leave you.'

Cincinnati, Ohio,
Saturday 15 August, 2.35 P.M.

'Kate?' Zimmerman came out of his office as she and Decker stepped out of the elevator onto their floor at the field office. 'A word, please?'

Kate squared her shoulders. This was the talk she'd been dreading for hours. 'Yes, sir. If you could give me a few seconds.' Zimmerman nodded and retreated to his office, and she looked up at Decker. 'If you can make flyers out of those pictures we took of Rawlings last night, we can go to the jail and try to get some real answers about Alice's murder when I'm done. Unless . . . y'know . . . I'm done.'

They'd had this talk on their way from the Kroger to the hospital, and again from the hospital to the field office. *I lost control of the situation and people got hurt. An officer was killed. And the Professor got away. Again.*

Decker gave her shoulder a light bump with his. 'It wasn't anything you could control. It was set up to be a clusterfuck from the word go.'

'Yeah. Right. I'll take my medicine.'

'If it makes you feel better, I think he's madder at me and Deacon.'

Her lips quirked up. 'If that *does* make me feel better, does that mean I'm a bitch?'

He grinned, making her insides . . . settle. 'Go. I'll get those photos done. Troy sent me Rawlings's booking photo too, so I'll add that in.'

Kate's answering grin disappeared like mist as she went into Zimmerman's office, closed the door, and sat down in front of his desk. She clenched her fists and wished for her knitting, but she'd left it in the car again. She swallowed, the gulp audible. 'I'm sorry, sir.'

Zimmerman rested his chin on his steepled fingers and studied her. 'For?'

Kate blinked rapidly and tried to quiet the sudden hurricane in her head. 'I don't even know where to start.'

Leaning back, he pulled something out of a drawer and tossed it to her. A protein bar. 'For starters, eat that.' He took a bottle of water from the same drawer and put it on the edge of his desk closest to her. When she was finished with the food and water, she twined her fingers together and waited.

A fraction calmer, actually. Surely he wouldn't feed her if he were planning to go all administrative discipline on her ass. She hoped.

'On a scale from one to five, how clear is your mind now?' he asked.

'I'm at about a Cat 4,' she answered honestly, and he chuckled.

'Then take this.' He tossed her a flat box, like old-fashioned lace hankies might come in.

She caught her breath when she lifted the lid. 'Origami paper,' she murmured, her throat going tight. 'Okay, so down to Cat 3 now. You've fed me and watered me and given me coping presents, so I don't think I'm in too much trouble.'

He chuckled again. 'Well, I wouldn't say that, but we'll share whatever blame comes down.' He shrugged, sobering. 'Decker was right, what he said in the hallway.'

'Which thing? That you're madder at him and Deacon than at me, or that the Kroger situation was a clusterfuck from the word go?'

'Both,' he said dryly. 'The truth is you all acted quickly to minimize the danger to civilians. It could have been worse.'

'We let him get away,' she murmured, petting the paper. It was so very nice. So textured and tactile under her fingertips.

'You didn't choose the venue. The girl did. He simply made the most of the knowledge that you wouldn't risk shooting an innocent bystander to stop him. I'll deal with the fallout. That's part of my job.' He gestured to the paper. 'That's from my wife. I mentioned the folding you do and she picked that up after she saw the report about the Kroger on the news. She thought you'd need it.'

Kate brushed her fingers over the thick paper, just waiting to be folded into something wonderful. 'You told her I fold paper? Why?'

'Because talking to her quiets the chaos in my mind at the end of my day. I don't tell her the nastier parts of my job. Like seeing a woman dismembered and shoved in matching luggage. I can't tell her the sensitive parts of our investigations, but I can tell her about my people, and she likes that because she's the mothering type.'

Kate was touched. Confused, but touched. 'I've never even met your wife.'

'Actually, you have. Twice. Once at Agent Symmes's funeral last week. You passed her your pack of Kleenex and smiled at her. Then yesterday you saw her outside in the parking lot. She was getting out of her car to bring me dinner as you were getting into your car muttering about men needing keepers. She said you took a moment from your rant to smile at her again. My wife likes you.' He shrugged. 'Go figure.'

Kate had to laugh. 'Gosh. Thank you. I'll have to write her an actual old-fashioned thank-you note.' She took the first piece of paper from the box, scooted her chair closer to Zimmerman's desk and started folding, sobering as she began to talk. 'So. The Kroger. The older woman is in bad shape with a broken rib and a fractured hip, but she'll live, barring any weird infections or complications. Officer Heinz – that's Kendra's partner – has been taken to the morgue. Deacon and his lieutenant did the death notification to his widow.' She drew a breath and sighed. 'And Mallory – that's Sunshine Suzie's real name – refuses to say a word.'

'I suppose we can hardly blame her at this point,' Zimmerman said quietly. Kate had called him from the ER to report the sparkly pink phone and the picture of the abducted Macy, and they'd immediately instituted an Amber Alert with only the photo and 'Macy' because they didn't yet know her last name or where she'd been abducted from.

'Nobody saw him put that phone down on Mallory's table,' she said. 'Deacon and Decker and I searched the security tapes, and we think we found him.' She looked up and met her boss's worried gaze. 'He was dressed like a cop, sir. No badge, but he wore the uniform shirt. Long-sleeved, which is how we picked him out of the crowd to begin with.'

'To cover the wound on his arm,' Zimmerman said, the beginnings of excitement in his voice. 'Could you see his face?'

She shrugged. 'Not really. He wore the standard-issue hat, brim pulled down. He had a mustache and a beard. Probably another disguise, but who knows?'

Zimmerman blew out a frustrated sigh. 'We found the cruiser. He abandoned it in a shopping mall. We couldn't trace the little girl's phone. It's a burner.'

She blinked, not expecting that. 'Who gives a little girl a burner phone?'

'Who makes a little girl's big sister do kiddie porn?' Zimmerman returned bitterly. 'So until Mallory talks, we're back to where we were this morning, pursuing leads to the Professor. I heard you and Decker discussing going to the jail.'

She finished the basket she'd been folding, set it aside, and began tearing the next sheet into even strips. 'Yes. We'll take the pictures of Rawlings and see what we can dig up. Hopefully something that tells us how he contacted the Professor or how he received the poison he used on Alice. As for the others, Deacon is staying at the hospital with Dani. Meredith is staying with Mallory, who's been moved to a regular room. We have a guard posted. Kendra went home with Wendi. She's a mess, sir. Kendra, I mean. And Adam and Troy came back here.'

Zimmerman nodded. 'Adam's back at trying to figure out where the filming was done on the later Suzie videos, and Troy's back to viewing the Alice videos. Hopefully Alice was banging someone who has some information about the traffickers' customers and suppliers.' He sighed wearily. 'Because we still have a lot of kids – teens and adolescents – unaccounted for.'

Kate focused on the paper and the way it felt as she folded each strip as she thought about the kids – the ones Decker and Wendi had identified from the neighborhood as well as the ones McCord had bought from Alice. 'I was thinking. Decker is right. McCord and the Professor crossed paths, probably five years ago – that's when the studio location changed. I keep wondering why he'd do that and why he'd remove those videos from the Internet, because that lost him money. It only makes sense if there was something in that first house . . . or in those first videos maybe. Something that could incriminate him or identify him.'

'So maybe Adam should be focusing on the first-year videos?' Zimmerman asked softly.

She nodded. 'Maybe McCord saw his video and said, "Dude, I found you this easy because you let this detail show up in your video. Let me show you how to do this gig right." And they became partners. Or maybe he found McCord because whatever happened in that first house almost got him caught and he was scared, but not so much that he'd stop making films. He sold drugs to kids he recognized from the videos, and they told him about McCord.'

'Or maybe McCord had a nicer place to film,' Zimmerman said.

She shook her head. 'If that was the case, the Professor would've left the videos up where they could continue making him money. He's moved everything to offshore servers now, based on the conversation that Alice had with her father. The one Decker taped with his bugs.'

'The conversation that started all this.'

She nodded. 'The conversation Decker thought important enough to risk his life to tell us about. "Tip of the iceberg", Alice said. McCord's operation was tiny. The Professor's the one with the reach. The traffickers' IT guy – Alice's half-brother – helped him move the servers offshore in exchange for a steady stream of revenue. He could have re-uploaded the first-year videos to that offshore server and made a mint, but he didn't.'

'You could very well be right,' Zimmerman said thoughtfully. 'I'll tell Adam to focus on the first-year Suzie films, the ones you got from Corey Addison's computer.'

'I'll help him when I'm done at the jail. Adam shouldn't have to shoulder that alone.'

'He isn't. I've been working with the head of ICAC to find their mole. We can't allow one bad apple to keep us from utilizing an entire department's resources. ICAC will cooperate with our own cybercrimes division and we'll ferret out whoever in there is dirty. In the meantime, they'll make tracing the Suzie filming location a priority, because you're right – the Professor is the one with the big reach. When I told ICAC what we were looking for, they found his other films right away. Not the server – too many proxies and too many foreign entities to navigate that quickly and easily. But progress.'

'Good. Then Decker and I will get to the jail.' Kate scooped up the flowers she'd folded from the torn strips of paper and placed them in the basket she'd made first. 'For Mrs Z,' she said with a smile. 'Until I have a free moment to write a proper thank-you card.'

Zimmerman picked up the basket, a slow smile of delight blooming on his face. 'She'll love it. Thank you.' He looked up, over Kate's shoulder. 'You can come in now, Decker.'

Kate startled, turning in her chair to find Decker leaning against the door frame, watching her. 'How long have you been standing there?'

'Since you started folding paper,' he said. 'I didn't want to interrupt when you were on a roll. But since you're done, there's something you should see. You too, boss.'

Kate and Zimmerman followed him, Kate holding the box of paper to her chest. Decker's tone had her worrying about what she was about to see. He led them to the private area where Kate had viewed Corey Addison's Sunshine Suzie videos the day before. 'Troy and Taylor have been examining the Alice videos in here,' he explained.

The two men were seated in front of a large monitor. 'Quincy here enlarged the picture,' Troy explained, 'so that his face fills the screen.'

'You won't have to see any more flesh than that if you don't want to,' Quincy added.

'I appreciate it,' Kate murmured, steeling herself for whatever it was they'd found.

It was a man, just his face as Quincy had promised. He was a handsome man, but . . . She wasn't sure what she was looking for. His face was lifted upwards, his head thrown back. His expression was tight with sexual concentration, his eyes closed. 'What are we supposed to—'

Zimmerman derailed her train of thought with a gasp of shock. 'Oh my God,' he breathed, sitting heavily in the chair next to Troy. 'That can't be who I think it is.'

'Oh, but it is,' Troy said soberly.

'Who?' Kate demanded. 'Who is he?'

Twenty-six

'Well?' Kate demanded again when no one answered her. 'Who is this guy?'

Troy looked up at her. 'Oh, right. You're new in town. You wouldn't recognize him. He's a local TV personality. He does the medical report on the news. Last time I saw him, he was discussing some new implant for controlling insulin delivery for diabetics.'

Zimmerman was shaking his head, trying to make sense of what they were seeing. '*He* was having sex with Alice?'

'In *many* different positions.' Troy grimaced. 'Alice was *quite* the athlete.'

'Holy shit.' Kate blinked at the image, her mind racing. 'He's a doctor?'

'Dr Brandon Edwards,' Zimmerman said numbly. 'He has a practice in the city.'

'A doctor would know chemistry,' Decker said, standing beside her, leaning heavily on his walking stick. 'Poisons. Drugs. Making ricin wouldn't be hard to do.'

She gaped at him. 'You're thinking that this is the Professor?'

Decker shrugged. 'Maybe. Maybe not. But he's the right height. The right body type.'

'And,' Troy added, 'so far he's the only one who's matched all the physical parameters.'

Zimmerman was still staring. 'I've met him. Shaken his hand.'

541

He shuddered hard. 'Oh my God. My kids went to him when they were in college.'

Kate wanted to shudder along with him. Considered trying to comfort him, but what could she say? She clutched the box of pretty paper tighter to her chest instead – kind of a talisman – and made herself think. 'I saw his eyes last night. I'd remember his eyes. Can you find a shot of him with his eyes open?'

'No,' Quincy said grimly. 'Not when he's facing the camera. He never actually makes eye contact with Alice while they're . . . doing it.'

'It's like he doesn't really want to be there.' Troy shrugged, an odd, almost hurt expression flickering across his face. 'He's imagining he's somewhere else. Or that she's someone else.'

'Okay, then . . .' Kate focused on the face frozen on the screen rather than on Zimmerman, who seemed to be pulling himself together. 'But his face is familiar to me, too, now that I look at it some more. I could have seen him in the crowd today at Kroger, but . . . I don't think that's it. It wouldn't have been from the TV news. I haven't watched any since I've been here. Maybe . . .' She drew a shocked breath as recognition smacked her hard. 'Quincy, can you bring the picture back to its original size?'

'You want to see him in all his flesh?' Quincy asked, surprised.

'Well, no, but do it anyway.' She practically snapped the command, then remembered herself and sighed. 'I'm sorry. I don't mean to be rude. Please reset the scale.'

Quincy complied, tapping his keyboard. 'The good doctor, in all his glory.'

Kate stilled, her body feeling suddenly heavy, her shoulders weighed down with the memory of what she'd witnessed the last time she'd been in this room. 'There,' she said hoarsely, pointing at the man's flank. 'Zoom there.'

Quincy obeyed immediately, and no one said a word.

Kate pursed her lips so tightly they hurt. 'Yeah. That's him. That's why he took them down. Sonofamother*fucking*bitch.'

'Kate?' Decker asked cautiously.

She didn't look at him. Her eyes were glued to the small tattoo on the doctor's left ass cheek. 'You know all those Sunshine Suzie videos that don't exist online anymore? The ones that were recorded when she was *twelve years old*?'

'Oh my God,' Decker breathed. 'He's in them? This doctor? The tattoo. That's what Stone saw when he was fourteen.'

Kate nodded grimly and opened her box of pretty paper.

Decker sat down next to her. 'I like lions,' he murmured. 'Tigers and bears are good too.'

Her smile was quick and forced, but she appreciated his attempt. *I gotta get this fixed. I can't keep folding paper and knitting blankets to cope with stress.* But that wasn't going to happen right now, so her hands started folding because her throat was closing up, a sob building at the thought of monsters who raped little girls. And then made money from it.

'That man, the one on the screen, was in all the videos. First, second, and third year.' Her hands faltered as she tried to swallow the baseball lodged in her throat. 'He was . . . raping her in all of them.' She drew a huge breath, her hands shaking too hard to fold paper. She hunched over, dropping her chin. 'Oh God.'

Decker splayed his hand on her back, rubbing big comforting circles. Saying nothing. Nor did anyone else.

She pulled the emotion back in and shoved it down. *I have to deal with this. It keeps surfacing, no matter how hard I shove it down.* She flattened her hands on the tabletop to stretch the muscles that had clenched. Then she began to fold again. 'He wore a wig, I think. In the videos. His hair didn't move right, like it was shellacked to his head. Like a big Ken doll. He was spray-tanned, and in the early videos this tattoo showed. In the later ones, it's not there.'

Decker kept rubbing her back. 'He must have learned how to cover it with makeup.'

She nodded. 'But here . . .' She jerked her chin toward the monitor. 'Here, he didn't know he was being recorded. Alice's camera was hidden. He didn't hide his tat. That's him.' Her voice hardened. 'And when we bring him in, we can prove that he raped a twelve-year-old in addition to tying him to production and distribution of child pornography.'

She glanced at Zimmerman, who looked green. 'I'm sorry to ask this, sir, but where did your kids go to college?'

He closed his eyes. 'King's College, just like Sidney Siler and Stone O'Bannion. Edwards's practice is near there. We had our own doctor, but both my kids played sports and needed physicals to play. His practice was convenient. They didn't have to miss class. He recruited customers out of his practice as their doctor. He sold them drugs as the fucking Professor. This keeps getting worse.'

'You don't know that he did anything to your kids,' she said gently, then recoiled when his eyes flew open, filled with rage.

'He touched them!' he roared. 'He looked at them!' He closed his eyes again, shaking his head. His hands clenched into fists, pounding his knees hard, just once, and when he spoke again, although it wasn't with his characteristic calm, he was under control. 'I'm sorry, Kate. I know you're trying to help, but that bastard had his *hands* on my *daughters*. I'm finding it difficult to be objective at the moment.'

Kate hesitated, then carefully covered one of his clenched fists with her palm. 'How could you be objective?' she asked softly. 'I'd want to kill him, too.'

Zimmerman's throat worked as he tried to swallow. He opened his eyes, but made no effort to shake her hand away, so she left it there, giving him whatever comfort she could. 'My kids are not the victims here. The victims are the kids he dragged into drugs when they were in middle school. And the kids that he and McCord somehow pulled into kiddie porn. We need to find out how he got his hands on Mallory. Maybe that will tell us how he recruited those victims.'

Decker took his hand off her back. 'I know where else I've seen him. Can I use the keyboard?' Quincy passed it down to him, and Decker typed fast, the sound like rifle fire. He opened a new window on the big monitor and Kate's heart sank.

'Oh no,' she whispered. Because now it made sense. A lot of things made sense.

'The Lorelle Meadows Shelter and Free Clinic,' Quincy said. 'That's the shelter down in Over-the-Rhine, right? But how does that factor into all of this?'

'Some of the child porn victims come from that neighborhood,' Decker said.

'And it's where Dani Novak was attacked,' Troy added. 'She said she volunteered there before getting offered a job. If he volunteered there too, he'd know the neighborhood kids. He'd know who was vulnerable. God, talk about being a kid in a candy store.'

Decker shook his head. 'He more than volunteered. I looked the website up yesterday when Dani said she'd been called into the shelter.' He clicked on *About Us*, and up popped a photo of Dr Brandon Edwards, polished and dignified. 'He's the director. Has been for years. And he's Dani's new boss.'

'Diesel said her attacker seemed to come out of nowhere,' Kate murmured. 'Because he came from inside the shelter itself. We need a positive ID from Mallory. She might be the only one, other than Alice, who's seen his real face.'

'Which is why he killed Alice,' Zimmerman said. 'But not before making sure she didn't have any written record of their transactions. All right. I want to do this fast and right. Nobody gets to be a cowboy. Got it?' They all nodded dutifully, and he went on. 'We mount a three-pronged attack. I'll send agents to his house and his office. They will sit there until I have a signed search warrant for both places. We'll likely need Mallory's ID to get a signature.'

'We can match the tattoos,' Kate said, protesting.

Zimmerman shook his head. 'He is a well-respected physician who has at least one cop in his pocket. Who knows who else he's blackmailing? I'm not going to risk a dirty judge, or even one who's star-struck because the bastard is on TV. We have to prove that's him. We might get a warrant for him specifically so that we can prove it, but not for his house and office, not right away, and that gives him time to destroy evidence. And perhaps even to harm Macy.'

'So where do you want us to go?' Kate asked.

'You and Decker go to the hospital. Get a positive ID from Mallory, even if it's only a video of her reaction when she sees his photo. I'll get the warrants drafted and have Edwards's home and office surrounded. As soon as you have the ID, tell me, and I'll get the warrant signed. Troy, I want you with the agents surrounding the office. Kate, Decker, you start for his home address as soon as you get that ID. Troy, I'll meet you at the office.'

'He films somewhere,' Kate said. 'His new studio. It could be in his house.'

Zimmerman nodded. 'Hopefully. But if it's not, maybe Meredith can convince Mallory to tell us where that is after she knows that we have him ID'd. Oh, and Kate, you tell that former partner of yours that if I or anyone else sees his white head anywhere, I will have it on a platter. He is to go nowhere near Edwards or any of the possible places he could be hiding. I'm serious. I will make sure he never works again. He's normally level-headed, but if he gets his hands on the man who attacked his sister, he'll kill him. And I can't protect him from that.'

Kate nodded. 'I'll tell him. Do I have permission to tie him up?' she added wryly.

Zimmerman nodded. 'You do. Better yet, call Faith. Tell her to keep him in line.'

'Yes, sir.'

Zimmerman waved them out the door. 'Go. Now. Vests on everybody. Be safe.'

Cincinnati, Ohio,
Saturday 15 August, 3.00 P.M.

He backed Gemma's minivan up to the kitchen door. He had to get those four teens out of his house, and with one good arm he wasn't planning to drag them any further than he had to. Once he had them someplace safe, he'd find a way to get closer to Mallory. That he'd be able to was not even a concern. He'd waltzed into the hospital and nobody had given him a second glance. He could be anyone he wanted to be and nobody could stop him.

He figured he could add a little GHB into the teens' drinks, like he had with JJ. None of them were terribly big, and he had a wheelchair in the basement from the last time he'd taken Roxy to the hospital for treatment. He'd just wheel them out and dump them in the back of the minivan. Once he had them tied up, it would be easy to offload them individually at the studio.

Because he was going to need the money those kids would make him even more now. It would be a long time before he could build his business back up to its current level without the Professor.

And the Professor, sadly, had to die.

Hm. Intriguing thought. He could actually kill one of his threats and make it look as if they'd been the Professor. That way he got rid of a threat and got the cops off his back. If the Professor was dead, they'd stop looking for him.

He'd have to give that one some serious consideration. He lifted the back hatch of the minivan and checked on Macy. She was awake and terrified. And crying. He patted her cheek.

'Don't cry. I'll have you someplace nice really soon.' He covered her back up with the blanket and entered his house through the kitchen door, and was immediately greeted by the heavy odor of pot. So the kids had found his stash.

Excellent. At least *something* was going according to plan.

He found them all in a happy daze around the TV, which was playing the very naughty, hard R, nearly porn movie he'd left out for them. They'd be easy to train once he got them hidden away and broken. He would have liked more time to soften them up, but thanks to Mallory, he no longer had that option.

Mallory was going to suffer. Death by ricin might be painful enough. No, nothing was painful enough. But he couldn't let himself focus on Mallory right now.

'Hi, sir!' Seth said happily.

'Hello, kids,' he said, feigning a scowl. Normally he wouldn't pretend to be angry. His ready acceptance of his victims' drug use was one thing that kept them coming back voluntarily. But since he wasn't going to let them go, he changed his approach on the fly. 'What the devil has been going on here? Are you all *high*?'

Sarah, the serious one, frowned. She did not appear to be high. *Figures.* There was always one goody-goody in every group. Once he got them to the studio, he'd have to break her first. The others would fall into line much faster without their moral spine.

'I tried to stop them, sir. Really. But they wouldn't listen to me.'

'This is not good, kids,' he said angrily. 'Your parents and grandparents trusted me to take care of you. I trusted you to behave.' He turned to Goody-Two-Shoes Sarah with a sigh. 'Maybe you can help me get them sober, then. I could use some help making coffee.' Into which he'd add liberal helpings of GHB.

She followed him into the kitchen, still frowning. 'I thought you were a doctor.'

He looked at her, eyebrows raised. 'I am.'

'Then why are you wearing that uniform? That's a policeman's uniform.'

I hate intelligent children. He handed her a bag of ground coffee and pointed to the machine. 'Because I stopped to help someone in a car accident while I was out. I got my clothes bloody and one of the officers offered me this shirt.'

That seemed to satisfy her. 'Oh. Okay. Should I make the coffee strong?'

'Please. They're pretty toasted.'

'I know,' she said, disgusted. 'I'm so sorry.'

'Don't be. I should have checked to make sure they hadn't brought any pot with them.'

She shook her head, one brow lifted. 'No, sir. They found it here. In the cookie jar.'

He sighed sadly. 'My niece lives with me. She has a drug problem. Sometimes she brings things into the house that she shouldn't. I'm sorry you had to see that.'

'Thank you for explaining it to me,' she said politely. 'I understand, but my gran would've gotten really mad. My mama brings in drugs. She's outta control.'

This he knew, because her mama was one of his better customers. He didn't know how the woman had been paying him all these years, but her most recent payment was Sarah herself. What he hadn't known was that there was a puritanical grandmother in the mix. 'Did you tell your gran?' he asked casually, relieved when she shook her head.

'My cell phone don't work here. Plus Mama told her that I'd be with her all day. She knew Gran wouldn't let me come here. Gran's real strict, on account of Mama's problem.'

Good. And that meant Sarah's gran would be one less person he'd have to kill. Sarah's mother, on the other hand . . . She had lied to him, told him that he'd have no trouble with Sarah. She hadn't mentioned Gran. So Mama would be dealt with.

He sighed to himself. He'd broken his number one rule: Never trust an addict. Next time he wouldn't be in such a hurry to make deals like the one he'd made with Sarah's mama.

He assessed Sarah's size. She didn't weigh more than a hundred pounds soaking wet. 'Do you drink coffee, Sarah?'

'No, but I like pop,' she said with a smile.

'Then let me get you some.' He poured cola into a glass, and while she was making the coffee for the others, he stirred in enough GHB to put her out fast. She guzzled it down and put out her glass for more. He refilled it, then asked her to get them some snacks. While her back was turned, he added the powder to the cups of coffee.

Sarah took the coffee in and scolded the others to drink it and sober up, sounding like a little mama herself. The other three kids fell into line, gulping the coffee down even though it was still very hot.

Oh yeah. I definitely have to break Sarah first. She's the kind who could lead an uprising.

He checked his watch, relieved when they all started to fade. He walked Sarah out first, holding her up as she staggered and stumbled. He pushed her into the back of the van, tying her firmly and taping her mouth before going back to get the others.

Everything worked as he'd hoped, and soon he had all four teenagers in the back of his van. He moved Macy to one of the middle seats so that she didn't get squashed by one of the bigger kids, then he locked up the house, got back in the minivan and was on his way, the ease of the operation a good omen. The horrible luck of this day was over.

He'd take them all to the studio, then rest a bit before he figured out how he'd deal with Mallory. And at some point he needed to get that antibiotic in his arm. It no longer throbbed. It was numb. And he didn't need to be a doctor to know that wasn't good at all.

Cincinnati, Ohio,
Saturday 15 August, 3.20 P.M.

Decker drew up a chair next to Agent Triplett, who'd pulled guard duty again, this time outside Mallory's room. Zimmerman had released all the security from the safe house, since nobody was using it to stay safe.

Meredith came out of Mallory's room, looking as tired as Decker felt.

'How is she?' Kate murmured.

Meredith shrugged. 'Physically, she's in pain. I've been watching her respiration and pulse like a hawk, just in case someone does try to put something in her IV other than pain meds. She drifts in and out. She kept asking for Kendra until I finally called Wendi and asked her to bring Kendra here. They're on their way.'

'She hasn't had any visitors,' Trip added. 'No one's tried anything. It's been quiet.'

'Not for much longer,' Decker said.

'That's for sure,' Kate agreed and quickly brought them up to speed, giving Meredith and Trip time to absorb the new information before telling them what they planned to do.

'You're going to videotape her reaction?' Meredith said uncertainly. 'That seems like a violation of her privacy to me. But I don't have a better plan. Did you tell her doctor so that they can be prepared if she goes into shock?'

Decker nodded. 'We did. Her doctor's on standby. It's more likely she'll need you to calm her down, Meredith.'

'Hopefully Kendra will be here soon. Mallory's got a one-track mind when it comes to wanting her here, which isn't uncommon for victims of abuse. They often attach themselves to a person – or the idea of a person. Kendra was her savior, her safety net all week. I think knowing someone had her back was what gave her the courage to come forward in the first place. That Kendra was there, waiting for her when she came out of the store – that's a powerful mental image. And one we really shouldn't try to make her give up.'

'We don't have time to wait for Kendra to get here,' Kate said. 'Zimmerman has a judge waiting to sign our warrant.'

Meredith's nod was weary. 'Then let's do this.'

'You and I are going to be in the room,' Kate told her. 'Decker's going to do the video.'

'And I'm just here to look pretty,' Trip said with a roll of his eyes.

Meredith patted his massive arm. 'You're here making her feel safe, even though she doesn't have the words to tell you that yet.'

Decker blew out a breath and forced himself to stand. 'I gotta say, I'm about done.'

'When did you two last eat?' Trip asked.

'I don't even remember,' Decker said with a short laugh. 'We'll have to grab something on our way out of here.'

Trip patted the cooler next to his foot. 'You can have my dinner. I got my eye on one of the nurses who I can sweet-talk into bringing me something later.'

Decker's stomach started growling at the thought. 'I'd say no thank you, but my stomach might just kill me.' He followed Kate into Mallory's room and hung by the door, waiting to see what the girl's reaction would be. He started recording, holding his phone so that it wasn't obvious what he was doing.

'Hi, Mallory,' Kate said, pulling one of the chairs close to the girl's bed. 'I'm back.'

Mallory blinked at her, half asleep. 'Kate.'

'That's right. That guy over there? He's one of my partners. His name is Agent Davenport.'

The girl seemed to wake up a little. 'Davenport?'

'Yes'm, but you can call me Decker. It's a nickname.'

'Why? Why is it a nickname?'

'Because I was a scrapper as a kid, and I decked everybody,' he answered with a smile. It was his stock answer for people who asked. But then something in his gut told him that he needed to give her more than that. He sobered, losing the smile. Losing the glossed-over version. 'I decked everybody because my mama would get high and we'd get put in foster care and sometimes it was good and sometimes it wasn't.' She watched him, suspicion flickering in her narrowed eyes, unsure whether she could trust that his story was true. So he gave her true, laying himself bare. 'She'd get clean long enough to get me and my sister back, and the cycle would begin again. Until my mama OD'd after letting some old pervert have my little sister.'

Mallory gasped, and from the corner of his eye he could see Meredith's eyes widen. Kate, on the other hand . . . She smiled at him encouragingly, making it so much easier to answer Mallory's next question. 'What happened to her? To both of them?'

'My mama died in a puddle of her own vomit, the needle still in her arm.' He drew a breath. 'My sister died too and . . . well, that was really hard because she suffered. A lot. She was a little girl and he . . . well, he was a grown man. He hurt her, so bad she died. But it wasn't like she even got to rest in peace, because the bastard who'd hurt her had taken pictures of her.'

Mallory went still, her eyes locked on Decker's. 'I'm so sorry,' she whispered.

He found a small smile for the young woman who'd also suffered. 'Thank you. But it got worse, because the bastard uploaded those pictures to the Internet. And some of the boys I knew found them. And they thought it was funny. I didn't agree.'

Mallory swallowed hard. 'So you decked them all?'

'Yes, ma'am, I did.'

The girl was trembling. 'Good,' she whispered. 'I'm glad.'

'Well, looking back, so am I. I got to fight back. At least I got to tell myself I was doing something, which is a lot better than doing nothing.'

Her eyes flashed, angry now. 'You want me to tell you things. I can't. He's got Macy. And he's here. I know he is. He knows.'

'Because he left the phone for you,' Kate murmured.

'You don't know what it's like to be watched. All the time. I thought if I got away I could tell the truth, I could do something, but he watches me here, just like at home. He's got eyes everywhere.

Spies, cameras, everywhere. I want to tell you everything. I do.' Tears filled Mallory's eyes and Decker's heart cracked. 'I really want to do the right thing. But I can't.'

'Can I come closer?' Decker asked.

Mallory nodded unsteadily. 'Yes. Thank you for asking.'

Decker handed off his phone to Trip, who moved to where Decker had been standing, continuing to record.

'Last thing I wanna do is make you afraid. More afraid,' Decker amended. He lowered himself into the chair on the other side of the bed, unable to silence his groan. 'Pardon the creaking, ma'am,' he drawled with a quiet smile, hoping to put her at ease. If there was ever a time to charm a lady, this was it. 'I was hurt last week. And then . . . well, someone tried to hurt me again.'

'Is your first name Griffin?' she asked, and it was Decker's turn to be surprised.

'Yes, it is. How do you know that?'

'I heard him talking about you. He was . . . afraid. It was the first time I ever heard him be afraid. He sent someone to kill you in the hospital. Then he was really mad when they failed.' Her lips curved in grim satisfaction. 'I'm glad they failed.'

'Me too. But I gotta thank my partner over there, Agent Coppola. She ran through the hospital like a damn crazy woman, jumping lunch carts like they were hurdles.'

'That must have been something to see,' Mallory murmured, then she pursed her lips, like she was thinking. She was silent for nearly a minute before she finally spoke. 'You need to warn someone named Dani. A lady. A doctor. He's going to try to kill her too.'

'He already tried,' Decker told her. 'He failed. Her friend was there and he stopped him. Threw a knife into his arm.'

'Oh,' Mallory breathed. '*That's* how he got the arm wound. It's infected. I . . . might have put something dirty in the bandage when he told me to fix him up. I was supposed to get him antibiotic, which I bought at Kroger today. But then he hit me with a car and I have no idea where the bottle is. That's karma, right?'

'It sure is,' Decker murmured. 'But sometimes karma isn't enough. Sometimes it needs help. Sometimes it needs somebody who's watching out for you, who jumps lunch carts like hurdles to save your life.'

'I don't have anyone like that. I just have me. And Macy just has me.'

'Now that's not true,' he said with mild reproach. 'You have me. And Kate. Kendra. Meredith. Agent Triplett over there. Anybody wants to get to you, they have to go through him. You have our whole team. You've been so brave. Making that first phone call. Taking that cab today so you could make the second call. You've trusted us, even before you knew us. We need you to trust us just a little more. We need you to look at a photo. Just one. Will you?'

'What is it of?'

'Six men,' Decker told her. 'We need to know if you know one of them.'

She looked at the door, saw Trip with Decker's phone, recording. 'You're taping me?'

'Yes,' Decker said honestly. 'Do you know what a search warrant is?'

'It's a paper that says you have the right to enter someone's house and search even if they don't want you to, right? Do you have one of those? On his house?'

'One thing at a time,' he said. 'Your definition is mostly right. But we can't just get a warrant any time we please. We have to get a judge to agree. To your second question, yes, we have a warrant waiting to be signed by the judge. He's waiting for you to tell us if we have the right man. We figured we'd tape this in case you continued not to want to talk to us, so that we could show him your reaction. But we also want to make sure that you're protected. We think this man has a lot of friends and we want to be sure nobody says we put words in your mouth.'

She stared at him, her expression wary, but clearly wanting so much to believe his words. 'Do I have to say anything?'

'Not if you don't want to.'

She bit her split lip. 'He'll find out. He'll hurt Macy. You don't know him like I do.'

She wants to be convinced, Decker thought. She was strong enough to take a little honesty right here. 'If you say nothing? We won't catch him and he'll still have Macy. But if you help us, our chances of getting her back are much better.' He held out his hand, palm up. 'Trust us.'

Mallory stared at his hand, then up at him. 'Do you promise to find her?'

'No,' he said quietly. 'I can't promise that. I won't lie to you. You deserve better than that and you're smart enough to know a lie anyway. I can't promise to find her. I can promise to do my best. And I can promise that my best is pretty damn good.' He hadn't moved his hand.

'He thinks I'm afraid of him,' she whispered. 'And he's right. I am. But if I say nothing and he turns Macy into me? I'd die.' She drew a breath, then slipped her hand in his. 'All right. Show me the pictures.'

Kate gave him a look that he'd remember for the rest of his life, no matter what happened next. It held pride and something more, something that made him so damn happy she'd jumped out of that tree and shoved her rifle in his back.

Kate had saved to her phone a photo array that included Dr Brandon Edwards. 'Did one of these men force you to make pornographic movies when you were twelve years old?'

Mallory froze. She nodded once.

Kate gentled her voice. 'I know this is hard, but can you point to which one?'

Mallory raised a trembling hand and pointed to the photo of Edwards.

Kate closed the photo window immediately. 'Thank you, Mallory. That's all we needed to know.'

'Wait,' Mallory said. She looked over at Trip. 'Are you still recording?'

'Yes, ma'am,' Trip said.

'Good.' She tightened her hold on Decker's hand until he nearly whimpered. But he didn't make a sound, because she was staring straight into the camera. 'Yes, Mr Judge, whoever you are,' she said loudly. 'The man in the top right corner is Dr Brandon Edwards. He forced me to make movies, starting when I was twelve until I was fifteen. He did horrible things. Sex things. I wanted to stop and he wouldn't let me. I tried to get help and he told lies about me. He made me look like I was crazy and a drug addict. He made my little sister afraid of me. And then he punished me by locking me in a closet for days, and when he let me out . . . he let other people . . . other men . . . do things too. He said that if I didn't do what he said, he'd make Macy do all those things, too. I thought about killing him so many times, but he said that if he died, his partner, Woody McCord, would take over, and that *he* wouldn't wait for Macy to get older.' She was breathing hard. 'He's had other kids during the time I've lived with him. Boys and girls. He made them do movies too. And today . . . he has four kids at his house. He was supposed to, anyway. I don't know if they came or not. I'll say this in court.' She lifted her chin. 'Unless he kills me first. Which he said he would do if I ever told.'

'We won't let him do that,' Decker said. 'We won't let him kill you.'

'I know you'll do your best not to let him,' she said, echoing his earlier words with a resignation that hurt to hear. She closed her eyes for a minute. 'Don't stop taping. I'm not finished.'

'Yes, ma'am,' Trip said respectfully.

'He killed his girlfriend. Her name was JJ. He . . .' She swallowed audibly. 'He cut her body up and put it in suitcases. Then he made me take the suitcases to the motel where she'd left her car, and put them in the trunk. He told me to leave the keys in the ignition, so I did. Maybe somebody took it, I don't know. And he's got a wife – Roxy – and she's really sick. She's at his house. Please help her, too.'

'Anything else, ma'am?' Trip asked.

'Um . . . he's got a sister, Nell. She's nice, but she thinks I'm bad. I don't think she knows about him. His other sister, Gemma, is an addict. And Macy's mom. He got us both from our real mother and he kept me and gave Macy to Gemma when she was a baby.' She licked her lips nervously. 'Gemma's husband is a policeman. His

556

name is Bob. I don't know his last name. I don't know where they live.'

A cop. That makes a lot of sense. 'Okay,' Decker said. 'We'll look for them. Bob's a common name, but Gemma's not. Her name will be in his personnel record.'

Her eyes opened wide and filled with tears. 'You believe me?' she whispered.

'Yes. Of course I believe you,' Decker said.

She choked on a sob. 'Nobody believed me. Nobody ever believed me.'

Decker's eyes stung. 'Who didn't believe you, honey?'

'Bob. I thought he'd help me. I thought he loved Macy and would want to protect her. But he didn't believe me and he hit me. Hard. He told me to stop lying and then he told Gemma, who told the doctor. That was the first time he locked me in a closet, but it wasn't the last time. He had everyone around us, all the neighbors, anyone who saw me, he had them believing that I was a mental case. That I hurt myself and that he was this wonderful guy for taking me in and giving me a home. Nobody would believe me if I said he was bad.'

Decker had to swallow hard. There was more, he knew. So many people who'd let this young woman down. Who'd betrayed her. Eventually he'd get the name of every one of them. But he needed to find the Professor first. That was his priority at the moment.

'Well, we believe you now,' he said hoarsely.

Meredith was standing at the head of the bed and now brushed Mallory's hair off her forehead. 'What happened to your mom, Mallory?'

'She gave us away because he sold her drugs. She was addicted to heroin and just wanted more and more. So she . . . sold us to him.' She blinked, sending the tears down her face. 'She sold us for drugs,' she sobbed brokenly. 'And nobody believed me.'

Decker wiped his eyes with his free hand, because he wasn't about to let go of Mallory, even if she broke every bone in his hand.

Trip cleared his throat roughly. 'Should I keep recording, Mallory?'

Mallory sucked in a breath, and damned if she didn't suck in her sobs too, just like Kate did. Tears continued to fall, but she quieted her crying through sheer will. 'Yes. You need to look in his basement. That's where he makes the drugs. Sometimes it smells really bad. I don't know what he's making. Sometimes I have to sleep outside because of the fumes. So check the basement.' She looked away, her brows furrowed. 'I think that's all.'

'I have one question,' Kate said. 'Well, maybe two. We know that he changed the place where he made the movies. Do you know where the new place is? Is it in his house?'

'No, it's not in his house, but I don't know where it is. I'm sorry. I really don't know. That's probably where he took Macy. He always gave me something that made me sleep and then blindfolded me in case I woke up before we got there. It's surrounded by trees. That's all I know. I'm sorry.'

'That's okay,' Kate said. 'You've helped us a lot. The last question – why did he change the place where he filmed?'

'Because of the second time I tried to tell. I borrowed a phone from a lady at the store and called the police. The police came to his house – his old house – and looked around, and one of them . . . he knew me. From the videos. He told the doctor that he'd tell. He wanted some of the money from the videos or he'd tell that movies were being made in his house. So the doctor sold the house and moved to where he is now. Do you need the address?'

'Tell us, just for the taped record,' Kate said.

Mallory recited the address, and it was the same one that Zimmerman had put on the warrant. The same one they'd search as soon as the girl had spoken her piece.

'But I don't know the cop's name,' she finished.

'Would you know him if you saw him again?' Decker asked.

Mallory's swollen red eyes narrowed. 'Yes. But only if . . . only if I saw him without clothes. Because he also made the doctor let him . . . have me. I never saw his face, but I remember his birthmark. So yes, I'd remember if I saw the birthmark again.'

Decker gritted his teeth against a sudden wave of fury that blazed through him. *Goddammit*. Another cop who should have protected her. No wonder she hadn't come forward sooner. 'Good. Because we believe you about that too.'

Her smile was weary. 'Thank you. There's a key to the house . . . it was in my pocket.'

Meredith pointed to a clear plastic bag that held Mallory's clothes. Kate pulled on a pair of gloves and searched the clothing, coming up with a key. 'It's new,' she said.

'He replaced the locks two days ago. JJ had made herself a key and was trying to steal drugs from him. He changed the alarm, too. The new code is 4655.' Mallory sagged back into the pillow. 'I'm all done. You can stop recording now.'

From the corner of his eye, Decker saw Trip lower the phone and take a swipe at his own eyes. Decker gave Mallory's hand a light squeeze. 'I have to go for a little while. I'll be back. We're going to do our best to find your sister. But you need to know that whatever happens, you are brave. And you are a good person. Nothing that's happened here is your fault. And Macy is lucky to have you for her big sister. Okay?'

'Okay,' she whispered. 'Thank you for telling me about your sister. What was her name?'

'Shelby Lynne. And I miss her, every day.'

'Then she was lucky to have you, too.'

Decker brought her hand to his cheek. 'Thank you. Now try to sleep. We'll be back.'

She let go of his hand and he stood up, his legs shaking beneath him. His whole body shook. He needed to get out of this room before he fell apart.

Kate led him to the door and took his phone from Trip. 'Did I hear you offer him food?'

'You did.' Trip handed her his cooler. 'Y'all be safe.'

'We will.' Not saying another word, Kate kept a firm hold on Decker's arm from the moment they left Mallory's room until he climbed into the passenger seat of her car. She gently buckled his seat belt and kissed his forehead. 'I was so proud of you in there. You're a good man, Griffin Davenport. Griff and Mama D would be proud too.'

He tried to smile and found he was too weary, physically and emotionally. 'You need to call Zimmerman.'

'I texted him while Mallory was talking. Told him it was a go. That the video was coming. I think I may have to upload it to a cloud somewhere, because it's way too big to email. Once you got her talking, she didn't want to stop, and I didn't want to stop her.'

'Kate?'

'What do you need, Decker?'

'You for one, but mostly right now I need a nap.'

She kissed his temple. 'Fine, but eat what's in the cooler first.'

Decker managed to eat all but the slice of apple pie before Kate made it to the interstate. Then he closed his eyes.

And let himself grieve for Mallory and Macy and for Shelby Lynne and all the other kids whose names they might never know. It wasn't until Kate pressed a pack of tissues into his hand that he realized he was crying, but he felt no embarrassment. No shame. Not with her. He wouldn't have let anyone else see him this . . . bare. No one but her. Because she was weeping too.

Twenty-seven

Decker woke with a start, fists clenched. Everything clenched. Because Kate was not there, her scent no longer in his head.

'Easy, soldier.' Troy sat in the driver's seat, his laptop balanced on the steering wheel while he typed. 'She went inside.'

Decker was in the passenger seat of her car, the seat tilted back as far as it would go. He wasn't sure how long he'd been asleep. It wasn't dark, but the sun had moved across the sky. He scrubbed his face, trying to wake up fully. 'Inside where?'

'Edwards's house. Damn, it feels good not to call him the Professor anymore.'

Decker grunted his agreement and hit the lever to straighten the seatback, glancing at the dashboard clock as he took stock of his surroundings. He'd been asleep for two and a half hours.

And felt surprisingly good. 'I thought you and Zimmerman went to the doctor's office.'

'We did. We picked up the doc's sister, Nell Edwards. She's a physician's assistant working under her brother's license.'

'Mallory mentioned her. Said she was nice and probably didn't know what her brother was doing.'

Troy's expression softened. 'Yeah. I saw the tape. That was a nice thing you did, Decker, telling her about your sister.'

Decker's face heated despite the cold air blowing from the A/C vents. 'Yeah, well. Anyway, what did Nell say?'

'That we were wrong. That her brother could never be involved

561

in any of that. That Mallory was mentally ill, unbalanced. That he had cared for the girl as a father and this was the thanks he got. And on and on. We left her in the interview room with an armed agent. She claims she doesn't know where her brother could be, but I'd lay good money that she's lying. Protecting him. We're getting ready to use the videos – him with Alice and him with Mallory – so we can convince her that he's a sociopathic pedophile, but I'm betting she finds an excuse for that too.'

'Probably. People are very good at believing what they want to believe. So Edwards wasn't in the house. What about the four kids?'

'Only thing remaining was the hovering cloud of an epic pot party. First guys in said they felt high just walking around the house. It's dissipated now, but you can still smell it in the carpet. There were cups of coffee in the living room and a half-drunk glass of pop in the kitchen. All positive for GHB.'

'So he drugged them and took them somewhere.'

'Farm boy's all woken up,' Troy said with sarcastic cheer. Decker gave him the finger, making Troy laugh.

'How long have we been here?'

'You've been here over an hour. I just got here twenty minutes ago. I took watch-Decker's-ass duty mainly because I wanted to sit in the A/C.'

'Nobody needs to watch my ass.'

Troy gave him a look of mild reproach. 'Less than twenty-four hours ago Kate was shot. Before that, Dani was assaulted because she knew where you were. We're not going anywhere alone. None of us. Z's orders. And speaking of the boss, we were happy to find out that it was Nell the PA who did their physicals a few years back, not Edwards himself.'

'That's good,' Decker said, profoundly relieved. 'What about Edwards's wife?'

Troy grimaced. 'That was pretty awful. They'd transported her by the time I got here, but she's sick. Maybe days from dying. Severe liver disease. Her skin was yellow and she wasn't coherent. The bedding was soiled . . . although it did appear she'd been cared for up until today.'

'Mallory,' Decker murmured. 'And no sign of Macy, I take it. Or any connection to a cop named Bob?'

'Not so far. And so far no one has reported Macy missing.'

'And the basement?'

'The door is set like a vault. We want to make sure we've collected all the evidence before we blow it off its hinges and send up a cloud of dust.'

'What if he's down there with Macy and the four kids?'

'There's no other way out. So if he's there, we've got him. But somehow I can't see him trapping himself like that.'

'I agree.' Decker was getting antsy. 'I'm going inside now. You coming?'

'Of course. I was just waiting for you to finish your beauty sleep.'

Troy gathered his things, and he and Decker found Kate with Adam and Quincy Taylor in Edwards's home office, gathered around his desktop computer.

Kate looked up, excitement in her eyes. 'You remember Mallory's comment about how he always watched her?'

'With spies and cameras,' Decker said. 'Did you find the cameras?'

'Did we ever,' Adam said. 'Took a while to figure out his password. We ended up asking Diesel how he'd broken into McCord's system nine months ago. Once he told us, it was straightforward.'

'Not really,' Quincy said. 'Diesel's kind of a fucking genius, which I did not expect.'

'I think he cultivates that Hell's Angels image on purpose,' Decker said, remembering how the man had broken down after giving him the flash drive. 'He's not what I expected either. So, what have you found?'

'We just started looking,' Kate said.

'The system records,' Quincy said eagerly, 'and it keeps the footage for years. This is a goldmine.' He tapped a few more keys, tabbing from camera to camera. The basement, the kitchen, the bathroom, Mallory's bedroom. 'God. He really was watching her. All the time. Poor kid.' He found the living room and rewound the tape until the four teens showed up. Three were smoking weed, their avid attention on what appeared to be an explicit movie on the big-screen TV.

'He's sexing them up,' Kate said, disgusted. 'Giving them drugs and edging them towards accepting porn. It would be only a matter of time before he pushed them into posing and having sex with each other. And him.'

Quincy fast-forwarded a bit to when Edwards returned to find the party going on. He was very matter-of-fact about it, then left the room with one of the teens. Quincy switched the camera view to the kitchen and they watched as Edwards mixed white powder into cups of coffee and one glass of cola. 'That's where he adds the GHB. We found it in the leftover drinks.'

One by one the teens began to get loopy and he walked them outside.

'Did he have a camera on the exterior?' Kate asked.

Quincy found it, and they watched Edwards putting the teens in an old minivan, then tying and gagging them.

'We just missed him,' Adam muttered. 'Goddammit.'

'What about the basement?' Decker asked.

Quincy found the camera and whistled. 'Wow.' The room was filled with chemistry equipment and had several large interior doors. Tabbing a few more times showed what was behind the doors – one was a storage room with big bags of powder marked *Heroin*, *Coke*, *Meth*, and bottles labeled *Steroid*. One door hid a cache of weapons – mostly semi-auto rifles and handguns.

'Jackpot,' Decker said, a grin nearly busting his face open. They had Edwards for the porn and the drugs. Now they had to put together all the evidence for the murders he'd committed. He was never getting out of prison.

'And he's got a very sophisticated wine cellar,' Troy added. 'We have an erudite sociopathic drug-dealing pedophile.'

Quincy tabbed a few more times and everyone did a double-take.

'That's his practice,' Troy said, edging closer to the screen. 'We were just there.'

Quincy hit a few buttons and the tape began to rewind. 'Yep.

There you are, Luther.' He stopped the rewind and hit play. 'The camera really does add ten pounds.'

'Fuck you,' Troy said, but without heat. 'That's Nell, the sister.' She was vigorously shaking her head. 'She was not going to believe her brother could do any wrong.'

'Does he have cameras anywhere else?' Decker asked. 'Like maybe in his studio?'

Kate gave him an approving look. 'Nap time served you well.'

'I gave him juice and a cookie,' Troy deadpanned, then his spine abruptly stiffened. 'What the hell? Stop. Oh my God. Quincy, stop tabbing.'

'I'm stopping, I'm stopping,' Quincy complained. They all stared at the screen. It was a different living room. 'This isn't here or the office. And who is that?' he asked as a man paced into camera range and crossed the room, shoving his hands through his hair and looking agitated. Panicked. Hysterical even. 'That looks like a CPD uniform.'

Decker got in close. 'Based on the photos of Macy on the book-shelves, I'd say that's a cop named Bob, Edwards's brother-in-law and Macy's adoptive father. Anybody recognize him?'

'No,' Adam answered, the only one from CPD in the room. 'But if we can send a still of his face to my lieutenant, she can pass it around. Somebody's got to know him. The photos on the bookshelf, there are some with a woman in them. Could be his wife. Get a copy of those, too.'

'In order to copy them, I have to figure out where he's keeping a hard copy of the tapes,' Quincy said. 'The file storage might not even be here on the premises. The surveillance system appears to be wireless. For now we may just have to snap a photo of this monitor.'

'For now, that'll do.' Decker watched as the man on screen continued to pace. 'Bob looks upset, but he hasn't reported Macy missing, has he? Or did he while I was sleeping?'

'No.' Kate frowned. 'Nobody's reported her missing. We have only the Amber Alert based on the photo Edwards left for Mallory. Why wouldn't Bob report it?'

'Or why wouldn't her mother?' Decker added, a bad feeling in his gut. 'Search the house, if you would, Quincy.'

Quincy tabbed slowly, viewing the study, the kitchen, the master bedroom. A child's room with the camera pointed straight at the bed.

'Oh God,' Decker breathed. A woman lay face up on the pink lace bedspread, her throat obscenely slit. Her eyes open and blank. The bedspread under her covered in blood. And a bullet hole in the center of her forehead. 'Gemma. Edwards's younger sister.'

'The kid's chair by the desk,' Kate said, pointing. 'It's kicked over. There was a struggle. That's where Macy was abducted. Can you rewind?'

Quincy did, and they watched in horror as a masked man came into the room, grabbed Macy from behind, and pressed a cloth against her mouth. She fought and kicked, knocking the chair over, but finally went limp. Seconds later, Gemma came in and there was a similar struggle, but the woman played possum, tricking the intruder into relaxing. Then she jumped to her feet and grabbed a lamp, but hesitated too long. She was overpowered but managed to rip the mask from the intruder's face. Edwards, his face plainly visible. Eyes huge, Gemma stared, then her expression became one of confused betrayal. Just before her throat was slit.

'That should be enough to convince Nell that her brother's not Mr Nice Guy,' Decker said. 'But just in case, can you look for the studio?'

Sure enough, there were cameras in the studio, externally and internally. The exterior of the house showed it to be isolated, with lots of trees surrounding it.

'This looks like the view through the back window of the newer Suzie films,' Adam confirmed. 'No neighbors. And no indication of its location. Dammit.'

'What about inside?' Decker pressed. 'Tab to the interior.'

The camera in the basement showed five children, tied and gagged. All still appeared to be breathing. One was Macy. The other four were adolescents.

Decker gripped the edge of Edwards's desk, his knees threatening to buckle in relief. 'They're still alive. All of them. Thank God. Where's Edwards?'

'Look.' Kate pointed. Quincy had tabbed past a few more rooms to a nice bedroom, where a man lay sleeping. He'd removed his shirt and his arm was bandaged – exactly where Diesel had made contact with his knife. 'Thank you, Diesel, for practicing your knife-throwing skills,' she murmured. 'What's that on the nightstand?'

'A prescription bottle,' Quincy said. 'But the camera doesn't zoom. I can't get a closer look at it. Some of the imaging software may be able to get some clarity, though.'

'It looks like a new bottle,' Decker said. 'Remember, Kate, that Mallory said she'd gotten a prescription filled for him at the Kroger right before he hit her with the car?'

'That bottle was found,' Troy said. 'It was an injectable antibiotic, not pills like that bottle. It had rolled into the street. One of the officers on the scene picked it up. It was written for Roxanne Edwards.'

'Maybe he wrote another one,' Decker said. 'If we call around to the pharmacies, find out if another prescription was filled for Roxanne, we'll at least know the direction he was traveling.'

'Very, very good,' Troy murmured. 'Maybe I'll try one of those naps, too. Where's the minivan? I didn't see it in any of the exterior shots.'

Quincy tabbed until he came to a garage where the minivan was parked. 'But the angle's wrong. I can't see the license plate.'

'Go back to Bob the cop's house,' Decker said. 'If Edwards stole the cruiser from the Kroger and parked it . . .' He frowned, thinking. 'It was a shopping mall where he left the cruiser, right?'

'It was,' Troy said. 'He either stole another car to get to Macy's or he walked. Either way, he may have taken the minivan from Bob's house. If we can get the license plate, we can get Bob's address, at least.'

Quincy had tabbed back to Bob's garage, a double garage where only one car was parked – a new Honda Accord. The camera was pointed at the car's hood. 'Still can't get the fucking license plate,' he growled. 'We could have tracked the address from that, too.'

'We still might be able to,' Troy said. 'Rewind to when Edwards got there.'

'No,' Decker said. 'Wait.' Because the door from the house had

567

opened and Bob the cop staggered out – in real time. He held a gun in his hand. 'Aw, shit. It's got a silencer on it. What the . . .' The bad feeling returned to his gut, amplifying by a million when Bob got in the Honda and closed his eyes, his expression one of freaked-out despair. 'Don't do it, Bob,' Decker muttered, half a plea, half a prayer. 'Just . . . don't.'

But Bob did do it. In full view of the camera, he put the gun in his mouth. And pulled the trigger.

For a moment there was nothing but silence around the monitor. 'Fuck,' Adam hissed. 'Goddammit.'

'Kate?' Troy's voice, filled with concern. 'You okay?'

Too late, Decker remembered Kate's nightmare. Jack's suicide. *Shit.* He turned to her just in time to hold her up. His arm went around her waist, taking her weight as her knees buckled, giving her time to regain her composure. Her face was pale, her lips parted and trembling. Her eyes wide and glassy with shock.

'Kate,' Decker whispered in her ear urgently, giving her a little shake. 'Not here.'

He knew she wouldn't want to break down in front of the others. The shake and the whisper were what she'd needed, and he watched as she pulled her composure back around her like a cloak. He held on to her waist until he felt her body stiffen and she stood on her own.

'God,' she whispered, still staring at the screen, where the cop's brains covered the interior of the Honda.

Troy gave Decker a knowing look before affecting a queasy grimace. 'Jesus, Quince, can you tab to a different room? I'm one second away from puking. And it won't be pretty.'

His movements jerky, Quincy moved the camera back to the sleeping Edwards.

'Thank you,' Troy said dramatically, then gave Kate's hand a quick squeeze.

She nodded her gratitude, and Decker was suddenly, fiercely glad that Troy was her partner. He knew that he himself couldn't be, not if he wanted to keep his sanity. *I'm way too close to her.* Way too close to falling for her.

568

But Troy . . . he'd watch Kate's back. So that was good.

Quincy huffed a mirthless chuckle. 'Sonofabitch is still asleep. I half expected him to wake up, just from the shock. Stupid, huh.'

'No,' Troy said kindly, not a hint of sarcasm. 'I've been on this job for nearly twenty years, and that's only the second time I've actually seen anyone blow his own brains out. It's not something we're likely to forget anytime soon.'

As a group, they stared at Edwards, everyone struggling to find their emotional footing. Because they had just seen a man die.

'We need to find him,' Decker said, 'before he wakes up. If we can surprise him . . .'

'But we still don't know where he is,' Adam snapped, frustrated. 'Either of them.'

Kate shuddered out a breath. 'But we have enough to convince someone who really is a good person to do the right thing,' she said grimly. 'Let's go see Nell.'

Cincinnati, Ohio,
Saturday 15 August, 7.50 P.M.

'Have you ever seen Kate do an interview?' Zimmerman asked as he and Decker stood in the observation area on the other side of the glass from the interview room. Kate and Troy sat at the interview table, reviewing their notes and finalizing strategy.

'Not a formal one like this,' Decker said.

'She's good. Of course, she has plenty of ammunition to wear down Ms Edwards's objections that her brother is a good boy, so this probably isn't a fair demonstration, but still.'

Zimmerman had decided that Kate and Troy should do the interview and Decker hadn't questioned the decision. He'd been so goddamn glad to leave Edwards's house.

It was the shock of seeing Bob the cop's suicide, live, in real time. The helplessness of the moments just before. And the pain of knowing that watching it had hurt Kate more than the rest of them put together.

But it was also that the pace of the last few days was getting to him. He'd pushed through the fatigue for two days, but in the last few hours he'd started craving the feel of a soft mattress cradling his body. And, of course, the feel of himself cradling Kate's body.

Soon. They were closing in on Edwards and soon they'd have him in custody. *Then we can sleep. And then we can have sex. Lots and lots of sex.* They'd make love, slow and sweet and . . . He needed to stop thinking about such things while standing next to their boss.

Decker pulled a chair close to the glass and sat down, forcing his mind back to the case. 'Quincy was able to make copies of the recorded security footage, and he and Adam will keep searching the tapes.'

'What we have is pretty damn powerful,' Zimmerman said. He seemed to hesitate for a moment, then sighed. 'I know about Kate's brother-in-law. I know she found his body.'

No, Decker thought. *She saw him pull the trigger, same as Bob the cop.*

'If she needs . . . anything,' Zimmerman went on, 'tell her it's okay. She probably won't tell me if she's having issues with her PTSD, but she might tell you.' He looked down at Decker, one brow raised. 'And that's *all* I have to say on the subject.'

Decker understood that 'the subject' meant both Kate's PTSD and the fact that Zimmerman was aware of their budding relationship. 'I'll let her know,' he said mildly.

The door to the observation room opened and Deacon Novak let himself in. 'Respectfully requesting permission to come aboard, sir,' he said, saluting Zimmerman smartly.

Zimmerman sighed. 'Deacon . . .'

'I'm not near the crime scene. I'm not going after Edwards.' Deacon's attitude fell away, leaving his face completely readable. He was angry and scared, but determined as well. 'Please. I just need to know. To hear.'

Zimmerman sighed again. 'Okay. But one outburst . . .'

'And you'll have my white head on a platter. Yeah, Kate told me. Um . . . Scarlett's outside. She wants to play in the sandbox, too.'

Zimmerman rolled his eyes and opened the door. 'Come in, Detective. Anyone else wanting to "play in the sandbox"?'

Scarlett grinned at him as she walked in. 'No, sir. Thank you, sir.' She and Deacon arranged a few more chairs and they all sat down to watch. 'Last time I saw Kate in action, she was in there with Alice. Good riddance and may she burn in hell,' she added in a mutter.

'On that we can agree,' Zimmerman said dryly. 'I guess you and Deacon deserve to be in on the end of it, since you were there at the beginning. And speaking of beginnings, I'm surprised you didn't bring Marcus O'Bannion along.'

Because Scarlett and Marcus had been the ones to unravel the traffickers from the outside while Decker had been working from the inside.

Scarlett grinned at Zimmerman again. 'Oh, Marcus wanted to come, but I didn't want to push my luck.'

Zimmerman snorted. '*Now* you don't want to push your luck? After all this?'

She winked at their boss. 'Well, Marcus did say he'd settle for an exclusive interview when all this is over.'

'Which will hopefully be soon,' Deacon said. 'Where is Nell Edwards?'

'In another room,' Decker said. 'They'll bring her in when Kate and Troy are ready.'

Deacon stared through the glass at Kate. 'I heard about Bob the cop. She okay?'

'What do you think?' Decker countered.

Deacon sighed. 'Right. Do we have an ID on Bob yet?'

'No,' Zimmerman answered. 'Nobody reported the gunshot because he used the silencer. Somewhere in the city a cop's sitting dead in his car. I don't get why he did it, though. He never reported Macy missing. Does he think she's dead?'

'Maybe,' Decker said, because he and Kate had discussed this as they'd driven from Edwards's house into the city. 'But Mallory said that Edwards gave Macy to his sister and her husband. Why would he need to do that? Did they try to adopt and couldn't? Macy would have been three years old at the time. How did they explain that all of a sudden they had a kid? Did she go to school? Nell will know something because she's in a few of the photos in

Bob's living room. She and Gemma and Macy. Kate's going to ask her about it.'

'Gemma isn't a common name,' Scarlett said, 'even though Bob is. Have we run a Robert, wife Gemma, through the CPD database?'

Zimmerman nodded. 'Your lieutenant did. But nada. We found Gemma Edwards in the birth records, but there's no marriage record for her, so maybe she and Bob were common law. They never filed taxes jointly. Gemma never filed at all.'

Decker's phone buzzed in his pocket. He checked the incoming text and Zimmerman did the same. 'From Adam,' Decker said. 'They tracked down the prescription Edwards picked up a few hours ago. It was filled at a CVS nowhere near his house. And the prescribing doctor was Nell Edwards.'

'Physician assistants can write scripts in certain situations,' Deacon said thoughtfully. 'If she called it in, she knows he's hurt. If not, he's forging her name.'

Kate and Troy were also reading from their phones. Kate looked up then and pointed upward, so Zimmerman turned up the volume for the room's speaker. 'We're having her escorted in now,' Kate said.

'You got the text about the prescription?' Zimmerman asked.

'Yep, we both did,' Troy answered for them. 'So we know the general vicinity where he is. Hopefully we can push Nell for more.'

'Cross your fingers and toes,' Kate said. 'Showtime, everyone.'

Twenty-eight

Cincinnati, Ohio,
Saturday 15 August, 8.05 P.M.

Nell Edwards was about fifty years old, but Kate thought she looked much older. Most of that was worry. And carefully banked rage. Hopefully she and Troy could use that rage to their advantage.

Nell narrowed her eyes when she saw Troy at the table. 'You again.'

'Yes, ma'am,' Troy said respectfully. 'I'm Special Agent Troy, in case you don't remember my name. This is my partner, Special Agent Coppola.'

'I remember your name,' Nell said coldly. 'I remember that you and your band of apes barged in and destroyed my office, telling lies.'

'We had a warrant, ma'am,' Troy said. 'Now we have a little more information.'

Kate took the lead, as they'd discussed. 'We have some videos we'd like you to watch.' She and Troy had carefully lined the videos up, hoping they wouldn't have to show all of them before Nell's resistance was chipped away. If she really was good, as Mallory had said, it seemed cruel to start by showing the video of her little sister being murdered. 'This was taken this afternoon, in the hospital.'

Nell's mouth pinched when she saw Mallory's battered face on the screen. 'That girl is delusional. She needs help, not for people to buy into her lies.'

'Just listen,' Kate said gently, and hit play. It was the part of the interview where Mallory had simply come forth, talking, telling all.

573

'Um . . . he's got a sister, Nell. She's nice, but she thinks I'm bad. I don't think she knows about him.'

'She's right,' Nell said. 'I believe she's a liar.'

'I only started there so that you'd know that Mallory believes you to be good,' Kate said. 'I'd like you to remember that.' She brought up the next video. It was one that Quincy Taylor had found when he'd rewound the view into the office at the Edwards practice.

Nell gasped. 'That's my office. Where did you get that?'

'In your brother's home office. He has cameras all over his own house, including the bedroom and bathroom that Mallory uses. He also has cameras in your practice and in your home.' Kate hit play. 'This was taken at your practice last night.'

Another gasp. 'He's . . . hurt. How did he get hurt? He didn't call me.' She grimaced as her brother began to stitch himself up. 'That's a bad cut. He should have called me.'

'He'd just attacked a doctor behind the free clinic,' Kate said.

'That is absurd!' Nell stood up, shaking. 'I won't hear any-more!'

'You will *sit down*,' Kate ordered in a voice she rarely used, but which always got results. Just like it did now, because Nell carefully lowered herself back to her seat. From the corner of her eye Kate watched Troy bend his mouth, impressed. 'Thank you,' she said to Nell.

'You're crazy,' Nell whispered. 'You're both crazy. I'm calling my lawyer.'

But she wouldn't, Kate knew. She wouldn't call her lawyer and she wouldn't walk out. Not yet. After years of dealing with people, as both an MP and an FBI agent, Kate could see that Nell was a woman easily cowed. Easily manipulated. It was probably how her brother had fooled her for so long, at least partially.

'You're not under arrest, ma'am,' Kate said politely. 'You're welcome to call your attorney if you like, but I don't have to wait until he or she gets here to continue.' She pulled out a few still photos and spread them on the table in front of Nell. 'These were taken at the ER last night. The victim is Dr Dani Novak.'

Nell's expression became horrified. 'Dani? We just hired her for the clinic. She was hurt? Who would *do* that? She wouldn't hurt a flea.'

'That's what I'm trying to tell you, ma'am,' Kate said. 'Dani was attacked last night as she left the clinic, but her attacker didn't know that someone was watching over her. That someone threw a knife at the attacker's right arm. The attacker took the knife out of his arm and stabbed Dani with it. She'll live, but only because the man watching out for her thought quickly and got her help. That man's knife made the wound that you just saw your brother stitching up.'

'That is absurd,' Nell said again, but her voice trembled.

Nell was second-guessing herself now, Kate could tell. She pressed harder. 'Why didn't he call you? Why didn't he ask for help? Why did he forge your name on a script for antibiotics?' She showed Nell her phone. Adam had obtained a copy of the script Edwards had used.

Nell stared at the document. 'There's an explanation. There has to be. That's not my handwriting. And the script is for Roxy, my sister-in-law.'

'Who is now in ICU.'

Nell rolled her eyes. 'She drank herself to death. I told Remy she needed help.'

'Why do you call your brother Remy?' Kate asked, genuinely interested.

A shrug. 'His name is Brandon. Kids called him Brandy, just to be snotty and cruel. Our father called him that too, to belittle him. So I told my brother that Remy was the best make of brandy. It was our little inside joke.' She lifted her chin defiantly. 'I *raised* that boy, Agent Coppola. There is no *way* I'll believe any of the things you've said to me.'

'I hear you,' Kate said. 'And I hope Mallory's assessment of you is valid, because I'm about to show you something that I'd hoped not to have to show.' She cued up the clip of Mallory at twelve years old. 'This is very serious, ma'am. I wouldn't show it to you ... I wouldn't possess it if it weren't so serious. My job at the FBI is stopping human traffickers, specifically those who force their victims into sexual slavery.'

Nell's eyes blazed. 'You're accusing my brother of being a sexual deviant. I've had enough!' She stood up and Kate rose with her, leaning in until they were nose to nose.

'I swear, ma'am, if you do not sit down, I will *sit* you down. This video is of a child being raped. And it's not the only one. You. Sit. Down.' She stared Nell down and the woman sank into her chair again, tears in her eyes.

'Why are you doing this?' she whispered. 'Why this witch hunt against my brother?'

Kate hit play and sat back, her arms folded over her chest. 'Watch.'

Nell turned away from the screen. 'I will not. That's disgusting.'

'That's Mallory,' Kate said coldly.

A scoffing sound. 'I'm . . . not surprised. She's a disturbed child. I can see her in a relationship with a grown man. She's too . . . alluring.'

Kate blinked at her. *Wow.* No wonder her brother had managed to fool her all these years. 'Look at the man, Miss Edwards. Look at him.'

Nell kept her eyes averted. Kate lifted the laptop and shoved it up to her face, forcing her to look at the screen. 'Open your eyes. Look. At. Him.'

Nell did, her mouth dropping open in horror. 'She . . . she seduced him.'

Kate put the laptop down carefully, because she wanted to throw it against the fucking wall. 'You are . . . Mallory was wrong. You are *not* good. You are not good at all.'

Nell lifted her chin, but it trembled. 'May I go now, Agent Coppola?'

'Two more clips,' Kate said. She hadn't wanted to show Nell these, but now . . . *Now I do. I want her to feel some serious pain.* She cued up the clip of Bob the cop coming into his garage. 'You know this man?'

'Of course. He's my brother-in-law. Why do you have this video?'

'I told you. Your brother has cameras everywhere. Including your bedroom, but that's not important now. Watch.'

Kate watched Nell's face because she couldn't watch the screen.

576

Not again. It had nearly destroyed her the first time. Thanks to Decker and Troy, she hadn't fallen apart in front of her colleagues.

I'll fall apart later.

'Oh my God.' Nell began breathing heavily. 'Oh my God. No. No!' She flinched at the moment Bob pulled the trigger, a sob barreling out of her mouth. 'Why? Why did he do this? Why would you make me see this?'

'Because I had to get your attention,' Kate said flatly. 'And because I had to watch hours of your brother raping a twelve-year-old girl.'

'He didn't. She seduced him. My brother is a good man!' She screamed the final words, her hands stretching into claws as she went for Kate's face.

Kate grabbed her wrists, holding the woman a few inches away. Thankfully Troy had leapt to his feet the moment Nell had started screaming, and he pulled the woman back, none too gently, then cuffed her hands behind her back and held her shoulders down so that she didn't jump out of her chair.

'Jesus,' he said, breathing hard. 'They're all fucking nuts.'

Kate shook her head. 'And she was supposed to be the sane one.' The door opened and Decker rushed in, his handsome face dark with fury.

'Do you need assistance, Agent Coppola?' he asked.

Kate smiled at him. 'No, but thank you, Agent Davenport. Oh, Davenport, I'd like to introduce you to Miss Nell Edwards. Her brother, Dr Brandon Edwards, is the one who tried to have you murdered while you were in the hospital.'

Decker had calmed himself while Kate made the tongue-in-cheek introduction, as she hoped he would. 'I'd like to say it was a pleasure, ma'am,' he drawled, 'but I'd be a damn liar.'

Nell stared wildly at them. 'You're all insane.' She looked back at the screen, which had ended with Bob the cop's brains all over the interior of his Honda, then closed her eyes. 'I can't believe any of this. Why would Bob do that? Why? He and Gemma have a good life. They have a daughter.' She stiffened. 'Where is Gemma? Where is Macy?'

'Ah,' Kate said. 'Segue.' She saw Decker tilt his head toward the table, asking if she needed him to stay. She gave him a nod and waited until he sat down. 'So, Nell, tell me about Bob and Gemma. Bob was a cop, we understand.'

Nell's eyes darted between Kate and Decker. Troy still stood behind her, ready to restrain her further if he needed to. 'Yes. He worked in the main office. He managed the dispatch office.'

Which explains a lot, Kate thought. 'So he'd see all incoming calls and be able to follow up on arrests.' *And warn his brother-in-law when young women called for help, like Mallory did today.*

'I guess so. You need to let me go. I have to find Gemma. I need to tell her. What if she finds him like that?'

'What is Bob's last name?' Kate asked.

Nell froze. 'I'm not telling you. I need to go. To find my sister and my niece.'

'Your niece has been abducted by your brother. We have video of that too,' Kate snapped. 'We've had an Amber Alert out since mid-afternoon. So maybe you could help us find her instead of calling us liars and standing in our way.'

Nell paled. 'Macy's gone? Abducted? How?'

'By. Your. Brother,' Kate repeated, leaning into the woman's space. 'And you're permitted to treat live people in your practice. Oh my God, woman! Wise up!'

'You are mean,' Nell said, sounding like a child now. 'Mean and awful and I'm going to report you to your supervisor.'

'Go ahead, he's behind the glass,' Kate said with a jerk of her head toward where Zimmerman watched. She drew a breath. Calmed her voice. 'Miss Edwards, your niece has been abducted and your sister is dead. Please don't make me show you those tapes too.'

Nell straightened in her chair, pulling her dignity around herself despite being cuffed. 'I don't believe you. I want to call my lawyer.'

Kate huffed, exasperated. 'And you are still not under arrest.'

'Then arrest me!' Nell snapped. 'I want my lawyer.'

Kate shrugged. 'I thought this would be easy. Because I thought you'd be a good person. All right, I'll arrest you so that you can call your lawyer, but watch this first.' She cued up the clip of Macy's abduction and Gemma's murder and hit play.

Nell, to her credit, did watch, horrified fascination on her face. When the masked man came in to drug Macy, she made a sound of real pain. And when Gemma pulled the hat off Edwards's face, she began to weep. 'Oh Remy, what have you done? What have you done?'

Kate hit pause. 'He slits her throat and then he shoots her in the head. That's why your brother-in-law took his own life. He found your sister's body. Do you really need to see that? Because I'll show it to you, simply because I do not like you, ma'am.'

Nell shook her head, sobbing. Rocking in her chair. 'Why are you doing this to me? To us?'

'Mary and Joseph,' Kate whispered, realizing that the woman would not believe until she saw it with her own eyes. 'Here. See for yourself.' She hit play.

Nell didn't breathe, flinching at the shot to Gemma's head. 'Remy,' she whispered. 'Why?'

'You can ask him yourself once we've rescued your niece and the other four kids he abducted,' Kate said, then showed the video of Macy and the children tied up in the basement. 'Your brother is in this house.' She spread stills from the studio on the table. 'Where is it?'

'I don't know. I really don't. If I knew, I'd tell you, for Macy, but I don't know.'

Kate wasn't sure if she believed the woman or not when she said she didn't know. But she did believe that Nell would go on protecting her brother. She caught Decker's eye, saw he thought the same. 'What is your brother-in-law's name?' she asked quietly.

'Seifert,' Nell sobbed. 'Robert Seifert.'

'And his address?' Kate pressed. 'We need to retrieve their bodies.'

Nell made a keening noise, like an animal in pain. She gave the address, rocking herself.

'Ma'am,' Decker said, and Nell looked up. 'Did Bob and Gemma drive a gray minivan?'

Nell's eyes were startled. 'Yes. A Chevy Traverse. It was a gift from Remy for their anniversary.'

'Thank you.' Decker stood up. 'I am sorry for your loss. But for you to accuse a twelve-year-old girl of seducing your brother . . . You, ma'am, are not a good person.'

He turned on his heel, leaning on his walking stick as he left the room. Kate and Troy followed, the three of them collapsing against the wall when they got to the hallway. Kate was trembling, but so were Troy and Decker. Some rage, some nerves, some the release of adrenaline.

Zimmerman joined them, pulling the door closed so that Nell couldn't hear them speak. 'I thought she'd tell you where the house was,' he said.

'She might not know,' Troy said, 'or she might have blocked it out. She seems comfortable with denial.'

'Run Robert Seifert through the DMV,' Decker said. 'It's a Chevy. Brand new.'

Kate could feel new energy bubbling up through her bones as she caught his train of thought. 'It might have OnStar. We can track it through the company.'

Decker met her eyes and nodded. 'Exactly.'

'And we can get a head start,' Troy added, 'by going to the drugstore where he picked up his prescription.'

'I'll have backup follow you,' Zimmerman said. 'Go.'

Cincinnati, Ohio,
Saturday 15 August, 9.35 P.M.

The worst part of any op, Decker thought, was waiting for it to start. The atmosphere in the van was tense, but at least it wasn't grim. They'd tracked the gray minivan with relative speed, although every minute they'd waited at the drugstore where Edwards had filled his prescription had felt like a year. They were still a few miles away, even with Troy driving like he was on a Formula One track.

Which had made for something of a bumpy ride.

The house belonged, ironically enough, to Bob Seifert, Edwards's brother-in-law. Or at least it was Bob's name on the deed and the mortgage and the bank account from which the mortgage payments were drawn. Whether or not he had known about the house – or what went on there – wasn't clear and might never be.

Because Bob had taken the coward's way out. Decker still hadn't processed that. He'd seen people die, too many times. He'd seen men's heads explode when hit by enemy fire. But today had been the first time he'd seen anyone take his own life like that. *Unlike Kate.*

He looked across the van, where Kate sat on the floor, legs stretched out in front of her. She was quietly knitting and had been for the last forty minutes, but every now and then she'd stiffen and suck in a breath, close her eyes and visibly regulate her breathing.

Decker would tap his foot against hers and she'd smile at him. It wasn't her real smile, but it seemed to anchor her enough to control her breathing. He fully expected her nightmares to continue making a regular appearance for a good long time.

Hell, he'd probably have nightmares too. And then they could wear each other out enough to hopefully go back to sleep. The thought brightened his mood considerably.

He glanced at the monitor mounted to the ceiling of the van. It was the feed from Edwards's camera system. Quincy had come through, finding a way to hijack the wireless feed and route it their way. The screen was filled with Edwards sleeping.

They crossed their fingers that he'd still be sleeping by the time they finally got there.

'We're coming up to the turnoff,' Troy called back. 'Is everybody suited up?'

A smattering of yeses sounded back – just Decker, Kate, Adam, and Triplett, who'd been relieved of guarding Mallory by one of the men who'd been on duty in the parking garage at the safe house. Zimmerman had wanted to keep the team small and tight – and staffed by people he knew he could trust.

With Bob the cop out of the picture, they were safer from leaks than they'd been with him on the job. But they were all very aware that a man like Edwards didn't operate for as long as he had without serious allies in CPD. Or maybe even the FBI. Until they knew for sure, Zimmerman wasn't going to risk the safety of five children.

Even the SWAT team that was on their way to cover them had been hand-picked. They'd left the city immediately after OnStar had provided the minivan's location. Zimmerman had held them back, just in case the drugstore where Edwards had gotten his meds wasn't on the way. So they were coming. Hopefully they were driving like the wind.

Kate put her knitting aside and began checking her weapons, including the rifle she now slung over her back. Just like the night she and Decker had met. She scrambled up on her knees and pressed a button on the communications console on the van's back wall directly below the monitor.

'Quincy, can you do a final sweep through the house, interior and exterior? I want to be sure I have my bearings.'

She'd find herself a tree to climb up as soon as they got there, a tree that would give her a direct line of sight to – hopefully – all the house's exits. They were hoping they could sneak the children out before Edwards woke up, and then restrain him in his sleep, but just in case he did wake up, they needed to be ready.

Because the man had shown a nasty willingness to throw ricin around, and they didn't want to have to rely on luck and cooperative winds again just to stay alive. Plus, they had no doubt that he'd kill those kids without a second of hesitation or an ounce of remorse.

The monitor above them flicked from room to room, all empty except the room where Edwards was sleeping and the basement where the five kids still lay tied and gagged. And still terrified, the three who were awake. Two of them had their eyes closed, hopefully asleep, because it was now too dark to be sure their chests were moving. *Let them be alive. Please let them be alive.*

'You need me to go through it again, Kate?' Quincy asked through the console. He was still in Edwards's house.

'Yes please,' she said. 'One more look around the outside.'

Quincy repeated the loop as the van began to slow. Troy made a turn onto a side road that led up to the house and brought the vehicle to a stop.

'This is as far as I want to go until we're sure he doesn't have the road booby-trapped. Kate, Adam? You two ready?'

They were the best shots of the group, so they were tapped to do the recon.

'As I'll ever be,' Kate said. She and Adam prepared to leave the van. Kate checked her weapons a final time and gave Decker a last smile. 'Be back in a jif.'

But she went no further, because Quincy had moved the camera back to where Edwards had been sleeping.

The bed was empty.

'Oh fuck,' Decker muttered. The monster was awake.

Cincinnati, Ohio,
Saturday 15 August, 9.40 P.M.

He staggered into the bathroom, splashing water on his face, trying to wake up completely as the alarm continued to whoop obnoxiously.

Someone is here. Someone had triggered the alarm at the end of the driveway. He gave his left cheek a stinging slap with his good hand, then tried the same with his right, relieved when the arm moved more fluidly. The antibiotic had started to work.

He ran to the studio where he did all his post-production editing and brought up his surveillance system, starting with the cameras at the end of the driveway.

A van. There was a black, windowless van sitting there, its engine idling. *Fuck.*

He changed views, checking the basement, and some of his tension subsided. The kids were still there, exactly as he'd left them. This house had not been breached.

But there was a van in his drive and that meant someone had figured it out. How had they known? How had they known to come *here*? Someone had told. His pulse started to race and he changed cameras to the one in his home office.

And his heart simply stopped. A man was in his office, sitting at his goddamn desk. Staring at his computer. From this camera angle he had no idea what the man was looking at, but did it matter? There were people in his house. *Cops.* Cops were in his house. Touching his things. He roared his outrage, tabbing the camera view from room to room.

They were in every room in his house except the basement, but they hadn't tripped the house's alarm. How the fuck had they not tripped the alarm? And then he knew.

'Mallory,' he said quietly. The girl was going to die, so damn painfully.

But he had to deal with the assholes on his property first.

He drew a breath and switched views to the office at the practice. Someone had been there too. File drawers were open and empty and all the computers had been removed.

They knew. Everyone knew.

Macy would be the first kid to die. *Let Mallory live with that.*

He switched to Gemma's house. Her body was no longer on the bed. His hand shaking, he picked up the phone and dialed Bob's cell. It rang and rang and then went to voicemail. Bob never let his phone go to voicemail. *Especially when I call.*

They'd gotten him, too. And Bob was such a spineless pussy, he'd probably spilled the beans right away. But Bob didn't know about this place. Nobody had known. How were they here? How had they found him?

It didn't matter. He needed to get away.

Just breathe, he commanded himself. *You've got leverage. Lots of leverage.*

But few weapons. He'd left everything back at home, in his basement. He had two guns – his own nine millimeter and the service weapon that had belonged to the cop he'd shot back at the Kroger.

Just focus on getting the hell out of here. Get the kids and get out of here.

He started to move, then froze. His monitor was changing views, and he wasn't doing it.

Someone had taken control of his surveillance system. *The guy sitting at my desk.*

Locking his jaw, he tapped a few keys. His self-destruct code. His screen went bright white then immediately dark. He couldn't see the van anymore, but they couldn't see him either.

Get the kids, he said to himself, *and then get the fuck out of here.*

Cincinnati, Ohio,
Saturday 15 August, 9.43 P.M.

'Quincy, what are you doing?' Kate asked as the monitor began cycling through Edwards's other properties, her heart sinking because she already knew the answer.

They'd been made.

'That's not me,' Quincy said through the console. 'He's taken control. I can't take it again until he lets go of his mouse or his keyboard or whatever he's using.' The monitor stopped on Macy's bedroom, Gemma's body no longer on the bed. The ME had taken her away.

The monitor went back to the studio house. 'That's me controlling now,' Quincy said, just as it blazed bright, then went dark. 'He's pulled the plug. We're blind.'

'Hold on,' Troy said grimly, and the van took off like a shot, bouncing them around like bobbers in a stream as the tires hit every damn pothole in the road. 'If he knows we're coming, we might as well get there as fast as possible.'

'At least if we're blind,' Decker said grimly, 'then he is too.'

'There's that,' Kate allowed. 'Okay, Troy, new plan. I'm going to find a tree with a view into the garage. He'll try to get away and he'll probably have at least one kid with him.'

'It'll be Macy,' Decker said. 'He has to know Mallory helped us.'

'Agreed.' Kate nodded. 'And that's the best of the worst, because she's small. She won't be the shield one of the older kids would have been. If I get a shot, I'm taking it. Okay?'

'Okay,' Troy said, swinging up to the house and pulling onto the grass. He did a quick three-point turn so that the front of the van was facing the road and the back was pointing towards the back of the house. He killed the van's lights, interior and exterior. 'Adam, you and I are going around back to break in through one of the basement windows. Other than Kate, I may be the only one skinny enough to get through those windows. I'll lift the kids out, hopefully before he gets down there. Quince, get us some ambulances. Have them wait at the end of the drive for our signal, because I don't want them driving into a firefight. Trip, you and Decker stay here. Trip, be ready to take any kids we're able to bring out through the window and put them in the van. Decker, you're the driver. We'll get the kids and get out. But if I give you the signal, you leave with as many kids as we can save, got it? Do not stick around and wait for us if I tell you to go. It means we're compromised. We save as many as we can. Everybody got it?'

To a person they nodded.

'Go,' Troy said grimly. 'Don't get killed.'

Kate took a last look at Decker. He was staring hard at her. *Be safe.*

She nodded. *You too.* Then she took off for the trees, hoping for the best.

Cincinnati, Ohio,
Saturday 15 August, 9.45 P.M.

Decker watched Kate run away from him, her rifle slung over her back. In less than a minute she'd disappeared up a tree with an agility he should have expected.

She'd been that graceful when she'd ridden him in bed. He prayed they'd make it out so that she could do it again.

He and Trip didn't speak, both of them on edge. From the driver's seat, Decker could see the front face of the house, including the garage door, which opened as they'd expected.

'He won't be able to start the minivan,' he said quietly to Trip. 'The OnStar security feature allows them to disable the ignition. Be prepared for some—'

An enraged roar came from the garage.

'Anger,' Decker finished.

'I've got her!' It was Edwards, and he was yelling. 'I have the cop's kid and I will kill her without blinking.'

Decker met Trip's eyes in the side mirror. Trip was pointing to the back corner of the house, where Adam had a bound teenager under one arm. Trip took off running towards Adam, neither of them visible to Edwards from the garage.

'*I am not coming out!*' Edwards screamed. 'I know you've got rifles out there. If you want this kid alive, you'll escort me out of here. You will be my cover. And you'll give me your van. I am not kidding! Otherwise the cop's kid dies and the rest die next. I have nothing to lose.'

And that was true.

Kate couldn't make her shot unless Edwards came out of the garage.

Trip laid the first teen in the back of the van with a tenderness and care that came as no surprise. 'I heard him,' he said. 'What're you gonna do?'

'I'm going to try to lure him out,' Decker said in a low whisper. 'You go back and tell Adam and Troy to hurry.'

He took the keys from the ignition. If Edwards managed to make a break for it, at least he wouldn't be able to drive away. *Not without taking me out first.* Then, drawing his gun in his left hand, and gripping his walking stick in his right, he edged across the house. He paused when he came to the open garage door, then peeked around the corner. Edwards stood next to the inoperable minivan, a bound and gagged Macy held against him, his left arm around the child's middle. He seemed to have regained some of the use of his right arm, because he had a good grip on the gun he held at Macy's head.

Macy was alive, but her eyes were glazed and glassy and she didn't even blink at Decker. She was either drugged, frozen with fear, or catatonic. *Or maybe all of the above.*

'I see you, Davenport,' Edwards said with a sneer. 'They sent their cripple? Really?'

'Really,' Decker said evenly. 'Everybody else was camped out in your house, playing with your toys, while I found this place. They're on their way.'

'Right,' Edwards scoffed. 'That bitch Coppola probably has her rifle trained on the door here, waiting for me to step outside.'

As if by design, the light in the garage door opener timed out and went dark.

Edwards laughed. 'Not going to be so easy to see me now, is it?'

Decker backed up a few inches, leaning the stick against the outer wall of the house long enough to depress the talk button on the radio hanging on his tactical vest. He grabbed the stick and leaned forward again, until he could see Edwards.

Now the others could hear and hopefully plan accordingly.

'Considering she's not here, it's immaterial.'

Edwards laughed again. 'You're a good liar. And that's a compliment coming from me.'

'Thank you. But I'm not lying. I figured out where you were and took off at warp speed. I told the others to follow.'

'Uh-huh. And just how did you figure out where I was?'

He's curious, Decker thought. That was good. And not completely unexpected. The man was a total narcissist. 'I'm an *accountant*, Edwards. I follow the goddamn money.'

'Huh. You're really an accountant? I thought that was a cover.'

'No, the bodyguard for drug-dealing, human-trafficking sociopathic killers part was a cover. I've got my CPA and everything, for real. I'm a card-carrying forensic accountant, so I started combing through your brother-in-law's accounts after we found he'd shot himself in the fucking head – which is really messy, by the way. He ruined the inside of the Honda that I'm guessing you bought for him because he wasn't making enough money to buy it on his own.'

Decker was talking off the top of his head. *Just need to give the others time to get the kids out of the basement.* But he'd just told a little girl that her father had killed himself. *Dammit.* He hoped Macy was too drugged to understand or remember what he'd just said.

'Ah, fuck,' Edwards spat. 'Bob killed himself? Well, that's better than getting caught. He could have spilled some serious secrets.'

'Yeah, but his social security number told secrets of its own. Like the houses he owned. Which included this one.'

Which wasn't true, but it occurred to him that they could have done it that way. Maybe even more easily than the whole OnStar tracking biz. So it apparently also made enough sense for Edwards to believe.

Edwards was quiet for several seconds, but Decker could no longer see his face. 'Well, they do say the geeks shall inherit the earth,' he said finally. 'Well done, Davenport. Now take me to your van, or I will splatter this child's brains all over these walls.'

From the corner of his eye, Decker saw movement in the trees. Just a flash of pale skin. Kate had jumped out of the tree. Changing her position to better attack.

Good girl. 'If I do what you say, I want you to leave Macy here with me.'

'Oh no,' Edwards said. 'You're coming with me. You'll be driving. I will continue to hold this pretty little girl just like this.'

'Okay. Just don't hurt her. Please.'

'Drop your gun. Kick it this way.'

Decker hesitated, then obeyed. 'There. Now you have my gun. It's the only one I'm carrying. You want to frisk me?'

Edwards chuckled. 'You're funny. I like that.' He kicked the gun under the minivan. 'Just in case you get second thoughts.'

Buddy, if I get second thoughts, I don't need a gun. I can break your neck like a fucking twig. But Decker didn't say that. 'That was my favorite gun,' he complained instead.

'Let me see the keys to the van,' Edwards snapped.

Decker held the key ring between his thumb and forefinger and jingled it. 'Where are we going?'

'I'll tell you when we get out of here.'

Decker laughed bitterly. 'You don't know where you're going because you got no place to hide. But that's fine. I guess you'll figure it out after I help you get away and then you kill me.'

'Aw, don't be like that,' Edwards mocked. 'Cover me, Davenport. I don't believe you're here alone, and if your bitch *is* out there, I don't want her to get a clear aim at anything vital. You're my shield, big guy, so spread those arms. Make yourself useful.'

Decker obeyed, extending one arm wide. 'I need the other hand for the cane. I just got out of a coma, you know,' he added sarcastically. 'No thanks to you.'

'Yeah, I know,' Edwards said, sounding disgruntled. 'No tricks.'

Decker looked over Edwards's head to see the door from the garage into the house creep open and Troy slip through. He had his gun drawn and pointed at Edwards.

But Troy could see the hold Edwards had on Macy. Edwards's finger was poised on the trigger, and the smallest twitch meant Macy would be dead. Being on the receiving end of a head shot could result in one hell of a twitch. So Troy stayed back. But he was there. Which meant all the kids were out and safe. Decker stepped back, giving Edwards just enough room to edge out of the garage. He used his body to guide Edwards so that the man's back was to the far side of his house.

Where Kate had crept. She showed herself to Decker then stepped back into the shadows, waiting for her opportunity. He needed to get Edwards's gun away from Macy's head so she could take her shot.

His hand clenched on the brass grip of his borrowed walking stick as a plan started forming in his mind. He hoped Kate was watching, then smiled to himself. Of course she was. She'd probably thought of the plan before he had.

He stumbled on purpose, pretending to overextend the arm that held the stick so he could keep his balance. Shifting his grip, he spun the stick, gripping with both hands as he swung upward, like it was a golf club. The brass ball at the end caught Edwards squarely on his elbow, and Decker followed through, using momentum to drive Edwards's arm up in an arc, taking the gun along for the ride.

Edwards screamed, stumbling for real, and Decker used the moment to snatch Macy from his left arm. Covering the child with his body, he twisted away, the stick still firmly clutched in one hand. He swung again, hitting Edwards in the back of the head, knocking him to his knees.

With Macy tucked tight against his chest, Decker had time to take only a few steps toward their van before a gun fired twice, both shots hitting him in the back. His vest absorbed them, but it still *hurt*. Swearing at the pain, he misstepped and staggered, his knees hitting the sidewalk pavers with an audible crack. Throwing his weight to one side, he landed on his shoulder so that he didn't squash Macy. Then he tucked his head down and gritted his teeth for the next shot.

Gunfire exploded in his ears. But none of it hit him.

It was over in the space of three heartbeats, the resulting silence deafening. Groaning, he rolled to his back to find Trip standing over him, bending to take Macy from his arms. Decker let the girl go and flopped both arms wide.

He hurt. All over. But he wasn't dead. Neither was Macy. So that was good, right?

He blinked up at the sky, trying to get his bearings. 'Kate!' he called. 'You okay?'

He exhaled, relieved when Kate's face appeared above his, her brown eyes filled with worry. 'If you say you're okay, I'm going to smack you,' she snapped.

He laughed up at her. 'I think I cracked my kneecaps, and my back just spasmed. I hurt all over. Does that satisfy you?'

Her hands shook as she brushed the hair from his face. 'Yes.'

'You're a hard woman, Kate.' He turned his face into her palm and let himself relax. Let her pet him. 'You got him?'

She relaxed too, her hands no longer shaking. 'I did. And Troy did. And Trip, too. But you got him first.' She grinned, her mood suddenly perking up. 'Nice moves with the walking stick, Decker. You went all Kung Fu Panda on his ass.'

Adrenaline had hit, leaving them both almost giddy. 'I most certainly did not,' he said, affronted. 'Bruce Lee maybe. Or even Jackie Chan. But no pandas, especially cartoon ones.'

'Hey, pandas are badass, Decker. They can eat your face.'

He gave her a hot look that made her catch her breath. 'I'd rather eat—'

'Decker!' She covered his mouth with her hand, looking up because Troy had joined them.

'Children, children,' Troy said mildly. 'Decker, do you need an ambulance? We've got several en route for the *actual* children.'

'God, no. No more ambulances for me.' He shuddered, suddenly sobered by the thought. 'Just help me sit up. The pain's already passing.' Which was a total lie, but neither of them called him on it.

Kate helped him sit, and he closed his eyes until the world stopped spinning. 'I could sleep for a week, but no ambulances.'

Triplett jogged over to pull him to his feet, and Decker reached for the stick to help keep his balance, but checked the movement even before Troy shook his head.

'Sorry. The stick's evidence now. Besides, it's covered in Professor Asshole's blood. You don't want it anymore.'

Kate put her arm around Decker's waist. 'I'll hold you up,' she said quietly, and he had no doubt that she could.

'I'll take you up on it.' Because he really just needed her hands on him. 'The kids?'

'The teenagers are physically okay,' Troy answered, relieved. 'They're scared and dehydrated and hungry. But they're in emotional shock. Lots of therapy in their future.'

'I think Macy's in physical shock,' Trip said, troubled. 'Adam's got her.'

Decker looked over at the van, where Adam had cut the bonds from Macy's hands and feet and was gently removing the tape from her mouth.

'I think Edwards gave her something so she wouldn't fight him,' he called over. 'Her heart's beating way too slowly. How long before the medics get here?'

'They were waiting at the end of the drive, like we told them to,' Troy said. 'I gave them the all-clear when the smoke cleared, so a minute tops.'

'Good.' Adam cradled the little girl in his arms. 'They need to tend to her first.'

Decker turned to the body slumped barely a yard from where he and Macy had fallen, realizing how close the man had come to firing at him a third time.

'He was aiming at your head,' Kate said quietly. Soberly.

'I figured as much, since the first two shots to my back bounced off. Fucker,' he muttered.

'Kate aimed *her* first shots at his hand after he got off *his* first two shots at you,' Troy said. 'She hit his hand and he dropped the first gun, but he had another. He tried to shoot with his left hand. Aimed at your head. He missed. But you'd hunkered down, so we could shoot him without hitting you and Macy by mistake.'

'I wanted him alive,' Kate said, more than sober now. 'I wanted to know what he did with all the kids he's taken all these years. But he was standing over you with his gun pointed at your head. And you . . .' Her voice cracked. 'You were protecting that little girl and . . . I couldn't let him hurt you. Either of you. But now we won't know. We won't know what he did with the others.' Her eyes filled as her voice broke completely. 'God, Decker. We can't bring them home if we don't even know who they were.'

Decker put his arm around her shoulders, pulled her close and kissed her temple, not caring that their team was watching or that the paramedics had just pulled up or that there was a dead body at their feet. He rocked her gently, suddenly so weary he could barely stand. 'But we brought five home tonight. Five kids. And Mallory, too. So six people, Kate. Six human beings get a second chance at a good life. Six human beings are safe because you did a hard thing, but it was the right thing for these six. Tonight we think about that. Tomorrow we'll worry about how to save all the others.'

'Seven,' she whispered. 'You too.'

'Right,' he whispered back. 'You saved me again. So seven.'

Troy and Trip had walked away to give them some privacy, directing the medics to Macy and the four teenagers.

Decker rested his cheek on top of Kate's head. 'You know what I think we should do?'

She hiccupped a laugh. 'Really, Decker?' she asked dryly.

He had to chuckle with her. 'Well, yeah, but that's not what I was going to say. I was *going* to say that I think we need to go to the hospital and see Mallory and tell her that her sister and those four kids are okay. And that the man who made her life a living hell for so many years will never do so again. And that she doesn't have to worry about him doing the same thing to anyone else. Ever. We tell her because she needs to hear it and because we need to hear ourselves say it. And then we go back to our borrowed bed and do that other thing. And then maybe we can sleep for a straight week.'

'I think that's an excellent idea. All of it.'

Twenty-nine

Cincinnati, Ohio,
Saturday 15 August, 11.25 P.M.

Meredith touched Mallory's hand gently, almost hating to wake her. She hadn't been asleep all that long. After making her statement for the record, she'd lain awake, staring at the ceiling. Knowing she'd done the right thing, but conscious of the potential cost. The life of the little sister she'd endured so much to protect lay in the balance, and Meredith had felt every moment of Mallory's pain and anxiety. If Macy had died . . .

But she hadn't. *And I get to tell her.* 'Mallory, honey, wake up.'

Mallory started, then relaxed a fraction when she realized where she was. Safe, but not secure. She might never be completely secure, but Meredith was determined to give her all the tools she'd need to build a life. Because this girl deserved a life.

Mallory licked dry lips. 'You came back,' she rasped.

Meredith poured a cup of water and gently put the straw to her cracked lips. 'I never left the hospital. I ate supper in the cafeteria and then went to sit with my friend in ICU.'

'The doctor. Dani Novak. Will she be okay?'

'Yeah. She's tough.' *God, please let Dani be tough. Just a little bit longer.* 'I have some good news for you.'

Mallory closed her eyes, but not before Meredith saw the flash of fear, followed by weary acceptance. She stiffened her shoulders, preparing herself. So sure the news was bad, even though Meredith had said it wasn't, because nothing in her life had ever been good. 'Go ahead. I'm ready.'

'Not all news is bad, Mallory,' Meredith said. 'Kate and Decker found Macy. She's alive and she'll be okay.' *Eventually.*

Mallory's body sagged, and a sob burst from her throat. 'I didn't think they would do it. I thought for sure I'd killed her by telling the truth.'

'Yet you did it anyway, because you trusted Decker. Don't forget that. Don't ever forget that you trusted, Mallory. Not everyone will let you down.'

'Where . . .' She shuddered out a sob. 'Where is she?'

'She's here, in the ER. They just brought her in.' Meredith had been in the ER to meet the ambulances, to make sure the four adolescents were settled with social workers. And then . . . Her heart squeezed so hard. The sight of Adam Kimble, walking alongside that stretcher, holding Macy's hand. The look on his face . . . She took a deep breath. It was sheer relief. Exultant thanksgiving. Quiet pride. He'd saved one. He'd saved five, actually.

Five wins. And when he'd met her eyes across the ER, he'd smiled at her.

Tomorrow he'd worry about the kids he hadn't saved and maybe he'd come back for more conversation and coloring. But tonight he'd smiled, and Meredith was going to hold on to that for as long as she could.

Mallory frowned. 'If she's okay, why do you look like you're going to cry?'

Meredith cleared her throat. 'Too often we worry and beat ourselves up for all the things we can't do, all the people we can't help. And then some days things go right. And that's . . . amazing. So these little tears here, they're good ones.'

Mallory nodded, but there was still suspicion in her eyes, so Meredith took out her phone. 'I took a photo of her.' Actually, it was a photo of Adam, but Mallory didn't need to know that. She handed Mallory her phone, and it was the young woman's turn for tears.

'Thank you.' Mallory's voice broke, her hands shaking as she held the phone, staring at the photo. 'Thank you so much.'

'I didn't do anything. I just got the privilege of telling you.' A knock on the door frame had both of them looking up.

Kate and Decker peeked around the door. 'Okay to come in?' Decker asked.

Mallory nodded, a smile quivering on her lips. 'Please. Meredith told me that Macy's okay.'

'Thanks to this guy,' Kate said. 'You know how I jumped hurdles to save him? He did some serious ninja moves to save Macy.'

Decker gave her a smile that spoke of private jokes. 'Ninjas are cool. I can get on the ninja train.' He came up to the bed, leaning on a wooden cane. 'Can I sit? I'm really tired.'

'Please.' Mallory frowned at the cane as Decker lowered himself into a chair. 'That's not what you had before. The one you had was shiny.'

'The one I had is now covered in Brandon Edwards's blood,' Decker said with satisfaction. 'He's dead, Mallory. He won't ever hurt you or Macy again.'

Mallory covered her mouth, overcome. 'How? Who?'

Kate leaned her hip against Decker's shoulder. 'Decker hit him with the stick, took your sister out of Edwards's arms, then . . . I shot him. Along with two other agents. So it was a group effort.'

Mallory shuddered out a breath. 'Oh God. But . . . Macy . . . Will she have to go back to Gemma and Bob? I'll take her. I'll do anything.' She leaned forward, earnest and tense and scared. 'I'll get a job. Please let me take her.'

Meredith rubbed Mallory's back. 'We'll figure all that out. But she's not going back to Bob and Gemma.'

Mallory studied their faces, then eased back against the pillow. 'They're dead, too?'

Decker nodded. 'Yes. The doctor killed Gemma, then Bob . . .' He hesitated, flicking his gaze up to Kate, who seemed to wilt.

'Bob killed himself,' Kate finished. 'So you don't have to worry about any of them.'

Mallory shook her head. 'There's still the other man. McCord. Edwards said McCord would take Macy if something happened to him. That he would put her in videos right now, because he liked little girls. That he wouldn't wait for her to grow up. I still have to keep her safe from him.'

Kate opened her mouth, then closed it, sighing softly. 'Well, I know you're safe from McCord, because he's been dead for nine months.'

Anger flared in Mallory's eyes. 'Did Edwards know that?'

'Yes,' Kate said.

Mallory's lips firmed. 'If I'd known, I would have killed Edwards nine months ago. I was more afraid of McCord because he liked really little girls, like Macy is now. At least Edwards was the devil I knew.'

'Well you don't have to worry about either of them anymore,' Kate said quietly. 'They're all gone. And you helped make that happen. You had the courage to make that first phone call, trying to find Kendra.' She looked around, frowning. 'I thought Kendra was going to come and sit with you.'

'I sent her home,' Mallory said softly. 'She was crying. She kept trying not to, but . . . her partner died and she was sad.'

'You're a good person, Mallory,' Decker said. 'You know that, right? I'm proud of you.'

Mallory drew a deep breath, her eyes growing shiny. She wiped them with the hem of the sheet, then looked at Meredith. 'I get it. Good tears.'

'Very good tears,' Meredith said. 'But I think Decker's falling asleep in that chair. Maybe we should send him home too.'

Decker smiled, but his exhaustion was clear. 'I don't have a home yet. But I will soon. I don't think anybody will mind if we use the safe house one more night.' He stood up and kissed Mallory's forehead. 'Thank you.'

Mallory blushed shyly. 'Thank me? For what?'

'For being so brave and for letting me tell you about my sister. Because someone told me recently that if I tell people about her, she won't be forgotten.'

'I won't ever forget her,' Mallory promised. 'Or you.' She leaned over to look up at Kate. 'Or you too, Kate.'

Kate laughed. 'Yeah, uh-huh. I know who the charming one in this relationship is. Come on, ninja man. Time to go sleep.'

Mallory watched them go, then turned to Meredith, troubled. 'I don't have a home either.'

'I have a place all ready for you. Don't worry. For now, know that Macy is safe and four other kids are safe because of you. Now, I do have a home that I'd really like to go sleep in. And, um, I hope it's not trashed. My little niece had a slumber party there last night and I might go home to find a mess.'

'I can clean,' Mallory offered. 'I'm good at that. I can clean your house and other people's houses, too. And maybe make money for a place for me and Macy.' But her voice trembled as she said it, and Meredith knew that her promise of home and security hadn't been believed.

'Did you know that Kendra's sister runs a home for young women just like you? Girls who've been forced to do many of the things you've had to do.'

'Why? Why would she have a home like that?'

'Because twenty years ago, Wendi was a Sunshine Suzie too.'

'Oh,' Mallory breathed. And then she believed. 'I have a place to live. For how long?'

'As long as you need it. Wendi already has a bed in a room just for you, and if I know her, which I do, she'll have clothes and shampoo and everything you need. When you leave here, I'll take you straight there. You can get all healed up at Wendi's place.'

'And Macy? Can she come live with me?'

'Maybe. Although she's going to need different things than you because she's so much younger. Either way, I promise we will find someplace wonderful for her, where they can help her get over the shock of what's happened. Because she's not going to know what to think. She's going to be scared too. Her world just exploded. We'll be there for her and for you.

'Now, about the house cleaning. If my niece messed my place up, she will clean it herself. But I'm pretty sure she's done that anyway. You do not have to work for me to pay me back for helping you. If you want to clean other people's houses for pay, there is nothing wrong with that. But I'd like to see you have some real choices, because you haven't had many of those in your life.'

'What kind of choices?'

'We're going to teach you a skill. You can choose the job you want to do or we'll find a way for you to go to college if that's what you want to do.'

'I can't go to college. I . . .' Mallory looked embarrassed. 'I never went to high school. He wouldn't let me. I read all the books in his house, but I wasn't allowed out to go to school. He told people that Roxy was home-schooling me, but that wasn't true either.'

'Then we'll figure that out too. There are options for you, Mallory. Lots of choices. But we can do all that later. Just know you're not alone.' Meredith squeezed her hand. 'I'll be back tomorrow. Get some sleep. You're gonna have a life.'

Mallory swallowed hard, her eyes narrowing in determination. 'I'm gonna have a *good* life.'

Cincinnati, Ohio,
Sunday 16 August, 3.45 P.M.

Chocolate. Decker drew a deep breath, smiling as he slid out of sleep into that in-between place where no one was expected to think clearly. He liked that place. Especially when it smelled so good. The last few times he'd woken, he'd pulled Kate's scent into his lungs, and the fact that he wasn't doing so now made him frown. He patted the pillow next to him and it was cold.

But the smell of chocolate got stronger. The next deep breath pulled him fully into wakefulness, and he opened his eyes. Kate stood next to the bed wearing a pair of faded jeans, a Baltimore Orioles T-shirt, and a puzzled frown. She held a plate of brownies in one hand and a handful of long sticks in the other. Three long wooden sticks with brass grips. Walking sticks with a red ribbon threaded around and criss-crossed, ending in a big red bow. Kind of like a bouquet. But not.

'Why are they wrapped with ribbon?' he asked, his voice raspy with sleep. He'd slept most of the day away, waking only to eat and make love with Kate. He hadn't done either one of them often enough, though, because right now he was starving – for food and for her.

'They're a present from Keith and Jeremy O'Bannion. There's a card.'

599

He pushed himself up, shoving at the pillows so he could sit against the headboard. He took the card, then a brownie, which he shoved into his mouth. 'Mmph. Good.'

She laughed. 'God, Decker, don't choke on it. I don't want to have to do the Heimlich.'

'Hungry,' he grunted.

'So what else is new?' She sat on the edge of the bed. 'What does the card say?'

'Why are you dressed?'

'I'm pretty sure the card does not say that,' she said dryly. 'I've been writing reports while you snored like a buzz saw.'

There was more to it, more than simply writing reports. He could see shadows in her eyes, but he didn't push it for the moment, opening the card instead. He grinned. '"We heard you fucked up the stick I loaned you. Here are three more, in case you get the opportunity to use them in similar fashion." Written in two different hands. I'm thinking Keith did the first bit.'

'I'm thinking that's a fair assumption.' She leaned into him, resting her chin on his shoulder. 'What else?'

His grin softened. 'Jeremy adds, "Thank you for eliminating the man who took advantage of a fourteen-year-old boy, selling him drugs when he was sad and vulnerable. The world is a better place today without Brandon Edwards in it." Then Keith says, "Next time, choke down on the stick. You get more power that way. Happy to show you how. If you already know how, the *Ledger*'s baseball team always needs power hitters."'

She chuckled. 'Bloodthirsty. I like it.'

'Too bad I won't need the sticks much longer.' Only until he'd completely recovered and didn't get so damn tired. 'They make me feel all dignified.'

'And they're an awesome weapon.'

'Hell, yeah.' He put the card aside, then wrapped his arm around her shoulders, cuddling her against him. 'What happened?'

'Troy stopped by to check on us and bring you your canes. Keith had dropped them off at the field office. Oh, Troy also brought you about six pounds of M&Ms from Deacon, his thanks for ending "the fucking bastard who hurt Dani".'

'Nice of him. And? Why else did Troy stop by?'

She sighed. 'To tell us what they found in the backyard of Edwards's studio.'

His heart sank. 'The kids he'd used up.'

'Yes. Quincy's done nothing but rewind Edwards's surveillance tapes, and he found footage of him burying several bodies. They did a scan with ground-penetrating radar. There are six bodies buried there. That doesn't account for all the kids, but Quincy found some evidence of . . . sales. So he'll keep digging. In the computer and in the ground, I guess. We might be able to save a few more. Or at least give closure to some of the parents who came forward to Wendi.'

Decker drew a breath and let it out. 'Dammit.'

'I know, but . . . we don't give up, right? What was it you said? Something like, it spreads to every dark corner and all we can do is go after the bastards that make it, one at a time, right? So that's what we'll do. And then we'll save who we can.'

'When?'

She was caressing his skin, little pats meant not to arouse but to comfort. 'When what?'

'When do we start?'

She pulled back to study his face. 'I start back Wednesday. With Troy. My partner, remember? You get a few weeks off. Boss's orders. Apparently Zimmerman took some flack from the powers-that-be for letting you participate the last few days. They said he should have cleared your participation with his superiors before letting you go into the field.'

'I feel a little bad about that.' He really did. He liked Zimmerman.

'Nah, don't worry about it. Troy says Zimmerman handled it. Made his apologies to the big cheeses, promised he'd do better next time, but Troy's known the guy for years. Says this isn't the first time Zimmerman's apologized versus asking permission and it's unlikely to be the last.'

'So if you start Wednesday, what are you going to do tomorrow and Tuesday?'

'Get my apartment ready. My furniture comes on Tuesday. And I might get a dog. Something small.'

He blinked. 'Really? From Delores?'

'Who else? It seems to be the thing to do.'

'How long's your lease on this apartment?'

Her patting hand stilled. 'Three months, then month to month. It's one of the short-term places for people on temporary assignment. Why?'

'Is this assignment temporary?' he countered warily.

'No. But I needed a place to live and I didn't have a lot of time to search. I was kind of busy, sitting next to your bedside and watching you sleep. Plus I didn't want to sign a big lease and find out I hated the neighborhood. Why?'

'Because if Cincinnati is my permanent assignment, I want a house. With a yard where I can have a garden. And a dog. A big one. I've never had a place of my own.'

'Then you should have one. You know, you could stay with me until you find a house. I have two bedrooms. We could have our space, take our time, get to know each other better.'

'And if it takes me three months to find the right house?'

'Why don't we wait and see? It's not a race.'

He snorted a laugh. It had quickly become their slow-down phrase when one of them got too revved up and wanted to rush sex and the other wanted it slow. They'd used it twice today alone. But a third time they'd both wanted hard and fast so there'd been no talking at all. 'Okay. Fair enough. Not a race.'

She pressed a kiss to his chest, over his heart. 'Nap time's over. You need to get dressed because we've been asked to dinner at Scarlett and Marcus's house. Scarlett's been playing with her new oven and Marcus supposedly has the grill going with the promise of steaks and beer. There's going to be a crowd. Something about helping Marcus build a gazebo.'

He brightened. 'Then he can help me build something when I get my house.'

'I'm told that's the way it works. Come on. I want to stop by the hospital first and I have a few things to buy on the way. Dani's been moved to a regular room and I wanted to check on Mallory and Macy, too.'

He wanted to grumble, but he had spent all day in bed. 'Where are we stopping?'

She winked at him. 'Yarn store. I'm going to try and convert me some knitters. That way I don't look like the odd man out.' She started backing out of the room. 'I'll wait for you in the living room. If I stay here, you won't get out of bed till tomorrow, and I want a steak.'

He wasn't fooled by the wink and the hasty retreat. It bothered her, the fact that she needed to be doing something with her hands in order to think. 'You said you'd teach me,' he called after her when she was almost to the door. 'Maybe I can use a pair of those really fat needles because I got . . . you know, big hands.'

A true smile bloomed. 'I thought you were just saying that. You'd really knit? In public?'

'Of course I would, for purely selfish reasons. It helps you make very smart connections, and I want that edge. Plus you'll have to sit really close to me to show me what to do. I'm playing all the angles.'

'Then maybe you could show me how to go undercover?'

He held up the blanket. 'You have an open invitation for that.'

'You're bad and I'm serious. I want to, you know, not scream *Fed*.'

He feigned a grimace. 'Well *that* won't be so easy. It's good that I like a challenge.'

She was laughing as she closed the door, and he felt proud of himself for making her smile. He felt happy. Just . . . happy to be here.

He'd finally have a home. And someone wonderful to share it with. It was more than enough. It was everything.

Cincinnati, Ohio,
Sunday 16 August, 6.00 P.M.

Decker kissed Kate's cheek when they reached Dani's room. 'Go in. I'll be a minute.'

603

Kate's smile was sad. When they'd passed the family waiting room, Diesel had been there, standing at the window, looking like he'd lost his best friend. 'See if you can get him to come with us to Scarlett and Marcus's. He looks like he could use some time away from here.'

'I'll try.' It was all Decker could promise. He peeked into Dani's room just to see with his own eyes how she seemed. And truthfully, she looked much better than he'd expected. She was sitting up in bed, pale but smiling. Especially when she saw it was Kate who'd come to visit.

'Finally, someone who'll give me the true scoop!' Dani exclaimed. 'Deacon won't tell me anything.' She rolled her unusual eyes. 'He doesn't want anyone to upset me.'

Kate sniffed as she sat in the chair by the bed. 'Deacon's had a bug shoved up his ass for days. I'll tell you whatever you want to know, and what *he* doesn't know won't hurt him.'

Decker backed away, his heart considerably lighter. He'd pictured Dani with tubes and masks and looking like death warmed over. There were tubes, but only a few, and she looked . . . okay. Not like herself, but definitely okay.

The death-warmed-over part, Decker thought as he entered the family waiting room, would be Diesel. The tattooed mountain looked positively grim.

Decker leaned next to the window so that he could see Diesel's face. 'You look like shit.'

Diesel just rolled his eyes and said nothing.

'Seriously, you look worse than she does. She's going to be okay. Her doctor said so.'

'I know.' The words rumbled out, rusty and pitched so low they were almost inaudible.

'Then why the attitude? And why aren't you sitting in there with her?'

'She has family to sit with her.'

Decker heard the bitter undercurrent, but wasn't sure where it came from, so he proceeded carefully. 'A lot of family. She's lucky in that respect.'

Diesel glanced sideways. 'What happened to *your* family? Your foster family?'

'They're gone. They were old when they took me in. But they loved me while they had me and I guess that makes me lucky too, huh?'

Diesel turned his attention back to the window. 'You don't have to babysit me. I'll be okay.'

'I wasn't babysitting. I thought I was standing here talking to a friend who might need me. But I can just stand here if you want. And not talk.'

Diesel snorted. 'I'd truly like to see that.'

Decker grinned, unoffended. 'Hell, man, I was in a fucking coma for a week, and before that, undercover with the biggest group of lowlifes you could *never* want to meet, and I wasn't about to talk to them if I didn't have to. So I have some words saved up. I can give 'em to you or to the universe in general, but they ain't stayin' in my mouth, I can tell you that much.'

Diesel's lips curved. 'Wow.'

'I'm sayin'.'

He dropped his gaze to Decker's walking stick. ' I heard you did some damage with that last night.'

'I did. But not with this one. This is a replacement for the one I used last night, which is in the evidence locker. Covered in Edwards's blood.'

'Thank you.' It was offered seriously, and Decker's grin faded to a smile of grim satisfaction.

'I wish I'd hit him hard enough to spread some brains, too, but Kate took care of that.'

'I'll thank her too.'

'Edwards hurt enough people that you'll have to stand in line.' Decker was quiet for a moment, then sighed. 'Why *are* you standing here alone? You don't have to be alone.'

'I know.' Diesel hesitated. 'I'm just not sure how to be with people.'

'I guess I understand that. It's like when you come back from deployment and civilians are all around and you don't fit in and you're not sure if you ever will. You walk and talk and look like normal people, but . . . we're not like them and we never will be.'

Diesel's big shoulders rose and fell on a sigh, but his expression never changed. 'No, I never will be.'

But there was so much more to it than being a fish out of water. Decker struggled for the right words. 'You just cracked open a can of worms that were overrun by maggots. By looking at those photos, I mean. And by bringing them to me. So maybe you're thinking that Dani has family to take care of her and that maybe she doesn't need or even want the company of someone whose headspace is filled with maggots.'

Finally, finally Diesel made eye contact and Decker's heart cracked yet again. 'Yes,' Diesel murmured. 'Incredibly disgusting visual, but yes.'

'I think Dani Novak's got some maggots of her own.'

Diesel glared at him. 'Not of her making,' he said stubbornly.

'Maybe, maybe not. You don't know where her maggots came from. I'm not saying they're her fault, though I can tell you that you don't become HIV positive from a fucking toilet seat, so she does have a story in there somewhere. You don't know what that story is. You don't know what's going on in her head. Not until you ask her.'

Diesel snorted his disbelief. 'And she'd just tell me?'

'Maybe. Maybe not today or even tomorrow, or maybe not ever because that's her choice. But just maybe she'd like to know you care, because she's as lonely as you are.'

'She's got family,' Diesel said again, harder this time.

'Okay, okay, I'll back off.'

Again the slight quirk of his lips. 'I'll believe that when I see it.'

Which wasn't a direct order to cease and desist, so that was good at least. 'Kate and I won't stay long. We're on our way to some shindig at Marcus's.'

'I know. I was invited too.'

'Then why are you here? I bet they've got food out right now.' And damned if Decker wasn't hungry again.

A grunt. 'Marcus is going to make us help him with that damn gazebo of his.'

'I know. But then he'll owe me when I have repairs to make on my house.'

A spark of interest. 'You got a house?'

'I'm going to. I plan to start looking at places tomorrow. I know what I want, but I also know what I can afford and it'll need some fixin'. I heard that you and Marcus build houses.'

'We have. But not in a while.'

'But you have a contractor's license, right? Maybe you could check out the houses I'm interested in and tell me if they're money pits or not.'

'They're all money pits, Davenport. Even the good ones.'

'Yeah,' Decker allowed, 'but I still want one. I want a home. And a dog. I want a place I can invite my friends, with a big-screen TV for ball games, and furniture we won't break if we sit on it. I figure if *you* can sit on a sofa and not break it, then it's safe for the rest of us.'

Diesel's grin was quick but real. 'I'm your canary in the mine, huh?'

'See, you got words, too. Come with me, we'll say hi to Dani and then we'll go to Marcus's for what I'm hoping will be really good steaks.'

He was surprised when Diesel fell into line behind him, the two of them too wide to walk side by side through the hallways.

Dani looked up with genuine delight at the sight of Decker, her smile growing softer when Diesel appeared behind him. 'Come in, please. Kate's just showing me how to knit.'

'Proselytizing, Kate?' Diesel asked.

'Absolutely,' Kate said with a hard nod. 'Because one knitter looks eccentric, but two look like a club.'

Decker leaned down to kiss Dani's cheek, before settling in the chair on the other side of the bed. 'My gift to you, Dr Novak, is that you were right. I needed to rest more before I went out in the field. I'm paying the price now.'

Dani gave him a prim look. 'You know I didn't want to be right.'

Decker chuckled. 'But you won't argue that you were.'

She smiled at him. 'Nope. Thank you, Decker. I heard what you did last night. Going all Kung Fu Panda and everything. Cute and cuddly but deadly.'

Diesel made a strangled sound, like he was trying not to laugh. Decker glared at Kate, who simply ignored them all, knitting serenely.

Decker sighed. 'Anyway, I'm taking it easy. Plenty of bed rest.'

'That's not what Kate said,' Dani said, brows lifted. 'Not about the rest part, anyway. Oh baby, oh baby!'

He didn't need a mirror to know that his face was turning red. 'God, Kate.'

Kate's head had jerked up, her eyes wide. 'I did not! I said no such thing! Kung Fu Panda, yes, but never oh baby, oh baby. Not even a *single* oh baby. Dani, stop causing trouble! Dammit, woman, you made me drop a stitch!'

Diesel actually snickered, and Dani's smile lit up her whole face. 'But it made Coach Diesel laugh and that was worth it.'

Kate gathered her things. 'That is the last time I bring you books from my collection,' she said, pretending to be annoyed.

'Um, which collection?' Decker asked, remembering the erotic book in her purse.

Kate lifted a brow. 'The one you're thinking about right now.'

Dani held up the book for them to see, and yes, it was one of the titles that Kate could read in public to be sure no one would meet her eyes or even notice her face. 'I've already read this one,' Dani said. 'But I'll pass it along to the nurses. It'll win me favors. Maybe even an extra helping of Jell-O.'

'It should be good for more than Jell-O,' Kate told her. 'I'll be back tomorrow. I'll bring you another book if you behave.'

Dani's smile dimmed, fatigue covering her like a lead blanket. 'That's okay. I can't focus enough to read right now. My head still hurts a bit.'

They'd all been so worried about the stab wound that they'd nearly forgotten about her head. Edwards had hit her hard enough to cause a concussion. 'An audio book, maybe,' Decker suggested. 'I know I enjoyed hearing voices when I was trying to wake up.'

'Maybe,' Dani said. 'That would be really sweet. Now, I don't mean to be rude, but I'm about to fall asleep. I heard you have a barbecue to go to, so eat a few burgers for me. Let me know if Deacon isn't there. I told him he had to go because he was driving me crazy. Coach, would you mind staying for just a minute?'

Diesel looked stunned, but he nodded. 'I'll meet you at Scarlett and Marcus's,' he said to Decker. 'I promise I'll be there.'

Cincinnati, Ohio,
Sunday 16 August, 7.15 P.M.

As it turned out, Diesel beat them there, because Kate had to make a stop on the way. Scarlett Bishop lived in a multicolored house at the top of a huge hill. Luckily someone had saved them a place in the driveway or Decker would have had to climb that hill, because there was a long line of cars parked in front.

'I think everyone in the city's here,' Decker murmured into her ear as they walked around the house to the backyard, and Kate thought he might just be right. The yard was packed with men and children. Most of the men – including Diesel – were working on a gazebo that was starting to take form. A country music radio station played from stereo speakers, background music to the pounding of hammers and the whine of an electric saw. There were burgers and beer, but no one had overindulged, much to Kate's relief. Unlike the barbecues she'd attended as a kid, this one was a nice friendly party.

She recognized about two thirds of the people. Marcus, of course, who was manning the grill. Stone was there too, looking better than he had the last time they'd seen him. Delores was around somewhere, because her big dog was curled up next to Stone's wheelchair. In fact, there were dogs everywhere – a sheltie at Marcus's feet, a three-legged bulldog chasing after a lab puppy whose teeth marks were probably a match for those in Deacon's ruined shoes.

Someone had set up a horseshoe pit, and several kids were trying to play. A little girl took her turn, missed, then looked up and saw Kate and Decker standing just inside the gate.

'Mr Decker!' With a smile she came running, stopping just short of throwing her arms round Decker's waist. She lowered her arms and put on a polite face. 'I'm glad you're here.'

Decker held out his free arm. 'Hug. Please.' Her smile reappearing, the girl obeyed, and Decker gave an obligatory 'Oof' when she squeezed him hard. 'Hope, this is Miss Kate. Kate, Hope Beardsley. She helped me find Alice's apartment.'

Kate shook the child's offered hand. 'It's nice to meet you. I've heard a lot about you.'

'I heard you're a crack shot,' Hope said guilelessly, and Kate wondered if she herself had ever been quite so innocent.

Probably not. But it didn't really matter, because who Kate was had brought her here, to this backyard in this town, standing beside a very good man.

'I'm pretty good,' she allowed. 'When you're older, if your parents agree, I'll teach you.'

Hope's eyes sparkled. 'My dad will say it's okay. He wants you to teach him too.'

'Well then, I guess it'll work out nicely. Where are the ladies?'

'Inside, getting away from the heat. We're playing horseshoes. Do you want to play?'

'I do,' Decker said. 'I used to be pretty good at it, years ago. You coming, Miss Kate?'

'In a bit. I want to find Deacon.'

'Mr Deacon's inside,' Hope confided. 'Said the light was hurting his eyes. He said he'd come out when it got dark and we could catch fireflies. We won't keep them, of course, because that's mean.' She pointed at the bag Kate held. 'What's that?'

'A present for Mr Deacon. You two have fun.' Kate watched as Decker made his way across the backyard, wondering if he knew that the small girl had her hands out, planning to catch him if he fell. *Better not fall, Davenport.* He'd squish that kid like a bug.

She found the house abuzz with voices, mostly the women she'd seen in the ER two days before as they'd waited for word about Dani's surgery. They were grouped around a banged-up table, a young brunette she'd never met at the head. Faith sat on one side of the woman, Wendi Cullen on the other. Meredith, Scarlett, Bailey, and Kendra all had their heads together, talking animatedly while pointing at the paper the brunette was furiously filling with notes.

They appeared to be planning something.

Deacon came up behind Kate with a cold bottle of water. 'Drink. You look parched.'

'I am. It's hotter than hell out there. What's going on here?'

'Ah. The fund-raising planning committee, led by Audrey O'Bannion.' Deacon pointed at the brunette sitting between Faith and Wendi. 'Audrey is Jeremy's daughter. Wendi's halfway house needs a new home, so Faith has donated the old house she inherited from her grandmother. They're doing a fund-raiser for the repairs that need to be made.' He smiled slyly. 'Those men out there have no idea that they're being volunteered to do all kinds of work.'

Kate chuckled. 'I think this is wonderful. Just what we need after the last week.'

'I agree. Too much sadness. And worry. We needed a little bit of hope, you know?'

'Yeah, I know. Especially since it's not over yet.'

'I know.' He sighed heavily. 'Adam and I went over Bob Seifert's phone logs. He never called Edwards the night of the McCord raid.'

'Damn,' she said softly. 'So we have another dirty cop somewhere.'

'Yeah. And we still don't know anything about the traffickers' network – who they bought from, who they sold to. Whether any of the victims they sold are still alive . . .'

'That's going to be Decker's job. He'll keep reproducing the ledgers he can remember, and eventually I'll be able to help him unwind all the transactions. Following the money is still our fallback plan.'

Deacon was quiet for a long moment. 'I talked to Troy. He told me about the graveyard they found behind Edwards's house. That's going to be a rough assignment: identifying bodies, informing the victims' families. I offered him my help.'

Which was a huge gesture, because Deacon knew exactly how hard a task that was. He'd done it before, back when they were in Baltimore, and Kate remembered what the experience had cost him. She'd helped him back then, brought him coffee on mornings when the bags under his eyes announced his nightmares.

But we all have our nightmares. Kate's new one would be seeing Edwards aiming for Decker's head while Decker protected an innocent child. A child who wasn't going to end up in that graveyard. Kate kept telling herself that, and the thought gave her the strength to square her shoulders.

'That was really nice of you to offer, Deacon, and I know Troy appreciated it. He told me so this afternoon when we discussed the work that has to be done to identify those victims.'

'So that'll be your assignment?' Deacon asked, looking distressed.

'He's my partner, just like you were. I helped you through it. Troy and I will figure it out. But if it gets to be too much, I'll come and find you. Just like you and me in the old days.'

His lips curved in a ghost of a smile. 'When we'd do a Marvel DVD marathon and then eat shawarma like the Avengers at the end of the movie. Remember?'

She smiled back at him. 'When they were so tired after saving the planet. Yeah, I remember.'

'Damn, that's how I feel right now, you know? I'm so damn tired. I feel like we just saved the planet. Again.'

'Or the city at the very least. You and Scarlett and Marcus and Decker and me. Adam and Meredith. And Troy and Quincy Taylor and Diesel, too. We should celebrate somehow.'

'Definitely Diesel too. Dani wouldn't be breathing if it weren't for him. Damn, I've got to find a shawarma restaurant around here. Faith wants Cincinnati chili all the time, and that's fine. That's her comfort food. But sometimes,' he said wistfully, 'sometimes you gotta eat shawarma with the guys you shared the trenches with, y'know?'

'I know.' Kate held up the bag she'd brought in from the car. 'So I found one. A shawarma restaurant, I mean. It's not too far from here and it's pretty damn good.'

His eyes brightened with excited amusement. 'You got hangry in the car again and ate some of it, didn't you?'

'And I have knitting needles in my bag that I'm not afraid to use,' she returned without heat. 'Wanna just sit and chill and enjoy the fact that we saved a bunch of lives?'

'I think that's an amazing idea. Trouble is, we've got a lot more people who pitched in.'

'I brought enough for everyone. We all get to be tired superheroes today.'

Deacon drew a deep breath, his eyes going abruptly shiny. He slid his shades on, hiding his emotion from the others, but Kate had seen and that was more than good enough.

'Then let's do it,' he said. 'Scar? Meredith? Ladies? Come with us,' he said. When they got outside, he shouted for the men. 'Even you, Davenport,' he called out, earning Decker's slow grin as he ambled back from the horseshoe pit, holding Hope's hand.

'So you like him now?' Kate asked as she and Deacon unloaded the bag onto a picnic table.

'Maybe. If he hasn't hurt you in ten or twenty years, maybe.'

Kate met Decker halfway, leaving Deacon to explain to the others what they were eating and why. 'He liked the idea?' Decker asked.

She slid her arm around his waist and rested her head on his shoulder. 'He did. Thanks for finding the place for me.' Decker had done the legwork, searching the Internet for the restaurant while she'd been in the yarn store.

'You're welcome. It's a team thing, right?'

Kate looked at the team, at the big smiles on their faces. 'Definitely a team thing.'

Decker kissed the top of her head. 'Them too. But I was talking about us. You and me.'

'You and me. I like the way that sounds in your Mississippi drawl. Yeah. You and me. Let's go have some celebration shawarma.'

'And then later . . . well, later we can celebrate some more. With our team of two. Okay?'

She had to laugh. 'That's a plan.'

About Karen Rose

Karen Rose was introduced to suspense and horror at the tender age of eight when she accidentally read Poe's *The Pit and the Pendulum* and was afraid to go to sleep for years. She now enjoys writing books that make other people afraid to go to sleep.

Karen lives in Florida with her family, their cat, Bella, and two dogs, Loki and Freya. When she's not writing, she enjoys reading, and her new hobby – knitting.